T0332820

EVERYMAN,
I WILL GO WITH THEE,
AND BE THY GUIDE,
IN THY MOST NEED
TO GO BY THY SIDE

.

RABINDRANATH TAGORE

THE BEST
OF
TAGORE

EDITED AND INTRODUCED
BY RUDRANGSHU MUKHERJEE

EVERYMAN'S LIBRARY
Alfred A. Knopf   New York   London   Toronto

415

THIS IS A BORZOI BOOK
PUBLISHED BY ALFRED A. KNOPF

First included in Everyman's Library, 2023
Introduction copyright © 2023 by Rudrangshu Mukherjee
Selection, Bibliography and Notes copyright © 2023 by Everyman's Library
Chronology by Frederick Holloway copyright © 2023 by Everyman's Library

Copyright material used with permission from the following:

Rabindranath Tagore: Selected Short Stories © William Radice, 1985 (year of first publication). Reproduced with permission of Johnson & Alcock Ltd.
Rabindranath Tagore: Selected Short Poems © William Radice, 1991 (year of first publication). Reproduced with permission of Johnson & Alcock Ltd.

The Essential Tagore by Rabindranath Tagore, edited by Fakrul Alam and Radha Chakravarty. Copyright © 2011 by the President and Fellows of Harvard College. Selections reprinted by arrangement with Harvard University Press.

Rabindranath Tagore: Selected Short Stories. Reproduced with permission of Oxford University Press India, © 2000
Rabindranath Tagore: Selected Writings for Children. Reproduced with permission of Oxford University Press India, © 2002
Rabdindranath Tagore: Selected Poems. Reproduced with permission of Oxford University Press India, © 2004

The English Writings of Rabindranath Tagore, vol. 1 (Poems), edited by Sisir Kumar Das, Sahitya Akademi, New Delhi, 1994.
The English Writings of Rabindranath Tagore, vol. 3 (A Miscellany), edited by Sisir Kumar Das, Sahitya Akademi, New Delhi, 1996.

History at the Limit of World-History, ed. Ranajit Guha. Copyright © 2002 Columbia University Press. Reprinted with permission of Columbia University Press.

Further details of sources can be found in the Notes at the back of this volume.

All rights reserved. Published in the United States by Alfred A. Knopf, a division of Penguin Random House LLC, New York, and in Canada by Penguin Random House Canada Limited, Toronto. Distributed by Penguin Random House LLC, New York. Published in the United Kingdom by Everyman's Library, 50 Albemarle Street, London W1S 4BD and distributed by Penguin Random House UK, 20 Vauxhall Bridge Road, London SW1V 2SA.

everymanslibrary.com
www.everymanslibrary.co.uk

ISBN: 978-1-101-90838-9 (US)
978-1-84159-415-6 (UK)

A CIP catalogue record for this book is available from the British Library

Typography by Peter B. Willberg
Book design by Barbara de Wilde and Carol Devine Carson
Typeset in the UK by Input Data Services Ltd, Bridgwater, Somerset
Printed and bound in Germany by GGP Media GmbH, Pössneck

C O N T E N T S

———

Introduction ix

Select Bibliography xxv

Chronology xxviii

SHORT STORIES
The Ghat's Story 5
The Postmaster 14
Little Master's Return 20
Wealth Surrendered 27
The Living and the Dead 35
Kabuliwallah 46
Holiday 53
Giribala 59
The Hungry Stones 66
Guest 76
The Haldar Family 90
The Wife's Letter 109
House Number One 123
The Parrot's Training 137
The Patriot 141
The Laboratory 146
The Story of a Mussalmani 186

NOVEL
The Home and the World 193

PLAYS
The Post Office 365
Red Oleanders 389

v

ESSAYS

Nationalism in the West	439
Nationalism in India	461
Construction versus Creation	478
East and West	489
A Vision of India's History	499
The Educational Mission of the Visva-Bharati	525
The Religion of Man	531
Crisis in Civilization	643
Historicality in Literature	650

POEMS FOR CHILDREN

The Captive Hero	657
The Hero	660
The Palm Tree	662
Our Little River	663
The Runaway City	665

SONGS

Nothing Has Worked Out	669
Only Coming and Going	669
Through Death and Sorrow	670
My Bengal of Gold	671
Suddenly from the Heart of Bengal	672
If They Answer Not to Thy Call	673
Blessed Am I to Have Been Born in This Land	673
This Stormy Night	674
I Know Not How Thou Singest, My Master	674
The Suit	675
When Life Has Withered	675
I'll Overcome You	676
Light of Mine, O Light	676
Thou Art the Ruler of the Minds of All People	677
Thou Hast Made Me Endless	678
You Stand on the Other Shore	679
The Night My Doors Were Shattered	679
My Lamp Blown Out	680

CONTENTS

Not Your Word Alone 680
Forgive My Languor, O Lord 681
The Cloud Says, 'I Am Going' 681
When My Footprints No Longer Mark This Road . . 682
Beyond Boundaries of Life and Death 683
My Time Flies 683
There – in the Lap of the Storm Clouds –
    the Rain Comes 684
Because I Would Sing 684
May Farewell's Platter Be Replete 685
Stars Fill the Sky 685
Has He Come? Or Hasn't He? 686
A Slight Caress, a Few Overheard Words 686

POEMS
The Spring Wakes From Its Dream 689
I Won't Let You Go 690
Swaying 694
The Golden Boat 698
Now Turn Me Back 699
The Lord of Life 702
A Half-acre of Land 704
Affliction 706
Snatched by the Gods 708
Where the Mind Is Without Fear 713
Death-wedding 713
Pilgrimage to India 715
The Flying Geese 718
In Praise of Trees 720
The Child 722
Question 731
Unyielding 732
I 733
Earth 735
Africa 738
The Day My Consciousness Was Freed 740
Concord 741
The Pall of the Self 743

They Work 744
On the Banks of the Rupnarayan 745
The First Day's Sun 746
The Path of Your Creation 746
Delusions I Did Cherish 747
I Thought I Had Something to Say 747
I Threw Away My Heart 748
My Heart, Like a Peacock 748
I Ask for an Audience 749
Our Master Is a Worker 749
The World Today 750
Why Deprive Me 751
An Oldish Upcountry Man 751
Though I Know, My Friend 752
At the Dusk of the Early Dawn 752
The Santal Woman 754
Through the Troubled History of Man 755
Those Who Struck Him Once 755

Notes 757

INTRODUCTION

Rabindranath Tagore, who was born in Calcutta on 7 May 1861 and died in the same city on 7 August 1941, has been known by many names. To those who do not speak Bengali he is simply Tagore – an anglicized version of the old family name of Thakur. To almost all educated Bengalis he is just Rabindranath. To many, in the course of a very a long life, Tagore was, as Mahatma Gandhi called him, 'Gurudev' (revered teacher). In the late nineteenth century and early twentieth century he was at times fondly referred to as Rabi Thakur in the urban literati circles of Bengal.

Tagore's family originally hailed from the district of Jessore, now in Bangladesh. The story went that they had lost their high-caste Brahmin status in Jessore when one of their number partook of food with a Muslim. As a consequence, they migrated to Calcutta – this was at the beginning of the eighteenth century when the British had begun to establish a trading hub and settlement there – and settled near fishermen on the banks of the river Hooghly. The poor fishermen needed Brahmins (even those who had lost their caste) to carry out Hindu rituals and they honoured the newcomers by calling them *thakur* (lord or master). Members of the family soon gave up their careers as priests and began to work as commercial agents of the British East India Company, making enormous amounts of money. Their wealth acquired legendary proportions under Rabindranath Tagore's grandfather, Dwarakanath Tagore (1794–1846), an entrepreneur, who like many others in late eighteenth-century and early nineteenth-century Calcutta, used his fortune to buy landed estates in Bengal and Orissa. Dwarakanath was a close friend of Rammohun Roy (1772–1833), who pioneered the movement post-1815 to reform orthodox Hindu society and religious practices. Rabindranath Tagore's father Debendranath (1817–1905) had a deep interest in India's spiritual and philosophical traditions and under his patriarchy the Tagore family mansion in Jorasanko (in north Calcutta) emerged as a major centre of cultural and literary activity.

Rabindranath Tagore was the fourteenth child of his parents and like all his siblings showed musical and literary talent at a very young age. He was only thirteen when he published his first poem ('Abhilasha' – Desire), and his first poetry book, *Kabikahini* (A Poet's Tale) followed three years later. His early songs, stories and dance-dramas also attracted attention. In his reminiscences, *Jivan Smriti*, Rabindranath recalls attending the wedding reception of the eldest daughter of Romesh Chandra Dutt (1848–1909, member of the Indian Civil Service and author), where his host had stepped forward to welcome and garland Bankim Chandra Chattopadhyay (1838–94, the foremost novelist and intellectual in Bengal in the late nineteenth century). Seeing Rabindranath, Bankim Chandra quickly took the garland and put it around his neck, saying that he deserved it. Bankim Chandra then asked Romesh Dutt if he had read Rabindranath's book of poems, *Sandhya Sangeet* (Evening Music). When Dutt answered in the negative, Bankim Chandra praised the poems. Rabindranath remembered that praise as a very special gift. He was a mere twenty years old at the time, and it would not be long before he was being recognized as a major poet in Bengali.

Rabindranath had little or no formal education. When he was twelve his father took him to the hill station Dalhousie and opened up his mind to the world of nature, to astronomy, to Indian music and to literature and Indian philosophy. When he was sixteen, his eldest brother, Dwijendranath (1840–1926) – mathematician, philosopher and poet – brought out a literary journal called *Bharati*, where Rabindranath published many pieces including essays on Dante and Petrarch, whose works he had got to know in the library of another of this brothers, Satyendranath, the first Indian to join the Indian Civil Service. In 1878, Rabindranath travelled to England to stay with Satyendranath and his wife Gyanadanandini. During his sojourn abroad for over a year Rabindranath was exposed to Western ways of life and to Western music and literature. Some of the tunes and melodies that he picked up in England were echoed in an opera, *Valmiki Prativa* (The Genius of Valmiki), which he composed in 1881. Rabindranath's education was thus somewhat unique. He always remembered that there were paths to education that lay beyond the boundaries of school walls. Late in life, in a book about his early years called *Chhelebela* (Childhood), he wrote, 'I wandered around the outskirts of schools. House tutors were appointed and I played truant. Whatever I managed to get was from the proximity to human beings.'

When he was twenty-two, Rabindranath was married to Bhabatarini, who was the daughter of a clerk on his father's estate. Once the young bride, aged ten, entered the Tagore household her name was changed to Mrinalini. Perhaps the name Bhabatarini seemed too rustic to the urban sophisticated Tagore household. A couple of months before his marriage, Rabindranath was asked by his father to look after the family estates. He took this responsibility very seriously and, after a period of training at the estate offices in Calcutta, went out to the heart of eastern Bengal where he travelled by boat as this was an area crisscrossed by rivers, the most important of which was the vast ocean-like Padma. Rabindranath's journey into the rural world had two momentous consequences for his intellectual and creative development.

First, he was brought close to nature, renewing and reaffirming the experiences that he had had as a boy at Dalhousie when he had walked among the woods and the hills and had watched the night sky with his father. In rural and riverine Bengal, his eyes, his senses and his mind were ravished by the beauty of the natural world, and soothed by a powerful feeling of connection to it. In a letter dated June 1891 during one of his trips, he wrote:

I cannot describe the wonderful moonlit nights I am now having here. It is not my purpose to say that the address where this letter will reach does not witness moonlit nights – there over the maidan, over the church spire and over the silent trees the moonlight establishes its quiet presence. But there, there are five other things. Here I have nothing but the silent night. I won't be able to express the infinite peace and beauty I experience all by myself . . . I put my head on the window sill, the wind caresses my hair, the river gurgles on, the moonlight shimmers and often the eyes are filled with tears.

Second, he observed the lives of the common people – their daily routine, their rituals, their ceremonies, their festivals and their entertainments. He discovered how the rhythm of every-day life served to sustain them in spite of the exploitation which they endured and the grinding poverty that dominated their existence. In his mind, he could fuse together his closeness to nature and his observation of the lives of the poor. In another letter, dated 10 May 1893, he expressed this coming together in a very moving way:

I see now large swollen clouds have gathered all around . . . here the play of sunshine and clouds is so important – how people stare at the sky . . . I feel very sad and compassionate seeing my poor peasant sub-jects. They are like the Almighty's helpless children. They have noth-ing unless the Almighty gives it to them. When the earth's milk dries up, they only know how to cry – when their hunger is assuaged, they forget everything.

This exposure to nature and the rural world found expression in a series of outstanding short stories which were published in the mid-1890s as *Galpaguccha* (Collection of Stories) and also in many memorable songs and poems. Of equal importance, however, was the awakening of Rabindranath's social conscience. The sufferings of human beings that he saw first-hand had touched him profoundly. In an unforgettable poem, 'Ebar Phirao More', loosely translated as 'Now Let Me Return' (1894), he wrote:

There standing, heads bowed and dumb, on their downcast faces writ-ten only the story of a hundred years of pain and sorrow. Great the burden on their shoulders, they move slowly as long as they have life – then they bequeath the burden to their children, generation after gen-eration. They do not display their anger at destiny, they do not abuse the gods, they do not blame humankind, they harbour no resentment; for their painful lives they eke out only a few grains of rice.

His acute awareness of people's helplessness brought him to a new commitment which he expressed in a prayer-like poem, published in 1901: 'Give me the strength never to disown the poor or bend my knees before insolent might.'

From the time he began touring parts of the Bengal country-side to look after his family's landed estates, he became concerned and then involved with the welfare of the people who lived in the villages. He wrote about their problems in his essays. Rabindranath's sympathy for the poor and his dedication to their service was also reflected in his creative work – especially in his short stories and in some of his novels. The very first story in *Galpaguccha*, 'The Ghat's Story', captures Tagore's close engagement with the rural world of Bengal.

The experience of witnessing the lives of the poor had a profound impact on Rabindranath's view of history. In 1904 he argued in an essay, 'Swadeshi Samaj' (Indian Society), that in India the warring and hunting of kings had never affected in any way the organization of rural society. The latter was the object of utter indifference and shameless exploitation by the government and the local landlords. He invoked the same idea with greater clarity in an essay entitled 'Sahitye Aitihasikata' (Historicality in Literature), written in May 1941 (possibly his last prose piece). Towards the end of that essay, he went back to his youthful travels:

Once when I used to travel by boat along the rivers of Bengal and came to sense its playful vitality, my inner soul delighted in gathering those wonderful impressions of weal and woe in my heart which were composed into sketches of country life month after month . . . There is no doubt that the rural scenes surveyed by the poet in those days were affected by the conflicts of political history. However . . . what came to be reflected in *Galpaguccha* was not the image of a feudal order nor indeed any political order at all, but that history of the weal and woe of human life which, with its everyday contentment and misery, has always been there in the peasants' fields and village festivals, manifesting their simple and abiding humanity across all of history – sometimes under Mughal rule, sometimes under British rule. I am not acquainted with at least three-quarters of that far-flung history in which the critics of today wander about so extensively. That is why I guess it upsets me so much. I have in my mind to say, 'Off with your history'.

History, for Rabindranath, was in the rhythms of the quotidian.

History, or the history that Rabindranath would come to loathe and reject, impinged on his life in a very significant way at the beginning of the twentieth century. In 1901, when he turned forty, his enormous creative output of twenty-one books were collected in one volume. But events in Bengal were soon to sweep him unexpectedly into politics. In 1905 the Viceroy, Lord Curzon, formally announced that Bengal would be partitioned into two provinces. The official reason given was that of administrative expediency. But the real reason was to separate Bengal into a Hindu-majority area and a Muslim-majority area so that Hindus and Muslims could not come together to oppose British rule. Rabindranath, together with other members of the Bengali intelligentsia, was steadfastly opposed to this proposal to divide Bengal and Bengalis. On 16 October 1905 – Partition Day, on which Calcutta observed a *hartal* (general strike) – a group which included several eminent people, Rabindranath to the fore, gathered early in the morning and went first to the river Hooghly to take a dip. After this, they tied *rakhis* (bands that symbolized brotherhood) on each other's wrists. Rabindranath recalled that he tied rakhis on the wrists of whoever he met; not even policemen were left out. On the same day, he was present at two large public meetings. He lent his support to build a national fund and on the very first day of the launch of the fund Rs 30,000 was raised. In the course of his involvement with the anti-Partition movement, Rabindranath composed a number of memorable patriotic songs. Among these were 'Amar sonar Bangla' (My Golden Bengal) which was to become in 1971 the national anthem of Bangladesh, and 'Jadi tor dak shune keu na ashe tobe ekla cholo re' (If no one listens to your call, walk alone) which became one of Gandhi's favourite songs. As Ezra Pound was to say later, Tagore 'has sung Bengal into a nation'.

One of the key elements in the movement was the idea of *swadeshi* – the boycott of foreign goods and the use of Indian ones. Rabindranath championed this idea. But he went a step further. He wrote:

The salt from Liverpool and the cloth from Manchester does not harm us so much. But voluntarily accepting foreign customs and getting tied to them distorts our mind . . . The last fortress of our freedom is our heart – the key to that is in our own hands, the king does not have the strength to enter there. If we ourselves allow foreign customs to work there, then we will be reduced to the plight of beggars and gain the humiliation of slaves.

As the movement gained momentum what dismayed Rabindranath was the deployment of coercion. He wrote about the various ways through which the boycott was being imposed on those who refused to obey the call – from threatening that their forefathers would rot in hell to stopping their essential services (barber, washerman, etc.), burning their houses and publicly thrashing them. He emphasized that the main victims of such acts of coercion were invariably the poor and members of the lower classes whose interests the movement had sought to suppress. Boycott, Rabindranath argued, was dividing the people because it was not based on voluntary consent. He raised the ethical question of ends and means and pointed out that something noble and good could not be accomplished by force and violence. His growing disillusionment made him turn away from the movement and focus on village reconstruction.

In 1906–7 he had spoken about the need to start from what he called, in some of his essays, 'village patriotism'. At the heart of this was the welfare of the villages – education, cleaning ponds, building roads, preventing the oppression of the weak by the strong. These activities he saw as the responsibility of the people themselves, not of external agencies such as the state. He practised what he preached and he pursued the project of village reconstruction on his own landed estates. The outcome of his efforts was considerable – on his estates in Kaligram and Selaidah, for example, three free health centres, more than two hundred primary schools, as well as night schools for adults, numerous public works and a rural bank to fight the moneylenders. It was this very close exposure to rural life that led to a disillusionment of a different kind. He expressed this in a letter written in July 1908: 'Having seen all this [caste-ridden Hindu society that hindered rural reconstruction], I no longer feel any desire to "idealize" the Hindu *samaj* [society] through delusions pleasant to the ear but ultimately suicidal.' The prayer-like poem quoted earlier, 'Give me the strength never to disown the poor . . .', began to acquire a salience in Rabindranath's activities. He became acutely conscious of the parasitical position of the zamindar. To his son-in-law, Nagendranath Gangopadhyay, whom he had sent abroad, along with his own son Rathindranath, to study agricultural science, Rabindranath wrote on

29 October 1907: 'Remember that the landlord's wealth is actually the peasants': they are bearing the cost of your education by starving or half-starving themselves. It is your responsibility to repay this debt in full. That is your first task, even before the welfare of your own family.'

The other area to which Rabindranath devoted his attention was education. In 1862 his father, Debendranath, had bought some property in Bolpur in the district of Birbhum in West Bengal. Debendranath had handed over the property to a board of trustees and had specified in the trust deed that the space was to be used for meditation on the formless supreme being. On the property had been established a temple of worship, a site for prayer and a dwelling-place called Santiniketan (the Abode of Peace). In 1901 Rabindranath decided to start an experimental school at Santiniketan, which would be modelled on the forest hermitages of ancient India. Pointing out where his 'school' differed from others, Rabindranath wrote:

From our very childhood habits are formed and knowledge is imparted in such a manner that our life is weaned away from nature and our mind and the world are set in opposition from the beginning of our days. Thus the greatest of educations for which we come prepared is neglected, and we are made to lose our world to find a bagful of information instead. We rob the child of his earth to teach him geography, of language to teach him grammar.

As the school expanded, Rabindranath's vision for Santiniketan took on global dimensions. Ideas about international co-operation on educational projects began to germinate in his mind when he visited England in 1912. His aim was to see and understand the educational methods of the West. He also wanted people to know of what he was trying to do at Santiniketan. One of the outstanding people he attracted to his cause was Charles Freer Andrews, an Anglican missionary (he had taught at St Stephen's College in Delhi), social reformer and supporter of Indian nationalism. In 1914 he gave up the priesthood and went to Santiniketan where he spent his life teaching and working alongside Rabindranath. In 1921 Rabindranath achieved his aim of establishing alongside his school a university, to which he gave the name Visva-Bharati, choosing its motto from a Vedic text, 'Yatra Visvam Bharati Ekanirham' – Where the world makes its home in a single nest. He was keen to attract the finest international scholars and a number responded to his call – Sylvain Lévi, the renowned French orientalist, who became the first Visiting Professor at Visva-Bharati, the young agricultural scientist Leonard Knight Elmhirst, the Viennese art historian Stella Kramrisch. The famous economist, Amartya Sen, who was a student at Visva-Bharati in the 1940s, recalls in his memoir, *Home in the World*, how classes were held in the open, close to nature and how there was no pressure to perform and do well.

In the villages around Santiniketan, Rabindranath pursued his project of reconstruction and social welfare. His aim was to structure the economy of these villages to make the people self-reliant in an environment where the guiding principle would not be self-interest but co-operation. He wrote:

The symptoms of our miseries cannot be removed from the outside; their causes must be extirpated from within. If we wish to do this, we must undertake two tasks; first, to educate everyone in the land, so as to unite them mentally with all the world . . . Secondly, to unite them among themselves in the sphere of their livelihood, so as to bring about their union with the world through their work.

Rabindranath's trip to England turned out to be momentous in an unexpected way unrelated to his educational enterprises. He had carried with him his own translations of some of his poems, mostly from *Gitanjali* (Song Offering). He showed these translations to the painter William Rothenstein (whom he had met in Calcutta in 1910) who in turn showed them to the poet William Butler Yeats. Yeats read the poems aloud to a gathering of writers and intellectuals at Rothenstein's and then again at a dinner for seventy people given for Tagore by the India Society and *The Nation*, proposing in his toast: 'I know of no man in my time who has done anything in the English language to equal these lyrics. Even as I read them in this literal prose translation, they are as exquisite in style as in thought.' That same year an English translation of *Gitanjali* was published in England. The next year the Nobel Prize in Literature was awarded to

Rabindranath – he was the first non-European to receive it – and two years later a knighthood was bestowed on him. After only four years he renounced his knighthood following the massacre on 13 April 1919 at Jallianwala Bagh in Amritsar where Brigadier-General Dyer ordered his soldiers to fire into a peaceful crowd in an enclosed garden, killing and injuring hundreds. In his letter of renunciation written at the end of May 1919 and addressed to Lord Chelmsford, the then Viceroy, Rabindranath described the massacre and the repressive measures that came in its aftermath as being 'without parallel in the history of civilized governments, barring some conspicuous exceptions, recent and remote'. He said the British Empire in India possessed the 'most terribly efficient organization for destruction of human lives . . .' Under these circumstances, he continued:

The time has come when badges of honour make our shame glaring in their incongruous context of humiliation, and I for my part wish to stand shorn of all special distinctions, by the side of those of my countrymen who for their so-called insignificance, are liable to suffer a degradation not fit for human beings. And these are the reasons which have painfully compelled me to ask Your Excellency, with due deference and regret, to relieve me of my title of Knighthood . . .

Through the 1920s and the 1930s, until age and ill health began to plague him, Rabindranath travelled within India and across the world – to the USA, to Japan, to Europe, to Latin America, to China and Soviet Russia – spreading his message of universal humanism and international co-operation. His message of universal humanism went hand in hand with a rejection of nationalism and blind patriotism. As early as 1908, he had written to a friend that

patriotism cannot be our final spiritual shelter. I will not buy glass for the price of diamonds, and I will never allow patriotism to triumph over humanity as long as I live. I took a few steps down that road and stopped: for when I cannot retain my faith in universal man standing over and above my country, when patriotic prejudices overshadow my God, I feel inwardly starved.

Wherever he went he gave lectures and raised funds for Visva-Bharati; towards the end of his life he became increasingly worried about the future of this cherished institution. Rabindranath's travels in no way affected his creative activity. He continued to write songs, novels, plays, essays and textbooks for children. Some of his most moving and profound poems were written in his last years. And in the late 1920s he added a new facet to his creativity. He began to paint.

Rabindranath had no formal training as a painter. His growing interest in visual expression can be traced through the doodles that he made in the margins of his manuscripts. These doodles over time began to acquire imaginary and grotesque forms. Instead of simply deleting words or sentences, Rabindranath would elaborate on the cancellations or emendations to create patterns or figures and then sometimes he would string them together so that a page of a manuscript was transformed into a visual image. From such beginnings, Rabindranath took to painting – sometimes abstract, sometimes inventing fantastical plants and animals. He also painted human figures – often women – portraits and landscapes. His landscapes were almost always dark, his colours were earthy but many of his paintings, as Satyajit Ray, the film-maker, remarked, 'evoked . . . . a joyous freedom'. His paintings and drawings, uninfluenced by any artist, Western or Eastern, numbered over two thousand. They were utterly original.

The diversity of Rabindranath's creative oeuvre matched that of his work in the sphere of education and social reform. He himself said that he was a 'messenger of variety' and on his seventy-fourth birthday described his life as 'a garland of many Rabindranaths'. In literature he made lyric poetry the anchor of his creativity. His poems range from Bengali verse-forms to sonnets and blank verse that he imbibed from Western literature and adapted for the Bengali language. Many of his later poems were composed in free verse. His themes are similarly varied: simple human concerns; love, both human and devotional; the natural world; politics. There is satire, humour, and even nonsense. He shows a sensitivity to the world of children and women. The mood of his poetry at times seems to reflect the various seasons, moving seamlessly from the uncomplicated to the philosophically profound. In the words of Professor Sukanta Chaudhuri, a leading authority on Rabindranath, he 'sets out to be the poet of everything there is, and succeeds in improbable measure in this impossible venture'.

Much of Rabindranath's poetry was inextricably linked to his songs. He had no formal training in music, but he was born with an unerring ear and, before age took its toll, a powerful and outstanding singing voice. His musical compositions were eclectic. He drew from Western tunes and ballads as well as from North Indian and Carnatic classical music and from various types of Bengali music-making, especially from the *bauls* (wandering folk singers). Many of his songs are stirring, moving and patriotic (one such song, 'Jana gana mana adhinayaka' – Thou art the ruler of the minds of all people – is the national anthem of India); others celebrate nature. His best songs are invariably touched by an ineffable poignancy. His love songs blur the distinction between the profane and the sacred. There has been no lyricist and music-maker like him in the Bengali language. Bengalis remember Rabindranath through his songs – in their festivals, in their joy and in their sorrow.

Rabindranath's prose fiction consists of his short stories, his novels and novellas. The immediate context of his early short stories has already been discussed. When he was barely twenty, he began his first novel, *Bauthakuranir hat* (The Young Queen's Market), inspired by the work of Bankim Chandra Chatto-padhyay, whose novels he read with great enthusiasm and attention. For Rabindranath, his prose fiction, like much of his creative endeavour, was a world of experimentation: in form, in themes and in narrative techniques. In the very first story of *Galpaguccha*, 'The Ghat's Story', he made the *ghat*, the steps or the landing site of a riverbank, the narrator. In *Ghare Baire* (The Home and the World), the novel unfolds through the narrative voices of the three principal characters, each of them presenting an account from their own perspective. In other novels, most notably in *Gora*, he followed a linear narrative. *Gora* traces the eponymous protagonist's journey from orthodox Hindu, working restlessly among the rural poor, to the discovery, first, of his true identity as the orphan child of Irish parents – his father had died during the 1857 revolt, his mother in childbirth – and then, in a moment of epiphany, of the rich plurality of Indian-ness represented by his adoptive mother Anandamayi, who had brought him up, eschewing all the caste taboos, as her own son. In his novels, as well as in some of his short stories, he examined the world of domesticity and the complex web of human relationships embedded within the home and the family. One of the most remarkable features of his fictional world was Rabindranath's exploration and depiction of the lives of women – their interiority, their anguish, the discrimination and neglect they suffered, and their strengths. All these are manifest most powerfully in 'Nashtanirh' (The Broken Nest, which Satyajit Ray made into a film called *Charulata*), and in 'Streer Patra' (The Wife's Letter). Rabindranath, however, did not restrict himself to merely representing the condition of women; through Damini, one of the main characters in *Chaturanga* (Quartet), he sought to portray the quest of a women to liberate herself from sorrow and seek independence and personal fulfilment. Her quest remains incomplete but is no less poignant and moving for that. In some ways, Rabindranath's own walks through what Umberto Eco has tellingly called 'the fictional woods' remain incomplete because he was forever experimenting with themes, form and language.

The mention of language is important: through his prose in both his fiction and his discursive essays, Rabindranath actually shaped and moulded the modern Bengali language. He built upon the legacy of Bankim Chandra but chose not to adopt the latter's highly Sanskritized Bengali. Rabindranath was a self-conscious stylist and his style never remained static. He broke from tradition and broke again and again from his own style. He refused to conform even with the standards he himself had set. All these features made him a supreme creative figure not just of his own time and his own country.

As the Second World War raged, Rabindranath, appalled by 'the orgy of terror' unleashed in Europe, wrote an address in Bengali for his eightieth birthday celebrations at Santiniketan in 1941. He titled the speech 'Sabhyatar Sankat' (Crisis in Civiliza-tion) and it is often and rightly considered his last testament. In this address, Rabindranath announced his complete disillusion-ment with Western civilization and its vehicle in India, British rule. He admitted that his initial fascination for things British had grown out of his profound admiration for English literature. But he had pulled himself away from his preoccupation with literature and, when faced with the reality that was India, had come to recognize that the standard-bearers of civilization could disown their standards when it suited their self-interest. The poverty of the people, the absence of basic amenities like food, clothes, water, education and health made it evident that the so-called civilized race was utterly and contemptuously indifferent to the sufferings of millions of Indians. He was forced to admit to himself that in no other state with a modern administration had such neglect occurred. Rabindranath was no longer willing to describe British civilization as civilization.

In spite of this disillusionment and the ruin and devastation that he saw all around the world, Rabindranath refused to abandon hope. The address ends, as the last article of his creed, with a cry of hope:

I had at one time believed that the springs of civilization would issue out of the heart of Europe. But today when I am about to quit the world that faith has gone bankrupt altogether. As I look around I see the crumbling ruins of a proud civilization strewn like a vast heap of futility. And yet I shall not commit the grievous sin of losing faith in Man. I would rather look forward to the opening of a new chapter in his history after the cataclysm is over and the atmosphere rendered clean with the spirit of service and sacrifice. Perhaps that dawn will come from this horizon, from the East where the sun rises. A day will come when unvanquished Man will retrace his path of conquest, despite all barriers, to win back his lost human heritage.

Rabindranath's faith in 'unvanquished Man' was an integral part of his world view which drew sustenance from the philosophy and the wisdom of the Upanishads. This faith had given him the strength to transcend great personal sorrow: the loss of his wife, Mrinalini, in 1902; the death of his second daughter, Renuka, the next year; and then the cruellest cut of all, the death of his youngest son, Samindranath, in 1907. (It needs to be underlined that it was precisely when Rabindranath was enduring this series of bereavements that he was involved in the anti-Partition protests.) It was from the Upanishads that Rabindranath derived his sense of piety and the idea that strength had to be organic and internal. But his faith and piety were not blind; they were capacious enough to admit questions and radical doubt. In 1926, as he witnessed religious riots, he wrote, 'Honest atheism is much better than this terrifying deluded religion . . . I cannot see any solution except to burn all India's misguided religious faith in the flames of atheism and make an absolute fresh start.' In 1939, when he heard an account about a young girl who had been raped and murdered, he cried out: 'The godly faith of the scriptures scatters with the dust. The sky rings out: there is no escape, no redress.'

The doubt was most starkly expressed in the poem 'Question' (1931). Addressing God, the poet begins, 'Era after era you have sent messengers who preached love and forgiveness . . .' but at the end he asks, 'Those who have made your air toxic, put out your light, have you forgiven them, have you loved them?' The question unanswered – and unanswerable – constitutes a radical doubt. Rabindranath lived with such unanswered questions. In one of his last poems composed on 27 July 1941, eleven days before his death – he posed yet another one:

> The sun of the first day
> Had asked the question
> At the new emergence of Being
> Who are you –
> No answer was found
> Years and years passed
> The day's last sun
> Uttered the last question on the shores of the western sea
> Who are you –
> Did not get an answer.

Perhaps because of his doubt, he could describe, in his very last poem, life and creation to be deceptive. Through his multi-faceted creativity, his questions and doubts and his unswerving hope in humanity, Rabindranath left behind a legacy which the world can ignore only at its own intellectual impoverishment and peril.

RABINDRANATH TAGORE

*

The selection that follows is of course a very small part of Rabindranath's prolific output. The attempt has been to present all the aspects of his creativity save his paintings and his letters. Each section is chronologically arranged. The notes at the back provide dates of publication, the names of the translators and the sources.

I am grateful to Gopalkrishna Gandhi for his most valuable comments on a draft of the Introduction.

Rudrangshu Mukherjee

RUDRANGSHU MUKHERJEE is Chancellor and Professor of History at Ashoka University of which he was the founding Vice Chancellor. He holds a D.Phil. in Modern History from the University of Oxford. He taught at the University of Calcutta and has held visiting appointments at Princeton University and the University of California, Santa Cruz amongst others. He was the Editor, Editorial Pages, *The Telegraph*. He is internationally acclaimed as a historian of the revolt of 1857 in India, on which he has published six books. He has also written on other themes relating to the history of modern India. His most recent book is *Tagore & Gandhi: Walking Alone, Walking Together*.

SELECT BIBLIOGRAPHY

(Only books in English)

ALAM, FAKRUL, and CHAKRAVARTY, RADHA (eds), *The Essential Tagore*, Harvard University Press, Cambridge MA and London, 2011.

BHATTACHARYA, SABYASACHI, *The Mahatma and the Poet: Letters and Debates Between Gandhi and Tagore*, National Book Trust, New Delhi, 1997.

CHATTERJEE, PARTHA, 'Tagore's Non-Nation' in the same author's *Lineages of Political Society: Studies in Postcolonial Democracy*, Permanent Black, Ranikhet, 2011.

CHAUDHURI, SUKANTA (ed.), *The Cambridge Companion to Rabindranath Tagore*, Cambridge University Press, Cambridge, 2020.

CHAUDHURI, SUKANTA (ed.), *Rabindranath Tagore: Selected Short Stories*; Oxford Tagore Translations, Oxford University Press, New Delhi, 2000.

CHAUDHURI, SUKANTA (ed.), *Rabindranath Tagore: Selected Writings for Children*, Oxford Tagore Translations, Oxford University Press, New Delhi, 2002.

CHAUDHURI, SUKANTA (ed.), *Rabindranath Tagore: Selected Poems*, Oxford Tagore Translations, Oxford University Press, New Delhi, 2004.

DAS, SISIR KUMAR (ed.), *The English Writings of Rabindranath Tagore*, 3 vols, Sahitya Akademi, New Delhi, 1994–6.

DAS GUPTA, UMA (ed.), *Friendships of 'Largeness and Freedom': Andrews, Tagore, and Gandhi: An Epistolary Account, 1912–1940*, Oxford University Press, New Delhi, 2018.

DUTTA, KRISHNA, and ROBINSON, ANDREW, *Rabindranath Tagore: The Myriad-Minded Man*, Bloomsbury, London, 1995.

GANGULY, SWATI, *Tagore's University: A History of Visva-Bharati, 1921–1961*, Permanent Black and Ashoka University, Ranikhet, 2022.

GHOSH, NITYAPRIYA, *The English Writings of Rabindranath Tagore*, vol. 4, Sahitya Akademi, New Delhi, 2007.

MUKHERJEE, RUDRANGSHU, 'The Last Testament', *Seminar*, No. 623, July 2011.

MUKHERJEE, RUDRANGSHU, *Tagore & Gandhi: Walking Alone, Walking Together*, Aleph Book Company, New Delhi, 2021.

RADICE, WILLIAM (edited and translated), *Rabindranath Tagore: Selected Poems*, Penguin, London, 1985 (reprinted 2005).

RADICE, WILLIAM (edited and translated), *Rabindranath Tagore: Selected Short Stories*, Penguin, London, 1991.

RAY, SATYAJIT, 'Portrait of a Man' in *The UNESCO Courier*, Dec. 1961.

SEN, AMARTYA, *The Argumentative Indian: Writings on Indian History, Culture and Identity*, Allen Lane, London, 2005.

SEN, AMARTYA, *Home in the World: A Memoir*, Allen Lane, London, 2021.

THOMPSON, E. P., *Alien Homage: Edward Thompson and Rabindranath Tagore*, Oxford University Press, New Delhi, 1993.

CHRONOLOGY

DATE	AUTHOR'S LIFE	LITERARY CONTEXT
1861	Born 7 May 1861 at Jorasanko, the Tagore family seat in north Calcutta (Kolkata), Bengal, the fourteenth, and youngest child of Maharshi Debendranath Tagore and Sarada Devi.	Michael Madhusudan Datta: *Meghnadbadh Kavya* and *Brajangana Kavya*. Charles Dickens: *Great Expectations*.
1862	His father buys land at Bolpur in West Bengal, which is later developed into Santiniketan, a place of meditation and worship.	Michael Madhusudan Datta: *Birangana Kavya*.
1863	His second-eldest brother, Satyendranath Tagore, enters the Indian Civil Service examinations in London and becomes the first Indian to qualify.	
1864		Bankim Chandra Chatterjee: *Rajmohan's Wife*. Alfred Tennyson: *Enoch Arden*.
1865		Bankim Chandra Chatterjee: *Durgesnandini*. Matthew Arnold: *Essays in Criticism* (and 1888). Dickens: *Our Mutual Friend*.
1866		Bankim Chandra Chatterjee: *Kapalkundala*.

Indian Councils Act 1861 reforms the Viceroy's Executive Council, which becomes a cabinet comprising 'ordinary members' heading separate departments, and also includes several non-official Indian members; the viceregal veto is retained.

Indian Civil Services Act passed, allowing Indians to compete in recruitment examinations. However, the examinations are held in Britain, and the syllabus favours British candidates.

American Civil War begins, increasing the market value of Indian raw cotton.

Lancashire Cotton Famine (to 1865).

Proclamation of the Kingdom of Italy.

Emancipation of serfs in Russia.

Lord Elgin replaces Lord Canning as Viceroy of India.

Death of Lord Elgin. Sir Robert Napier and subsequently Sir William Denison appointed as acting Viceroys.

Death of Dost Mohammad Khan, Emir of Afghanistan, triggering a civil war between his sons.

Abraham Lincoln's Emancipation Proclamation.

Sir John Lawrence becomes Viceroy of India.

Shimla made the 'summer capital' of the British Raj.

Duar (Anglo-Bhutan) War (to 1865).

Indian customs duty, introduced in 1860 to contribute towards repayment of lost revenue in the 1857–9 Rebellion, reduced from 10 to 7%.

International Working Men's Association (First International) founded in London.

First Geneva Convention.

American Civil War ends (with Union victory), leading to decreased demand for Indian raw cotton and a consequent market crash.

Beginning of cycle of famines in India following market downturns in commercial agriculture.

Assassination of US President Abraham Lincoln. Thirteenth Amendment abolishes non-penal slavery.

Keshab Chunder Sen leaves the Brahmo Samaj after doctrinal disagreement with Debendranath Tagore; forms the rival Bharatvarshiya Brahmo Samaj.

Orissa Famine, and laissez-faire British policy, lead to over one million deaths.

Fenians active in Ireland: Habeas Corpus suspended in Ireland.

Ku Klux Klan started in US.

DATE	AUTHOR'S LIFE	LITERARY CONTEXT
1867	Attends the first Hindu Mela.	
1868	Formal schooling begins at the Oriental Seminary, then the Normal School, Calcutta.	Robert Browning: *The Ring and the Book* (to 1869). Wilkie Collins: *The Moonstone*. William Wilson Hunter: *The Annals of Rural Bengal*.
1869		Bankim Chandra Chatterjee: *Mrinalini*. Alfonse Daudet: *Letters from My Windmill*. Tennyson: *The Holy Grail*. Leo Tolstoy: *War and Peace*.
1870		Death of Charles Dickens. *The Mystery of Edwin Drood* (unfinished) published.
1871	Begins to attend the Anglo-Indian Bengal Academy.	Charles Darwin: *The Descent of Man*. Fyodor Dostoevsky: *Demons* (to 1872).
1872		George Eliot: *Middlemarch*. Thomas Hardy: *Under the Greenwood Tree*.

CHRONOLOGY

Proportion of British to Indian soldiers in the armies reaches 65,000 to 140,000 following efforts to increase British troop numbers as part of post-1857 restructuring.

Nabagopal Mitra founds the Hindu Mela, a festival in Calcutta promoting indigenous religion and culture. It is supported by the Tagore family; Ganendranath Tagore becomes its first secretary.

Fenian Rising in Ireland, and subsequent attacks in England.

Second Reform Act in Britain.

Shir 'Ali Khan becomes Emir of Afghanistan following the civil war, and is endorsed by the Viceroy, Sir John Lawrence.

British expedition to Abyssinia and victory at the Battle of Magdala.

Gladstone's first Liberal ministry (to 1874).

Lord Mayo replaces Sir John Lawrence as Viceroy of India.

Ambala meeting between Lord Mayo and Shir 'Ali Khan, at which the latter's call for increased British support is unheeded.

India's railway network reaches over 5,000 miles (8,000 km).

Rajputana Famine.

Opening of the Suez Canal, enabling steamers to travel between Britain and India in approximately three weeks.

Disestablishment of the Protestant Church of Ireland.

Poona Sarvajanik Sabha (Poona Public Society) established to take up Indian grievances with the British government. Mahadev Govind Ranade becomes a leading figure.

England and India linked by telegraph, transforming communications.

Gladstone's first Irish Land Act.

Elementary Education Act in England and Wales.

Competitive examination introduced in the Civil Service in Britain.

Franco-Prussian War (to 1871).

Rome and the Papal States incorporated into the Kingdom of Italy.

Fifth Buddhist Council at Mandalay called by Mindon, King of Burma (Myanmar).

Paris Commune suppressed. Wilhelm I of Prussia declared German Emperor at Versailles; Bismarck becomes Chancellor. Third Republic created in France.

Meeting of Stanley and Livingstone at Ujiji.

Edward Burnett Tylor's *Primitive Culture* applies Darwin's methods to the science of anthropology.

Indian census records a population of around 200 million.

Assassination of Lord Mayo at the Andaman Islands penal colony by the Afghan Sher Ali Afridi, who is subsequently executed.

Lord Northbrook becomes Viceroy.

Bankim Chandra Chatterjee founds the newspaper *Bangadarsan*.

Secret ballot in British elections imposed by law.

Disraeli's Crystal Palace speech exalting the Crown as focus of the new imperialism.

DATE	AUTHOR'S LIFE	LITERARY CONTEXT
1873	First acquaintance with the Sanskrit Upanishads. Partakes in the Upanayan (sacred thread) ceremony, inducting him into Brahminism. Expedition to Dalhousie in the Himalayas with his father. En route visits Santiniketan for the first time, and the Sikh Golden Temple at Amritsar.	Bankim Chandra Chatterjee: *Bishabriksha* and *Indira*. Sayyid Ahmad Khan: *Causes of the Indian Revolt*.
1874	Publishes first poem, 'Abhilasha' (Desire) in *Tattwabodhini Patrika*, a newspaper established by his father.	Bankim Chandra Chatterjee: *Yugalanguriya*.
1875	Attends St Xavier's School, Calcutta. Reads his poem 'Hindu Mela's Gift' at the Hindu Mela (Feb), attracting the attention of the playwright Nabinchandra Sen. Death of his mother (March). Composes first song for his brother Jyotirindranath's play, *Sarojini*.	Bankim Chandra Chatterjee: *Radharani* and *Chandrasekhar*. Nabinchandra Sen: *Palashir Yuddha*.
1876	Henceforward educated by tutors at home. Participates in Jyotirindranath's fledgling clandestine revolutionary society, Sanjibani Sabha.	Swarnakumari Devi: (Tagore's sister) *Dipnirban*.
1877	Joins editorial staff of *Bharati*, a journal newly founded by Jyotirindranath; his own contributions include his debut long poem *Kabikahini* (A Poet's Tale), a short story *Bhikharini* (The Beggar Woman) and his (unfinished) first novel *Karuna* (Pity, to 1878). Recites poem satirizing Lord Lytton's Delhi Durbar at the Hindu Mela.	Bankim Chandra Chatterjee: *Rajani*. Helena Blavatsky: *Isis Unveiled*.
1878	*Kabikahini* published as a book. Stays for four months at Ahmedabad with his brother Satyendranath, now a judge, improving his English by	Bankim Chandra Chatterjee: *Krishnakanter Will*. Blavatsky: *From the Caves and Jungles of Hindustan* (to 1886). Tolstoy: *Anna Karenina*.

CHRONOLOGY

HISTORICAL EVENTS

Bihar Famine (to 1874). Pabna Peasant Uprisings in Bengal (to 1876).
Irish Home Rule League founded.

Disraeli Prime Minister (to 1880), following aggressive imperial and military
policy in South Africa, the Balkans and the Mediterranean.
First Impressionist exhibition in Paris.

Swami Dayananda Sarasvati establishes the Arya Samaj, a reformist Hindu
organization in Bombay (Mumbai).
Sir Sayyid Ahmad Khan establishes the Anglo-Muhammadan Oriental
College at Aligarh.
Theosophical Society founded by Helena Blavatsky and Henry Steel Olcott.

Lord Northbrook resigns as Viceroy over the British government's opposition
to his non-interventionist stance on Afghanistan; replaced by Lord Lytton.
Madras Famine (to 1878), in which 4–5 million people die.
Royal Titles Act, Queen Victoria styled Empress of India.
Indian Association established in Bengal by Surendranath Banerjea and
Ananda Mohan Bose.
Alexander Graham Bell invents the telephone.
The first Delhi Durbar, celebrating the proclamation of Queen Victoria as
Empress of India.
Jamsetji Nusserwanji Tata opens the Empress Mills in Nagpur.
Russo–Turkish War (to 1878).

Second Anglo-Afghan War (to 1880).
Death of Mindon, King of Burma; succession of Thibaw.
The Sadharan Brahmo Samaj breaks away from Keshab Chunder Sen's
Brahmo Samaj of India.
Vernacular Press Act allows government of India to censor English-language

DATE	AUTHOR'S LIFE	LITERARY CONTEXT
1878 cont.	reading English literature. They travel to England (Sept), with a view to his studying law. Based in Hove with his sister-in-law and her young children, he briefly attends Brighton Proprietary School.	
1879	Moved to lodgings in London (Jan); private tutors engaged. Attends several sessions of the House of Commons, hearing Gladstone speak and witnessing Frank Hugh O'Donnell's opposition to the Press Act in India. Writes poem 'Bhagna Tari' (The Wrecked Boat) and 'Chatterton, the Boy-poet', literary criticism, published in *Bharati*. From June lodges with Dr Scott and his family in London. Enters Faculty of Arts and Law at University College London (Nov), where he admires the teaching of Henry Morley.	Dostoevesky: *The Brothers Karamazov* (to 1880). Henry James: *Daisy Miller*.
1880	Summoned home by his father, he arrives in India (March) having gained no qualifications.	
1881	Publishes *Letters from an Expatriate in Europe* and his first non-fiction collection, *Vividha Prasanga* (Miscellaneous Topics). Writes and stages *Valmiki Pratibha* (Genius of Valmiki), an operetta. Delivers his debut public lecture, on music, for the Bethune Society in Calcutta. Attempt to return to England to study law aborted at Madras when the nephew accompanying him falls ill (April); visits his father at Mussoorie. Stays with Jyotirindranath and his wife Kadambari in Chandernagore and Calcutta.	Bankim Chandra Chatterjee: *Rajsimha*. James: *The Portrait of a Lady*. William Wilson Hunter: *The Imperial Gazetteer of India*.

papers; meets with major opposition, particularly from the Indian
Association.
Congress of Berlin.
Cyprus becomes a British protectorate.

Viceroy Lytton, rejecting the unanimous advice of the Executive Council,
removes tax on processed British cotton imports.
Death of Shir 'Ali Khan, Emir of Afghanistan.
Treaty of Gandamak agreed with his successor, Ya'qub Khan.
Assassination of Sir Louis Cavagnari, British resident in Kabul; second
British invasion deposes Ya'qub Khan.
Visit of Helena Blavatsky to India; meets Swami Dayananda Sarasvati.
Bethune College founded in Calcutta, the first women's college in Asia.
Gladstone's Midlothian Campaign (to 1880).
Anglo-Zulu War.

Lord Ripon replaces Lord Lytton as Viceroy of India.
'Abd al-Rahman Khan becomes Emir of Afghanistan.
Liberals win majority in general election; Gladstone Prime Minister (to 1885).
Charles Stewart Parnell elected leader of the Irish Parliamentary Party
(Home Rule Party).
First Boer War (to 1881).
Viceroy Ripon repeals the Vernacular Press Act.
Bal Gangadhar Tilak founds the newspapers *Mahratta*, published in English,
and *Kesari* (Lion), published in Marathi.
Licences granted to Oriental Telephone Company to establish telephone
exchanges in Calcutta, Madras, Bombay and Rangoon (Yangon).
Gladstone's second Irish Land Act.
Tsar Alexander II assassinated in Russia.
Fenian dynamite campaign in Britain (to 1885).

DATE	AUTHOR'S LIFE	LITERARY CONTEXT
1882	Publishes *Sandhya Sangeet* (Evening Songs) – praised by Bankim Chandra Chatterjee. Ultimately unsuccessful efforts with Jyotirindranath and Rajendrahal Mitra to found a Bengali Literary Academy. The brothers visit Darjeeling.	Bankim Chandra Chatterjee: *Anandamath*.
1883	Publishes *Prabhat Sangeet* (Morning Songs) and *Bou-Thakuranir Haat* (The Young Queen's Market), a novel. His father puts him in charge of the family estates, subject to successful training. The family select Bhabatarini, aged 10, daughter of an estate employee, as his bride. After wedding (9 Dec) she lives at Jorasanko and her name is changed to Mrinalini.	Tr. Richard Burton & F. F. Arbuthnot: *The Kama Sutra of Vatsyayana*.
1884	Publishes *Prakritir Pratishodh* (Nature's Revenge), a play, and *Chhabi o Gan* (Pictures and Songs). Deeply affected by the suicide of his sister-in-law Kadambari, aged 25. Writes, though does not publish, *Pushpanjali* (Offering of Flowers), addressed to Kadambari. Death of his brother, Hemendranath.	Bankim Chandra Chatterjee: *Debi Chaudhurani*. Henrik Ibsen: *The Wild Duck*.
1885	Publishes *Alochona* (Discussions), a collection of essays.	Tennyson: *Tiresias*.
1886	Birth of his first child, his daughter Madhurilata (Bela). Publishes *Karhi o Kamal* (Sharps and Flats), a collection of poetry.	Bankim Chandra Chatterjee: *Sitaram*. Prafulla Chandra Ray: *India Before and After the Mutiny*. Rudyard Kipling: *Departmental Ditties*.

HISTORICAL EVENTS

Headquarters of the Theosophical Society established at Adyar, near Madras (Chennai).
Murder of the British Chief Secretary for Ireland and the Permanent Under-Secretary in Phoenix Park, Dublin.
Egypt becomes a de facto British protectorate.
Germany, Austria-Hungary and Italy sign Triple Alliance.

The Indian National Conference in Bengal established by Surendranath Banerjea.

Lord Dufferin replaces Lord Ripon as Viceroy.
Third Reform Act in Britain.
Fabian Society founded in London.
Berlin Conference called to regulate European colonization of Africa; the 'scramble for Africa' nonetheless continues.

Indian National Congress (Congress Party) founded; first meeting in Bombay with 73 official and 10 unofficial representatives. Demands for increase in elected non-official representatives to the regional and national councils, equal access to the Indian Civil Service, retrenchment, and customs duties on imported British industrial goods.
Bengal Tenancy Act.
Trade treaty between Thibaw's Kingdom of Burma and France. Third Anglo-Burmese War.
Death of General Gordon at Khartoum.
British annexation of Upper Burma.
Gladstone's third ministry (Feb–July). First Irish Home Rule Bill defeated; Liberal Party splits. After general election Lord Salisbury forms a Unionist government (to 1892) of Conservatives in alliance with Liberal Unionists.

DATE	AUTHOR'S LIFE	LITERARY CONTEXT
1887	Delivers a public lecture on Hindu Marriage for the Savitri Sabha organization in Calcutta, criticizing child marriage.	Nabinchandra Sen: *Raivatak*. Stopford Brooke: *Poems* Hardy: *The Woodlanders*.
1888	Birth of his son, Rathindranath. *Mayar Khela* (Play of Illusion), written at the request of the Women's Theosophical Society, published and performed. His father sets up the Santiniketan Trust.	Anton Chekhov: *The Steppe*. Kipling: *Plain Tales from the Hills* and *The Phantom Rickshaw*. Oscar Wilde: *The Happy Prince*.
1889	The Emerald Theatre, Calcutta, produces his play *Raja o Rani* (King and Queen). Assumes the role of *zamindar*, with responsibility for the family estates in East Bengal (Nov), and stays at Selaidah on the houseboat *Padma*.	Blavatsky: *The Key to Theosophy*. Gerhart Hauptmann: *Before Dawn*. Tennyson: *Demeter*. Alfred Russel Wallace: *Darwinism*. W. B. Yeats: *The Wanderings of Oisin*.
1890	Publishes *Manasi* (Mind's Creation), poetry, and *Visarjan* (Sacrifice), a drama. Travels to England with Satyendranath and a friend (Aug), via Italy and France. Spends a short time in London. Interest in Western music. Homesick, returns to India (Oct).	Sylvain Lévi: *The Indian Theatre*.
1891	Birth of his daughter Renuka (Rani). Plays major role in new journal, *Sadhana*, founded by his brother Dwijendranath (to 1895). Completes verse drama *Chitrangada*. Festivities at Santiniketan marking the opening of the Brahmo Prayer Hall (Dec).	Hardy: *Tess of the D'Urbervilles*. Ibsen: *Hedda Gabler*. Wilde: *The Picture of Dorian Gray* and *Lord Arthur Savile's Crime*.
1892	During the 1890s embarks on judiciary reforms on his East Bengal estates, and sets up co-operative and self-reliance projects. Close contact with	Hauptmann: *The Weavers*. Kipling: *Barrack-Room Ballads*. Wilde: *Lady Windermere's Fan*.

HISTORICAL EVENTS

Pandit Shiv Narayan Agnihotri establishes the Dev Samaj (Divine Society) following split with the Brahmo Samaj.
Mahadev Govind Ranade establishes the Indian National Social Conference.
Queen Victoria's Golden Jubilee.
'Bloody Sunday': prohibited rally of radicals and Irish militants in Trafalgar Square broken up by police and troops.
Lord Lansdowne replaces Lord Dufferin as Viceroy.
Congress Party meeting attracts 1,248 delegates.
Fabian socialist Annie Besant champions the cause of the 'match girls' at the Bryant and May factory in London.

British Committee of the Indian National Congress established.

Cecil Rhodes becomes Prime Minister of Cape Colony.
Split in Irish Home Rule Party following Parnell's involvement in O'Shea divorce case.
Kaiser Wilhelm II dismisses Bismarck.

Bill to raise the age of consent for unmarried and married Indian girls from 10 to 12 years becomes law.
Death of Charles Stewart Parnell.

Indian Councils Act 1892, increasing the number of non-official members of the Central and Provincial Legislative Councils. More Indians were thereby included.
Gladstone forms fourth administration.

DATE	AUTHOR'S LIFE	LITERARY CONTEXT
1892 cont.	rural people and the natural world has profound effect on his literary work.	
1893	Increasing involvement with nationalist movement; writes around 35 major political essays between 1893 and 1908.	Alice Meynell: *Poems* and *The Rhythm of Life*.
1894	Birth of daughter Mira. Publishes *Chhoto Galpo*, his first short-story collection, and *Sonar Tari* (The Golden Boat), poems. Becomes Vice-President of the newly founded Bangiya Sahitya Parishad (Academy of Bengali Letters).	Kipling: *The Jungle Book*. Tolstoy: *The Kingdom of God is Within You*.
1895	Publishes *Galpa-Dasak*, a collection of short stories.	James: 'The Altar of the Dead'. H. G. Wells: *The Time Machine*. Wilde: *The Importance of Being Earnest*.
1896	Birth of son Samindranath (Sami). *Chaitali* (poems).	Abanindranath Tagore: *Khirer Putul*. Wells: *The Island of Doctor Moreau*.
1897	Sets up Swadeshi Bhandar to foster handicrafts in his Calcutta locality. Starts to build his own house on the Jorasanka estate. Raises money for Bal Gangadhar Tilak's defence, and reads a paper, 'Kantharodh' (The Throttle), at a public meeting in Calcutta, criticizing the Seditions Act.	Kipling: *Captains Courageous*. Mark Twain: *Following the Equator*. Wells: *The Invisible Man*.

Sir Mortimer Durand begins negotiations with the Emir of Afghanistan to determine the Indo-Afghan border.
First World's Parliament of Religions in Chicago, Vivekananda representing Hinduism. His opening speech (11 Sept), addressing 'Sisters and Brothers of America' and calling for religious toleration and an end to fanaticism, creates a sensation.
Independent Labour Party formed under Keir Hardie.
Second Irish Home Rule Bill is passed by the House of Commons but defeated in the Lords.
First Matabele War (to 1894).
Women enfranchised in New Zealand.
Reintroduction of customs duty on processed British cotton imports following a crash in the silver market.
Lord Elgin replaces Lord Lansdowne as Viceroy.
Gandhi (in South Africa 1893–1914) founds the Natal Indian Congress to oppose discrimination against Indians in the British colony.
Resignation of Gladstone.
Dreyfus case begins in France.

Jagadish Chandra Bose demonstrates wireless transmission via electromagnetic waves in Calcutta,
Salisbury forms Unionist ministry (to 1902), with Joseph Chamberlain as Colonial Secretary.
Rhodesia founded. Jameson Raid on the Transvaal.
Freud's *Studien über Hysterie* inaugurates psychoanalysis.
Trial and imprisonment of Oscar Wilde.
Bubonic plague arrives in Bombay.
Indian Famine (to 1897).
Establishment of the Durand Line, ceding some Afghan territory to British India following negotiations.
Second Matabele War (to 1897).
Anglo-Egyptian conquest of Sudan (to 1899).
Imprisonment of Bal Gangadhar Tilak on a charge of seditious writings.
Vivekananda establishes the Ramakrishna mission at Belur Math monastery near Calcutta.
Queen Victoria's Diamond Jubilee.
British punitive expedition destroys Benin City.

DATE	AUTHOR'S LIFE	LITERARY CONTEXT
1898	Becomes editor of *Bharati* (to 1903). Assists in plague relief efforts in Calcutta.	Swarnakumari Devi: *Kahake*. Lévi: *The Doctrine of Sacrifice in the Brahmanas*.
1899	Publishes *Katha* (Ballads). Death of his nephew Balendranath, who had worked with him at Selaidah and Santiniketan.	Chekhov: *Uncle Vanya*. Joseph Conrad: *Heart of Darkness*. Meynell: *The Spirit of Place*. Thomas Sturge Moore: *The Vinedresser*. Yeats: *The Wind Among the Reeds*.
1900	Publishes *Kahini* (Tales), *Kalpana* (Imaginings) and *Kshanika* (Moments), poetry collections.	Mahadev Govind Ranade: *Rise of the Maratha Power*. Conrad: *Lord Jim*. Sister Nivedita (Margaret Noble): *Kali the Mother*.
1901	Becomes editor of the literary journal *Bangadarshan*, owned by Bankimchandra Chatterjee (to 1905). Publishes *Naivedya* (Offering), poems, and *Nastanirh* (A Broken Nest), a novella. Two of his daughters are married – Bela, not quite 15, and Rani, aged 10. Opens a small school, Bamhacharya Ashram, at Santiniketan. Undertakes fundraising to support the scientific research of Jagadish Chandra Bose.	Goldsworthy Lowes Dickinson: *Letters from John Chinaman*. Kipling: *Kim*. Thomas Mann: *Buddenbrooks*. Bernard Shaw: *Three Plays for Puritans*.
1902	Death of his wife, Mrinalini, aged 29. Composes *Smaran* (In Remembrance), a series of poems in her memory.	Jagadish Chandra Bose: *Response in the Living and Non-Living*. Jane Addams: *Democracy and Social Ethics*. André Gide: *The Immoralist*. Kipling: *Just So Stories*. John Masefield: *Salt-Water Ballads*. Yeats: *Cathleen ni Houlihan*.

CHRONOLOGY

Amendment to Indian Penal Code expands definition of sedition.
Plague in Calcutta.
Sister Nivedita (Margaret Noble) opens her school for girls in Calcutta.
Death of Gladstone.
Britain and France clash in the Sudan (Fashoda incident).
Britain granted 99-year lease on Hong Kong by Chinese government.
First German Navy Law: arms race with Britain begins.
Indian Famine (to 1900).
Lord Curzon becomes Viceroy. During his period of office (to 1905) sets up numerous commissions resulting in a series of administrative, judicial, economic, industrial, agricultural and educational reforms. Police and railways reorganized. Causes of famine investigated.
Tribal uprising in the Chotanagpur region of West Bengal (to 1900) led by Birsa Munda, a religious visionary.
Second Boer War (to 1902).
Opening of the Irish Literary Theatre in Dublin (renamed the Abbey Theatre in 1904).
After a century of expansion the British Empire covers one fifth of the globe, home to one quarter of the world's population.
India's railway network reaches approximately 25,000 miles (40,000 km).
'Khaki' election backs Lord Salisbury's Unionist administration.
Irish Home Rule Party reunited under leadership of John Redmond.
Death of Queen Victoria, accession of King Edward VII.
North-West Frontier Province established by Lord Curzon, removing it from jurisdiction of the Punjab Province.
First Nobel prizes awarded.
Guglielmo Marconi successfully transmits first wireless signal across the Atlantic, from Cornwall to Newfoundland.

Beginning of the second Delhi Durbar (to 1903), celebrating the accession of King Edward VII as Emperor of India.
Peace of Vereeniging: Second Boer War ends with British victory.
At convention of Cumann na nGaedheal ('Party of the Irish') Arthur Griffith advocates passive resistance to British rule, a policy later known as 'Sinn Féin'.

DATE	AUTHOR'S LIFE	LITERARY CONTEXT
1903	Death of Rani, aged 12, of tuberculosis. Publishes *Shishu* (The Child), poems for children, and the novel *Chokher Bali* (Grit in the Eye).	James: *The Ambassadors* and 'The Beast in the Jungle'. Okakura Kakuzo: *The Ideals of the East*. Helen Keller: *The Story of My Life*.
1904	Delivers lecture *Swadeshi Samaj* (Society and State) at the Minerva Theatre in Calcutta.	Sister Nivedita (Margaret Noble): *Web of Indian Life*. A. C. Bradley: *Shakespearean Tragedy*. Okakura Kakuzo: *The Awakening of Japan*. Rudyard Kipling: *Traffics and Discoveries* Romain Rolland: *Jean-Christophe* (10 vols, to 1912).
1905	Death of his father (19 Jan), aged 87. Tagore leads a procession through Calcutta (16 Oct) in protest at the partition of Bengal, proclaiming it the day of *Rakhi-bandhan* (tying the knot of friendship). Speaks at meetings in support of the Swadeshi movement. Composes many patriotic songs, some performed in processions, including 'Amar sonar Bangla' (My Golden Bengal), later adopted as the national anthem of Bangladesh.	Begum Rokeya Sakhawat Hossain: *Sultana's Dream*. Lévi: *Nepal: Historical Study of a Hindu Kingdom* (3 vols, to 1908). Wells: *Kipps*.
1906	Publishes *Kheya* (The Ferry), a poetry collection and *Nauka Dubi* (Boat-Wreck), a novel. Briefly involved in a National Council of Education to establish a national university. Sends his son Rathindranath and son-in-law Nagendranath Gangopadhyay to study agriculture at the University of Illinois.	John Galsworthy: *The Forsyte Saga* (to 1921). Okakura Kakuzo: *The Book of Tea*. Kipling: *Puck of Pook's Hill*. Selma Lagerlöf: *The Wonderful Adventures of Nils* (to 1907). Albert Schweitzer: *The Quest of the Historical Jesus*.

CHRONOLOGY

Younghusband Expedition to Tibet (to 1904).
Lord Curzon proposes the partition of the province of Bengal (*Gazette of India*, 12 Dec). Irish Land Purchase Act introduced by Conservative George Wyndham, in an effort to weaken support for home rule through incentivizing the sale of land to tenants.

Lord Curzon's Monuments Act establishes an Archaeological Deparment which is responsible for the restoration and protection of historical monuments.
Unpopular Indian Universities Act brings universities under closer supervision of government.
Official Secrets Act in India.
Entente Cordiale between Britain and France.
Russo-Japanese War; Japanese victory in 1905 forces Russia to abandon expansionist programme in East Asia.

Announcement of partition plan for Bengal (19 July), implemented on 16 October, opposed by Tagore and the *bhadralok* Hindu elite of Calcutta. Mass demonstrations in protest. Formal proclamation of the Swadeshi movement (7 Aug) at the Calcutta Town Hall. Resolution to boycott British manufactured goods, especially cotton, and to promote Indian industries. Bonfires of British textiles. Public demonstrations are dealt with aggressively by police; student nationalism repressed.
Bande Mataram, radical English-language newspaper supporting Indian independence, founded in Calcutta, and edited by Aurobindo Ghosh.
Gopal Krishna Gokhale becomes president of the Indian National Congress.
Resignation of Lord Curzon as Viceroy as a result of a disagreement with his Commander-in-Chief, Lord Kitchener. Lord Minto becomes Viceroy. John Morley becomes Secretary of State for India.
Sinn Féin ('We Ourselves') established by Arthur Griffith. Ulster Unionist Council founded.
Suffragette militant campaign begins in Britain (to 1914).
First Russian Revolution.
Persian Constitutional Revolution (to 1911).
National Council of Education formed with the aim of placing education under Bengali control. Bengal National College and the Bengal Institute of Technology established.
Communal riots in eastern Bengal (to 1907), as an impoverished, predominantly Muslim peasantry rejects being forced to buy costly and inferior Indian *swadeshi* goods.
Revolutionary Jugantar party established by Aurobindo Ghosh and Barin Ghosh.
Dadabhai Naoroji, president of the Indian National Congress, calls for *swaraj* (home rule) in Calcutta.
Sultan Sir Mohammad Shah, Aga Khan III, leads a delegation of

DATE	AUTHOR'S LIFE	LITERARY CONTEXT
1906 *cont.*		
1907	Death of his son Samindranath, aged nearly 11, of cholera. Withdraws from Swadeshi movement over the religious violence it provokes.	Rudyard Kipling awarded the Nobel Prize in Literature. Sarat Chandra Chattopadhyay: *Badadidi*. Addams: *Newer Ideals of Peace*.
1908	Publishes four collections of political essays: *Raja o Praja* (The King and the Subjects), *Samuha*, *Swadesh* (My Country) and *Samaj* (Society).	Charles Freer Andrews: *North India*. Keller: *The World I Live In*. Tolstoy: 'Letter to a Hindu'.
1909	Publishes *Prayashchitta* (Atonement), a play. *Modern Review*, a Calcutta magazine, begins to publish English translations of some of Tagore's works.	Nobel Prize awarded to the Swedish novelist Selma Lagerlöf, the first female laureate. Rolland: *Theatre of the Revolution* (3 plays). Kipling: *Actions and Reactions*.
1910	Publishes *Gora*, a novel, and *Gitanjali* (Song Offerings).	Addams: *Twenty Years at Hull-House*. Arnold Bennett: *Clayhanger* (to 1918). E. M. Forster: *Howards End*. Sturge Moore: *Art and Life*. Wells: *The History of Mr Polly*.

prominent Muslims which obtains a commitment from Lord Minto not to jeopardize Muslim interests.

Muslim League established in Dacca (Dhaka); professes approval for the partition of Bengal and criticizes the Swadeshi movement.

Gandhi organizes resistance to the 'Black Act' in Transvaal, requiring Indians to carry identity cards, his first campaign of mass civil disobedience.

General election in Britain results in Liberal landslide; policies of New Liberalism (social welfare reform) introduced (to 1914).

Seditious Meetings Act, followed by a series of repressive acts (to 1910). Calcutta riots (1–4 October).

Attempted assassination of Sir Andrew Fraser, Lieutenant Governor of Bengal.

John Morley assigns Sayyid Husain Bilgrami, a founder of the Muslim League, and Krishna Govinda Gupta, the senior Hindu member of the Indian Civil Service, to the Council of India.

Fractious meeting of the Indian National Congress in Surat, leading to a split between moderate and revolutionary factions.

Annie Besant becomes president of the Theosophical Society.

Anglo-Russian Entente, bringing about the Triple Entente between Britain, France and Russia.

Tilak imprisoned in Mandalay (to 1914).

Hemchandra Das begins the manufacture of bombs in Bengal. Alipore Bomb Case. Terrorist attacks increase.

H. H. Asquith's Liberal ministry (to 1916).

Young Turk Revolution.

Indian Councils Act 1909 (the Morley-Minto Reforms) provides for elections of legislative councils on a narrow franchise, and institutes distinct Muslim electorates, though the executive veto remains.

Morley pressures Minto to appoint Satyendra Prassano Sinha, Advocate General of Bengal, as the first Indian official member of the Executive Council.

Constitutional crisis following rejection by House of Lords of Lloyd George's 'People's Budget' (passed in 1910).

The private Banaras Hindu University established by Pandit Madan Mohan Malaviya.

135 Indian delegates elected to legislative councils.

Lord Hardinge replaces Lord Minto as Viceroy.

Edwin Samuel Montagu becomes Parliamentary Under Secretary of State for India (to 1914).

India Society founded in London to promote Indian art.

Irish Home Rule Party holds balance of power in the Commons after two general elections (Jan and Nov).

Formation of the Union of South Africa as a self-governing dominion within the British Empire.

Death of King Edward VII (6 May); accession of King George V.

First Post-Impressionist exhibition in London.

DATE	AUTHOR'S LIFE	LITERARY CONTEXT
1911	William Rothenstein, British artist and patron of the India Society, London, visits Jorasanko. Tagore publishes *Raja*, a play and writes *Dak Ghar* (The Post Office), one of his best-known plays. Composes 'Jana gana mana', performed at the 26th Indian National Congress, and later to be India's national anthem.	Ajit Kumar Chakravarty: *Brahmavidyalaya*. G. K. Chesterton: *Appreciations and Criticisms of the Works of Charles Dickens*.
1912	Begins journey to England (March), but turns back due to ill health. While convalescing, translates some of his songs into English. Resumes journey (May) with his son and wife. Stays in Hampstead, London. Through William Rothenstein he is introduced to literary figures including W. B. Yeats, Ezra Pound, Ernest Rhys, Robert Bridges, Arthur Fox-Strangways, May Sinclair and Alice Meynell. The India Society publishes *Gitanjali* in an English limited edition, introduced by Yeats (Nov). Tagore's first trip to the US (Oct–May 1913), visiting Urbana and Chicago, New York and Harvard and giving lectures. Publishes *Jibansmitri* (published in English *as My Reminiscences*, 1917).	Ajit Kumar Chakravarty: *Rabindranath*. Sarojini Naidu: *The Bird of Time*. Robert Bridges: *Poetical Works*. Mann: *Death in Venice*. Ezra Pound: *Ripostes*.
1913	Macmillan edition of *Gitanjali* published (March). Returns to London (April) and is fêted. *The Post Office* (tr. Devabrata Mukerjea) is performed at the Abbey Theatre, Dublin and in London. Returns to India (Sept). Wins the Nobel Prize in Literature (Nov), following nomination by Thomas Sturge Moore, becoming the first	James Elroy Flecker: *The Golden Journey to Samarkand*. D. H. Lawrence: *Sons and Lovers*. John Maynard Keynes: *Indian Currency and Finance*.

CHRONOLOGY

HISTORICAL EVENTS

The third Delhi Durbar, celebrating the accession of King George V as Emperor of India.
Partition of Bengal reversed, on the advice of Lord Hardinge.
Decree that Calcutta be replaced by Delhi as capital of British India.
The Tata Iron and Steel Company commences operations in Bihar.
Irish Home Rule Party supports Liberals' Parliament Act to reduce power of House of Lords in return for a Home Rule bill.
Agadir crisis.

Construction of New Delhi commences.
Formation of the new province of Bihar and Orissa through separation from Bengal.
Assassination attempt on Lord Hardinge in Delhi.
Captain Scott's Antarctic expedition ends in tragedy.
Sinking of RMS *Titanic* on maiden voyage.
Third Irish Home Rule Bill introduced by Asquith. Ulster Covenant signed by Sir Edward Carson in Belfast and by nearly 500,000 others, engaging to oppose implementation of Home Rule.
South African Native National Congress founded (renamed African National Congress in 1923).
Balkan Wars (to 1913).

The Ghadr (Revolution) party founded by Punjabi Sikhs.
Third Irish Home Rule Bill passed by House of Commons, but Lords still able to delay it temporarily (Jan).
Dublin Lock-out (Aug–Jan 1914); 'Bloody Sunday' clashes between police and strikers (31 Aug).
Sir Edward Carson threatens to set up provisional government for Ulster should Home Rule be implemented (Sept).

DATE	AUTHOR'S LIFE	LITERARY CONTEXT
1913 cont.	person of non-Western origin to do so. Publishes *Glimpses of Bengal Life*, his first English story anthology (tr. Rajani Rajan Sen), *Chitra*, an English version of *Chitrangada*, and *Sadhana: The Realization of Life*, a collection of his American lectures. Receives honorary degree from Calcutta University.	
1914	Publishes *Gitimalya* (Garland of Songs). André Gide's French translation of *Gitanjali* published. Charles Freer Andrews joins community at Santiniketan. Boys from Gandhi's Phoenix Ashram in South Africa temporarily join the school (Nov).	Sarat Chandra Chattopadhyay: *Parineeta*. Ajit Kumar Chakravarty: *Kabyaparikrama*. A. H. Fox Strangways: *The Music of Hindostan*, Hardy: *Satires of Circumstance*. James Joyce: *Dubliners*. Lawrence: *The Prussian Officer*. Pound (ed.): *Des Imagistes*. May Sinclair: *The Three Sisters*. Yeats: *Responsibilities*.
1915	Meets Gandhi for the first time at Santiniketan (March). Lord Carmichael, Governor of Bengal, visits the school (March). Tagore receives a knighthood in the Birthday Honours of King George V (June).	Ford Madox Ford: *The Good Soldier*. Patrick Geddes: *Cities in Evolution*. Rolland: *Above the Battle*. Romain Rolland, the French pacificist writer, awarded the Nobel Prize in Literature.
1916	Publishes *Ghare Baire* (*The Home and the World*, 1919) and *Chaturanga* (Quartet), novels; *Balaka* (Wild Geese), poetry; *Phalguini*, a play (Play of Phalgun, the Month of Spring). *The Hungry Stone*, his second story collection in English; *Stray Birds* and *Fruit-Gathering*, poetry anthologies. Lecture	Ajit Kumar Chakravarty: *Maharshi Debendranath Tagore* and *Raja Ram Mohan*. Dickinson: *The European Anarchy*. Joyce: *A Portrait of the Artist as a Young Man*. William Winstanley Pearson: *For India and Shantiniketan: The Bolpur School of Rabindranath Tagore*.

1

India's railway network reaches approximately 35,000 miles (56,000 km).
Assassination of Archduke Franz Ferdinand (28 June). Beginning of the
First World War. Widespread initial support in India, including from many
nationalist leaders such as Tilak and Gandhi.
Indian divisions suffer major casualties in the First Battle of Ypres (Oct–Nov)
and the winter campaigns on the Western Front (to 1915).
British Indian Army captures Basra from the Ottoman Empire (Dec).
Komagata Maru incident.
Both Ulster Volunteer Force and Irish Volunteers obtain arms from Germany.
Hindu–German Conspiracy (to 1917); expatriate nationalists, notably the
Ghadr party in the US, try to create a Pan-India rebellion against the British
Empire, but their activities are known to British intelligence.
Third Irish Home Rule Bill hurried through (Sept) but Suspensory Act
delays its execution for duration of war; problem of Ulster similarly shelved.
Indian Relief Act and Smuts–Gandhi Agreement in South Africa.
Sir Satyendra Prassano Sinha becomes president of the Indian National
Congress.
Lala Har Dayal, leader of the Ghadr party, works in the Berlin India
Committee against the British.
Major General Sir Charles Townshend's 6th (Poona) Division of the British
Indian army besieged at Kut al-'Amarah (Dec).
Deaths of Gopal Krishna Gokhale and Sir Pherozeshah Mehta, weakening
the moderates in the Indian National Congress.
Defence of India Act.
Gandhi establishes the Kochrab Ashram in Gujarat.
Gallipoli campaign (Feb 1915–Feb 1916).
Lord Chelmsford replaces Lord Hardinge as Viceroy.
Fall of Kut al-'Amarah to Ottoman forces (April).
Indian National Congress reunites, with Tilak in the vanguard. Lucknow Pact
between the Congress and the Muslim League (Dec).
Tilak establishes the Home Rule League in Bombay (April).
Annie Besant establishes the All-India Home Rule League in Madras (Sept).
Easter Rising (24–29 April) begins with seizure of General Post Office in
Dublin; Patrick Pearse proclaims Irish Republic. After defeat by British
forces, thousands of suspects arrested and 15 leaders of the Rising executed,
outraging Irish public opinion.

DATE	AUTHOR'S LIFE	LITERARY CONTEXT
1916 cont.	tour to Japan (May–Sept) and the USA (including Seattle, New York, Denver, Salt Lake City and San Francisco), his main theme nationalism and internationalism.	
1917	Returns to India (Jan). Publishes *Nationalism* and *Personality* (based on American lectures). Publicly criticizes the detention of the socialist and theosophist Annie Besant, who called for Irish and Indian Home Rule.	Sarat Chandra Chattopadhyay: *Devdas.* Sarojini Naidu: *The Broken Wing.* T. S. Eliot: *Prufrock and Other Observations.* Knut Hamsun: *Growth of the Soil.* Hardy: *Moments of Vision.* Yeats: *The Wild Swans at Coole.*
1918	Death of his daughter Madhurilata (Bela) of tuberculosis, aged 31. His aim to create 'an international centre of humanistic studies', he lays the cornerstone of Visva-Bharati, a new university at Santiniketan (18 Dec). *Tota Kahini* (The Parrot's Training), a short story, published in Bengali and English; *Palataka* (The Fugitive), prose poems; *Mashi*, his third story collection in English.	Prafulla Chandra Ray: *Essays and Discourses.* Otto Spengler: *The Decline of the West* (to 1922).
1919	Travel in south and western India (Jan–March). Writes letter to the Viceroy, Lord Chelmsford (31 May), published in India and England, denouncing the massacre at Amritsar and renouncing his knighthood	John Maynard Keynes: *The Economic Consequences of the Peace.* Hermann von Keyserling: *The Travel Diary of a Philosopher.* Pound: *Quia Pauper Amavi.*

HISTORICAL EVENTS

Asquith resigns; Lloyd George becomes Prime Minister (Dec).
Naval Battle of Jutland (31 May–1 June).
Battle of the Somme (1 July–13 Nov).
Einstein publishes his theory of general relativity.

Annie Besant under house arrest (June–Sept); becomes president of the
Congress Party (Dec).
Indians allowed to become commissioned officers.
British Indian Army takes Baghdad (March).
Resignation of Austen Chamberlain, Secretary of State for India following
criticism by the Mesopotamia Commission. Replaced by Edwin Montagu,
who tours India (to 1918).
Factional tensions weaken the pact between the Congress Party and the
Muslim League.
Sir Jagadish Chandra Bose founds the Bose Institute for scientific research.
Irish constitutional convention set up in Dublin. Eamon de Valera becomes
president of Sinn Féin, now an avowedly republican party.
United States declares war on Germany (April).
Battle of Passchendaele (31 July–6 Nov).
Balfour Declaration favouring establishment of Jewish state in Palestine.
Tsar Nicholas II deposed in February Revolution in Russia (March).
Bolshevik Revolution in Russia (Nov).
Montagu–Chelmsford Report, recommending a role in provincial
administration for elected Indian ministers.
Influenza pandemic ('Spanish flu') (to 1919); Indian casualties represent
around half of global deaths.
Treaty of Brest-Litovsk: Russia withdraws from war (March).
German Spring Offensive on Western Front. Battle of Amiens and Allied
'Hundred Days' Offensive. Collapse of German and Habsburg empires.
Allied armies occupy Constantinople (to 1923). Armistice (11 Nov) ends
World War 1.
In general election (Dec) Sinn Féin triumph, winning 73 out of 105 Irish
seats in House of Commons.
Representation of the People Act in the United Kingdom: women over 30
gain the vote, universal male suffrage granted.
Execution of Tsar Nicholas II and his family. Russian Civil War (to 1921).
US President Wilson's Fourteen Points for word peace and statement on
national self-determination.
Rowlatt Act, extending wartime emergency powers acts. Opposed by all
Indian members of the Supreme Legislative Council; Mohammed Ali
Jinnah and others resign in protest. Gandhi calls for a national strike (*hartal*)
and non-violent protests (the Rowlatt *satyagraha*) to take place on 6 April.
Mass demonstrations in Lahore and Amritsar in the Punjab. Gandhi
arrested on the way to a demonstration in the Punjab. Saifuddin Kitchlew
and Dr Satyapal arrested in Amritsar, leading to a protest at the residence of

DATE	AUTHOR'S LIFE	LITERARY CONTEXT
1919 cont.	(this is never recognized by the Crown). Sangit Bhavana, institute of dance, drama and music, and Kala Bhavana, an institute of fine arts, founded at Santiniketan. Publishes *Lipika* (Sketches) and *Japanjatri* (A Traveller in Japan). Signs Romain Rolland's 'Declaration of Independence of the Human Spirit'.	
1920	Gandhi invites him to Gujarat. Lectures there and in Bombay (March–April). Lecture tour to Europe (May) to raise money for Visva-Bharati: Britain, the Netherlands, Belgium, France (meets Rolland, Gide, poet Anna de Noailles, and indologist Sylvain Lévi whom he invites to Santiniketan). Continues to the US (Oct), his third visit. Meets the British agronomist Leonard Elmhirst, inviting him to direct his rural reconstruction project at Surul. Death of his eldest sister, Saudamini.	Katherine Mansfield: *Bliss.* Sturge Moore: *Medea* and *Tragic Mothers: Medea, Niobe, Tyrfing.* Anna de Noailles: *Eternal Forces.* Wilfred Owen: *Poems.* Pound: *Hugh Selwyn Mauberley.* Shaw: *Heartbreak House.* Wells: *The Outline of History.*
1921	Publishes *Glimpses of Bengal*, a translation of letters written by Tagore from East Bengal 1885–95 (*Chhinnapatra*, 1913). Return to Europe from the US (March), visiting Britain,	Edward John Thompson: *Rabindranath Tagore: His Life and Work.* W. Somerset Maugham: *The Trembling of a Leaf.*

CHRONOLOGY

Deputy Commissioner Miles Irving. Several demonstrators killed by British troops, leading to rioting.

Jallianwala Bagh Massacre in Amritsar: Brigadier General Reginald Dyer's soldiers kill 379 civilians and wound 1,200 (13 April). Martial law declared in the Punjab by Lieutenant Governor Sir Michael O'Dwyer (15 April).

Hunter Commission (to 1920) criticizes Dyer's actions. He is forced to retire from the army.

Khilafat movement develops, led by Shaukat and Muhammad Ali and Abul Kalam Azad, and supported by Gandhi.

Government of India Act 1919 (Montagu-Chelmsford Reforms), creating a Legislative Assembly and Council of State, with an increased franchise determined by property and education; dyarchy introduced in provincial administration.

Third Anglo-Afghan War.

Sinn Féin refuse to assume House of Commons seats, instead forming Dáil Éireann ('Irish Assembly'), which elects a republican provisional government. Irish Republican Army (IRA) formed. Outbreak of Irish War of Independence.

Versailles Peace Conference.

Egyptian Revolution.

Sir Jagadish Chandra Bose elected fellow of the Royal Society, the third Indian to be so.

Lord Sinha becomes Governor of Bihar and Orissa.

Hijrat, spurred by the Khilafat movement, sees the attempted migration of around 18,000 Muslim peasants from India to Afghanistan.

Gandhi begins his non-cooperation movement with his *satyagraha* ('holding onto truth') campaign on a national scale.

Increased Hindu–Muslim tensions in the nationalist movement. Jinnah leaves the Indian National Congress session at Nagpur (Dec).

'Black and Tans' (Royal Irish Constabulary Special Reserve) raised in Britain to assist Irish police force. 'Bloody Sunday' in Dublin (21 Nov): IRA kill 14 British intelligence agents, and Black and Tans subsequently kill 14 civilians at a football match in Croke Park stadium.

Government of Ireland Act (Dec), partitioning Ireland to form Northern Ireland, composed of six of the nine counties of Ulster, and Southern Ireland, granting each a devolved parliament.

League of Nations founded.

Division of Ottoman Middle-Eastern territories in Treaty of Sèvres: France given a mandate for Syria and Lebanon, Britain for Palestine and Mesopotamia (Iraq). Iraqi revolt against British authorities in Mesopotamia.

Indian census records a population of over 319 million.

Lord Reading replaces Lord Chelmsford as Viceroy.

University of Dacca founded.

Muslim Malabar rebellion in south India.

Albert Einstein wins the Nobel Prize in Physics.

Devolved parliament of Northern Ireland assembles in Belfast (June).

DATE	AUTHOR'S LIFE	LITERARY CONTEXT
1921 cont.	France, Switzerland, Germany, Denmark, Sweden, Austria, Czechoslovakia. First round of debates in the *Modern Review* with Gandhi (who replies in *Young India*), expressing reservations about the non-cooperation movement. Arrives in India (July). Visva-Bharati formally established (23 Dec).	Bertrand Russell: *The Analysis of Mind*.
1922	Elmhirst commences work on the rural reconstruction project at Surul, named Sriniketan (Abode of Wellbeing) by Tagore. First visit to Ceylon (Sri Lanka) (Oct–Nov). Publishes *Muktadhara* (The Freed Stream), a play, and *Creative Unity* (10 philosophical lectures). Death of brother Somendranath.	Sri Aurobindo (Ghosh): *Essays on the Gita*. Kazi Nuzrul Islam: *Agnibeena* (poems and songs). Eliot: *The Waste Land*. Forster: *Alexandria: A History and a Guide*. Joyce: *Ulysses*. Pearson: *The Dawn of a New Age*.
1923	Death of his brother, pioneering civil servant Satyendranath Tagore. Death of W. W. Pearson, a teacher at Santiniketan and his friend, secretary and translator, in an accident in Italy. Fundraising trip to Karachi, Hyderabad, Porbandar and Bombay in support of Kala Bhavana.	W. B. Yeats awarded the Nobel Prize in Literature. Dickinson: *War: Its Nature. Cause and Cure*. Kahlil Gibran: *The Prophet*. Schweitzer: *Philosophy of Civilization*. Shaw: *Saint Joan*.
1924	Journey to Burma, China and Japan (March–Aug). Hosted by General Ch'i in Nanking, and received by the deposed emperor Xuantong (Puyi) in the Forbidden City. Visit to Argentina (Nov–Jan), forming a close friendship with the writer Victoria Ocampo.	Kaza Nuzrul Islam: *Bisher Banshi* (polemic, banned by government). Forster: *A Passage to India*. Hemingway: *In Our Time*. Sean O'Casey: *Juno and the Paycock*. Rolland: *Mahatma Gandhi*.
1925	Death of his brother, the playwright and painter Jyotirindranath Tagore. Meets Gandhi at Santiniketan (May) in attempt to resolve their	Chesterton: *The Everlasting Man*. F. Scott Fitzgerald: *The Great Gatsby*. Pound: *Cantos I–XVI*.

HISTORICAL EVENTS

Anglo-Irish Treaty, establishing the Irish Free State with dominion status (Dec), dismays republicans.

Massacre of 22 policemen at Chauri Chaura (Feb), prompting Gandhi to pause the non-cooperation movement.
Gandhi charged with sedition (based on three articles in *Young India*) in March; sentenced to six years' imprisonment.
Lord Lytton replaces the Earl of Ronaldshay as Governor of Bengal.
Deposition of the Ottoman Sultan Mehmed VI; election of Abdülmecid II as caliph by the Turkish Grand National Assembly.
Outbreak of Irish Civil War (to 1923). Irish Free State Constitution Act passed (Dec). W. B. Yeats becomes a senator.
Chanak crisis; fall of Lloyd George (Oct).
Mussolini's fascist march on Rome.
USSR established.
Establishment of the Swaraj Party under the leadership of Motilal Nehru and Chitta Ranjan Das with the aim of obstructing the reformed legislature from within (Jan). Participates in 1923 elections with some success particularly in Bengal where they are able to paralyse the legislature for two years.
IRA calls ceasefire and arms dump (April–May). Éamon De Valera arrested and imprisoned (to 1924).
German hyperinflation. Reparations crisis: French troops occupy the Ruhr. Hitler's Munich Putsch fails.

Gandhi released from prison (Feb).
British Empire Exhibition in London (to 1925).
Abolition of the caliphate by the Turkish Grand National Assembly (March).
Intercommunal rioting amongst Hindus and Muslims on the Malabar Coast and in northern Indian cities.
First Labour (minority) government in United Kingdom under Ramsay MacDonald (Jan–Nov).

Keshav Baliram Hedgewar establishes the Rashtriya Swayamsevak Sangh for the protection of Hindu political, cultural and religious interests.
Locarno Pact.

DATE	AUTHOR'S LIFE	LITERARY CONTEXT
1925 cont.	political disagreements. Debates continue, Gandhi responding in *Young India* to two *Modern Review* essays of Tagore, 'The Cult of the Charkha' and 'Striving for Swaraj'. First English version, largely by Tagore, of his play *Red Oleanders* (*Rakta Karabi*, 1926). Publishes *Broken Ties* (story collection) and *Purabi*, poems dedicated to Victoria Ocampo.	Thompson: *The Other Side of the Medal*. Virginia Woolf: *Mrs Dalloway*.
1926	Death of his eldest brother, the philosopher and polymath Dwijendranath Tagore. Travels to Europe (May–Dec). In Italy, is received by Mussolini but also meets the ostracized philosopher and politician Benedetto Croce. Initially impressed by Mussolini, he subsequently publishes a letter in the *Manchester Guardian* (5 Aug) criticizing his fascist regime. Extensive travels in Europe. Meets Albert Einstein for the first time, in Berlin.	Thompson: *Rabindranath Tagore: Poet and Dramatist*. Jagadish Chandra Bose: *The Nervous Mechanism of Plants*. Yasunari Kawabata: *The Izu Dancer*. T. E. Lawrence: *The Seven Pillars of Wisdom*. Lévi: *India and the World*.
1927	Travels in South-East Asia.	Hemingway: *Men Without Women*. Thompson: *A History of India* and *An Indian Day*.
1928	Takes up painting. Publishes *Fireflies* (epigrams).	Kaza Nuzrul Islam: 'Chol, chol, chol', later national marching song of Bangladesh. Thompson: *Suttee*. Yeats: *The Tower*.
1929	Following a curtailed North American lecture tour, makes third trip to Japan. Publishes two novels, *Shesher Kabita* (The Last Poem) and *Yogayog* (Relationships), and *Mahua* (a plant with an intoxicating nectar), poems. Devoting much time to painting.	Thomas Mann awarded the Nobel Prize in Literature. Mann: *Mario and the Magician*. Shaw: *The Apple Cart*. Thompson: *Atonement*. Yeats: *The Winding Stair*.

HISTORICAL EVENTS

Lord Irwin replaces Lord Reading as Viceroy.
April Riots in Calcutta.
Anti-treaty faction of Sinn Féin splits: De Valera forms Fianna Fáil
('Soldiers of Destiny').
General Strike in UK.
John Logie Baird demonstrates television.

Sir Francis Stanley Jackson replaces Lord Lytton as Governor of Bengal.

Simon Commission of 7 British MPs on constitutional reform in India
(to 1930); protests in response.
Representation of the People (Equal Franchise) Act grants universal female
suffrage in Britain.
Kellogg–Briand Pact outlawing war signed in Paris.
Stalin's first Five-Year Plan.
Alexander Fleming discovers penicillin.
Jawaharlal Nehru elected president of the Indian Congress (Dec).
Lord Goschen acts as Viceroy of India.
Ramsay MacDonald heads a second Labour minority government as Prime
Minister.
Wall Street Crash and onset of Great Depression.

DATE	AUTHOR'S LIFE	LITERARY CONTEXT
1930	Exhibits his paintings in France, England, Germany, Denmark, Russia and the USA (Mar–Jan 1931). Meets Einstein again in Berlin and New York; their conversations are featured in *The New York Times*. In conversation with H. G. Wells in Geneva (June). In Moscow (Sept) he is impressed by the achievements of Communism but deplores the violent suppression of dissent. Fifth and final visit to the US (Oct–Dec), meeting President Herbert Hoover and lecturing at Carnegie Hall, returning via England. Participates in the Round Table Conference, and delivers the Hibbert Lectures in Oxford. Publishes *The Child*, a long poem in English.	Kaza Nuzrul Islam: *Pralaya Shikha* (poems and songs; proscribed) and *Mrityukshuda* (novel). Eliot: *Ash Wednesday*. Thompson: *The Reconstruction of India*.
1931	Long talk with Bernard Shaw at a *Spectator* luncheon (Jan). Seventieth birthday: publication of *The Golden Book of Tagore*, a compilation of tributes from luminaries from around the world. Publishes *The Religion of Man*; *Vanavani* (Voice of the Forest), poems; *Russiar Chithi* (Letters from Russia). Exhibits his paintings in Calcutta (Dec).	Kaza Nuzrul Islam: *Shiulimala* (stories). Jiddu Krishnamurti: *The Songs of Life*. William Rothenstein: *Men and Memories* (3 vols, to 1939). Ernest Rhys: *Everyman Remembers*. Thompson: *A Farewell to India*.
1932	Death of his sister, the novelist Swarnakumari Tagore. Cables PM Ramsay MacDonald to protest against Gandhi's arrest (4 Jan). Visits Gandhi in Yervada prison in Poona. Publishes 'An Appeal to My Countrymen: After Mahatma Gandhi's Epic Fast'. Travels to Iraq and Persia. Publishes *Parasye* (In Persia)	Prafulla Chandra Ray: *Life and Experiences of a Bengali Chemist* (to 1935). Andrews: *What I Owe to Christ* (autobiography, royalties donated to Santiniketan). Evelyn Waugh: *Black Mischief*. Wells: *The Work, Wealth and Happiness of Mankind*.

HISTORICAL EVENTS

Proclamation of the Congress Party's Purna Swaraj ('complete self-rule')
resolution (26 Jan).
Chittagong Armoury Raid, mounted by Surya Sen.
Gandhi's Salt March from Sabarmati to Dandi in protest at the salt tax
(March–April). Arrested and imprisoned (to Jan 1931).
First Round Table Conference held in Westminster (Nov 1930–Jan 1931)
without Congress Party representatives.
Sir Muhammad Iqbal proposes a Muslim state in north-western India.

Lord Willingdon becomes Viceroy.
Dedication of New Delhi as capital of British India.
Japanese invasion of Manchuria (to 1932).
Ramsay MacDonald forms National government in response to economic
situation.
Gandhi agrees to suspend the civil disobedience campaign and represents
the Congress Party at the Second Round Table Conference (Sept). When
it ends (Dec), MacDonald announces government's intention to proceed
with a federal plan for India with two Muslim-majority states in Sind and
North-West Frontier Province; Indians to work out a Minorities agreement
but a Communal Award to be imposed by the British if they failed to do so.
Gandhi returns to India and resumes disobedience campaign.
Statute of Westminster establishes legislative independence of dominions
within the British Empire; British Commonwealth inaugurated.
Britain gives up Gold Standard.
Sir John Anderson becomes Governor of Bengal.
Third Round Table Conference (Nov–Dec), without Congress Party or
British Labour Party representation. Creation of separate provinces of
Orissa and Sind, and distinct colony status give to Burma.
Communal Award announced by MacDonald (Aug), proposing separate
electorates for other minority communities and interest groups, including
low-caste groups. Gandhi, again in prison, goes on hunger strike in protest.
He negotiates an alternative arrangement, the Poona Pact, with B. R.
Ambedkar, representing 'the depressed classes' (Sept).
Ottawa Agreements institute British 'imperial preference' in trade (to 1937).

DATE	AUTHOR'S LIFE	LITERARY CONTEXT
1932 cont.	and two poetry books, *Punascha* (Postscript) and *Parishesh* (The End). Appointed Ramtanu Lahiri Professor in History, University of Calcutta.	
1933	Participates in the Tagore Festival in Bombay, arranged by Sarojini Naidu. Publishes the novella *Dui Bon* (Two Sisters) and the dance dramas *Chandalika* (The Untouchable Girl) and *Tasher Desh* (Card Country).	Hemingway: *Winner Take Nothing.* Maugham: *Ah King.* Wells: *The Shape of Things to Come.*
1934	Visits Ceylon, his last trip overseas. Publishes *Char Adhyay* (Four Chapters), his last novel, and *Malancha* (The Orchard), essays. Nehru visits Sanitiniketan where his daughter is studying.	Thompson: *The Rise and Fulfilment of British Rule in India.* Waugh: *A Handful of Dust.*
1935	Publishes *Shesh Saptak* (The Last Octave) and *Bithika* (The Avenue), poems.	Mulk Raj Anand: *Untouchable.* R. K. Narayan: *Swami and Friends.*
1936	Publishes *Patraput* (Platter of Leaves) and *Shyamali* (The Verdant), poems. Produces new dance-drama version of *Chitrangada* and goes with it on a fundraising tour in north India (April–May). Writes poem 'Africa' after Mussolini's invasion of Abyssinia, a critique of European imperialism. Speaks out against Spanish Civil War.	Mulk Raj Anand: *Coolie.* Jawaharlal Nehru: *An Autobiography.* Keynes: *The General Theory of Employment, Interest and Money.* Yeats includes 7 poems by Tagore in *The Oxford Book of Modern Verse.*
1937	Delivers the first convocation address at Calcutta University to be given in Bengali. League against Fascism and War set up with Tagore as president.	Narayan: *The Bachelor of Arts.* Thompson: *Burmese Silver* and *The Life of Charles, Lord Metcalfe.*

CHRONOLOGY

Nazis become largest party in German Reichstag.
Oswald Mosley founds British Union of Fascists.

Nazi raid on Einstein's house at Caputh, Brandenburg.
Choudhary Rahmat Ali calls for a separate Muslim state to be named
Pakistan, composed of the north-western and north-eastern territories of
British India.
Hitler becomes German Chancellor.
US President Franklin Roosevelt announces New Deal.

Execution of Surya Sen.
Bihar–Nepal earthquake, one of the worst in Indian history (Gandhi–Tagore
polemic, Gandhi interpreting the earthquake as an act if God, Tagore
insisting on its natural causes).
Attempted assassination of Sir John Anderson, Governor of Bengal.

Silver Jubilee of George V.
Government of India Act 1935, further expanding the franchise and the
autonomy of elected provincial governments, though maintaining *de jure*
the viceregal legislative veto; federation to include Princely states not
implemented due to opposition.
Baldwin takes over from Ramsay MacDonald as Prime Minister heading
National government.
Hitler announces German re-armament. In Germany Nuremberg Laws
deprive Jews of citizenship.
Italy invades Abyssinia.
Lord Linlithgow replaces Lord Willingdon as Viceroy.
Death of King George V, accession of King Edward VIII. Abdication crisis;
accession of King George VI.
Spanish Civil War begins (ending with victory for Nationalists under
General Franco in 1939). Moscow show trials (to 1938).

Congress Party success in Indian provincial elections, gaining outright
majorities in six of the eleven provinces (and able to form coalitions in two
more). Muslim League seek to participate in government in the United
Provinces, which the Congress Party rejects unless the League merges
completely with the Congress Party. Jinnah condemns 'Hindu Raj'. Nehru

DATE	AUTHOR'S LIFE	LITERARY CONTEXT
1937 *cont.*	China Bhavana, an institute for Chinese studies, established at Visva-Bharati under the auspices of Tan Yun Shan. Death of his friend, the scientist Jagadish Chandra Bose. Tagore's health begins to deteriorate.	
1938	His letter to Chiang-Kai-Shek (1937) expressing solidarity is widely published and provokes anger in Japan. Publishes *Prantik* (On the Border) and *Snejuti* (Evening Lamp), poetry. Death of his nephew, the artist Gaganendranath Tagore.	Raja Rao: *Kanthapura*. Maud Gonne MacBride: *A Servant of the Queen*. Harriet Monroe: *A Poet's Life: Seventy Years in a Changing World*. Stefan Zweig: *Beware of Pity*.
1939	Preparations for first volume of his collected works, the Visva-Bharati Edition. Publishes *Shyama*, a dance drama; *Prahasini* (The Smiling One) and *Akashpradip* (Skylamp), poetry. Continues political involvement; both Nehru and Subhas Chandra Bose visit him in Santinikehtan (Jan–Feb).	Sri Aurobindo (Ghosh): *The Life Divine*. Andrews: *The True India: A Plea for Understanding*. Eliot: *The Idea of a Christian Society*; *The Family Reunion*; *Old Possum's Book of Practical Cats*. Rumer Godden: *Black Narcissus*.
1940	Gandhi's last visit to Santiniketan; Tagore requests that he strive to ensure the future of Visva-Bharati. Deaths of his friends C. F. Andrews and Kalimohan Ghosh, and his nephew, author and translator Surendranath Tagore. Letter to Roosevelt (June) calling on US 'to stand against the universal disaster'. Publishes *Chhelebela /Boyhood Days*, his second childhood memoir and *Nabajatak* (Newborn) and *Sanai* (The Shehnai), poems. Oxford D. Litt (honorary) conferred on him at Santiniketan.	Graham Greene: *The Power and the Glory*. Hemingway: *For Whom the Bell Tolls*. Keynes: *How to Pay for the War*.

launches Muslim Mass Contact campaign with considerable success initially, but within two years abandoned as counter-productive.

New Irish Constitution implemented (Dec) after endorsement by referendum, renaming the state Éire ('Ireland'), ignoring the British Crown and introducing an elected, septennial president to replace the Governor-General, and the post of 'taoiseach' as head of government.

In Britain Baldwin retires as Prime Minister and is replaced by Neville Chamberlain.

Bombing of Guernica by German planes. Hitler and Mussolini form Rome–Berlin Axis.

Marco Polo Bridge incident, following which Japan invades China.

Subhas Chandra Bose elected president of the Congress Party, defeating Gandhi's preferred candidate. Bose is an advocate of armed struggle against the British.

Pirpur and Shareef Reports detail Muslim grievances against Congress Party majority rule.

Germany annexes Austria. Munich crisis.

Subhas Chandra Bose elected president of the Congress Party for the second time. Subsequent resignation of Bose (April), forming the Forward Bloc party together with his brother Sarat Chandra Bose.

Molotov–Ribbentrop Pact. Nazi Germany invades Poland. Britain and France declare war on Germany. Outbreak of World War II (Sept). Éire declares neutrality.

Declaration of war announced without consultation by Lord Linlithgow, leading the Congress Party to urge the resignation of its members in provincial governments. Jinnah announces a 'Day of Deliverance' (22 Dec) from the Congress Party's control of provincial administration.

Assassination in London of Sir Michael O'Dwyer, Lieutenant Governor of Punjab during the Amritsar Massacre, and injury of Lord Zetland, Secretary of State for India, by Udham Singh (13 March), for which Singh is executed.

Lahore meeting of the Muslim Congress, producing the Lahore Resolution calling for a single Muslim state of Pakistan (March).

Resignation of Neville Chamberlain (May). Winston Churchill leads coalition government. Fall of France (June). Dunkirk evacuation. Battle of Britain. Blitz bombardment campaign by the Luftwaffe against British cities (Sept–May 1941).

Tripartite Pact between Japan, Germany and Italy.

Bose demands formation of a Provisional National Government in India. Arrested (July) and imprisoned for six months.

August Offer by Linlithgow, promising to include more Indian members on the Executive Council, to establish an advisory war council with Indian participation and (after the war) to set up a representative Indian body to frame a new constitution for India as a dominion. Both Congress and the Muslim League reject it.

DATE	AUTHOR'S LIFE	LITERARY CONTEXT
1941	Health continues to decline. 'Shabhyatar Shankat' (Crisis in Civilization) delivered as a public address at Santiniketan (14 April) then translated and published. Celebrates 80th birthday (7 May). Writes story 'Musalmanir Galpa'. Death at Jorasanko (7 August) following an operation.	Kipling: *Something of Myself.*

HISTORICAL EVENTS

On release from prison, Bose escapes to Germany, where he recruits Indian prisoners-of-war to join an Indian Legion to fight for India's independence.

By June, over 20,000 supporters of Gandhi's *satyagraha* campaign held in prison.

Nazi Germany invades the USSR in Operation Barbarossa (June).

Japanese attack on Pearl Harbor (Dec); US enters World War II. Japanese invasion of Malaya. Fall of Hong Kong. Burma campaign begins (Dec).

Rabindranath Tagore

For
SATYAJIT RAY
In Memoriam

and for

AMARTYA SEN
In Admiration

SHORT STORIES

The Ghat's Story

IF EVENTS WERE etched in stone, you could have read many stories of many ages on each of my steps. If you wish to hear tales of the past, sit down on one of these steps and listen attentively to the murmuring of the waters; you will be able to hear so many forgotten stories of long ago.

I remember another day, a day like this one. It was a few days to the month of Ashwin. In the early morning, a sweet light breeze carrying the approaching winter's chill was bringing new life to the limbs of those risen from slumber. The leaves on the trees, like them, were shivering slightly.

The Ganga was full. Only four of my steps remained above water. Land and water had embraced: on the bank, the Ganga's water had reached even the lush undergrowth of taro below the mango grove. Near that bend of the river, three ancient stacks of bricks raised their heads above the water. The fishing-boats tied to the trunks of the babul trees near the river's edge were rocking on the morning tide; the restless youthful tide-water was splashing teasingly around them, as if tweaking their ears in gentle sport.

The light of the early autumn morning, falling on the swollen river, was like raw gold, like the champak flower. At no other time do the rays of the sun have this colour. The sunlight fell on the sandbanks, on the fields of kash. The kash was not yet in full bloom, it had just begun to blossom.

The boatmen, uttering Lord Rama's name, released the boats. Just as the birds had joyously spread their wings at first light and flown into the blue sky, so too did the little boats spread their little sails and emerge into the sun's rays. They seemed like birds: floating, like swans, on the water, but spreading their wings out into the sky in delight.

The brahman Bhattacharya, carrying his kosha-kushi, had come to bathe in the Ganga at his appointed time. Women were coming in ones and twos to draw water.

All this happened not very long ago. You may think that a great deal of time has passed, but to me it seems just the other day. For me, in my age-long unchanging vigil, the days toss by on the waves of the flowing Ganga – and so the time seems short. For me the light of day, the shadow of night, falls daily on the surface of the river, and is daily erased, leaving no impression behind. Therefore, although I look old, my heart is ever young. For me the sun's rays have not been blotted out by the heavy weight of the algae of long-held memories. By some turn of fate, a single clump of algae may be carried by the current to knock against me, and then swept on again. But I cannot say that there is none at all that comes to rest.

The creepers and weeds and moss which have sprung up in my crevices, where the Ganga's current does not reach, are witnesses to my past: it is they who have bound the past in their loving embrace, keeping it for ever sweet, green and fresh. Every day the Ganga moves a step further away from me; every day I too become a step older.

That old woman from the Chakrabarti household who is now going home, a namabali around her shoulders, shivering after her bath and counting her beads: her mother's mother was then a young girl. I remember she used to play a special game; every day she would set an aloe leaf afloat on the Ganga. On my right hand there was a sort of eddy in the current; the leaf would keep on circling there, while she put down her pitcher on the ground to look at it. When I saw her some time later, now grown to maturity, bringing her own daughter with her to fetch water; when I saw that girl in her turn grow older, rebuking the other girls when they splashed water and teaching them manners – then I used to remember the aloe-leaf boat with amusement.

The story that I had set out to tell escapes me. As I begin one tale, another floats up on the stream: stories come, stories go, I cannot hold on to them. Only one or two, like those aloe-leaf boats, fall into the eddy and keep coming round again and again. Just such a story, today, is circling round my steps with its load of wares, as if on the brink of being swallowed up by the current every moment. Like the aloe leaf, it is very small, and bears very little – only two flowers to play with. Should it drown, a gentle-hearted girl will only let fall a sigh before returning home.

There, beside the temple, where you now see the fence around the Gosains' cattle-shed, there used to be a babul tree. An open-air market would be set up once a week below it. The Gosains had not yet begun to live here. Where they now have their family shrine, there used to be only a leaf-thatched shelter.

This peepal tree, which has now spread its limbs through my ribs, its roots like monstrous, elongated fingers holding in their hard grasp my cracked stone soul, was then a tiny sapling. It had just begun to rear its head of fresh green leaves. When the sun shone, the shadows of the leaves played all day on my stones; its young roots would tickle my breast like a child's fingers. If anyone plucked even a single leaf, I felt the pain as my own.

Though I was old, I was still straight and erect in those days; not broken-backed as I am now, crooked and uneven, with a thousand cracks like deep wrinkles, my hollows the haunt of countless frogs preparing for their long winter sleep. Only my left arm lacked a couple of bricks, making a hole in which a drongo had nested. When it awoke with a rustle at dawn, dipping its tail forked like the tail of a fish, and whistling as it flew up into the sky, I knew that it was time for Kusum to visit the ghat.

The girl I speak of was called Kusum by the other women at the ghat. I think that must have been her name. When her little shadow fell on the water, I wanted to hold on to it for ever. If only I could have bound it to my stones! She had this quality of sweetness. When she trod on my stones, her four-fold anklets tinkling, my clumps of moss and weeds seemed to tremble in delight. It was not as if Kusum played or chatted to excess, or laughed and joked very much: yet the strange thing was that she had more companions than anyone else. Even the naughtiest girls could not do without her. Some called her Kusi, some Khusi or Joy, some Rakshusi or Demoness. Her mother called her Kusmi. Every now and then I would see Kusum sitting by the water's edge. There was a strange affinity between her heart and the water. She loved the water.

After some time I saw Kusum no longer. Bhuban and Swarna would come and shed tears at the ghat. I heard that their Kusi-Khusi-Rakshusi had been taken away to her in-laws' home. It seemed there was no Ganga there. There, everyone was new to her: the house was new, so were the surroundings. It was as if a lotus had been taken out of the water to be planted on the land.

In course of time, I had almost forgotten about Kusum. A year had passed. Even the girls at the ghat did not talk about her very much. One evening, I was suddenly startled by the touch of long-familiar feet. It seemed to me that they were Kusum's feet. Indeed they were, but no anklets tinkled upon them any more. They lacked their old melody. I had always felt the touch of Kusum's feet together with the ringing of her anklets. Today, suddenly, the absence of that music made the evening murmur of the waters sound melancholy; the breeze rustling the leaves in the mango grove seemed to lament a loss.

Kusum had been widowed. I heard that her husband used to work in a far-off place; she had seen him only for a day or two. She received the news of her widowhood by post; at the age of eight, she had wiped away the vermilion from her forehead, taken off her ornaments, and returned again to her native place on the bank of the Ganga. But few of her companions were left. Bhuban, Swarna, Amala had gone to their in-laws' homes. Only Sharat was left, but I had heard that she too was to be married in the coming month of Agrahayan. Kusum was quite alone. But when she sat quietly on my steps, resting her head on her knees, it seemed to me as if all the waves in the river were waving to her together, calling to her, 'Kusi – Khusi – Rakshusi!'

Just as the Ganga swells day by day at the beginning of the rains, so too did Kusum fill day by day with youthful beauty. But her faded clothes, her sad face, her quiet nature cast so shadowy a veil over her youth that this flowering beauty was not evident to everyone's eyes. It seemed as though no one could see that Kusum had grown up. Certainly I did not notice it. To me Kusum had always remained the same little girl. True, she wore no anklets now, but I could hear the anklets tinkling in her step. Ten years passed in this way, but no one in the village seemed to have paid heed.

That year, just such a day as this one dawned towards the end of the month of Bhadra. Your great-grandmothers rose in the morning to see just this gentle sunlight. When they veiled their faces with their sari-ends, picked up their pitchers and walked through the trees down the uneven paths, talking among themselves, lighting still further the early morning light on my stones, no thought of you had even formed in any corner of their minds. Just as you cannot imagine that your mothers' mothers once ran about and played, that those days were as vibrant and real as these ones, that they too, with young and tender hearts like yours, swayed between joys and sorrows; so too this autumn day, this picture of happiness lit by the radiance of the autumn sun – without them, without the least trace or memory of their joys and griefs – was still more unknown to their imaginations.

That day, the first northerly breeze of the season had begun blowing gently since dawn, shaking one or two of the blossoming babul flowers down upon me. A few streaks of dew could be seen on my stones. That morning, a tall, fair young ascetic with a grave yet radiant face came to take shelter in the Shiva temple opposite. The news of his arrival spread through the village. The women put down their pitchers and crowded the temple to touch the holy man's feet.

The crowd increased daily. In the first place, a sannyasin; moreover, one of incomparable beauty; and on top of all, neglecting no one, seating the children on his lap, asking the mothers about their households. Within a short time he gained immense standing among the women. Many men also came to visit him. Some days he would read from the *Bhagavat Purana*, on others expound the *Bhagavadgita* or sit in the temple and discuss various religious texts. Some came to him for advice, some for a sacred mantra, some to cure their illnesses. The women at the ghat would exclaim among themselves, 'Oh, what beauty! It seems as though Shiva himself has come to dwell in his temple.'

Every day at dawn, just before sunrise, when the sannyasin stood immersed in the water of the Ganga, facing the morning star, and singing the hymn to dawn in slow deep tones, I could not hear the murmur of the waves. Every morning the sky over the Ganga's eastern bank would redden to the music of his voice, streaks of crimson would fall on the edges of the clouds, the darkness would fall away like the burst calyx of a blossoming bud and the red flower of morning bloom little by little in the pool of the sky. To me it would seem that at each syllable of the great incantation pronounced by this holy man, standing in the midst of the Ganga with his gaze towards the east, the spell of night was broken, the moon and stars descended to the west, the sun ascended in the east, and the aspect of the universe was transformed. Who was this enchanter? When the sannyasin rose from the river after bathing, his long, fair, pure body like a flame of some sacrificial fire, water streaming from his knotted hair, the first rays of the morning sun would fall on his limbs, and, it seemed, be reflected from them.

A few more months passed in this way. At the time of the solar eclipse in the month of Chaitra, many people came to bathe in the Ganga. A huge fair sprang up below the babul tree. Many people took this opportunity to catch a glimpse of the sannyasin. Among them were several women from the village where Kusum's husband's family lived.

The sannyasin was seated in meditation on my steps in the morning. Upon seeing him, one of the women suddenly pinched her neighbour and cried out, 'Look, isn't this our Kusum's husband?'

Another woman parted her veil with two fingers and exclaimed, 'Yes – indeed it is. That's the Chatterjees' younger son.' Yet another, who did not bother overmuch about her veil, said, 'Ah, just his forehead, just his nose, just his eyes.'

Another woman, not looking at the sannyasin, let fall a sigh, pushed her pitcher against the water and said, 'Alas, how can he be alive? How could he come back again? Can Kusum be so lucky?'

Then one said, 'He didn't have such a beard'; another said, 'He wasn't so thin'; yet another, 'I don't think he was so tall.'

In this way, the question was settled after a fashion, and was not raised again.

Everyone in the village had seen the sannyasin, Kusum alone excepted. Because of the crowd, Kusum had altogether given up coming to me. One evening, on the date of the full moon, the sight of the rising moon perhaps reminded her of our old association.

There was no one at the ghat at that time. The crickets were calling. The temple gongs had ceased a short while ago; the last wave of sound, fainter and fainter, had faded like a shadow into the shadowy line of trees on the further bank. There was bright moonlight; the tide was lapping at the banks. Kusum's shadow fell on me as she sat. There was very little wind; the trees and bushes were hushed. In front of Kusum, the moon's rays spread full and unbroken on the waters of the Ganga; behind her, beside her, the darkness lay hiding, huddled in a shroud, among the trees and bushes, the shadow of the temple, the foundations of the ruined house, the banks of the pond, the grove of palm trees. Bats hung from the chhatim tree. An owl cried out, as though weeping, from its perch on the temple spire. Closer to the houses, the jackals' howl rose sharply, then died out.

The sannyasin slowly emerged from the temple. Approaching the ghat, he had descended a couple of steps but was about to return, having noticed the solitary woman, when Kusum suddenly lifted her face and looked behind her.

The end of her sari had slipped off her head. The moonlight fell on her upturned face just as it falls on an upturned, blossoming flower. At that moment, the two looked at each other. It seemed as though they came to know each other; as if they had known each other from a previous birth.

An owl flew screeching overhead. Startled at the sound, Kusum gathered herself together and pulled her sari over her head. She rose and prostrated herself at the sannyasin's feet.

The sannyasin blessed her and asked, 'What is your name?'

Kusum answered, 'My name is Kusum.'

No further words were exchanged that night. Kusum's house was close by; with slow steps, she returned home. That night, the sannyasin sat for a long time on my steps. At last, when the moon had travelled all the way from the east to the west, when the sannyasin's shadow no longer fell behind but before him, he rose and went into the temple.

The following day onwards, I would see Kusum come daily to take the dust of the sannyasin's feet. When the sannyasin expounded the scriptures, she would stand to one side and listen. After completing his morning prayers, the sannyasin would call Kusum and discourse to her on religion. Was Kusum able to understand all he said? But she would listen silently, with deep attention. She would obey to the letter every word of advice he gave her. Every day she would carry out the temple tasks, never neglecting the service of the deity; she would pick flowers for the puja, fetch water from the Ganga and wash the temple floor.

Whatever the sannyasin told her, she would think about as she sat on my steps. Slowly, her vision seemed to expand, her heart to unfold: she began to see what she had not seen before, to hear what she had never heard previously. The dark shadow that had fallen across her serene face disappeared. Every morning, when she prostrated herself in reverence at the sannyasin's feet, she seemed like a dew-washed flower, offered to the deity in worship. A chaste radiant bloom seemed to light up her entire body.

At this time, near winter's end, there is a cold wind, yet sometimes towards the evening, a spring breeze blows from the south and the chill in the air is entirely gone. After many days, flutes play in the village, songs can be heard. The boatmen rest their oars, let their boats run free on the current, and sing of Krishna.

From branch to branch, suddenly, joyfully, the birds begin calling to each other. It was then that time of the year.

It seemed as though the touch of the spring breeze had in-
fused a youthfulness, little by little, into my stony heart. The
plants and creepers that covered me seemed to have drawn that
effervescence of youth into themselves and burst out in blossom.
At this time, Kusum was no longer to be seen. For some days
now she had not been coming to the temple, not to the ghat; nor
was she to be seen near the sannyasin.

I did not know what had happened meanwhile. Some time
later, Kusum and the sannyasin met on my steps one evening.

Kusum bowed her head and asked, 'Master, did you summon me?'

'Yes. Why don't I see you any more? Why do you now
neglect the service of the god?'

Kusum was silent.

'Tell me frankly what is in your mind.'

Kusum turned her face aside a little and said, 'Master, I am a
sinful woman. That's why I'm neglectful.'

The sannyasin said in a tone of deep affection, 'Kusum, I can
tell that your heart is unquiet.'

Kusum gave a start. Perhaps she thought, 'Who knows how
much the sannyasin has understood?' Her eyes slowly filled with
tears, and she sat down at that very spot. Covering her face with
the end of her sari, she sat on the steps near the sannyasin's feet
and began to weep.

The sannyasin moved away a little and said, 'Tell me frankly
why you are not at peace, and I will show you the path to peace.'

Kusum began to speak in tones of unshaken reverence, but
she halted from time to time; from time to time, words failed
her. 'If you command me, I shall certainly tell you. But I won't
be able to explain fully; I believe you have already understood
everything. Master, I revered someone like a god. I worshipped
him, and my heart was filled with that joy. But one night I saw
him in a dream as the lord of my heart, as though we were sitting
somewhere in a bakul grove; he had clasped my right hand in his
left, and was speaking to me of love. This seemed to me neither
impossible nor extraordinary. The dream ended, but my trance
did not. When I saw him the next day, I no longer saw him as
before. The image of that dream arose again and again in my
mind. I fled in fear, but the image remained with me. Since then

my heart has known no peace – everything has become dark to me.'

While Kusum said these words, repeatedly wiping away her tears, I could feel the sannyasin pressing his right foot down hard on my stone surface.

When Kusum had finished speaking, the sannyasin said, 'You must tell me who you saw in your dream.'

Kusum raised her clasped hands in plea and said, 'I cannot tell you that.'

The sannyasin said, 'I am asking you for your own good. Tell me plainly who it was.'

Kusum wrung her two soft hands violently, joined them again and asked, 'Must I say who it was?'

The sannyasin said, 'Yes, you must.'

Kusum answered on the instant, 'Master, it was you.'

As soon as her words reached her own ears, she fell in a faint on my hard lap. The sannyasin stood like a stone image.

When Kusum woke from her swoon, the sannyasin said in measured tones, 'You have obeyed me in everything; now you must obey my last command. I am leaving this place immediately. We must not meet again. You must forget me. Promise me that you will strive to do so.'

Kusum stood up, looked into the sannyasin's face and said in a calm voice, 'Master, it will be done.'

The sannyasin said, 'Then I go.'

Kusum said nothing more. Bowing to the sannyasin, she placed the dust of his feet on her head. The sannyasin departed.

Kusum said, 'He has commanded that I forget him.' So saying, she descended slowly into the waters of the Ganga.

From her earliest youth, she had lived beside these waters; now that she was weary, if the water were not to reach out to draw her to its lap, who else would do so? The moon set, the night passed into deep darkness. I heard a splash; I could make out nothing else. The wind rose and fell in the darkness; it seemed as though it wanted to blow out the stars for fear that the least thing would be visible.

She who used to play on my lap ended her sport that day and moved away, I could not learn where.

The Postmaster

FOR HIS FIRST JOB, the postmaster came to the village of Ulapur. It was a very humble village. There was an indigo-factory near by, and the British manager had with much effort established a new post office.

The postmaster was a Calcutta boy – he was a fish out of water in a village like this. His office was in a dark thatched hut; there was a pond next to it, scummed over with weeds, and jungle all around. The indigo agents and employees had hardly any spare time, and were not suitable company for an educated man. Or rather, his Calcutta background made him a bad mixer – in an unfamiliar place he was either arrogant or ill-at-ease. So there was not much contact between him and the residents in the area.

But he had very little work to do. Sometimes he tried to write poems. The bliss of spending one's life watching the leaves trembling in the trees or the clouds in the sky – that was what the poems expressed. God knew, however, that if a genie out of an Arab tale had come and cut down all the leafy trees overnight, made a road, and blocked out the sky with rows of tall buildings, this half-dead, well-bred young man would have come alive again.

The postmaster's salary was meagre. He had to cook for himself, and an orphaned village-girl did housework for him in return for a little food. Her name was Ratan, and she was about twelve or thirteen. It seemed unlikely that she would get married. In the evenings, when smoke curled up from the village cowsheds, crickets grated in the bushes, a band of intoxicated Baul singers in a far village sang raucously to drums and cymbals, and even a poet if seated alone on a dark verandah might have shuddered a little at the trembling leaves, the postmaster would go inside, light a dim lamp in a corner of the room and call for Ratan. Ratan would be waiting at the door for this, but she did not come at the first call – she would call back, 'What is it, Dadababu, what do you want?'

'What are you doing?' the postmaster would say.

'I must go and light the kitchen fire –'

'You can do your kitchen work later. Get my hookah ready for me.'

Soon Ratan came in, puffing out her cheeks as she blew on the bowl of the hookah. Taking it from her, the postmaster would say abruptly, 'So, Ratan, do you remember your mother?' She had lots to tell him: some things she remembered, others she did not. Her father loved her more than her mother did – she remembered him a little. He used to come home in the evening after working hard all day, and one or two evenings were clearly etched in her memory. As she talked, Ratan edged nearer to the postmaster, and would end up sitting on the ground at his feet. She remembered her little brother: one distant day, during the rainy season, they had stood on the edge of a small pond and played at catching fish with sticks broken off trees – this memory was far more vividly fixed in her mind than many more important things. Sometimes these conversations went on late into the night, and the postmaster then felt too sleepy to cook. There would be some vegetable curry left over from midday, and Ratan would quickly light the fire and cook some chapati: they made their supper out of that.

Occasionally, sitting on a low wooden office-stool in a corner of his large hut, the postmaster would speak of his family – his younger brother, mother and elder sister – all those for whom his heart ached, alone and exiled as he was. He told this illiterate young girl things which were often in his mind but which he would never have dreamt of divulging to the indigo employees – and it seemed quite natural to do so. Eventually Ratan referred to the postmaster's family – his mother, sister and brother – as if they were her own. She even formed affectionate imaginary pictures of them in her mind.

It was a fine afternoon in the rainy season. The breeze was softly warm; there was a smell of sunshine on wet grass and leaves. Earth's breath – hot with fatigue – seemed to brush against the skin. A persistent bird cried out monotonously somewhere, making repeated and pathetic appeals at Nature's midday durbar. The postmaster had hardly any work: truly the only things to look at were the smooth, shiny, rain-washed leaves quivering, the layers of sun-whitened, broken-up clouds left over from the rain. He watched, and felt how it would be to have a close companion here, a human object for the heart's most intimate affections. Gradually it seemed that the bird was saying precisely this, again and again; that in the afternoon shade and solitude the same meaning was in the rustle of the leaves. Few would believe or imagine that a poorly paid sub-postmaster in a small village could have such feelings in the deep, idle stillness of the afternoon.

Sighing heavily, the postmaster called for Ratan. Ratan was at that moment stretched out under a guava tree, eating unripe guavas. At the sound of her master's call she got up at once and ran to him.

'Yes, Dadababu, you called?' she said, breathlessly.

'I'm going to teach you to read, a little bit each day,' said the postmaster. He taught her daily at midday from then on, starting with the vowels but quickly progressing to the consonants and conjuncts.

During the month of Śrābaṇ, the rain was continuous. Ditches, pits and channels filled to overflowing with water. The croaking of frogs and the patter of rain went on day and night. It was virtually impossible to get about on foot – one had to go to market by boat. One day it rained torrentially from dawn. The postmaster's pupil waited for a long time at the door, but when the usual call failed to come, she quietly entered the room, with her bundle of books. She saw the postmaster lying on his bed: thinking that he was resting, she began to tip-toe out again. Suddenly she heard him call her. She turned round and quickly went up to him saying, 'Weren't you asleep, Dadababu?'

'I don't feel well,' said the postmaster painfully. 'Have a look – feel my forehead.'

He felt in need of comfort, ill and miserable as he was, in this isolated place, the rain pouring down. He remembered the touch on his forehead of soft hands, conch-shell bangles. He wished his mother or sister were sitting here next to him, soothing his illness and loneliness with feminine tenderness. And his longings did not stay unfulfilled. The young girl Ratan was a young girl no longer. From that moment on she took on the role of a mother, calling the doctor, giving him pills at the right time, staying awake at his bedside all night long, cooking him convalescent meals, and saying a hundred times, 'Are you feeling a bit better, Dadababu?'

Many days later, the postmaster got up from his bed, thin and weak. He had decided that enough was enough: somehow he would have to leave. He wrote at once to his head office in Calcutta, applying for a transfer because of the unhealthiness of the place.

Released from nursing the postmaster, Ratan once again took up her normal place outside his door. But his call did not come for her as before. Sometimes she would peep in and see the postmaster sitting distractedly on his stool or lying on his bed. While she sat expecting his summons, he was anxiously awaiting a reply to his application. She sat outside the door going over her old lessons numerous times. She was terrified that if he suddenly summoned her again one day, the conjunct consonants would all be muddled up in her mind. Eventually, after several weeks, his call came again one evening. With eager heart, Ratan rushed into the room. 'Did you call, Dadababu?' she asked.

'I'm leaving tomorrow, Ratan,' said the postmaster.

'Where are you going, Dadababu?'

'I'm going home.'

'When are you coming back?'

'I shan't come back again.'

Ratan did not question him further. The postmaster himself told her that he had applied for a transfer, but his application had been rejected; so he was resigning from his post and returning home. For several minutes, neither of them spoke. The lamp flickered weakly; through a hole in the crumbling thatched roof, rain-water steadily dripped on to an earthenware dish. Ratan then went slowly out to the kitchen to make some chapati. She made them with none of her usual energy. No doubt her thoughts distracted her. When the postmaster had had his meal, she suddenly asked, 'Dadababu, will you take me home with you?'

'How could I do that!' said the postmaster, laughing. He saw no need to explain to the girl why the idea was impossible.

All night long, whether dreaming or awake, Ratan felt the postmaster's laugh ringing in her ears. 'How could I do that!'

When he rose at dawn, the postmaster saw that his bath-water had been put out ready for him (he bathed according to his Calcutta habit, in water brought in a bucket). Ratan had not been able to bring herself to ask him what time he would be leaving; she had carried the bath-water up from the river late at night, in case he needed it early in the morning. As soon as he finished his bath, the postmaster called her. She entered the

room softly and looked at him once without speaking, ready for
her orders. 'Ratan,' he said, 'I'll tell the man who replaces me
that he should look after you as I have; you mustn't worry just
because I'm going.'

No doubt this remark was inspired by kind and generous
feelings, but who can fathom the feelings of a woman? Ratan
had meekly suffered many scoldings from her master, but these
kindly words were more than she could bear. The passion in her
heart exploded, and she cried, 'No, no, you mustn't say anything
to anyone – I don't want to stay here.' The postmaster was taken
aback: he had never seen Ratan behave like that before.

A new postmaster came. After handing over his charge to
him, the resigning postmaster got ready to leave. Before going,
he called Ratan and said, 'Ratan, I've never been able to pay you
anything. Today before I go I want to give you something, to
last you for a few days.' Except for the little that he needed for
the journey, he took out all the salary that was in his pocket. But
Ratan sank to the ground and clung to his feet, saying, 'I beg
you, Dadababu, I beg you – don't give me any money. Please,
no one need bother about me.' Then she fled, running.

The departing postmaster sighed, picked up his carpet-bag,
put his umbrella over his shoulder, and, with a coolie carrying
his blue-and-white-striped tin trunk on his head, slowly made
his way towards the boat.

When he was on the boat and it had set sail, when the swollen flood-waters of the river started to heave like the Earth's
brimming tears, the postmaster felt a huge anguish: the image
of a simple young village-girl's grief-stricken face seemed to
speak a great inarticulate universal sorrow. He felt a sharp desire
to go back: should he not fetch that orphaned girl, whom the
world had abandoned? But the wind was filling the sails by then,
the swollen river was flowing fiercely, the village had been left
behind, the riverside burning-ground was in view. Detached by
the current of the river, he reflected philosophically that in life
there are many separations, many deaths. What point was there
in going back? Who belonged to whom in this world?

But Ratan had no such philosophy to console her. All she
could do was wander near the post office, weeping copiously.
Maybe a faint hope lingered in her mind that Dadababu might
return; and this was enough to tie her to the spot, prevent her
from going far. O poor, unthinking human heart! Error will

not go away, logic and reason are slow to penetrate. We cling
with both arms to false hope, refusing to believe the weightiest
proofs against it, embracing it with all our strength. In the end it
escapes, ripping our veins and draining our heart's blood; until,
regaining consciousness, we rush to fall into snares of delusion
all over again.

Little Master's Return

I

RAICHARAN WAS TWELVE when he first came to work in the house. He was from Jessore district and had long hair and large eyes; a slender boy with gleaming dark skin. His employers, like him, were Kaisthas. His main duty was to help with looking after their one-year-old son – who in time progressed from Raicharan's arms to school, from school to college, and from college to being munsiff in the local court. Raicharan had remained his servant. But now there was a mistress as well as a master in the household, and most of the rights that Raicharan had hitherto had over Anukul Babu passed to her.

Although his former responsibilities were diminished by her presence, she largely replaced them with a new one. A son to Anukul was soon born, and was won over completely by the sheer force of Raicharan's devotion. He swung him about with such enthusiasm, tossed him in the air with such dexterity, cooed and shook his head in his face so vigorously, chanted so many meaningless random questions for which there could be no reply, that the very sight of Raicharan sent the little master into raptures.

When the boy learnt to crawl stealthily over a door-sill, giggling with merriment if anyone tried to catch him, and speedily making for somewhere safe to hide, Raicharan was entranced by such uncommon skill and quickness of decision. He would go to the child's mother and say admiringly, '*Mā*, your son will be a judge when he grows up – he'll earn a fortune.' That there were other children in the world who could at this young age dart over a door-sill was beyond Raicharan's imagination; only future judges could perform such feats. His first faltering steps were amazing too, and when he began to call his mother 'Ma', his *pisimā* 'Pishi', and Raicharan 'Channa', Raicharan proclaimed these staggering achievements to everyone he met. How astonishing it was that he should not only call his mother 'Ma', his aunt 'Pishi', but also Raicharan 'Channa'! Really, it was hard to understand where such intelligence had sprung from. Certainly no adult could ever show such extraordinary intelligence, and people would be unsure of his fitness to be a judge even if he could.

Before long, Raicharan had to put a string round his neck and pretend to be a horse; or he had to be a wrestler and fight with the boy – and if he failed to let himself be defeated and thrown to the ground, there would be hell to pay. By now, Anukul had been transferred to a Padma river district. He had brought a push-chair from Calcutta for his son. Raicharan would dress him in a satin shirt, gold-embroidered cap, golden bangles and a pair of anklets, and take the young prince out in his push-chair twice a day for some air.

The rainy season came. The Padma began to swallow up gardens, villages and fields in great hungry gulps. Thickets and bushes disappeared from the sandbanks. The menacing gurgle of water was all around, and the splashing of crumbling banks; and swirling, rushing foam showed how fierce the river's current had become.

One afternoon, when it was cloudy but did not look like rain, Raicharan's capricious young master refused to stay at home. He climbed into his push-chair and Raicharan gingerly pushed it to the river-bank beyond the paddy-fields. There were no boats on the river, no people working in the fields: through gaps in the clouds, the sun could be seen preparing with silent fiery ceremony to set behind the deserted sandbanks across the river. Suddenly peace was broken by the boy pointing and calling, 'Fowers, Channa, fowers!' A little way off there was a huge *kadamba* tree on a wet, muddy stretch of land, with some flowers on its upper branches: these were what had caught the boy's attention. (A few days previously, Raicharan had strung some flowers on to sticks and made him a '*kadamba*-cart'; he had had such fun pulling it along with a string that Raicharan did not have to put on reins that day – an instant promotion from horse to groom.)

'Channa' was not very willing to squelch through the mud to pick the flowers. He quickly pointed in the other direction and said, 'Look, look at that bird – flying – now it's gone. Come, bird, come!' He pushed the chair forward fast, burbling on in this way. But it was futile: to try to distract by so simple a device a boy who would one day become a judge – especially as there was nothing particular to attract his attention anywhere, and imaginary birds would not work for very long. 'All right,' said Raicharan, 'you sit in the chair and I'll get you the flowers. Be good now, don't go near the water.' Tucking his dhoti up above his knees, he headed for the *kadamba* tree.

But the fact that he had been forbidden to go near the water immediately attracted the boy's mind away from the *kadamba*-flowers and towards the water. He saw it gurgling and swirling along, as if a thousand wavelets were naughtily, merrily escaping to a forbidden place beyond the reach of some mighty Raicharan. The boy was thrilled by their mischievous example. He gently stepped down from his chair, and edged his way to the water. Picking a long reed, he leant forward, pretending the reed was a fishing-rod: the romping gurgling wavelets seemed to be murmuring an invitation to the boy to come and join their game.

There was a single plopping sound, but on the bank of the Padma river in monsoon spate many such sounds can be heard. Raicharan had filled the fold of his dhoti with *kadamba*-flowers. Climbing down from the tree, he made his way back towards the push-chair, smiling – but then he saw that the child was not there. Looking all around, he saw no sign of him anywhere. His blood froze: the universe was suddenly unreal – pale and murky as smoke. A single desperate cry burst from his breaking heart: 'Master, little master, my sweet, good little master!' But no one called out 'Channa' in reply, no childish mischievous laugh came back. The Padma went on rushing and swirling and gurgling as before, as if it knew nothing and had no time to attend to the world's minor occurrences.

As evening fell the boy's mother grew anxious and sent people out to search with lanterns. When they reached the river-bank, they found Raicharan wandering over the fields like a midnight storm-wind, sobbing, 'Master, my little master!' At last he returned home and threw himself at his mistress's feet, crying in reply to all her questions, 'I don't know, *Mā*, I don't know.'

Although everyone knew in their hearts that the Padma was the culprit, suspicion fell on a group of gypsies encamped at the edge of the village. The mistress of the house even began to suspect that Raicharan had stolen the boy – so much so that she called him and entreated, 'Bring back my child! I'll give you whatever money you want.' But Raicharan could only beat his brow, and she ordered him from her sight. Anukul Babu tried to dispel his wife's unfounded suspicion: what motive could Raicharan have had for so vile an act? 'What do you mean?' said his wife. 'The boy had gold ornaments on him.'

II

RAICHARAN WENT BACK to his home village. His wife had not borne him a child, and he had long ceased to hope for one. But it so happened that before the year had ended his ageing wife gave birth to a son – and then soon afterwards died.

At first Raicharan had nothing but hatred for the newly born child, who he felt had somehow taken the little master's place by deceit. It seemed a deadly sin to delight in his own son after allowing his master's only son to be washed away. If his widowed sister had not been there, the child would not have breathed Earth's air for long.

Amazing it was, but after a few months the child began to crawl over the door-sill and show a merry ability to evade all sorts of restrictions. He chuckled and wailed just as the little master had done. Sometimes when Raicharan heard him cry his heart missed a beat; it was just as if the little master were crying somewhere for his lost Raicharan. Phelna – that was what Raicharan's sister called the boy – began in due course to call her 'Pishi'. When Raicharan heard that familiar name one day, he suddenly thought, 'The little master cannot do without my love: he has been born again in my house.'

There were several convincing proofs in favour of this belief. First, there was the short interval between the death and the birth. Second, his wife could not, at so advanced an age, have conceived a son merely through her own fecundity. Third, the child crawled, toddled and called his aunt 'Pishi' just as the little master had done. There was much to indicate that he too would grow up to become a judge. Raicharan then remembered the strong suspicions the mistress of the house had had, and he realized with astonishment that her maternal instinct had rightly told her that someone had stolen her son. He now felt deeply ashamed of the way he had neglected the child: devotion took hold of him again. From now on he brought him up like a rich man's son. He bought him satin shirts and a gold-embroidered cap. His dead wife's ornaments were melted down to make bangles and bracelets for him. He forbade him from playing with the local children; all day long he himself was the child's sole playmate. Whenever they got the chance, the local boys would mock Phelna for being a 'prince', and the villagers marvelled at Raicharan's odd behaviour.

When Phelna was old enough to go to school, Raicharan sold
his land and took the boy to Calcutta. With great difficulty he
found a job, and sent Phelna to a high-class school. He skimped
and scraped to get the boy good food and clothing and a decent
education, saying to himself, 'If it was love for me that brought
you into my house, dear child, then you must have nothing but
the best.'

Twelve years passed in this way. The boy did well at his studies and was fine to behold: sturdily built, with a dark, glossy
complexion. He took great trouble over his hair; his tastes were
refined and cultured. He could never think of his father quite
as his father, because Raicharan treated him with a father's affection but a servant's devotion. To his discredit, Phelna never
told anyone that Raicharan *was* his father. The students in the
hostel where Phelna lived were always making fun of the rustic
Raicharan; and it cannot be denied that when his father was
not present Phelna joined in the fun. But everyone was fond
of the mild, doting Raicharan, and Phelna also loved him – but
(to repeat) not quite as his father: affection was mixed with
condescension.

Raicharan grew old. His employer was perpetually finding
fault with him. His health was deteriorating, and he could not
concentrate on his work: he was getting forgetful. But no employer who pays full wages will accept old age as an excuse.
Moreover, the cash that Raicharan had raised by selling off his
possessions was nearly at an end. Phelna was always complaining
now that he was short of proper clothes and luxuries.

III

ONE DAY RAICHARAN suddenly resigned from his job, and
giving Phelna some money said, 'Something has happened – I
need to go back to the village for a few days.' He then set off for
Barasat, where Anukul Babu was now munsiff.

Anukul had had no other child. His wife still grieved for
her son.

One evening Anukul was resting after returning from the
court, while his wife, at great expense, purchased from a *sannyāsī*
a holy root and a blessing that would bring her a child. A voice
was heard in the yard: 'Greetings, *Mā.*'

'Who's there?' said Anukul Babu.

Raicharan appeared. 'I am Raicharan,' he said, taking the dust of his former master's feet.

Anukul's heart melted at the sight of the old man. He asked him numerous questions about his present circumstances, and invited him to work for him again.

Raicharan smiled weakly and said, 'Let me pay my respects to *Māṭhākrun*.'

Anukul Babu took him through to the inner rooms of his house. His wife was not nearly so pleased to see Raicharan, but Raicharan took no notice of this and said with clasped hands, 'Master, *Mā*, it was I who stole your son. It was not the Padma, it was no one else, it was I, ungrateful wretch that I am.'

'What are you saying?' said Anukul. 'Where is he?'

'He lives with me,' said Raicharan. 'I'll bring him the day after tomorrow.'

That was Sunday, and the courts were closed. Husband and wife watched the road anxiously from dawn. At ten o'clock, Raicharan arrived with Phelna.

Anukul's wife without thought or question drew him on to her lap, touched him, sniffed him, eyed his face intently, cried and laughed nervously. Truly, the boy was fine to look at – nothing in his looks or dress suggested a poor background. There was a very loving, modest, bashful expression in his face. At the sight of him, Anukul's heart too swelled with love. But keeping his composure, he asked, 'What proof have you?'

'How can such an act be proved?' said Raicharan. 'Only God knows that I stole your son; no one else in the world knows.'

Anukul thought the matter over and decided that since his wife had embraced the boy as her own with such fervour it would not be appropriate to search for proof now; whatever the truth might be, it was best to believe. In any case, how could Raicharan have acquired such a boy? And why should the old servant wish to mislead them now? Questioning the boy, he learnt that he had lived with Raicharan from an early age and had called him Father, but that Raicharan had never behaved towards him like a father – he had been more like a servant. Driving all doubt from his mind, Anukul said, 'But, Raicharan, you must not darken our door again now.'

With clasped hands and quavering voice Raicharan replied, 'I am old now, Master. Where shall I go?'

'Let him stay,' said the mistress of the house. 'I have forgiven him. Let our son be blessed.'

'He cannot be forgiven for what he has done,' said the righteous Anukul.

'I didn't do it,' cried Raicharan, embracing his master's feet. 'God did it.'

Even angrier now that Raicharan should lay the blame for his own sin on to God, Anukul said, 'One should not place trust in someone who has betrayed trust so heinously.'

Rising from Anukul's feet, Raicharan said, 'It was not I, Master.'

'Then who was it?'

'It was my Fate.'

No educated man could be satisfied by such an explanation.

'I have no one else in the world,' said Raicharan.

Phelna was certainly rather annoyed that Raicharan had stolen him – a munsiff's son – and dishonourably claimed him as his own. But he said generously to Anukul, 'Father, please pardon him. If you won't let him stay in the house, then give him a monthly allowance.'

Raicharan, saying nothing, looked once at his son and made an obeisance to all; then he went out through the door and disappeared into the world's multitude. At the end of the month, when Anukul sent a small sum to Raicharan at his village address, the money came back. No one of that name was known there.

Wealth Surrendered

I

BRINDABAN KUNDA WAS furious. He announced to his father, 'I'm leaving – right now.'

'You ungrateful scoundrel,' said Yajnanath Kunda. 'All I've spent feeding and clothing you over the years, with not a paisa back – and now see how you turn on me.'

In fact, the amount spent on food and clothing in Yajnanath's house had never been great. The sages of old survived on impossibly little; Yajnanath presented an equally noble example. He could not go quite as far as he liked, partly because of the demands of modern life, partly because of the unreasonable rules for keeping body and soul together which Nature imposes. His son had put up with this while he was unmarried; but after marrying, his standards of food and dress began to clash with his father's extreme austerity. Brindaban's standards were material rather than spiritual. His requirements were in line with society's changing response to cold, heat, hunger and thirst. There were frequent rows between father and son, and matters came to a head when Brindaban's wife fell seriously ill. The *kabirāj* wanted to prescribe an expensive medicine for her, but Yajnanath questioned his competence and dismissed him. Brindaban pleaded with his father at first, then grew angry, but to no avail. When his wife died, he accused his father of murdering her. 'What do you mean?' said Yajnanath. 'Do you suppose that no one who takes medicine dies? If expensive medicine were the answer, kings and emperors would be immortal. Why should your wife die with any more pomp than your mother or grandmother?'

Truly if Brindaban had not been blinded with grief and seen things objectively, he would have found much consolation in this thought. Neither his mother nor grandmother had taken medicine when they were dying. It was an ancient custom in the household not to do so. But modern people do not want to die according to ancient rules. (I am speaking of the time when the British had newly arrived in this country, but the behaviour of the younger generation was already causing consternation among the elders.)

This was why up-to-date Brindaban quarrelled with old-fashioned Yajnanath and said, 'I'm leaving.'

Giving him instant permission to go, his father said for all to hear that to give his son a single paisa would be as sinful as shedding a cow's blood. Brindaban, for his part, said that to take any of his father's money would be like shedding his mother's blood. They then parted company.

After so many undisturbed years, the people of the village were rather excited by this mini-revolution. And because Brind-aban had been deprived of his inheritance, they all tried – as hard as they could – to distract Yajnanath from remorse at the rift with his son. They said that to quarrel with one's father over a mere wife could happen only in this day and age. After all, if a wife goes she can quickly be replaced by another – but if a father goes a second father cannot be found for love or money! This was a sound argument; but in my view (Brindaban being what he was) it would have cheered him somewhat rather than making him penitent.

It is unlikely that Yajnanath felt much distress at his son's departure. It was a considerable financial saving, and furthermore it removed a dread that had plagued him constantly – that Brind-aban might one day poison him: what little food he ate was tainted by this morbid notion. It lessened somewhat when his daughter-in-law died; and now that his son had left he felt much more relaxed.

Only one thing pained him. Brindaban had taken his four-year-old son Gokulchandra with him. Gokul had cost relatively little to feed and clothe, so Yajnanath had felt quite easy towards him. (Despite his regret at the boy's removal, however, he could not help making some rapid calculations: how much he would save each month now that they had both gone, how much each year, and how much capital would earn an equivalent amount of interest.) It became difficult living in an empty house, with-out Gokul's mischief to disturb it. Yajnanath missed having no one to pester him during the *pūjās*, no one pinching his food at mealtimes, no one running away with the inkpot when he did his accounts. Washing and eating with no one to disturb him was a melancholy business. Such undisturbed emptiness was what people gained after death, he thought. It tugged at his heart to see, in his bedding and quilt, holes made by his grandson, and on the mat he sat on ink-blots made by the same artist. For making his dhoti unfit to wear in less than two years, the pampered boy had been severely scolded by his grandfather. Now Yajnanath felt tears in his eyes when he saw that dhoti in Gokul's bedroom, dirty, torn, abandoned, knotted all over. Instead of using it to make wicks for lamps or for some other domestic purpose, he carefully stored it in a trunk, and promised that if Gokul returned and ruined a dhoti in even a single year, he would not scold him. But Gokul did not return. Yajnanath seemed to be ageing much faster than before, and the empty house felt emptier every day.

Yajnanath could not stay peacefully at home. Even in the afternoon, when all high-born people take a siesta, he roamed about the village with a hookah in his hand. During these silent afternoon walks, the village-boys would abandon their games and, retreating to a safe distance, bellow out locally composed rhymes about Yajnanath's miserliness. They none of them dared − in case their next meal was spoiled by so bad an omen − to utter his real name: they gave him names of their choosing. Old folk called him 'Yajna*nash*';[1] why exactly the boys should have called him 'Bat' is hard to explain. Perhaps they saw some resemblance in his pale, sickly skin.

II

ONE DAY YAJNANATH was wandering along mango-tree-shaded paths in this way, when he saw a boy he had not previously seen taking command of the others and directing them in entirely new sorts of mischief. The boys were quite carried away by his forceful character and fresh imagination. Instead of retreating like them at the sight of the old man, the new boy went smartly right up to Yajnanath, and shaking out his chadar released a chameleon, which ran over Yajnanath's body and off into the bushes − leaving him quivering and smarting at the shock. The boys roared with amusement. A few paces on, Yajnanath's *gāmchā* was suddenly whipped off his shoulders, to reappear as a turban on the new boy's head.

Yajnanath was rather impressed by this novel kind of courtesy from a young stranger. He had not had such daring familiarity from any boy for a long time. By much shouting and coaxing, he managed to bring him to heel.

1. 'Destroyer of sacrifice' as opposed to 'lord of sacrifice' (Yajna*nath*).

'What's your name?' he asked.

'Nitai Pal.'

'Where are you from?'

'Shan't tell you.'

'Who's your father?'

'Shan't tell you.'

'Why won't you tell me?'

'I've run away from home.'

'Why?'

'My father wanted to send me to school.'

Yajnanath felt immediately that to send such a boy to school would be a waste of money and that his father must be a fool.

'Will you come and live in my house?' he asked.

Raising no objection, the boy came along and settled in there as easily as under the shade of a roadside tree. Not only that, he issued barefaced orders for food and dress as if paid for in advance – and roundly disputed such matters with the master of the house. It had been easy to win arguments with his own son; but with someone else's, Yajnanath had to give in.

III

THE VILLAGERS WERE amazed at the unprecedented affection that Yajnanath showed for Nitai Pal. 'The old man has not got much longer to live,' they thought, 'and this strange boy will inherit all his wealth.' They were all very envious of him, and were determined to do him down. But the old man hid him as closely as the ribs of his chest.

Sometimes the boy fretted and talked of leaving. Yajnanath would appeal to his greed, saying, 'You'll get all my wealth when I die.' The boy was still young, but he knew the measure of this promise.

Then the villagers started to search for Nitai's father. 'How sore his parents must be about him!' they said. 'What a wicked boy he is!' They hurled unrepeatable abuse at him – but their feelings were fired more by selfish malice than moral outrage.

One day Yajnanath heard from a passer-by that a man called Damodar Pal was looking for his lost son, and was on his way to the village. Nitai was alarmed at this news – he was about to abandon his prospects and flee; but Yajnanath reassured him, saying, 'I'll hide you where no one will be able to find you. Not even the people in this village.'

'Show me where,' said the boy, very intrigued.

'If I show you now, we'll be found out,' said Yajnanath. 'I'll show you tonight.'

Nitai was excited by this promise of a new adventure. He vowed that as soon as his father had gone, having failed to find him, he would use the place to challenge his friends in a game of hide-and-seek. No one would find him! It would be great fun. It amused him greatly that his father had scoured the whole country for him and had failed to find him.

At midday Yajnanath locked the boy into the house and went out somewhere. When he returned, Nitai pestered him with questions; and as soon as dusk fell he asked if they could go.

'It's not night yet,' said Yajnanath.

A little later Nitai said, 'It's night now, *Dādā* – let's go.'

'People are not asleep yet,' said Yajnanath.

'They're asleep now – let's go,' said Nitai a few moments later.

The night wore on. Though he was doing his utmost to stay awake, Nitai began to nod as he sat. At one in the morning, Yajnanath took Nitai by the hand and led him along the dark paths of the sleeping village. There was no sound anywhere, except for a dog barking from time to time, answered loudly by other dogs near and far. Sometimes nocturnal birds, startled by the sound of footsteps, flapped away through the forest. Nitai nervously clasped Yajnanath's hand.

After crossing several fields, they came at last to a tumble-down, god-forsaken temple surrounded by jungle. 'Here?' said Nitai, rather crossly. It was not at all as he had imagined. There was no mystery here. He had sometimes had to spend nights in ruined temples like this after he had run away from home. The place was not bad for hide-and-seek, but not totally beyond discovery.

Yajnanath lifted a slab in the middle of the temple. The boy saw that beneath it there was a kind of cellar, with a lamp flickering. He was surprised and intrigued by this, but rather frightened too. Yajnanath climbed down a ladder into the cellar, and Nitai nervously followed him.

Down in the cellar, there were brass water-pots everywhere. There was a mat for a deity in the midst of them, with vermilion, sandal-paste, garlands and other *pūjā*-materials laid out in front. Nitai noticed with amazement that the pots were full of rupee-coins and gold *mohars*.

'Nitai,' said Yajnanath, 'I told you that I would give you all my money. I haven't got much – just these few pitcherfuls. Today I place it all in your hands.'

Nitai jumped. 'All? Aren't you going to keep a single rupee for yourself?'

'It would bring leprosy to my hand if I took any of it. But one more thing: if my long-lost grandson Gokulchandra, or his son or grandson or great-grandson or any of his descendants come, then all this money must be given to him or to them.'

Nitai decided that Yajnanath had gone mad. 'All right,' he agreed.

'Now sit on this *āsan*,' said Yajnanath.

'Why?'

'You must be worshipped.'

'Why?'

'It is the custom.'

The boy sat on the *āsan*. Yajnanath smeared sandalwood on his forehead, and a spot of vermilion, and put a garland round his neck. Then, sitting before him, he began to mutter mantras. Nitai was terrified at finding himself worshipped as a god, terrified by the mantras. '*Dādā*,' he cried.

Yajnanath continued reading the mantras, without replying. At length he dragged the heavy pitchers, one by one, in front of the boy and dedicated them, making him say each time: 'I count and bequeath this money to Gokulchandra Kunda son of Brindaban Kunda son of Yajnanath Kunda son of Paramananda Kunda son of Prankrishna Kunda son of Gadadhar Kunda son of Yudhisthira Kunda; or to Gokulchandra's son or grandson or great-grandson or any of his true descendants.'

The repetition of this formula over and over again had a stupefying effect on the boy. His tongue gradually lost all movement. By the time the ceremony was over, the air of the little cave-like room was thick with smoke from the lamp and the breath of the two of them. Nitai's palate was dry; his arms and legs were feverishly hot; he was finding it difficult to breathe. The lamp guttered and went out. In the darkness, the boy sensed Yajnanath climbing up the ladder.

'Where are you going, *Dādā*?' he cried in alarm.

'I'm leaving you,' said Yajnanath. 'You stay here: no one will find you. But remember Gokulchandra son of Brindaban son of Yajnanath.'

He climbed out of the cellar and pulled the ladder up after him. '*Dādā*,' gasped Nitai, barely able to speak, 'I want to go back to my father.'

Yajnanath put the slab back into place, and straining his ears just managed to hear Nitai gasping the word, 'Father.' Then there was a thud, and after that no sound at all.

Consigning his wealth in this way to the care of a *yakṣa*, Yajnanath pressed some soil over the slab, and heaped it over with sand and broken bricks from the temple. He covered the heap with clumps of grass, and heeled in bushes from the forest. The night was almost over, but he could not bring himself to leave the place. Every now and then he put his ear to the ground. He imagined that he heard a crying from the innermost depths of the Earth; that the night sky was filled with that one sound; that all the people asleep in the world had been woken by it, and were sitting on their beds, listening. The old man went on frenziedly piling up more and more soil, as if trying to stop Earth's mouth. But somebody called out, 'Father' – and Yajnanath thumped the ground and hissed, 'Be quiet, everyone will hear you.'

Again, somebody called out, 'Father.'

The old man noticed dawn arriving. Fearfully he left the temple and emerged into open country. Even there someone was calling, 'Father.' He turned in great alarm: there in front of him was his son Brindaban.

'Father,' said Brindaban, 'I hear that my son has been hiding in your house. Give him back to me.'

The old man lurched towards Brindaban. His eyes and face were horribly distorted as he leant forward and said, '*Your* son?'

'Yes,' said Brindaban, 'Gokul. Now his name is Nitai Pal and my name is Damodar. You have a bad name with every-one round about, so we changed our names – otherwise no one would have talked to us.'

The old man clawed at the sky with all his fingers, as if struggling to clasp the air; then fell to the ground, fainting. When he came round again, he hurried Brindaban to the temple. 'Can you hear the crying?' he asked.

'No,' said Brindaban.

'If you strain your ears, can't you hear someone crying "Father"?'

'No,' said Brindaban.

The old man seemed relieved at this. From then on, he would go round asking everyone 'Can you hear the crying?' – and they all laughed at his madman's words.

About four years later, Yajnanath was on his death-bed. When the world's light grew dim in his eyes and breath began to fail, he suddenly sat up in delirium; groping with both hands, he murmured, 'Nitai – someone has taken my ladder away.' When he found no ladder out of the vast, lightless, airless cellar he was in, he slumped back against the pillows. Then he vanished, to the place which no one playing hide-and-seek on earth can discover.

The Living and the Dead

I

THE WIDOW LIVING with the zamindar Sharadashankar's family, in the big house at Ranihat, had no blood-relatives left. One by one they had died. In her husband's family, too, there was no one she could call her own, having no husband or son. But there was a little boy – her brother-in-law's son – who was the apple of her eye. His mother had been very ill for a long time after his birth, so his Aunt Kadambini had brought him up. Anyone who brings up someone else's son becomes specially devoted: there are no rights, no social claims – nothing but ties of affection. Affection cannot prove itself with a legal document; nor does it wish to. All it can do is love with doubled intensity, because it owns so uncertainly.

Kadambini poured her frustrated widow's love on to this boy, till one night in Śrābaṇ she suddenly died. For some strange reason her heartbeat stopped. Everywhere else, Time continued; yet in this one, small, tender, loving heart its clock's tick ceased. Keeping the matter quiet, in case the police took notice, four Brahmin employees of the zamindar quickly carried off the body to be burnt.

The cremation-ground at Ranihat was a long way from human habitation. There was a hut on the edge of a tank there, and next to it an immense banyan tree: nothing else at all on the wide open plain. Formerly a river had flowed here – the tank had been made by digging out part of the dried-up course of the river. The local people now regarded this tank as a sacred spring. The four men placed the corpse inside the hut and sat down to wait for the wood for the pyre to arrive. The wait seemed so long that they grew restless: Nitai and Gurucharan went off to see why the firewood was so long coming, while Bidhu and Banamali sat guarding the corpse.

It was a dark monsoon night. The clouds were swollen; not a star could be seen in the sky. The two men sat silently in the dark hut. One of them had matches and a candle, wrapped up in his chadar. They could not get the matches to light in the damp air, and the lantern they had brought with them had gone out as well. After sitting in silence for a long time, one of them said,

'I could do with a puff of tobacco, *bhāi*. We forgot everything in the rush.'

'I'll run and get some,' said the other. 'I won't be a minute.'

'That's nice!' said Bidhu, perceiving his motive. 'I suppose I'm to stay here on my own?'

They fell silent again. Five minutes seemed like an hour. They began inwardly to curse the two who had gone to trace the firewood – no doubt they were sitting comfortably somewhere having a smoke and chatting. They were soon convinced that this must be so. There was no sound anywhere – just the steady murmur of crickets and frogs round the tank. Suddenly the bed seemed to stir a little, as if the dead body had turned on to its side. Bidhu and Banamali began to shudder and mutter prayers. Next moment a long sigh was heard: the two immediately fled outside and ran off towards the village.

A couple of miles along the path they met their two companions returning with lanterns in their hands. They had actually just been for a smoke, and had found out nothing about the firewood. They claimed it was being chopped up now and would not be long coming. Bidhu and Banamali then described what had happened in the hut. Nitai and Gurucharan dismissed this as nonsense, and rebuked the other two angrily for deserting their post.

The four of them swiftly returned to the hut at the cremation-ground. When they went in, they found that the corpse had gone: the bed was empty. They stared at one another. Could jackals have made off with it? But even the garment that covered it had gone. Searching about outside the hut they noticed in a patch of mud by the door some recent, small, woman's footprints.

The zamindar, Sharadashankar, was not a fool: to try to tell him a ghost-story would get them nowhere. After long discussion, the four decided they had best say simply that the cremation had taken place.

When, towards dawn, the wood arrived at last, those who brought it were told that in view of the delay the job had already been done, using firewood stored in the hut. They had no reason to doubt this. A dead body was not a valuable object: why should anyone wish to steal it?

II

IT IS WELL known that an apparently lifeless body can harbour dormant life which in time may bring the body back to life. Kadambini had not died: for some reason, her life-function had been suspended – that was all.

When she regained consciousness, she saw dense darkness all around her. She realized that the place where she was lying was not her usual bedroom. She called out '*Didi*' once, but no one in the dark room replied. She sat up in alarm, recalling her death-bed – that sudden pain in her chest, the choking for breath. Her eldest sister-in-law had been squatting in a corner of the room warming her little son's milk on a stove – Kadambini had collapsed on to the bed, no longer able to stand. Gasping, she had called, '*Didi*, bring the little boy to me – I think I'm dying.' Then everything had gone black, as if an inkpot had been poured over a page of writing. Kadambini's entire memory and consciousness, all the letters in her book of life, became at that moment indistinguishable. She had no recollection of whether her nephew had called out '*Kākimā*' for the last time, in his sweet loving voice; whether she had been given that final viaticum of love, to sustain her as she travelled from the world she knew, along Death's strange and endless path.

Her first feeling was that the land of death must be one of total darkness and desolation. There was nothing to see there, nothing to hear, nothing to do except sit and wait, forever awake. Then she suddenly felt a chilly, rainy wind through an open door, and heard the croaking of monsoon frogs; and all her memories of the monsoon, from childhood right through her short life, rose in her mind. She felt the touch of the world again. There was a flash of lightning: for an instant the tank, the banyan tree, the vast plain and a distant row of trees showed themselves before her eyes. She remembered how she had sometimes bathed in the tank on sacred occasions; how seeing dead bodies in the cremation-ground there had made her aware of the awesomeness of death.

Her immediate idea was that she should return home. But then she thought, 'I'm not alive – they won't take me back. It would be a curse on them. I am exiled from the land of the living – I am my own ghost.' If that were not so, how had she come at dead of night from the safe inner quarters of Sharadashankar's house to this remote cremation-ground? But if her funeral rites had not yet been completed, then what had become of the people who should have burned her? She recalled her last moments before dying, in the well-lit Sharadashankar residence; then, finding herself alone in this distant, deserted, dark cremation-ground, she again said to herself, 'I no longer belong to the world of living people. I am fearsome, a bringer of evil; I am my own ghost.'

As this realization struck, all ties and conventions seemed to snap. It was as if she had weird power, boundless liberty – to go where she liked, do what she liked; and with the onset of this feeling she dashed out of the hut like a madwoman, like a gust of wind – ran out into the dark burning-ground with not the slightest shame, fear or worry in her mind.

But her legs were tired as she walked, and her body began to weaken. The plain stretched on endlessly, with paddy-fields here and there and knee-deep pools of water. As dawn broke slowly, village bamboo-groves could be seen, and one or two birds called. She now felt very afraid. She had no idea where she stood in the world, what her relation to living people would be. So long as she was in the wide open plain, in the burning-ground, in the darkness of the Śrābaṇ night, she remained fearless, as if in her own realm. Daylight and human habitation were what terrified her. Men fear ghosts, but ghosts fear men: they are two separate races, living on opposite sides of the river of death.

III

WANDERING AROUND AT night like a madwoman, with her mud-smeared clothes and weird demeanour, Kadambini would have terrified anyone, and boys would probably have run away and thrown pebbles at her from a distance. Fortunately the first passer-by to see her in this condition was a gentleman.

'Mā,' he said, approaching her, 'you look as though you come from a good family: where are you going to, alone on the road like this?'

At first Kadambini did not reply, and merely stared blankly at him. She felt totally at a loss. That she was out in the world, that she looked well-born, that a passer-by was asking her questions – all this was beyond her grasp.

The gentleman spoke again. 'Come along, *Mā*, I'll take you home. Tell me where you live.'

Kadambini began to think. She could not imagine returning to her in-laws' house, and she had no parental home; but then she remembered her childhood friend Yogmaya. Although she had not seen her since childhood, they had sometimes exchanged letters. At times there had been an affectionate rivalry between them, with Kadambini asserting that nothing was greater than her love for Yogmaya, while Yogmaya suggested that Kadambini was not responding sufficiently to her own affection. But neither doubted that if opportunity to meet arose again, neither would wish to lose sight of the other. 'I'm going to Shripaticharan's house at Nishindapur,' said Kadambini to the gentleman.

The man was going to Calcutta. Nishindapur was not near by, but it was not out of his way. He personally saw Kadambini to Shripaticharan Babu's house.

The two friends were a little slow to recognize each other, but soon their eyes lit up as each saw a childhood resemblance in the other. 'Well I never,' said Yogmaya. 'I never thought that I would see you again. But what brings you here? Did your in-laws kick you out?'

Kadambini was silent at first, then said, '*Bhāi*, don't ask me about my in-laws. Give me a corner in your house, as a servant. I'll work for you.'

'What an idea!' said Yogmaya. 'How can you be a servant? You're my friend, you're like –' and so on. Then Shripati came into the room. Kadambini gazed at him for a moment, then slowly walked out, without covering her head or showing any other sign of modesty or respect. Afraid that Shripati would take offence at her friend's behaviour, Yogmaya made apologies for her. But so little explanation was necessary – indeed, Shripati accepted her excuses so easily – that she felt uneasy.

Kadambini joined her friend's household, but she could not be intimate with her – Death stood between them. If one doubts or is conscious of oneself, one cannot unite with another. Kadambini looked at Yogmaya as if she and her house and husband were in a different, distant world. 'They are people of the world,' she felt, 'with their loves and feelings and duties, and I am an empty shadow. They are in the land of the living, whereas I belong to Eternity.'

Yogmaya was also puzzled, could not understand anything.

Women cannot bear mystery, for this reason: that poetry, hero-ism or learning can thrive on uncertainty but household arts cannot. Therefore women thrust aside what they don't under-stand, maintaining no connection with it, or else they replace it with something they themselves have made – something more useful. If they cannot do either of these, they get angry. The more impenetrable Kadambini became, the more resentful Yogmaya became towards her, wondering why she had been burdened with such trouble.

There was a further problem. Kadambini was terrified of her-self. Yet she could not run away from herself. Those who are frightened of ghosts look backwards in terror – they are fright-ened of what they cannot see. But Kadambini was terrified of her inner self – nothing outside frightened her. Thus, in the silence of midday, she would sit alone in her room and sometimes shout out loud; and in the evening, the sight of her shadow in the lamplight made her quiver all over. Everyone in the house was alarmed by her fear. The maids and servants and Yogmaya herself began to see ghosts all over the place. Eventually, in the middle of the night, Kadambini came out of her bedroom, wailing; she came right up to the door of Yogmaya's room and cried, '*Didi, Didi*, I beg you! Do not leave me alone!'

Yogmaya was as angry as she was frightened. She would have driven Kadambini out of the house, there and then. The kindly Shripati, with great effort, managed to calm Kadambini down and settle her in an adjoining room.

The next day Shripati received an unexpected summons from the inner part of the house. Yogmaya burst into a torrent of accusation: 'So! A fine man you are. A woman leaves her own husband's home and takes up residence in your house – months have gone by but she shows no sign of leaving – and I've heard not the slightest objection from you. What are you thinking of? You men are a fine lot.'

In fact, of course, men are unthinkingly weak about women, and women can accuse them all the more because of this. Even if he had been willing to swear on his life that his concern for the pathetic yet beautiful Kadambini was no more than was proper, his behaviour suggested otherwise. He had said to himself, 'The people in her husband's house must have treated this childless widow with great injustice and cruelty, so that she was forced to flee and take refuge with me. She has no father or mother –

so how can I desert her?' He had refrained from inquiring about her background, not wishing to upset her by questioning her on this unwelcome subject. But his wife was now objecting strongly to his passive, charitable attitude; and he realized he would have to inform Kadambini's in-laws of her whereabouts, if he was to keep the peace in his household. In the end he decided it would not be fruitful to write a letter; it would be better to go to Ranihat personally to find out what he could.

Shripati set off, and Yogmaya went to Kadambini and said, 'My dear, it doesn't seem advisable for you to stay here any more. What will people say?'

'I have no connection with people,' said Kadambini, looking solemnly at Yogmaya.

Yogmaya was nonplussed. '*You* may not have,' she said irritably, 'but *we* have. How can we go on putting up someone else's widow?'

'Where is my husband's house?' said Kadambini.

'Hell!' thought Yogmaya. 'What is the woman on about?'

'Who am I to you?' said Kadambini slowly. 'Am I of this world? All of you here smile, weep, love, possess things; I merely look on. You are human beings; I am a shadow. I do not understand why God has put me in your midst. You're worried that I'll damage your happiness – I in turn cannot understand what my relation is to you. But since the Almighty has kept no other place for the likes of me, I shall wander round you and haunt you even if you cut me off.'

Her stare and the tone of her words were such that Yogmaya understood their import, even if she did not understand them literally and was unable to reply. She could not manage any more questions. Gloomy and oppressed, she left the room.

IV

SHRIPATI DID NOT return from Ranihat until nearly ten at night. The whole world seemed awash with torrential rain. With its thudding sound, it gave the impression that it would never end, that the night would never end.

'What happened?' asked Yogmaya.

'It's a long story,' said Shripati. 'I'll tell you later.' He took off his wet clothes, had something to eat and after smoking for a bit went to bed. He seemed very preoccupied. Yogmaya suppressed her curiosity all this while, but when she got into bed she asked, 'What did you find out? Tell me.'

'You are certainly mistaken,' said Shripati.

Yogmaya was rather annoyed at this. Women do not make mistakes, or if they do men are wiser not to mention them; it is safest to let them pass without complaining. 'In what way?' asked Yogmaya heatedly.

'The woman you have accepted into your house,' said Shripati, 'is not your friend Kadambini.'

Such a remark – especially from one's husband – might reasonably cause offence. 'So I don't know my own friend?' said Yogmaya. 'I have to wait for you to identify her? What an absurd thing to say!'

Shripati replied that its absurdity or otherwise was not the point: proof was what counted. There was no doubt whatsoever that Kadambini had died.

'Listen,' said Yogmaya. 'You've got into a complete muddle. Whatever you heard in whatever place you went to can't be right. Who asked you to go anyway? If you had written a letter, everything would have been made clear.'

Distressed by his wife's lack of confidence in his efficiency, Shripati started to explain all the proofs in detail – but to no avail. They went on arguing into the small hours. Shripati believed their guest had been deceiving his wife all this time, and Yogmaya believed she had deserted her family; so both were agreed that Kadambini should be evicted from the house immediately. But neither was willing to admit defeat in the argument. Their voices rose higher and higher, and they forgot that Kadambini was lying in the next room.

'It's a terrible thing,' said one voice. 'I heard what happened with my own ears.'

'How can I accept that?' shouted the other. 'I can see her with my own eyes.'

Eventually Yogmaya said, 'All right, tell me when Kadambini died.' She hoped, by finding a discrepancy with the date of one of Kadambini's letters, to prove that Shripati was wrong. But they worked out that the date given to Shripati was exactly one day before Kadambini had come to their house. Yogmaya felt a racing in her heart at this, and Shripati too began to feel unnerved. Suddenly the door of their room blew open, and a damp wind put out their lamp. The darkness outside instantly filled their whole room from floor to ceiling. Kadambini came and stood right inside their room. It was half past two in the morning: the rain outside was relentless.

'Friend,' said Kadambini, 'I am your Kadambini, but I am no longer alive. I am dead.'

Yogmaya yelled out in terror; Shripati was speechless.

'But other than being dead, what harm have I done to you? If I have no place in this world, or in the next world, then where shall I go?' And again, in the rain and the night, as if to wake God from his sleep, she screamed, 'Oh, tell me, where shall I go?' Then, leaving the dumbfounded husband and wife in the dark house, Kadambini fled in search of her place in or beyond the world.

V

IT IS HARD to say how Kadambini returned to Ranihat. She did not show herself to anyone at first: she spent the whole day, without food, in a ruined deserted temple. When evening came – early, as it does in the monsoon, and oppressively dark – and the villagers, fearing a storm, had retreated into their houses, Kadambini emerged on to the road again. As she approached her in-laws' house, her heart started to pound; but she pulled her heavy veil round her head like a servant, and the gate-keepers did not prevent her from entering. Meanwhile the rain had come on even harder, and the wind blew more fiercely.

The mistress of the house – Sharadashankar's wife – was play-ing cards with her widowed sister-in-law. The maid was in the kitchen, and the little boy was lying in the bedroom, sleeping after a bout of fever. Kadambini entered the bedroom, without anyone noticing. It was impossible to say why she had returned to her in-laws' house – she herself did not know why – but she knew that she wanted to see the little boy again. She gave no thought to where she would go after that, or what would happen to her.

She saw, in the lamplight, the thin, frail little boy lying asleep with his fists clenched. Her racing heart thirsted when she saw him: how she longed to clasp him to her breast one last time, to protect him from all misfortune! But then she thought, 'Now that I am not here, who will look after him? His mother loves company, gossiping, playing cards; for a long time she was happy

to leave him in my care; she never had to bother with his upbringing. Who will take care of him, as I did?' The little boy
suddenly turned over and, half-asleep, said, '*Kākimā*, give me
some water.' 'O my darling,' she inwardly replied, 'my treasure:
you haven't yet forgotten your *Kākimā*.' At once she poured
out some water from the pitcher and, raising him up against her
breast, helped him to drink.

While he remained half-asleep, the little boy showed no surprise at taking water from his aunt as he had been used to doing.
But when Kadambini – fulfilling her longstanding desire – kissed
him, and then laid him down again, he came out of his sleep and
hugged her, asking, '*Kākimā*, did you die?'

'Yes, my darling,' she said.

'Have you come back to me? You won't die again?'

Before she could reply an uproar broke out: a maid had
come into the room with a bowl of sago in her hand, but had
then screamed and fallen down in a faint. Hearing her scream,
Sharadashankar's wife dropped her cards and came running: she
stiffened like wood when she was in the room, unable either to
flee or utter a word. Seeing all this, the boy himself took fright.
'*Kākimā*, you must go,' he said, wailing.

Kadambini felt for the first time now that she had not died.
The ancient house, everything in it, the little boy, his affection
– they were all equally alive to her; there was no gulf intervening between her and them. When she had been in her friend's
house she had felt dead, felt that the person whom her friend had
known had died. But now that she was in her nephew's room,
she realized that his *Kākimā* had never died at all.

'*Didi*,' she said pathetically, 'why are you frightened of me?
See – I am just as I was.'

Her sister-in-law could not keep her balance any longer; she
collapsed unconscious.

Informed by his sister, Sharadashankar Babu himself came
into the inner quarters. Clasping his hands he begged, 'Sister-in-
law, it is not right of you to do this. Shatish is the only son in the
family: why are you casting your eye on him? Are we strangers
to you? Ever since you went, he has wasted away day by day;
he has been constantly ill, calling out "*Kākimā, Kākimā*" day and
night. Now that you have bid farewell to the world, please stop
attaching yourself to him, please go away – we'll perform your
proper funerary rites.'

Kadambini could bear no more. She screamed out, 'I did not die, I did not die, I tell you! How can I make you understand – I did not die! Can't you see: I am *alive*.' She seized the bell-metal bowl that had been dropped on the ground and dashed it against her brow: blood gushed out from the impact. 'See here, I am alive!'

Sharadashankar stood like a statue; the little boy whimpered for his father; the two stricken women lay on the ground. Crying out, 'I did not die, I did not die, I did not die,' Kadambini fled from the room and down the stairs, and threw herself into the tank in the inner courtyard of the house. Sharadashankar heard, from the upper floor, a splashing sound.

It went on raining all night, and it was still raining the next morning; even in the afternoon there was no let-up. Kadambini had proved, by dying, that she had not died.

Kabuliwallah

MY FIVE-YEAR-OLD daughter Mini can't stop talking for a minute. It only took her a year to learn to speak, after coming into the world, and ever since she has not wasted a minute of her waking hours by keeping silent. Her mother often scolds her and makes her shut up, but I can't do that. When Mini is quiet, it is so unnatural that I cannot bear it. So she's rather keen on chatting to me.

One morning, as I was starting the seventeenth chapter of my novel, Mini came up to me and said, 'Father, Ramdoyal the gatekeeper calls a crow a *kauyā* instead of a *kāk*. He doesn't know anything, does he!'

Before I had a chance to enlighten her about the multiplicity of languages in the world, she brought up another subject. 'Guess what, Father, Bhola says it rains when an elephant in the sky squirts water through its trunk. What nonsense he talks! On and on, all day.'

Without waiting for my opinion on this matter either, she suddenly asked, 'Father, what relation is Mother to you?'

'Good question,'[1] I said to myself, but to Mini I said, 'Run off and play with Bhola. I've got work to do.'

But she then sat down near my feet beside my writing-table, and, slapping her knees, began to recite '*āgḍum bāgḍum*' at top speed. Meanwhile, in my seventeenth chapter, Pratap Singh was leaping under cover of night from his high prison-window into the river below, with Kanchanmala in his arms.

My study looks out on to the road. Mini suddenly abandoned the '*āgḍum bāgḍum*' game, ran over to the window and shouted, 'Kabuliwallah, Kabuliwallah!'

Dressed in dirty baggy clothes, pugree on his head, bag hanging from his shoulder, and with three or four boxes of grapes in his hands, a tall Kabuliwallah was ambling along the road. It was hard to say exactly what thoughts the sight of him had put into my beloved daughter's mind, but she began to shout and shriek at him. That swinging bag spells trouble, I thought: my

1. Lit. 'In my mind I said "sister-in-law".'

seventeenth chapter won't get finished today. But just as the Kabuliwallah, attracted by Mini's yells, looked towards us with a smile and started to approach our house, Mini gasped and ran into the inner rooms, disappearing from view. She had a blind conviction that if one looked inside that swinging bag one would find three or four live children like her.

Meanwhile the Kabuliwallah came up to the window and smilingly salaamed. I decided that although the plight of Pratap Singh and Kanchanmala was extremely critical, it would be churlish not to invite the fellow inside and buy something from him.

I bought something. Then I chatted to him for a bit. We talked about Abdur Rahman's efforts to preserve the integrity of Afghanistan against the Russians and the British. When he got up to leave, he asked, 'Babu, where did your little girl go?'

To dispel her groundless fears, I called Mini to come out. She clung to me and looked suspiciously at the Kabuliwallah and his bag. The Kabuliwallah took some raisins and apricots out and offered them to her, but she would not take them, and clung to my knees with doubled suspicion. Thus passed her first meeting with the Kabuliwallah.

A few days later when for some reason I was on my way out of the house one morning, I saw my daughter sitting on a bench in front of the door, nattering unrestrainedly; and the Kabuliwallah was sitting at her feet listening – grinning broadly, and from time to time making comments in his hybrid sort of Bengali. In all her five years of life, Mini had never found so patient a listener, apart from her father. I also saw that the fold of her little sari was crammed with raisins and nuts. I said to the Kabuliwallah, 'Why have you given all these? Don't give her any more.' I then took a half-rupee out of my pocket and gave it to him. He unhesitatingly took the coin and put it in his bag.

When I returned home, I found that this half-rupee had caused a full-scale row. Mini's mother was holding up a round shining object and saying crossly to Mini, 'Where did you get this half-rupee from?'

'The Kabuliwallah gave it to me,' said Mini.

'Why did you take it from the Kabuliwallah?' said her mother.

'I didn't ask for it,' said Mini tearfully. 'He gave it to me himself.'

I rescued Mini from her mother's wrath, and took her outside. I learnt that this was not just the second time that Mini and the Kabuliwallah had met: he had been coming nearly every day and, by bribing her eager little heart with pistachio-nuts, had quite won her over. I found that they now had certain fixed jokes and routines: for example as soon as Mini saw Rahamat, she giggled and asked, 'Kabuliwallah, O Kabuliwallah, what have you got in your bag?' Rahamat would laugh back and say – giving the word a peculiar nasal twang – 'An *elephant*.' The notion of an elephant in his bag was the source of immense hilarity; it might not be a very subtle joke, but they both seemed to find it very funny, and it gave me pleasure to see, on an autumn morning, a young child and a grown man laughing so heartily.

They had a couple of other jokes. Rahamat would say to Mini, 'Little one, don't ever go off to your *śvaśur-bāṛi*.' Most Bengali girls grow up hearing frequent references to their *śvaśur-bāṛi*, but my wife and I are rather progressive people and we don't keep talking to our young daughter about her future marriage. She therefore couldn't clearly understand what Rahamat meant; yet to remain silent and give no reply was wholly against her nature, so she would turn the idea round and say, 'Are *you* going to your *śvaśur-bāṛi*?' Shaking his huge fist at an imaginary father-in-law Rahamat said, 'I'll settle him!' Mini laughed merrily as she imagined the fate awaiting this unknown creature called a *śvaśur*.

It was perfect autumn weather. In ancient times, kings used to set out on their world-conquests in autumn. I have never been away from Calcutta; precisely because of that, my mind roves all over the world. I seem to be condemned to my house, but I constantly yearn for the world outside. If I hear the name of a foreign land, at once my heart races towards it; and if I see a foreigner, at once an image of a cottage on some far bank or wooded mountainside forms in my mind, and I think of the free and pleasant life I would lead there. At the same time, I am such a rooted sort of individual that whenever I have to leave my familiar spot I practically collapse. So a morning spent sitting at my table in my little study, chatting with this Kabuliwallah, was quite enough wandering for me. High, scorched, blood-coloured, forbidding mountains on either side of a narrow desert path; laden camels passing; turbaned merchants and wayfarers, some on camels, some walking, some with spears in their hands, some with old-fashioned flintlock guns: my friend would talk of his native land in his booming, broken Bengali, and a mental picture of it would pass before my eyes.

Mini's mother is very easily alarmed. The slightest noise in the street makes her think that all the world's drunkards are charging straight at our house. She cannot dispel from her mind – despite her experience of life (which isn't great) – the apprehension that the world is overrun with thieves, bandits, drunkards, snakes, tigers, malaria, caterpillars, cockroaches and white-skinned marauders. She was not too happy about Rahamat the Kabuliwallah. She repeatedly told me to keep a close eye on him. If I tried to laugh off her suspicions, she would launch into a succession of questions: 'So do people's children never go missing? And is there no slavery in Afghanistan? Is it completely impossible for a huge Afghan to kidnap a little child?' I had to admit that it was not impossible, but I found it hard to believe. People are suggestible to varying degrees; this was why my wife remained so edgy. But I still saw nothing wrong in letting Rahamat come to our house.

Every year, about the middle of the month of Māgh, Rahamat went home. He was always very busy before he left, collecting money owed to him. He had to go from house to house; but he still made time to visit Mini. To see them together, one might well suppose that they were plotting something. If he couldn't come in the morning he would come in the evening; to see his lanky figure in a corner of the darkened house, with his baggy pyjamas hanging loosely around him, was indeed a little frightening. But my heart would light up as Mini ran to meet him, smiling and calling, 'O Kabuliwallah, Kabuliwallah,' and the usual innocent jokes passed between the two friends, unequal in age though they were.

One morning I was sitting in my little study correcting proof-sheets. The last days of winter had been very cold, shiveringly so. The morning sun was shining through the window on to my feet below my table, and this touch of warmth was very pleasant. It must have been about eight o'clock – early morning walkers, swathed in scarves, had mostly finished their dawn stroll and had returned to their homes. It was then that there was a sudden commotion in the street.

I looked out and saw our Rahamat in handcuffs, being

marched along by two policemen, and behind him a crowd of
curious boys. Rahamat's clothes were blood-stained, and one of
the policemen was holding a blood-soaked knife. I went outside
and stopped him, asking what was up. I heard partly from him
and partly from Rahamat himself that a neighbour of ours had
owed Rahamat something for a Rampuri chadar; he had tried to
lie his way out of the debt, and in the ensuing brawl Rahamat
had stabbed him.

Rahamat was mouthing various unrepeatable curses against
the lying debtor, when Mini ran out of the house calling, 'Kabuliwallah, O Kabuliwallah.' For a moment Rahamat's face lit up
with pleasure. He had no bag over his shoulder today, so they
couldn't have their usual discussion about it. Mini came straight
out with her 'Are *you* going to your *śvaśur-bāṛi*?'

'Yes, I'm going there now,' said Rahamat with a smile. But
when he saw that his reply had failed to amuse Mini, he bran-
dished his handcuffed fists and said, 'I would have killed my
śvaśur, but how can I with these on?'

Rahamat was convicted of assault, and sent to prison for several years. He virtually faded from our minds. Living at home,
carrying on day by day with our routine tasks, we gave no
thought to how a free-spirited mountain-dweller was passing
his years behind prison-walls. As for the fickle Mini, even her
father would have to admit that her behaviour was not very
praiseworthy. She swiftly forgot her old friend. At first Nabi the
groom replaced him in her affections; later, as she grew up, girls
rather than little boys became her favourite companions. She
even stopped coming to her father's study. And I, in a sense,
dropped her.

Several years went by. It was autumn again. Mini's marriage had
been decided, and the wedding was fixed for the *pūjā*-holiday.
Our pride and joy would soon, like Durga going to Mount
Kailas, darken her parents' house by moving to her husband's.

It was a most beautiful morning. Sunlight, washed clean by
monsoon rains, seemed to shine with the purity of smelted gold.
Its radiance lent an extraordinary grace to Calcutta's back-streets,
with their squalid, tumbledown, cheek-by-jowl dwellings. The
sānāi started to play in our house when night was scarcely over. Its
wailing vibrations seemed to rise from deep within my rib-cage.
Its sad Bhairavī *rāga* joined forces with the autumn sunshine, in

spreading through the world the grief of my imminent separation. Today my Mini would be married.

From dawn on there was uproar, endless coming and going. A canopy was being erected in the yard of the house, by binding bamboo-poles together; chandeliers tinkled as they were hung in the rooms and verandahs; there was constant loud talk.

I was sitting in my study doing accounts, when Rahamat suddenly appeared and salaamed before me. At first I didn't recognize him. He had no bag; he had lost his long hair; his former vigour had gone. But when he smiled, I recognized him.

'How are you, Rahamat?' I said. 'When did you come?'

'I was let out of prison yesterday evening,' he replied.

His words startled me. I had never confronted a would-be murderer before; I shrank back at the sight of him. I began to feel that on this auspicious morning it would be better to have the man out of the way. 'We've got something on in our house today,' I said. 'I'm rather busy. Please go now.'

He was ready to go at once, but just as he reached the door he hesitated a little and said, 'Can't I see your little girl for a moment?'

It seemed he thought that Mini was still just as she was when he had known her: that she would come running as before, calling 'Kabuliwallah, O Kabuliwallah!'; that their old merry banter would resume. He had even brought (remembering their old friendship) a box of grapes and a few nuts and raisins wrapped in paper – extracted, no doubt, from some Afghan friend of his, having no bag of his own now.

'There's something on in the house today,' I said. 'You can't see anyone.'

He looked rather crestfallen. He stood silently for a moment longer, casting a solemn glance at me; then, saying 'Babu salaam', he walked towards the door. I felt a sudden pang. I thought of calling him back, but then I saw that he himself was returning.

'I brought this box of grapes and these nuts and raisins for the little one,' he said. 'Please give them to her.' Taking them from him, I was about to pay him for them when he suddenly clasped my arm and said, 'Please, don't give me any money – I shall always be grateful, Babu. Just as you have a daughter, so do I have one, in my own country. It is with her in mind that I came with a few raisins for your daughter: I didn't come to trade with you.'

Then he put a hand inside his big loose shirt and took out from somewhere close to his heart a crumpled piece of paper. Unfolding it very carefully, he spread it out on my table. There was a small handprint on the paper: not a photograph, not a painting – the hand had been rubbed with some soot and pressed down on to the paper. Every year Rahamat carried this memento of his daughter in his breast-pocket when he came to sell raisins in Calcutta's streets: as if the touch of that soft, small, childish hand brought solace to his huge, homesick breast. My eyes swam at the sight of it. I forgot then that he was an Afghan raisin-seller and I was a Bengali Babu. I understood then that he was as I am, that he was a father just as I am a father. The handprint of his little mountain-dwelling Parvati reminded me of my own Mini.

At once I sent for her from the inner part of the house. Objections came back: I refused to listen to them. Mini, dressed as a bride – sandal-paste pattern on her brow, red silk sari – came timidly into the room and stood close by me.

The Kabuliwallah was confused at first when he saw her: he couldn't bring himself to utter his old greeting. But at last he smiled and said, 'Little one, are you going to your *śvaśur-bāṛi*?'

Mini now knew the meaning of *śvaśur-bāṛi*; she couldn't reply as before – she blushed at Rahamat's question and looked away. I recalled the day when Mini and the Kabuliwallah had first met. My heart ached.

Mini left the room, and Rahamat, sighing deeply, sat down on the floor. He suddenly understood clearly that his own daughter would have grown up too since he last saw her, and with her too he would have to become re-acquainted: he would not find her exactly as she was before. Who knew what had happened to her these eight years? In the cool autumn morning sunshine the *sānāi* went on playing, and Rahamat sat in a Calcutta lane and pictured to himself the barren mountains of Afghanistan.

I took out a banknote and gave it to him. 'Rahamat,' I said, 'go back to your homeland and your daughter; by your blessed reunion, Mini will be blessed.'

By giving him this money, I had to trim certain items from the wedding-festivities. I wasn't able to afford the electric illuminations I had planned, nor did the trumpet-and-drum band come. The womenfolk were very displeased at this; but for me, the ceremony was lit by a kinder, more gracious light.

Holiday

PHATIK CHAKRABARTI, leader of the gang, suddenly had a bright idea. Lying by the river was a huge *sāl*-tree log, just waiting to be made into a mast. Everyone must help to roll it along! Without giving a thought to the surprise, annoyance and inconvenience that would be caused to the person who needed the log for timber, all the boys fell in with this suggestion. They got down to the task with a will; but just then Phatik's younger brother Makhanlal came and solemnly sat on the log. The boys were rather nonplussed by his haughty, dismissive attitude.

One of them went up to him and nervously tried to push him off, but he refused to budge. Wise beyond his years, he continued to ponder the vanity of all childish games.

'You'll pay for this,' said Phatik, brandishing his fist. 'Clear off.'

But Makhanlal merely adjusted his perch and settled down even more immovably on the log.

In this kind of situation, Phatik ought to have preserved his supremacy over the other boys by delivering immediately a hearty slap on his wayward brother's cheek – but he didn't dare. Instead he assumed a manner implying that he could, had he so wished, have meted out this customary punishment, but he wasn't going to, because a more amusing idea had occurred to him. Why not, he proposed, roll the log over with Makhanlal on it?

Makhan at first saw glory in this; he did not think (nor did anyone else) that like other worldly glories it might carry dangers. The boys rolled up their sleeves and began to push – 'Heave ho! Heave ho! Over we go!' With one spin of the log, Makhan's solemnity, glory and wisdom crashed to the ground.

The other boys were delighted at such an unexpectedly quick outcome, but Phatik was rather embarrassed. Makhan immediately jumped up and threw himself on to him, hitting him with blind rage and scratching his nose and cheeks. Then he made his way home tearfully.

The game having been spoilt, Phatik pulled up a few reeds, and climbing on to the prow of a half-sunk boat sat quietly chewing them. A boat – not a local one – came up to the mooring-place. A middle-aged gentleman with a black moustache but grey hair stepped ashore. 'Where is the Chakrabartis' house?' he asked the boy.

'Over there,' replied Phatik, still chewing the reed-stalks. But no one would have been able to understand which direction to take.

'Where?' asked the gentleman again.

'Don't know,' said Phatik, and he carried on as before, sucking juice from the stalks. The gentleman had to ask others to help him find the house.

Suddenly Bagha Bagdi (a servant) appeared and said, 'Phatik-*dādā*, Mother's calling you.'

'Shan't go,' said Phatik.

He struggled and kicked helplessly as Bagha picked him up bodily and carried him home. His mother shouted furiously when she saw him: 'You've beaten up Makhan again!'

'I didn't beat him up.'

'How dare you lie to me?'

'I did *not* beat him up. Ask him.'

When Makhan was questioned he stuck to his earlier accusation, saying, 'He *did* beat me up.' Phatik could not stand this any more. He charged at Makhan and thumped him hard, shouting, 'So who's lying now?' His mother, taking Makhan's part, rushed and slapped Phatik's back several times heavily. He pushed her away. 'So you'd lay hands on your own mother?' she screamed.

At that moment the black-grey gentleman entered the house and said, 'What's going on here?'

'*Dādā!*' said Phatik's mother, overwhelmed with surprise and joy. 'When did you come?' She bent down and took the dust of his feet.

Many years previously her elder brother had gone to the west of India to work, and in the meantime she had had two children; they had grown, her husband had died – but all this time she had never seen her brother. At long last Bishvambhar Babu had returned home, and had now come to see his sister.

There were celebrations for several days. At length, a couple of days before his departure, Bishvambhar questioned his sister about the schooling and progress of her two sons. In reply, he was given a description of Phatik's uncontrollable wildness and inattention to study; while Makhan, by contrast, was perfectly behaved and a model student. 'Phatik drives me mad,' she said.

Bishvambhar then proposed that he take Phatik to Calcutta, keep him with him and supervise his education. The widow easily agreed to this. 'Well, Phatik,' he asked the boy, 'how would you like to go to Calcutta with your uncle?' 'I'd love to,' said Phatik, jumping up and down.

His mother did not object to seeing her son off, because she always lived in dread that Makhan might be pushed into the river by him or might split his head open in some terrible accident; but she was a little cast down by the eagerness with which Phatik seized the idea of going. He pestered his uncle with 'When are we going? When are we going?' – and couldn't sleep at night for excitement.

When at last the day to leave came, he was moved to a joyous display of generosity. He bestowed on Makhan his fishing-rod, kite and reel, with permanent right of inheritance.

When he arrived at his uncle's house in Calcutta, he first had to be introduced to his aunt. I cannot say she was over-pleased at this unnecessary addition to her family. She was used to looking after her house and three children as they were, and suddenly to loose into their midst an unknown, uneducated country boy would probably be most disruptive. If only Bishvambhar had insight commensurate with his years! Moreover, there is no greater nuisance in the world than a boy of thirteen or fourteen. There is no beauty in him, and he does nothing useful either. He arouses no affection; nor is his company welcome. If he speaks modestly he sounds false; if he speaks sense he sounds arrogant; if he speaks at all he is felt to be intrusive. He suddenly shoots up in height so that his clothes no longer fit him – which is an ugly affront to other people. His childish grace and sweetness of voice suddenly disappear, and people find it impossible not to blame him for this. Many faults can be forgiven in a child or a young man, but at this age even natural and unavoidable faults are felt to be unbearable.

He himself is fully aware that he does not fit properly into the world; so he is perpetually ashamed of his existence and seeks forgiveness for it. Yet this is the age at which a rather greater longing for affection develops in him. If he gets at this time love and companionship from some sympathetic person, he will do anything in return. But no one dares show affection, in case others condemn this as pampering. So he looks and behaves like a stray street-dog.

To leave home and mother and go to a strange place is hell for a boy of this age. To live with loveless indifference all around is like walking on thorns. This is the age when normally a conception forms of women as wonderful, heavenly creatures; to be cold-shouldered by them is terribly hard to bear. It was therefore especially painful to Phatik that his aunt saw him as an evil star. If she happened to ask him to do a job for her and – meaning well – he did more than was strictly necessary, his aunt would stamp on his enthusiasm, saying, 'That's quite enough, quite enough. I don't want you meddling any more. Go and get on with your own work. Do some studying.' His aunt's excessive concern for his mental improvement would then seem terribly cruel and unjust.

He so lacked love in this household, and it seemed he could breathe freely nowhere. Stuck behind its walls, he thought constantly of his home village. The fields where he would let his 'monster-kite' fly and flap in the wind; the river-bank where he wandered aimlessly, singing a *rāga* of his own invention at the top of his voice; the small stream in which he would jump and swim now and then in the heat of the day; his gang of followers; the mischief they would get up to; the freedom; above all his harsh, impetuous mother; all this tugged continually at his helpless heart. A kind of instinctive love, like an animal's; a blind longing to be near; an unspoken distress at being far; a heartfelt, anguished cry of '*Mā, Mā*' like a motherless calf at dusk; such feelings perpetually afflicted this gawky, nervous, thin, lanky, ungainly boy.

At school there was no one more stupid and inattentive than he. If asked a question he would just stare back vacantly. If the teacher cuffed him, he would silently bear it like a laden, exhausted ass. At break-time, he would stand at the window staring at the roofs of distant houses, while his classmates played outside. If a child or two appeared for a moment on one of the roofs, in the midday sunshine, playing some game, his misery intensified.

One day he plucked up courage to ask his uncle, 'Uncle, when will I be going home to see Mother?'

'When the school holiday comes,' said his uncle. The *pūjā*-holiday in the month of Kartik – that was a long way off!

One day Phatik lost his school-books. He never found it easy to prepare his lessons, and now, with his books lost, he was completely helpless. The teacher started to beat and humiliate him every day. His standing in school sank so low that his cousins were ashamed to admit their connection with him. Whenever he was punished, they showed even greater glee than the other boys. It became too much to bear, and one day he went to his aunt and confessed like a criminal that he had lost his school-books. 'Well, well,' said his aunt, lines of annoyance curling round her lips, 'and do you suppose I can buy you new books five times a month?' He said no more. That he should have wasted *someone else*'s money made him feel even more hurt and rejected by his mother. His misery and sense of inferiority dragged him down to the very earth.

That night, when he returned from school, he had a pain in his head and was shivering. He could tell he was getting a fever. He also knew that his aunt would not take kindly to his being ill. He had a clear sense of what an unnecessary, unjustifiable nuisance it would be to her. He felt he had no right to expect that an odd, useless, stupid boy such as he should be nursed by anyone other than his mother.

The next morning Phatik was nowhere to be seen. He was searched for in all the neighbours' houses round about, but there was no trace of him. In the evening torrential rain began, so in searching for him many people got soaked to the skin – to no avail. In the end, finding him nowhere, Bishvambhar Babu informed the police.

A whole day later, in the evening, a carriage drew up outside Bishvambhar's house. Rain was still thudding down relentlessly, and the street was flooded to a knee's depth. Two policemen bundled Phatik out of the carriage and put him down in front of Bishvambhar. He was soaked from head to foot, covered with mud, his eyes and cheeks were flushed, he was trembling violently. Bishvambhar virtually had to carry him into the house.

'You see what happens,' snapped his wife, 'when you take in someone else's child. You must send him home.' But in fact the whole of that day she had hardly been able to eat for worry, and had been unreasonably tetchy with her own children.

'I was going to go to my mother,' said Phatik, weeping, 'but they brought me back.'

The boy's fever climbed alarmingly. He was delirious all

night. Bishvambhar fetched the doctor. Opening his bloodshot eyes for a moment and staring blankly at the ceiling joists, Phatik said, 'Uncle, has my holiday-time come?' Bishvambhar, dabbing his own eyes with a handkerchief, tenderly took Phatik's thin, hot hand in his and sat down beside him. He spoke again, mumbling incoherently: 'Mother, don't beat me, Mother. I didn't do anything wrong, honest!'

The next day, during the short time when he was conscious, Phatik kept looking bewilderedly round the room, as if expecting someone. When no one came, he turned and lay mutely with his face towards the wall. Understanding what was on his mind, Bishvambhar bent down and said softly in his ear, 'Phatik, I've sent for your mother.'

Another day passed. The doctor, looking solemn and gloomy, pronounced the boy's condition to be critical. Bishvambhar sat at the bedside in the dim lamplight, waiting minute by minute for Phatik's mother's arrival. Phatik started to shout out, like a boatman, 'More than one fathom deep, more than two fathoms deep!' To come to Calcutta they had had to travel some of the way by steamer. The boatmen had lowered the hawser into the stream and bellowed out its depth. In his delirium, Phatik was imitating them, calling out the depth in pathetic tones; except that the endless sea he was about to cross had no bottom that his measuring-rope could touch.

It was then that his mother stormed into the room, bursting into loud wails of grief. When, with difficulty, Bishvambhar managed to calm her down, she threw herself on to the bed and sobbed, 'Phatik, my darling, my treasure.'

'Yes?' said Phatik, seemingly quite relaxed.

'Phatik, darling boy,' cried his mother again.

Turning slowly on to his side, and looking at no one, Phatik said softly, 'Mother, my holiday has come now. I'm going home.'

Giribala

GIRIBALA IS OVERFLOWING with exuberance of youth that seems spilling over in spray all around her, – in the folds of her soft dress, the turning of her neck, the motion of her hands, in the rhythm of her steps, now quick now languid, in her tinkling anklets and ringing laughter, in her voice and glances. She would often been seen, wrapt in a blue silk, walking on her terrace, in an impulse of unaccountable restlessness. Her limbs seem eager to dance to the time of an inner music unceasing and unheard. She takes pleasure in merely moving her body, causing ripples to break out in the flood of her young life. She would suddenly pluck a leaf from a plant in the flower-pot and throw it up in the sky, and her bangles would give a sudden tinkle, and the careless grace of her hand, like a bird freed from its cage, would fly unseen in the air. With her swift fingers she would brush away from her dress a mere nothing; standing on tiptoe she would peep over her terrace walls for no cause whatever, and then with a rapid motion turn round to go to another direction, swinging her bunch of keys tied to a corner of her garment. She would loosen her hair in an untimely caprice, sitting before her mirror to do it up again, and then in a fit of laziness would fling herself upon her bed, like a line of stray moonlight slipping through some opening of the leaves, idling in the shadow.

She has no children and, having been married in a wealthy family, has very little work to do. Thus she seems to be daily accumulating her own self without expenditure, till the vessel is brimming over with the seething surplus. She has her husband, but not under her control. She has grown up from a girl into a woman, yet escaping, through familiarity, her husband's notice.

When she was newly married and her husband, Gopinath, was attending his college, he would often play the truant and under cover of the midday siesta of his elders secretly come to make love to Giribala. Though they lived under the same roof, he would create occasions to send her letters on tinted paper perfumed with rosewater, and would even gloat upon some exaggerated grievances of imaginary neglect of love.

Just then his father died and he became the sole owner of his property. Like an unseasoned piece of timber, the immature youth of Gopinath attracted parasites which began to bore into his substance. From now his movements took the course that led him in a contrary direction from his wife.

There is a dangerous fascination to be leaders of men, to which many strong minds have succumbed. To be accepted as the leader of a small circle of sycophants, in his own parlour, has the same fearful attraction for a man who suffers from a scarcity of brains and character. Gopinath assumed the part of a hero among his friends and acquaintances, and tried daily to invent new wonders in all manner of extravagance. He won a reputation among his followers for his audacity of excesses, which goaded him not only to keep up his fame, but to surpass himself at all costs.

In the meanwhile, Giribala, in the seclusion of her lonely youth, felt like a queen who had her throne, but no subjects. She knew she had the power in her hand which could make the world of men her captive; only that world itself was wanting.

Giribala has a maidservant whose name is Sudha. She can sing and dance and improvise verses, and she freely gives expression to her regret that such a beauty as that of her mistress should be dedicated to a fool who forgets to enjoy what he owns. Giribala is never tired of hearing from her the details of her charms, while at the same time contradicting her, calling her a liar and a flatterer, exciting her to swear by all that is sacred that she is earnest in her admiration, which statement, even without the accompaniment of a solemn oath, is not difficult for Giribala to believe.

Sudha used to sing to her a song beginning with the line, 'Let me write myself a slave upon the soles of thy feet,' and Giribala in her imagination could feel that her beautiful feet were fully worthy of bearing inscriptions of everlasting slavery from conquered hearts, if only they could be free in their career of conquest.

But the woman to whom her husband Gopinath has surrendered himself as a slave is Lavanga, the actress, who has the reputation of playing to perfection the part of a maiden languishing in hopeless love and swooning on the stage with an exquisite naturalness. When her husband had not altogether vanished from her sphere of influence, Giribala had often heard from him about the wonderful histrionic powers of this woman and in her jealous curiosity had greatly desired to see Lavanga on the stage. But she could not secure her husband's consent, because Gopinath was firm in his opinion that the theatre was a place not fit for any decent woman to visit.

At last she paid for a seat and sent Sudha to see this famous actress in one of her best parts. The account that she received from her on her return was far from flattering to Lavanga, both as to her personal appearance and her stage accomplishments. As, for obvious reasons, she had great faith in Sudha's power of appreciation, where it was due, Giribala did not hesitate to believe her in her description of Lavanga, which was accompanied by a mimicry of a ludicrous mannerism.

When at last her husband deserted her in his infatuation for this woman, she began to feel qualms of doubt. But as Sudha repeatedly asserted her former opinion with ever greater vehemence, comparing Lavanga to a piece of burnt log dressed up in a woman's clothes, Giribala determined secretly to go to the theatre herself and settle this question for good.

And she *did* go there one night with all the excitement of a forbidden entry. Her very trepidation of heart lent a special charm to what she saw. She gazed at the faces of the spectators, lit up with an unnatural shine of lamplight; and, with the magic of its music and the painted canvas of its scenery, the theatre seemed to her like a world where society was suddenly freed from its law of gravitation.

Coming from her walled up terrace and joyless home, she had entered a region where dreams and reality had clasped their hands in friendship, over the wine cup of art.

The bell rang, the orchestra music stopped, the audience sat still in their seats, the stage-lights shone brighter, and the curtain was drawn up. Suddenly appeared in the light, from the mystery of the unseen, the shepherd girls of the Vrinda forest, and with the accompaniment of songs commenced their dance, punctuated with the uproarious applause of the audience. The blood began to throb all over Giribala's body, and she forgot for the moment that her life was limited to the circumstances and that she was not free in a world where all laws had melted in music.

Sudha came occasionally to interrupt her with her anxious whispers urging her to hasten back home for the fear of being detected. But she paid no heed to her warning, for her sense of fear had gone.

The play goes on. Krishna has given offence to his beloved
Radha and she in her wounded pride refuses to recognize him.
He is entreating her, abasing himself at her feet, but in vain.
Giribala's heart seems to swell. She imagines herself as offended
Radha; and feels that she also has in her this woman's power to
vindicate her pride. She had heard what a force was woman's
beauty in the world but to-night it became to her palpable.

At last the curtain dropped, the light grew dim, the audience
got ready to leave the theatre, but Giribala sat still like one in a
dream. The thought that she would have to go home had vanished from her mind. She waited for the curtain to rise again and
the eternal theme of Krishna's humiliation at the feet of Radha
to continue. But Sudha came to remind her that the play had
ended and the lamps would soon be put out.

It was late when Giribala came back home. A kerosene lamp
was dimly burning in the melancholy solitude and silence of her
room. Near the window upon her lonely bed a mosquito curtain was gently moving in the breeze. Her world seemed to her
distasteful and mean like a rotten fruit swept into the dustbin.

From now she regularly visited the theatre every Saturday.
The fascination of her first sight of it lost much of its glamour.
The painted vulgarity of the actresses and the falseness of their
affectation became more and more evident, yet the habit grew
upon her. Every time the curtain rose the window of her life's
prison-house seemed to open before her and the stage, bordered
off from the world of reality by its gilded frame and scenic display, by its array of lights and even its flimsiness of conventionalism, appeared to her like a fairyland where it was not impossible
for herself to occupy the throne of the fairy queen.

When for the first time she saw her husband among the
audience shouting his drunken admiration for a certain actress
she felt an intense disgust and prayed in her mind that a day
might come when she might have an opportunity to spurn him
away with her contempt. But the opportunity became rarer
every day, for Gopinath was hardly ever to be seen at his home
now, being carried away, one knew not where, in the centre of
a dust-storm of dissipation.

One evening in the month of March, in the light of the full
moon, Giribala was sitting on her terrace dressed in her cream-
coloured robe. It was her habit daily to deck herself with jewellery as if for some festive occasion. For these costly gems were

like wine to her – they sent heightened consciousness of beauty to her limbs; she felt like a plant in spring tingling with the impulse of flowers in all its branches. She wore a pair of diamond bracelets on her arms, a necklace of rubies and pearls on her neck, and a ring with a big sapphire on the little finger of her left hand. Sudha was sitting near her bare feet admiringly touching them with her hand and expressing her wish that she were a man privileged to offer her life as homage to such a pair of feet.

Sudha gently hummed a lovesong to her and the evening wore on to night. Every body in the household had finished their evening meal, and gone to sleep. When suddenly Gopinath appeared reeking with scent and liquor, and Sudha drawing her cloth-end over her face, hastily ran away from the terrace.

Giribala thought for a moment that her day had come at last. She turned away her face and sat silent.

But the curtain in her stage did not rise and no song of entreaty came from her hero, with the words – 'Listen to the pleading of the moon-light, my love, and hide not thy face.'

In his dry unmusical voice Gopinath said, 'Give me your keys.'

A gust of south wind like a sigh of the insulted romance of the poetic world scattered all over the terrace the smell of the night-blooming jasmines and loosened some wisp of hair on Giribala's cheek. She let go her pride, and got up and said, 'You shall have your keys if you listen to what I have to say.'

Gopinath said, 'I cannot delay. Give me your keys.'

Giribala said, 'I will give you the keys and everything that is in the safe, but you must not leave me.'

Gopinath said, 'That cannot be. I have urgent business.'

'Then you shan't have the keys,' said Giribala.

Gopinath began to search for them. He opened the drawers of the dressing table, broke open the lid of the box that contained Giribala's toilet requisites, smashed the glass panes of her almirah, groped under the pillows and mattress of the bed, but the keys he could not find. Giribala stood near the door stiff and silent like a marble image gazing at vacancy. Trembling with rage Gopinath came to her and said with an angry growl, 'Give me your keys or you will repent.'

Giribala did not answer and Gopinath, pinning her to the wall, snatched away by force her bracelets, necklace and ring, and, giving her a parting kick, went away.

Nobody in the house woke up from his sleep, none in the neighbourhood knew of this outrage, the moonlight remained placid and the peace of the night undisturbed. Hearts can be rent never to heal again amidst such serene silence.

The next morning Giribala said she was going to see her father and left home. As Gopinath's present destination was not known and she was not responsible to anybody else in the house her absence was not noticed.

2

THE NEW PLAY of 'Manorama' was on rehearsal in the theatre where Gopinath was a constant visitor. Lavanga was practising for the part of the heroine Manorama, and Gopinath, sitting in the front seat with his rabble of followers, would vociferously encourage his favourite actress with his approbation. This greatly disturbed the rehearsal but the proprietors of the theatre did not dare to annoy their patron of whose vindictiveness they were afraid. But one day he went so far as to molest an actress in the greenroom and he had to be turned away by the aid of the police.

Gopinath determined to take his revenge, – and when, after a great deal of preparation and shrieking advertisements, the new play 'Manorama' was about to be produced, Gopinath took away the principal actress Lavanga with him and disappeared. It was a great shock to the manager, who had to postpone the opening night, and, getting hold of a new actress, taught her the part, and brought out the play before the public with considerable misgivings in his mind.

But the success was as unexpected as it was unprecedented. When its news reached Gopinath he could not resist his curiosity to come and see the performance.

The play opens with Manorama living in her husband's house neglected and hardly noticed. Near the end of the drama her husband deserts her and concealing his first marriage manages to marry a millionaire's daughter. When the wedding ceremony is over and the bridal veil is raised from her face she is discovered to be the same Manorama, only no longer the former drudge, but queenly in her beauty and splendour of dress and ornaments. In her infancy she had been brought up in a poor home being kidnapped from the house of her rich father, who having traced her to her husband's home, has brought her back to him and celebrates her marriage once again in a fitting manner.

In the concluding scene, when the husband is going through his period of penitence and humiliation, as is fit in a play which has its moral, a sudden disturbance arose among the audience. So long as Manorama appeared obscured in her position of drudgery Gopinath showed no sign of perturbation. But when after the wedding ceremony she came out dressed in her red bridal robe and took her veil off, when with a majestic pride of her overwhelming beauty she turned her face towards the audience and, slightly bending her neck, shot a fiery glance of exultation at Gopinath, applause broke out in wave after wave and the enthusiasm of the spectators became unbounded.

Suddenly Gopinath cried out in a thick voice, 'Giribala', and like a madman tried to rush upon the stage. The audience shouted, 'Turn him out,' the police came to drag him away and he struggled and screamed, 'I will kill her,' while the curtain dropped.

The Hungry Stones

I WENT AWAY during the *pūjā* holiday, touring the country with a theosophist relative. It was on the train back to Calcutta that we met the man. He was a Bengali Babu, but his dress made us think at first that he was a Muslim from Northern India – and his conversation was even more surprising. He spoke on every subject with such authority, that one might have taken him for God's personal adviser. We had been quite content not to know about the world's secret happenings: how far the Russians had advanced, what the British were plotting, or the bungling machinations of the Native States. But our informant said with a slight smile, 'There happen more things in heaven and earth, Horatio, than are reported in your newspapers.' It was the first time we had been away from home, so the man's whole style was a revelation to us. He could jump, at the drop of a hat, from science to the Veda to recitations of Persian couplets; having no such command ourselves, we admired him more and more. So much so, that my theosophist relative grew sure there was supernatural aura around the man – a strange sort of magnetism, a divine power, an astral body, or something of that sort. He listened to every little thing he said with rapt attention, and made surreptitious notes. I suspected that our strange companion was not unaware of this, and was rather flattered.

The train came to a junction, and we sat in a waiting-room for a connection. It was half past ten at night. We heard that some kind of disruption on the line had delayed the train badly. I decided to spread my bed-roll out on the table and get some sleep, but it was then that the man began the following story. I got no more sleep that night . . .

'Because of some disagreements over policy, I left my employ in the state of Junagar and entered the service of the Nizam of Hyderabad. I was young and sturdy at that time, so I was first of all given the job of collecting the cotton-tax at Barich.

'Barich is a most romantic place. The Shusta river there (the name is derived from the Sanskrit *svacchatoyā*[1]) flows through large forests with desolate mountains above, snaking its pebbly way over rocks like a skilful dancer picking her feet. A white marble palace stands alone on high rocks beneath the mountains, with 150 steep stone steps leading up from the river. There is no other house near by. The village of Barich with its cotton-market is a long way off.

'About 250 years ago Shah Mahmud II built the palace as a private pleasure-dome. In those days there were rose-scented fountains in the bathrooms: young Persian concubines sat in seclusion on cool marble, with their hair unplaited for bathing, dipping their soft, naked feet in pools of pure water, sitars in their laps, singing vineyard ghazals. Those fountains play no longer, the songs are heard no more, fair feet no longer fall on white stone: there is no one to inhabit the palatial emptiness of the place but a single, lonely tax-collector. But the old clerk in the office, Karim Khan, told me over and over again not to live there. "If you want, go there during the day," he said, "but don't ever spend a night." I scoffed at him. The servants, likewise, were willing to work there till dusk, but not to sleep there. "Suit yourselves," I said. The building had such a bad name that even thieves didn't venture there at night.

'At first the desolation of the palace oppressed me like a weight on my chest. I kept away from it as much as I could, working continuously, returning exhausted to my room to sleep. But after a few weeks, it began to exert a strange attraction. It is difficult to describe my state of mind and equally hard to convince people of it. The whole building seemed alive: it was sucking me in, its powerful stomach-juices were digesting me slowly. Probably it started to work on me from the moment I first set foot in it, but I clearly remember the day when I first became conscious of its power.

'It was the beginning of the summer: the market was sluggish, and I had little work to do. I had sat down in a comfortable chair by the river at the bottom of the steps, a little before sunset. The Shusta was depleted; its many sandbanks opposite were ruddy in the afternoon light; near me, pebbles glittered in the clear, shallow water at the bottom of the steps. There was not a breath of wind. The scent of wild basil, spearmint and aniseed in the hillside woods made the air oppressive.

1. 'Clear water.'

'When the sun went down behind the crags, a long shadow fell, like a curtain abruptly ending the drama of the day. Here in this cleft between mountains there was no real dusk, no mingling of light and dark. I was about to mount my horse and ride away, when I heard footsteps on the stairway. I turned round – but there was no one there.

'Thinking that my senses were deceiving me, I settled in my chair again; but now lots of footsteps could be heard – as if a crowd of people were rushing down the steps together. Slight fear mixed with a peculiar pleasure filled my body. Even though there was no physical presence before me, I had a clear impression of a crowd of jubilant women rushing down the steps this summer evening to bathe in the Shusta. There was no actual sound this evening on the silent slopes and river-bank, or inside the empty palace, but I could none the less hear bathers passing me, chasing one another with merry laughter like the waters of a spring. They didn't seem to notice me. I was as invisible to them as they were to me. The river was as undisturbed as before, but I had a clear feeling that its shallow stream was being ruffled by jingling, braceleted arms, that friends were splashing each other and shrieking with laughter, that kicking swimmers were scattering spray like fistfuls of pearls.

'I felt a kind of trembling in my chest: I can't say if the feeling was of fear or delight or curiosity. I longed to see what was happening, but there was nothing in front of me to see. I felt that if I strained to listen, I would hear all that was spoken – but when I *did* try to listen, I only heard scraping crickets! I felt that a 250-year-old black curtain was dangling in front of me; if only I could lift one corner and peer behind it, what a splendid royal scene would be revealed! But in the deep darkness nothing could be seen.

'Suddenly the sultriness of the air was broken by a sharp gust of wind: the calm Shusta shook like the tresses of a nymph, and the whole shadowy forest stirred as if waking from a bad dream. Whether dream or not, the invisible pageant from a world of 250 years ago was whisked away in a trice. The magic women who brushed past me with bodiless footsteps and noiseless laughter to jump into the Shusta did not return up the steps, wringing the water from their clothes. The spring breeze blew them away like a scent, in a single gust.

'Had the ruinous Goddess of Poetry landed on my shoulders,

finding me all on my own? Had she come to clobber me, for being such a slave to tax-collection? I decided I had better eat: an empty stomach can play havoc with one's health. I called my cook and ordered a full, spicy Moglai meal, swimming in ghee.

'The next morning the whole affair seemed ridiculous. I cheerfully trundled about, driving my pony-trap myself, wearing a pith helmet like a *sāheb*, making routine inquiries. I had my tri-monthly report to write, so I meant to stay late at my office. But as soon as it was dusk, I found myself drawn to the palace. I cannot say *who* was drawing me; but I felt it unwise to delay. I felt I was expected. Instead of completing my report, I put on my helmet again and returned to the huge, rock-bound palace, disturbing the deserted, shadowy path with my rattling pony-trap's wheels.

'The room at the top of the steps was immense. Its huge decorated, vaulted ceiling rested on three rows of pillars. It echoed all the time with its own emptiness. Evening was well-advanced, but no lamps had been lit. As I pushed open the door and entered that vast room, I felt a tremendous upheaval, like a court breaking up – people dispersing through doors, windows, rooms, passages, verandahs. I stood astonished; there was nothing I could *see*. I shuddered, went gooseflesh all over. A lingering scent of age-old shampoo and *ātar* caught my nostrils. I stood in the gloom between the pillars, and heard all round me the gush of fountains on stone, the sound of a sitar (but what the tune was I did not know), the tinkle of gold ornaments, the jingle of anklets, the noise of a gong striking the hour, a distant *ālāp* on a *sānāi*, the chinking of chandeliers swinging in the breeze, the song of a caged nightingale on the verandah, the cry of tame cranes in the gardens: all combining to create the music of the dead. I was transfixed: I felt that this impalpable, unreal scene was the only truth in the world, that everything else was a mirage. Was I really the Honourable Mr So-and-So, eldest son of the late Mr So-and-So, earning 450 rupees a month for collecting cotton-taxes? Did I really wear a pith helmet and short kurta, drive a pony-trap to the office? It seemed so odd and absurd and false, that I burst out laughing as I stood in that great, dark room.

'My Muslim servant then came in with a flaming kerosene lamp. I don't know whether he thought I was mad – but I suddenly remembered that I *was* the Honourable Mr So-and-So, eldest son of the late Mr So-and-So. Our great poets and artists could maybe say whether disembodied fountains played eternally in this world or somewhere outside it, or whether endless *rāgas* were plucked on a magic sitar by invisible fingers, but this was true for sure, that I earned 450 rupees a month collecting taxes in the Barich cotton-market! Sitting at my lamplit camp-table with my newspaper, I recalled my strange hallucination of a little while ago, and laughed boisterously.

'I finished the newspaper, ate my Moglai food, turned out the lamp, and lay down in my small corner bedroom. Through the open window in front of me, a brilliant star above the darkly wooded Arali hills looked down from millions and millions of miles away at the Honourable Tax-collector on his measly camp-bed. I cannot say when I fell asleep, reflecting on the wonder and absurdity of that. And I don't know how long I slept. But suddenly I awoke with a start – not that there was any sound in the room, or any person that I could see. The bright star had set behind the dark hills, and the thin light of the new moon shone wanly through my window as if afraid to enter. I couldn't see anyone. But I seemed to feel someone gently pushing me. I sat up; whoever it was said nothing, but five ring-studded fingers pressed me firmly to follow.

'I stood up gingerly. Although there was not a soul but me in that palace with its hundreds of rooms and immense emptiness, where sound slept and only echoes were awake, I still walked in fear of waking someone. Most of the rooms in the palace were kept closed, and I had never been in them before; so I cannot say where and by which route I went that night, following with soundless steps and bated breath that urgent, unseen guide! I couldn't keep track of the narrow dark passages, the long verandahs, the huge solemn audience-chambers, the airless and obscure cells.

'Although I could not see my guide with my eyes, I had an image of her in my mind. She was an Arab woman, whose marble-white hands emerged from voluminous sleeves – hard and flawless hands. A fine veil hung down from her head-dress; a curved knife was tied to her waist. It was as if a night had come floating from *One Thousand and One Nights*. I felt I was making my way through the narrow unlit alleyways of sleeping Baghdad, towards some dangerous assignation.

'At last my guide stopped before a dark blue curtain and seemed to point to something underneath. There was nothing there, but the blood in my chest froze with fear. In front of the curtain a fearsome African eunuch sat with drawn sword in his lap, legs sprawled out, dozing. The guide tiptoed over his legs and lifted a corner of the curtain. Behind it was a room spread with Persian carpets: I could not see who was sitting on the couch, but I saw two feet lazily resting on a pink velvet footstool, beautiful feet in brocade slippers peeping out of loose saffron pyjamas. On the floor near by was a bluish crystal bowl with apples, pears, oranges and grapes; and next to this there were two small goblets and a glass decanter of golden wine ready for a guest. From within the room, a strange intoxicating incense enthralled me.

'I was nerving myself to step over the sprawled legs of the eunuch, but he suddenly woke – his sword fell on to the stone floor with a clatter. There was then a horrible yell, and I found myself sitting on my camp-bed, soaked with sweat. It was dawn: the thin moon was pale as a sleepless invalid, and our local madman, Meher Ali, was walking as usual down the empty early-morning road shouting, "Keep away, keep away!"

'My first Arabian Night ended in this way – but a thousand more nights were to follow. A gulf between my days and my nights developed. During the day I would go about my work in a state of exhaustion, cursing my nights with their empty delusions and dreams; but at night it was my work-bound existence that seemed trivial, false and ridiculous. After dark I lived in a trance, in a maze of intoxication. I took on a strange *alter ego*, hidden in an unwritten history of hundreds of years ago. My short English jacket and tight trousers ill-befitted that person. So I dressed very carefully in baggy pyjamas, flower-patterned kurta, red velvet fez, a long silk choga; I perfumed my handkerchief with *ātar*; instead of cigarettes I smoked an enormous many-coiled hubble-bubble filled with rose-water; I sat in a large cushioned *kedārā* – waiting, it seemed, for a grand romantic tryst. But as darkness thickened a weird thing happened which I cannot describe. It was as if some torn pages from a marvellous story were blown by a sudden spring breeze to flutter around the various rooms of that vast palace. They could be followed so far, but never right to the end. I spent my nights wandering from room to room chasing those swirling torn pages.

'Amidst the swirling, tattered dreams, the whiffs of henna, the snatches of sitar-music, the gusts of wind spattered with

scented water, I caught from time to time, like flashes of lightning, glimpses of a beautiful woman. She was dressed in saffron
pyjamas; brocade sandals curving at the toe on her soft pink feet;
a richly embroidered bodice tight round her breast; a red cap on
her head with a fringe of golden tassels framing her forehead and
cheeks. She made me mad. I spent my nethermost dreams each
night wandering through the streets and dwellings of an intricate
fantasy realm, in quest of her.

'On some evenings, I would light two lamps either side of a
large mirror and carefully dress myself like a prince. Suddenly
next to my own reflection in the mirror, the spectre of that same
Persian girl appeared for a moment. She would bend her neck
and direct her deep black eyes at me, full of a fierce, plaintive
passion, while unspoken phrases hovered on her moist, beautiful
lips. Then, nimbly twisting her buxom body round and up in
a light and exquisite dance, she would vanish into the mirror –
smile, gaze, ornaments, pain, longing, confusion flashing like a
shower of sparks – whereupon a wild gust of wind, scented with
woodland plunder, blew out my two lamps. I would undress
and stretch myself on the bed next to my dressing-room, eyes
closed, tingling with delight. The air all around me – laden with
mixed scents from the Arali hills – swam with kisses and caresses;
the touch of soft hands seemed to fill the secretive dark. I felt
murmurs in my ear, perfumed breath on my brow, and the end
of a delicate veil fragrantly brushing my cheeks. Ravishing, serpentine coils seemed to grip me ever more tightly – until, with a
heavy sigh, limp with fatigue, I sank into deep slumber.

'One afternoon I decided to ride out – someone told me
not to, I forget who, but I insisted on going. My *sāheb*'s hat
and jacket were hanging on a wooden hook: I snatched them
and was going to put them on, but a tremendous whirlwind,
sweeping before it sand from the Shusta banks and dry leaves
from the Arali hills, whisked them away from me, and a sweet
peal of laughter, hitting every note of mirth, driven higher and
higher up the scale by the wind, soared to where the sun sets,
and spiralled away.

'I did not go riding that day; and from then on I gave up
wearing the short jacket and *sāheb*'s hat that had been so ridiculed. That night I sat up in bed and heard someone groaning
and wailing: beneath the bed, under the floor, from within a
dark tomb in the stone foundations of the palace, someone was

crying, "Release me; break down the doors of futile fantasy, deep slumber, cruel illusion; lift me on to your horse, press me to your breast, carry me away through forests, over mountains, over rivers to your daylit abode!"

'Who was I? How could I rescue her? *Which* lovely, drowning projection of desire should I drag ashore from a whirlpool of swirling dreams? Divinely beautiful, where and when did you live? By which cool spring, and in which palm-shade, and to which desert nomad were you born? To which slave-market were you taken to be sold, crossing hot sands, riding on a lightning horse, torn from your mother's lap by a Bedouin brigand, like a flower from a wild creeper? Which royal servant studied your blooming bashful beauty, counted out gold *mudrās*, took you overseas, placed you in a golden palanquin, gave you to his master's harem? What was your story there? Amidst the *sārangī*-music, the tinkling anklets, the cruelly glittering wine, did there not lurk the flash of daggers, the bite of poisons, the savagery of covert glances! Unlimited wealth; eternal imprisonment! Two maids either side of you, waving fly-whisks, diamond bracelets twinkling! Kings and princes sprawling before the jewel-and-pearl-studded slippers encasing your fair feet! At the entrance-door, a Negro like Hell's messenger but in Heaven's garb, standing with sword unsheathed! Did you, O desert-flower, float away on that stream of wealth so horribly gleaming, so fraught with conspiracy, foaming with envy and smirched with blood, to meet a cruel death or to land on an even more regal, even more abominable shore?

'Suddenly Meher Ali, the madman, was shouting, "Keep away, keep away! All is false! All is false!" I saw that it was dawn; the chaprassi was giving me the mail; the cook was salaaming and asking what he should cook today. "No," I announced, "I can't stay in this palace any more." That very day I moved all my things to the office. The old clerk Karim Khan smiled slightly when he saw me. Annoyed at his smile, I said nothing to him and settled down to my work.

'As the day wore on, the more distracted I became. I wondered what point there was in going anywhere. Tax-assessment seemed pointless; the Nizam and his government meant little; everything coming and going and happening around me was wretched, worthless, senseless!

'I threw aside my pen, slammed my ledger shut, and quickly

climbed into my pony-trap. As if of its own accord it took me
to the palace, arriving as dusk fell. I rapidly climbed the steps and
went in.

'Today everything was still. The dark rooms seemed sullen.
My heart was swelling with repentance, but nowhere was there
anyone to speak to, anyone to ask for forgiveness. I roamed
around the dark rooms blankly. I wished I could find a musical
instrument, sing a song to someone. I would have sung, "O fire,
the insect that tried to flee you has returned to die. Have pity
on it now, burn its wings, shrivel it to ashes." Suddenly two
tears fell on my forehead from above. That day thick clouds had
gathered over the Arali hills. The dark forest and the inky Shusta
seemed paralysed with dread. But now, water and land and sky
shuddered; and a lightning-fanged storm unleashed itself through
distant trackless forests, roaring and howling and rushing hither.
Doors in the palace slammed; huge empty rooms boomed with
a note of despair.

'The servants were all at the office; there was no one to light
the lamps. I distinctly felt, on that cloudy moonless night, in the
jet-black darkness of the rooms, that a woman was lying face-
down on a carpet at the foot of a bed, tearing her unkempt hair
with tight-clenched fists; blood was pouring from her pale brow;
sometimes she was laughing fiercely and hysterically; sometimes
she was sobbing wildly; she had ripped off her bodice and was
beating her naked breasts; the wind was roaring through the
window, driving in rain that soaked her to the skin.

'The storm went on all night, and the weeping too. I went
on wandering through pitch-black rooms in fruitless remorse.
There was no one anywhere; no one whom I could comfort.
Who was it who was so distressed? Where was this inconsolable
grief coming from?

'Once again the madman was shouting, "Keep away! Keep
away! All is false! All is false!" I saw that it was dawn, and Meher
Ali even on this storm-swept day was circling the palace shouting his usual cry. I wondered now if Meher Ali too had at one
time lived in this palace; even though he was mad now and lived
outside, he was daily lured by its monstrous stony charm, and
every morning came to walk round it. I immediately ran up to
the madman through the rain and asked, "Meher Ali, what is
false?"

'He gave no answer, pushed me aside and, like a wheeling

bird transfixed by the leer of a huge snake, continued to shout and wander round the palace, continued to warn himself over and over again with all his might, "Keep away! Keep away! All is false!"

'Dashing through the rain and storm like a man possessed, I returned to the office. I called Karim Khan and said, "Tell me what all of this means."

'The gist of what he told me was this. Once upon a time the palace had been churned by insatiable lust, by the flames of wild pleasure. Cursed by those passions, those vain desires, every stone now hungered and thirsted, strove like a vampire to consume every soul who came near. Of those who had stayed for more than three nights in the palace, only Meher Ali had emerged, with his wits gone. No one else till now had escaped its grasp.

'I asked, "Is there no escape for me?"

'The old man answered, "There is only one way and that is very hard. I can tell it to you, but first I must tell you the ancient story of one who lived there, a Persian slave-girl. A stranger and sadder tale was never heard." '

At that moment, the coolies came and told us that the train was coming. So soon? We rolled up our bedding, and the train arrived. A sleepy Englishman stuck his head out of a first-class compartment to read the name of the station. 'Hello,' he shouted, recognizing our companion, and he let him into his carriage. We got into the second class. We never found out who the gentleman was, and we never heard the end of the story either.

I said, 'The fellow took us for fools and was pulling our legs; he made the whole thing up.' My theosophist relative disagreed, and our dispute caused a rift which was never healed.

Guest

I

MATILAL BABU, ZAMINDAR of Kathaliya, was returning home with his family by boat. One afternoon he moored the boat near a riverside market so that their meal could be prepared. A Brahmin boy came over and asked, 'Where are you going, Babu?' The boy was not more than fifteen or sixteen.

'Kathaliya,' replied Matilal Babu.

'Could you drop me at Nandigram on the way?'

Matilal consented. 'What's your name?' he asked.

'Tarapada,' said the boy.

The fair-skinned boy was beautiful to look at. His smile and his large eyes had the grace of youth. His body – bare except for a stained dhoti – was free of any excess: as if lovingly carved by a sculptor, or as if in a previous life he had been a young sage whose pure religious devotion had removed all grossness, honed him to gleaming, Brahminical perfection.

'Come and wash, *bābā*,' said Matilal Babu tenderly. 'You can eat with us.'

'Leave that to me,' said Tarapada, and without a moment's hesitation he joined in the cooking. Matilal's servant was Hindusthani: he was not very good at cutting up fish.[1] Tarapada took over, and soon had the dish ready, and had cooked some vegetables too with practised skill. He then took a dip in the river, and, opening his bundle, produced a clean white garment and a small wooden comb. He sleeked his long hair away from his forehead and down to his neck, adjusted his glistening sacred thread, and stepped on to the boat.

Matilal Babu invited him into the cabin. His wife and his nine-year-old daughter were there. His wife Annapurna was tenderly attracted to the boy when she saw him, and wondered, 'Whose child is he? Where has he come from? How could his mother bear to abandon him?' She placed mats for Matilal and the boy to sit on, side by side. The boy was not a big eater. Annapurna felt he must be shy, and tried to get him to eat this or that; but when he had finished, he would not be tempted to

---

1. Fish is eaten much less in North India than in Bengal.

more. He clearly did everything according to his own wishes –
but with such ease that there was nothing assertive about him.
He was not at all shy.

When everyone had eaten, Annapurna sat him next to her
and asked him about his background. She didn't gather much.
All she could establish was that the boy had run away from home
of his own volition at the age of seven or eight.

'Isn't your mother alive?' asked Annapurna.

'She is,' said Tarapada.

'Doesn't she love you?' asked Annapurna.

Tarapada seemed to find this question peculiar. 'Why
shouldn't she love me?' he said, laughing.

'Then why did you leave her?' said Annapurna.

'She has four more sons and three daughters,' said Tarapada.

Pained by this odd reply, Annapurna said, 'What a thing to
say! Just because I have five fingers, does it mean that I want to
chop one off?'

Tarapada was young, so his life-story was brief; but the boy
was a complete original. He was his parents' fourth son, and was
still a baby when his father died. Despite there being so many
in the house, Tarapada was the darling of all; mother, brothers,
sisters and neighbours doted on him. So much so, that his tutor
never beat him – everyone would have been appalled if he had.
There was no reason for him to leave. Half-starved boys who
constantly stole fruit from trees and were thrashed by the owners
of the trees – *they* never strayed from the village or their scolding
mothers! But this darling of everyone joined a touring *yātrā*-
troupe and left his village without a thought.

Search-parties went out and he was brought back. His mother
pressed him to her breast and drenched him with tears; his sisters
wept too. His elder brother tried to perform his duty as guardian;
but he soon abandoned his feeble attempts at discipline, and welcomed him back with open arms. Women invited him to their
houses, plied him with even greater displays of affection. But he
would not accept ties, even ties of love: his stars had made him
a wanderer. If he saw strange boats on the river, or a *sannyāsī*
from a distant region under the local peepul tree, or if gypsies sat
by the river, making mats or wicker baskets, his heart would stir
with longing to be free, to explore the outside world. And after
he had run away two or three times, family and villagers gave up
hope of him.

Again he joined a *yātrā*-troupe at first. But when the master of
the troupe began to treat him almost as a son, and the members
of the troupe, young and old, had all fallen for him – and even
the people in the houses where they performed (especially the
women) began to make a special fuss of him – one day, without
saying a word, he disappeared, and could not be found.

Tarapada was as wary of ties as a young fawn, and was also
like a deer in his love of music.[1] The songs of the *yātrā* were
what had first lured him away from home. Melodies sent a trembling through his veins, and rhythms made his body swing. Even
as a baby he had shown such solemn, grown-up attention at
musical gatherings, sitting and swaying and forgetting himself,
that his elders could hardly restrain their amusement. Not only
music: when the rains of Śrābaṇ fell on the thick leaves, when the
clouds thundered, when the wind moaned in the woods like a
motherless demon-child, his heart was swept away. The call of a
kite high in the sky in the still heat of noon, the croaking of frogs
on rainy evenings, the howling of jackals at night, all entranced
him. Impelled by this passion for music, it was not long before
he had joined a group of *pā̃cāli*-singers. The leader of the group
carefully taught him songs and trained him to recite *pā̃cāli* by
heart. He too began to love him as his own. Like a pet cage-bird,
Tarapada learnt a few songs, and then one morning flew away.

Finally he joined a troupe of gymnasts. From Jyaiṣṭha to
Āṣāṛh a fair toured the district. *Yātrā*-troupes, *pā̃cāli*-singers,
bards, dancers and stallholders travelled by boat from one site
to another. For the second year running this round of entertainment included a small gymnastics-troupe from Calcutta. At
first Tarapada joined the stallholders – sold *pān* at the fair. But
then his natural curiosity drew him to the wonderful skills of
the gymnasts, and he joined their troupe. He had taught himself
to play the flute very well: during the gymnastic display he had
to play Lucknow *ṭhumṛi*s at top speed on the flute – this was his
only task.

It was from this troupe that he had most recently absconded.
He had heard that the zamindars at Nandigram had founded, on
a lavish scale, an amateur *yātrā*-group, so he tied up his bundle
and headed for the place, meeting Matilal Babu on the way.

1. There is a traditional belief in India that deer are musical. In Rajput paintings,
deer are shown dumbstruck before a musician.

Despite these connections with various groups, his nature had not been corrupted by any. He was, deep down, entirely detached and free. The foul language he had heard, the dreadful sights he had seen, had not fixed themselves in his mind. They passed him by. He remained unbound by any kind of habit or custom. He swam in the murky waters of the world with pure white wings, like a swan. However many times his curiosity made him dive in, his wings could not be soaked or soiled. There was a pure and natural innocence in this runaway boy's expression. So much so, that the worldly-wise Matilal Babu invited him in without doubt or question, and with great tenderness.

II

IN THE AFTERNOON the boat set sail. Annapurna continued to ask the boy kind questions about his home and family; he answered laconically, and then went out on deck to escape. The monsoon river, swollen to maximum fullness, seemed to harry the earth with its reckless turbulence. In the cloudless sunshine, the half-sunk reeds along the bank, the fields of succulent sugar-cane beyond, and the far-off bluey-green woods kissing the horizon, seemed transformed by the touch of a golden wand into new beauty. The speechless sky gazed down in wonder: everything was alive, throbbing, awash with confident light, shiny with newness, bursting with plenty.

Tarapada took refuge on the roof of the boat in the shade of the sail. Sloping pastures, flooded jute-fields, green, rippling late-autumn paddy, narrow paths leading from the *ghā*ṭs, and villages shaded by encircling foliage, came one by one into view. To this water, earth and sky, this movement of life and sound, these varied levels and vast vistas, to this huge, immovable, mute, unblinking, natural world, the boy was intimately linked. Yet not for a moment did it try to hold him with its loving embrace. Calves running on the banks with tails up-raised; ponies grazing and hopping about with hobbled legs; kingfishers swooping from fishing-net poles to plop into the water to catch fish; boys splashing; women shrilly chatting as they stood chest-deep, floating their saris out in front to rub them clean; fish-wives with baskets, saris tucked up, buying fish from the fishermen: all of this Tarapada watched with unflagging curiosity – never were his eyes sated.

As he sat, he soon got talking with the helmsman and oarsmen. Sometimes he took the *lagi* and punted the boat himself.
When the helmsman needed a smoke, he would take the tiller;
when the sail needed to be turned, he helped skilfully.

Just before dusk Annapurna called Tarapada and asked, 'What
do you like to eat at night?'

'Whatever I get,' said Tarapada. 'I don't eat every day.'

She felt disturbed by this beautiful Brahmin boy's indifference
to her hospitality. She longed to feed, clothe and give succour to
him. But she could not discover how to please him. She osten-
tatiously sent her servants to buy milk and sweets: Tarapada ate
the sweets willingly enough, but he would not touch the milk.
Even the taciturn Matilal urged him to drink it, but he simply
replied, 'I don't like it.'

Three days passed. Tarapada expertly joined in everything,
from the cooking and shopping to the sailing of the boat. Anything he saw interested him; any work that he did absorbed
him. His sight, his hands and his mind were ever-active: like
Nature herself he was always serene and detached, yet always
busy. People usually dwell in a fixed place, but Tarapada was like
a joyous wave on life's unending stream: past or future meant
nothing – moving forward was the only thing that mattered.

By mixing with various groups, he had learnt all sorts of
delightful accomplishments. Things were stamped on his mind
with astonishing ease, unclouded as it was by any kind of worry.
He knew *pācāli*, folk-tales, *kīrtan*, and long pieces from *yātrās*.
Matilal Babu habitually read the *Rāmāyaṇa* to his wife and daughter. One evening he had just got to the story of Kush and Lab
when Tarapada, unable to restrain himself, came down from the
roof of the boat and said, 'Put the book away. I know a song
about Kush and Lab – listen!'

He began a *pācāli*. Dashu Ray's verse, sweet as a flute, flowed
on swiftly; the helmsman and oarsmen came and peered through
the door of the cabin; as dusk fell, a stream of laughter, pathos
and music spread through the evening air: the banks became
alert, and people in passing boats were lured for a moment and
strained their ears to listen. When the *pācāli* had finished, everyone sighed deeply, wishing it would last forever. The tearful
Annapurna longed to take the boy and press him to her breast
and bury her face in his hair. Matilal Babu thought, 'If I could
somehow keep this boy, he would make up for my having no

son.' The little girl Charushashi, though, was full of envy and
jealousy.

III

SHE WAS HER parents' only child, sole claimant on their affection. There was no end to her wilfulness and obstinacy. She had
her own opinions about food, clothes and hair-styles, but there
was no consistency in them. Whenever she was invited out, her
mother was terrified that she would make impossible demands
over dress. If her hair-style displeased her, to do and redo it made
no difference, and merely led to a tantrum. She was like this with
everything. But if she was in a good mood, she was amenable
to anything – and would show excessive love for her mother,
hugging her, kissing her, laughing in an unbalanced way. The
girl was a puzzle.

But now her volatile feelings began to concentrate in fierce
animosity towards Tarapada, and she caused exceptional trouble
to her parents. At meals she scowled and pushed her plate away:
she would complain about the cooking, slap the maid, and object
to everything. The more that Tarapada's accomplishments impressed her and others, the more angry she became. She would
not admit that he had any virtues at all; undeniable evidence of
them made her even more critical. On the night that Tarapada
sang about Kush and Lab, Annapurna thought, 'Wild animals
can be tamed by music, so perhaps my daughter will soften.'

'How did you like it, Charu?' she asked. She gave no answer,
merely tossed her head, implying: 'I didn't like it at all and shall
never like it.'

Realizing that Charu was jealous, her mother stopped showing affection for Tarapada in front of her. After dark, when
Charu had gone to bed after eating early, Annapurna would sit
by the door of the cabin and Matilal Babu and Tarapada would
sit outside, and at Annapurna's request Tarapada would sing.
With his singing, the goddess of the sleeping, darkened homes
on the bank would sink into a trance, and Annapurna's heart
swelled with love and appreciation. But Charu would get up
and shout tearfully and angrily, 'Mother, I can't get to sleep with
this noise!' She found it quite unbearable to be sent to bed on
her own while her parents sat and listened to Tarapada singing.

The natural fierceness of this fiery black-eyed girl fascinated

Tarapada. He would tell her stories, sing her songs, play her the
flute, make great efforts to win her round – but with no success
at all. Only in the afternoons when he bathed in the swollen
river, sporting his fair, pure body in a swimming display worthy
of a young water-god – only then could she not help being
attracted just a little bit. She would watch him then. But she
didn't reveal her interest to anyone, and – born actress that she
was – carried on knitting a woollen scarf with apparent indifference to Tarapada's water-sports.

IV

TARAPADA TOOK NO notice of Nandigram when they passed
it. The large boat – sometimes with its sails up, sometimes towed
– proceeded slowly on down rivers and tributaries, and the days
of the passengers too flowed with a soft and easy pace through
the peace and beauty of the scene. No one was in any kind of
hurry; long afternoons were spent bathing and eating; and as
soon as dusk fell the boat was moored at a village *ghāṭ*, by trees
buzzing with crickets and aglow with fireflies.

After about ten days of this the boat arrived at Kathaliya.
Ponies and a palanquin were sent from the house to receive the
zamindar; a guard of honour (with bamboo *lāṭhis*) fired rounds of
blanks – raucously echoed by the village crows.

Meanwhile Tarapada slipped off the boat and quickly looked
round the village. Calling one villager *Dādā*, another *Khuṛā*, another *Didi*, and another *Māsī*, he established friendly relations
with everyone in a couple of hours. Because he had no normal
ties, he could get to know people with amazing ease and speed.
Within a few days he had won all hearts.

He mixed with everyone on equal terms. He was unconven-
tional, yet able to adapt to any situation or work. With boys he
was a boy, yet somehow separate and special; with older people
he was not a boy, yet not too precocious either; with herders he
was a herder, yet also a Brahmin. He joined in with things as if
used to them all his life. He'd be chatting in the sweet-shop: the
sweet-maker would say, 'Could you mind the shop for a while?
I shan't be long.' Cool as a cucumber, Tarapada sat there keeping
the flies off the *sandeś* with a *śāl*-leaf. He could even make sweets
himself, knew something of weaving, and was not completely
ignorant of how to turn a potter's wheel.

Tarapada reigned over the whole village; there was just one young girl whose hatred he simply could not overcome. Perhaps it was because this girl so fiercely wished him to leave that he stayed on so long. But Charushashi now proved how hard it is to fathom even a juvenile female mind.

Bāmunthākrun's[1] daughter Sonamani had been widowed at the age of five; she was Charu's playmate. She had been ill for a while, and had not been able to go out to see her friend. When she was recovered and came to see her again, a rift between them came about for almost no reason.

Charu had been speaking at length about Tarapada: she hoped, by saying what a precious asset he was, to astonish and intrigue her friend. But when she discovered he was known to Sonamani, that he called Bāmunthākrun *Māsī* and that Sonamani called him *Dādā*; when she heard that he not only treated mother and daughter to *kīrtan*-tunes on his flute but had, at Sonamani's request, made her a bamboo flute; that he'd picked her fruits from high branches and flowers from thorny ones; when she heard all this, darts of fire stabbed her. She had thought of Tara-pada as *their* Tarapada – guarded closely, so that ordinary people might glimpse him yet never be able to grasp him: they would admire his beauty and talents from a distance, and Charushashi's family would gain glory thereby. Why should Sonamani have such easy contact with this singular, divinely favoured Brahmin boy? If Charu's family had not taken him in, had not looked after him so, how would Sonamani ever have seen him? Sonamani's *Dādā* indeed! She burned all over at the thought.

Why was the Charu who had tried to strike the boy down with arrows of hatred so anxious to claim sole rights over him? Understand this who will.

Later that day Charu had a serious rift with Sonamani over another trivial matter. She marched into Tarapada's room, found his beloved flute, and callously jumped and stamped on it. She was still doing so when Tarapada came in. He was amazed by the image of destruction that the girl presented.

'Charu, why are you smashing my flute?' he asked.

'I *want* to smash it! I'm *going* to smash it!' shouted Charu with red eyes and flushed face; and, stamping unnecessarily on the already smashed flute, she burst into loud sobs and ran from the

1. A title rather than a name, often given to Brahmin widows.

room. Tarapada picked up the pieces, turned them this way and that, but it was useless. To wreak destruction on his old, innocent flute was so absurd that he burst out laughing. Charushashi intrigued him more every day.

He was also intrigued by the English illustrated books in Matilal Babu's library. Tarapada had considerable knowledge of the world, but he could not enter the world of these pictures at all. He tried to do so in his imagination, but found no satisfaction in this. Seeing his interest in these books, Matilal said one day, 'Would you like to learn English? You'll understand these pictures then.'

'I *would* like to learn it,' he replied at once.

Matilal Babu happily engaged the headmaster of the village secondary school – Ramratan Babu – to teach the boy English each evening.

V

TARAPADA SET ABOUT learning English with great concentration and retention. It released him into a hitherto inaccessible realm, unconnected with his former world. The local people saw no more of him; at dusk, when he went to the empty riverside to pace swiftly up and down reciting his lessons, his boyish devotees mournfully watched from a distance; they dared not disturb his studies.

Charu too did not see much of him now. Formerly Tarapada ate in the women's quarters, under Annapurna's loving gaze; but because this could take a long time he asked Matilal Babu to arrange for him to eat outside them. Annapurna was hurt by this and objected, but Matilal was so pleased by Tarapada's keenness to learn that he agreed to the new arrangement.

Charu now insisted that she too wanted to learn English. At first her parents were amused by their wayward daughter's new idea, lovingly laughed at it; but its absurdity was soon washed away by tears. Doting parents that they were, they were forced to give in, and she started to study alongside Tarapada with the same tutor.

Study, however, was alien to her restless nature. She learned nothing herself – merely disrupted Tarapada's learning. She fell far behind, couldn't learn anything by heart, but couldn't bear to be behind! If Tarapada overtook her and moved on to a new lesson, she was furious and burst into tears. When he finished an old book and bought a new one, she had to buy the new book too. In his spare time he would sit in his room learning and writing his lessons: the jealous girl couldn't stand this – she would secretly come and pour ink on his exercise-book, steal his pen, even tear from the book the passage he had been set to learn. Tarapada bore most of this with amusement: if she went too far he slapped her, but he was quite unable to control her.

A chance occurrence saved him. One day, truly annoyed, he tore up his ink-spilled exercise-book and sat gloomily. Charu came to the door, and prepared herself for a beating. But nothing happened: Tarapada went on sitting in silence. The girl went in and out of the room. Several times she came so close that Tarapada could, if he had wished, easily have thwacked her on the back. But he did not do that, and remained solemn. The girl was in a quandary. How to ask for forgiveness was some-thing she had never learnt; yet she was extremely anxious for forgiveness. Finally, seeing no other way, she took a piece of the torn exercise-book, sat down next to Tarapada and wrote in large round letters, 'I will never pour ink on your exercise-book again.' She then made elaborate efforts to attract his attention. At this Tarapada could not contain himself any more, and he burst out laughing. The girl dashed from the room, overcome with shame and anger. Only if she had been able to expunge from all time the paper on which she had humbled herself, would her fury have been eased.

During this period Sonamani had once or twice, with her heart in her mouth, lurked outside the lesson-room. She was close to her friend Charushashi in most matters, but with regard to Tarapada she feared and distrusted her. At moments when Charu was in the women's quarters, she would stand timidly outside Tarapada's door. He would look up from his book and say tenderly, 'What is it, Sona, what's up? How is *Māsī*?' Son-amani would say, 'You haven't been to see us for a long time – Mother wishes you would sometime. She has backache, so she can't come to you.'

Charu would perhaps now appear. Sonamani was flustered: she felt like a thief. Charu would scowl and shriek at her, 'Well, Sona – coming to disturb our studies! I'll tell my father!' As if she herself was Tarapada's guardian, whose sole object was to watch him day and night in case his studies were disturbed! But

God was not unaware of what her actual motive was in coming to Tarapada's room at this odd time, and Tarapada also knew it well. Poor Sonamani fumbled for false explanations; when Charu venomously called her a liar she withdrew, sick at heart, defeated. The kindly Tarapada would call her and say, 'Sona, I'll come to your house this evening.' Charu hissed back like a snake, 'How can you go? What about your lessons? I'll tell *Māṣṭārmaśāy!*'

Undaunted by Charu's threat, Tarapada spent a couple of evenings at Bāmunṭhākrun's house. On the third day Charu, without further warning, quietly bolted his door; and, fetching the padlock from her mother's spice-box, locked him in. She kept him prisoner for the whole evening, only opening the door when it was time to eat. Tarapada was angrily silent, and was about to go out without eating. Then the passionate, overwrought girl clasped her hands and cried out repeatedly, 'I promise you – cross my heart – that I won't do it again. Please, I beg you, eat before you go!' When even this had no effect she began to wail, and he was forced to turn back and eat.

Charu many times promised herself that she would behave properly towards Tarapada, that she would not annoy him again; but when Sonamani and others turned up it put her into such a rage that she could not control herself. If she was good for a few days, Tarapada would steel himself for another tempest. No one could say how the attack would come or on what grounds. There would be a mighty storm, and floods of tears to follow, and after that peace and affection again.

VI

ALMOST TWO YEARS passed like this. Tarapada had never moored himself to anyone for so long. Maybe his studies had a hold on him; or maybe he was changing as he grew up, and a stable existence in a comfortable house had more appeal than before. Maybe the beauty of his study-companion – even if she had been constantly bad-tempered – was exerting unconscious influence.

Meanwhile Charu had reached the age of eleven. Matilal Babu had sought out two or three good marriage-offers. Now that she had reached marriageable age, he placed a ban on English books and outside visits. She kicked up a terrible fuss at these new restrictions.

Then one day Annapurna called Matilal and said, 'Why search outside for a groom? Tarapada would make a fine husband. And your daughter likes him.'

Matilal Babu was astonished at this suggestion. 'That's impossible,' he said. 'We don't know anything about his family. She's my only daughter: I want to marry her well.'

Some people came from the zamindar's house at Raydanga to look at the girl. Efforts were made to dress Charu up: she shut herself in her room and refused to come out. Matilal Babu begged and rebuked her from outside, but without result. Finally he had to lie to the delegation from Raydanga: his daughter had suddenly fallen ill, and could not be seen today. They assumed from this lame excuse that the girl had some kind of defect.

Matilal Babu started to reflect that Tarapada was indeed good to look at, good in every outward aspect; he could keep him at home, so his only daughter would not have to go to someone else's house. He realized that his truculent daughter's foibles, which he and his wife could smile at, would not be received so well by in-laws.

After lengthy discussion, Matilal and Annapurna sent a man to Tarapada's village to find out about his family. The information came that it was poor, but high-caste. Matilal Babu then sent a marriage-proposal to the boy's mother and brothers. They were well-pleased, and agreed to it at once.

Back at Kathaliya, Matilal and Annapurna discussed the day and hour of the wedding, but the naturally cautious Matilal kept the whole matter secret.

Charu, though, could not be restricted. She sometimes burst into Tarapada's room like a cavalry-charge, disturbing his studies with crossness, eagerness or scorn. Sometimes, detached and independent though he was, he felt a strange stirring in his heart at this, a sort of electrical impulse. Till now he had floated lightly and serenely without impediment on Time's stream: sometimes now he was snared by strange distracting day-dreams. He would leave his studies and go into Matilal Babu's library and flick through the pages of the illustrated books; the imaginary world which he mixed with these pictures was much changed – much more highly-coloured than before. He could not laugh at Charu's strange behaviour quite as he had done in the past. When she was bad he never thought of beating her now. This deep change, this powerful feeling of attraction, was like a new dream.

Matilal Babu fixed the wedding for the month of Śrāban, and sent word to Tarapada's mother and brothers; but he did not inform Tarapada himself. He told his *moktār* in Calcutta to hire a trumpet-and-drum band, and he ordered everything else that would be needed for the wedding.

Early monsoon clouds formed in the sky. The village-river had been dried up for weeks; there was water only in holes here and there; small boats lay stuck in these pools of muddy water, and the dry river-bed was rutted with bullock-cart tracks. But now, like Parvati returning to her parents' home, gurgling waters returned to the empty arms of the village: naked children danced and shouted on the river-bank, jumped into the water with voracious joy as if trying to embrace the river; the villagers gazed at the river like a dear friend; a huge wave of life and delight rolled through the parched village. There were boats big and small with cargoes from far and wide; in the evenings the *ghāṭ* resounded with the songs of foreign boatmen. The villages along the river had spent the whole year confined to their own small worlds: now, with the rains, the vast outside world had come in its earth-coloured watery chariot, carrying wondrous gifts to the villages, as if on a visit to its daughters. Rustic smallness was temporarily subsumed by pride of contact with the world; everything became more active; the bustle of distant cities came to this sleepy region, and the whole sky rang.

Meanwhile at Kurulkata, on the Nag family estate, a famous chariot-festival was due to be held. One moonlit evening Tarapada went to the *ghāṭ* and saw, on the swift flood-tide, boats with merry-go-rounds and *yātrā*-troupes, and cargo-boats rapidly making for the fair. An orchestra from Calcutta was practising loudly as it passed; the *yātrā*-troupe was singing to violin accompaniment, shouting out the beats; boatmen from lands to the west split the sky with cymbals and thudding drums. Such excitement! Then clouds from the east covered the moon with their huge black sails; an east wind blew sharply; cloud after cloud rolled by; the river gushed and swelled; darkness thickened in the swaying riverside trees; frogs croaked; crickets rasped like wood-saws. To Tarapada the whole world seemed like a chariot-festival: wheels turning, flags flying, earth trembling, clouds swirling, wind rushing, river flowing, boats sailing, songs rising! There were rumbles of thunder, and slashes of lightning in the sky: the smell of torrential rain approached from the dark distance. But Kathaliya village next to the river ignored all this: she shut her doors, turned out her lamps and went to sleep.

The following morning Tarapada's mother and brothers arrived at Kathaliya; and that same morning three large boats from Calcutta, laden with things for the wedding, moored at the zamindar's *ghāt*; and very early, that same morning, Sonamani brought some mango-juice preserve[1] in paper and some pickle wrapped in a leaf, and timidly stood outside Tarapada's room – but Tarapada was not to be seen. In a cloudy monsoon night, before love and emotional ties could encircle him completely, this Brahmin boy, thief of all hearts in the village, had returned to the unconstraining, unemotional arms of his mother Earth.

---

1. *āmsattva*; a great delicacy, made by drying mango-juice in the sun.

The Haldar Family

HERE WAS A FAMILY with no apparent reason for discord. It was well-to-do, and its members were all quite good people. Yet a conflict arose.

If human affairs were governed by reason, society would be like a book of sums. If you were careful, your calculations would never turn out wrong; or if they did, you could correct them simply by applying an eraser.

But the god of human destiny has a fine sense of humour. Whether he is skilled in mathematics I cannot say, but he shows no taste for it. He has no concern for an accurate calculation of the debits and credits of human existence. Hence his plans allow for an element of incongruity, which can intrude without warning and play havoc with the normal course of events. This is what heightens the drama and sends floods of tears and laughter to breach the banks of life's stream.

And so it happened in this instance too. A rogue elephant overran a lotus grove, and the lotus was commingled with the slime in which it grew. Were it not so, this story would not have been written.

In this family of which I speak, Banwarilal was undoubtedly the worthiest member. He knew this very well himself, and it caused him much agitation. His sense of worth impelled him from within like a steam engine. If the road ahead was clear, well and good; if not, he would ram into whatever stood in his way.

His father Manoharlal still kept up the old aristocratic style. He saw himself as the jewel in the crown of his particular society; there was thus no reason for him to be concerned with its arms and legs. Ordinary mortals went about their appointed duties; he alone remained idle and motionless, at the centre of this immense enterprise of living.

One often sees such people attracting to themselves, as though magnetically and without effort, at least one or two strong and genuine souls. The reason is simple. There is a type of people on this earth who seem to have been born with a devotion to service. To fulfil their natural instinct, they seek out some help-less person over whom they can take complete charge. These natural-born benefactors do not enjoy serving their own ends half as much as going about someone else's: keeping that person in comfort, guarding him against every adversity, enhancing his prestige in society – that is what gives them utmost satisfaction. They are a species of male mothers, and that too not with their own sons but other people's.

Manoharlal's personal servant Ramcharan was of this nature. The whole object of his existence, the only reason he worked his body to exhaustion, was to look after his master's physical well-being. He would willingly have huffed and puffed all night and day like a smith's bellows, if his master could thereby be spared the strain of breathing for himself. Outsiders might think that Manoharlal drove his retainer unduly hard. If the mouthpiece of his hookah were to fall on the floor, it seemed grotesque to make Ramcharan come running to spare Manohar the labour of picking it up. But for Ramcharan, making himself indispensable in a host of such dispensable matters was a cause of supreme satisfaction.

As with Ramcharan, so with another of Manoharlal's hench-men, Nilkantha. He was entrusted with all the affairs of the estate. But while Ramcharan, thanks to his master's largesse, looked extremely well-nourished, Nilkantha's bones scarcely bore flesh enough to hide their nakedness. He stood guard over his master's treasure trove like the very image of Famine. The wealth was all Manoharlal's; but the attachment to it was entirely Nilkantha's.

Nilkantha and Banwarilal had long had their differences. For instance, Banwarilal, having received permission from his father to order some new piece of jewellery for his wife, would expect to be disbursed the money and commission the jeweller himself; but that was not to be. All expenses had to be handled by Nil-kantha alone; and the ornament, when finally delivered, would be to no one's liking. Banwari would be convinced that the jeweller had given Nilkantha a cut. Men of strict principles do not lack enemies. Banwari had been warned by many that the more close-fisted Nilkantha was with others, the more he raked in for himself.

Yet the animosities that had built up on both sides were over quite petty sums. Nilkantha, being a shrewd man, realized well enough that if he were not on good terms with Banwarilal, he would be inviting trouble at a future date. But his parsimony over his master's wealth had become an obsession with him. If he believed some expenditure to be unjustified, he would flout even his master's express orders.

On the other hand, Banwarilal was feeling more and more need for unjustified expenditure. The root cause that provokes irrational behaviour in males was present here too in strong measure. There might be various opinions about the beauty of Banwari's wife Kiranlekha; we need not go into that. It is Banwari's own opinion that concerns us here. The attachment he displayed for his wife was considered quite excessive by the rest of his womenfolk. In other words, all the attention they would have liked to receive from their own husbands but did not, was lavished here.

Whatever her age might have been, Kiranlekha still looked a young girl, with nothing of the matronly demeanour expected of the eldest son's wife. All in all, she seemed just a slip of a thing. He called her 'Anu', his little speck; and sometimes even more lovingly, 'Paramanu', his atom. Those well-versed in the physical sciences know how powerful such minute portions of matter can be.

Kiran never asked for anything from her husband. She had a detached air, as if she needed nothing in particular. Her houseful of sisters-in-law took up all her time and attention; she showed no apparent need for the solitary contemplation evinced in the first flush of young love. There were no signs of enthusiasm in her interactions with Banwarilal: she accepted what he gave her with good grace, but never made any demands. It was left to Banwari to think out ways to please her. When a wife comes out with open demands, one can argue and cut back on a few things; but one can hardly bargain with oneself. In such a situation, unasked-for gifts inevitably prove costlier than those supplied on demand.

In Kiran's case, moreover, there was no telling how pleased she actually was with her husband's love-offerings. If asked, she would say, 'Yes, it's nice.' But Banwari would remain in doubt. 'Did she really like it?' he would keep wondering. Then Kiran would scold him gently: 'What a habit you have! Why must you fuss so? It's fine, just fine.'

Banwari knew from his schoolbooks that to be satisfied with one's lot is a great virtue. But this virtue in his wife caused him much pain. His wife did not merely satisfy him; she totally enchanted him, and he wanted her to be enchanted by him too.

She did not have to try too hard; her youthful charm brimmed over, her caring touch came out spontaneously. But for a man, such opportunities are rare. He must do something concrete to demonstrate his manliness. Unless he can prove his strength, his love seems pallid. If nothing else serves, he can display his wealth as an expression of power, parade it like a peacock's train; that might give him some consolation. Yet this project too was repeatedly thwarted by Nilkantha. He, Banwarilal, the eldest son of the family, had no real authority, while Nilkantha lorded it over him because of his master's indulgence! It was awkward and insulting: all the more so because it scuttled all Banwari's plans for loading the quiver of the God of Love.

One day Banwari would be the rightful owner of all this wealth. But his youth would not last forever: the rainbow cup of summer would not always fill of itself with nectar. His wealth would harden and congeal, as it did with all men of property, like ice on mountain peaks: no carefree flow of spendthrift folly then. He needed the money now, while he still had the vigour to throw it round in joyful abandon.

Banwari had three principal hobbies – wrestling, hunting and the study of Sanskrit. His notebook was crammed with Sanskrit verses. They came in very handy on rainy days, full-moon nights, or when the south wind was blowing. Thankfully, Nilkantha had no authority to cut back on their rhetorical ornaments. No bookkeeper or accountant could question the extravagance of their hyperboles. They might have stinted on the gold in Kiran's earrings; not so with the stream of verse poured into her ears – never short in measure, and in terms of feeling, quite measureless.

Banwari was tall and robust, with the physique of a wrestler. When he lost his temper, people would tremble with fear. But this young stalwart had a very tender heart. When Bangshilal, his younger brother, was a little child, Banwari had cared for him like a mother. He seemed to feel a deep-seated need to nurture others.

In his love for his wife, too, there was this same nurturing instinct. Kiranlekha seemed like a tiny ray of light seeking a path through thick foliage. Her very minuteness evoked a special tenderness in him: he wished to deck her up in many ways, with fine clothes and ornaments. This was more a creative joy than a mere desire to enjoy or possess: the joy of making the one into the various, of seeing the one Kiranlekha in many hues and garbs.

But reciting Sanskrit poetry in her ears could hardly satisfy Banwari's craving. His male instinct for dominance remained unfulfilled; so did his wish to enrich the object of his love with opulent gifts.

And so it came to pass that this favourite of fortune, in the full blossom of his youth, with his wealth and prestige and his beautiful wife, gradually turned into a menace.

Madhu the fisherman was a tenant of Manoharlal's. His wife Sukhada came to see Kiranlekha one day, fell at her feet and wept. The trouble was that a few years ago, Madhu and some other fishermen had borrowed a thousand rupees from Mano-harlal to buy nets and fish the river as they always did. While the catch was good, paying back the loan had never been a problem, so they had not minded the high rate of interest. But that year the catch was poor; and as luck would have it, the fish had hardly showed up at their bend of the river for three consecutive years. The fishermen suffered a loss, and were themselves entangled in a net of debts. Those who had come from other places simply disappeared; but Madhu, being a local tenant, had no means of escape. As a result, the whole burden of debt had fallen on him. Sukhada had come to plead with Kiran to save them from ruin. Going to Kiran's mother-in-law would serve no purpose, since that lady could not dream that any decision by Nilkan-tha could ever be challenged; whereas knowing of Banwari's grudge against Nilkantha, Madhu had sent Sukhada to appeal to his wife.

Kiran knew that however much Banwari might rant and rave against Nilkantha, he had no authority to override the latter's decisions. She tried to make this clear to Sukhada over and over again. 'How can I help you? We have no say in this. Tell Madhu to appeal directly to the master himself.'

That had been tried already. But complaints made to Mano-harlal were referred back to Nilkantha, which only made mat-ters worse for the complainant. If he lodged a second appeal, Manoharlal would be furious. What pleasure was there in being wealthy, if he had to take on the bother of managing his wealth?

While Sukhada was recounting her woes to Kiran, Banwari

happened to be in the next room, greasing the barrel of his rifle. He heard every word that passed. Kiran's pathetic plea of help-lessness, repeated over and over again, cut him to the quick.

That night marked the full moon of Magh, just before the advent of spring. The oppressive heat of the day had given way in the evening to a sudden crazy wind. A koel was singing his heart out, trying to overcome some deep indifference with his song. The air was filled with the fragrance of many flowers. From the garden outside the window, the heady perfume of the muchkunda intoxicated the spring sky. Kiran was wearing a red-dyed sari, with a garland of white jasmine in her hair. For Ban-wari too, as was customary with this couple, a wrap of identical hue and a thick jasmine garland had been laid out to celebrate the season. The evening rolled by, but there was no sign of Ban-wari. The brimming cup of youth held no savour for him that night. How could he step into the heaven of romance with such a heavy heart? He had no power to relieve Madhu Kaibarta's distress; Nilkantha alone did. Who ever wove a garland for a coward like him?

The first thing he did was to call Nilkantha to his outer cham-ber and forbid him from ruining Madhu for his debts. Nilkantha retorted that letting Madhu off would induce others to follow his example, and many other such debts would have to be written off too. Unable to win his point, Banwari then started cursing and swearing. He called Nilkantha low-bred; to which Nilkan-tha replied, 'If I were not low-born, would I be here serving the high-born?' Banwari then called him a thief; to which Nilkantha replied, 'To be sure, those to whom God has given nothing of their own must survive by others' wealth.' He endured every insult humbly. Finally he said, 'The lawyer's waiting, I must go now. If you need me, I'll come later.'

Banwari then decided to win his younger brother Bangshi over to his side and confront their father together. Going alone would be of no use: they had had arguments over Nilkantha before this. The old man was already annoyed with Banwari. At one time, everyone had thought that Manoharlal loved his first-born best. Now it seemed Bangshi was his favourite; so Banwari wanted Bangshi to be a party to his quarrel.

Bangshi was the model of a good boy. He alone in the family had passed a couple of examinations. He was now preparing for the law degree – studying all day, staying up night after night.

God knows whether he retained anything in his head; physically at any rate, he was exhausted.

Even on this spring evening, Bangshi's windows were closed. The change of season caused him alarm; the breeze had little charm for him. A kerosene lamp burnt on his table. Books lay in piles on the floor, on his bed, on the table. In an alcove on one wall stood an array of medicine bottles.

Bangshi would not be persuaded to go along with his brother's proposal. 'You're scared of Nilkantha!' thundered Banwari. Bangshi remained silent. He did in fact try to stay in Nilkantha's good books at all times. He spent most of the year in lodgings in Calcutta, where he invariably fell short of funds. So keeping Nilkantha happy had become a habit with him.

Banwari flung some more insults at him, called him a coward, a toady and a wimp, and went off to confront his father on his own. Manoharlal was sitting by the garden pool, his corpulent pampered body bared to the evening breeze. Around him sat a bunch of flatterers, regaling him with a highly-coloured account of how a neighbouring landowner, Akhil Majumdar, had recently been put out of countenance at the District Court by a barrister from Calcutta. This delightful tale seemed all the more pleasurable in the perfumed evening air.

Banwari's sudden arrival on the scene marred this mood. No preface, no leisurely development of theme: Banwari was in no mood for niceties. He plunged straight in, declaring loudly that Nilkantha was damaging their interests: he was a thief, lining his pockets with his master's wealth. This allegation was without proof and indeed without basis. On the contrary, their affairs were flourishing under Nilkantha's care, nor was he a thief. Banwari had thought that it was his father's firm faith in Nilkantha's honesty which led him to trust the man so. This was not at all the case. In fact Manoharlal was quite convinced that Nilkantha stole whenever he had the chance. But that, to him, was no reason to think less of the man, because such had ever been the way of the world. Great houses had always survived on the leftovers of thieving underlings. If he were not smart enough to steal, would he have brains enough to manage his master's affairs? Managing an estate was not a task for the righteous Yudhisthir.

'That's quite enough!' Manoharlal broke in with marked irritation. 'You don't have to worry about what Nilkantha does or does not do.' He added: 'Look at Bangshi, he doesn't bother about such things. He busies himself with his studies. That boy at least is turning out well.'

After this interruption, Akhil Majumdar's woeful plight lost its power to entertain; and so for Manoharlal, the spring breeze blew in vain, and the moonlight, glittering on the dark waters of the pool, served no purpose. The only two people for whom the evening was not wasted were Bangshi and Nilkantha. Bangshi studied till late behind closed windows; Nilkantha was busy half the night discussing legal matters with the lawyer.

Kiran had put out the bedroom lamp, and sat waiting by the window. She had finished her chores early that evening. Dinner had to wait, because Banwari had not arrived. Madhu the fisherman had gone out of her thoughts. The fact that Banwari had no power to help him in any way did not bother her at all. She had never been eager for her husband to demonstrate any particular power. It was his illustrious family that made him great in her eyes. Enough that he was her father-in-law's eldest son: she did not envisage any greater distinction for him. They were the famous Haldars of Gosainganj, no less!

Banwari paced the front porch till late at night, then finally came in. He had forgotten all about his evening meal. That Kiran had stayed hungry because of him, pained him all the more that night. She put up with so much, and he was so utterly useless: it did not make sense. Every mouthful he ate seemed to stick in his throat. 'I must save Madhu, whatever it takes,' he told his wife in great agitation. Kiran was taken aback at this uncalled-for vehemence. 'Just listen to him!' she said. 'How can you of all people save Madhu?'

Banwari resolved to pay off Madhu's debts himself; but the trouble was, he could never save any money. So he planned to sell off one of his three best guns and a costly diamond ring. But he could not hope to get a good price for these in the village; moreover, tongues would wag if he even tried. So Banwari made out a pretext to go to Calcutta. Before he left, he called Madhu aside and told him not to worry.

Meanwhile, Nilkantha came to know that Madhu had approached Banwari. He was furious. His guards began terrorizing the fishermen so vindictively as to threaten their self-respect.

The very day Banwari returned from Calcutta, Madhu's son Swarup ran up panting and fell wailing at his feet. 'What's the matter?' asked Banwari. Swarup explained that his father had been put in the zamindar's lock-up the previous night. Banwari trembled with rage. 'Go and report this to the police right away!' he said.

Go to the police! Complain against Nilkantha! Swarup was terrified. Finally, under pressure from Banwari, he did as he was told. The police swooped down on the lock-up, released Madhu, arrested Nilkantha and a few guards, and produced them before the magistrate.

Manohar's life was thrown in turmoil. His lawyers fleeced him of money on the pretext of paying bribes, then split the cash with the police. A barrister arrived from Calcutta, a greenhorn who had just taken his robes. He had this advantage, that what was recorded as his fees did not all reach his pocket. Madhu, on the other hand, had one of the best lawyers from the District Court to argue his case. Who exactly was footing his bills was not clear. Nilkantha was sentenced to six months' imprisonment. They appealed to the High Court, but the verdict was upheld.

The good prices fetched by the ring and the gun had not been spent in vain. Madhu was safe for the present, and Nilkantha was in prison. But after such an interlude, how was Madhu to stay on at his old home? Banwari reassured him once again: 'Stay just where you are; you have nothing to fear.' How he could give such an assurance, no one knew but himself: maybe in the pride of his virile courage.

Banwari made no secret of the fact that he was at the bottom of all this; it even reached the master's ears. Manoharlal sent word through his servant that Banwari was not to come before him. Banwari did not flout his father's orders.

Kiran was stunned at her husband's behaviour. What was this! A first-born son not on speaking terms with his own father! Moreover, he had sent their own employee to prison and disgraced the family name before all the world. That too for such small fry as Madhu the fisherman!

Strange indeed. This family had seen so many first-borns over the years, nor was there ever a lack of Nilkanthas to serve them. The Nilkanthas took charge of the estate, and the heads of the household simply preserved the great family tradition, expending no effort in the process. Never had there been such topsy-turvy goings-on.

The elder son's loss of authority hurt the elder daughter-in-law's sense of prestige. After all these years, Kiran truly found reason to disrespect her husband. After all these years, her red springtime sari seemed pale, and the jasmine garland in her hair wilted with shame.

Kiran was a mature woman, yet childless still. This very Nilkantha had once, with her father-in-law's permission, almost arranged for Banwari to take a second wife. That Banwari was the heir-apparent had to be kept in mind above all things: his being without a male child was unthinkable. Kiran's heart had trembled then. But she had to admit that it was a justifiable decision. She had not been angry with Nilkantha, but rather blamed her own fate. If her husband had not raved at Nilkantha, almost laid hands on him, quarrelled with his parents and forced them to cancel the proposed match, Kiran would still not have thought it unjust. In fact, she had secretly thought him rather unmanly for not heeding the family's interests. The compulsions of a great family were themselves great. They had the right to be cruel. The joys and sorrows of a young wife, or some poor fisherman, were nothing in comparison.

Any departure from the customary is considered unforgivable by one and all; yet Banwari simply could not get this into his head. He should have played his role as heir apparent to the hilt; to act by any other criteria of right and wrong, disturbing the settled continuity, was utterly irresponsible. This was clear to everyone except himself.

Kiran carried her woes to her young brother-in-law. Bangshi was clever; dyspeptic as well, and ready to wheeze and cough at the slightest breeze, but sagacious and level-headed. He put his open law-book face down on the table and said: 'This is nothing but sheer madness.'

Kiran nodded in agreement, greatly disturbed. 'You know your brother, Thakurpo. When he's in a good mood he's fine, but once he loses his temper there's no stopping him. Tell me, what am I to do?'

What most hurt Banwari was that Kiran's views should so exactly match those of every sensible member of the family. This fragile young woman, tender as a champak bud – yet with all his masculine powers, he still failed to draw her to his aching heart. If Kiran had been fully in accord with him at the present juncture, his wounded heart would not have festered as it did.

Fanned by opposition from every quarter, the simple duty of protecting Madhu now became an obsession with Banwari. All

other matters seemed trivial by comparison. Meanwhile, Nilkantha came back from prison looking healthy and well-fed, as if
he had been an honoured guest at his father-in-law's house. He
resumed his duties again as composedly as ever.

Now Madhu simply had to be evicted, or else Nilkantha
would lose face among the tenant farmers. It was not so much a
matter of prestige as of discipline: if the peasants got out of hand,
it would hinder Nilkantha's work, so he had to take measures.
Nilkantha started readying his trowel to remove Madhu like
a weed.

This time Banwari did not stay in the background. He told
Nilkantha in very clear terms that he would stop Madhu's evic-
tion by whatever means. First, he settled Madhu's debts fully out
of his own pocket. Next, finding no other way, he personally
went to the magistrate and informed him that Nilkantha was
scheming against Madhu.

His well-wishers tried to warn him that if he continued in this
way, Manoharlal might disinherit him any day. He might have
done so already but for the trouble it would entail. There was
Banwari's mother to think of, and various relatives with their
various opinions: they would create just the kind of fuss and
bother Manohar hated. That was why he still held his peace.

And so things sped, till one morning Madhu's door was found
padlocked. He had disappeared overnight, no one knew where.
Nilkantha, concerned at the unseemly turn of events, had given
Madhu money from the estate coffers and sent him off with his
family to Varanasi. The police were aware of this, so they made
no trouble. But Nilkantha cleverly spread the rumour that on the
night of the dark moon, Madhu with his wife and children had
been sacrificed to the goddess Kali; their bodies had been stuffed
into sacks and drowned in the middle of the Ganga. The people
shook in terror, and their respect for Nilkantha rose higher than
ever.

Banwari's obsession was thereby laid at rest; but his life was
no longer the same.

He had been extremely fond of his brother once; now Bangshi seemed nothing to him, merely one of the Haldar family.
And his own Kiran, whose image had lodged in his heart from
the days of his youth and entwined his whole being – she was
not his either, she was one of them. There was a time when he
would fret because the ornaments ordered by Nilkantha seemed

unsuitable for his beloved. Now he felt that all those verses with which he had lovingly adorned her, from Kalidasa to Amaru and Chaura, did not suit this senior wife of the Haldar family.

The summer breeze still blew, the rain still thrilled the monsoon nights, and the pain of unrequited love wandered weeping through the passages of a desolate heart.

Not everyone feels the need for passionate romance. For most people, the daily portion doled out by life's little measuring-basket serves well enough. This frugal dispensation leaves the wider world undisturbed. But for some people that is just not sufficient. They cannot, like unborn chicks, survive on the sustenance within the egg; having hatched out of the shell, they seek nourishment from the world outside. Banwari was born with such a hunger. He needed to fulfil his own love by his own masculinity; but whichever way he turned, he found his path blocked by the solid edifice of the Haldar family, against which he knocked his head in vain.

Life slipped back to normal again. Banwari now spent more time hunting; except for this there was no great outward change. He went to the inner quarters for his meals, talked as usual with his wife. Kiran had still not forgiven Madhu: he was the root cause of her husband's loss of status within the family. Her anger against him burst forth every now and then: Madhu was a rascal, a villain of the first order; to show him any kindness was to prove oneself a dupe. She carried on endlessly in this vein but still found no peace. At first Banwari had tried to protest, thereby agitating Kiran even more; after that he uttered no word on the subject. He carried on with his family duties. Kiran did not seem to feel any lack, but Banwari's inner being remained dry, lacklustre and perpetually starved.

Around this time, news broke that the younger daughter-in-law, Bangshi's wife, would soon be a mother. The whole household was overjoyed. The duty to their noble house which Kiran had failed to perform stood to be fulfilled at long last. Now they hoped and prayed that the goddess Shasthi would grant them a boy and not a girl.

A boy it was. The younger master had passed his college exams; now he won full marks in the family examination too. They had already made much of him for some time; their attentions now passed all bounds.

Every member of the household was taken up with the baby.

Kiran seldom put him down from her lap. So rapt was she that even Madhu Kaibarta's vile nature no longer engaged her mind.

Banwari was extremely fond of children. Small, helpless, pretty things always aroused his love and pity. God must plant in every human being some little trait that goes against his basic nature: or else how could Banwari ever bear to shoot birds?

His desire to see Kiran blessed with a child had remained unfulfilled all this time. So when Bangshi had a son, Banwari was a little jealous at first, but he did not take long to put such feelings aside. He would have loved this child very much indeed, but for the fact that Kiran's preoccupation with the baby grew more and more excessive. The gap between Banwari and his wife grew wider. It was clear to him that Kiran had at last found something that could truly fulfil her heart's desire. All these years, Banwari had been like a lodger in her heart, allowed entry only because the rightful owner was absent. Now that the owner had arrived in person, Banwari had been relegated to a corner of the house. He saw how deeply engrossed Kiran could be in her affection, with what intensity she gave of herself; and his mind shook its head and said, 'Never could I touch her heart so, though I tried with all my powers.'

Not only that: thanks to the boy, Kiran seemed to be more at home in Bangshi's room. All her plans and discussions went off better with Bangshi. Banwari began despising that sharp-witted, frail-bodied, sapless coward of a man more and more. Everyone around him thought Bangshi to be worthier than him in every way. Banwari could put up with that; but when his own wife made it clear that she valued Bangshi more as a man, Banwari could not be content with his fate, or with the world at large.

Then one day, just before Bangshi's exams, word came from Calcutta that he was grievously ill. The doctors feared for his life. Banwari rushed to Calcutta and nursed his brother day and night, but to no avail.

Death drew out every thorn from Banwari's memory. He only remembered, more brightly now that his memories were washed by tears, that Bangshi had been his little brother. As an infant, he had been sheltered and cherished in his Dada's lap.

He came back fully determined to look after the child with all his heart. But Kiran did not trust him in this regard. She had noticed his hostility to the baby right from the start. She had moreover concluded that whatever was natural in other people would be unnatural in her husband's case. This child was the family's sole heir: everyone realized how precious he was; therefore her husband could not comprehend it. Kiran was eternally afraid that his malicious eye would bring the child ill luck. Her brother-in-law was no more, and there was no hope of her bearing a child herself; so this little one had to be guarded against all evil. Caring for Bangshi's son was thus no easy prospect for Banwari.

The boy began to grow up, showered with affection from all quarters. He was named Haridas. All that attention seemed to have left him rather weak and sickly. Protective charms and amulets were strung all over his body. His zealous guardians continually surrounded him.

With all this, the boy still managed to spend time with Banwari. He loved to swagger about with his uncle's riding-crop. It was the first thing he would lispingly ask for when they met. Banwari would bring it out and swish it around, to the child's immense delight. Sometimes Banwari placed him on his own horse, which brought the whole household running to the rescue in great alarm. Or Banwari might bring out his guns and play with his nephew. If Kiran caught sight of this, she would whisk the boy away. But these forbidden games were the very ones that thrilled Haridas most. So in spite of every obstacle, his uncle became a great favourite with him.

After a long time, death became a frequent visitor to the family. Manohar's wife was the first to go. Nilkantha began looking for a suitable bride for the old master; but Manohar himself died before the auspicious day could arrive. Haridas was then eight years old. On his deathbed, Manohar entrusted his little grandson to the care of Kiran and Nilkantha. To Banwari he had nothing to say.

When his will was retrieved from his chest, it was found that Manohar had bequeathed his estate to little Haridas. Banwari was entitled to a monthly stipend of two hundred rupees for life. Nilkantha was executor, and would be in full charge of all the affairs of the Haldar family as long as he lived.

It was clear to Banwari that no one in the family trusted him, either with the child or with the property. He was good for nothing and would damage anything he laid his hands on: there were no two opinions about that. It was therefore his lot to eat whatever meals they served him, then go quietly to sleep in the corner room.

'I'm not going to live as Nilkantha's pensioner. Let's leave this house and go to live in Calcutta,' he said to Kiran.

'What are you saying?' rejoined Kiran. 'It's your own father's house, and Haridas is like your own son. Why should you resent his being left the property?'

How hard-hearted her husband could be! He was jealous of that tiny little boy! Kiran had no doubt that her father-in-law had made a sound decision. She was sure that had Banwari been left the estate, he would have been cheated right, left and centre by every Jadu and Madhu, every low-bred fisherman or Mussulman weaver: the Haldar's future heir would have been cast adrift on a boundless sea. This boy was the lamp to light up their line, and Nilkantha was the right man to keep the oil supply secure.

Banwari watched as Nilkantha entered the women's quarters and went through every room, listing each item, locking up every chest and cupboard. Finally he came to Banwari's bedroom and started listing each item of daily use. Kiran was not embarrassed by his presence, since he visited these quarters quite often. In a voice choking with tears for her departed father-in-law, she helped with the inventory in the intervals of wiping her eyes.

'Get out of my room this minute!' Banwari roared like a lion.

'I'm not doing anything wrong, Bara Babu,' Nilkantha said humbly. 'Master's will requires me to take full stock of his possessions. All this furniture is Haridas's after all.'

'Just look at that,' thought Kiran to herself. 'Haridas is no stranger. What's so demeaning about living on your son's property? Besides, do we take our possessions with us when we pass on? Sooner or later, our children get to enjoy them anyway.'

For Banwari, the very floors of this house were like thorns under his feet; the walls burnt into his eyes. And there was no one in this vast household to whom he could confide his feelings.

He wished desperately to leave everything at once and simply walk away. But his anger still smouldered within him. The thought of Nilkantha lording it over the household in his absence was more than he could bear. He had to inflict some grievous damage right away.

'I'll see how Nilkantha protects this property,' he said.

He strode into his father's room and found it empty. They were all busy in the inner quarters, making an inventory of the jewellery and utensils. Even the most careful of persons can slip up sometimes. Nilkantha had forgotten to lock the chest where the will had been stored. There were fat bundles of documents inside it, substantiating the titles to the family estates.

Banwari knew nothing of the contents of these documents; but he knew they were of vital importance, and that their absence would cripple them in any legal dispute. So he wrapped the documents in a large handkerchief, slipped out into the garden and sat thoughtfully for a long time on a platform under a champak tree.

Nilkantha came out to him to discuss the arrangements for the funeral next day. Nilkantha's posture was full of humility, but something in his expression – or maybe Banwari imagined it – infuriated the latter. Nilkantha's unctuousness seemed simply a way of mocking him.

Nilkantha started saying, 'About the funeral arrangements –'

'What do I know about such things?' Banwari broke in.

'How can you say that? It's your prerogative to perform the rites.'

'What a prerogative! To perform the last rites! That's all I'm needed for, nothing else!' Banwari roared. 'Go away! Get out! Don't disturb me.'

Nilkantha did get out, but Banwari thought he was laughing as he walked away. Every servant in the house seemed to Banwari to be laughing behind his back at his slighted and discarded self. One of the family, yet not really so – what sharper irony could fate inflict on him? He was worse off than a beggar on the street.

Banwari left the house with his bundle of documents. The Banerjees of Pratappur were their neighbours and rival landowners. 'I'll hand over all these papers to them,' Banwari had decided. 'Let the estate be ruined.'

On his way out, he heard Haridas calling to him from upstairs in his boyish trill, 'Uncle, are you going out? I want to come too!'

It's the boy's unlucky star that makes him say that, thought Banwari. 'I'm taking to the streets; let him come with me. So be it: let everything be destroyed.'

As he reached the outer garden, he heard a great commotion. A widow's hut was on fire near the marketplace. Such disasters had always stirred Banwari to action. This time too he went running to the rescue, dropping his bundle under the champak tree.

When he came back, the bundle was missing. The first

thought that pierced his heart like steel was: 'I've lost to Nilkantha once again! Compared to this, what harm would there have been if the widow's hut had burnt to ashes?' He was convinced that the cunning Nilkantha had retrieved the papers.

He stormed into the office there and then. Nilkantha hurriedly closed a box beside him, stood up respectfully and touched Banwari's feet. Banwari thought he had hidden the documents in that very box. With no words wasted, he flung it open and started rummaging inside. All he found was a ledger-book and some related bills. He upturned the box and shook it, but it yielded nothing further.

'Did you go out to the champak tree?' he asked, his voice nearly choking.

'Yes, of course I did, sir. I saw you rushing off, so I went to see what the matter was.'

'So you must have picked up the papers I had wrapped in my handkerchief.'

'No, sir, I did not,' said Nilkantha, looking quite innocent.

'That's a lie!' said Banwari. 'Give them back at once, or I warn you you'll be in trouble.'

Banwari raved and ranted, but to no effect. He could not explain what exactly he was looking for; and since he knew he had no right to the stolen goods, all he could do was to curse himself inwardly for his foolish negligence.

Having created this scene in the office, he went back to the garden to search all over again. He swore by his mother that he would not give up till he had found those papers. He had no idea how he would go about it; all he could do was stamp his feet like an angry little boy and mutter, 'I will, I will, I will!'

He sat down under the tree, quite exhausted. There was no one there: he had no one and nothing to call his own. From now on, he would have to fight it out alone with no resources, battling his destiny and the world at large. He had no prestige, no respectability, no love, no affection – nothing at all. All he had was the determination to destroy and be destroyed.

He sat there a long time, seething and chafing within him, until he fell asleep from exhaustion. When he woke again, he was not sure where he was at first. Once his head cleared, he sat up and found Haridas beside him. 'What have you lost, Uncle? Tell me.'

Banwari was stunned. What answer could he give?

'If I get it back for you, what'll you give me?' asked Haridas.

He must be referring to something else, thought Banwari. 'I'll give you everything I have,' he said.

He meant it as a joke. He knew he had nothing to give.

Haridas now unwrapped a fold of his dhoti and took out the bundle. The handkerchief had the picture of a tiger printed on it. His uncle had often shown it to him, and Haridas longed to have it. When all the servants had rushed off to the scene of the fire, Haridas had come down and spotted the bundle right away.

Banwari gathered the child into his arms and sat there in silence. His eyes were streaming with tears. He remembered how once he had had to whip a newly-bought dog repeatedly to subdue it. One day he had misplaced the whip and was searching high and low, when the dog itself brought it in its mouth to its master, happily wagging its tail. He could never bring himself to whip a dog again.

Banwari quickly wiped his eyes. 'Tell me what you would like to have, Haridas.'

'I want this handkerchief, Uncle!'

'Let's go, then! Up you get on my shoulders!'

He lifted up the child and went indoors. Entering his bed-room, he saw Kiran laying out a blanket that had aired all day on the verandah. The minute she saw them she cried out anxiously, 'Put him down, put him down, you'll drop him!'

Banwari looked steadily into her eyes and said, 'Don't be afraid about me any more. I won't drop him.'

He took the child down and put him on Kiran's lap. Then he took out the bundle of papers and handed them to her too, saying, 'Put these away safely. They're the titles to Haridas's property.'

Kiran looked surprised. 'How did you get hold of them?'

'I stole them,' replied Banwari.

With that, he hugged Haridas close and said, 'Here you are, son. You can have this precious possession of your uncle's that you'd set your heart on.' And he put the handkerchief into the boy's hands.

Then he turned and took another good look at Kiran. She was no longer the slim young woman he had known. Unobserved by him, she had put on weight: her appearance now matched her senior role in the Haldar household. Banwari's treasured collection of Sanskrit love poetry could now go the way of all his other property.

He disappeared that very night. He left only a scribbled note to say he was going to look for a job.

He couldn't even wait for his father's funeral rites! Everyone in the land condemned him bitterly.

The Wife's Letter

My submission at your lotus feet –

WE HAVE BEEN married for fifteen years, but to this day I have never written you a letter. I have always been at hand – you have heard so many words from my lips, and I too have listened to you – but there has never been an interval in which a letter might have been written.

Today I have come on a pilgrimage to the seat of Lord Jagannath in Puri, while you remain tied to your work in your office. Your bond with Calcutta is like that of a snail with its shell; the city has grown into your body and soul. That is why you did not apply for leave from the office. Such was the wish of the Almighty; he granted *my* application for leave.

I am the second daughter-in-law of your father's house. Today, after fifteen years, standing by the ocean's shore, I have learnt that I have a different relation as well with the world and the Lord of the world. That is why I have taken courage to write this letter; it is not a letter from the second daughter-in-law of your family.

In infancy – when no one but God, who had fated my relation with your family, knew of its possibility – my brother and I were struck down together by typhoid. My brother died; I survived. The women of the neighbourhood began to say, 'Mrinal lived because she's a girl; if she'd been a boy, would she have been spared?' The god of death is skilled in the art of theft; he covets what is precious.

Death will not come for me. It is to explain this properly that I have sat down to write this letter.

When a distant uncle of yours came with your friend Nirad to our house to inspect the prospective bride, I was twelve years old. We lived in an inaccessible village, where you could hear the jackals howl by day. To reach it you had to take a carriage from the railway station for fourteen miles, and cover the last three miles of dirt road in a palanquin. How sorely were they harassed that day! And on top of that, our East Bengal cooking – your uncle has still not forgotten the farce of that meal.

Your mother was determined that her second daughter-in-law's looks should make good the elder one's deficiency in beauty. Otherwise why should you take so much trouble to visit our village? In Bengal, no one has to hunt out diseases of the spleen, the liver, or the stomach, nor need you search for a bride; they come and fasten on you themselves, they will not let you go.

My father's heart began to quake, my mother called on the goddess Durga. How was a rustic worshipper to appease the gods of the city? Their hope lay solely in the beauty of their daughter. But their daughter took no pride in that beauty – it was priced at whatever the buyer offered. It is for this reason that women never lose their diffidence, whatever their beauty or virtues.

The anxiety of the entire household, indeed of the entire neighbourhood, lay on my heart like a stone. That day it seemed as though all the light in the sky and all the powers of the universe were joint bailiffs firmly holding up a twelve-year-old country girl for the scrutiny of her two examiners' two pairs of eyes. I had nowhere to hide.

The whole sky wept to the strains of flute-music as I entered your house. Even after a minute scrutiny of my imperfections, the crowd of housewives acknowledged that on the whole I was indeed beautiful. This verdict made my elder sister-in-law grave. But I wonder what use my beauty was! If some ancient pedant had created beauty out of holy Ganga silt, then you would have valued it; but as it is, it was created by God for His own pleasure, and so it has no value in your righteous household.

It did not take long for you to forget that I had beauty – but you were forced to remember at each step that I had brains. This intelligence is so much a part of my nature that it has survived even fifteen years in your household. My mother feared for this cleverness of mine; for a woman it was an impediment. If one who must follow the limits laid down by rule seeks to follow her intelligence, she will stumble repeatedly and come to grief. But what was I to do? God had carelessly given me much more intelligence than I needed to be a wife in your household; to whom was I now to return it? Your family have abused me daily as an over-clever female. Harsh words are the consolation of the weak – so I forgive them.

I had one possession beyond your household, which none of you knew about. I used to write poems in secret. Whatever rubbish they were, the walls of your women's quarters had not grown round them. In them lay my freedom – I was myself in them. You and your family never liked, never even recognized, whatever in me exceeded the 'second daughter-in-law' of your household. In fifteen years, you never discovered that I am a poet.

The most vivid of my first memories of your house is of the cattle-shed. The cattle were housed in a shed just next to the stairs leading to the women's quarters; they had no room to move in except for the courtyard in front. In a corner of that courtyard stood the wooden trough for their fodder. The servant had much to do in the mornings; meanwhile the starving cows would lick and chew the sides of the trough to a pulp. My heart wept for them. I was a country girl – when I first entered your house, those two cows and three calves seemed to me as my only familiar relatives in the whole city. When I was a new bride, I would feed them secretly out of my own food. When I grew up, my evident fondness for the cows led those of my in-laws on jesting terms with me to express doubts about my lineage.

My daughter died almost immediately after she was born. She called to me, too, to go with her. If she had lived, she would have brought to my life whatever is great and true: from being the second daughter-in-law, I would then have become a mother. A mother, even within the confines of her own family, belongs to the family of the world. I suffered only the pain of motherhood; I never experienced its freedom.

I remember that the English doctor was astonished at the sight of our women's quarters, and scolded us angrily about the state of the lying-in room. There is a garden to the front of your house; your outer rooms lack nothing by way of furniture and ornaments. The inner rooms are like the reverse of a piece of work in wool; they have neither decorum, nor grace, nor ornament. There lights burn dimly; the air enters by stealth, like a thief; the courtyard is immovably choked with rubbish; the stains on the walls and floors reign undisturbed. But the doctor made a mistake: he thought that this caused us constant suffering. In fact the reverse was true. Neglect is like the ashes which cover a fire: perhaps keeping it alive, but preventing its heat from being outwardly felt. When self-respect dwindles, neglect does not seem unjust; for this reason, it causes no suffering. That is also why women are ashamed to feel pain. I say, therefore, if it is your decree that women must suffer, then it is best to keep them in as neglected a state as possible; in comfort, the pain of suffering becomes greater.

Whatever the condition in which you kept me, it never occurred to me that there was any suffering involved. In the lying-in room, death came and stood at my head, yet I felt no fear at all. What is life to us, that we should fear death? Death is unwelcome only to those whose hold on life has been strengthened by love and care. If death, that day, had pulled me by the hand, I would have come away roots and all, like a clump of grass from loose earth. A Bengali woman speaks of dying in every second utterance. But where is the glory in such death? I am ashamed to die, so easy is death for the likes of me.

My daughter was like the evening star, appearing briefly only to fade away. I became occupied again with my daily chores and the cows and their calves. Life would have rolled on in this way to the very end, and there would have been no need, today, to write you this letter. But a tiny seed is blown by the wind to take root as a peepal shoot in a mortared house; in the end its ribs of brick and timber are cracked apart by that tiny seed. From somewhere a little speck of life blew into the firmly mortared arrangements of my household existence, and from that day the cracks began to appear.

After the death of their widowed mother, my elder sister-in-law's young sister Bindu was driven by her cousins' ill-treatment to seek refuge in her elder sister's house. All of you thought: what a nuisance! So vexatious is my nature that there was no helping it, the moment I saw all of you growing irritated and angry, my whole heart ranged itself to do battle by the side of the helpless girl. To have to take shelter with strangers against their wishes – how immense a humiliation! Is it possible to push aside one who has been forced to submit even to this?

I then became aware of my sister-in-law's situation. The claim of affection alone had prompted her to give shelter to her sister. But when she realized her husband's unwillingness, she began to pretend that the whole matter was a great nuisance – that she would do anything to be rid of this burden. She lacked the courage to show her love openly, from the heart, to her orphaned sister. She is an obedient wife.

Her dilemma grieved me still further. I saw that she made a point of demonstrating to everyone the coarseness of the clothes and food she provided for Bindu, as well as the fact that Bindu was put to work at the most menial of household chores. At this I felt not only pain but shame. My sister-in-law was anxious to prove to everyone that our household, by some fluke, had secured Bindu at a bargain price. She yielded much labour but cost very little.

My elder sister-in-law's family had little to boast of beyond its lineage: they possessed neither wealth nor good looks. You know how they pleaded with and importuned your father to agree to the marriage. My sister-in-law had always thought of her marriage as a great offence to your family. For this reason she tried, in every way, so to restrict herself as to take up very little space in your house.

But her wise example makes life difficult for us women. It is impossible for me to so limit myself in every point. When I decide that something is right, it is not my nature to be persuaded for someone else's sake that it is wrong. You too have had many proofs of this.

I drew Bindu to my rooms. Sister-in-law said: 'Meja Bou is simply spoiling a poor man's daughter.' She went around complaining to everyone as though I had brought about some terrible disaster. But I know that in her heart, she was relieved. Now the burden of blame would fall on me alone. Her heart was at peace in the knowledge that I was providing her sister with the love she herself could not show her.

My sister-in-law had tried to strike a few years off her sister's age. But it would not have been wrong to say, if only in secret, that she was no younger than fourteen. You know that the girl was so ill-favoured that if she fell and hurt her head, people would be worried that the floor had suffered some damage. As a result, in the absence of her parents, there was no one to arrange a marriage for her, and who would be so hardy as to want to marry such a girl?

Bindu came to me in great trepidation of heart, as if she thought that I would not survive the contagion of her touch: as though there was no need for her to have been born at all in this world, as though she must pass by unobtrusively, avoiding people's eyes. In her father's house, her cousins had been unwilling to give up to her even a corner where some unwanted thing might lie forgotten. Inessential rubbish can easily find a place around our houses, because people forget it, but an inessential girl is in the first place unwanted, and moreover impossible to overlook; hence she does not find a place even in the rubbish-heap. One cannot say that Bindu's cousins are utterly necessary to this world either; but they do well enough.

So when I called Bindu to my rooms, there was a trembling in her heart. Her fear filled me with sadness. I conveyed to her in many loving ways that there was a little place for her in my household.

But my household, after all, was not mine alone, and so my task was not easy. After a few days with me she developed a red rash on her skin: perhaps a heat rash, perhaps something else. All of you said it was smallpox – because it was Bindu. An inexperienced doctor from the neighbourhood came and said that he could not tell what it was until a day or two had passed. But who was prepared to wait that day or two? Bindu herself was ready to die of shame at her illness. I said, 'Never mind if she has smallpox, I'll stay with her in the lying-in room. No one else need be troubled.' When all of you were in a fury at me over this, and even Bindu's sister was putting on a show of extreme irritation and proposing to send the poor girl to hospital, suddenly the rash disappeared completely. At this you became even more concerned. You said that undoubtedly the smallpox had settled deep into her. For she was Bindu.

One great virtue of being reared in neglect is that one's constitution becomes virtually indestructible. Ailments refuse to visit you – the highways to death are wholly shut off. So illness mocked at Bindu and passed on – nothing happened to her. But it grew abundantly clear that the most insignificant person in the world was the one that was hardest to give shelter to. One who has most need of shelter finds the greatest obstacles to it.

When Bindu lost her fear of me, she tied herself in yet another knot. She developed so great a love for me that it made me afraid. I had never seen such an image of love in my household. I had read of such love in books, but that was love between men and women. For a long time, there had been no occasion for me to recall that I was beautiful – now, after so many years, this ugly girl became obsessed with my beauty. It was as if her eyes could never have enough of gazing on my face. She would say, 'Didi, no one but me has ever seen this face of yours.' On the days when I braided my hair myself, she would be hurt and offended. She loved to handle the weight of my hair. I did not need to dress up unless we were invited out; but Bindu would plague me to dress up every day. The girl was infatuated with me.

There is not even the smallest patch of earth in the women's quarters in your house. A gab tree has somehow taken root by the north wall near the gutter. When I saw the leaves of that tree flush red, I would realize that spring had come to the earth. In the midst of my household cares, when I saw this unloved girl's heart one day glow with colour, I realized that in the heart's world too, there is a breeze of spring-time – a breeze which comes from some far-off heaven, not from the end of the lane.

The unbearable force of Bindu's love made me restless and uneasy. I confess that sometimes I felt angry with her. Yet that love made me glimpse a true image of myself, one that I had never seen before. This was the image of my free self.

Meanwhile, all of you thought it excessive that I should lavish such care on a girl like Bindu. As a result, there were endless complaints and objections. When my armlets were stolen from my room, you were not ashamed to suggest that Bindu was somehow involved in the theft. When the police started searching people's houses during the Swadeshi Movement, you began to suspect that Bindu was a female informer in the pay of the police. There was no other proof of this than that she was Bindu.

The maids in your house refused to do any work for her. Bindu herself would grow rigid with embarrassment if I asked any of them to do something for her. As a result, my expenditure on her behalf went up. I had to keep a maid especially for her. You did not like this. When you saw the clothes I gave her, you became so angry that you stopped my allowance. From the very next day, I began to wear the coarsest mill-produced dhotis at twenty annas a pair. I also forbade Mati's mother to take out the dishes after my meal; I would myself feed the leftover rice to the calves and scrub the dishes at the pump in the courtyard. You were not very pleased by the sight when you saw me at these tasks one day. Yet I never learned this wisdom: whether I was pleased or not did not matter, but you had to be pleased at all costs.

Meanwhile, as your anger increased, so did Bindu's age. This natural event made you unnaturally concerned. I am still amazed at one thing: why did you not send Bindu away from your house by force? I know very well that you are secretly afraid of me. Inwardly, you cannot but respect the intelligence that God gave me.

In the end, unable to get rid of Bindu by your own means, you had recourse to Prajapati, the god of marriage. A bridegroom was arranged for Bindu. My sister-in-law said, 'Thank heavens, Mother Kali has saved the reputation of our family.'

I did not know what the groom was like; I heard from you that he was eligible in every respect. Bindu clasped my feet and wept, saying 'Didi, why need I get married?'

I tried to persuade her, telling her, 'Bindu, don't be afraid, I've heard he's a good groom.'

Bindu answered, 'If he's so eligible, what have I got that might please him?'

The groom's family did not even come to see Bindu. My sister-in-law was greatly relieved at this.

But Bindu's tears continued incessantly, day and night. I know what she suffered. I had fought many battles for Bindu in my household, but I did not have the courage to say that her marriage must be stopped. How should I say this? What would happen to her if I died?

In the first place she was a girl, and on top of that she was dark-complexioned. It was better not to think of where she was going or what might happen to her. The thought sent shudders through my heart.

Bindu said, 'Didi, there are still five days to the wedding. Mightn't I die in this time?'

I scolded her severely, but God knows that I would have been relieved if there had been an easy means of death for Bindu.

The day before the wedding, Bindu went to her sister and asked her, 'Didi, I'll live in your cattle-shed, I'll do whatever you ask of me. I beg of you, don't throw me away like this.'

Her sister had been shedding tears in secret for the past few days; she wept then as well. But we do not have hearts only, we have the scriptures too; she said, 'Bindi, you know that a husband is the sole end of a woman's life. If you are fated to suffer, no one can avert it.'

The truth was that there was no escape anywhere. Bindu must marry, whatever befell her.

I had wanted the wedding to take place in our house. But you announced that it must be held in the groom's house – this was the custom in their family.

I realized that your household deity would never endure it if your family were forced to spend on Bindu's wedding. So I

had to fall silent. But there is one thing you did not know. I had
wanted to tell my sister-in-law, but I did not, because she would
have died of fear. I adorned Bindu with some of my jewellery.
Perhaps my sister-in-law saw this but pretended not to notice.
I beg you in the name of righteousness, forgive her for this.

Before leaving, Bindu embraced me, asking, 'Didi, are you all
abandoning me?'

I answered 'No, Bindi, whatever happens to you, I'll never
abandon you.'

Three days passed. In one corner of the coal-shed on the
ground floor of your house, I had reared a lamb which one of
your tenants had sent as a gift for your table, and which I had rescued from the flames of your appetite. Every morning I would
feed it gram with my own hands; for a few days I had tried relying on your servants, but found that they were more interested
in eating it than in feeding it.

That morning, when I entered the coal-shed, I found Bindu
crouched in a corner. On seeing me she collapsed on the floor,
clasped my feet and began to weep silently.

Bindu's husband was mad.

'Are you telling the truth, Bindi?'

'Could I tell you such a big lie, Didi? He is mad. My father-
in-law did not want this marriage; but he is mortally afraid of
my mother-in-law. He left for Varanasi before the wedding. My
mother-in-law had set her heart on marrying her son off; she
went ahead with it.'

I sat down, overcome, on the heap of coal. Women have no
pity for women. They say, 'She's only a woman. So what if the
groom's mad, he's a man, isn't he?'

One could not tell at first sight that Bindu's husband was
insane; but he would sometimes grow so violent that he had to
be locked up in a room. He had seemed normal on the night
of the wedding, but staying up at night and all the excitement
had brought on an attack the next day. In the afternoon, Bindu
had sat down to her meal of rice, served on a brass platter, when
suddenly her husband snatched the platter and threw it, rice and
all, into the courtyard. He had got it into his head that Bindu
was Rani Rasmani; the servant must have stolen her golden plate
and served her on his own brass platter. This was the reason for
his anger.

Bindu was terrified. On the third night, when Bindu's

mother-in-law commanded her to sleep in her husband's room, she shrivelled up in fear. Her mother-in-law had a vicious temper; in a rage, she lost control of her senses. She too was insane, though not so completely as her son, and therefore she was more terrible. Bindu was forced to enter her husband's room. That night he was quiet, but Bindu's entire body grew stiff with fear. Very late at night, when he had fallen asleep, Bindu found a means to flee the house and come here. I need not describe in detail how she managed this.

My whole body burned with anger and disgust. I said, 'Such a fraudulent marriage isn't a marriage at all. Bindu, stay with me as you used to. Let me see who dares take you away.'

You said, 'Bindu is lying.'

I answered, 'Bindu has never lied.'

You asked, 'How do you know?'

I answered, 'I'm certain of this.'

You tried to frighten me by saying that if Bindu's in-laws lodged a case with the police, we would be in trouble.

I answered, 'They deceived us by marrying her to a madman. Will the court not listen to us?'

You said, 'Must we go to court, then? What obligation is it of ours?'

I replied, 'I'll sell my jewellery and do what needs to be done.'

You asked, 'So are *you* going to go to the lawyer's chambers?'

There was no answer to this. I could beat my forehead in despair, but what more could I do?

Meanwhile, Bindu's brother-in-law had arrived and was kicking up a great row in the outer rooms. He was threatening to go to the police.

I do not know where I got the strength; but I could not bring myself to send back to the slaughter-house the calf that had run away from there to take shelter with me. I said defiantly, 'Let him go to the police, then!'

Saying this, I decided to take Bindu to my bedroom, lock the door, and stay there with her. But when I looked for her, Bindu was gone. While I had been exchanging words with you, she had gone out of her own accord and turned herself over to her brother-in-law. She had realized that if she stayed in this house, I would be in great trouble.

By running away Bindu had simply added to her suffering. Her mother-in-law's argument was, that her son had not after all tried to eat Bindu up. The world had many instances of bad husbands; compared to them her son was pure gold.

My sister-in-law said, 'She's an ill-fated girl. What's the point of being sorry for her? He might be a madman or a stupid goat, but he's her husband all the same.'

You recalled the supreme instance of wifely devotion: how a wife carried her leprosy-stricken husband herself to his whore's house. You never felt the least embarrassment about proclaiming this tale of the greatest cowardice in the world. Hence being born a human being never prevented you from being angry at Bindu's behaviour: you felt no shame. My heart burst with pity for Bindu, but I could not contain my shame for you. I was a village girl, and cast moreover into your household: through what crack had God filled me with such sense? I could not bear this righteous talk of yours.

I knew for certain that Bindu would die rather than come back to our house. Yet had I not given her my word, the day before she was married, that I would never abandon her? My younger brother Sharat was at college in Calcutta. You know that he was so enthusiastic a volunteer for every kind of social mission, from killing rats in the plague quarter to relief work in the Damodar floods, that even two successive failures in the First Arts Examination had not curbed his zeal. I called him and said, 'You must arrange to bring me news of Bindu, Sharat. Bindu will not dare write to me – and even if she does, the letter would never reach me.'

Rather than this, if I had told him to abduct Bindu from her house and bring her to me, or to beat her mad husband's head, Sharat would have been better pleased.

As I was talking to Sharat, you came into the room and asked, 'What trouble are you starting now?'

I said, 'It's the same trouble that I began when I entered your household – but that was your doing.'

You asked, 'Have you brought Bindu here again and hidden her somewhere?'

I answered, 'If Bindu came, I would certainly hide her here. But she won't come: you need have no fear.'

Your suspicion grew at seeing Sharat with me. I knew that you had never liked Sharat's visits to our house. You were afraid that the police were watching him; some day he would get involved in a political case, and drag the lot of you into it as well. For this reason I was even forced to send him my blessings through a messenger on Brothers' Day; I did not invite him to the house.

I heard from you that Bindu had run away again, and so her brother-in-law had come to enquire at your house. It was as though I had been pierced to the heart. I realized how terrible was the unfortunate girl's suffering, yet there was nothing I could do about it.

Sharat hurried off to bring news. He returned in the evening and told me, 'Bindu had gone to her cousins' house, but they flew into a terrible rage and took her back immediately to her in-laws. They still haven't got over the sting of the expense and carriage-hire she cost them.'

Your aunt was staying in your house on her way to Puri on pilgrimage. I said to you, 'I'll go with her.'

You were so delighted by this sudden evidence of piety in me, that you made not the least objection. The thought was also in your mind that if I remained in Calcutta, I would again create a problem over Bindu some day. I was myself a terrible problem.

We were to leave on the Wednesday; by Sunday it had all been decided. I called Sharat and told him, 'By whatever means, you must put Bindu on the train to Puri on Wednesday.'

Sharat's face lit up; he said, 'Never fear, Didi, I'll put her on the train and go to Puri myself as well. I'll get to see Lord Jagannath into the bargain.'

That evening Sharat came again. The look on his face stopped my heart. I asked, 'What is it, Sharat? Couldn't you manage it?'

He said, 'No.'

I asked, 'Weren't you able to persuade her?'

He said, 'There's no need any longer. Yesterday night she set her clothes on fire and killed herself. I got word from one of the nephews of the house, with whom I'd struck up a friendship, that she'd left a letter for you, but they've destroyed it.'

Peace at last!

Everyone in the land was annoyed. They began to say, 'It's now the fashion for girls to set their saris on fire and kill themselves.'

You said, 'This is all play-acting.' That may be so. But one should reflect why this play-acting takes its toll only of the saris of Bengali women, not of the dhotis of brave Bengali gentlemen.

Bindi was always unlucky! So long as she was alive, she was

never known for beauty or talent; even in dying, it never occurred to her to work out some novel means of dying which all the men in the land could applaud! In death, too, she made people angry.

My sister-in-law hid herself in her room and wept. But there was some consolation in her tears. Whatever befell, the family was saved; Bindu had only died. If she had lived, who knows what might have happened!

I have come on pilgrimage. Bindu did not need to come after all, but for me there was need.

I did not suffer in your household, as suffering is commonly understood. In your house there is no lack of food or clothes. Whatever be your elder brother's character, you have no vices of which I can complain to the Almighty. Even if your nature had been like your brother's, I might have passed my days somehow or other, and like that devoted wife my sister-in-law, might have tried to blame not my lord and husband but only the Lord of the Universe. And so I have no complaint to make against you – that is not the purpose of my letter.

But I will never again return to your house at number 27, Makhan Baral Lane. I have seen Bindu. I have learnt what it means to be a woman in this domestic world. I need no more of it.

And I have also seen that though she was a woman, God did not abandon her. Whatever the powers you exercised over her, there was a limit to them. She was greater than her wretched human birth. Your feet were not long enough to tread her life underfoot for ever, at your wish and by your custom. Death is more powerful than you. In that death, she has attained greatness. There, she is no longer simply the daughter of a Bengali household, the young 'sister' of her tyrannical cousins, the deceived wife of an unknown, mad husband. There she is infinite.

When the flute-call of that death sounded through the broken heart of a young girl to the Yamuna-bank of my own life, it seemed at first as though I had been struck by an arrow. I asked God, 'Why should the most petty things in life prove the most difficult? Why should the fragile bubble of a joyless life, immured in this little lane, be so terrible an obstacle? When Your whole earth beckons me, holding out the nectar-bowl of the six seasons, why can I not, even for a moment, cross the tiny threshold of these women's quarters? In this universe You have created, with this life I have been given, why must I die inch by inch in this petty shelter of brick and wood? How trivial is this daily commerce of my life, how trivial are its set rules, set habits, set phrases, set blows – yet in the end, must the stranglehold of this pettiness triumph, and Your creation, this universe of joy, be defeated?'

But death sounded its flute-call: 'What are these walls of masonry, these thorny hedges of your domestic laws? By what suffering or humiliation can they still imprison human beings? See, the triumphal flag of life waves in the hands of death! O second daughter-in-law, you need have no fear! It takes not even a second to cast off your wifely slough.'

I am no longer afraid of your lane. The blue ocean is before me today, and the rain-clouds of Asharh are gathered overhead.

You had shrouded me over in the darkness of your habits and customs. For a short space, Bindu came and stole a glimpse of me through the rents in that shroud. And it was this very girl who, through her death, tore my shroud to tatters. Today, having come out, I find no vessel to contain my glory. He who found my slighted beauty pleasing, that Beauteous One is gazing at me through the whole sky. The second daughter-in-law is dead at last.

Do you think I am going to kill myself? Have no fear, I shan't indulge in such a stale jest with you. Mirabai too was a woman like me. Her fetters were not light either, but she did not need to die in order to live. Mirabai said in her song, 'Let father, mother, everyone abandon her, O Lord, but Mira will never let you go, whatever befalls her!' It is this holding on which is life.

I too shall live. At last, I live.

Bereft of the shelter of your family's feet,
Mrinal.

House Number One

I DO NOT EVEN smoke. I have one addiction which soars beyond the skies; under its shadow, all other addictions have dried to their very roots. It is my addiction to books. The sacred motto of my life has been 'Borrow in order to read books as long as you live, or even if you don't live.'

In my younger days, when my resources were meagre, I used to read publishers' catalogues, like people who read railway time-tables because they love to travel but lack the means. My elder brother had an uncle by marriage who used to buy every Bengali book, undiscriminatingly, as soon as it was published. It was his special point of pride that he had never lost even a single volume. Perhaps no one else in Bengal was ever so lucky: because among the things that tend to disappear – wealth, life, careless men's umbrellas – Bengali books occupy the prime place. Clearly, the keys to this uncle-in-law's book-case were inaccessible even to the aunt-in-law. In my boyhood, when I sometimes went with my brother to his in-laws' house – 'like a poor man accompanying the king of kings', I spent my time there gazing at those locked book-cases. My eyes' tongue would water at the sight.

It will suffice to say that I failed my examinations because from childhood onward, I had read too much. I had no time for the very little reading needed to pass.

Having failed my examinations, I enjoy a great privilege. I do not bathe in the water of learning stored in university pitchers; it has been my habit to plunge into the running stream. Many BAs and MAs visit me these days. However modern, they are still under the surveillance of the Victorian age. Like the earth in the Ptolemaic system, their world of knowledge is firmly screwed to the eighteenth and nineteenth centuries, as if students in Bengal must revolve round that point for ever, generation after generation. Their intellectual chariot has travelled laboriously beyond Mill and Bentham, but tilted to one side as it reached Carlyle and Ruskin. They dare not take the air beyond the fence of their teachers' jargon.

We have turned English literature into a peg to which our minds can be tethered to chew the cud; but in its own country, this literature has not stood still. There, it has moved along with the life of the land. I may not share that life, but I have tried to follow that movement. I learnt French, German and Italian on my own. I started learning Russian a short while ago. I have bought a ticket on the express train of modernism, which covers more than sixty miles an hour. That is why I did not get stuck even at Huxley and Darwin, nor did I fear to examine Tennyson critically. I even feel ashamed to follow the boat bearing Ibsen and Maeterlinck's names, to carry on a secure trade in easy fame among our literary monthlies.

I had never dreamt that a group of people might seek out someone like me. I find that in Bengal there are a handful of youths who do not abandon college, yet grow restless and are drawn beyond the confines of their college by the sound of Saraswati's veena. A few such young men began trickling into my room in ones and twos.

And thus I acquired my second addiction – that is, talking. In polite language, it could be termed discourse. The discourse we hear around us in the nation's literature, periodical or unseasonal, is so naive and inept yet so worn and stale that from time to time, I feel like dispelling its damp stuffiness by the free air of unconstrained thought. Yet I am too lazy to write down my ideas. To have eager listeners within my reach is a great comfort to me.

My group began increasing in number. I lived in house number 2 in our lane and my first name is Adwaitacharan, 'believer in the oneness of God and universe'. So our group came to be called the Sect of Two and One. No one in our sect had the least sense of time. One of them would turn up in the morning with a new English book, the pages flagged with punched tram tickets. The discussion would last till one o'clock and still find no end. Someone else would arrive in the evening with his fresh college notes and show no sign of leaving even at two in the morning.

I often asked them to meals, for I knew that like their brains, the palates of literary enthusiasts have great powers to taste and savour. But I never heeded the plight of the person on whom I relied to feed these hungry guests. How could the stir of housework, the flicker of the kitchen fire, divert one's eyes from the great potter's wheels of universal thought and learning whereby some human cultures were baked hard while others disintegrated when still soft?

I have read in the poets that only Shiva can interpret the enigmatic frowns of his consort. But Shiva has three eyes. I have only two, whose vision has been dimmed by constant reading. So I never noticed how the arch of my wife's eyebrows quivered when she had to arrange a feast at an odd hour. Gradually she came to accept that the system in my house was a lack of system, and indiscipline its order of rule. My domestic clock lacked rhythm; discomposing winds blew through every cranny of my house. All my money and energy went down the single open drain of acquiring books. My wife knew better than I how our other needs were sustained on the money left over from my hobby, like a stray cur licking and sniffing at the left-overs of a pedigreed dog of foreign breed.

A person like me urgently needs to talk on various scholarly subjects; not to show off one's learning, or to benefit others, but as a way of assisting thought, an exercise to aid the digestion of knowledge. Had I been a writer or a teacher, it would have been a redundant exercise. People with regular work do not have to devise aids to digestion; those who stay at home need at least to walk briskly on the terrace. My situation was of the latter kind. Until I acquired my entourage, my only accessory had been my wife. She endured silently and for long the noisy process of my mental digestion. Though her saris were cheap mill-woven stuff and her ornaments not of pure or solid gold, whatever she heard from her husband – be it eugenics or Mendelism or mathematical logic – had nothing cheap or spurious about it. She was deprived of this discourse when my followers increased in number; but I never heard her complain about it.

My wife's name is Anila. I do not know what the word means, nor did my father-in-law when he named her. The word sounds sweet and seems to have a meaning. Whatever the dictionary says, what the name really meant was that my wife was her father's darling. My mother-in-law died leaving a son aged two and a half. As a pleasant way to solve the problem of his upbringing, my father-in-law married again. How far his intentions were fulfilled can be seen from his request to Anila two days before his death. He held her hands and said, 'I am going, my child. You are the only person left to look after Saroj.' I do not know for certain how he provided for his wife and the children of his second marriage. But he secretly handed over to Anila almost seven and a half thousand rupees out of his savings.

He said, 'You need not invest it. Spend the principal to pay for Saroj's education.'

I was somewhat taken by surprise at this. My father-in-law was not only intelligent, he was what men call wise. That is to say, he never did anything out of impulse, but acted with deliberation. I had therefore never doubted that if he had to entrust his son's education to anyone, it should be me. I really cannot say what made him adjudge his daughter fitter than his son-in-law in this matter. Yet had he not known me to be utterly trustworthy in money matters, he would not have left so much cash with my wife. In fact he was a Philistine of the Victorian era and, till the last, could not recognize my worth.

I was piqued, and at first decided not to say a word on the subject. Nor did I. I was confident that Anila would have to approach me, since she had no other option. When she did not come to me for advice, I thought she could not summon the courage.

At last one day, I asked her in course of conversation, 'What are you doing about Saroj's education?'

Anila said, 'I've found a tutor for him, and he's going to school as well.'

I gave her to understand that I was willing to take charge of Saroj's education. I tried to explain to her some of the new methods of teaching. Anila said neither yes nor no.

After all these years, I suspected for the first time that Anila did not respect me. I did not have a college degree: maybe that was why she thought I had neither the right nor the ability to advise her on education. Anila must have failed to recognize the worth of all I had told her so long about eugenics, evolution and radio waves. Perhaps she thought that even boys in the Second Class knew more than me because their knowledge had been driven firmly into their skulls, as by so many turns of a screw, each time their teacher boxed their ears. I felt deeply annoyed. I reflected that a person whose chief asset is knowledge and intelligence should give up all hope of proving his worth to women.

Most great dramas of human life proceed behind the curtain, which suddenly lifts at the end of the fifth act. While my cronies and I were preoccupied with Bergsonian philosophy and Ibsenian psychology, I thought that no flame had been lit on the altar of Anila's life. But as I look back today, I realize clearly that the Maker who shapes living images with fire and hammer was very much at work in Anila's heart. A constant tussle was being enacted there between a younger brother, an elder sister and a stepmother.

The mythical serpent Vasuki holds up a mythical earth which is at least static. But for the woman who bears a world of pain, that world is re-created each moment by fresh buffets. She has to negotiate her small everyday domestic trials with that shifting load of pain pressed to her heart. Who but the Omniscient can fully understand what she feels? At least I realized nothing. I never knew what anxiety, what spurned efforts, what deep longings of hurt affection were stirring so near me behind a screen of silence. I used to think that the chief event in Anila's life was preparing for our group's scheduled feast-days. Now I understand clearly that through profound suffering, the younger brother had become the person closest to his Didi. I never took the least interest in the matter, since they had totally rejected my advice and help in the matter of Saroj's upbringing. I did not even ask how things were with him.

In the meantime, tenants arrived at house number 1 in our lane. This house had been built long ago by the well-known, rich moneylender Uddhab Baral. Over the next two generations, his family lost its wealth and its people. Only one or two widows were left: they did not live here, and the house was in disrepair. Once in a while, it would be rented out briefly for a wedding or other such occasion. No long-term tenants were interested in such a big house. The person who came to live here now was, let us say, Raja Sitangshumouli; he was, let us assume, the zamindar of Narottampur.

I might have remained in the dark about such a great arrival just next door. Like Karna, who was born with a protective amulet, I too had a protection gifted me by providence: this was my habitual absentmindedness. It was a thick, strong armour. It afforded me the means of protecting myself from the perpetual jostling, clamour and abuse all around me.

Rich men of modern times are, however, nuisances beyond the natural: they are preternatural nuisances. Creatures that possess two hands, two legs and one head are human beings. Those who have suddenly acquired a few more such limbs are demons. They continually break their natural bounds with fearsome noise and torment heaven and earth by their excesses. It is impossible not to take notice of them. Such people, who do not merit attention yet whom you cannot ignore, are an illness afflicting the world. Even the king of the gods fears them.

I could see that Sitangshumouli was of this type. I had never known that a single person could bear so much of superfluity. With his carriages, horses and attendants, he seemed to be playing a stage role with ten heads and twenty arms. The fences around my scholarly paradise were broken every day by his depredations.

I first met him at the corner of our lane. The chief advantage of this narrow lane was that an absentminded person like me could walk along without bothering to look ahead or behind him, right or left. One ran no risk of untimely death even while debating inwardly on a story by Meredith, a poem by Browning, or the work of some modern Bengali poet. But on that day, suddenly, I heard a loud warning cry. I turned around to find a pair of huge chestnut horses, drawing an open brougham, about to descend on me from behind. The owner himself was driving; the coachman sat beside him. The babu was pulling sharply at the reins with both hands. I somehow saved myself by clutching at the wall of a tobacco shop. The babu was angry with me. The man who drives carelessly cannot pardon a careless pedestrian. I have already mentioned the reason for this. The pedestrian has only two legs and is thus a normal man. The man who rides in a coach has eight legs: he is a demon. He creates trouble in the world by this unnatural excess. The guardian god of the two-legged man was not prepared for the sudden emergence of the eight-legged.

By the salutary law of my nature, I would have forgotten both carriage and rider in course of time. They were not specially worth remembering in this world full of marvels. But such people usurp much more than a man's natural part in making a noise. Hence though I could remain oblivious of my neighbour in house number 3 for days and months if I so wished, it was hard to forget the neighbour at number 1 even for a second. At night, the unmusical stamping of his eight or ten horses on the wooden stable floor left dents all over my sleep. And it was impossible to remain courteously disposed when in the early morning, eight to ten grooms massaged those eight to ten horses. Besides, none among his retinue of footmen and door-keepers from Orissa or Bihar was inclined to restrain his voice or moderate his talk. So, one man though he was, he commanded a large number of noise machines. This is the hallmark of a demon. It may not cause him disturbance. Perhaps Ravana could sleep soundly when he snored out of twenty nostrils; but consider the plight of his neighbours. The chief feature of paradise is the beauty of its proportions, whereas the demons who devastated its beauty were chiefly distinguished by excess. That demon of excess is now attacking human habitations, riding on a moneybag. If we try to evade him, he descends upon us in a four-horse carriage – and, moreover, browbeats us.

That afternoon, my followers had not yet arrived. I was reading a book on tides. Suddenly a missive from my neighbour knocked loudly against my window-pane, having flown over my compound wall and front gate. It was a tennis ball. The attraction of the moon, the stirrings of the earth, the metrics of the universal lyric order were all eclipsed by the recollection that I had a neighbour – had him in excess of requirement, redundantly yet inescapably. The very next moment, my old servant Ajodhya ran up panting. He was my only attendant. He would not appear when called, and remained unmoved by my shouts. If asked why he was not to be found, he said he had too much to do for one man. But that day I saw him pick up the ball without any urging and run next door. I came to know that he was paid four paise for each ball that he fetched.

I found that not only were my peace and my window-panes shattered, my followers too were destabilized. It was not so surprising that Ajodhya's contempt for my insignificance should grow by the day; but even Kanailal, the leading member of my group, grew curious about the adjacent house. I had been secure that his devotion to me was based on mental wealth and not outward accessories. But one day I saw him beat Ajodhya to pick up a runaway tennis ball and run next door. Obviously, he wanted an excuse to make my neighbour's acquaintance. I realized that his mind was not quite like that of Brahma-worshipping Maitreyi: immortal truth alone would not satisfy his hunger.

I tried to be fiercely sarcastic about the epicurean ways of Number One. I said that his efforts to cover his empty mind with external trappings were as futile as trying to cover the sky with coloured clouds: even a mild breeze drives them away and exposes the empty sky. One day, Kanailal protested and said that the man was not wholly worthless: he had a BA degree.

Kanailal was himself a graduate, so I could not say anything about that degree.

Number One's chief accomplishments were clamorous in nature. He could play three instruments – the cornet, the esraj and the cello. This was made evident at all hours. I do not pride myself as an authority on music, but I do not look upon music as an exalted branch of wisdom. Music came into existence when man lacked language and was dumb: he could not think, so he would shout. Even today, primitive races love to make unnecessary noise. But I discovered at least four young men in my group who could not concentrate even on the latest advance in mathematical logic when Number One played the cello.

About the time when quite a few of the boys felt drawn towards house number 1, Anila told me one day, 'The people next door are becoming a nuisance. Let's move to some other house.'

I was very pleased to hear this. I told my group, 'You see how women have a natural acumen. They fail to understand what needs rational proof, but don't even take a minute to understand what lacks proof.' Kanailal laughed and added: 'For example, evil spirits, ghosts, the efficacy of the dust of a brahman's feet, divine reward for worshipping one's husband, etc. etc.'

'Not at all,' I said. 'Just look at this: we are overwhelmed by the pomp and display next door, but Anila hasn't been taken in by it.'

Anila suggested two or three times that we change house. I too liked the idea, but I did not have the patience to hunt for a house among the lanes of Calcutta. At last one day, Kanailal and Satish were seen playing tennis at house number 1. I next heard a rumour that Jati and Haren were playing in the musical soirées there, one on the box harmonium and the other on the tabla, while Arun had won great acclaim among them by singing comic songs. I had known them all for five or six years but never suspected them of such accomplishments. Arun, in particular, I had known as an enthusiast in comparative religion. How could I have guessed that he was adept at comic songs?

To tell the truth, I was envious of Number One, however much I slighted him publicly. I could think and judge, grasp the inner meaning of everything and solve great problems; hence it was impossible for me to consider Sitangshumouli as my intellectual equal. Even so I was envious of him. People will laugh if I explain the reason. In the morning, Sitangshu used to ride out on a spirited horse. With what admirable skill he would ply the reins and control the animal! I watched the scene every day and thought, 'I wish I could cut a figure on a horse with such aplomb!' I had a secret longing for the practical efficiency that I totally lacked.

I do not understand music very well, but I would often look out surreptitiously from my window to see Sitangshu playing the esraj. His effortless, elegant mastery over the instrument fascinated me. The esraj seemed to love him like a woman and willingly surrender all its music to him. The natural sway that Sitangshu had over everything – objects, houses, men, animals – spread a charm and grace all around him. It was something indescribable, and I could not but consider it to be rare. I felt he did not need to ask for anything; everything would come to him of its own, and he would make a place for himself wherever he chose to go.

So one after another, a number of my followers started visiting house number 1, to play tennis or join in concerts. I could think of no way to rescue these tempted souls except by leaving the place. An estate agent told me of a suitable house somewhere around Baranagar or Kashipur. I agreed to take it. It was half past nine in the morning. I went to tell my wife to get ready. She was neither in the pantry nor in the kitchen. I found her in the bedroom, sitting silently with her head against the window bars. She got up as soon as she saw me. I told her, 'We can move to our new house the day after tomorrow.'

'Let's wait for about a fortnight,' she said.

'Why?' I asked her.

Anila said, 'Saroj's exam results will be out soon. I'm worried about it, I don't feel like moving house just now.'

This was a subject that, among many others, I never discussed with my wife. So we put off moving house for the time being. In the meantime, I heard that Sitangshu would leave soon on a trip to south India. So the big shadow looming over house number 2 would be removed.

The unseen drama of life suddenly becomes visible in the fifth act. My wife had gone to her late father's house. She returned the next day and shut herself in the bedroom. There was going to be a full moon that night, and our group would have a moonlight feast. I knocked on the door to discuss the arrangements.

There was no response at first. 'Anu,' I called. After a while, Anila opened the door. 'Have you made the arrangements for dinner?' I asked.

She nodded silently.

I told her, 'Don't forget that they're very fond of your fish kachuris and amra chutney.'

I came out and found Kanailal waiting.

'Come a little early this evening, Kanai,' I said to him.

Kanai looked amazed. 'What are you saying? Are we going to have our meeting today?'

'Of course,' I said. 'Everything's ready – the latest novel by Maxim Gorky, Russell's discussion of Bergson, fish kachuris and even amra chutney.'

Kanai stared at me in astonishment. After some time he said, 'Adwaita Babu, let's not meet today.'

Finally, I learnt by asking him that my brother-in-law Saroj had taken his own life last evening. He had failed in the examination and been reviled by his stepmother. He could not bear it, and had hanged himself with a length of cloth.

I asked him, 'How did you learn all this?'

He answered, 'From number 1.'

From Number One! It had happened like this. When the news reached Anila towards evening, she had not waited for a carriage to be called. Taking Ajodhya with her, she had gone out and hired a carriage on the way. Having learnt the news from Ajodhya that night, Sitangshu had gone to my in-laws', squared the police and personally supervised the cremation.

I anxiously went back into the house. I had thought Anila would again have retreated to the bedroom and locked the door. Instead I found her making chutney on the verandah adjoining the pantry. As I studied her face, I realized that her life had been overturned in the course of a single night.

'Why didn't you tell me anything?' I asked accusingly.

She lifted her large eyes and looked at me once, but said nothing.

I felt humbled and deeply ashamed. If Anila had told me, 'What good would that have done?' I would have had no answer. I am utterly ignorant about coping with the upheavals of life, with worldly joys and sorrows. I told her, 'Anila, forget about all this. We're not having our meeting this evening.'

With her eyes fixed on the amra she was peeling, she said,

'Why not? You must. I've made all these arrangements – I can't let it all go to waste.'

'We can't possibly hold our meeting today,' I said.

'You may not hold your meeting,' she replied, 'but I'm inviting them today.'

I felt somewhat reassured. I concluded that Anila had not been affected too badly by her bereavement. I thought she had developed a certain detachment of mind because of the lofty doctrines I once used to tell her about. Though she lacked the training and ability to understand it all, there was such a thing as *personal magnetism*.

A few members of my group were absent that evening. Kanai did not turn up at all, nor any of those who had joined the tennis group at house number 1. They had gone there for a farewell dinner: Sitangshumouli was leaving the next day by the early morning train. On the other hand, Anila that day prepared a much more elaborate dinner than she had ever done before. Even a spendthrift like me could not help feeling it was rather extravagant.

Our group dispersed at one o'clock if not later. I was tired and went to bed at once. 'Won't you go to bed?' I asked Anila.

She answered, 'I've got to put away the dishes.'

I woke up next morning at about eight. There was a small table in my bedroom on which I used to keep my spectacles. I found a piece of paper under them. On it was written, in Anila's writing, 'I am leaving. Don't try to find me. You won't succeed even if you try.'

I was mystified. There was a tin box on the table. I opened it and found all Anila's jewels, even the bangles she always wore – everything except the conchshell bracelets and iron bangle indicating her married state. In one compartment was her bunch of keys, in others various coins in paper packets. Whatever money remained from the monthly household expenses was accounted for to the last paisa. A notebook contained a list of utensils and other household goods, as well as of the clothes sent to the washerman. The milkman's and grocer's accounts were also there. Only her own address was missing.

I understood this much, that Anila was gone. I searched all the rooms thoroughly.

I enquired at my in-laws' house. She was nowhere.

I was never good at planning special measures when something

extraordinary happened. I felt utterly desolated. On a sudden, I
turned my eyes to house number 1. It was shut up; the doorman
sat smoking a hookah at the gate. Raja Babu had left early in the
morning.

My heart gave a jump. Suddenly I realized that while I was
discoursing on the latest theories of right logic, an ancient wrong
had been spreading its net in my household. I had read of such
incidents in Flaubert, Tolstoy, Turgenev and other great story-
tellers. I had analysed their implications with great zest and infinite subtlety. I had never dreamt that such a thing could happen
in my own house.

After the initial shock, I tried to take the whole thing lightly,
like a veteran philosopher. I remembered my wedding day and
smiled wryly. I pondered how we waste so much of hope, effort
and emotion. How many days and nights, how many years had
I spent without the least anxiety, my eyes shut in the secure
conviction that there was a living object called a wife. All of a
sudden, I had opened my eyes to find that the bubble had burst.
Let it be. But everything in the world was not like a bubble.
Had I not learnt to recognize things which lasted down the ages,
beyond birth and death?

I discovered, however, that the modern sage in me had fainted
at the shock, while the primitive animal had woken up and was
wandering about, crying with hunger. I kept pacing the terrace
and the balcony, roaming through the empty house. At last one
day I went into my bedroom, where I had so often seen my
wife sitting alone by the window. I started rummaging through
everything in a frenzy. Suddenly, on opening the drawer where
Anila used to keep her mirror, I discovered a packet of letters
tied with red silk ribbon. They had come from house number 1.

My breast seemed to be on fire. My first impulse was to burn
the lot. But things that hurt us deeply also attract us fearfully. I
could not help reading all those letters.

I have now read them fifty times over. The first letter was in
three or four pieces. It seemed that the reader had torn it up immediately on reading it and then carefully pasted the fragments
on a sheet of paper. The letter ran as follows.

> If you tear this letter up before you read it, I shall not be
> sorry; but I must say what I have to say.
>   I have seen you. I have moved about this world all this

time with my eyes open, but only now at the age of thirty-two have I really seen something. A curtain of sleep had been drawn across my eyes all this time. You have touched me with a golden wand, and I have seen you with my newly-awakened vision: indescribable, an object of wonder to your very Creator. I have found what I desired. I want nothing else, only to chant your praises to you. Were I a poet, I would not need to write them to you in a letter; I would set them up in verse to be sung by the world's voice. I know you will not reply to this letter, but please do not misunderstand me. Please accept my adoration silently, in the trust that I can do you no harm. If you can respect my respect for you, it will benefit you as well. I need not write who I am but it will not remain a secret from your heart.

There were twenty-five such letters. There was no indication that Anila had replied to any of them. Had she done so, a discordant note would have sounded at that point – the spell of the golden wand been broken, the hymn of praise silenced.

But how very strange it was. After eight years of intimacy, I saw my wife for the first time through the letters of a stranger who had had only a moment's glimpse of her. How very thick had been the curtain of sleep over my eyes: I had received Anila from the priest, but I had not paid the price to receive her from her Creator. The new school of logic and my Sect of Two and One had been far more important than she ever was. Since I had never really seen her, never possessed her even for a moment, how could I complain if someone else had won her by offering her his life's worth?

This was the last letter:

I hardly know you externally, but in my heart I have seen your pain. Here I have to face a severe test. My man's arms refuse to remain passive. I feel an urge to defy the constraints set by heaven and earth and rescue you from your futile life. But then I reflect that the God within you has His seat amidst your suffering. I do not have the right to steal it away. I am allowing myself till daybreak tomorrow. If by then some divine oracle dispels my doubt, something will surely happen. The gale of desire quenches the light that leads us. So I shall restrain my heart and pray intently for your good.

It was clear that their doubts had been dispelled and their paths merged into one. In the process, Sitangshu's letters had become my own – the praise chanted by my heart.

A long time passed. Books no longer held me. I felt such a painful longing to see Anila once, somehow, that I could not restrain myself. I learnt on enquiry that Sitangshu was in the Mussouri hills.

On going there, I often saw Sitangshu pass by; but Anila was not with him. I was afraid that he might have abused and deserted her. I could not hold myself back: I confronted him directly. It is needless to recount the details. Sitangshu said, 'I got only one letter from her – here it is.'

He drew from his pocket a small enamelled card-case of gold and extracted a piece of paper. It read, 'I am leaving. Don't try to find out where I am. You won't succed even if you try.'

It was the same handwriting, the same words, the same date. The piece of blue paper was the other half of that in my possession.

The Parrot's Training

ONCE UPON A time there was a bird. It was ignorant. It sang all right, but never recited scriptures. It hopped pretty frequently, but lacked manners.

Said the Raja to himself: 'Ignorance is costly in the long run. For fools consume as much food as their betters, and yet give nothing in return.'

He called his nephews to his presence and told them that the bird must have a sound schooling.

The pundits were summoned, and at once went to the root of the matter. They decided that the ignorance of birds was due to their natural habit of living in poor nests. Therefore, according to the pundits, the first thing necessary for this bird's education was a suitable cage.

The pundits had their rewards and went home happy.

A golden cage was built with gorgeous decorations. Crowds came to see it from all parts of the world. 'Culture, captured and caged!' exclaimed some, in a rapture of ecstasy, and burst into tears. Others remarked: 'Even if culture be missed, the cage will remain, to the end, a substantial fact. How fortunate for the bird!'

The goldsmith filled his bag with money and lost no time in sailing homewards.

The pundit sat down to educate the bird. With proper deliberation he took his pinch of snuff, as he said: 'Text-books can never be too many for our purpose!'

The nephews brought together an enormous crowd of scribes. They copied from books, and copied from copies, till the manuscripts were piled up to an unreachable height. Men murmured in amazement: 'Oh, the tower of culture, egregiously high! The end of it lost in the clouds!'

The scribes, with light hearts, hurried home, their pockets heavily laden.

The nephews were furiously busy keeping the cage in proper trim. As their constant scrubbing and polishing went on, the people said with satisfaction: 'This is progress indeed!'

Men were employed in large numbers, and supervisors were

still more numerous. These, with their cousins of all different degrees of distance, built a palace for themselves and lived there happily ever after.

Whatever may be its other deficiencies, the world is never in want of fault-finders; and they went about saying that every creature remotely connected with the cage flourished beyond words, excepting only the bird.

When this remark reached the Raja's ears, he summoned his nephews before him and said: 'My dear nephews, what is this that we hear?'

The nephews said in answer: 'Sire, let the testimony of the goldsmiths and the pundits, the scribes and the supervisors, be taken, if the truth is to be known. Food is scarce with the fault-finders, and that is why their tongues have gained in sharpness.'

The explanation was so luminously satisfactory that the Raja decorated each one of his nephews with his own rare jewels.

The Raja at length, being desirous of seeing with his own eyes how his Education Department busied itself with the little bird, made his appearance one day at the great Hall of Learning.

From the gate rose the sounds of conch-shells and gongs, horns, bugles and trumpets, cymbals, drums and kettle-drums, tomtoms, tambourines, flutes, fifes, barrel-organs and bagpipes. The pundits began chanting *mantras* with their topmost voices, while the goldsmiths, scribes, supervisors, and their numberless cousins of all different degrees of distance, loudly raised a round of cheers.

The nephews smiled and said: 'Sire, what do you think of it all?'

The Raja said: 'It does seem so fearfully like a sound principle of Education!'

Mightily pleased, the Raja was about to remount his elephant, when the fault-finder, from behind some bush, cried out: 'Maharaja, have you seen the bird?'

'Indeed, I have not!' exclaimed the Raja, 'I completely forgot about the bird.'

Turning back, he asked the pundits about the method they followed in instructing the bird. It was shown to him. He was immensely impressed. The method was so stupendous that the bird looked ridiculously unimportant in comparison. The Raja was satisfied that there was no flaw in the arrangements. As for any complaint from the bird itself, that simply could not be expected. Its throat was so completely choked with the leaves from the books that it could neither whistle nor whisper. It sent a thrill through one's body to watch the process.

This time, while remounting his elephant, the Raja ordered his State ear-puller to give a thorough good pull at both the ears of the fault-finder.

The bird thus crawled on, duly and properly, to the safest verge of inanity. In fact, its progress was satisfactory in the extreme. Nevertheless, nature occasionally triumphed over training, and when the morning light peeped into the bird's cage it sometimes fluttered its wings in a reprehensible manner. And, though it is hard to believe, it pitifully pecked at its bars with its feeble beak.

'What impertinence!' growled the kotwal.

The blacksmith, with his forge and hammer, took his place in the Raja's Department of Education. Oh, what resounding blows! The iron chain was soon completed, and the bird's wings were clipped.

The Raja's brothers-in-law looked black, and shook their heads, saying: 'These birds not only lack good sense, but also gratitude!'

With text-book in one hand and baton in the other, the pundits gave the poor bird what may fitly be called lessons!

The kotwal was honoured with a title for his watchfulness, and the blacksmith for his skill in forging chains.

The bird died.

Nobody had the least notion how long ago this had happened. The fault-finder was the first man to spread the rumour.

The Raja called his nephews and asked them, 'My dear nephews, what is this that we hear?'

The nephews said: 'Sire, the bird's education has been completed.'

'Does it hop?' the Raja enquired.

'Never!' said the nephews.

'Does it fly?'

'No.'

'Bring me the bird,' said the Raja.

The bird was brought to him, guarded by the kotwal and the sepoys and the sowars. The Raja poked its body with his finger. Only its inner stuffing of book-leaves rustled.

Outside the window, the murmur of the spring breeze amongst the newly budded *asoka* leaves made the April morning wistful.

The Patriot

I AM SURE that Chitragupta, who keeps strict record at the gate of Death, must have noted down in big letters accusations against me, which had escaped my attention altogether. On the other hand many of my sins, that have passed unnoticed by others, loom large in my own memory. The story of my transgression, that I am going to relate, belongs to the latter kind, and I hope that a frank confession of it, before it is finally entered in the Book of Doom, may lessen its culpability.

It all happened yesterday afternoon, on a day of festival for the Jains in our neighbourhood. I was going out with my wife, Kalika, to tea at the house of my friend Nayanmohan.

My wife's name means literally a 'bud'. It was given by my father-in-law, who is thus solely responsible for any discrepancy between its implication and the reality to which it is attached. There is not the least tremor of hesitancy in my wife's nature; her opinions on most subjects have reached their terminus. Once, when she had been vigorously engaged in picketing against British cloth in Burrabazar, the awe-struck members of her party in a fit of excessive admiration gave her the name, *Dhruva-vrata*, the woman of unwavering vows.

My name is Girindra, the Lord of the Rocks, so common among my countrymen, whose character generally fails to act up to it. Kalika's admirers simply know me as the husband of my wife and pay no heed to my name. By good luck inherited from my ancestors I have, however, some kind of significance, which is considered to be convenient by her followers at the time of collecting subscriptions.

There is a greater chance of harmony between husband and wife, when they are different in character, like the shower of rain and the dry earth, than when they are of a uniform constitution. I am somewhat slipshod by nature, having no grip over things, while my wife has a tenacity of mind which never allows her to let go the thing which it has in its clutches. This very dissimilarity helps to preserve peace in our household.

But there is one point of difference between us, regarding

which no adjustment has yet become possible. Kalika believes that I am unpatriotic.

This is very disconcerting, because according to her, truth is what she proclaims to be true. She has numerous internal evidences of my love for my country; but as it disdains to don the livery of the brand of nationalism, professed by her own party, she fiercely refuses to acknowledge it.

From my younger days, I have continued to be a confirmed book-lover: indeed, I am hopelessly addicted to buying books. Even my enemies would not dare to deny that I read them; and my friends know only too well how fond I am of discussing their contents. This had the effect of eliminating most of my friends, till I have left to me Banbihari, the sole companion of my lonely debates. We have just passed through a period, when our police authorities, on the one hand, have associated the worst form of sedition with the presence of the Gita in our possession; and our patriots, on their side, have found it impossible to reconcile appreciation of foreign literature with devotion to one's Motherland. Our traditional Goddess of culture, Saraswati, because of her white complexion, has come to be regarded with suspicion by our young nationalists. It was openly declared, when the students shunned their College lectures, that the water of the divine lake, on which Saraswati had her white lotus seat, had no efficacy in extinguishing the fire of ill-fortune that has been raging for centuries round the throne of our Mother, Bharat-Lakshmi. In any case, intellectual culture was considered to be a superfluity in the proper growth of our political life.

In spite of my wife's excellent example and powerful urgings I do not wear Khaddar, – not because there is anything wrong in it, nor because I am too fastidious in the choice of my wardrobe. On the contrary, among those of my traits, which are not in perfect consonance with our own national habits, I cannot include a scrupulous care as to how I dress. Once upon a time, before Kalika had her modern transformation, I used to wear broad-toed shoes from Chinese shops and forgot to have them polished. I had a dread of putting on socks: I preferred *Punjabis* to English shirts, and overlooked their accidental deficiency in buttons. These habits of mine constantly produced domestic cataclysms, threatening our permanent separation. Kalika declared that she felt ashamed to appear before the public in my company. I readily absolved her from the wifely duty of accompanying me to those parties where my presence would be discordant.

The times have changed, but my evil fortune persists. Kalika still has the habit of repeating: 'I am ashamed to go out with you.' Formerly, I hesitated to adopt the uniform of her set, when she belonged to the pre-nationalist age; and I still feel reluctant to adopt the uniform of the present regime, to which she owns her allegiance.

The fault lies deep in my own nature. I shrink from all conscious display of sectarian marks about my person. This shyness on my part leads to incessant verbal explosions in our domestic world, because of the inherent incapacity of Kalika to accept as final any natural difference, which her partner in life may possess. Her mind is like a mountain stream, that boisterously goes round and round a rock, pushing against it in a vain effort to make it flow with its own current. Her contact with a different point of view from her own seems to exercise an irresistible reflex action upon her nerves, throwing her into involuntary convulsions.

While getting ready to go out yesterday, the tone with which Kalika protested against my non-Khaddar dress was anything but sweet. Unfortunately, I had my inveterate pride of intellect, that forced me into a discussion with my wife. It was unpleasant, and what's more, futile.

'Women find it convenient,' I said to her, 'to veil their eyes and walk tied to the leading strings of authority. They feel safe when they deprive their thoughts of all freedom, and confine them in the strict Zenana of conformity. Our ladies today have easily developed their devotion to Khaddar, because it has added to the over-burdened list of our outward criterion's of propriety, which seem to comfort them.'

Kalika replied with almost fanatical fury: 'It will be a great day for my country, when the sanctity of wearing Khaddar is as blindly believed in as a dip in the holy water of the Ganges. Reason crystallized becomes custom. Free thoughts are like ghosts, which find their bodies in convention. Then alone they have their solid work, and no longer float about in a thin atmosphere of vacillation.'

I could see that these were the wise sayings of Nayanmohan, with the quotation marks worn out; Kalika found no difficulty in imagining that they were her own.

The man who invented the proverb, 'The silent silence all antagonists', must have been unmarried. It made my wife all the more furious, when I offered her no answer. 'Your protest against caste', she explained, 'is only confined to your mouth. We, on the contrary, carry it out in practice by imposing a uniformly white cover over all colour distinctions.'

I was about to reply, that my protest against caste did truly have its origin in my mouth, whenever I accepted with relish the excellent food cooked by a Muhammadan. It was certainly oral, but not verbal; and its movements were truly inward. An external cover hides distinctions, but does not remove them.

I am sure my argument deserved utterance, but being a helpless male, I timidly sought safety in a speechless neutrality; for, I knew, from repeated experience, that such discussions, started in our domestic seclusion, are invariably carried by my wife, like soiled linen, to her friendly circle to be ruthlessly beaten and mangled. She has the unpleasant habit of collecting counterarguments from the mouth of Professor Nayanmohan, exultantly flinging them in my face, and then rushing away from the arena without waiting for my answer.

I was perfectly certain about what was in store for me at the Professor's tea-table. There would be some abstruse dissertation on the relative position in Hindu culture of tradition and free thought, the inherited experience of ages and reason which is volatile, inconclusive, and colourlessly universal. In the meanwhile, the vision floated before my mind's eye of the newly-brought books, redolent of Morocco leather, mysteriously veiled in a brown paper cover, waiting for me by my cushions, with their shy virginity of uncut pages. All the same, I was compelled to keep my engagement by the dread of words, uttered and un-uttered, and gestures suggestive of trouble.

We had travelled only a short distance from our house. Passing by the street-hydrant, we had reached the tiled hut occupied by an up-country shopkeeper, who was giving various forms to indigestibility in his cauldron of boiling mustard oil, when we were obstructed by a fearful uproar.

The Marwaris, proceeding to their temple, carrying their costly paraphernalia of worship, had suddenly stopped at this place. There were angry shouts, mingled with the sound of thrashing, and I thought that the crowd were dealing with some pickpocket, enjoying the vigour of their own indignation, which gave them the delightful freedom to be merciless towards one of their own fellow beings. When, by dint of impatient tooting of horn, our motor car reached the centre of the excited crowd, we found that the old municipal sweeper of our district was being beaten. He had just taken his afternoon bath and was carrying a bucket of clean water in his right hand with a broom under his arm. Dressed in a check-patterned vest, with carefully combed hair still wet, he was walking home, holding his seven-year-old grandson by his left hand, when accidentally he came in contact with somebody, or something, which gave rise to this violent outburst. The boy was piteously imploring everybody not to hurt his grandfather; and the old man himself with joined hands uplifted, was asking forgiveness for his unintentional offence. Tears were streaming from his frightened eyes, and blood was smeared across his grey beard.

The sight was intolerable to me. I decided at once to take up the sweeper into my car and thereby demonstrate to the pious party, that I was not of their cult.

Noticing my restlessness, Kalika guessed what was in my mind. Gripping my arm, she whispered: 'What are you doing? Don't you see he is a sweeper?'

'He may be a sweeper,' said I, 'but those people have no right to beat him in this brutal manner.'

'It's his own fault,' Kalika answered. 'Would it have hurt his dignity, if he had avoided the middle of the road?'

'I don't know,' I said impatiently. 'Anyhow, I am going to take him into my car.'

'Then I leave your car this moment,' said Kalika angrily. 'I refuse to travel with a sweeper.'

'Can't you see,' I argued, 'that he has just bathed, and his clothes are clean, – in fact, much cleaner than those of the people who are beating him?'

'He's a sweeper!' she said decisively. Then she called to the chauffeur, 'Gangadin, drive on.'

I was defeated. It was my cowardice.

Nayanmohan, I am told, brought out some very profound sociological arguments, at the tea-table, specially dealing with the inevitable inequality imposed upon men by their profession and the natural humiliation which is inherent in the scheme of things. But his words did not reach my ears, and I sat silent all through the evening.

The Laboratory

[*In this story, italics have been used very frequently to indicate English words embedded in the original Bengali text, especially the dialogue, reflecting the common speaking practice of anglicized Bengalis. However, English words without any special social nuance – technical terms in particular – have not been italicized.*]

NANDAKISHORE WAS AN engineer with a degree from the University of London. As a student he had always been shining, *brilliant*, ranked in the first class right from school in every examination he ever took.

He had brains in plenty. His needs were extensive, but his means were limited.

He managed to involve himself with two large bridge-building projects for the Railways. Such projects allow much scope for increasing income and lowering expenditure, though not by entirely honourable means. When he started raking it in with the left hand as well as the right, his conscience did not prick him. Where the profit and loss pertain to an *abstract* entity called a company, the pains are not accredited to the stock of any individual.

Work-wise, his superiors called him a *genius*, so perfect were his calculations. Yet being a native Bengali, he never got his due rewards. When Sahib colleagues of lower calibre stood over him, their hands in their well-lined pockets and their legs apart, and patted him familiarly on the back with a 'Hallo, Mr Mallik', he did not like it one bit: the more so because it was he who did the work, and they who took the cash as well as the credit. As a result, he had made his own *private* valuation of the rewards due to him; and he knew perfectly well how to make up the difference.

Whatever money he may have made, legitimately and otherwise, Nandakishore never lived like a lord. He had a little house of one-and-a-half storeys in a narrow lane in Shikdarpara. He found no time to change out of his factory-soiled clothes. If anyone made fun of him, he would reply, 'The livery of His Majesty the Labourer – that's my dress.'

He did however build a massive mansion for scientific research and development. So preoccupied was he with this hobby, that he paid no heed when tongues started wagging. Where did this skyscraper come from? Where did he find Aladdin's lamp?

Some hobbies can become obsessive, like an alcoholic addiction: one pays no heed to what people might be saying. Nandakishore had a curious cast of mind. He was crazy about science. He would flip through the pages of a scientific catalogue and clutch the arms of his chair in shivers of excitement. He would order such expensive instruments from Germany and America as were not to be found even in the big universities of India. It was this that most saddened the seeker after knowledge: his poor country had to survive on the left-overs from the feast of learning. Not having the opportunity to use the fine equipment available abroad, our young people had to make do with scraps of knowledge out of dry textbooks. 'We're not short of brains, we're simply short of money,' he would roar. His life's ambition was to open up the highway of science to our young men.

The more of priceless equipment he collected, the more his colleagues' moral conscience rose against him. At this point his English boss stepped in to bail him out of trouble. This man had great respect for Nandakishore's professional competence. Besides, he was aware of the scale on which Railway funds were routinely siphoned off.

Nandakishore was forced to resign. With the boss's blessings, he was able to buy up scrap from the Railways at a bargain price and start a factory of his own. That was during the First World War in Europe, when the market was flourishing. The man was exceptionally clever. He found various new channels through which his profits flowed in a flood tide.

At this time, he developed another passion.

He had once spent some time in the Punjab on business. He came upon a female companion there. He was sitting on his verandah one morning, drinking tea, when a young woman of twenty years came up to him boldly, her ghagra swinging – bright eyes, smiling lips, sharp as a whetted knife. She sidled up to his feet and said, 'Babuji, I've been watching you morning and evening over the last few days. I'm quite amazed.'

Nandakishore laughed and said, 'Why, don't you have a zoo in these parts?'

She said, 'I don't need a zoo. Those that should be caged are all roaming outside. So I'm looking for real men.'

'Found any?'

She pointed to Nandakishore and said, 'Here's one.'

Nandakishore laughed. 'Tell me what virtues you have found in me.'

She said, 'I saw all the big local businessmen come crowding round you with their thick gold chains and diamond rings. They thought they'd found a stranger, a Bengali, who knew nothing about trade: you'd be easy prey. But I saw all their tricks come to nothing. In fact they're the ones who've fallen into your trap. They haven't realized this as yet, but I have.'

Nandakishore was startled at her words. Some girl this! Not a simpleton by any means.

The girl said, 'Let me tell you about myself. Listen carefully. There's a well-known astrologer in our area. He read my horoscope and said that I'd be a famous person one day. He said my birth-house was aspected by Satan.'

'Really!' exclaimed Nandakishore. 'By Satan himself?'

The girl said, 'You know, Babuji, Satan is the most famous presence in the whole world. Some people speak ill of him, but he's really quite honourable. Our heavenly father Bholanath is always so doped, he's not capable of running this world. Just look how our rulers have conquered the world – by their devilry, not by any Christian power. But they honour their commitments: that's why they can hold on to what they have. The day they go back on their word, they'll find themselves thrown out on their ear by the devil himself.'

Nandakishore was truly amazed. The girl continued, 'Don't mind my saying so, Babu, but you have the devil's inspiration too, so you're bound to succeed. I've charmed a lot of men, but this is the first time I've met a man who can beat me at my own game. Don't let go of me, Babu, or you'll be the loser.'

Nandakishore laughed and said, 'What must I do?'

'My grandmother's debts are forcing her to sell her house. You must pay them off.'

'How much does she owe?'

'Seven thousand rupees.'

Nandakishore was surprised at her audacious demand. He said, 'Very well, I'll pay; but what then?'

'Then I will never leave your side.'

'What will you do?'

'I'll see that no one ever manages to cheat you, except myself.'

Nandakishore laughed again. 'Very well, that's settled then. Here you are: wear this ring.'

He had a mental touchstone by which he had detected valuable metal here. He saw the lustre of genuine *character* shining through this girl, and how aware and confident she was of her own worth. Nandakishore had no hesitation in paying the aged grandmother seven thousand rupees.

The girl was called Sohini. She had strong, beautiful features of north Indian cast. But Nandakishore was not the kind of man to be swayed by good looks. He had no time to be playing the market of youthful hearts.

The situation from which Nandakishore had raised her was neither secluded nor very pure. But this obstinate and indomitable man cared nothing for society's norms and strictures. His friends asked whether he had married her. 'Not overly married,' he would answer, 'only to a tolerable degree.' People were amused to see him spend a great deal of effort to educate her after his own model. 'Does she intend to be a professor?' they would ask. Nanda's reply was, 'No, she has to be a she-Nandakishore. No ordinary girl can ever be that.' Or he would say, 'I'm not in favour of inter-caste marriages.'

'What do you mean?'

'For the husband to be an engineer and the wife to peel vegetables is not permissible by human law. I see such unequal marriages all the time, but I'm trying to match our castes. If you want a faithful wife, see that you share the same faith.'

II

NANDAKISHORE DIED IN late middle age during a daring scientific experiment that went awry.

Sohini shut down all his affairs. Sharpers, practised at cheating a vulnerable widow, began swarming round her in force. Those who could claim the remotest tie of blood filed lawsuits. Sohini started learning up the finer points of law herself. On top of that, she spread her womanly charms in the right quarters of the legal community. Her skills were well developed in that department, and she had no concern for propriety. She won all the cases, one after another. A distant cousin-in-law was sent to prison for having forged a document.

They had a daughter whom they had named Nilima. The girl herself changed the name to Nila. Let no one imagine that the parents of a dark-skinned daughter had covered the ignominy of her complexion with a euphemism. She was extremely fair. Her mother said their ancestors had come from Kashmir. Her skin glowed like the white lotus of that land, her eyes were like blue lotuses, her hair was a glossy golden-brown.

When it came to getting her married, there was no question of going by caste or pedigree. The only way was to steal someone's heart: a means whose magic efficacy surpassed all the hallowed texts. A young Marwari boy, with inherited wealth and modern education, fell suddenly into the Love-God's invisible trap. One day, Nila was at the school gate waiting for her car. The boy had happened to see her. Thereafter, he had strolled down that street quite a few times. Following her natural female instincts, the girl had taken to waiting at the gate far ahead of time. Not just the Marwari boy: there were youths from several other communities who practised strolling round that spot. But it was the Marwari who jumped into the net with eyes closed, never to return. They were married under civil law, beyond the social pale; but not for very long. Fate first brought him a bride; and then, to draw a permanent line across their conjugal life, he contracted typhoid, and was free.

By various tactics, good and bad, the suitors persisted. The mother could see how restless her daughter had become. She recalled her own burning agitation at the same age, and felt deeply anxious. She built strong barricades around Nila by the process of her education. No male tutors were to be hired: a learned lady was found instead. Nila's youthful charms affected her too, stirring up steamy chambers of undefined desire. Scores of stricken admirers continued to hover around, but found the doors closed. Other women wishing to befriend Nila invited her to tea, or to tennis, or to the cinema; but the invitations never reached their destination. The honeyed air attracted many buzzing lovers, but none of these poor beggars could get a visa out of Sohini. The girl, on the other hand, eagerly looked round for an opportunity, however unsuitable. She read books not approved by the textbook committee, acquired pictures disingenuously passed off as material for art lessons. Her learned tutoress was herself distracted by such activity. On her way back from the Diocesan School one day, a young man, with tousled hair and the hint of a moustache on his handsome face, had thrown a letter into Nila's car that made her veins throb when she read it. She had hidden the letter among her clothes. Her mother found out. Nila was locked up in her room for a whole day without food.

Sohini searched for a suitable match among the bright students who had received scholarships from her late husband. They all seemed to have an eye on her moneybags. One of them even dedicated his thesis to Sohini. She said to him, 'Dear me, how very unfortunate! You embarrass me. I hear your postgraduate course is nearly over, yet you're making your offerings of sandal-paste and flowers in quite an unsuitable quarter. You must worship with greater care, you know, or you'll never get on in life.'

There was one particular young man Sohini had had her eyes on for some time. He was clearly a desirable match. His name was Rebati Bhattacharya. He was already a Doctor of Science, and some of his papers had been favourably reviewed abroad.

III

SOHINI WAS GOOD at the arts of socializing. She picked out Manmatha Choudhuri, one of Rebati's earlier teachers. She had him under her spell in no time. She asked him over frequently for tea, toast and omelettes, or sometimes fried hilsa roe, and brought up the topic one day. She said, 'You must have wondered why I ask you over to tea so often.'

'That doesn't worry me at all, Mrs Mallik, I assure you.'

Sohini said, 'People think we make friends to serve our selfish interests.'

'Well, Mrs Mallik, let me tell you what I think. Whoever's interest it may serve, it's the friendship itself that is of value. And besides, for a simple professor like me, it's no small honour to be of any use to anyone. Our brains get no chance to be exercised outside our textbooks, so they turn rather pale. I can see you're amused to hear me say this. Well, though I'm a teacher, I have a sense of humour. Take note of that before you call me over for tea another time.'

'I've taken note, and I'm relieved. I've seen so many professors with whom you have to call in a doctor to make them smile.'

'Splendid! I can see you're one of us. So let's get down to what's really on your mind.'

'Perhaps you know that my husband's laboratory was his life's only joy. I don't have a son, so I'm looking for a young man whom I could put in charge of that laboratory. I have Rebati Bhattacharya in mind.'

'A deserving young man. But the field he's chosen will need a great deal of capital to carry his research through to the end.'

Sohini said, 'I have heaps of money gathering mould. Widows of my age lavish it on the brokers of various gods and goddesses to ensure their entry to heaven. You may not like to hear this, but I don't believe in such things.'

Choudhuri opened his eyes very wide at this. 'What do you believe in then?'

'If I find a truly worthy man, I'd like to pay off his debts as far as I can. That's my idea of religious works.'

Choudhuri said, 'Hooray! A stone floating in water! It seems one can sometimes find intelligence even among women. I know of a silly Bachelor of Science: I saw him touching a guru's feet the other day and turning back-somersaults, enough to send his brains flying like cotton fluff. So you want to set Rebati up right here in your laboratory. Wouldn't it be better to keep him at some distance?'

'Make no mistake, Mr Choudhuri. I'm a woman after all. This laboratory was my husband's place of worship. If I can find the right man to keep the flame alight on his very altar, he will be well pleased, no matter where he may be now.'

Choudhuri said, '*By Jove*, I hear the voice of a woman speaking at last. It's not an unpleasant sound. But remember, supporting Rebati through to the end would entail more than a lakh of rupees.'

'I'd still have some scraps left over.'

'But will the person you're trying to please in the other world, really be happy? I've heard such creatures have the habit of jumping onto anyone's neck if they so please.'

'Don't you read the papers? When a man dies, all his virtues are listed in paragraph after paragraph. It can't be wrong to pin some faith on that man's graciousness. A man who has piled up wealth has also piled up a load of sins with it. What are we wives here for if we can't shake out the money bags and help lighten that burden? Let the money go; I don't need it.'

The professor sat up excitedly. 'What can I say? We take gold out of mines. It's genuine gold, even though it has many admixtures. You are such a disguised nugget. I've spotted you at last. Now tell me what I have to do.'

'Get that young man to agree.'

'I'll try, but it won't be easy. Anyone else would have jumped at your offer.'

'What might hold him back?'

'A female planet has been straddling his horoscope right from childhood, crossing his path with relentless lack of good sense.'

'You don't say! You mean –'

'It's no use getting excited, Mrs Mallik. You know what *matriarchial* society means. Women are superior to men in such societies. The wave of that Dravidian culture once flowed through Bengal.'

'But that golden age is past,' said Sohini. 'It may still survive somewhere deep down and create whirlpools of folly, but the rudder is firmly in men's hands now. They're the ones who whisper in our ears – and box our ears too, almost pulling them off at times.'

'What a way you have with words! If women like you were to set up a new *matriarchy*, I wouldn't mind keeping laundry lists of your saris, and sending our college principal off to grind corn. Psychologists say that *matriarchy* doesn't exist outwardly in Bengal, but it runs in our blood. Have you heard such pathetic moos of "Ma, Ma" so persistently among men of any other race? Let me inform you that there's a formidable female sitting atop Rebati's sprouting tree of wisdom.'

'Is he in love with someone?'

'That would have made sense; it would mean he had some life in him. Losing his head for a young woman – that's how it should be at his age. Instead of which he's become a prayer-bead in the hands of a pious old woman. Nothing can save him – neither his youth, nor his brains, nor his science.'

'Suppose I were to invite him to tea one day. Would he eat with unclean beings like us?'

'Unclean! If he refuses, I'll give him a thrashing good cleansing, a dhobi-wash that'll take every speck of brahmanical nonsense out of him. One other thing: I believe you have a beautiful daughter.'

'I do. And the wretched girl is indeed beautiful. There's nothing I can do about that.'

'Oh no, don't get me wrong. Speaking for myself, I'm all for beautiful girls. It's like an ailment with me, I can't help it. But Rebati's relatives are rather humourless, you see: they might take fright.'

'Don't worry, I've decided to fix her up with someone of our own caste.'

This was a blatant lie.

'You yourself have married outside your caste.'

'And I've suffered no end for it. I've had to fight endless legal battles to keep my property. How I managed to win is best left unsaid.'

'I've heard something of it. There was gossip about you and the articled clerk on your adversary's side. You won the case and made off, and the poor man nearly hanged himself.'

'How else have women survived through the ages? Feminine wiles need clever planning, just like the rules of battle; but of course one needs to top it up with some honey as well. That's a woman's natural fighting style.'

'There you go misunderstanding me again. We're scientists, not judges. We observe the play of nature quite dispassionately. The outcome of the play takes its own course. In your case, the results were just as expected, and I said, "All praise to her." I also thought that being a professor and not an articled clerk is what has saved me. Mercury's distance from the sun is just great enough to save that planet. It's a matter of mathematics: there's nothing either good or evil about it. I think you've learnt about such things.'

'That I have. The planets follow the laws of attraction and repulsion – that's something one ought to know.'

'I must confess to something else. I was making a mental calculation just now while talking to you: that's mathematics too. Just think, if I had been at least ten years younger, I'd have got into needless trouble today. I've missed *collision* by an inch. But the steam is rising inside me nonetheless. Imagine, what a mathematical puzzle the whole of creation really is!'

Choudhuri slapped his knees and burst into hearty laughter. There was one thing he had failed to realize, however. Sohini had spent a good two hours before his arrival making herself up so carefully as to cheat her very Creator.

IV

NEXT DAY, THE professor arrived to find Sohini bathing and towelling a bony, mangy dog.

'Why such honour for this ill-omened creature?' he asked.

'Because I've rescued him. He broke his leg in a car accident. I bandaged it up and cured him. Now I have a *share* in his life.'

'Won't it make you sad to see this wretch every day?'

'I haven't kept him to admire his looks. I like the way he's gaining back his health, after coming so close to death. Because I sustain his urge to live, I don't need to drag a goat to the Kali Temple for religion's sake. I've decided to build a hospital for the lame and blind dogs and rabbits in your biology lab.'

'The more I see you, Mrs Mallik, the more amazed I am.'

'You'll get over it if you see even more. You'd said you'd bring news of Rebati Babu, so tell me.'

'We're distantly related, so I know all about his family. His mother died when he was born. His father's sister brought him up. This aunt is a great stickler for rules and rituals: the slightest lapse, and she'll bring the house down. Not a soul in the family that isn't scared of her. Rebati's manly vigour was beaten to dust, thanks to this aunt. Five minutes late from school, and he'd have to explain himself for all of twenty-five minutes.'

Sohini said, 'I thought men did the disciplining, and women the loving and caring: that keeps the balance.'

'Women strut like swans. They don't keep their balance; they sway from side to side. Sorry, Mrs Mallik. There are rare exceptions, of course, who can keep their heads up and walk straight, like –'

'Say no more. But I too have a good deal of the woman about my roots. Look at this latest fixation I've developed: catching young men. Otherwise, would I have bothered you like this?'

'Now don't keep saying that. Do you know, I've come here even without preparing for my classes? That's how much I'm enjoying neglecting my duties.'

'Perhaps you have a soft spot for the whole female race.'

'Not impossible at all. But there are distinctions to be made there too. Anyway, we'll take that up some other time.'

Sohini laughed and said, 'Or never at all. For now, just finish what you were saying. How did Rebati Babu do so well for himself?'

'Not nearly as well as he might have. He needed to go up to the mountains in connexion with his *research*. He decided to go to Badrinath. Shock and horror! His aunt's aunt had gone and died on that very road, years ago. So his aunt said, "No mountains for you so long as I'm alive." What I've hoped and prayed for ever since is best left unsaid. Let's drop the subject.'

'But why blame the aunts alone? Will their darling nephews never develop solid bones?'

'I've told you already. *Matriarchy* infects their very blood and addles their brains, so that they start mooing "Ma, Ma." It's a crying shame. That was episode *number one*. Later, when Rebati was going to Cambridge on a government scholarship, up comes the aunt again, weeping and howling. She was convinced he was going there to marry a memsahib. I said, "Suppose he does, what then?"'

'Disaster! What had been a hypothetical fear became a certainty. She said, "If he goes abroad, I'll hang myself." Being an atheist, I didn't know which particular god to pray to for the rope to be spun; so I couldn't procure it for her. I ranted at Rebati, called him *stupid*, *dunce*, *imbecile*. That was it. Now Rebu is busy extracting drops of oil from the Indian mill.'

Sohini was quite roused on hearing this. 'I feel like dashing my brains out against the wall. Well, one woman has dragged Rebati down; now another woman will pull him back to shore. I vow it.'

'To tell you the truth, *madam*, I think you yourself have perfected the art of taking such beasts by the horn and drowning them; but I doubt whether you're as adept at pulling them up by the tail. You'd better start practising. How do you happen to be so keen on *science*, may I ask?'

'My husband had an abiding interest in all branches of *science* all his life. He had two addictions, burma cheroots and his laboratory. He got me hooked on cheroots and almost made a Burmese woman out of me. I gave it up because men seemed to find it odd. He converted me to his other passion too. Other men make fools of women to entrap them; he entrapped me by imparting knowledge day and night. You know, Choudhuri Mashai, a husband's faults can never be hidden from his wife; but I tell you I've never detected the least dross in his make-up. When I saw him close at hand, I thought he was a great man; now from a distance, he seems even greater.'

'What do you see as his greatest strength?' asked Choudhuri.

'Shall I tell you? Not his learning, but his total, dispassionate reverence for learning. There was an atmosphere of worship around him. We women need a visible, tangible object to worship; so his laboratory is now my god. Sometimes I feel like lighting lamps and incense, blowing conch shells and beating gongs in it; but then I'm afraid my husband would despise that. When he worshipped here daily, college students would crowd round these instruments to hear him teach, and I sat down with them too.'

'Were the boys able to concentrate?'

'The ones who could were marked out. I've seen some real ascetics among them. Others would pretend to take notes while writing long letters to their fair neighbour, practising their literary skills.'

'How did you like that?'

'Shall I tell you the truth? I rather liked it. My husband would go off to work, and the romantic ones would hang around here.'

'Don't mind my asking this, but I like to study psychology. Did they have any luck?'

'I don't like saying this, but I'm an impure woman. I got to know a few of them well; in fact I still feel a wrench in my heart to think of them.'

'Quite a few?'

'Don't you know the heart is greedy? It hides its fire under flesh and blood, but it flares up with a little prodding. I started out with a bad name, so I have no qualms about talking frankly. We women are not lifelong ascetics. We have a tough time trying to keep up a pretence. Draupadis and Kuntis have to pretend to be Sitas and Savitris. I must tell you this, Choudhuri Mashai, and you must remember, that since childhood I've never had a very clear sense of right and wrong. I never had a guru, you see. So I've plunged into bad ways quite easily, and swum through easily too. I've been smirched in body but not in mind. Nothing could take a hold on me. Anyway, with my husband's death, my desires have been cast on the flames of his funeral pyre: my heaped-up sins are being burnt away one by one. The sacrificial fire is burning right here in this laboratory.'

'*Bravo*! you speak the truth with such courage.'

'It's easy when you find someone who can get you to speak the truth. You yourself are so frank, so genuine.'

'And do those favoured correspondents still cultivate you?'

'That's how they've cleansed my heart. I saw them gathering round with an eye on my cheque book. They thought women can't get over their infatuations, so they'd break in by romancing me and burgle their way to my strongbox. They didn't realize that I don't have so much sentiment in my arid Punjabi heart. I can flout all the strictures of society for my physical pleasure, but not on my life will I betray my faith. They couldn't draw a paisa away from my laboratory. So I'm guarding my temple door with the rock of my heart. They don't have the strength to melt that stone. The man who picked me out wasn't mistaken.'

'I bow to his memory, and wish I could box those fellows' ears.'

He made a round of the laboratory with Sohini before taking his leave. He said, 'Here the womanly intelligence has been distilled: the evil demons expelled as dregs, and the pure *spirit* recovered.'

'Say what you will, I can't help being worried,' said Sohini. 'Womanly intelligence is the Almighty's original creation. When we're young and have strength of will, it hides in the bushes; when our blood cools down, the traditional aunt in all of us comes out. I hope I die before that.'

'Don't worry, I predict you'll be in full possession of your faculties when you die,' said the professor.

V

DRESSED IN A white sari, with her greying hair well-powdered, Sohini managed to put on an aura of chaste piety. She took her daughter with her by motor launch to the Botanical Gardens. The girl was dressed in a blue-green Benarasi sari, with a light yellow choli showing through a dot of red kumkum on her forehead, a fine line of kajal round her eyes, her hair in a loose bun below her neck, her feet in black leather sandals worked in red velvet.

Sohini tracked Rebati down in the grove of trees where, she had ascertained, he normally spent his Sundays. She came and made her obeisance, actually touching his feet with her forehead. Rebati jumped up in extreme embarrassment.

Sohini said, 'Forgive me, son, but you're a brahman and I'm just a kshatri's daughter. Mr Choudhuri may have told you about me.'

'Yes, but where can I make place for you to sit?'

'Here's fresh green grass: what better seat can there be? You must be wondering what brings me here. I'm here to keep a vow. I won't find another brahman like you anywhere.'

Rebati showed surprise. 'A brahman like me?'

'But of course. My guru has told me that the best brahman is one who has best command of the best learning of our times.'

Rebati was acutely embarrassed. 'My father was a practising priest, but I don't know any of the prayers and rituals.'

'How can you say that? The mantras you have learnt are the incantations by which man has tamed the universe. You're wondering how a mere woman can talk in this way. I learnt it from one who was a real man indeed. He was my husband. Please promise, my son, that you'll visit the seat of his worship.'

'I'm free tomorrow morning: I'll go then.'

'I see you're fond of plants. I'm delighted. My husband's search for plants took him all the way to Burma, and I went along with him.'

She had gone along indeed, but not at the call of science. The dross in her own nature made her suspect the same in her husband. She was suspicious to the core. Once when Nandakishore was seriously ill, he had told his wife, 'The one good thing about dying is that you won't be able to hunt me out and haul me back with you.'

'But I might go along with you,' Sohini had replied.

'God forbid!' Nandakishore had retorted with a smile.

Now Sohini told Rebati, 'I brought back a seedling from Burma. "Kozaitaniyeng" they call it. It had lovely flowers – but I couldn't keep it alive.'

She had looked up the name in her husband's library that morning for the first time. She had never set eyes on the plant. She was weaving a net of learning to trap a learned man.

Rebati was impressed. 'Do you know its Latin name?'

'It's *Millettia*,' said Sohini with supreme ease.

She continued: 'My husband set no store by most of our traditional beliefs; but one thing he had blind faith in. He was convinced that if women in a special condition were to fill their minds with all that is beautiful in nature, they would surely give birth to beautiful children. Do you believe that?'

Needless to say, Nandakishore had held no such belief.

Rebati scratched his head and said, 'We haven't found enough evidence as yet to support the idea.'

Sohini said, 'Well, I've found at least one proof of it in my own family. From where did my daughter get such amazing beauty? Like a bouquet of spring flowers – well you'll know what I mean when you see her for yourself.'

Rebati grew eager to see her. No element of drama was lacking.

Sohini had dressed up her brahman cook like a temple priest in a silk dhoti, with sandalwood paste on his forehead, a flower tied to his topknot, the holy thread across his chest freshly furbished with wood-apple resin. She called him and said, 'Thakur, it's time now, bring Nilu over.'

Her mother had instructed Nila to wait inside the steam-launch. She was to make her entrance with a basket of flowers, letting the soft morning light and shadow play on her for quite a while.

Sohini used this interval to examine Rebati in great detail. His complexion was dark but smooth, with a touch of pale ochre. His forehead was broad, his hair stroked upwards with his fingers. His eyes were not large, but they were bright and clear: in fact, they were his most prominent feature. His face was smooth and rounded, like a woman's. Of all the information she had gathered about Rebati, one item had struck her the most. All his childhood friends seemed to have a tearfully *sentimental* affection for him. He had a weak-spirited charm which could fascinate immature males.

Sohini was a little disturbed. She believed it was not necessary for a man to be handsome to cast anchor in a woman's heart. Knowledge and intelligence, too, were no more than minor factors. What mattered most was his male *magnetism*, like radio waves signalling from within his nerves and muscles. It expressed itself in the arrogance of unspoken desire.

She remembered her own youthful excesses. The man she was drawn to, or who was drawn to her, was neither handsome nor learned nor high-born. But he radiated a strange invisible heat that had taken her unawares in body and mind, touching her intensely with his masculine appeal. The thought that her daughter, too, would be tossed by that irresistible agitation gave her no peace. The last phase of youth is the most dangerous of all; luckily for Sohini, she had been largely engaged in a relentless search for knowledge during those years. But Sohini's mind happened to be fertile soil for such studies. Not every girl has the same interest in abstract knowledge. Nila was not equally enlightened.

Nila came up gradually from the landing-stage. The sunlight fell on her forehead, her hair; the gold threadwork in her sari glittered and shone. Rebati took her in at a glance. The very next moment he lowered his eyes: that is how he had been trained from childhood. Beautiful young girls, those heart-stealing examples of the Mother-Goddess's pleasure, had been hidden from his view by his aunt's minatory finger. So when he did get a chance, he had to be content with a quick stolen sip of visual nectar.

Sohini cursed him silently and said, 'Look, look: oh do take a look.'

Rebati looked up startled.

Sohini said, 'Just see, Doctor of Science, how wonderfully the colour of her sari blends with the colour of the leaves.'

'Wonderful,' said Rebati diffidently.

'Oh, he's quite impossible,' said Sohini to herself. Aloud she said, 'That faint hint of yellow picking through the bluish-green – now which flower does that remind you of?'

With such encouragement, Rebati took a good look at last. He said, 'There's one flower I'm thinking of, but its outer petals are brown not blue.'

'Which flower is it?'

'*Gmelina*,' said Rebati.

'Ah yes. It has five petals, one bright yellow and the other four dark.'

Rebati was surprised. 'How do you know so much about flowers?'

Sohini laughed. 'I know I shouldn't, my son. Any flowers not used in worship should be like strange men we have nothing to do with.'

Nila approached slowly with her basket of flowers. Her mother said, 'Don't stand there so shyly, come here and touch his feet.'

'Not at all, not at all,' cried Rebati, greatly agitated. He was sitting with his legs crossed under him. Nila had to fumble for a while to locate his feet. Rebati's whole body shivered at her touch. There were rare orchids in her basket, and a silver platter with sweets; nut wafers, pistachio fudge, coconut and milk delights, squares of steamed yoghurt.

'These are all made by Nila,' said Sohini.

This was an absolute lie. Nila had neither skill nor interest in such work.

Sohini said, 'You must taste some, my son. She made them at home, all in your honour.'

They had actually been ordered from a reliable shop in Barabazar.

Rebati apologized with joined palms: 'I never eat at this time of day. I can take it home if you permit me.'

'That's a good idea,' said Sohini. 'My husband was against forcing food on anyone. He'd say, "People are not pythons, you know."'

She took out a large tiffin carrier and stacked the food neatly in each compartment. She told Nila to arrange the flowers in a basket. 'Don't mix up the separate kinds, my dear. And take that silk scarf from your hair and cover the flowers with it.'

The scientist's eyes took on the thirsting look of the art lover. This was something outside the material world of weights and measures. Nila's delicate fingers played rhythmically among the flowers of many colours: Rebati could not take his eyes off them. He looked up at her face now and then. A chain of rubies, pearls and emeralds, clipped to her hair like a rainbow, framed it on one side; the red piping of her yellow choli peeped out on the other. Sohini was looking downwards to arrange the sweets, but she had something like a third eye. She did not miss the magic spell being cast in front of her.

Going by her experience with her husband, she had thought that scholars had a strong fence guarding their pasture, which no common cattle could cross. Now she realized that not all such fences were equally strong. The discovery did not please her.

VI

SHE ASKED THE professor to come and see her the next day. She said, 'I keep bothering you by calling you over like this for my selfish needs. Maybe your work suffers too.'

'Call me more often, I beg you. If there's a need, well and good; if there's none, that's even better.'

'You know how my husband was crazy about collecting

expensive equipment. He cheated his employers out of that dispassionate greed. The finest laboratory in Asia – that's what he
was working towards, and I got drawn into it too. It was this
craze that has kept me going all these years, or my heady blood
would have fermented and spilt over. Choudhuri Mashai, you're
the only friend with whom I can talk frankly about the evil that
clings to my nature. Finding an outlet for the scandalous side of
my being is a great relief.'

Choudhuri said, 'With someone who can see the total person,
you don't need to hide the truth. It's the half-truths that are
shameful. We scientists are in the habit of seeing things in their
entirety.'

'My husband used to say that people are desperate to protect
their lives, but life can't be protected. So to satisfy the urge for
life, they look for something of greater value than life itself. That
something is what he found in this laboratory. If I can't keep this
laboratory alive, that will truly kill him, and I'll be a wife guilty
of murdering her husband. I need someone to protect it. That's
why I was looking for Rebati.'

'Did you make a try?'

'I did, and I think I'll succeed quite readily; but not for good.'

'Why?'

'The minute his aunt hears that he's being drawn to me, she'll
swoop down and snatch him away. She'll think I've set up a trap
to marry him to my daughter.'

'What's wrong with that? It would be a good thing. But
didn't you say you wouldn't marry your daughter to someone
outside your own caste?'

'I didn't know your views on the matter then, so I lied. Yes,
I had wanted them to marry, very much. But I've given up the
idea now.'

'Why?'

'I've realized how ruinous my girl can be. She'll break whatever she touches.'

'But she's your own daughter.'

'Indeed she is; so I know her inside out.'

The professor said, 'But women can be a great source of *inspiration* for men. Don't forget that.'

'I know it. Men thrive by adding meat and fish to their diet;
but go beyond that to alcohol and they're ruined. My daughter
is a veritable decanter filled to the brim.'

'What would you like to do then?'

'I wish to gift my laboratory to the *public*.'

'Depriving your only daughter?'

'My daughter! If I left it to her, I don't know to what pits she might let it sink. I'll make Rebati the President of the Trust. His aunt shouldn't object to that.'

'If I could tell what women might object to, I wouldn't have been born a man. But there's one thing I don't understand. If you don't want him as a son-in-law, why make him President?'

'What good are these machines by themselves? You need a man to give them life. There's something else as well. We haven't bought a single new instrument since my husband died. It's not for lack of funds, but lack of a clear objective. I hear Rebati is working on *magnetism*. Let him focus his purchases in that direction. Never mind the expense.'

'What should I say? If you were a man, I'd have danced about, carrying you on my shoulders. Your husband stole Railway funds, and you've stolen his male cast of mind. I've never come across such a remarkable grafting of one mind upon another. I can't imagine why you think it necessary to consult me.'

'It's because you're such a genuine person. You can say exactly what's right.'

'You make me laugh. Do you think I'm so stupid that I'd say the wrong thing and risk being caught out by you? Well then, let's get down to business. We must make a list of all the assets, have them valued, get a good lawyer to settle your rights, frame the regulations – all sorts of formalities.'

'You must take charge of all that, please.'

'Only in name, yes. You know very well that I'll say just what you make me say, do exactly what you make me do. What I gain is the chance to meet you twice a day. You've no idea with what eyes I regard you.'

Sohini rose from her seat, darted up to Choudhuri, put an arm round his neck, kissed his cheek, and returned demurely to her place.

'Goodness! I see the beginning of my ruin.'

'If there was any danger of that, I'd come nowhere near you. You'll have your ration of this now and then.'

'You're sure?'

'I'm very sure. It doesn't cost me anything; and judging by your expression, you don't expect much more either.'

'You mean it's like a woodpecker pecking on dead wood.
Well – I'm off to see the lawyer.'

'Come this way tomorrow.'

'To do what?'

'To wind Rebati up a bit.'

'And lose my own heart in the bargain.'

'Are you the only one with a heart?'

'Do you have anything left of yours?'

'Yes, a lot of leftovers.'

'You can set a lot of monkeys dancing with that.'

VII

THE NEXT DAY Rebati arrived at the laboratory at least twenty
minutes ahead of time. Sohini was not ready; she came out hurriedly in her everyday wear. Rebati realized he had made a *faux
pas*. He said, 'My watch doesn't seem to be running properly.'

'No doubt,' replied Sohini curtly.

Rebati thought he heard a sound at the door and looked up
eagerly. It was Sukhan the servant, come to deliver the keys to
the glass cases.

Sohini asked, 'Shall I ask him to bring you a cup of tea?'

Rebati thought he ought to accept the offer. 'Why not?' he
said.

He was not used to having tea, poor fellow. At most, at the
signs of a coming cold, he would sip hot water boiled with
wood-apple leaves. He was hoping in his heart that Nila herself
would bring the tea.

'Do you like your tea strong?' asked Sohini.

'Yes,' he said without thinking.

He thought that was the smart thing to say. The tea arrived,
and it was strong indeed: black as ink, bitter as neem leaves. It
was brought in by the Mussalman cook. This too was to test
him. He could not utter a word of protest. Sohini did not ap-
prove of such diffidence. She said, 'Why don't you pour out the
tea, Mubarak? It's getting cold.'

Surely Rebati had not come twenty minutes too early to be
served tea by the Muslim cook!

Only God and Sohini knew with what a heavy heart he raised
the spoon to his lips. Being a woman after all, Sohini took pity
on him and said, 'Let that cup be. Let me pour you some milk

instead, and have some fruit with it. You've come here so early. I'm sure you haven't eaten anything this morning.'

That was a fact. Rebati had expected a repetition of the feast at the Botanical Gardens. This came nowhere near it: only the taste of that bitter tea in his mouth, and in his heart the bitter experience of broken hopes.

Just then, the professor walked in. He slapped Rebati on the back and said, 'What's happened to you, man? Frozen cold, I see. Sitting there drinking milk like a little girl! Are these children's toys you see around you? Men of vision have seen Lord Shiva's crew enact the destructive dance of eternal time in this place.'

'Come, come, why are you scolding him? He's come on an empty stomach. He was looking rather wan when he arrived.'

'Oh dear, here comes Aunt the Second: one aunt to slap him on this cheek, a second to kiss him on the other. Between them, the poor fellow will disintegrate like soggy earth. You know how it is. When Lakshmi the goddess of wealth comes to you unasked, you don't notice her presence; those who roam the world to seek her out make her their own. There's no better way to be deprived than to receive something without asking for it. Tell me something, Mrs – oh, never mind the "Mrs", I'm going to call you Sohini, whether you like it or not.'

'Why should I mind? Call me Sohini by all means. And if you call me Suhi, it'll be music to my ears.'

'Let me tell you a secret. There's another word that rhymes with your name. It has such a lucid meaning that I keep repeating both words to myself all day, in rhythm with cymbals tinkling in my head.'

'You match things together in your chemical *research*: this must be a fall-out of that.'

'Matching chemicals can sometimes lead to death. It's best not to stir up things too much – highly flammable stuff.'

And he burst into hearty laughter.

'No, one shouldn't discuss such things in front of this youngster. He isn't even an *apprentice* yet in the gunpowder factory. His aunt's sari-end is shielding him still, and it's *non-combustible*.'

Rebati's girlish face slowly reddened.

'Sohini, I was about to ask you whether you've given him any opium this morning. Why is he looking so drowsy?'

'If I have, it must have been by accident.'

'Come on, Rebu! Wake up, I say. You shouldn't be so

tongue-tied in female company, it makes them more bold. They're like a disease: they look out for any signs of weakness in a man, and the minute they spot a chink they slip through and make your *temperature* shoot up. I'm an authority on the *subject*, so I have to warn these youngsters. They've got to learn from people like me, who've been wounded and lived to tell the tale. Don't mind me, Rebu my boy, but the silent ones are the most dangerous. Come on, let me show you round the place. Look at those two galvanometers – the very latest model. And here's a high vacuum pump, and a microphotometer. They aren't light rafts to steer you through your exams. Once you set yourself up here, we'll see how sick that bald-pated professor of yours begins to look. I name no names. When you started out as my student, didn't I tell you that there was a great future dangling in front of your nose? Don't spoil it through your own negligence. If I'm mentioned even in a minuscule note in the first *chapter* of your biography, I'll consider it a great tribute.'

The scientist began to wake from his stupor. His eyes glowed. His whole expression was transformed from within. Sohini looked at him with admiration. She said, 'Everyone who knows you wishes you the greatest success, something extraordinary and everlasting. But the greater the hope, the stronger the obstacles, inward and outward.'

The professor gave Rebati another great thump on the back. His spine tingled from the impact. The professor said in his booming voice, 'Look, Rebu, the kind of future we're talking of should come riding the elephant of the gods; but these miserly times dump it onto a wretched bullock cart, that gets stuck in the mud and refuses to move. Did you hear that, Sohini, Suhi? – No, no, don't worry: I'm not going to slap you on the back. Tell me frankly, didn't I put that rather well?'

'Excellently.'

'Write it down in your diary.'

'I will.'

'Did you get my meaning, Rebi?'

'I think so.'

'Remember, great talent means a great responsibility. It's not your personal property. You have to answer for it to eternity. Did you hear that, Suhi? How's that for phrasing?'

'Wonderful. In olden times, kings would take off their neck-laces and honour you.'

'They're all dead, but –'

'That "but" hasn't died. I'll keep it in mind.'

Rebati said, 'Don't worry, nothing will weaken my resolve.'

He bent down to touch Sohini's feet. Sohini hurriedly stopped him.

'Now why did you do that?' said Choudhuri. 'Not to perform a good act is a sin; to prevent someone from doing so is even worse.'

Sohini said, 'If he has to pay his respects anywhere, it should be there.' She pointed to a platform with a bust of Nandakishore. There was incense burning there, and a tray full of flowers.

She said, 'I have read in the Puranas of sinners being saved. That's the great man who saved this sinner. He had to stoop very low to do it, but he was able to pull me up in the end: not to sit beside him – I would be lying if I said so – but beneath his feet. He initiated me into the path of salvation through learning. He warned me not to throw away the precious stones he had mined all his life on the ash-heap of a daughter and son-in-law's pride. He said, "This is where I'm entrusting my salvation, and the salvation of my country."'

'Did you hear that, Rebu?' said the professor. 'This is going to be trust property, and you'll be put in charge.'

Rebati was quick to protest. 'I'm not worthy of such an honour. I could never manage.'

'Can't manage!' said Sohini. 'Shame on you, that's no way for a man to talk.'

Rebati said, 'I've always been an academic, I've never taken on such responsibilities.'

Choudhuri said, 'A duck can't swim until it's hatched out of the egg. That shell of yours will be cracking today.'

Sohini said, 'Don't worry, I'll be there to help you.'

Rebati felt reassured and took his leave.

Sohini looked at the professor. He said, 'There are many kinds of fools on earth, and the foolish male is their paragon. But you must remember that one can't prove one's worth until one's entrusted with responsibility. Man was first endowed with a pair of hands: that's what made him human. If he had been given hooves instead, he'd also have grown a tail to be twisted. Do you think you saw hooves on Rebati instead of hands?'

'I still don't like it. Men brought up by women alone never

seem to lose their milk teeth. It's just my bad luck. Why did I think of anyone else when you're around?'

'I'm glad to hear that. Tell me what good you've seen in me.'

'You don't have the least bit of covetousness in you.'

'That's a big insult! You mean I don't covet what ought to be coveted? Of course I do –'

Sohini stopped him short by putting her arms round his neck, kissing him on both cheeks, and quickly moving away.

'Under which account does that go down, Sohini?'

'I can never repay the debt I owe you, so here's the interest.'

'I got just one the first day; today it's two. Will it keep increasing like this?'

'Of course it will, with compound interest.'

VIII

CHOUDHURI SAID, 'Sohini, did you have to make me the priest to conduct your husband's funeral? That's a grave responsibility, to please someone whose life one can't even grope towards comprehending. It's not the usual line of ritual offering, so that –'

'You're not the usual kind of priest either. Whatever you think best will be the line to follow. You've arranged for the offerings, I hope.'

'That's exactly what I've been doing all these days. I've shopped around quite a bit. All the stuff has been laid out in the big room downstairs. The souls that live in this world will surely imbibe them and be satisfied.'

Sohini went downstairs with the professor, and saw the gifts he had bought for science students: all kinds of instruments, models, costly books, slides for microscopes, biology specimens. Each gift had a tag with a name and address. Two hundred and fifty cheques had been made out, each to cover a year's grant for a student. No expense had been spared. It added up to much more than the money spent on feeding brahmans at rich men's funerals, yet it did not seem so lavish to the eye.

'And what will be the priest's fee? You haven't mentioned that.'

'Your satisfaction is my fee.'

'Together with that, I've kept this chronometer aside for you. My husband had ordered it from Germany, for his *research*.'

Choudhuri said, 'I can't express what I feel. I don't want to speak empty words. My priestly duties have been well compensated.'

'There's one other person whom I can't forget today – our Manik's widow.'

'Who's this Manik?'

'He was the chief mechanic of this laboratory. He had marvellously skilful hands. He could make delicate adjustments to a hair's breadth, and he had an infallible head for machinery. My husband looked on him as a very dear friend. He took him along in his car to visit big factories. But he was an alcoholic, and the lab assistants looked down on him because of his humble origins. My husband said, "He has real talent, something you can't just pick up anywhere or achieve by training." He treated Manik with the greatest respect. You'll understand from this why he gave me such honour too. The good that he saw in me far outweighed the bad. Where he trusted me most – a foundling like me – that's one trust I've never betrayed, and that I'm trying to maintain still with my heart and soul. He would never have got this from anyone else. He ignored my weaknesses and gave full honour to my strengths. If he hadn't seen my worth, can you imagine to what depths I might have sunk? I'm a degenerate person; but I'm also very good, though I say this myself, or else he could not have tolerated me at all.'

'Well, I can boast that I knew from the very first day that you were an especially good person, Sohini. Had you been good in a cheap sort of way, any stain you took would never have come off.'

'Anyway, whatever others may think about me, the honour that one man gave me remains to this day, and will remain till I die.'

'The more I see of you, Sohini, the more I realize you're not the simple kind of woman who melts at the mention of her husband's name.'

'No, I'm not. I saw the strength in him, I knew from the first day that he was a man indeed. I didn't have to go by the scriptures to play the devoted wife. I'll say this proudly, that the precious jewels I have in me are worthy to adorn his neck and his alone.'

Nila entered the room at this point. 'Excuse me, Professor,' she said, 'I'd like a word with my mother.'

'By all means, my dear. I was on my way to the laboratory. I want to check how Rebati is doing.'

'Don't worry,' said Nila. 'His work's progressing quite well. I've been watching him through the window now and then. He has his head in his books all the time, writing away, taking notes, biting his pen in deep thought. I'm not allowed to enter, in case Sir Isaac's *gravitation* is upset. Ma was telling someone the other day that he's working on *magnetism*. That's why his needle gets deflected if anyone passes by, particularly women.'

Choudhuri guffawed. 'The laboratory is right inside us, my dear. Research on *magnetism* is an ongoing project there: we can't but be wary of people who deflect the needle. It confuses our sense of direction. I'll be off.'

When he had left, Nila said to her mother, 'How long will you keep me tied to your sari-end? You know you won't be able to: you'll only end up being sorry.'

'What exactly would you like to do?'

Nila said, 'You know about the *Higher Study Movement* for girls: you've donated a lot of money to it. Why don't you find something for me to do there?'

'I'm worried that you won't set about it in the right way.'

'Do you think that stopping all movement is the best way to move forward?'

'Of course not. I realize that, and that's just what worries me.'

'Why don't you let me worry about that myself? You'll have to ultimately. I'm not a child any more. You think those are public places where all kinds of people come and go, so it's dangerous. Well, the world won't stop moving just to please you. And you can't stop my meeting them, under any law at your disposal.'

'I know, I know. I realize that my fears won't remove the causes of fear. So you want to join the *Higher Study Circle*, do you?'

'Yes I do.'

'Very well. I know you'll send all the male professors to perdition, one after another. But you must promise me one thing: you mustn't go anywhere near Rebati, and you mustn't enter the laboratory under any pretext.'

'Really, Ma, I don't know what you think of me. Approach that miniature Sir Isaac Newton of yours! Is that what you think of my taste? I'd rather die.'

She mimicked the way Rebati writhed when he was embarrassed, and said, 'That's not the *style* I like in a man. You can save him up for the kind of woman who likes mothering adult little boys. He's just not worth the hunting.'

'I think you're exaggerating. It makes me suspect you're not speaking your mind. Anyway, whatever your feelings about him, if you try to ruin him, you'll be in bad trouble.'

'I never know what you really want. You wanted to get me married to him at one point, so you began decking me up like a doll: did you think I couldn't tell? Is that why you don't want me to go near him, in case the gloss wears off by contact?'

'Look, Nila, let me tell you this straight. You're not going to marry him by any means.'

'Should I marry the Rajkumar of Motigarh then?'

'If you so please.'

'It'll be quite convenient. He has three wives already, so I'll have a lighter load. And he's usually found drunk and disorderly at various *night-clubs* – so I'll get time off then.'

'Very well, go ahead. But I won't let you marry Rebati.'

'Why, do you think I'll muddle Sir Isaac Newton's brains?'

'Let's not argue about that. Just remember what I've told you.'

'Suppose he comes drooling after me himself?'

'He'll have to quit this place then. You can feed him out of your own larder, he won't get a paisa of your father's fortune.'

'Consternation! Then good-bye, Sir Isaac.'

This act of the drama ended here that day.

IX

'EVERYTHING ELSE IS going smoothly, Choudhuri Mashai. It's my daughter who has me worried. I can't make out what she's angling after.'

Choudhuri said, 'And what about the people who are angling for her? That should be a cause for worry too. The word's got round that your husband left a huge fortune for the upkeep of his laboratory. The figure keeps increasing as tongues wag on. So everyone's laying bets on both the kingdom and the princess.'

'The princess will be sold dirt cheap, I know. But as long as I'm alive, the kingdom won't be so easy to get.'

'But the bidders have started flocking already. I saw our

Professor Majumdar the other day, walking out of a cinema hand in hand with the princess herself. He looked away when he saw me. He goes around lecturing on edifying subjects all over the place: he's very articulate about the good of the country. But when he turned his head away, he had me seriously worried about our motherland.'

'Choudhuri Mashai, the doors have burst open.'

'They have indeed. Now even this poor fellow will have to guard his chattels carefully.'

'Let a plague take the whole Majumdar clan! All I'm worried about is our Rebati.'

'There's no danger at present,' said Choudhuri. 'He's immersed in his work. It's going wonderfully well.'

'You know what his problem is, Choudhuri Mashai? He might be the greatest expert in *science*, but when it comes to what you call *matriarchy*, he's a rank amateur.'

'Very true. He hasn't been vaccinated even once. If he catches the infection, it'll be hard to save him.'

'You must come and check his health every day.'

'If he picks up a germ from God knows where and I catch it at my age, it'll be the death of me. But have no fear. I hope you can take a joke, even though you're a woman. I've crossed the *epidemic* zone. Now I don't get infected even on contagion. But there's a problem. I have to leave for Gujranwala the day after tomorrow.'

'Is that another joke? Spare this poor woman, please.'

'I'm serious. An old friend of mine, Amulya Addy, was a doctor there for some twenty-five years. He had a good practice, invested in property too. He died recently of apoplexy, leaving a widow and children. I'll have to sort out his affairs, sell his property and bring the family back here. I'm not sure how long that'll take.'

'One can't have anything to say to that.'

'We have no say over anything that happens in this world, Sohini. All you can do is to keep up your courage and take things as they come. Those who believe in fate are not wrong, you know. We *scientists* too believe that what is inevitable cannot be altered by even a hair. Do what you can for as long as you can; when there's nothing you can do, just call a halt.'

'Very well. I'll go by that.'

'This Majumdar I told you of, is not the most dangerous of

the lot. They keep him in their gang to lend themselves respectability. The others I've heard about are, as Chanakya would say,
dangerous even at a hundred hands' distance. There's Bankubihari the attorney: having resort to him is like embracing an octopus. Such men relish the hot blood of wealthy widows. Store
away that information and use it as you might. And above all,
remember my *philosophy*.'

'You can keep your *philosophy*, Choudhury Mashai. If anyone
touches my laboratory, I'll defy your fate, I'll defy your doctrine
of immutable cause and effect. I'm a Punjabi woman: I can wield
a knife quite readily. I can kill anyone, even my own daughter or
any aspiring son-in-law.'

She had a knife tucked into a belt under her sari. She drew it
out with a single quick motion and displayed its glittering blade.
She said, 'He singled me out. I'm not a Bengali woman, to do
nothing but weep her eyes out for love. I can give my life for
love, and take life too. Between my laboratory and my heart, I
place this knife.'

Choudhuri said, 'I used to write poetry once. Now I feel
I can write it again.'

'Write poetry if you like, but take back your *philosophy*. I'll
never accept what is unacceptable. I'll fight alone. And I'll say
proudly, "I'll win. I'll win, I'll win." '

'*Bravo*! I take back my *philosophy*. From now on, I'll be the
drummer in your triumphal march. For the present, I'll take
leave of you for some time. But I'll be back soon.'

Amazingly, Sohini's eyes filled with tears. 'Don't mind me,'
she said, and put her arms around Choudhuri's neck. 'No ties
last for ever in this world. This too is just a momentary bond.'

With that, she loosened her embrace, fell at his feet, and made
a pranam.

X

WHAT NEWSPAPERS CALL 'situations' happen all of a sudden,
and always in a cluster. The story of life, with its joys and sorrows, proceeds at a gradual pace. Suddenly in the final chapter, a
collision shatters everything; then all is still. The creator builds up
his story bit by bit, then breaks it with a single blow.

Sohini's grandmother lived in Ambala. She sent her a telegram: 'If you wish to see me, come at once.'

This grandmother was her only living relation. It was from her that Nandakishore had bought Sohini.

Nila's mother said to her, 'You must come with me.'

Nila said, 'That's impossible.'

'Why?'

'They want to hold a reception in my honour.'

'Who are "they"?'

'The *members* of the Awakeners' Club. Don't worry, it's perfectly respectable. You can see the list of *members*: very exclusive.'

'What are your aims and objectives?'

'They're hard to define. The name itself gives you an indication. It has all kinds of meanings hidden deep in it – spiritual, literary, *artistic*. Nabakumar Babu gave a very good interpretation of it the other day. They're going to ask you for a donation.'

'But I find they've already taken a donation to end all donations. You've fallen completely into their hands. But that will be all. They've got what I consider dispensable. There's nothing else they can get out of me.'

'Why are you getting so angry, Ma? They want to serve the country quite selflessly.'

'Let's not go into that. Your friends must have told you by now that you're independent.'

'They have.'

'Those selfless people must have also informed you that the money your husband left you is yours to spend as you wish.'

'I know that.'

'I've heard you're planning to get a probate on the will. Is that true?'

'Yes it's true. Banku Babu is my solicitor.'

'Has he given you any more advice, held out any more hopes?'

Nila was silent.

'I'll straighten out your Banku Babu if he trespasses on my territory. If I can't do it within the law, I'll break the law. I'll come back from Ambala via Peshawar. The laboratory will be guarded day and night by four Sikh guards. And let me show you this before I go – I'm a Punjabi woman.'

She brought out the knife from her belt and said, 'This knife recognizes neither my daughter nor her solicitor. Keep that in mind. If I need to settle accounts when I get back, I will.'

XI

THE LABORATORY WAS surrounded by extensive open grounds, to insulate it from sound and vibrations as much as possible. Rebati found the peaceful atmosphere ideal for his work, so he often came back at night.

The clock downstairs had struck two. Rebati was gazing through the window at the night sky, deep in thought, when he suddenly noticed a shadow on the wall.

He turned round and found Nila in the room. She was in her nightwear, a thin silk *chemise*. A startled Rebati was about to leap up from his chair, when Nila came, sat in his lap, and wrapped him in her arms. Rebati started trembling all over; his chest heaved violently. He said in a thick choking voice, 'Go away: please go away from this room.'

'Why?' she asked.

'I can't bear it,' said Rebati. 'Why did you come here?'

Nila held him even closer and said, 'Why, don't you love me?'

'I do, I do,' said Rebati. 'But you must go now.'

Suddenly, a Punjabi guard came into the room. He addressed her sternly in Hindi, 'Shame on you, Maiji! Please go away at once.'

Unknown to his consciousness, Rebati had pressed the electric bell at his side.

The man turned to Rebati. 'Babuji, don't betray your trust.'

Rebati pushed Nila off his lap and stood up. The guard warned Nila once again, 'Please go away, or I'll have to carry out the mistress's orders.'

In other words, he would lay hands on her and throw her out. Nila moved towards the door with a parting shot. 'Do you hear me, Sir Isaac Newton? – You're invited to tea at our place tomorrow – at 4.45 sharp. Did you hear that? Or have you fainted away?' She turned round to look at him.

'I've heard,' said Rebati in a steamy mumble.

Nila's flawless body was sharply defined through her nightwear, like a sculpted statue. Rebati could not help but look on, totally spellbound. Nila left. Rebati laid his head on the table and slumped. Such amazing beauty was beyond his dreams. An electric shower coursed through his veins like a startled stream of fire. He clenched his fists and kept repeating to himself that he would not go to the tea party the next day. He wanted to take a strong vow, but the words wouldn't escape his lips. 'I won't go. I won't go. I won't go,' he wrote on the blotting paper in front of him. Suddenly he noticed a deep red handkerchief lying on the table, with 'Nila' embroidered in one corner. He pressed it to his face. The perfume went to his head, and an intoxicated feeling spread through his body.

Nila came back into the room. She said, 'I had an errand which I'd forgotten.'

The guard tried to stop her. 'Don't worry,' she told him, 'I haven't come to steal anything. I just want a signature. I want to make you President of the Awakeners' Club: you're a famous person.'

Rebati protested shrinkingly, 'But I know nothing about the Club.'

'You don't need to know anything. It's enough for you to know that Brajendra Babu is a *patron*.'

'I don't know who Brajendra Babu is.'

'You need know just this much, that he's the Director of the Metropolitan Bank. Now be a dear – just one signature, nothing more.' She engirded his shoulder with her right arm, held his hand and said, 'Sign here.'

He put down his signature, like a man in a dream.

Nila was folding up the paper when the guard intervened. 'I must see that paper.'

'You won't understand what's in it,' said Nila.

'I don't have to understand,' said the guard. He snatched the paper out of her hands and tore it into little bits. 'If you need to draw up any documents, do it outside, not in here.'

Inwardly, Rebati breathed a sigh of relief. The guard said, 'Come, Maiji, let me take you home.' And he steered her out once more.

After a while, the man was back again. He said, 'I keep all the doors locked. You must have let her in.'

To be suspected like this! It was insulting. Rebati denied it repeatedly. 'I did not open any door.'

'Then how did she come in?'

That was indeed puzzling. The scientist started inspecting every room. Finally, he found a window facing the road which had been latched from inside. Someone had opened the latch sometime during the day.

The guard could not credit Rebati with such cunning. He viewed him as a simpleton, with just strength enough to ply his books. He struck his forehead. 'Women! It's destiny that makes them so devilish.'

For the little that was left of the night, Rebati kept on resolving that he would not go to the tea party.

The crows started to call. Rebati went home.

XII

THE NEXT DAY there was no mistake in timing. Rebati arrived at the tea party at 4.45 sharp. He had thought the tea would be *tête-à-tête*. He had not mastered the art of *fashionable* dressing. He was wearing a freshly laundered dhoti and kurta, with a folded chaddar across one shoulder. On arriving, he realized it was a big garden party with crowds of unknown people, all very fashionably turned out. His heart sank, and he looked for a corner to hide in. Just as he had found such a place and was about to sit down, the whole company stood up in a body. 'Welcome, Dr Bhattacharya, this seat is for you.'

They showed him to a velvet-lined chair right at the centre. He realized he was the chief object of attention. Nila came forward, placed a garland round his neck, and a dot of sandalwood paste on his forehead. Brajendra Babu proposed that he be made president of the Awakeners' Club. Banku Babu seconded the proposal, and there was loud applause all round. Haridas Babu the writer made a speech on the *international* fame of Dr Bhattacharya. He said, 'With our sails filled with the wind of Rebati Babu's fame, the Awakeners' Club will voyage from port to port along the Western ocean.'

The organizers whispered to the press reporters that every metaphor should be carefully noted.

As the speakers continued one after another, saying things like 'At last Dr Bhattacharya has put the mark of victory in *science* on the Motherland's brow', Rebati's heart filled with pride. He saw himself blazing in the noon sky of the civilized world. He immediately discounted all the unsavoury rumours he had heard about the Awakeners' Club. When Haridas Babu said, 'Rebati Babu's name, which works like a charm everywhere, is being lent to this gathering as a protective amulet, indicating how noble our aims are', Rebati was overwhelmed by the glory of his name and the onus it laid upon him. He cast aside the slough of his earlier diffidence. Women lowered cigarettes from their lips and leaned over his chair, saying with the sweetest smiles, 'Sorry to bother you, but you simply must give us your *autograph*.'

Rebati felt he had been living in a dream all these years. He had emerged from the cocoon of those dreams, and was now a full-grown butterfly.

The guests left one by one. Nila held on to Rebati's hand and said, 'You mustn't go just yet.'

She poured heady wine through his veins.

The daylight was dwindling; green shadows of evening spread through the grove.

They sat close to each other on a garden bench. She took his hand in hers and said, 'Dr Bhattacharya, being a man, why are you so afraid of women?'

'Afraid of them? Never!' said Rebati very confidently.

'Aren't you afraid of my mother?'

'Why should I be afraid of her? I respect her.'

'And me?'

'I'm definitely afraid of you.'

'That's good news. My mother said she'll never let you marry me. I'll kill myself then.'

'I won't let anything stop us. We'll certainly get married.'

She put her head on his shoulder and said, 'Perhaps you don't know how much I want you.'

Rebati drew her head closer to his chest and said, 'No power on earth can snatch you away from me.'

'What about caste?'

'Let caste go to the blazes.'

'Then you must notify the Registrar tomorrow.'

'Right. Tomorrow it shall be.'

Rebati had begun displaying male brashness.

The consequences followed rapidly.

Sohini's grandmother had developed signs of paralysis. She was on her deathbed, and would not let go of Sohini till the last. This was an opportunity Nila seized with both hands, giving full play to the turbulence of youth.

Rebati's masculine appeal had been weakened by the weight of his learning: Nila did not find him attractive enough. But he was a safe bet as a husband: she could carry on as wildly as ever after their marriage, and he would not have the strength to protest. Not only that, the assets of the laboratory were such as to excite her avarice. Her well-wishers opined that there was no fitter candidate than Rebati to take charge of the laboratory. All wise men surmised that Sohini would never let him slip her grasp.

Meanwhile, goaded by the taunts of his associates, Rebati was persuaded to let the newspapers announce his presidentship of the Awakeners' Club. When Nila teased him and asked, 'Are you scared?' he said, 'I just don't *care*.' He was determined to remove any doubts about his manliness. 'Eddington and I are in regular correspondence, I'll invite him to the Club one of these days,' he announced. 'Bravo!' said the members.

Rebati's real work had come to a halt. The flow of his inquiry had been broken. His mind would be intent on Nila's arrival: how she would appear behind him of a sudden and cover his eyes with her hands. She would sit on the arm of his chair and put her left arm around his neck. He tried to assure himself that the break in his work was only temporary, that the broken ends would join up once he had composed himself a little. But there were no signs of returning composure. Nila did not think that the damage to his work was damaging the world in any way. She thought it all to be a huge joke.

The web entangled Rebati more and more every day. The Awakeners' Club pressed around him, determined to make him a complete male. He still could not bring himself to utter their foul language, but he forced himself to laugh when he heard foul talk. Dr Bhattacharya had become a great source of amusement for the Club.

Rebati was often plagued by jealousy. Nila lit her cheroot from the one between the bank director's lips. Rebati would never be able to match that. Cigar smoke made his head reel; but seeing Nila acting up in this manner made him feel still more sick. Besides, he could not but protest at all the hugging and tugging. Nila would say, 'It's just my body after all: it doesn't engage us, we put no value on it. What matters is the love one feels inside, and that's something I don't fling around.' Here she would clutch Rebati's hand firmly. At that moment Rebati would think of the others as a deprived lot. All they were getting was the outer shell, not the rich kernel.

The entrance to the laboratory went on being guarded round

the clock. Inside, the work lay unfinished, and there was nobody to be seen.

XIII

NILA SAT IN the drawing-room, her feet up on the sofa, her back reclining on the cushions. On the floor, leaning against the sofa near her feet, sat Rebati with a bunch of closely-written foolscap pages.

Rebati shook his head and said, 'The language is too florid. I'll feel embarrassed to read this.'

'Are you such a great authority on style? This is not one of your chemical formulas. Now don't grumble, just learn it off by heart. Do you know who's written this? Our man of letters, Pramadaranjan Babu himself.'

'All these long *sentences* and big fancy words! I'll never re-member them.'

'What's so difficult about them? I've got it all by heart al-ready, what with reading it aloud to you so many times: "In the finest, most auspicious hour of my life, this honour bestowed on me by the Awakeners' Club, like a garland of flowers from the celestial garden . . ." – Grand! Don't worry, I'll be right next to you, prompting you discreetly.'

'I'm not too familiar with Bengali literary style, but I can't help feeling that the whole thing sounds like a joke against me. Why can't I say it in simple English? *Dear friends, allow me to offer you my heartiest thanks for the honour you have conferred upon me on behalf of the Awakeners' Club – the great Awakener – etc. etc.* Just one or two sentences, that's all.'

'Never! It's so amusing to hear you speak in Bengali. Take that bit where you say, "O you Youth of Bengal, who drive the chariot of freedom, pioneers on the road strewn with the broken chains of past bondage" – could you ever put that across so elegantly in English? Such words from the lips of a scientist like you will make all the young men raise their hoods and dance like snakes. Come, there's still time. I'll help you learn it.'

Heavy of weight, tall of stature, and attired like an English-man, Brajendra Haldar, the bank manager, came scrunching up the stairs at that moment. 'This is intolerable!' he said. 'When-ever I come, I find you in possession of Nila. You have nothing better to do than to stand like a thorn hedge keeping her away from us.'

Rebati cringed. 'I'm here on specially important work today, that's why –'

'Of course you have work. You've invited the *members* over today. That's why I took a chance and dropped in for half an hour on my way to office. I'd thought you'd be busy elsewhere. And what do I find? You're stuck here with your work. Wonderful! When there's no work, you spend your leisure here; and when there is work, that brings you here too. How do we working men keep up with such a dogged character? Nila, *is it fair?*'

Nila said, 'Dr Bhattacharya's problem is that he can't come out with the truth confidently enough. He hasn't come here on work: that's rubbish. He's come because he can't keep away from me. That's the truth, and it's worth hearing. He takes up all my time through sheer persistence. That's where his manliness lies. And the rest of you are beaten by his crude rustic ways.'

'Very well then, we'll use our manly strength too. From now on the members of the Awakeners' Club will practise the art of abducting women. We'll revive the Puranic Age.'

'That seems rather amusing,' said Nila. ' "Abduction" sounds better than "accepting one's hand". But how do you go about it?'

'Do you want me to demonstrate?' asked Haldar.

'Right now?'

'Yes, right away.'

He swept her up from the sofa in his arms. Nila screamed and giggled and clung to his neck.

Rebati's face grew dark with anger, yet he lacked the strength either to imitate this conduct or to put a stop to it. He was more angry with Nila than with Haldar: why did she encourage these headstrong boors?

'The car's ready,' said Haldar. 'I'm taking you off to Diamond Harbour. I'll bring you back in time for the dinner-party. I had some work at the bank, but that can go to hell. I'll be doing a good turn, giving Dr Bhattacharya a chance to work quietly on his own. It's best to remove a big distraction like you. He'll thank me for it.'

Rebati noticed that Nila did not struggle or try to extricate herself. She lay quite comfortably against his chest, encircling his neck amorously. 'Don't worry, Scientist-Sahib,' she said on their way out. 'This is just the *rehearsal* of an abduction. I'm not going across to Lanka – I'll be back in time for your party.'

Rebati tore up the piece of writing he held. Haldar's physical strength, and the way he asserted his rights, made Rebati's vaunted scholarship seem futile by contrast.

The dinner that evening was at a well-known restaurant. The host was Rebati Bhattacharya himself; beside him sat his honoured guest Nila. A famous film actress was there to sing. Bankubihari had risen to *propose* a *toast*; Rebati's praises were being sung, and Nila's along with his. The women were drawing on cigarettes with a vengeance, to prove they were not entirely women. Middle-aged women in masks of youth were vying to beat the younger ones in the race, nudging and jostling, flaunting their gestures and postures, their loud laughter and high voices.

All of a sudden, Sohini entered the room. Silence fell on the gathering. She looked at Rebati and said, 'I don't seem to recognize you. Dr Bhattacharya, is it? You had asked for money for your necessary expenses, and I sent it to you last Friday. I can see quite clearly that you're not short of funds. You'll have to come right away. I want to take stock tonight of every item in the laboratory.'

'Do you distrust me?'

'I didn't till now. But if you have any shame, don't mention the word "trust" ever again.'

Rebati was about to get up. Nila tugged at his clothes and forced him down again. 'He has asked his friends over tonight,' she said. 'Let them first take their leave. He'll go afterwards.'

There was a cruel sting in what she said. Sir Isaac had been her mother's favourite: there was no one she trusted more. That is why he had been chosen among the rest to take charge of the laboratory. To rub it in further, Nila continued, 'Ma, do you know how many people have been invited this evening? Sixty-five. They wouldn't all fit in here, so half of them are in the next room: can't you hear the din? Twenty-five rupees a head, whether you drink or not. There'll be a hefty sum to pay for empty glasses. Any other person would have turned pale at the sum. The Bank Director was amazed at this gentleman's generosity. Do you know how much he paid the film star? Four hundred rupees for a single night!'

Rebati's heart was floundering like a catfish being cut up alive. His dry mouth could not utter a word.

'What's today's celebration in aid of?' asked Sohini.

'Don't you know? It's out in the Associated Press. He's become President of the Awakeners' Club, that's why. He'll pay the six hundred rupees for *life membership* later on at his convenience.'

'That won't be for a long time.'

There was a steamroller trundling through Rebati's heart.

'So it won't be convenient for you to get up now?' Sohini asked him.

Rebati looked at Nila. Her arch frown roused his manly pride. 'How can I, with all the guests here —' he said.

'Right. I'll sit here and wait for you. Naserullah, go and wait at the door.'

'That can't be, Ma,' said Nila. 'We have some confidential matters to discuss. You shouldn't be present.'

'Nila, you're just a beginner in the game of wits: you can't beat me yet. You think I don't know what your discussions are about? I need to stay right here for that very reason.'

'What have you heard, and from whom?'

'The trick of getting news lies in one's moneybag, like a snake in its hole. You have three legal experts here, ferreting through documents to see whether they can find any chink through which you can siphon off the laboratory funds. Isn't that so, Nilu?'

'It's quite true. It's unnatural that a father should leave all that money and his daughter have no *share* in it. That's why everyone suspects —'

Sohini rose from her seat. 'The real reason for suspicion goes much further back in time,' she said. 'Who is your father? In whose property are you claiming a *share*? Aren't you ashamed to say you're the daughter of such a man?'

Nila jumped up. 'What are you saying, Ma?'

'The truth, that's what. It was no secret to him; he knew everything. He got everything he expected from me, and he will, even now. He cared for nothing else.'

Barrister Ghosh intervened. 'Your word of mouth is not sufficient proof,' he said.

'He was aware of that too. So he put it down very carefully in a registered document.'

'Come on, Banku, it's getting late. Why wait any longer? Let's go.'

The Peshawari guard's demeanour was a clear signal for all sixty-five guests to disappear in a hurry.

Just then, Choudhuri entered, suitcase in hand. 'I received your telegram and came running back. What's this, Rebi Baby, your face looks as white as *parchment*. Where's baby's bowl of milk, then?'

Sohini pointed to Nila. 'Here's the one who's supplying that.'

'So you're a dairymaid now, are you, my dear?'

'She's hunting for a dairyman. There's her quarry.'

'Not our Rebi, surely!'

'This time my daughter has saved my laboratory. I couldn't judge this man properly; my daughter spotted how I was turning my laboratory into a cowshed. A little longer and it would have been buried in a cowdung-pit.'

'Since you're the one who discovered this cowherd, my dear, you must take charge of the creature yourself,' said the professor. 'He is blessed with all things except intelligence. With you beside him, no one will notice the lack. Stupid males are easily led by the nose on a rope.'

'What do you say, Sir Isaac Newton?' asked Nila. 'You've already given notice to the marriage registrar. Would you like to withdraw it now?'

'Not on my life,' said Rebati, puffing out his chest.

'The marriage will be at an inauspicious moment then.'

'It will happen, it will!'

'But far away from the laboratory,' said Sohini.

The professor said, 'Nilu, my dear, he's stupid, but he's not totally useless. Once he comes out of his stupor, you won't have to worry about his feed and upkeep.'

'Sir Isaac, you must find yourself a better tailor then, or else I'll have to cover my face in your presence.'

Suddenly another shadow fell upon the wall. Rebati's aunt came and stood before him.

'Rebi, come along,' she said.

Rebati slunk out after his aunt, very meekly. He did not look back even once.

The Story of a Mussalmani

A DRAFT

[*'The Story of a Mussalmani'* was not published in Rabindranath's lifetime, nor is there any manuscript in his own hand. He dictated the story on 24–25 June 1941, some month and a half before his death. The transcription does not carry any revisions in his own hand. It is clearly not a finished story but a draft. Nonetheless, it is important as Rabindranath's last attempt at a short story.

It has another importance as well. As the pieces in this collection testify, Rabindranath was a bold lifelong critic of the ills of contemporary Hindu society. In this draft too, he lashes out at the cowardice and prejudice of a society that cannot protect its women but is inhumanly insistent on their purity. The story also bears a relevance to the destructive communal politics of its period of composition. Its message takes on a special resonance on the lips of a Hindu woman converted to Islam.

We cannot tell how Rabindranath might have modified his draft. But even as a draft, it is a significant text.]

THOSE WERE THE times when agents of anarchy were menacing the functioning of the state, when each day and each night was swayed by blows of unforeseen violence. Daily life was enmeshed in nightmares. Householders looked up to the gods, and people were afflicted by imaginary terrors of demons. It was hard to trust anyone, man or god: one had constantly to resort to tears. The consequences of good deeds and of bad deeds were hardly distinguishable. People stumbled into misfortune all the time.

In such a situation, having a beautiful daughter at home was like a curse of fate. The parents and relatives of any such girl would say, 'The sooner we're rid of her the better.' Bangshibadan, the landlord of Teen Mahala, had acquired such a curse in his house.

It was the beautiful Kamala, whose parents had died, and it would have pleased her other relatives if she had died at the same time. She had not, and her uncle Bangshi had brought her up with great care and affection ever since. But her aunt used to tell her neighbours, 'Look at the injustice of it! Her parents died, leaving all the trouble to us. Who knows what might happen at any moment? After all, we have our own children. And she's set in the midst of us like a burning torch of destruction: she invites all sorts of evil stares. I'm afraid some day our whole family will be ruined just because of her. It keeps me awake at night!'

Still, the time passed by after a fashion. Then along came a proposal of marriage, and Kamala could not be hidden from the public eye any longer. Her uncle used to say, 'That's why I'm looking for a match with a family who'll be able to protect the girl.' The match that he found was the second son of Paramananda Seth of Mochakhali. The boy was sitting on huge sums of money which would probably disappear once his father died. He was a man of luxurious tastes. He proudly flaunted various ways of wasting money – falconry, gambling, bulbul fights. He was very proud about his wealth, of which he had a good deal. He had gigantic bodyguards from Bhojpur, skilled in fighting with lathis. He would openly challenge anyone in any quarter to lay hands on him. He was particularly fastidious about women. He already had one wife and was looking for a young one to be his second. He came to know about Kamala's beauty. The Seths were very rich and powerful. They were determined to bring her home as their bride.

Kamala burst into tears and said, 'Uncle, must you really send me to perdition in this way?'

'You know, my child, that if I had the strength to protect you, I would have held you to my heart all my life.'

After the marriage contract was settled, the groom came to the wedding with a lot of fanfare. There were plenty of musicians, and a great deal of pomp and show. Kamala's uncle said pleadingly, 'My son, maybe it isn't wise to make such a show. These are bad times.'

At this, the groom swore and said, 'Let's see who has the guts to mess around with me!'

The uncle said, 'The girl was ours until the marriage ceremony was over. Now she is yours, you have the responsibility of escorting her safely to your home. We cannot do it, we are weak.'

The groom said loftily, 'Don't worry.'

The bodyguards from Bhojpur twirled their moustaches and stood with lathis in hand. The groom set out with his bride,

through the famed fields of Taltari. Madhu-Mollar was the captain of a band of brigands. At about midnight, he attacked the
caravan with his men, shouting and brandishing torches. Most
of the Bhojpuris vanished. Madhu-Mollar was a well-known
bandit, there was no escape from his hands.

Kamala was about to leave her palanquin and hide in the
bushes when old Habir Khan appeared behind her. Everyone
venerated Habir Khan like a prophet. Habir stood firmly there
and shouted, 'Go away, my sons. This is Habir Khan.'

The bandits said, 'Khan Sahib, of course we cannot argue
with you, but why are you spoiling our trade?'

However, they had to leave.

Habir told Kamala, 'You are a daughter to me. Don't be
afraid. Let us leave this dangerous place and go to my home.'

Kamala shrank visibly. Habir said, 'I understand. You're a
Hindu brahman's daughter, so you're hesitating to go to a
Muslim home. But don't forget that true Muslims respect devout
brahmans as well. You can stay at my home like a girl of a Hindu
family. My name is Habir Khan. My house is nearby. Come with
me, I'll keep you safe.'

Kamala was a brahman girl; she could not overcome her diffidence. Habir sensed that and said, 'Look, as long as I am alive,
nobody in these parts will offend against your faith. Come with
me, don't be afraid.'

Habir Khan took Kamala home with him. Surprisingly, in
one of the eight wings of that house, there was a Shiva temple
and all arrangements for practising the Hindu faith.

An old Hindu brahman appeared and told Kamala, 'This
place is just like a Hindu home, you won't lose your caste here.'

Kamala cried and said, 'Please send word to my uncle. Ask
him to come here and take me home.'

Habir said, 'You are mistaken, my child. Your people won't
take you back. They'll abandon you on the road. You can test it
for yourself if you like.'

Habir Khan took Kamala as far as the back door of her uncle's
house and said, 'I'll wait here.'

Kamala went inside the house, clung to her uncle and said,
'Please don't desert me.'

The tears rolled down her uncle's eyes.

Her aunt came, saw her and shouted, 'Show her the door!
Show the door to this ill-omened creature! You ruinous girl,

aren't you ashamed to come here after staying with infidels?'

Her uncle said, 'I am helpless, my child. This is a Hindu home, nobody can take you back. If we do, we'll lose caste ourselves.'

Kamala stood there for a while with lowered head, then slowly went out of the back door and left with Habir. The doors of her uncle's house closed for ever behind her.

She could follow her accustomed rituals at Habir Khan's house. Habir Khan said, 'My sons will not come to this wing of the house. You can freely exercise your customs and rituals with the help of this old brahman.'

This house had a history. That wing was called the 'The Raj-putani's wing'. Some time in the past, a Nawab had brought home a Rajput woman, but made separate arrangements for her to preserve her religion. She worshipped Shiva, and sometimes even went on pilgrimage. Aristocratic Muslims of that time had a respect for devout Hindus. The Rajput woman lived there and sheltered all the Hindu begums, who continued their religious practices as before. It was said that Habir Khan was that Rajput woman's son. He did not take up his mother's religion, but he worshipped his mother at heart. Now that his mother was no more, he had taken on a mission to commemorate his mother – by providing a special shelter for Hindu women oppressed or ostracized by society.

Here Kamala found something she had never got at her own home. There, her aunt used to berate her, and she had to hear all the time that she was mischievous and ill-omened, that she had brought misfortune to the family, and that they would be saved only by her death. Her uncle sometimes brought clothes for her, but it had to be done secretly for fear of her aunt. In the Rajputani's wing, she was treated like a queen, with utmost respect and care. She had servants all around her, all of them from Hindu families.

At last the emotions of youth stirred in her body. A boy from the family started visiting her wing secretly from time to time, and Kamala was attracted to him. One day she told Habir Khan, 'Father, I have no religion. My only religion rests in the fortu-nate person whom I love. I have never found the providence of God in the religion which has deprived me of all kinds of love all through my life and finally flung me upon the garbage-heap of ignominy. To this day I cannot forget that the gods of that religion have insulted me every single day. Dear father, I have tasted love and affection for the first time at your home. Only now have I understood that life is precious even for a wretched woman like me. By revering that love, I worship the god who has given me shelter. That god is my god, neither Hindu nor Muslim. I have given my heart to your second son Karim, I have conjoined my life and faith with his. Make me a Muslim: I won't object. Maybe I can preserve both religions.'

Thus their life flowed on. There was no possibility of their encountering Kamala's former kin. On the other hand, Habir Khan tried to help Kamala forget that she was not of their people. She was named Meherjan.

The time came for the marriage of Kamala's uncle's second daughter, Sarala. The arrangements were made as before, and the same trouble befell. The same band of brigands attacked them on their way. They had once been deprived of their prey, so this time they were determined to have their own back.

But from behind them came a thunderous voice, 'Watch out!'

'Damn, Habir Khan's men have come to spoil everything.' The bride's folk left her alone in the palanquin and tried frantically to run away. A spear now appeared in the midst of them, its tip decorated with Habir Khan's crescent-marked pennant. A fearless woman stood holding the spear.

She said to Sarala, 'Don't be afraid, sister. I have brought you the assurance of shelter from someone who shelters everyone, someone who isn't concerned with caste or religion.

'Uncle, my pranams to you. Don't worry, I shan't actually touch your feet. Now take Sarala back to your home. She has not been contaminated by any touch. Tell Aunt that when I grew up with the food and clothes that she unwillingly gave me, I never dreamed I would be able to repay my debts in this way. Please take this red silk sari I have brought for Sarala, and this brocade cushion. And if ever she is in distress, remember she has a Mussalman sister to protect her.'

NOVEL

THE HOME
AND THE WORLD

CHAPTER ONE

Bimala's Story

I

MOTHER, TODAY THERE comes back to mind the vermilion mark[1] at the parting of your hair, the *sari*[2] which you used to wear, with its wide red border, and those wonderful eyes of yours, full of depth and peace. They came at the start of my life's journey, like the first streak of dawn, giving me golden provision to carry me on my way.

The sky which gives light is blue, and my mother's face was dark, but she had the radiance of holiness, and her beauty would put to shame all the vanity of the beautiful.

Everyone says that I resemble my mother. In my childhood I used to resent this. It made me angry with my mirror. I thought that it was God's unfairness which was wrapped round my limbs – that my dark features were not my due, but had come to me by some misunderstanding. All that remained for me to ask of my God in reparation was, that I might grow up to be a model of what woman should be, as one reads it in some epic poem.

When the proposal came for my marriage, an astrologer was sent, who consulted my palm and said, 'This girl has good signs. She will become an ideal wife.'

And all the women who heard it said: 'No wonder, for she resembles her mother.'

I was married into a Rajah's house. When I was a child, I was quite familiar with the description of the Prince of the fairy story. But my husband's face was not of a kind that one's imagination would place in fairyland. It was dark, even as mine was. The feeling of shrinking, which I had about my own lack of physical beauty, was lifted a little; at the same time a touch of regret was left lingering in my heart.

But when the physical appearance evades the scrutiny of our senses and enters the sanctuary of our hearts, then it can forget itself. I know, from my childhood's experience, how devotion is

1. The mark of Hindu wifehood and the symbol of all the devotion that it implies.
2. The *sari* is the dress of the Hindu woman.

beauty itself, in its inner aspect. When my mother arranged the different fruits, carefully peeled by her own loving hands, on the white stone plate, and gently waved her fan to drive away the flies while my father sat down to his meals, her service would lose itself in a beauty which passed beyond outward forms. Even in my infancy I could feel its power. It transcended all debates, or doubts, or calculations: it was pure music.

I distinctly remember after my marriage, when, early in the morning, I would cautiously and silently get up and take the dust[1] of my husband's feet without waking him, how at such moments I could feel the vermilion mark upon my forehead shining out like the morning star.

One day, he happened to awake, and smiled as he asked me: 'What is that, Bimala? What *are* you doing?'

I can never forget the shame of being detected by him. He might possibly have thought that I was trying to earn merit secretly. But no, no! That had nothing to do with merit. It was my woman's heart, which must worship in order to love.

My father–in–law's house was old in dignity from the days of the *Badshahs*. Some of its manners were of the Moguls and Pathans, some of its customs of Manu and Parashar. But my husband was absolutely modern. He was the first of the house to go through a college course and take his M.A. degree. His elder brother had died young, of drink, and had left no children. My husband did not drink and was not given to dissipation. So foreign to the family was this abstinence, that to many it hardly seemed decent! Purity, they imagined, was only becoming in those on whom fortune had not smiled. It is the moon which has room for stains, not the stars.

My husband's parents had died long ago, and his old grand-mother was mistress of the house. My husband was the apple of her eye, the jewel on her bosom. And so he never met with much difficulty in overstepping any of the ancient usages. When he brought in Miss Gilby, to teach me and be my companion, he stuck to his resolve in spite of the poison secreted by all the wagging tongues at home and outside.

My husband had then just got through his B.A. examination and was reading for his M.A. degree; so he had to stay in Calcutta

1. Taking the dust of the feet is a formal offering of reverence and is done by lightly touching the feet of the revered one and then one's own head with the same hand. The wife does not ordinarily do this to the husband.

to attend college. He used to write to me almost every day, a few lines only, and simple words, but his bold, round handwriting would look up into my face, oh, so tenderly! I kept his letters in a sandalwood box and covered them every day with the flowers I gathered in the garden.

At that time the Prince of the fairy tale had faded, like the moon in the morning light. I had the Prince of my real world enthroned in my heart. I was his queen. I had my seat by his side. But my real joy was, that my true place was at his feet.

Since then, I have been educated, and introduced to the modern age in its own language, and therefore these words that I write seem to blush with shame in their prose setting. Except for my acquaintance with this modern standard of life, I should know, quite naturally, that just as my being born a woman was not in my own hands, so the element of devotion in woman's love is not like a hackneyed passage quoted from a romantic poem to be piously written down in round hand in a schoolgirl's copy-book.

But my husband would not give me any opportunity for worship. That was his greatness. They are cowards who claim absolute devotion from their wives as their right; that is a humiliation for both.

His love for me seemed to overflow my limits by its flood of wealth and service. But my necessity was more for giving than for receiving; for love is a vagabond, who can make his flowers bloom in the wayside dust, better than in the crystal jars kept in the drawing-room.

My husband could not break completely with the old-time traditions which prevailed in our family. It was difficult, therefore, for us to meet at any hour of the day we pleased.[1] I knew exactly the time that he could come to me, and therefore our meeting had all the care of loving preparation. It was like the rhyming of a poem; it had to come through the path of the metre.

After finishing the day's work and taking my afternoon bath, I would do up my hair and renew my vermilion mark and put on my *sari*, carefully crinkled; and then, bringing back my body and mind from all distractions of household duties, I would

---

1. It would not be reckoned good form for the husband to be continually going into the zenana, except at particular hours for meals or rest.

dedicate it at this special hour, with special ceremonies, to one individual. That time, each day, with him was short; but it was infinite.

My husband used to say, that man and wife are equal in love because of their equal claim on each other. I never argued the point with him, but my heart said that devotion never stands in the way of true equality; it only raises the level of the ground of meeting. Therefore the joy of the higher equality remains permanent; it never slides down to the vulgar level of triviality.

My beloved, it was worthy of you that you never expected worship from me. But if you had accepted it, you would have done me a real service. You showed your love by decorating me, by educating me, by giving me what I asked for, and what I did not. I have seen what depth of love there was in your eyes when you gazed at me. I have known the secret sigh of pain you suppressed in your love for me. You loved my body as if it were a flower of paradise. You loved my whole nature as if it had been given you by some rare providence.

Such lavish devotion made me proud to think that the wealth was all my own which drove you to my gate. But vanity such as this only checks the flow of free surrender in a woman's love. When I sit on the queen's throne and claim homage, then the claim only goes on magnifying itself; it is never satisfied. Can there be any real happiness for a woman in merely feeling that she has power over a man? To surrender one's pride in devotion is woman's only salvation.

It comes back to me today how, in the days of our happiness, the fires of envy sprung up all around us. That was only natural, for had I not stepped into my good fortune by a mere chance, and without deserving it? But providence does not allow a run of luck to last for ever, unless its debt of honour be fully paid, day by day, through many a long day, and thus made secure. God may grant us gifts, but the merit of being able to take and hold them must be our own. Alas for the boons that slip through unworthy hands!

My husband's grandmother and mother were both renowned for their beauty. And my widowed sister-in-law was also of a beauty rarely to be seen. When, in turn, fate left them deso-late, the grandmother vowed she would not insist on having beauty for her remaining grandson when he married. Only the auspicious marks with which I was endowed gained me an entry into this family – otherwise, I had no claim to be here.

In this house of luxury, but few of its ladies had received their meed of respect. They had, however, got used to the ways of the family, and managed to keep their heads above water, buoyed up by their dignity as *Ranis* of an ancient house, in spite of their daily tears being drowned in the foam of wine, and by the tinkle of the dancing girls' anklets. Was the credit due to me that my husband did not touch liquor, nor squander his manhood in the markets of woman's flesh? What charm did I know to soothe the wild and wandering mind of men? It was my good luck, nothing else. For fate proved utterly callous to my sister-in-law. Her festivity died out, while yet the evening was early, leaving the light of her beauty shining in vain over empty halls – burning and burning, with no accompanying music!

His sister-in-law affected a contempt for my husband's modern notions. How absurd to keep the family ship, laden with all the weight of its time-honoured glory, sailing under the colours of his slip of a girl-wife alone! Often have I felt the lash of scorn. 'A thief who had stolen a husband's love!' 'A sham hidden in the shamelessness of her new-fangled finery!' The many-coloured garments of modern fashion with which my husband loved to adorn me roused jealous wrath. 'Is not she ashamed to make a show-window of herself – and with her looks, too!'

My husband was aware of all this, but his gentleness knew no bounds. He used to implore me to forgive her.

I remember I once told him: 'Women's minds are so petty, so crooked!' 'Like the feet of Chinese women,' he replied. 'Has not the pressure of society cramped them into pettiness and crooked-ness? They are but pawns of the fate which gambles with them. What responsibility have they of their own?'

My sister-in-law never failed to get from my husband what-ever she wanted. He did not stop to consider whether her re-quests were right or reasonable. But what exasperated me most was that she was not grateful for this. I had promised my husband that I would not talk back at her, but this set me raging all the more, inwardly. I used to feel that goodness has a limit, which, if passed, somehow seems to make men cowardly. Shall I tell the whole truth? I have often wished that my husband had the manliness to be a little less good.

My sister-in-law, the Bara Rani,[1] was still young and had no pretensions to saintliness. Rather, her talk and jest and laugh inclined to be forward. The young maids with whom she surrounded herself were also impudent to a degree. But there was none to gainsay her – for was not this the custom of the house? It seemed to me that my good fortune in having a stainless husband was a special eyesore to her. He, however, felt more the sorrow of her lot than the defects of her character.

II

MY HUSBAND WAS very eager to take me out of *purdah*.[2]

One day I said to him: 'What do I want with the outside world?'

'The outside world may want you,' he replied.

'If the outside world has got on so long without me, it may go on for some time longer. It need not pine to death for want of me.'

'Let it perish, for all I care! That is not troubling me. I am thinking about myself.'

'Oh, indeed. Tell me what about yourself?'

My husband was silent, with a smile.

I knew his way, and protested at once: 'No, no, you are not going to run away from me like that! I want to have this out with you.'

'Can one ever finish a subject with words?'

'Do stop speaking in riddles. Tell me . . .'

'What I want is, that I should have you, and you should have me, more fully in the outside world. That is where we are still in debt to each other.'

'Is anything wanting, then, in the love we have here at home?'

'Here you are wrapped up in me. You know neither what you have, nor what you want.'

'I cannot bear to hear you talk like this.'

'I would have you come into the heart of the outer world

---

1. *Bara* = Senior; *Chota* = Junior. In joint families of rank, though the widows remain entitled only to a life-interest in their husbands' share, their rank remains to them according to seniority, and the titles 'Senior' and 'Junior' continue to distinguish the elder and younger branches, even though the Junior branch be the one in power.

2. The seclusion of the zenana, and all the customs peculiar to it, are designated by the general term 'Purdah', which means Screen.

and meet reality. Merely going on with your household duties, living all your life in the world of household conventions and the drudgery of household tasks – you were not made for that! If we meet, and recognize each other, in the real world, then only will our love be true.'

'If there be any drawback here to our full recognition of each other, then I have nothing to say. But as for myself, I feel no want.'

'Well, even if the drawback is only on my side, why shouldn't you help to remove it?'

Such discussions repeatedly occurred. One day he said: 'The greedy man who is fond of his fish stew has no compunction in cutting up the fish according to his need. But the man who loves the fish wants to enjoy it in the water; and if that is impossible he waits on the bank; and even if he comes back home without a sight of it he has the consolation of knowing that the fish is all right. Perfect gain is the best of all; but if that is impossible, then the next best gain is perfect losing.'

I never liked the way my husband had of talking on this subject, but that is not the reason why I refused to leave the zenana. His grandmother was still alive. My husband had filled more than a hundred and twenty per cent of the house with the twentieth century, against her taste; but she had borne it uncomplaining. She would have borne it, likewise, if the daughter-in-law[1] of the Rajah's house had left its seclusion. She was even prepared for this happening. But I did not consider it important enough to give her the pain of it. I have read in books that we are called 'caged birds'. I cannot speak for others, but I had so much in this cage of mine that there was not room for it in the universe – at least that is what I then felt.

The grandmother, in her old age, was very fond of me. At the bottom of her fondness was the thought that, with the conspiracy of favourable stars which attended me, I had been able to attract my husband's love. Were not men naturally inclined to plunge downwards? None of the others, for all their beauty, had been able to prevent their husbands going headlong into the burning depths which consumed and destroyed them. She believed that I had been the means of extinguishing this fire, so deadly to the

---

1. The prestige of the daughter-in-law is of the first importance in a Hindu household of rank.

men of the family. So she kept me in the shelter of her bosom, and trembled if I was in the least bit unwell.

His grandmother did not like the dresses and ornaments my husband brought from European shops to deck me with. But she reflected: 'Men will have some absurd hobby or other, which is sure to be expensive. It is no use trying to check their extravagance; one is glad enough if they stop short of ruin. If my Nikhil had not been busy dressing up his wife there is no knowing whom else he might have spent his money on!' So whenever any new dress of mine arrived she used to send for my husband and make merry over it.

Thus it came about that it was her taste which changed. The influence of the modern age fell so strongly upon her, that her evenings refused to pass if I did not tell her stories out of English books.

After his grandmother's death, my husband wanted me to go and live with him in Calcutta. But I could not bring myself to do that. Was not this our House, which she had kept under her sheltering care through all her trials and troubles? Would not a curse come upon me if I deserted it and went off to town? This was the thought that kept me back, as her empty seat reproachfully looked up at me. That noble lady had come into this house at the age of eight, and had died in her seventy-ninth year. She had not spent a happy life. Fate had hurled shaft after shaft at her breast, only to draw out more and more the imperishable spirit within. This great house was hallowed with her tears. What should I do in the dust of Calcutta, away from it?

My husband's idea was that this would be a good opportunity for leaving to my sister-in-law the consolation of ruling over the household, giving our life, at the same time, more room to branch out in Calcutta. That is just where my difficulty came in. She had worried my life out, she ill brooked my husband's happiness, and for this she was to be rewarded! And what of the day when we should have to come back here? Should I then get back my seat at the head?

'What do you want with that seat?' my husband would say. 'Are there not more precious things in life?'

Men never understand these things. They have their nests in the outside world; they little know the whole of what the household stands for. In these matters they ought to follow womanly guidance. Such were my thoughts at that time.

I felt the real point was, that one ought to stand up for one's rights. To go away, and leave everything in the hands of the enemy, would be nothing short of owning defeat.

But why did not my husband compel me to go with him to Calcutta? I know the reason. He did not use his power, just because he had it.

III

IF ONE HAD to fill in, little by little, the gap between day and night, it would take an eternity to do it. But the sun rises and the darkness is dispelled – a moment is sufficient to overcome an infinite distance.

One day there came the new era of *Swadeshi*[1] in Bengal; but as to how it happened, we had no distinct vision. There was no gradual slope connecting the past with the present. For that reason, I imagine, the new epoch came in like a flood, breaking down the dykes and sweeping all our prudence and fear before it. We had no time even to think about, or understand, what had happened, or what was about to happen.

My sight and my mind, my hopes and my desires, became red with the passion of this new age. Though, up to this time, the walls of the home – which was the ultimate world to my mind – remained unbroken, yet I stood looking over into the distance, and I heard a voice from the far horizon, whose meaning was not perfectly clear to me, but whose call went straight to my heart.

From the time my husband had been a college student he had been trying to get the things required by our people produced in our own country. There are plenty of date trees in our district. He tried to invent an apparatus for extracting the juice and boiling it into sugar and treacle. I heard that it was a great success, only it extracted more money than juice. After a while he came to the conclusion that our attempts at reviving our industries were not succeeding for want of a bank of our own. He was, at the time, trying to teach me political economy. This alone would not have done much harm, but he also took it into his head to teach his countrymen ideas of thrift, so as to pave the way for a bank; and then he actually started a small bank. Its high rate of interest, which made the villagers flock so enthusiastically

1. The Nationalist movement, which began more as an economic than a political one, having as its main object the encouragement of indigenous industries.

to put in their money, ended by swamping the bank altogether.

The old officers of the estate felt troubled and frightened. There was jubilation in the enemy's camp. Of all the family, only my husband's grandmother remained unmoved. She would scold me, saying: 'Why are you all plaguing him so? Is it the fate of the estate that is worrying you? How many times have I seen this estate in the hands of the court receiver! Are men like women? Men are born spendthrifts and only know how to waste. Look here, child, count yourself fortunate that your husband is not wasting himself as well!'

My husband's list of charities was a long one. He would assist to the bitter end of utter failure anyone who wanted to invent a new loom or rice-husking machine. But what annoyed me most was the way that Sandip Babu used to fleece him on the pretext of *Swadeshi* work. Whenever he wanted to start a newspaper, or travel about preaching the Cause, or take a change of air by the advice of his doctor, my husband would unquestioningly supply him with the money. This was over and above the regular living allowance which Sandip Babu also received from him. The strangest part of it was that my husband and Sandip Babu did not agree in their opinions.

As soon as the *Swadeshi* storm reached my blood, I said to my husband: 'I must burn all my foreign clothes.'

'Why burn them?' said he. 'You need not wear them as long as you please.'

'As long as I please! Not in this life . . .'

'Very well, do not wear them for the rest of your life, then. But why this bonfire business?'

'Would you thwart me in my resolve?'

'What I want to say is this: Why not try to build up something? You should not waste even a tenth part of your energies in this destructive excitement.'

'Such excitement will give us the energy to build.'

'That is as much as to say, that you cannot light the house unless you set fire to it.'

Then there came another trouble. When Miss Gilby first came to our house there was a great flutter, which afterwards calmed down when they got used to her. Now the whole thing was stirred up afresh. I had never bothered myself before as to whether Miss Gilby was European or Indian, but I began to do so now. I said to my husband: 'We must get rid of Miss Gilby.'

He kept silent.

I talked to him wildly, and he went away sad at heart.

After a fit of weeping, I felt in a more reasonable mood when we met at night. 'I cannot,' my husband said, 'look upon Miss Gilby through a mist of abstraction, just because she is English. Cannot you get over the barrier of her name after such a long acquaintance? Cannot you realize that she loves you?'

I felt a little ashamed and replied with some sharpness: 'Let her remain. I am not over anxious to send her away.'

And Miss Gilby remained.

But one day I was told that she had been insulted by a young fellow on her way to church. This was a boy whom we were supporting. My husband turned him out of the house. There was not a single soul, that day, who could forgive my husband for that act – not even I. This time Miss Gilby left of her own accord. She shed tears when she came to say goodbye, but my mood would not melt. To slander the poor boy so – and such a fine boy, too, who would forget his daily bath and food in his enthusiasm for *Swadeshi*.

My husband escorted Miss Gilby to the railway station in his own carriage. I was sure he was going too far. When exaggerated accounts of the incident gave rise to a public scandal, which found its way to the newspapers, I felt he had been rightly served.

I had often become anxious at my husband's doings, but had never before been ashamed; yet now I had to blush for him! I did not know exactly, nor did I care, what wrong poor Noren might, or might not, have done to Miss Gilby, but the idea of sitting in judgement on such a matter at such a time! I should have refused to damp the spirit which prompted young Noren to defy the Englishwoman. I could not but look upon it as a sign of cowardice in my husband, that he should fail to understand this simple thing. And so I blushed for him.

And yet it was not that my husband refused to support *Swadeshi*, or was in any way against the Cause. Only he had not been able whole-heartedly to accept the spirit of *Bande Mataram*.[1]

'I am willing,' he said, 'to serve my country; but my worship I reserve for Right which is far greater than my country. To worship my country as a god is to bring a curse upon it.'

1. Lit.: 'Hail Mother'; the opening words of a song by Bankim Chatterjee, the famous Bengali novelist. The song has now become the national anthem, and *Bande Mataram* the national cry, since the days of the *Swadeshi* movement.

CHAPTER TWO

Bimala's Story

THIS WAS THE time when Sandip Babu with his followers came
to our neighbourhood to preach *Swadeshi*.

There is to be a big meeting in our temple pavilion. We
women are sitting there, on one side, behind a screen. Triumphant shouts of *Bande Mataram* come nearer: and to them I am
thrilling through and through. Suddenly a stream of barefooted
youths in turbans, clad in ascetic ochre, rushes into the quadrangle, like a silt-reddened freshet into a dry river-bed at the first
burst of the rains. The whole place is filled with an immense
crowd, through which Sandip Babu is borne, seated in a big
chair hoisted on the shoulders of ten or twelve of the youths.

Bande Mataram! Bande Mataram! Bande Mataram! It seems as
though the skies would be rent and scattered into a thousand
fragments.

I had seen Sandip Babu's photograph before. There was
something in his features which I did not quite like. Not that
he was bad-looking – far from it: he had a splendidly handsome
face. Yet, I know not why, it seemed to me, in spite of all its
brilliance, that too much of base alloy had gone into its making.
The light in his eyes somehow did not shine true. That was why
I did not like it when my husband unquestioningly gave in to all
his demands. I could bear the waste of money; but it vexed me
to think that he was imposing on my husband, taking advantage
of friendship. His bearing was not that of an ascetic, nor even of a
person of moderate means, but foppish all over. Love of comfort
seemed to . . . any number of such reflections come back to me
today, but let them be.

When, however, Sandip Babu began to speak that afternoon,
and the hearts of the crowd swayed and surged to his words, as
though they would break all bounds, I saw him wonderfully
transformed. Especially when his features were suddenly lit up by
a shaft of light from the slowly setting sun, as it sunk below the
roof-line of the pavilion, he seemed to me to be marked out by
the gods as their messenger to mortal men and women.

From beginning to end of his speech, each one of his utterances was a stormy outburst. There was no limit to the confidence of his assurance. I do not know how it happened, but I found I had impatiently pushed away the screen from before me and had fixed my gaze upon him. Yet there was none in that crowd who paid any heed to my doings. Only once, I noticed, his eyes, like stars in fateful Orion, flashed full on my face.

I was utterly unconscious of myself. I was no longer the lady of the Rajah's house, but the sole representative of Bengal's womanhood. And he was the champion of Bengal. As the sky had shed its light over him, so he must receive the consecration of a woman's benediction . . .

It seemed clear to me that, since he had caught sight of me, the fire in his words had flamed up more fiercely. Indra's[1] steed refused to be reined in, and there came the roar of thunder and the flash of lightning. I said within myself that his language had caught fire from my eyes; for we women are not only the deities of the household fire, but the flame of the soul itself.

I returned home that evening radiant with a new pride and joy. The storm within me had shifted my whole being from one centre to another. Like the Greek maidens of old, I fain would cut off my long, resplendent tresses to make a bowstring for my hero. Had my outward ornaments been connected with my inner feelings, then my necklet, my armlets, my bracelets, would all have burst their bonds and flung themselves over that assembly like a shower of meteors. Only some personal sacrifice, I felt, could help me to bear the tumult of my exaltation.

When my husband came home later, I was trembling lest he should utter a sound out of tune with the triumphant paean which was still ringing in my ears, lest his fanaticism for truth should lead him to express disapproval of anything that had been said that afternoon. For then I should have openly defied and humiliated him. But he did not say a word . . . which I did not like either.

He should have said: 'Sandip has brought me to my senses. I now realize how mistaken I have been all this time.'

I somehow felt that he was spitefully silent, that he obstinately refused to be enthusiastic. I asked how long Sandip Babu was going to be with us.

1. The Jupiter Pluvius of Hindu mythology.

'He is off to Rangpur early tomorrow morning,' said my husband.

'Must it be tomorrow?'

'Yes, he is already engaged to speak there.'

I was silent for a while and then asked again: 'Could he not possibly stay a day longer?'

'That may hardly be possible, but why?'

'I want to invite him to dinner and attend on him myself.'

My husband was surprised. He had often entreated me to be present when he had particular friends to dinner, but I had never let myself be persuaded. He gazed at me curiously, in silence, with a look I did not quite understand.

I was suddenly overcome with a sense of shame. 'No, no,' I exclaimed, 'that would never do!'

'Why not!' said he. 'I will ask him myself, and if it is at all possible he will surely stay on for tomorrow.'

It turned out to be quite possible.

I will tell the exact truth. That day I reproached my Creator because he had not made me surpassingly beautiful – not to steal any heart away, but because beauty is glory. In this great day the men of the country should realize its goddess in its womanhood. But, alas, the eyes of men fail to discern the goddess, if outward beauty be lacking. Would Sandip Babu find the *Shakti* of the Motherland manifest in me? Or would he simply take me to be an ordinary, domestic woman?

That morning I scented my flowing hair and tied it in a loose knot, bound by a cunningly intertwined red silk ribbon. Dinner, you see, was to be served at midday, and there was no time to dry my hair after my bath and do it up plaited in the ordinary way. I put on a gold-bordered white *sari*, and my short-sleeve muslin jacket was also gold-bordered.

I felt that there was a certain restraint about my costume and that nothing could well have been simpler. But my sister-in-law, who happened to be passing by, stopped dead before me, surveyed me from head to foot and with compressed lips smiled a meaning smile. When I asked her the reason, 'I am admiring your get-up!' she said.

'What is there so entertaining about it?' I enquired, consider-ably annoyed.

'It's superb,' she said. 'I was only thinking that one of those low-necked English bodices would have made it perfect.' Not only her mouth and eyes, but her whole body seemed to ripple with suppressed laughter as she left the room.

I was very, very angry, and wanted to change everything and put on my everyday clothes. But I cannot tell exactly why I could not carry out my impulse. Women are the ornaments of society – thus I reasoned with myself – and my husband would never like it, if I appeared before Sandip Babu unworthily clad.

My idea had been to make my appearance after they had sat down to dinner. In the bustle of looking after the serving the first awkwardness would have passed off. But dinner was not ready in time, and it was getting late. Meanwhile my husband had sent for me to introduce the guest.

I was feeling horribly shy about looking Sandip Babu in the face. However, I managed to recover myself enough to say: 'I am so sorry dinner is getting late.'

He boldly came and sat right beside me as he replied: 'I get a dinner of some kind every day, but the Goddess of Plenty keeps behind the scenes. Now that the goddess herself has appeared, it matters little if the dinner lags behind.'

He was just as emphatic in his manners as he was in his public speaking. He had no hesitation and seemed to be accustomed to occupy, unchallenged, his chosen seat. He claimed the right to intimacy so confidently, that the blame would seem to belong to those who should dispute it.

I was in terror lest Sandip Babu should take me for a shrinking, old-fashioned bundle of inanity. But, for the life of me, I could not sparkle in repartees such as might charm or dazzle him. What could have possessed me, I angrily wondered, to appear before him in such an absurd way?

I was about to retire when dinner was over, but Sandip Babu, as bold as ever, placed himself in my way.

'You must not,' he said, 'think me greedy. It was not the dinner that kept me staying on, it was your invitation. If you were to run away now, that would not be playing fair with your guest.'

If he had not said these words with a careless ease, they would have been out of tune. But, after all, he was such a great friend of my husband that I was like his sister.

While I was struggling to climb up this high wave of intimacy, my husband came to the rescue, saying: 'Why not come back to us after you have taken your dinner?'

'But you must give your word,' said Sandip Babu, 'before we let you off.'

'I will come,' said I, with a slight smile.

'Let me tell you,' continued Sandip Babu, 'why I cannot trust you. Nikhil has been married these nine years, and all this while you have eluded me. If you do this again for another nine years, we shall never meet again.'

I took up the spirit of his remark as I dropped my voice to reply: 'Why even then should we not meet?'

'My horoscope tells me I am to die early. None of my fore-fathers have survived their thirtieth year. I am now twenty-seven.'

He knew this would go home. This time there must have been a shade of concern in my low voice as I said: 'The blessings of the whole country are sure to avert the evil influence of the stars.'

'Then the blessings of the country must be voiced by its god-dess. This is the reason for my anxiety that you should return, so that my talisman may begin to work from today.'

Sandip Babu had such a way of taking things by storm that I got no opportunity of resenting what I never should have per-mitted in another.

'So,' he concluded with a laugh, 'I am going to hold this husband of yours as a hostage till you come back.'

As I was coming away, he exclaimed: 'May I trouble you for a trifle?'

I started and turned round.

'Don't be alarmed,' he said. 'It's merely a glass of water. You might have noticed that I did not drink any water with my dinner. I take it a little later.'

Upon this I had to make a show of interest and ask him the reason. He began to give the history of his dyspepsia. I was told how he had been a martyr to it for seven months, and how, after the usual course of nuisances, which included different al-lopathic and homoeopathic misadventures, he had obtained the most wonderful results by indigenous methods.

'Do you know,' he added, with a smile, 'God has built even my infirmities in such a manner that they yield only under the bombardment of *Swadeshi* pills.'

My husband, at this, broke his silence. 'You must confess,' said he, 'that you have as immense an attraction for foreign medicine as the earth has for meteors. You have three shelves in your sitting-room full of . . .'

Sandip Babu broke in: 'Do you know what they are? They are the punitive police. They come, not because they are wanted, but because they are imposed on us by the rule of this modern age, exacting fines and inflicting injuries.'

My husband could not bear exaggerations, and I could see he disliked this. But all ornaments are exaggerations. They are not made by God, but by man. Once I remember in defence of some untruth of mine I said to my husband: 'Only the trees and beasts and birds tell unmitigated truths, because these poor things have not the power to invent. In this men show their superiority to the lower creatures, and women beat even men. Neither is a profusion of ornament unbecoming for a woman, nor a profusion of untruth.'

As I came out into the passage leading to the zenana I found my sister-in-law, standing near a window overlooking the reception rooms, peeping through the venetian shutter.

'You here?' I asked in surprise.

'Eavesdropping!' she replied.

V

WHEN I RETURNED, Sandip Babu was tenderly apologetic. 'I am afraid we have spoilt your appetite,' he said.

I felt greatly ashamed. Indeed, I had been too indecently quick over my dinner. With a little calculation, it would become quite evident that my non-eating had surpassed the eating. But I had no idea that anyone could have been deliberately calculating.

I suppose Sandip Babu detected my feeling of shame, which only augmented it. 'I was sure,' he said, 'that you had the impulse of the wild deer to run away, but it is a great boon that you took the trouble to keep your promise with me.'

I could not think of any suitable reply and so I sat down, blushing and uncomfortable, at one end of the sofa. The vision that I had of myself, as the *Shakti* of Womanhood, incarnate, crowning Sandip Babu simply with my presence, majestic and unashamed, failed me altogether.

Sandip Babu deliberately started a discussion with my husband. He knew that his keen wit flashed to the best effect in an argument. I have often since observed, that he never lost an opportunity for a passage at arms whenever I happened to be present.

He was familiar with my husband's views on the cult of *Bande Mataram*, and began in a provoking way: 'So you do not allow that there is room for an appeal to the imagination in patriotic work?'

'It has its place, Sandip, I admit, but I do not believe in giving it the whole place. I would know my country in its frank reality, and for this I am both afraid and ashamed to make use of hypnotic texts of patriotism.'

'What you call hypnotic texts I call truth. I truly believe my country to be my God. I worship Humanity. God manifests Himself both in man and in his country.'

'If that is what you really believe, there should be no difference for you between man and man, and so between country and country.'

'Quite true. But my powers are limited, so my worship of Humanity is continued in the worship of my country.'

'I have nothing against your worship as such, but how is it you propose to conduct your worship of God by hating other countries in which He is equally manifest?'

'Hate is also an adjunct of worship. Arjuna won Mahadeva's favour by wrestling with him. God will be with us in the end, if we are prepared to give Him battle.'

'If that be so, then those who are serving and those who are harming the country are both His devotees. Why, then, trouble to preach patriotism?'

'In the case of one's own country, it is different. There the heart clearly demands worship.'

'If you push the same argument further you can say that since God is manifested in us, our *self* has to be worshipped before all else; because our natural instinct claims it.'

'Look here, Nikhil, this is all merely dry logic. Can't you recognize that there is such a thing as feeling?'

'I tell you the truth, Sandip,' my husband replied. 'It is my feelings that are outraged, whenever you try to pass off injustice as a duty, and unrighteousness as a moral ideal. The fact, that I am incapable of stealing, is not due to my possessing logical faculties, but to my having some feeling of respect for myself and love for ideals.'

I was raging inwardly. At last I could keep silent no longer.

'Is not the history of every country,' I cried, 'whether England, France, Germany, or Russia, the history of stealing for the sake of one's own country?'

'They have to answer for these thefts; they are doing so even now; their history is not yet ended.'

'At any rate,' interposed Sandip Babu, 'why should we not follow suit? Let us first fill our country's coffers with stolen goods and then take centuries, like these other countries, to answer for them, if we must. But, I ask you, where do you find this "answering" in history?'

'When Rome was answering for her sin no one knew it. All that time, there was apparently no limit to her prosperity. But do you not see one thing: how these political bags of theirs are bursting with lies and treacheries, breaking their backs under their weight?'

Never before had I had any opportunity of being present at a discussion between my husband and his men friends. Whenever he argued with me I could feel his reluctance to push me into a corner. This arose out of the very love he bore me. Today for the first time I saw his fencer's skill in debate.

Nevertheless, my heart refused to accept my husband's position. I was struggling to find some answer, but it would not come. When the word 'righteousness' comes into an argument, it sounds ugly to say that a thing can be too good to be useful.

All of a sudden Sandip Babu turned to me with the question: 'What do *you* say to this?'

'I do not care about fine distinctions,' I broke out. 'I will tell you broadly what I feel. I am only human. I am covetous, I would have good things for my country. If I am obliged, I would snatch them and filch them. I have anger. I would be angry for my country's sake. If necessary, I would smite and slay to avenge her insults. I have my desire to be fascinated, and fascination must be supplied to me in bodily shape by my country. She must have some visible symbol casting its spell upon my mind. I would make my country a Person, and call her Mother, Goddess, Durga – for whom I would redden the earth with sacrificial offerings. I am human, not divine.'

Sandip Babu leapt to his feet with uplifted arms and shouted 'Hurrah!' – The next moment he corrected himself and cried: '*Bande Mataram.*'

A shadow of pain passed over the face of my husband. He said to me in a very gentle voice: 'Neither am I divine: I am human. And therefore I dare not permit the evil which is in me to be exaggerated into an image of my country – never, never!'

Sandip Babu cried out: 'See, Nikhil, how in the heart of a woman Truth takes flesh and blood. Woman knows how to be cruel: her virulence is like a blind storm. It is beautifully fearful. In man it is ugly, because it harbours in its centre the gnawing worms of reason and thought. I tell you, Nikhil, it is our women who will save the country. This is not the time for nice scruples. We must be unswervingly, unreasoningly brutal. We must sin. We must give our women red sandal paste with which to anoint and enthrone our sin. Don't you remember what the poet says:

> Come, Sin, O beautiful Sin,
> Let thy stinging red kisses pour down fiery red wine into our
>   blood.
> Sound the trumpet of imperious evil
> And cross our forehead with the wreath of exulting lawlessness,
> O Deity of Desecration,
> Smear our breasts with the blackest mud of disrepute,
>   unashamed.

Down with that righteousness, which cannot smilingly bring rack and ruin.'

When Sandip Babu, standing with his head high, insulted at a moment's impulse all that men have cherished as their highest, in all countries and in all times, a shiver went right through my body.

But, with a stamp of his foot, he continued his declamation: 'I can see that you are that beautiful spirit of fire, which burns the home to ashes and lights up the larger world with its flame. Give to us the indomitable courage to go to the bottom of Ruin itself. Impart grace to all that is baneful.'

It was not clear to whom Sandip Babu addressed his last appeal. It might have been She whom he worshipped with his *Bande Mataram*. It might have been the Womanhood of his country. Or it might have been its representative, the woman before him. He would have gone further in the same strain, but my husband suddenly rose from his seat and touched him lightly on the shoulder saying: 'Sandip, Chandranath Babu is here.'

I started and turned round, to find an aged gentleman at the door, calm and dignified, in doubt as to whether he should come in or retire. His face was touched with a gentle light like that of the setting sun.

My husband came up to me and whispered: 'This is my master, of whom I have so often told you. Make your obeisance to him.'

I bent reverently and took the dust of his feet. He gave me his blessing saying: 'May God protect you always, my little mother.'

I was sorely in need of such a blessing at that moment.

Nikhil's Story

I

ONE DAY I had the faith to believe that I should be able to bear whatever came from my God. I never had the trial. Now I think it has come.

I used to test my strength of mind by imagining all kinds of evil which might happen to me – poverty, imprisonment, dishonour, death – even Bimala's. And when I said to myself that I should be able to receive these with firmness, I am sure I did not exaggerate. Only I could never even imagine one thing, and today it is that of which I am thinking, and wondering whether I can really bear it. There is a thorn somewhere pricking in my heart, constantly giving me pain while I am about my daily work. It seems to persist even when I am asleep. The very moment I wake up in the morning, I find that the bloom has gone from the face of the sky. What is it? What has happened?

My mind has become so sensitive, that even my past life, which came to me in the disguise of happiness, seems to wring my very heart with its falsehood; and the shame and sorrow which are coming close to me are losing their cover of privacy, all the more because they try to veil their faces. My heart has become all eyes. The things that should not be seen, the things I do not want to see – these I must see.

The day has come at last when my ill-starred life has to reveal its destitution in a long-drawn series of exposures. This penury, all unexpected, has taken its seat in the heart where plenitude seemed to reign. The fees which I paid to delusion for just nine years of my youth have now to be returned with interest to Truth till the end of my days.

What is the use of straining to keep up my pride? What harm if I confess that I have something lacking in me? Possibly it is that unreasoning forcefulness which women love to find in men. But is strength a mere display of muscularity? Must strength have no scruples in treading the weak underfoot?

But why all these arguments? Worthiness cannot be earned merely by disputing about it. And I am unworthy, unworthy, unworthy.

What if I *am* unworthy? The true value of love is this, that it can ever bless the unworthy with its own prodigality. For the worthy there are many rewards on God's earth, but God has specially reserved love for the unworthy.

Up till now Bimala was my home-made Bimala, the product of the confined space and the daily routine of small duties. Did the love which I received from her, I asked myself, come from the deep spring of her heart, or was it merely like the daily provision of pipe water pumped up by the municipal steam-engine of society?

I longed to find Bimala blossoming fully in all her truth and power. But the thing I forgot to calculate was, that one must give up all claims based on conventional rights, if one would find a person freely revealed in truth.

Why did I fail to think of this? Was it because of the husband's pride of possession over his wife? No. It was because I placed the fullest trust upon love. I was vain enough to think that I had the power in me to bear the sight of truth in its awful nakedness. It was tempting Providence, but still I clung to my proud determination to come out victorious in the trial.

Bimala had failed to understand me in one thing. She could not fully realize that I held as weakness all imposition of force. Only the weak dare not be just. They shirk their responsibility of fairness and try quickly to get at results through the short-cuts of injustice. Bimala has no patience with patience. She loves to find in men the turbulent, the angry, the unjust. Her respect must have its element of fear.

I had hoped that when Bimala found herself free in the outer world she would be rescued from her infatuation for tyranny. But now I feel sure that this infatuation is deep down in her nature. Her love is for the boisterous. From the tip of her tongue to the pit of her stomach she must tingle with red pepper in order to enjoy the simple fare of life. But my determination was, never to do my duty with frantic impetuosity, helped on by the fiery liquor of excitement. I know Bimala finds it difficult to respect me for this, taking my scruples for feebleness – and she is quite angry with me because I am not running amuck crying *Bande Mataram*.

For the matter of that, I have become unpopular with all my countrymen because I have not joined them in their carousals. They are certain that either I have a longing for some title, or else that I am afraid of the police. The police on their side suspect me of harbouring some hidden design and protesting too much in my mildness.

What I really feel is this, that those who cannot find food for their enthusiasm in a knowledge of their country as it actually is, or those who cannot love men just because they are men – who needs must shout and deify their country in order to keep up their excitement – these love excitement more than their country.

To try to give our infatuation a higher place than Truth is a sign of inherent slavishness. Where our minds are free we find ourselves lost. Our moribund vitality must have for its rider either some fantasy, or someone in authority, or a sanction from the pundits, in order to make it move. So long as we are impervious to truth and have to be moved by some hypnotic stimulus, we must know that we lack the capacity for self-government. Whatever may be our condition, we shall either need some imaginary ghost or some actual medicine-man to terrorize over us.

The other day when Sandip accused me of lack of imagination, saying that this prevented me from realizing my country in a visible image, Bimala agreed with him. I did not say anything in my defence, because to win in argument does not lead to happiness. Her difference of opinion is not due to any inequality of intelligence, but rather to dissimilarity of nature.

They accuse me of being unimaginative – that is, according to them, I may have oil in my lamp, but no flame. Now this is exactly the accusation which I bring against them. I would say to them: 'You are dark, even as the flints are. You must come to violent conflicts and make a noise in order to produce your sparks. But their disconnected flashes merely assist your pride, and not your clear vision.'

I have been noticing for some time that there is a gross cupidity about Sandip. His fleshly feelings make him harbour delusions about his religion and impel him into a tyrannical attitude in his patriotism. His intellect is keen, but his nature is coarse, and so he glorifies his selfish lusts under high-sounding names. The cheap consolations of hatred are as urgently necessary for him as the satisfaction of his appetites. Bimala has often warned me, in the old days, of his hankering after money. I understood this, but I could not bring myself to haggle with Sandip. I felt ashamed even to own to myself that he was trying to take advantage of me.

It will, however, be difficult to explain to Bimala today that Sandip's love of country is but a different phase of his covetous self-love. Bimala's hero-worship of Sandip makes me hesitate all the more to talk to her about him, lest some touch of jealousy may lead me unwittingly into exaggeration. It may be that the pain at my heart is already making me see a distorted picture of Sandip. And yet it is better perhaps to speak out than to keep my feelings gnawing within me.

II

I HAVE KNOWN my master these thirty years. Neither calumny, nor disaster, nor death itself has any terrors for him. Nothing could have saved me, born as I was into the traditions of this family of ours, but that he has established his own life in the centre of mine, with its peace and truth and spiritual vision, thus making it possible for me to realize goodness in its truth.

My master came to me that day and said: 'Is it necessary to detain Sandip here any longer?'

His nature was so sensitive to all omens of evil that he had at once understood. He was not easily moved, but that day he felt the dark shadow of trouble ahead. Do I not know how well he loves me?

At tea-time I said to Sandip: 'I have just had a letter from Rangpur. They are complaining that I am selfishly detaining you. When will you be going there?'

Bimala was pouring out the tea. Her face fell at once. She threw just one enquiring glance at Sandip.

'I have been thinking,' said Sandip, 'that this wandering up and down means a tremendous waste of energy. I feel that if I could work from a centre I could achieve more permanent results.'

With this he looked up at Bimala and asked: 'Do you not think so too?'

Bimala hesitated for a reply and then said: 'Both ways seem

good – to do the work from a centre, as well as by travelling about. That in which you find greater satisfaction is the way for you.'

'Then let me speak out my mind,' said Sandip. 'I have never yet found any one source of inspiration suffice me for good. That is why I have been constantly moving about, rousing enthusiasm in the people, from which in turn I draw my own store of energy. Today you have given me the message of my country. Such fire I have never beheld in any man. I shall be able to spread the fire of enthusiasm in my country by borrowing it from you. No, do not be ashamed. You are far above all modesty and diffidence. You are the Queen Bee of our hive, and we the workers shall rally around you. You shall be our centre, our inspiration.'

Bimala flushed all over with bashful pride and her hand shook as she went on pouring out the tea.

Another day my master came to me and said: 'Why don't you two go up to Darjeeling for a change? You are not looking well. Have you been getting enough sleep?'

I asked Bimala in the evening whether she would care to have a trip to the Hills. I knew she had a great longing to see the Himalayas. But she refused . . . The country's Cause, I suppose!

I must not lose my faith: I shall wait. The passage from the narrow to the larger world is stormy. When she is familiar with this freedom, then I shall know where my place is. If I discover that I do not fit in with the arrangement of the outer world, then I shall not quarrel with my fate, but silently take my leave . . . Use force? But for what? Can force prevail against Truth?

Sandip's Story

I

THE IMPOTENT MAN says: 'That which has come to my share is mine.' And the weak man assents. But the lesson of the whole world is: 'That is really mine which I can snatch away.' My country does not become mine simply because it is the country of my birth. It becomes mine on the day when I am able to win it by force.

Every man has a natural right to possess, and therefore greed is natural. It is not in the wisdom of nature that we should be content to be deprived. What my mind covets, my surroundings must supply. This is the only true understanding between our inner and outer nature in this world. Let moral ideals remain merely for those poor anaemic creatures of starved desire whose grasp is weak. Those who can desire with all their soul and enjoy with all their heart, those who have no hesitation or scruple, it is they who are the anointed of Providence. Nature spreads out her riches and loveliest treasures for their benefit. They swim across streams, leap over walls, kick open doors, to help themselves to whatever is worth taking. In such a getting one can rejoice; such wresting as this gives value to the thing taken.

Nature surrenders herself, but only to the robber. For she delights in this forceful desire, this forceful abduction. And so she does not put the garland of her acceptance round the lean, scraggy neck of the ascetic. The music of the wedding march is struck. The time of the wedding I must not let pass. My heart therefore is eager. For, who is the bridegroom? It is I. The bridegroom's place belongs to him who, torch in hand, can come in time. The bridegroom in Nature's wedding hall comes unexpected and uninvited.

Ashamed? No, I am never ashamed! I ask for whatever I want, and I do not always wait to ask before I take it. Those who are deprived by their own diffidence dignify their privation by the name of modesty. The world into which we are born is the world of reality. When a man goes away from the market of real things with empty hands and empty stomach, merely filling his bag with big sounding words, I wonder why he ever came into this hard world at all. Did these men get their appointment from the epicures of the religious world, to play set tunes on sweet, pious texts in that pleasure garden where blossom airy nothings? I neither affect those tunes nor do I find any sustenance in those blossoms.

What I desire, I desire positively, superlatively. I want to knead it with both my hands and both my feet; I want to smear it all over my body; I want to gorge myself with it to the full. The scrannel pipes of those who have worn themselves out by their moral fastings, till they have become flat and pale like starved vermin infesting a long-deserted bed, will never reach my ear.

I would conceal nothing, because that would be cowardly. But if I cannot bring myself to conceal when concealment is needful, that also is cowardly. Because you have your greed, you build your walls. Because I have my greed, I break through them. You use your power: I use my craft. These are the realities of life. On these depend kingdoms and empires and all the great enterprises of men.

As for those *avatars* who come down from their paradise to talk to us in some holy jargon – their words are not real. Therefore, in spite of all the applause they get, these sayings of theirs only find a place in the hiding corners of the weak. They are despised by those who are strong, the rulers of the world. Those who have had the courage to see this have won success, while those poor wretches who are dragged one way by nature and the other way by these *avatars*, they set one foot in the boat of the real and the other in the boat of the unreal, and thus are in a pitiable plight, able neither to advance nor to keep their place.

There are many men who seem to have been born only with an obsession to die. Possibly there is a beauty, like that of a sunset, in this lingering death in life which seems to fascinate them. Nikhil lives this kind of life, if life it may be called. Years ago, I had a great argument with him on this point.

'It is true,' he said, 'that you cannot get anything except by force. But then what *is* this force? And then also, what *is* this getting? The strength I believe in is the strength of renouncing.'

'So you,' I exclaimed, 'are infatuated with the glory of bankruptcy.'

'Just as desperately as the chick is infatuated about the bankruptcy of its shell,' he replied. 'The shell is real enough, yet it is given up in exchange for intangible light and air. A sorry exchange, I suppose you would call it?

When once Nikhil gets on to metaphor, there is no hope of making him see that he is merely dealing with words, not with realities. Well, well, let him be happy with his metaphors. We are the flesh-eaters of the world; we have teeth and nails; we pursue and grab and tear. We are not satisfied with chewing in the evening the cud of the grass we have eaten in the morning. Anyhow, we cannot allow your metaphor-mongers to bar the door to our sustenance. In that case we shall simply steal or rob, for we must live.

People will say that I am starting some novel theory just because those who are moving in this world are in the habit of talking differently though they are really acting up to it all the time. Therefore they fail to understand, as I do, that this is the only working moral principle. In point of fact, I know that my idea is not an empty theory at all, for it has been proved in practical life.

I have found that my way always wins over the hearts of women, who are creatures of this world of reality and do not roam about in cloud-land, as men do, in idea-filled balloons.

Women find in my features, my manner, my gait, my speech, a masterful passion – not a passion dried thin with the heat of asceticism, not a passion with its face turned back at every step in doubt and debate, but a full-blooded passion. It roars and rolls on, like a flood, with the cry: '*I want, I want, I want.*' Women feel, in their own heart of hearts, that this indomitable passion is the lifeblood of the world, acknowledging no law but itself, and therefore victorious. For this reason they have so often abandoned themselves to be swept away on the flood-tide of my passion, recking naught as to whether it takes them to life or to death. This power which wins these women is the power of mighty men, the power which wins the world of reality.

Those who imagine the greater desirability of another world merely shift their desires from the earth to the skies. It remains to be seen how high their gushing fountain will play, and for how long. But this much is certain: women were not created for these pale creatures – these lotus-eaters of idealism.

'Affinity!' When it suited my need, I have often said that God has created special pairs of men and women, and that the union of such is the only legitimate union, higher than all unions made by law. The reason of it is, that though man wants to follow nature, he can find no pleasure in it unless he screens himself with some phrase – and that is why this world is so overflowing with lies.

'Affinity!' Why should there be only *one*? There may be affinity with thousands. It was never in my agreement with nature that I should overlook all my innumerable affinities for the sake of only one. I have discovered many in my own life up to now, yet that has not closed the door to one more – and that one is clearly visible to my eyes. She has also discovered her own affinity to me.

And then?

Then, if I do not win I am a coward.

CHAPTER THREE

Bimala's Story

VI

I WONDER WHAT could have happened to my feeling of shame. The fact is, I had no time to think about myself. My days and nights were passing in a whirl, like an eddy with myself in the centre. No gap was left for hesitation or delicacy to enter.

One day my sister-in-law remarked to my husband: 'Up to now the women of this house have been kept weeping. Here comes the men's turn.

'We must see that they do not miss it,' she continued, turning to me. 'I see you are out for the fray, Chota¹ Rani! Hurl your shafts straight at their hearts.'

Her keen eyes looked me up and down. Not one of the colours into which my toilet, my dress, my manners, my speech, had blossomed out had escaped her. I am ashamed to speak of it today, but I felt no shame then. Something within me was at work of which I was not even conscious. I used to overdress, it is true, but more like an automaton, with no particular design. No doubt I knew which effort of mine would prove specially pleasing to Sandip Babu, but that required no intuition, for he would discuss it openly before all of them.

One day he said to my husband: 'Do you know, Nikhil, when I first saw our Queen Bee, she was sitting there so demurely in her gold-bordered *sari*. Her eyes were gazing inquiringly into space, like stars which had lost their way, just as if she had been for ages standing on the edge of some darkness, looking out for something unknown. But when I saw her, I felt a quiver run through me. It seemed to me that the gold border of her *sari* was her own inner fire flaming out and twining round her. That is the flame we want, visible fire! Look here, Queen Bee, you really must do us the favour of dressing once more as a living flame.'

So long I had been like a small river at the border of a village. My rhythm and my language were different from what they are now. But the tide came up from the sea, and my breast

---

1. Bimala, the younger brother's wife, was the *Chota* or Junior Rani.

heaved; my banks gave way and the great drumbeats of the sea waves echoed in my mad current. I could not understand the meaning of that sound in my blood. Where was that former self of mine? Whence came foaming into me this surging flood of glory? Sandip's hungry eyes burnt like the lamps of worship before my shrine. All his gaze proclaimed that I was a wonder in beauty and power; and the loudness of his praise, spoken and unspoken, drowned all other voices in my world. Had the Creator created me afresh, I wondered? Did he wish to make up now for neglecting me so long? I who before was plain had become suddenly beautiful. I who before had been of no account now felt in myself all the splendour of Bengal itself.

For Sandip Babu was not a mere individual. In him was the confluence of millions of minds of the country. When he called me the Queen Bee of the hive, I was acclaimed with a chorus of praise by all our patriot workers. After that, the loud jests of my sister-in-law could not touch me any longer. My relations with all the world underwent a change. Sandip Babu made it clear how all the country was in need of me. I had no difficulty in believing this at the time, for I felt that I had the power to do everything. Divine strength had come to me. It was something which I had never felt before, which was beyond myself. I had no time to question it to find out what was its nature. It seemed to belong to me, and yet to transcend me. It comprehended the whole of Bengal.

Sandip Babu would consult me about every little thing touching the Cause. At first I felt very awkward and would hang back, but that soon wore off. Whatever I suggested seemed to astonish him. He would go into raptures and say: 'Men can only think. You women have a way of understanding without thinking. Woman was created out of God's own fancy. Man, He had to hammer into shape.'

Letters used to come to Sandip Babu from all parts of the country which were submitted to me for my opinion. Occasionally he disagreed with me. But I would not argue with him. Then after a day or two – as if a new light had suddenly dawned upon him – he would send for me and say: 'It was my mistake. Your suggestion was the correct one.' He would often confess to me that wherever he had taken steps contrary to my advice he had gone wrong. Thus I gradually came to be convinced that behind whatever was taking place was Sandip Babu, and behind

Sandip Babu was the plain common sense of a woman. The glory of a great responsibility filled my being.

My husband had no place in our counsels. Sandip Babu treated him as a younger brother, of whom personally one may be very fond and yet have no use for his business advice. He would tenderly and smilingly talk about my husband's childlike innocence, saying that his curious doctrine and perversities of mind had a flavour of humour which made them all the more lovable. It was seemingly this very affection for Nikhil which led Sandip Babu to forbear from troubling him with the burden of the country.

Nature has many anodynes in her pharmacy, which she secretly administers when vital relations are being insidiously severed, so that none may know of the operation, till at last one awakes to know what a great rent has been made. When the knife was busy with my life's most intimate tie, my mind was so clouded with fumes of intoxicating gas that I was not in the least aware of what a cruel thing was happening. Possibly this is woman's nature. When her passion is roused she loses her sensibility for all that is outside it. When, like the river, we women keep to our banks, we give nourishment with all that we have: when we overflow them we destroy with all that we are.

Sandip's Story

II

I CAN SEE that something has gone wrong. I got an inkling of it the other day.

Ever since my arrival, Nikhil's sitting-room had become a thing amphibious – half women's apartment, half men's: Bimala had access to it from the zenana, it was not barred to me from the outer side. If we had only gone slow, and made use of our privileges with some restraint, we might not have fallen foul of other people. But we went ahead so vehemently that we could not think of the consequences.

Whenever Bee comes into Nikhil's room, I somehow get to know of it from mine. There are the tinkle of bangles and other little sounds; the door is perhaps shut with a shade of unnecessary vehemence; the bookcase is a trifle stiff and creaks if jerked open. When I enter I find Bee, with her back to the door, ever so busy selecting a book from the shelves. And as I offer to assist her in this difficult task she starts and protests; and then we naturally get on to other topics.

The other day, on an inauspicious[1] Thursday afternoon, I sallied forth from my room at the call of these same sounds. There was a man on guard in the passage. I walked on without so much as glancing at him, but as I approached the door he put himself in my way saying: 'Not that way, sir.'

'Not that way! Why?'

'The Rani Mother is there.'

'Oh, very well. Tell your Rani Mother that Sandip Babu wants to see her.'

'That cannot be, sir. It is against orders.'

I felt highly indignant. 'I order you!' I said in a raised voice. 'Go and announce me.'

The fellow was somewhat taken aback at my attitude. In the meantime I had neared the door. I was on the point of reaching it, when he followed after me and took me by the arm saying: 'No, sir, you must not.'

What! To be touched by a flunkey! I snatched away my arm and gave the man a sounding blow. At this moment Bee came out of the room to find the man about to insult me.

I shall never forget the picture of her wrath! That Bee is beautiful is a discovery of my own. Most of our people would see nothing in her. Her tall, slim figure these boors would call 'lanky'. But it is just this lithesomeness of hers that I admire – like an up-leaping fountain of life, coming direct out of the depths of the Creator's heart. Her complexion is dark, but it is the lustrous darkness of a sword-blade, keen and scintillating.

'Nanku!' she commanded, as she stood in the doorway, pointing with her finger, 'leave us.'

'Do not be angry with him,' said I. 'If it is against orders, it is I who should retire.'

Bee's voice was still trembling as she replied: 'You must not go. Come in.'

It was not a request, but again a command! I followed her in, and taking a chair fanned myself with a fan which was on the table. Bee scribbled something with a pencil on a sheet of paper and, summoning a servant, handed it to him saying: 'Take this to the Maharaja.'

---

1. According to the Hindu calendar.

'Forgive me,' I resumed. 'I was unable to control myself, and hit that man of yours.'

'You served him right,' said Bee.

'But it was not the poor fellow's fault, after all. He was only obeying his orders.'

Here Nikhil came in, and as he did so I left my seat with a rapid movement and went and stood near the window with my back to the room.

'Nanku, the guard, has insulted Sandip Babu,' said Bee to Nikhil.

Nikhil seemed to be so genuinely surprised that I had to turn round and stare at him. Even an outrageously good man fails in keeping up his pride of truthfulness before his wife – if she be the proper kind of woman.

'He insolently stood in the way when Sandip Babu was coming in here,' continued Bee. 'He said he had orders . . .'

'Whose orders?' asked Nikhil.

'How am I to know?' exclaimed Bee impatiently, her eyes brimming over with mortification.

Nikhil sent for the man and questioned him. 'It was not my fault,' Nanku repeated sullenly. 'I had my orders.'

'Who gave you the order?'

'The Bara Rani Mother.'

We were all silent for a while. After the man had left, Bee said: 'Nanku must go!'

Nikhil remained silent. I could see that his sense of justice would not allow this. There was no end to his qualms. But this time he was up against a tough problem. Bee was not the woman to take things lying down. She would have to get even with her sister-in-law by punishing this fellow. And as Nikhil remained silent, her eyes flashed fire. She knew not how to pour her scorn upon her husband's feebleness of spirit. Nikhil left the room after a while without another word.

The next day Nanku was not to be seen. On inquiry, I learnt that he had been sent off to some other part of the estates, and that his wages had not suffered by such transfer.

I could catch glimpses of the ravages of the storm raging over this, behind the scenes. All I can say is, that Nikhil is a curious creature, quite out of the common.

The upshot was, that after this Bee began to send for me to the sitting-room, for a chat, without any contrivance, or pretence of its being an accident. Thus from bare suggestion we came to broad hint: the implied came to be expressed. The daughter-in-law of a princely house lives in a starry region so remote from the ordinary outsider that there is not even a regular road for his approach. What a triumphal progress of Truth was this which, gradually but persistently, thrust aside veil after veil of obscuring custom, till at length Nature herself was laid bare.

Truth? Of course it was the truth! The attraction of man and woman for each other is fundamental. The whole world of matter, from the speck of dust upwards, is ranged on its side. And yet men would keep it hidden away out of sight, behind a tissue of words; and with home-made sanctions and pro-hibitions make of it a domestic utensil. Why, it's as absurd as melting down the solar system to make a watch-chain for one's son-in-law![1]

When, in spite of all, reality awakes at the call of what is but naked truth, what a gnashing of teeth and beating of breasts is there! But can one carry on a quarrel with a storm? It never takes the trouble to reply, it only gives a shaking.

I am enjoying the sight of this truth, as it gradually reveals itself. These tremblings of steps, these turnings of the face, are sweet to me: and sweet are the deceptions which deceive not only others, but also Bee herself. When Reality has to meet the unreal, deception is its principal weapon; for its enemies always try to shame Reality by calling it gross, and so it needs must hide itself, or else put on some disguise. The circumstances are such that it dare not frankly avow: 'Yes, I am gross, because I am true. I am flesh. I am passion. I am hunger, unashamed and cruel.'

All is now clear to me. The curtain flaps, and through it I can see the preparations for the catastrophe. The little red ribbon, which peeps through the luxuriant masses of her hair, with its flush of secret longing, it is the lolling tongue of the red storm cloud. I feel the warmth of each turn of her *sari*, each sugges-tion of her raiment, of which even the wearer may not be fully conscious.

Bee was not conscious, because she was ashamed of the real-ity; to which men have given a bad name, calling it Satan; and so it has to steal into the garden of paradise in the guise of a snake, and whisper secrets into the ears of man's chosen consort

1. The son-in-law is the pet of a Hindu household.

and make her rebellious; then farewell to all ease; and after that comes death!

My poor little Queen Bee is living in a dream. She knows not which way she is treading. It would not be safe to awaken her before the time. It is best for me to pretend to be equally unconscious.

The other day, at dinner, she was gazing at me in a curious sort of way, little realizing what such glances mean! As my eyes met hers, she turned away with a flush. 'You are surprised at my appetite,' I remarked. 'I can hide everything, except that I am greedy! Anyhow, why trouble to blush for me, since I am shameless?'

This only made her colour more furiously, as she stammered: 'No, no, I was only . . .'

'I know,' I interrupted. 'Women have a weakness for greedy men; for it is this greed of ours which gives them the upper hand. The indulgence which I have always received at their hands has made me all the more shameless. I do not mind your watching the good things disappear, not one bit. I mean to enjoy every one of them.'

The other day I was reading an English book in which sex-problems were treated in an audaciously realistic manner. I had left it lying in the sitting-room. As I went there the next after-noon, for something or other, I found Bee seated with this book in her hand. When she heard my footsteps she hurriedly put it down and placed another book over it – a volume of Mrs Hemans's poems.

'I have never been able to make out,' I began, 'why women are so shy about being caught reading poetry. We men – lawyers, mechanics, or what not – may well feel ashamed. If we must read poetry, it should be at dead of night, within closed doors. But you women are so akin to poesy. The Creator Himself is a lyric poet, and Jayadeva[1] must have practised the divine art seated at His feet.'

Bee made no reply, but only blushed uncomfortably. She made as if she would leave the room. Whereupon I protested: 'No, no, pray read on. I will just take a book I left here, and run away.' With which I took up my book from the table. 'Lucky

---

1. A Vaishnava poet (Sanskrit) whose lyrics of the adoration of the Divinity serve as well to express all shades of human passion.

you did not think of glancing over its pages,' I continued, 'or you would have wanted to chastise me.'

'Indeed! Why?' asked Bee.

'Because it is not poetey,' said I. 'Only blunt things, bluntly put, without any finicking niceness. I wish Nikhil would read it.'

Bee frowned a little as she murmured: 'What makes you wish that?'

'He is a man, you see, one of us. My only quarrel with him is that he delights in a misty vision of this world. Have you not observed how this trait of his makes him look on *Swadeshi* as if it was some poem of which the metre must be kept correct at every step? We, with the clubs of our prose, are the iconoclasts of metre.'

'What has your book to do with *Swadeshi*?'

'You would know if you only read it. Nikhil wants to go by made-up maxims, in *Swadeshi* as in everything else; so he knocks up against human nature at every turn, and then falls to abusing it. He never will realize that human nature was created long before phrases were, and will survive them too.'

Bee was silent for a while and then gravely said: 'Is it not a part of human nature to try and rise superior to itself?'

I smiled inwardly. 'These are not your words', I thought to myself. 'You have learnt them from Nikhil. *You* are a healthy human being. Your flesh and blood have responded to the call of reality. You are burning in every vein with life-fire — do I not know it? How long should they keep you cool with the wet towel of moral precepts?'

'The weak are in the majority,' I said aloud. 'They are continually poisoning the ears of men by repeating these shibboleths. Nature has denied them strength — it is thus that they try to enfeeble others.'

'We women are weak,' replied Bimala. 'So I suppose we must join in the conspiracy of the weak.'

'Women weak!' I exclaimed with a laugh. 'Men belaud you as delicate and fragile, so as to delude you into thinking yourselves weak. But it is you women who are strong. Men make a great outward show of their so-called freedom, but those who know their inner minds are aware of their bondage. They have manufactured scriptures with their own hands to bind themselves; with their very idealism they have made golden fetters of women to wind round their body and mind. If men had not that extraordinary faculty of entangling themselves in meshes of their own contriving, nothing could have kept them bound. But as for you women, you have desired to conceive reality with body and soul. You have given birth to reality. You have suckled reality at your breasts.'

Bee was well read for a woman, and would not easily give in to my arguments. 'If that were true,' she objected, 'men would not have found women attractive.'

'Women realize the danger,' I replied. 'They know that men love delusions, so they give them full measure by borrowing their own phrases. They know that man, the drunkard, values intoxication more than food, and so they try to pass themselves off as an intoxicant. As a matter of fact, but for the sake of man, woman has no need for any make-believe.'

'Why, then, are you troubling to destroy the illusion?'

'For freedom. I want the country to be free. I want human relations to be free.'

III

I WAS AWARE that it is unsafe suddenly to awake a sleepwalker. But I am so impetuous by nature, a halting gait does not suit me. I knew I was overbold that day. I knew that the first shock of such ideas is apt to be almost intolerable. But with women it is always audacity that wins.

Just as we were getting on nicely, who should walk in but Nikhil's old tutor Chandranath Babu. The world would have been not half a bad place to live in but for these schoolmasters, who make one want to quit in disgust. The Nikhil type wants to keep the world always a school. This incarnation of a school turned up that afternoon at the psychological moment.

We all remain schoolboys in some corner of our hearts, and I, even I, felt somewhat pulled up. As for poor Bee, she at once took her place solemnly, like the topmost girl of the class on the front bench. All of a sudden she seemed to remember that she had to face her examination.

Some people are so like eternal pointsmen lying in wait by the line, to shunt one's train of thought from one rail to another.

Chandranath Babu had no sooner come in than he cast about for some excuse to retire, mumbling: 'I beg your pardon, I . . .'

Before he could finish, Bee went up to him and made a

profound obeisance, saying: 'Pray do not leave us, sir. Will you not take a seat?' She looked like a drowning person clutching at him for support – the little coward!

But possibly I was mistaken. It is quite likely that there was a touch of womanly wile in it. She wanted, perhaps, to raise her value in my eyes. She might have been pointedly saying to me: 'Please don't imagine for a moment that I am entirely overcome by you. My respect for Chandranath Babu is even greater.'

Well, indulge in your respect by all means! Schoolmasters thrive on it. But not being one of them, I have no use for that empty compliment.

Chandranath Babu began to talk about *Swadeshi*. I thought I would let him go on with his monologues. There is nothing like letting an old man talk himself out. It makes him feel that he is winding up the world, forgetting all the while how far away the real world is from his wagging tongue.

But even my worst enemy would not accuse me of patience. And when Chandranath Babu went on to say: 'If we expect to gather fruit where we have sown no seed, then we . . .' I had to interrupt him.

'Who wants fruit?' I cried. 'We go by the Author of the *Gita* who says that we are concerned only with the doing, not with the fruit of our deeds.'

'What is it then that you *do* want?' asked Chandranath Babu.

'Thorns!' I exclaimed, 'which cost nothing to plant.'

'Thorns do not obstruct others only,' he replied. 'They have a way of hurting one's own feet.'

'That is all right for a copy-book,' I retorted. 'But the real thing is that we have this burning at heart. Now we have only to cultivate thorns for others' soles; afterwards when they hurt us we shall find leisure to repent. But why be frightened even of that? When at last we have to die it will be time enough to get cold. While we are on fire let us seethe and boil.'

Chandranath Babu smiled. 'Seethe by all means,' he said, 'but do not mistake it for work, or heroism. Nations which have got on in the world have done so by action, not by ebullition. Those who have always lain in dread of work, when with a start they awake to their sorry plight, they look to short-cuts and scamping for their deliverance.'

I was girding up my loins to deliver a crushing reply, when Nikhil came back. Chandranath Babu rose, and looking towards

Bee, said: 'Let me go now, my little mother, I have some work to attend to.'

As he left, I showed Nikhil the book in my hand. 'I was telling Queen Bee about this book,' I said.

Ninety-nine per cent of people have to be deluded with lies, but it is easier to delude this perpetual pupil of the schoolmaster with the truth. He is best cheated openly. So, in playing with him, the simplest course was to lay my cards on the table.

Nikhil read the title on the cover, but said nothing. 'These writers,' I continued, 'are busy with their brooms, sweeping away the dust of epithets with which men have covered up this world of ours. So, as I was saying, I wish you would read it.'

'I have read it,' said Nikhil.

'Well, what do you say?'

'It is all very well for those who really care to think, but poison for those who shirk thought.'

'What do you mean?'

'Those who preach "Equal Rights of Property" should not be thieves. For, if they are, they would be preaching lies. When passion is in the ascendant, this kind of book is not rightly understood.'

'Passion,' I replied, 'is the street lamp which guides us. To call it untrue is as hopeless as to expect to see better by plucking out our natural eyes.'

Nikhil was visibly growing excited. 'I accept the truth of passion,' he said, 'only when I recognize the truth of restraint. By pressing what we want to see right into our eyes we only injure them: we do not see. So does the violence of passion, which would leave no space between the mind and its object, defeat its purpose.'

'It is simply your intellectual foppery,' I replied, 'which makes you indulge in moral delicacy, ignoring the savage side of truth. This merely helps you to mystify things, and so you fail to do your work with any degree of strength.'

'The intrusion of strength,' said Nikhil impatiently, 'where strength is out of place, does not help you in your work . . . But why are we arguing about these things? Vain arguments only brush off the fresh bloom of truth.'

I wanted Bee to join in the discussion, but she had not said a word up to now. Could I have given her too rude a shock, leaving her assailed with doubts and wanting to learn her lesson afresh from the schoolmaster? Still, a thorough shaking-up is essential. One must begin by realizing that things supposed to be unshakeable can be shaken.

'I am glad I had this talk with you,' I said to Nikhil, 'for I was on the point of lending this book to Queen Bee to read.'

'What harm?' said Nikhil. 'If I could read the book, why not Bimala too? All I want to say is, that in Europe people look at everything from the viewpoint of science. But man is neither mere physiology, nor biology, nor psychology, nor even sociology. For God's sake don't forget that. Man is infinitely more than the natural science of himself. You laugh at me, calling me the schoolmaster's pupil, but that is what you are, not I. You want to find the truth of man from your science teachers, and not from your own inner being.'

'But why all this excitement?' I mocked.

'Because I see you are bent on insulting man and making him petty.'

'Where on earth do you see all that?'

'In the air, in my outraged feelings. You would go on wounding the great, the unselfish, the beautiful in man.'

'What mad idea is this of yours?'

Nikhil suddenly stood up. 'I tell you plainly, Sandip,' he said, 'man may be wounded unto death, but he will not die. This is the reason why I am ready to suffer all, knowing all, with eyes open.'

With these words he hurriedly left the room.

I was staring blankly at his retreating figure, when the sound of a book, falling from the table, made me turn to find Bee following him with quick, nervous steps, making a detour to avoid passing too near me.

A curious creature, that Nikhil! He feels the danger threatening his home, and yet why does he not turn me out? I know, he is waiting for Bimal to give him the cue. If Bimal tells him that their mating has been a misfit, he will bow his head and admit that it may have been a blunder! He has not the strength of mind to understand that to acknowledge a mistake is the greatest of all mistakes. He is a typical example of how ideas make for weakness. I have not seen another like him – so whimsical a product of nature! He would hardly do as a character in a novel or drama, to say nothing of real life.

And Bee? I am afraid her dream-life is over from today. She

has at length understood the nature of the current which is bearing her along. Now she must either advance or retreat, openeyed. The chances are she will now advance a step, and then retreat a step. But that does not disturb me. When one is on fire, this rushing to and fro makes the blaze all the fiercer. The fright she has got will only fan her passion.

Perhaps I had better not say much to her, but simply select some modern books for her to read. Let her gradually come to the conviction that to acknowledge and respect passion as the supreme reality, is to be modern – not to be ashamed of it, not to glorify restraint. If she finds shelter in some such word as 'modern', she will find strength.

Be that as it may, I must see this out to the end of the Fifth Act. I cannot, unfortunately, boast of being merely a spectator, seated in the royal box, applauding now and again. There is a wrench at my heart, a pang in every nerve. When I have put out the light and am in my bed, little touches, little glances, little words flit about and fill the darkness. When I get up in the morning, I thrill with lively anticipations, my blood seems to course through me to the strains of music . . .

There was a double photo-frame on the table with Bee's photograph by the side of Nikhil's. I had taken out hers. Yesterday I showed Bee the empty side and said: 'Theft becomes necessary only because of miserliness, so its sin must be divided between the miser and the thief. Do you not think so?'

'It was not a good one,' observed Bee simply, with a little smile.

'What is to be done?' said I. 'A portrait cannot be better than a portrait. I must be content with it, such as it is.'

Bee took up a book and began to turn over the pages. 'If you are annoyed,' I went on, 'I must make a shift to fill up the vacancy.'

Today I have filled it up. This photograph of mine was taken in my early youth. My face was then fresher, and so was my mind. Then I still cherished some illusions about this world and the next. Faith deceives men, but it has one great merit: it imparts a radiance to the features.

My portrait now reposes next to Nikhil's, for are not the two of us old friends?

CHAPTER FOUR

Nikhil's Story

III

I WAS NEVER self-conscious. But nowadays I often try to take an outside view – to see myself as Bimal sees me. What a dismally solemn picture it makes, my habit of taking things too seriously!

Better, surely, to laugh away the world than flood it with tears. That is, in fact, how the world gets on. We relish our food and rest, only because we can dismiss, as so many empty shadows, the sorrows scattered everywhere, both in the home and in the outer world. If we took them as true, even for a moment, where would be our appetite, our sleep?

But I cannot dismiss myself as one of these shadows, and so the load of my sorrow lies eternally heavy on the heart of my world.

Why not stand out aloof in the highway of the universe, and feel yourself to be part of the all? In the midst of the immense, age-long concourse of humanity, what is Bimal to you? Your wife? What is a wife? A bubble of a name blown big with your own breath, so carefully guarded night and day, yet ready to burst at any pin-prick from outside.

My wife – and so, forsooth, my very own! If she says: 'No, I am myself' – am I to reply: 'How can that be? Are you not mine?'

'My wife' – Does that amount to an argument, much less the truth? Can one imprison a whole personality within that name?

My wife! – Have I not cherished in this little world all that is purest and sweetest in my life, never for a moment letting it down from my bosom to the dust? What incense of worship, what music of passion, what flowers of my spring and of my autumn, have I not offered up at its shrine? If, like a toy paper-boat, she be swept along into the muddy waters of the gutter – would I not also . . .?

There it is again, my incorrigible solemnity! Why 'muddy'? What 'gutter'? Names, called in a fit of jealousy, do not change the facts of the world. If Bimal is not mine, she is not; and no fuming, or fretting, or arguing will serve to prove that she is. If my heart is breaking – let it break! That will not make the world bankrupt – nor even me; for man is so much greater than the things he loses in this life. The very ocean of tears has its other shore, else none would have ever wept.

But then there is Society to be considerd . . . which let Society consider! If I weep it is for myself, not for Society. If Bimal should say she is not mine, what care I where my Society wife may be?

Suffering there must be; but I must save myself, by any means in my power, from one form of self-torture: I must never think that my life loses its value because of any neglect it may suffer. The full value of my life does not all go to buy my narrow domestic world; its great commerce does not stand or fall with some petty success or failure in the bartering of my personal joys and sorrows.

The time has come when I must divest Bimala of all the ideal decorations with which I decked her. It was owing to my own weakness that I indulged in such idolatry. I was too greedy. I created an angel of Bimala, in order to exaggerate my own enjoyment. But Bimala is what she is. It is preposterous to expect that she should assume the rôle of an angel for my pleasure. The Creator is under no obligation to supply me with angels, just because I have an avidity for imaginary perfection.

I must acknowledge that I have merely been an accident in Bimala's life. Her nature, perhaps, can only find true union with one like Sandip. At the same time, I must not, in false modesty, accept my rejection as my desert. Sandip certainly has attractive qualities, which had their sway also upon myself; but yet, I feel sure, he is not a greater man than I. If the wreath of victory falls to his lot today, and I am overlooked, then the dispenser of the wreath will be called to judgement.

I say this in no spirit of boasting. Sheer necessity has driven me to the pass, that to secure myself from utter desolation I must recognize all the value that I truly possess. Therefore, through the terrible experience of suffering let there come upon me the joy of deliverance – deliverance from self-distrust.

I have come to distinguish what is really in me from what I foolishly imagined to be there. The profit and loss account has been settled, and that which remains is myself – not a crippled self, dressed in rags and tatters, not a sick self to be nursed on invalid diet, but a spirit which has gone through the worst, and has survived.

My master passed through my room a moment ago and said with his hand on my shoulder: 'Get away to bed, Nikhil, the night is far advanced.'

The fact is, it has become so difficult for me to go to bed till late – till Bimal is fast asleep. In the day-time we meet, and even converse, but what am I to say when we are alone together, in the silence of the night? – so ashamed do I feel in mind and body.

'How is it, sir, you have not yet retired?' I asked in my turn. My master smiled a little, as he left me, saying: 'My sleeping days are over. I have now attained the waking age.'

I had written thus far, and was about to rise to go off bedwards when, through the window before me, I saw the heavy pall of July cloud suddenly part a little, and a big star shine through. It seemed to say to me: 'Dreamland ties are made, and dreamland ties are broken, but I am here for ever – the everlasting lamp of the bridal night.'

All at once my heart was full with the thought that my Eternal Love was steadfastly waiting for me through the ages, behind the veil of material things. Through many a life, in many a mirror, have I seen her image – broken mirrors, crooked mirrors, dusty mirrors. Whenever I have sought to make the mirror my very own, and shut it up within my box, I have lost sight of the image. But what of that. What have I to do with the mirror, or even the image?

My beloved, your smile shall never fade, and every dawn there shall appear fresh for me the vermilion mark on your forehead!

'What childish cajolery of self-deception,' mocks some devil from his dark corner – 'silly prattle to make children quiet!'

That may be. But millions and millions of children, with their million cries, have to be kept quiet. Can it be that all this multitude is quieted with only a lie? No, my Eternal Love cannot deceive me, for she is true!

She is true; that is why I have seen her and shall see her so often, even in my mistakes, even through the thickest mist of tears. I have seen her and lost her in the crowd of life's market-place, and found her again; and I shall find her once more when I have escaped through the loophole of death.

Ah, cruel one, play with me no longer! If I have failed to track you by the marks of your footsteps on the way, by the scent of your tresses lingering in the air, make me not weep for that for ever. The unveiled star tells me not to fear. That which is eternal must always be there.

Now let me go and see my Bimala. She must have spread her tired limbs on the bed, limp after her struggles, and be asleep. I will leave a kiss on her forehead without waking her – that shall be the flower-offering of my worship. I believe I could forget everything after death – all my mistakes, all my sufferings – but some vibration of the memory of that kiss would remain; for the wreath which is being woven out of the kisses of many a successive birth is to crown the Eternal Beloved.

As the gong of the watch rang out, sounding the hour of two, my sister-in-law came into the room. 'Whatever are you doing, brother dear?'[1] she cried. 'For pity's sake go to bed and stop worrying so. I cannot bear to look on that awful shadow of pain on your face.' Tears welled up in her eyes and overflowed as she entreated me thus.

I could not utter a word, but took the dust of her feet, as I went off to bed.

Bimala's Story

VII

AT FIRST I suspected nothing, feared nothing; I simply felt dedicated to my country. What a stupendous joy there was in this unquestioning surrender. Verily had I realized how, in thoroughness of self-destruction, man can find supreme bliss.

For aught I know, this frenzy of mine might have come to a gradual, natural end. But Sandip Babu would not have it so, he would insist on revealing himself. The tone of his voice became as intimate as a touch, every look flung itself on its knees in beggary. And, through it all, there burned a passion which in its violence made as though it would tear me up by the roots, and drag me along by the hair.

I will not shirk the truth. This cataclysmal desire drew me by day and by night. It seemed desperately alluring – this making havoc of myself. What a shame it seemed, how terrible, and yet how sweet! Then there was my overpowering curiosity; to which there seemed no limit. He of whom I knew but little,

1. When a relationship is established by marriage, or by mutual understanding arising out of special friendship or affection, the persons so related call each other in terms of such relationship, and not by name.

who never could assuredly be mine, whose youth flared so vigorously in a hundred points of flame – oh, the mystery of his
seething passions, so immense, so tumultuous!

I began with a feeling of worship, but that soon passed away.
I ceased even to respect Sandip; on the contrary, I began to look
down upon him. Nevertheless this flesh-and-blood lute of mine,
fashioned with my feeling and fancy, found in him a master-
player. What though I shrank from his touch, and even came
to loathe the lute itself; its music was conjured up all the same.

I must confess there was something in me which . . . what
shall I say? . . . which makes me wish I could have died!

Chandranath Babu, when he finds leisure, comes to me. He
has the power to lift my mind up to an eminence from where
I can see in a moment the boundary of my life extended on all
sides and so realize that the lines, which I took from my bounds,
were merely imaginary.

But what is the use of it all? Do I really desire emancipation?
Let suffering come to our house; let the best in me shrivel up and
become black; but let this infatuation not leave me – such seems
to be my prayer.

When, before my marriage, I used to see a brother-in-law of
mine, now dead, mad with drink – beating his wife in his frenzy,
and then sobbing and howling in maudlin repentance, vowing
never to touch liquor again, and yet, the very same evening,
sitting down to drink and drink – it would fill me with disgust.
But my intoxication today is still more fearful. The stuff has not
to be procured or poured out: it springs within my veins, and I
know not how to resist it.

Must this continue to the end of my days? Now and again
I start and look upon myself, and think my life to be a nightmare which will vanish all of a sudden with all its untruth. It has
become so frightfully incongruous. It has no connection with its
past. What it is, how it could have come to this pass, I cannot
understand.

One day my sister-in-law remarked with a cutting laugh:
'What a wonderfully hospitable Chota Rani we have! Her guest
absolutely will not budge. In our time there used to be guests,
too; but they had not such lavish looking after – we were so
absurdly taken up with our husbands. Poor brother Nikhil is
paying the penalty of being born too modern. He should have
come as a guest if he wanted to stay on. Now it looks as if it were

time for him to quit . . . O you little demon, do your glances
never fall, by chance, on his agonized face?'

This sarcasm did not touch me; for I knew that these women
had it not in them to understand the nature of the cause of my
devotion. I was then wrapped in the protecting armour of the
exaltation of sacrifice, through which such shafts were powerless
to reach and shame me.

VIII

FOR SOME TIME all talk of the country's cause has been
dropped. Our conversation nowadays has become full of modern
sex-problems, and various other matters, with a sprinkling of
poetry, both old Vaishnava and modern English, accompanied
by a running undertone of melody, low down in the bass, such
as I have never in my life heard before, which seems to me to
sound the true manly note, the note of power.

The day had come when all cover was gone. There was no
longer even the pretence of a reason why Sandip Babu should
linger on, or why I should have confidential talks with him every
now and then. I felt thoroughly vexed with myself, with my
sister-in-law, with the ways of the world, and I vowed I would
never again go to the outer apartments, not if I were to die
for it.

For two whole days I did not stir out. Then, for the first time,
I discovered how far I had travelled. My life felt utterly tasteless.
Whatever I touched I wanted to thrust away. I felt myself waiting – from the crown of my head to the tips of my toes – waiting
for something, somebody; my blood kept tingling with some
expectation.

I tried busying myself with extra work. The bedroom floor
was clean enough but I insisted on its being scrubbed over again
under my eyes. Things were arranged in the cabinets in one kind
of order; I pulled them all out and rearranged them in a different
way. I found no time that afternoon even to do up my hair; I
hurriedly tied it into a loose knot, and went and worried everybody, fussing about the store-room. The stores seemed short,
and pilfering must have been going on of late, but I could not
muster up the courage to take any particular person to task – for
might not the thought have crossed somebody's mind: 'Where
were your eyes all these days!'

In short, I behaved that day as one possessed. The next day I tried to do some reading. What I read I have no idea, but after a spell of absentmindedness I found I had wandered away, book in hand, along the passage leading towards the outer apartments, and was standing by a window looking out upon the verandah running along the row of rooms on the opposite side of the quadrangle. One of these rooms, I felt, had crossed over to another shore, and the ferry had ceased to ply. I felt like the ghost of myself of two days ago, doomed to remain where I was, and yet not really there, blankly looking out for ever.

As I stood there, I saw Sandip come out of his room into the verandah, a newspaper in his hand. I could see that he looked extraordinarily disturbed. The courtyard, the railings, in front, seemed to rouse his wrath. He flung away his newspaper with a gesture which seemed to want to rend the space before him.

I felt I could no longer keep my vow. I was about to move on towards the sitting-room, when I found my sister-in-law behind me. 'O Lord, this beats everything!' she ejaculated, as she glided away. I could not proceed to the outer apartments.

The next morning when my maid came calling, 'Rani Mother, it is getting late for giving out the stores,' I flung the keys to her, saying, 'Tell Harimati to see to it,' and went on with some embroidery of English pattern on which I was engaged, seated near the window.

Then came a servant with a letter. 'From Sandip Babu,' said he. What unbounded boldness! What must the messenger have thought? There was a tremor within my breast as I opened the envelope. There was no address on the letter, only the words: *An urgent matter – touching the Cause. Sandip.*

I flung aside the embroidery. I was up on my feet in a moment, giving a touch or two to my hair by the mirror. I kept the *sari* I had on, changing only my jacket – for one of my jackets had its associations.

I had to pass through one of the verandahs, where my sister-in-law used to sit in the morning slicing betel-nut. I refused to feel awkward. 'Whither away, Chota Rani?' she cried.

'To the sitting-room outside.'

'So early! A matinée, eh?'

And, as I passed on without further reply, she hummed after me a flippant song.

IX

WHEN I WAS about to enter the sitting-room, I saw Sandip immersed in an illustrated catalogue of British Academy pictures, with his back to the door. He has a great notion of himself as an expert in matters of Art.

One day my husband said to him: 'If the artists ever want a teacher, they need never lack for one so long as you are there.' It had not been my husband's habit to speak cuttingly, but latterly there has been a change and he never spares Sandip.

'What makes you suppose that artists need no teachers?' Sandip retorted.

'Art is a creation,' my husband replied. 'So we should humbly be content to receive our lessons about Art from the work of the artist.'

Sandip laughed at this modesty, saying: 'You think that meekness is a kind of capital which increases your wealth the more you use it. It is my conviction that those who lack pride only float about like water reeds which have no roots in the soil.'

My mind used to be full of contradictions when they talked thus. On the one hand I was eager that my husband should win in argument and that Sandip's pride should be shamed. Yet, on the other, it was Sandip's unabashed pride which attracted me so. It shone like a precious diamond, which knows no diffidence, and sparkles in the face of the sun itself.

I entered the room. I knew Sandip could hear my footsteps as I went forward, but he pretended not to, and kept his eyes on the book.

I dreaded his Art talks, for I could not overcome my delicacy about the pictures he talked of, and the things he said, and had much ado in putting on an air of overdone insensibility to hide my qualms. So, I was almost on the point of retracing my steps, when, with a deep sigh, Sandip raised his eyes, and affected to be startled at the sight of me. 'Ah, you have come!' he said.

In his words, in his tone, in his eyes, there was a world of suppressed reproach, as if the claims he had acquired over me made my absence, even for these two or three days, a grievous wrong. I knew this attitude was an insult to me, but, alas, I had not the power to resent it.

I made no reply, but though I was looking another way, I could not help feeling that Sandip's plaintive gaze had planted itself right on my face, and would take no denial. I did so wish he would say something, so that I could shelter myself behind his words. I cannot tell how long this went on, but at last I could stand it no longer. 'What is this matter,' I asked, 'you are wanting to tell me about?'

Sandip again affected surprise as he said: 'Must there always be some matter? Is friendship by itself a crime? Oh, Queen Bee, to think that you should make so light of the greatest thing on earth! Is the heart's worship to be shut out like a stray cur?'

There was again that tremor within me. I could feel the crisis coming, too importunate to be put off. Joy and fear struggled for the mastery. Would my shoulders, I wondered, be broad enough to stand its shock, or would it not leave me overthrown, with my face in the dust?

I was trembling all over. Steadying myself with an effort I repeated: 'You summoned me for something touching the Cause, so I have left my household duties to attend to it.'

'That is just what I was trying to explain,' he said, with a dry laugh. 'Do you not know that I come to worship? Have I not told you that, in you, I visualize the *Shakti* of our country? The Geography of a country is not the whole truth. No one can give up his life for a map! When I see you before me, then only do I realize how lovely my country is. When you have anointed me with your own hands, then shall I know I have the sanction of my country; and if, with that in my heart, I fall fighting, it shall not be on the dust of some map-made land, but on a lovingly spread skirt – do you know what kind of skirt? – like that of the earthen-red *sari* you wore the other day, with a broad blood-red border. Can I ever forget it? Such are the visions which give vigour to life, and joy to death!'

Sandip's eyes took fire as he went on, but whether it was the fire of worship, or of passion, I could not tell. I was reminded of the day on which I first heard him speak, when I could not be sure whether he was a person, or just a living flame.

I had not the power to utter a word. You cannot take shelter behind the walls of decorum when in a moment the fire leaps up and, with the flash of its sword and the roar of its laughter, destroys all the miser's stores. I was in terror lest he should forget himself and take me by the hand. For he shook like a quivering tongue of fire; his eyes showered scorching sparks on me.

'Are you for ever determined,' he cried after a pause, 'to make

gods of your petty household duties – you who have it in you
to send us to life or to death? Is this power of yours to be kept
veiled in a zenana? Cast away all false shame, I pray you; snap
your fingers at the whispering around. Take your plunge today
into the freedom of the outer world.'

When, in Sandip's appeals, his worship of the country gets
to be subtly interwoven with his worship of me, then does my
blood dance, indeed, and the barriers of my hesitation totter.
His talks about Art and Sex, his distinctions between Real and
Unreal, had but clogged my attempts at response with some re-
volting nastiness. This, however, now burst again into a glow
before which my repugnance faded away. I felt that my resplendent womanhood made me indeed a goddess. Why should not its
glory flash from my forehead with visible brilliance? Why does
not my voice find a word, some audible cry, which would be
like a sacred spell to my country for its fire initiation?

All of a sudden my maid Khema rushed into the room, dis-
hevelled. 'Give me my wages and let me go,' she screamed.
'Never in all my life have I been so . . .' The rest of her speech
was drowned in sobs.

'What is the matter?'

Thako, the Bara Rani's maid, it appeared, had for no rhyme
or reason reviled her in unmeasured terms. She was in such a
state, it was no manner of use trying to pacify her by saying I
would look into the matter afterwards.

The slime of domestic life that lay beneath the lotus bank of
womanhood came to the surface. Rather than allow Sandip a
prolonged vision of it, I had to hurry back within.

X

MY SISTER-IN-LAW was absorbed in her betel-nuts, the suspicion of a smile playing about her lips, as if nothing untoward had
happened. She was still humming the same song.

'Why has your Thako been calling poor Khema names?' I
burst out.

'Indeed? The wretch! I will have her broomed out of the
house. What a shame to spoil your morning out like this! As for
Khema, where are the hussy's manners to go and disturb you
when you are engaged? Anyhow, Chota Rani, don't you worry
yourself with these domestic squabbles. Leave them to me, and
return to your friend.'

How suddenly the wind in the sails of our mind veers round! This going to meet Sandip outside seemed, in the light of the zenana code, such an extraordinarily out-of-the-way thing to do that I went off to my own room, at a loss for a reply. I knew this was my sister-in-law's doing and that she had egged her maid on to contrive this scene. But I had brought myself to such an unstable poise that I dared not have my fling.

Why, it was only the other day that I found I could not keep up to the last the unbending hauteur with which I had demanded from my husband the dismissal of the man Nanku. I felt suddenly abashed when the Bara Rani came up and said: 'It is really all my fault, brother dear. We are old-fashioned folk, and I did not quite like the ways of your Sandip Babu, so I only told the guard . . . but how was I to know that our Chota Rani would take this as an insult? – I thought it would be the other way about! Just my incorrigible silliness!'

The thing which seems so glorious when viewed from the heights of the country's cause, looks so muddy when seen from the bottom. One begins by getting angry, and then feels disgusted.

I shut myself into my room, sitting by the window, thinking how easy life would be if only one could keep in harmony with one's surroundings. How simply the senior Rani sits in her verandah with her betel-nuts and how inaccessible to me has become my natural seat beside my daily duties! Where will it all end, I asked myself? Shall I ever recover, as from a delirium, and forget it all; or am I to be dragged to depths from which there can be no escape in this life? How on earth did I manage to let my good fortune escape me, and spoil my life so? Every wall of this bedroom of mine, which I first entered nine years ago as a bride, stares at me in dismay.

When my husband came home, after his M.A. examination, he brought for me this orchid belonging to some far-away land beyond the seas. From beneath these few little leaves sprang such a cascade of blossoms, it looked as if they were pouring forth from some overturned urn of Beauty. We decided, together, to hang it here, over this window. It flowered only that once, but we have always been in hope of its doing so once more. Curiously enough I have kept on watering it these days, from force of habit, and it is still green.

It is now four years since I framed a photograph of my

husband in ivory and put it in the niche over there. If I happen to look that way I have to lower my eyes. Up to last week I used regularly to put there the flowers of my worship, every morning after my bath. My husband has often chided me over this.

'It shames me to see you place me on a height to which I do not belong,' he said one day.

'What nonsense!'

'I am not only ashamed, but also jealous!'

'Just hear him! Jealous of whom, pray?'

'Of that false me. It only shows that I am too petty for you, that you want some extraordinary man who can overpower you with his superiority, and so you needs must take refuge in making for yourself another "me".'

'This kind of talk only makes me angry,' said I.

'What is the use of being angry with me?' he replied. 'Blame your fate which allowed you no choice, but made you take me blindfold. This keeps you trying to retrieve its blunder by making me out a paragon.'

I felt so hurt at the bare idea that tears started to my eyes that day. And whenever I think of that now, I cannot raise my eyes to the niche.

For now there is another photograph in my jewel case. The other day, when arranging the sitting-room, I brought away that double photo frame, the one in which Sandip's portrait was next to my husband's. To this portrait I have no flowers of worship to offer, but it remains hidden away under my gems. It has all the greater fascination because kept secret. I look at it now and then with doors closed. At night I turn up the lamp, and sit with it in my hand, gazing and gazing. And every night I think of burning it in the flame of the lamp, to be done with it for ever; but every night I heave a sigh and smother it again in my pearls and diamonds.

Ah, wretched woman! What a wealth of love was twined round each one of those jewels! Oh, why am I not dead?

Sandip had impressed it on me that hesitation is not in the nature of woman. For her, neither right nor left has any existence – she only moves forward. When the women of our country wake up, he repeatedly insisted, their voice will be unmistakably confident in its utterance of the cry: 'I *want*.'

'I want!' Sandip went on one day – this was the primal word at the root of all creation. It had no maxim to guide it, but it became fire and wrought itself into suns and stars. Its partiality is terrible. Because it had a desire for man, it ruthlessly sacrificed millions of beasts for millions of years to achieve that desire. That terrible word 'I want' has taken flesh in woman, and therefore men, who are cowards, try with all their might to keep back this primeval flood with their earthen dykes. They are afraid lest, laughing and dancing as it goes, it should wash away all the hedges and props of their pumpkin field. Men, in every age, flatter themselves that they have secured this force within the bounds of their convenience, but it gathers and grows. Now it is calm and deep like a lake, but gradually its pressure will increase, the dykes will give way, and the force which has so long been dumb will rush forward with the roar: 'I want!'

These words of Sandip echo in my heart-beats like a war-drum. They shame into silence all my conflicts with myself. What do I care what people may think of me? Of what value are that orchid and that niche in my bedroom? What power have they to belittle me, to put me to shame? The primal fire of creation burns in me.

I felt a strong desire to snatch down the orchid and fling it out of the window, to denude the niche of its picture, to lay bare and naked the unashamed spirit of destruction that raged within me. My arm was raised to do it, but a sudden pang passed through my breast, tears started to my eyes. I threw myself down and sobbed: 'What is the end of all this, what is the end?'

Sandip's Story

IV

WHEN I READ these pages of the story of my life I seriously question myself: Is this Sandip? Am I made of words? Am I merely a book with a covering of flesh and blood?

The earth is not a dead thing like the moon. She breathes. Her rivers and oceans send up vapours in which she is clothed. She is covered with a mantle of her own dust which flies about the air. The onlooker, gazing upon the earth from the outside, can see only the light reflected from this vapour and this dust. The tracks of the mighty continents are not distinctly visible.

The man, who is alive as this earth is, is likewise always en-veloped in the mist of the ideas which he is breathing out. His real land and water remain hidden, and he appears to be made of only lights and shadows.

It seems to me, in this story of my life, that, like a living plant, I am displaying the picture of an ideal world. But I am not merely what I want, what I think – I am also what I do not love, what I do *not* wish to be. My creation had begun before I was born. I had no choice in regard to my surroundings and so must make the best of such material as comes to my hand.

My theory of life makes me certain that the Great is cruel. To be just is for ordinary men – it is reserved for the great to be unjust. The surface of the earth was even. The volcano butted it with its fiery horn and found its own eminence – its justice was not towards its obstacle, but towards itself. Successful injustice and genuine cruelty have been the only forces by which individual or nation has become millionaire or monarch.

That is why I preach the great discipline of Injustice. I say to everyone: Deliverance is based upon injustice. Injustice is the fire which must keep on burning something in order to save itself from becoming ashes. Whenever an individual or nation becomes incapable of perpetrating injustice it is swept into the dust-bin of the world.

As yet this is only my idea – it is not completely myself. There are rifts in the armour through which something peeps out which is extremely soft and sensitive. Because, as I say, the best part of myself was created before I came to this stage of existence.

From time to time I try my followers in their lesson of cruelty. One day we went on a picnic. A goat was grazing by. I asked them: 'Who is there among you that can cut off a leg of that goat, alive, with this knife, and bring it to me?' While they all hesitated, I went myself and did it. One of them fainted at the sight. But when they saw me unmoved they took the dust of my feet, saying that I was above all human weaknesses. That is to say, they saw that day the vaporous envelope which was my idea, but failed to perceive the inner me, which by a curious freak of fate has been created tender and merciful.

In the present chapter of my life, which is growing in interest every day round Bimala and Nikhil, there is also much that remains hidden underneath. This malady of ideas which afflicts me is shaping my life within: nevertheless a great part of my life remains outside its influence; and so there is set up a discrepancy between my outward life and its inner design which I try my best to keep concealed even from myself; otherwise it may wreck not only my plans, but my very life.

Life is indefinite – a bundle of contradictions. We men, with our ideas, strive to give it a particular shape by melting it into a particular mould – into the definiteness of success. All the world-conquerors, from Alexander down to the American millionaires, mould themselves into a sword or a mint, and thus find that distinct image of themselves which is the source of their success.

The chief controversy between Nikhil and myself arises from this: that though I say 'know thyself', and Nikhil also says 'know thyself', his interpretation makes this 'knowing' tantamount to 'not knowing'.

'Winning your kind of success,' Nikhil once objected, 'is success gained at the cost of the soul: but the soul is greater than success.'

I simply said in answer: 'Your words are too vague.'

'That I cannot help,' Nikhil replied. 'A machine is distinct enough, but not so life. If to gain distinctness you try to know life as a machine, then such mere distinctness cannot stand for truth. The soul is not as distinct as success, and so you only lose your soul if you seek it in your success.'

'Where, then, is this wonderful soul?'

'Where it knows itself in the infinite and transcends its success.'

'But how does all this apply to our work for the country?'

'It is the same thing. Where our country makes itself the final object, it gains success at the cost of the soul. Where it recognizes the Greatest as greater than all, there it may miss success, but gains its soul.'

'Is there any example of this in history?'

'Man is so great that he can despise not only the success, but also the example. Possibly example is lacking, just as there is no example of the flower in the seed. But there is the urgence of the flower in the seed all the same.'

It is not that I do not at all understand Nikhil's point of view; that is rather where my danger lies. I was born in India and the poison of its spirituality runs in my blood. However loudly I may proclaim the madness of walking in the path of self-abnegation, I cannot avoid it altogether.

This is exactly how such curious anomalies happen nowadays in our country. We must have our religion and also our nation-alism; our *Bhagavadgita* and also our *Bande Mataram*. The result is that both of them suffer. It is like performing with an English military band, side by side with our Indian festive pipes. I must make it the purpose of my life to put an end to this hideous confusion.

I want the western military style to prevail, not the Indian. We shall then not be ashamed of the flag of our passion, which mother Nature has sent with us as our standard into the battle-field of life. Passion is beautiful and pure – pure as the lily that comes out of the slimy soil. It rises superior to its defilement and needs no Pears' soap to wash it clean.

V

A QUESTION HAS been worrying me the last few days. Why am I allowing my life to become entangled with Bimala's? Am I a drifting log to be caught up at any and every obstacle?

Not that I have any false shame at Bimala becoming an object of my desire. It is only too clear how she wants me, and so I look on her as quite legitimately mine. The fruit hangs on the branch by the stem, but that is no reason why the claim of the stem should be eternal. Ripe fruit cannot for ever swear by its slacken-ing stem-hold. All its sweetness has been accumulated for me; to surrender itself to my hand is the reason of its existence, its very nature, its true morality. So I must pluck it, for it becomes me not to make it futile.

But what is teasing me is that I am getting entangled. Am I not born to rule? – to bestride my proper steed, the crowd, and drive it as I will; the reins in my hand, the destination known only to me, and for it the thorns, the mire, on the road? This steed now awaits me at the door, pawing and champing its bit, its neighing filling the skies. But where am I, and what am I about, letting day after day of golden opportunity slip by?

I used to think I was like a storm – that the torn flowers with which I strewed my path would not impede my progress. But I am only wandering round and round a flower like a bee – not a storm. So, as I was saying, the colouring of ideas which man gives himself is only superficial. The inner man remains as ordi-nary as ever. If someone, who could see right into me, were to write my biography, he would make me out to be no different from that lout of a Panchu, or even from Nikhil!

Last night I was turning over the pages of my old diary . . . I had just graduated, and my brain was bursting with philosophy. Even so early I had vowed not to harbour any illusions, whether of my own or others' imagining, but to build my life on a solid basis of reality. But what has since been its actual story? Where is its solidity? It has rather been a network, where, though the thread be continuous, more space is taken up by the holes. Fight as I may, these will not own defeat. Just as I was congratulating myself on steadily following the thread, here I am badly caught in a hole! For I have become susceptible to compunctions.

'I want it; it is here; let me take it' – This is a clear-cut, straightforward policy. Those who can pursue its course with vigour needs must win through in the end. But the gods would not have it that such journey should be easy, so they have deputed the siren Sympathy to distract the wayfarer, to dim his vision with her tearful mist.

I can see that poor Bimala is struggling like a snared deer. What a piteous alarm there is in her eyes! How she is torn with straining at her bonds! This sight, of course, should gladden the heart of a true hunter. And so do I rejoice; but, then, I am also touched; and therefore I dally, and standing on the brink I am hesitating to pull the noose fast.

There have been moments, I know, when I could have bounded up to her, clasped her hands and folded her to my breast, unresisting. Had I done so, she would not have said one word. She was aware that some crisis was impending, which in a moment would change the meaning of the whole world. Standing before that cavern of the incalculable but yet expected, her face went pale and her eyes glowed with a fearful ecstasy. Within that moment, when it arrives, an eternity will take shape, which our destiny awaits, holding its breath.

But I have let this moment slip by. I did not, with uncompromising strength, press the almost certain into the absolutely assured. I now see clearly that some hidden elements in my nature have openly ranged themselves as obstacles in my path.

That is exactly how Ravana, whom I look upon as the real hero of the *Ramayana*, met with his doom. He kept Sita in his Asoka garden, awaiting her pleasure, instead of taking her straight into his harem. This weak spot in his otherwise grand character made the whole of the abduction episode futile. Another such touch of compunction made him disregard, and be lenient to, his traitorous brother Bibhisan, only to get himself killed for his pains.

Thus does the tragic in life come by its own. In the beginning it lies, a little thing, in some dark under-vault, and ends by over-throwing the whole superstructure. The real tragedy is, that man does not know himself for what he really is.

VI

THEN AGAIN THERE is Nikhil. Crank though he be, laugh at him as I may, I cannot get rid of the idea that he is my friend. At first I gave no thought to his point of view, but of late it has begun to shame and hurt me. Therefore I have been trying to talk and argue with him in the same enthusiastic way as of old, but it does not ring true. It is even leading me at times into such a length of unnaturalness as to pretend to agree with him. But such hypocrisy is not in my nature, nor in that of Nikhil either. This, at least, is something we have in common. That is why, nowadays, I would rather not come across him, and have taken to fighting shy of his presence.

All these are signs of weakness. No sooner is the possibility of a wrong admitted than it becomes actual, and clutches you by the throat, however you may then try to shake off all belief in it. What I should like to be able to tell Nikhil frankly is, that happenings such as these must be looked in the face – as great Realities – and that which is the Truth should not be allowed to stand between true friends.

There is no denying that I have really weakened. It was not this weakness which won over Bimala; she burnt her wings in the blaze of the full strength of my unhesitating manliness. Whenever smoke obscures its lustre she also becomes confused, and draws back. Then comes a thorough revulsion of feeling, and she fain would take back the garland she has put round my neck, but cannot; and so she only closes her eyes, to shut it out of sight.

But all the same I must not swerve from the path I have chalked out. It would never do to abandon the cause of the country, especially at the present time. I shall simply make Bimala one with my country. The turbulent west wind which has swept away the country's veil of conscience, will sweep away the veil of the wife from Bimala's face, and in that uncovering there will be no shame. The ship will rock as it bears the crowd across the ocean, flying the pennant of *Bande Mataram*, and it will serve as the cradle to my power, as well as to my love.

Bimala will see such a majestic vision of deliverance, that her bonds will slip from about her, without shame, without her even being aware of it. Fascinated by the beauty of this terrible wrecking power, she will not hesitate a moment to be cruel. I have seen in Bimala's nature the cruelty which is the inherent force of existence – the cruelty which with its unrelenting might keeps the world beautiful.

If only women could be set free from the artificial fetters put round them by men, we could see on earth the living image of Kali, the shameless, pitiless goddess. I am a worshipper of Kali, and one day I shall truly worship her, setting Bimala on her altar of Destruction. For this let me get ready.

The way of retreat is absolutely closed for both of us. We shall despoil each other: get to hate each other: but never more be free.

CHAPTER FIVE

Nikhil's Story

IV

EVERYTHING IS RIPPLING and waving with the flood of August. The young shoots of rice have the sheen of an infant's limbs. The water has invaded the garden next to our house. The morning light, like the love of the blue sky, is lavished upon the earth . . . Why cannot I sing? The water of the distant river is shimmering with light; the leaves are glistening; the rice-fields, with their fitful shivers, break into gleams of gold; and in this symphony of Autumn, only I remain voiceless. The sunshine of the world strikes my heart, but is not reflected back.

When I realize the lack of expressiveness in myself, I know why I am deprived. Who could bear my company day and night without a break? Bimala is full of the energy of life, and so she has never become stale to me for a moment, in all these nine years of our wedded life.

My life has only its dumb depths; but no murmuring rush. I can only receive: not impart movement. And therefore my company is like fasting. I recognize clearly today that Bimala has been languishing because of a famine of companionship.

Then whom shall I blame? Like Vidyapati I can only lament:

> It is August, the sky breaks into a passionate rain;
> Alas, empty is my house.

My house, I now see, was built to remain empty, because its doors cannot open. But I never knew till now that its divinity had been sitting outside. I had fondly believed that she had accepted my sacrifice, and granted in return her boon. But, alas, my house has all along been empty.

Every year, about this time, it was our practice to go in a house-boat over the broads of Samalda. I used to tell Bimala that a song must come back to its refrain over and over again. The original refrain of every song is in Nature, where the rain-laden wind passes over the rippling stream, where the green earth, drawing its shadow-veil over its face, keeps its ear close to the speaking water. There, at the beginning of time, a man and a woman first met – not within walls. And therefore we two must come back to Nature, at least once a year, to tune our love anew to the first pure note of the meeting of hearts.

The first two anniversaries of our married life I spent in Calcutta, where I went through my examinations. But from the next year onwards, for seven years without a break, we have celebrated our union among the blossoming water-lilies. Now begins the next octave of my life.

It was difficult for me to ignore the fact that the same month of August had come round again this year. Does Bimala remember it, I wonder? – she has given me no reminder. Everything is mute about me.

> It is August, the sky breaks into a passionate rain;
>   And empty is my house.

The house which becomes empty through the parting of lovers, still has music left in the heart of its emptiness. But the house that is empty because hearts are asunder, is awful in its silence. Even the cry of pain is out of place there.

This cry of pain must be silenced in me. So long as I continue to suffer, Bimala will never have true freedom. I *must* free her completely, otherwise I shall never gain *my* freedom from untruth . . .

I think I have come to the verge of understanding one thing. Man has so fanned the flame of the loves of men and women, as to make it overpass its rightful domain, and now, even in the name of humanity itself, he cannot bring it back under control. Man's worship has idolized his passion. But there must be no more human sacrifices at its shrine . . .

I went into my bedroom this morning, to fetch a book. It is long since I have been there in the day-time. A pang passed through me as I looked round it today, in the morning light. On the clothes rack was hanging a *sari* of Bimala's, crinkled ready for wear. On the dressing-table were her perfumes, her comb, her hair-pins, and with them, still, her vermilion box! Underneath were her tiny gold-embroidered slippers.

Once, in the old days, when Bimala had not yet overcome her objections to shoes, I had got these out from Lucknow, to tempt her. The first time she was ready to drop for very shame, to go in them even from the room to the verandah. Since then she has worn out many shoes, but has treasured up this pair. When first showing her the slippers, I chaffed her over a curious practice of hers; 'I have caught you taking the dust of my feet, thinking me asleep! These are the offerings of my worship to ward the dust off the feet of my wakeful divinity.' 'You must not say such things,' she protested, 'or I will never wear your shoes!'

This bedroom of mine — it has a subtle atmosphere which goes straight to my heart. I was never aware, as I am today, how my thirsting heart has been sending out its roots to cling round each and every familiar object. The severing of the main root, I see, is not enough to set life free. Even these little slippers serve to hold one back.

My wandering eyes fall on the niche. My portrait there is looking the same as ever, in spite of the flowers scattered around it having been withered black! Of all the things in the room their greeting strikes me as sincere. They are still here simply because it was not felt worth while even to remove them. Never mind; let me welcome truth, albeit in such sere and sorry garb, and look forward to the time when I shall be able to do so unmoved, as does my photograph.

As I stood there, Bimal came in from behind. I hastily turned my eyes from the niche to the shelves as I muttered: 'I came to get Amiel's Journal.' What need had I to volunteer an explanation? I felt like a wrong-doer, a trespasser, prying into a secret not meant for me. I could not look Bimal in the face, but hurried away.

V

I HAD JUST made the discovery that it was useless to keep up a pretence of reading in my room outside, and also that it was equally beyond me to busy myself attending to anything at all — so that all the days of my future bid fair to congeal into one solid mass and settle heavily on my breast for good — when Panchu, the tenant of a neighbouring *zamindar*, came up to me with a basketful of cocoa-nuts and greeted me with a profound obeisance.

'Well, Panchu,' said I. 'What is all this for?'

I had got to know Panchu through my master. He was extremely poor, nor was I in a position to do anything for him; so I supposed this present was intended to procure a tip to help the poor fellow to make both ends meet. I took some money from my purse and held it out towards him, but with folded hands he protested: 'I cannot take that, sir!'

'Why, what is the matter?'

'Let me make a clean breast of it, sir. Once, when I was hard pressed, I stole some cocoa-nuts from the garden here. I am getting old, and may die any day, so I have come to pay them back.'

Amiel's Journal could not have done me any good that day. But these words of Panchu lightened my heart. There are more things in life than the union or separation of man and woman. The great world stretches far beyond, and one can truly measure one's joys and sorrows when standing in its midst.

Panchu was devoted to my master. I know well enough how he manages to eke out a livelihood. He is up before dawn every day, and with a basket of *pan* leaves, twists of tobacco, coloured cotton yarn, little combs, looking-glasses, and other trinkets beloved of the village women, he wades through the knee-deep water of the marsh and goes over to the *Namasudra* quarters. There he barters his goods for rice, which fetches him a little more than their price in money. If he can get back soon enough he goes out again, after a hurried meal, to the sweetmeat seller's, where he assists in beating sugar for wafers. As soon as he comes home he sits at his shell-bangle making, plodding on often till midnight. All this cruel toil does not earn, for himself and his family, a bare two meals a day during much more than half the year. His method of eating is to begin with a good filling draught of water, and his staple food is the cheapest kind of seedy banana. And yet the family has to go with only one meal a day for the rest of the year.

At one time I had an idea of making him a charity allowance, 'But,' said my master, 'your gift may destroy the man, it cannot destroy the hardship of his lot. Mother Bengal has not only this one Panchu. If the milk in her breasts has run dry, that cannot be supplied from the outside.'

These are thoughts which give one pause, and I decided to devote myself to working it out. That very day I said to Bimal: 'Let us dedicate our lives to removing the root of this sorrow in our country.'

'You are my Prince Siddharta,[1] I see,' she replied with a smile. 'But do not let the torrent of your feelings end by sweeping me away also!'

---

1. The name by which Buddha was known when a Prince, before renouncing the world.

'Siddharta took his vows alone. I want ours to be a joint arrangement.'

The idea passed away in talk. The fact is, Bimala is at heart what is called a 'lady'. Though her own people are not well off, she was born a Rani. She has no doubts in her mind that there is a lower unit of measure for the trials and troubles of the 'lower classes'. Want is, of course, a permanent feature of their lives, but does not necessarily mean 'want' to them. Their very smallness protects them, as the banks protect the pool; by widening bounds only the slime is exposed.

The real fact is that Bimala has only come into my home, not into my life. I had magnified her so, leaving her such a large place, that when I lost her, my whole way of life became narrow and confined. I had thrust aside all other objects into a corner to make room for Bimala – taken up as I was with decorating her and dressing her and educating her and moving round her day and night; forgetting how great is humanity and how nobly precious is man's life. When the actualities of everyday things get the better of the man, then is Truth lost sight of and freedom missed. So painfully important did Bimala make the mere actualities, that the truth remained concealed from me. That is why I find no gap in my misery, and spread this minute point of my emptiness over all the world. And so, for hours on this Autumn morning, the refrain has been humming in my ears:

> It is the month of August, and the sky breaks into a passionate
>   rain;
>   Alas, my house is empty.

Bimala's Story

XI

THE CHANGE WHICH had, in a moment, come over the mind of Bengal was tremendous. It was as if the Ganges had touched the ashes of the sixty thousand sons of Sagar[1] which no fire could enkindle, no other water knead again into living clay. The ashes of lifeless Bengal suddenly spoke up: 'Here am I.'

I have read somewhere that in ancient Greece a sculptor had

---

1. The condition of the curse which had reduced them to ashes was such that they could only be restored to life if the stream of the Ganges was brought down to them.

the good fortune to impart life to the image made by his own hand. Even in that miracle, however, there was the process of form preceding life. But where was the unity in this heap of barren ashes? Had they been hard like stone, we might have had hopes of some form emerging, even as Ahalya, though turned to stone, at last won back her humanity. But these scattered ashes must have dropped to the dust through gaps in the Creator's fingers, to be blown hither and thither by the wind. They had become heaped up, but were never before united. Yet in this day which had come to Bengal, even this collection of looseness had taken shape, and proclaimed in a thundering voice, at our very door: 'Here I am.'

How could we help thinking that it was all supenatural? This moment of our history seemed to have dropped into our hand like a jewel from the crown of some drunken god. It had no resemblance to our past; and so we were led to hope that all our wants and miseries would disappear by the spell of some magic charm, that for us there was no longer any boundary line between the possible and the impossible. Everything seemed to be saying to us: 'It is coming; it has come!'

Thus we came to cherish the belief that our history needed no steed, but that like heaven's chariot it would move with its own inherent power – At least no wages would have to be paid to the charioteer; only his wine cup would have to be filled again and again. And then in some impossible paradise the goal of our hopes would be reached.

My husband was not altogether unmoved, but through all our excitement it was the strain of sadness in him which deepened and deepened. He seemed to have a vision of something beyond the surging present.

I remember one day, in the course of the arguments he continually had with Sandip, he said: 'Good fortune comes to our gate and announces itself, only to prove that we have not the power to receive it – that we have not kept things ready to be able to invite it into our house.'

'No,' was Sandip's answer. 'You talk like an atheist because you do not believe in our gods. To us it has been made quite visible that the Goddess has come with her boon, yet you distrust the obvious signs of her presence.'

'It is because I strongly believe in my God,' said my husband, 'that I feel so certain that our preparations for his worship are lacking. God has power to give the boon, but we must have power to accept it.'

This kind of talk from my husband would only annoy me. I could not keep from joining in: 'You think this excitement is only a fire of drunkenness, but does not drunkenness, up to a point, give strength?'

'Yes,' my husband replied. 'It may give strength, but not weapons.'

'But strength is the gift of God,' I went on. 'Weapons can be supplied by mere mechanics.'

My husband smiled. 'The mechanics will claim their wages before they deliver their supplies,' he said.

Sandip swelled his chest as he retorted: 'Don't you trouble about that. Their wages shall be paid.'

'I shall bespeak the festive music when the payment has been made, not before,' my husband answered.

'You needn't imagine that we are depending on your bounty for the music,' said Sandip scornfully. 'Our festival is above all money payments.'

And in his thick voice he began to sing:

'My lover of the unpriced love, spurning payments,
Plays upon the simple pipe, bought for nothing,
*   Drawing my heart away.'*

Then with a smile he turned to me and said: 'If I sing, Queen Bee, it is only to prove that when music comes into one's life, the lack of a good voice is no matter. When we sing merely on the strength of our tunefulness, the song is belittled. Now that a full flood of music has swept over our country, let Nikhil practise his scales, while we rouse the land with our cracked voices:

'My house cries to me: Why go out to lose your all?
My life says: All that you have, fling to the winds!
If we must lose our all, let us lose it: what is it worth after all?
If I must court ruin, let me do it smilingly:
For my quest is the death-draught of immortality.

'The truth is, Nikhil, that we have all lost our hearts. None can hold us any longer within the bounds of the easily possible, in our forward rush to the hopelessly impossible.

'Those who would draw us back,
They know not the fearful joy of recklessness.
They know not that we have had our call
From the end of the crooked path.
All that is good and straight and trim –
Let it topple over in the dust.'

I thought that my husband was going to continue the discussion, but he rose silently from his seat and left us.

The thing that was agitating me within was merely a variation of the stormy passion outside, which swept the country from one end to the other. The car of the wielder of my destiny was fast approaching, and the sound of its wheels reverberated in my being. I had a constant feeling that something extraordinary might happen any moment, for which, however, the responsibility would not be mine. Was I not removed from the plane in which right and wrong, and the feelings of others, have to be considered? Had I ever wanted this – had I ever been waiting or hoping for any such thing? Look at my whole life and tell me then, if I was in any way accountable.

Through all my past I had been consistent in my devotion – but when at length it came to receiving the boon, a different god appeared! And just as the awakened country, with its *Bande Mataram*, thrills in salutation to the unrealized future before it, so do all my veins and nerves send forth shocks of welcome to the unthought-of, the unknown, the importunate Stranger.

One night I left my bed and slipped out of my room on to the open terrace. Beyond our garden wall are fields of ripening rice. Through the gaps in the village groves to the North, glimpses of the river are seen. The whole scene slept in the darkness like the vague embryo of some future creation.

In that future I saw my country, a woman like myself, standing expectant. She has been drawn forth from her home corner by the sudden call of some Unknown. She has had no time to pause or ponder, or to light herself a torch, as she rushes forward into the darkness ahead. I know well how her very soul responds to the distant flute-strains which call her; how her breast rises and falls; how she feels she nears it, nay it is already hers, so that it matters not even if she run blindfold. She is no mother. There is no call to her of children in their hunger, no home to be lighted of an evening, no household work to be done. So; she

hies to her tryst, for this is the land of the Vaishnava Poets. She
has left home, forgotten domestic duties; she has nothing but an
unfathomable yearning which hurries her on – by what road, to
what goal, she recks not.

I, also, am possessed of just such a yearning. I likewise have
lost my home and also lost my way. Both the end and the means
have become equally shadowy to me. There remain only the
yearning and the hurrying on. Ah! wretched wanderer through
the night, when the dawn reddens you will see no trace of a
way to return. But why return? Death will serve as well. If the
Dark which sounded the flute should lead to destruction, why
trouble about the hereafter? When I am merged in its blackness,
neither I, nor good and bad, nor laughter, nor tears, shall be
any more!

XII

IN BENGAL THE machinery of time being thus suddenly run
at full pressure, things which were difficult became easy, one
following soon after another. Nothing could be held back any
more, even in our corner of the country. In the beginning our
district was backward, for my husband was unwilling to put any
compulsion on the villagers. 'Those who make sacrifices for their
country's sake are indeed her servants,' he would say, 'but those
who compel others to make them in her name are her enemies.
They would cut freedom at the root, to gain it at the top.'

But when Sandip came and settled here, and his followers
began to move about the country, speaking in towns and market-
places, waves of excitement came rolling up to us as well. A band
of young fellows of the locality attached themselves to him, some
even who had been known as a disgrace to the village. But the
glow of their genuine enthusiasm lighted them up, within as well
as without. It became quite clear that when the pure breezes
of a great joy and hope sweep through the land, all dirt and
decay are cleansed away. It is hard, indeed, for men to be frank
and straight and healthy, when their country is in the throes
of dejection.

Then were all eyes turned on my husband, from whose estates
alone foreign sugar and salt and cloths had not been banished.
Even the estate officers began to feel awkward and ashamed over
it. And yet, some time ago, when my husband began to import
country-made articles into our village, he had been secretly

and openly twitted for his folly, by old and young alike. When *Swadeshi* had not yet become a boast, we had despised it with all our hearts.

My husband still sharpens his Indian-made pencils with his Indian-made knife, does his writing with reed pens, drinks his water out of a bell-metal vessel, and works at night in the light of an old-fashioned castor-oil lamp. But this dull, milk-and-water *Swadeshi* of his never appealed to us. Rather, we had always felt ashamed of the inelegant, unfashionable furniture of his reception-rooms, especially when he had the magistrate, or any other European, as his guest.

My husband used to make light of my protests. 'Why allow such trifles to upset you?' he would say with a smile.

'They will think us barbarians, or at all events wanting in refinement.'

'If they do, I will pay them back by thinking that their refinement does not go deeper than their white skins.'

My husband had an ordinary brass pot on his writing-table which he used as a flower-vase. It has often happened that, when I had news of some European guest, I would steal into his room and put in its place a crystal vase of European make. 'Look here, Bimala,' he objected at length, 'that brass pot is as unconscious of itself as those blossoms are; but this thing protests its purpose so loudly, it is only fit for artificial flowers.'

The Bara Rani, alone, pandered to my husband's whims. Once she comes panting to say: 'Oh, brother, have you heard? Such lovely Indian soaps have come out! My days of luxury are gone by; still, if they contain no animal fat, I should like to try some.'

This sort of thing makes my husband beam all over, and the house is deluged with Indian scents and soaps. Soaps indeed! They are more like lumps of caustic soda. And do I not know that what my sister-in-law uses on herself are the European soaps of old, while these are made over to the maids for washing clothes?

Another time it is: 'Oh, brother dear, do get me some of these new Indian pen-holders.'

Her 'brother' bubbles up as usual, and the Bara Rani's room becomes littered with all kinds of awful sticks that go by the name of *Swadeshi* pen-holders. Not that it makes any difference to her, for reading and writing are out of her line. Still, in her writing-case, lies the selfsame ivory pen-holder, the only one ever handled.

The fact is, all this was intended as a hit at me, because I would not keep my husband company in his vagaries. It was no good trying to show up my sister-in-law's insincerity; my husband's face would set so hard, if I barely touched on it. One only gets into trouble, trying to save such people from being imposed upon!

The Bara Rani loves sewing. One day I could not help blurting out: 'What a humbug you are, sister! When your "brother" is present, your mouth waters at the very mention of *Swadeshi* scissors, but it is the English-made article every time when you work.'

'What harm?' she replied. 'Do you not see what pleasure it gives him? We have grown up together in this house, since he was a boy. I simply cannot bear, as you can, the sight of the smile leaving his face. Poor dear, he has no amusement except this playing at shop-keeping. You are his only dissipation, and you will yet be his ruin!'

'Whatever you may say, it is not right to be double-faced,' I retorted.

My sister-in-law laughed out in my face. 'Oh, our artless little Chota Rani! – straight as a schoolmaster's rod, eh? But a woman is not built that way. She is soft and supple, so that she may bend without being crooked.'

I could not forget those words: 'You are his dissipation, and will be his ruin!' Today I feel – if a man needs must have some intoxicant, let it not be a woman.

XIII

SUKSAR, WITHIN OUR estates, is one of the biggest trade centres in the district. On one side of a stretch of water there is held a daily bazar; on the other, a weekly market. During the rains when this piece of water gets connected with the river, and boats can come through, great quantities of cotton yarns, and woollen stuffs for the coming winter, are brought in for sale.

At the height of our enthusiasm, Sandip laid it down that all foreign articles, together with the demon of foreign influence, must be driven out of our territory.

'Of course!' said I, girding myself up for a fight.

'I have had words with Nikhil about it,' said Sandip. 'He

tells me, he does not mind speechifying, but he will not have coercion.'

'I will see to that,' I said, with a proud sense of power. I knew how deep was my husband's love for me. Had I been in my senses I should have allowed myself to be torn to pieces rather than assert my claim to that, at such a time. But Sandip had to be impressed with the full strength of my *Shakti*.

Sandip had brought home to me, in his irresistible way, how the cosmic Energy was revealed for each individual in the shape of some special affinity. Vaishnava Philosophy, he said, speaks of the Shakti of Delight that dwells in the heart of creation, ever attracting the heart of her Eternal Lover. Men have a perpetual longing to bring out this *Shakti* from the hidden depths of their own nature, and those of us who succeed in doing so at once clearly understand the meaning of the music coming to us from the Dark. He broke out singing:

> '*My flute, that was busy with its song,*
> *Is silent now when we stand face to face.*
> *My call went seeking you from sky to sky*
> > *When you lay hidden;*
> *But now all my cry finds its smile*
> > *In the face of my beloved.'*

Listening to his allegories, I had forgotten that I was plain and simple Bimala. I was *Shakti*; also an embodiment of Universal joy. Nothing could fetter me, nothing was impossible for me; whatever I touched would gain new life. The world around me was a fresh creation of mine; for behold, before my heart's response had touched it, there had not been this wealth of gold in the Autumn sky! And this hero, this true servant of the country, this devotee of mine – this flaming intelligence, this burning energy, this shining genius – him also was I creating from moment to moment. Have I not seen how my presence pours fresh life into him time after time?

The other day Sandip begged me to receive a young lad, Amulya, an ardent disciple of his. In a moment I could see a new light flash out from the boy's eyes, and knew that he, too, had a vision of *Shakti* manifest, that my creative force had begun its work in his blood. 'What sorcery is this of yours!' exclaimed Sandip next day. 'Amulya is a boy no longer, the wick of his life is all ablaze. Who can hide your fire under your home-roof?

Every one of them must be touched up by it, sooner or later, and when every lamp is alight what a grand carnival of a *Dewali* we shall have in the country!'

Blinded with the brilliance of my own glory I had decided to grant my devotee this boon. I was overweeningly confident that none could baulk me of what I really wanted. When I returned to my room after my talk with Sandip, I loosed my hair and tied it up over again. Miss Gilby had taught me a way of brushing it up from the neck and piling it in a knot over my head. This style was a favourite one with my husband. 'It is a pity,' he once said, 'that Providence should have chosen poor me, instead of poet Kalidas, for revealing all the wonders of a woman's neck. The poet would probably have likened it to a flower-stem; but I feel it to be a torch, holding aloft the black flame of your hair.' With which he . . . but why, oh why, do I go back to all that?

I sent for my husband. In the old days I could contrive a hundred and one excuses, good or bad, to get him to come to me. Now that all this had stopped for days I had lost the art of contriving.

Nikhil's Story

VI

PANCHU'S WIFE HAS just died of a lingering consumption. Panchu must undergo a purification ceremony to cleanse himself of sin and to propitiate his community. The community has calculated and informed him that it will cost one hundred and twenty-three rupees.

'How absurd!' I cried, highly indignant. 'Don't submit to this, Panchu. What can they do to you?'

Raising to me his patient eyes like those of a tired-out beast of burden, he said: 'There is my eldest girl, sir, she will have to be married. And my poor wife's last rites have to be put through.'

'Even if the sin were yours, Panchu,' I mused aloud, 'you have surely suffered enough for it already.'

'That is so, sir,' he naïvely assented. 'I had to sell part of my land and mortgage the rest to meet the doctor's bills. But there is no escape from the offerings I have to make the Brahmins.'

What was the use of arguing? When will come the time, I wondered, for the purification of the Brahmins themselves who can accept such offerings?

After his wife's illness and funeral, Panchu, who had been tottering on the brink of starvation, went altogether beyond his depth. In a desperate attempt to gain consolation of some sort he took to sitting at the feet of a wandering ascetic, and succeeded in acquiring philosophy enough to forget that his children went hungry. He kept himself steeped for a time in the idea that the world is vanity, and if of pleasure it has none, pain also is a delusion. Then, at last, one night he left his little ones in their tumble-down hovel, and started off wandering on his own account.

I knew nothing of this at the time, for just then a veritable ocean-churning by gods and demons was going on in my mind. Nor did my master tell me that he had taken Panchu's deserted children under his own roof and was caring for them, though alone in the house, with his school to attend to the whole day.

After a month Panchu came back, his ascetic fervour considerably worn off. His eldest boy and girl nestled up to him, crying: 'Where have you been all this time, father?' His youngest boy filled his lap; his second girl leant over his back with her arms around his neck; and they all wept together. 'O sir!' sobbed Panchu, at length, to my master. 'I have not the power to give these little ones enough to eat – I am not free to run away from them. What has been my sin that I should be scourged so, bound hand and foot?'

In the meantime the thread of Panchu's little trade connections had snapped and he found he could not resume them. He clung on to the shelter of my master's roof, which had first received him on his return, and said not a word of going back home. 'Look here, Panchu,' my master was at last driven to say. 'If you don't take care of your cottage, it will tumble down altogether. I will lend you some money with which you can do a bit of peddling and return it me little by little.'

Panchu was not excessively pleased – was there then no such thing as charity on earth? And when my master asked him to write out a receipt for the money, he felt that this favour, demanding a return, was hardly worth having. My master, however, did not care to make an outward gift which would leave an inward obligation. To destroy self-respect is to destroy caste, was his idea.

After signing the note, Panchu's obeisance to my master fell off considerably in its reverence – the dust-taking was left out. It made my master smile; he asked nothing better than that courtesy should stoop less low. 'Respect given and taken truly balances the account between man and man,' was the way he put it, 'but veneration is overpayment.'

Panchu began to buy cloth at the market and peddle it about the village. He did not get much of cash payment, it is true, but what he could realize in kind, in the way of rice, jute, and other field produce, went towards settlement of his account. In two months' time he was able to pay back an instalment of my master's debt, and with it there was a corresponding reduction in the depth of his bow. He must have begun to feel that he had been revering as a saint a mere man, who had not even risen superior to the lure of lucre.

While Panchu was thus engaged, the full shock of the *Swadeshi* flood fell on him.

VII

IT WAS VACATION time, and many youths of our village and its neighbourhood had come home from their schools and colleges. They attached themselves to Sandip's leadership with enthusiasm, and some, in their excess of zeal, gave up their studies altogether. Many of the boys had been free pupils of my school here, and some held college scholarships from me in Calcutta. They came up in a body, and demanded that I should banish foreign goods from my Suksar market.

I told them I could not do it.

They were sarcastic: 'Why, Maharaja, will the loss be too much for you?'

I took no notice of the insult in their tone, and was about to reply that the loss would fall on the poor traders and their customers, not on me, when my master, who was present, interposed.

'Yes, the loss will be his – not yours, that is clear enough,' he said.

'But for one's country . . .'

'The country does not mean the soil, but the men on it,' interrupted my master again. 'Have you yet wasted so much as a glance on what was happening to them? But now you would dictate what salt they shall eat, what clothes they shall wear. Why should they put up with such tyranny, and why should we let them?'

'But we have taken to Indian salt and sugar and cloth ourselves.'

'You may do as you please to work off your irritation, to keep up your fanaticism. You are well off, you need not mind the cost. The poor do not want to stand in your way, but you insist on their submitting to your compulsion. As it is, every moment of theirs is a life-and-death struggle for a bare living; you cannot even imagine the difference a few pice means to them – so little have you in common. You have spent your whole past in a superior compartment, and now you come down to use them as tools for the wreaking of your wrath. I call it cowardly.'

They were all old pupils of my master, so they did not venture to be disrespectful, though they were quivering with indignation. They turned to me. 'Will you then be the only one, Maharaja, to put obstacles in the way of what the country would achieve?'

'Who am I, that I should dare do such a thing? Would I not rather lay down my life to help it?'

The M.A. student smiled a crooked smile, as he asked: 'May we enquire what you are actually doing to help?'

'I have imported Indian mill-made yarn and kept it for sale in my Suksar market, and also sent bales of it to markets belonging to neighbouring *zamindars*.'

'But we have been to your market, Maharaja,' the same student exclaimed, 'and found nobody buying this yarn.'

'That is neither my fault nor the fault of my market. It only shows the whole country has not taken your vow.'

'That is not all,' my master went on. 'It shows that what you have pledged yourselves to do is only to pester others. You want dealers, who have not taken your vow, to buy that yarn; weavers, who have not taken your vow, to make it up; then their wares eventually to be foisted on to consumers who, also, have not taken your vow. The method? Your clamour, and the *zamindars'* oppression. The result: all righteousness yours, all privations theirs!'

'And may we venture to ask, further, what your share of the privation has been?' pursued a science student.

'You want to know, do you?' replied my master. 'It is Nikhil himself who has to buy up that Indian mill yarn; he has had to start a weaving school to get it woven; and to judge by his past brilliant business exploits, by the time his cotton fabrics leave the loom their cost will be that of cloth-of-gold; so they will only find a use, perhaps, as curtains for his drawing-room, even though their flimsiness may fail to screen him. When you get tired of your vow, you will laugh the loudest at their artistic effect. And if their workmanship is ever truly appreciated at all, it will be by foreigners.'

I have known my master all my life, but have never seen him so agitated. I could see that the pain had been silently accumulating in his heart for some time, because of his surpassing love for me, and that his habitual self-possession had become secretly undermined to the breaking point.

'You are our elders,' said the medical student. 'It is unseemly that we should bandy words with you. But tell us, pray, finally, are you determined not to oust foreign articles from your market?'

'I will not,' I said, 'because they are not mine.'

'Because that will cause you a loss!' smiled the M.A. student.

'Because he, whose is the loss, is the best judge,' retorted my master.

With a shout of *Bande Mataram* they left us.

CHAPTER SIX

Nikhil's Story

VIII

A FEW DAYS LATER, my master brought Panchu round to me. His *zamindar*, it appeared, had fined him a hundred rupees, and was threatening him with ejectment.

'For what fault?' I enquired.

'Because,' I was told, 'he has been found selling foreign cloths. He begged and prayed Harish Kundu, his *zamindar*, to let him sell off his stock, bought with borrowed money, promising faithfully never to do it again; but the *zamindar* would not hear of it, and insisted on his burning the foreign stuff there and then, if he wanted to be let off. Panchu in his desperation blurted out defiantly: "I can't afford it! You are rich; why not buy it up and burn it?" This only made Harish Kundu red in the face as he shouted: "The scoundrel must be taught manners, give him a shoe-beating!" So poor Panchu got insulted as well as fined.'

'What happened to the cloth?'

'The whole bale was burnt.'

'Who else was there?'

'Any number of people, who all kept shouting *Bande Mataram*. Sandip was also there. He took up some of the ashes, crying: "Brothers! This is the first funeral pyre lighted by your village in celebration of the last rites of foreign commerce. These are sacred ashes. Smear yourselves with them in token of your *Swadeshi* vow." '

'Panchu,' said I, turning to him, 'you must lodge a complaint.'

'No one will bear me witness,' he replied.

'None bear witness? – Sandip! Sandip!'

Sandip came out of his room at my call. 'What is the matter?' he asked.

'Won't you bear witness to the burning of this man's cloth?'

Sandip smiled. 'Of course I shall be a witness in the case,' he said. 'But I shall be on the opposite side.'

'What do you mean,' I exclaimed, 'by being a witness on this or that side? Will you not bear witness to the truth?'

'Is the thing which happens the only truth?'

'What other truths can there be?'

'The things that ought to happen! The truth we must build up will require a great deal of untruth in the process. Those who have made their way in the world have created truth, not blindly followed it.'

'And so –'

'And so I will bear what you people are pleased to call false witness, as they have done who have created empires, built up social systems, founded religious organizations. Those who would rule do not dread untruths; the shackles of truth are reserved for those who will fall under their sway. Have you not read history? Do you not know that in the immense cauldrons, where vast political developments are simmering, untruths are the main ingredients?'

'Political cookery on a large scale is doubtless going on, but –'

'Oh, I know! You, of course, will never do any of the cooking. You prefer to be one of those down whose throats the hotchpotch which is being cooked will be crammed. They will partition Bengal and say it is for your benefit. They will seal the doors of education and call it raising the standard. But you will always remain good boys, snivelling in your corners. We bad men, however, must see whether we cannot erect a defensive fortification of untruth.'

'It is no use arguing about these things, Nikhil,' my master interposed. 'How can they who do not feel the truth within them, realize that to bring it out from its obscurity into the light is man's highest aim – not to keep on heaping material outside?'

Sandip laughed. 'Right, sir!' said he. 'Quite a correct speech for a schoolmaster. That is the kind of stuff I have read in books; but in the real world I have seen that man's chief business is the accumulation of outside material. Those who are masters in the art, advertise the biggest lies in their business, enter false accounts in their political ledgers with their broadest-pointed pens, launch their newspapers daily laden with untruths, and send preachers abroad to disseminate falsehood like flies carrying pestilential germs. I am a humble follower of these great ones. When I was attached to the Congress party I never hesitated to dilute ten per cent of truth with ninety per cent of untruth. And now, merely because I have ceased to belong to that party, I have not forgotten the basic fact that man's goal is not truth but success.'

'True success,' corrected my master.

'Maybe,' replied Sandip, 'but the fruit of true success ripens only by cultivating the field of untruth, after tearing up the soil and pounding it into dust. Truth grows up by itself like weeds and thorns, and only worms can expect to get fruit from it!' With this he flung out of the room.

My master smiled as he looked towards me. 'Do you know, Nikhil,' he said, 'I believe Sandip is not irreligious – his religion is of the obverse side of truth, like the dark moon, which is still a moon, for all that its light has gone over to the wrong side.'

'That is why,' I assented, 'I have always had an affection for him, though we have never been able to agree. I cannot contemn him, even now; though he has hurt me sorely, and may yet hurt me more.'

'I have begun to realize that,' said my master. 'I have long wondered how you could go on putting up with him. I have, at times, even suspected you of weakness. I now see that though you two do not rhyme, your rhythm is the same.'

'Fate seems bent on writing *Paradise Lost* in blank verse, in my case, and so has no use for a rhyming friend!' I remarked, pursuing his conceit.

'But what of Panchu?' resumed my master.

'You say Harish Kundu wants to eject him from his ancestral holding. Supposing I buy it up and then keep him on as my tenant?'

'And his fine?'

'How can the *zamindar* realize that if he becomes my tenant?'

'His burnt bale of cloth?'

'I will procure him another. I should like to see anyone interfering with a tenant of mine, for trading as he pleases!'

'I am afraid, sir,' interposed Panchu despondently, 'while you big folk are doing the fighting, the police and the law vultures will merrily gather round, and the crowd will enjoy the fun, but when it comes to getting killed, it will be the turn of only poor me!'

'Why, what harm can come to you?'

'They will burn down my house, sir, children and all!'

'Very well, I will take charge of your children,' said my master. 'You may go on with any trade you like. They shan't touch you.'

That very day I bought up Panchu's holding and entered into formal possession. Then the trouble began.

Panchu had inherited the holding of his grandfather as his sole surviving heir. Everybody knew this. But at this juncture an aunt turned up from somewhere, with her boxes and bundles, her rosary, and a widowed niece. She ensconced herself in Panchu's home and laid claim to a life interest in all he had.

Panchu was dumbfounded. 'My aunt died long ago,' he protested.

In reply he was told that he was thinking of his uncle's first wife, but that the former had lost no time in taking to himself a second.

'But my uncle died before my aunt,' exclaimed Panchu, still more mystified. 'Where was the time for him to marry again?'

This was not denied. But Panchu was reminded that it had never been asserted that the second wife had come after the death of the first, but the former had been married by his uncle during the latter's lifetime. Not relishing the idea of living with a co-wife she had remained in her father's house till her husband's death, after which she had got religion and retired to holy Brindaban, whence she was now coming. These facts were well known to the officers of Harish Kundu, as well as to some of his tenants. And if the *zamindar*'s summons should be peremptory enough, even some of those who had partaken of the marriage feast would be forthcoming!

IX

ONE AFTERNOON, when I happened to be specially busy, word came to my office room that Bimala had sent for me. I was startled.

'Who did you say had sent for me?' I asked the messenger.

'The Rani Mother.'

'The Bara Rani?'

'No, sir, the Chota Rani Mother.'

The Chota Rani! It seemed a century since I had been sent for by her. I kept them all waiting there, and went off into the inner apartments. When I stepped into our room I had another shock of surprise to find Bimala there with a distinct suggestion of being dressed up. The room, which from persistent neglect had latterly acquired an air of having grown absent-minded, had regained something of its old order this afternoon. I stood there silently, looking enquiringly at Bimala.

She flushed a little and the fingers of her right hand toyed for a time with the bangles on her left arm. Then she abruptly broke the silence. 'Look here! Is it right that ours should be the only market in all Bengal which allows foreign goods?'

'What, then, would be the right thing to do?' I asked.

'Order them to be cleared out!'

'But the goods are not mine.'

'Is not the market yours?'

'It is much more theirs who use it for trade.'

'Let them trade in Indian goods, then.'

'Nothing would please me better. But suppose they do not?'

'Nonsense! How dare they be so insolent? Are you not . . .'

'I am very busy this afternoon and cannot stop to argue it out. But I must refuse to tyrannize.'

'It would not be tyranny for selfish gain, but for the sake of the country.'

'To tyrannize for the country is to tyrannize over the country. But that I am afraid you will never understand.' With this I came away.

All of a sudden the world shone out for me with a fresh clearness. I seemed to feel it in my blood, that the Earth had lost the weight of its earthiness, and its daily task of sustaining life no longer appeared a burden, as with a wonderful access of power it whirled through space telling its beads of days and nights. What endless work, and withal what illimitable energy of freedom! None shall check it, oh, none can ever check it! From the depths of my being an uprush of joy, like a waterspout, sprang high to storm the skies.

I repeatedly asked myself the meaning of this outburst of feeling. At first there was no intelligible answer. Then it became clear that the bond against which I had been fretting inwardly, night and day, had broken. To my surprise I discovered that my mind was freed from all mistiness. I could see everything relating to Bimala as if vividly pictured on a camera screen. It was palpable that she had specially dressed herself up to coax that order out of me. Till that moment, I had never viewed Bimala's adornment as a thing apart from herself. But today the elaborate manner in which she had done up her hair, in the English fashion, made it appear a mere decoration. That which before had the mystery of her personality about it, and was priceless to me, was now out to sell itself cheap.

As I came away from that broken cage of a bedroom, out into the golden sunlight of the open, there was the avenue of bauhinias, along the gravelled path in front of my verandah, suffusing the sky with a rosy flush. A group of starlings beneath the trees were noisily chattering away. In the distance an empty bullock cart, with its nose on the ground, held up its tail aloft – one of its unharnessed bullocks grazing, the other resting on the grass, its eyes dropping for very comfort, while a crow on its back was pecking away at the insects on its body.

I seemed to have come closer to the heartbeats of the great earth in all the simplicity of its daily life; its warm breath fell on me with the perfume of the bauhinia blossoms; and an anthem, inexpressibly sweet, seemed to peal forth from this world, where I, in my freedom, live in the freedom of all else.

We, men, are knights whose quest is that freedom to which our ideals call us. She who makes for us the banner under which we fare forth is the true Woman for us. We must tear away the disguise of her who weaves our net of enchantment at home, and know her for what she is. We must beware of clothing her in the witchery of our own longings and imaginings, and thus allow her to distract us from our true quest.

Today I feel that I shall win through. I have come to the gateway of the simple; I am now content to see things as they are. I have gained freedom myself; I shall allow freedom to others. In my work will be my salvation.

I know that, time and again, my heart will ache, but now that I understand its pain in all its truth, I can disregard it. Now that I know it concerns only me, what after all can be its value? The suffering which belongs to all mankind shall be my crown.

Save me, Truth! Never again let me hanker after the false paradise of Illusion. If I must walk alone, let me at least tread your path. Let the drum-beats of Truth lead me to Victory.

Sandip's Story

VII

BIMALA SENT FOR me that day, but for a time she could not utter a word; her eyes kept brimming up to the verge of overflowing. I could see at once that she had been unsuccessful with Nikhil. She had been so proudly confident that she would have her own way – but I had never shared her confidence. Woman knows man well enough where he is weak, but she is quite unable to fathom him where he is strong. The fact is that man is as much a mystery to woman as woman is to man. If that were not so, the separation of the sexes would only have been a waste of Nature's energy.

Ah pride, pride! The trouble was, not that the necessary thing had failed of accomplishment, but that the entreaty, which had cost her such a struggle to make, should have been refused. What a wealth of colour and movement, suggestion and deception, group themselves round this 'me' and 'mine' in woman. That is just where her beauty lies – she is ever so much more personal than man. When man was being made, the Creator was a school-master – His bag full of commandments and principles; but when He came to woman, He resigned His headmastership and turned artist, with only His brush and paint-box.

When Bimala stood silently there, flushed and tearful in her broken pride, like a storm-cloud, laden with rain and charged with lightning, lowering over the horizon, she looked so abso-lutely sweet that I had to go right up to her and take her by the hand. It was trembling, but she did not snatch it away. 'Bee,' said I, 'we two are colleagues: for our aims are one. Let us sit down and talk it over.'

I led her, unresisting, to a seat. But strange! at that very point the rush of my impetuosity suffered an unaccountable check – just as the current of the mighty Padma, roaring on in its irresist-ible course, all of a sudden gets turned away from the bank it is crumbling by some trifling obstacle beneath the surface. When I pressed Bimala's hand my nerves rang music, like tuned-up strings; but the symphony stopped short at the first movement.

What stood in the way? Nothing singly; it was a tangle of a multitude of things – nothing definitely palpable, but only that unaccountable sense of obstruction. Anyhow, this much has become plain to me, that I cannot swear to what I really am. It is because I am such a mystery to my own mind that my attrac-tion for myself is so strong! If once the whole of myself should become known to me, I would then fling it all away – and reach beatitude!

As she sat down, Bimala went ashy pale. She, too, must have realized what a crisis had come and gone, leaving her unscathed. The comet had passed by, but the brush of its burning tail had overcome her. To help her to recover herself I said: 'Obstacles there will be, but let us fight them through, and not be down-hearted. Is not that best, Queen?'

Bimala cleared her throat with a little cough, but simply to murmur: 'Yes.'

'Let us sketch out our plan of action,' I continued, as I drew a piece of paper and a pencil from my pocket.

I began to make a list of the workers who had joined us from Calcutta and to assign their duties to each. Bimala interrupted me before I was through, saying wearily: 'Leave it now; I will join you again this evening'; and then she hurried out of the room. It was evident she was not in a state to attend to anything. She must be alone with herself for a while – perhaps lie down on her bed and have a good cry!

When she left me, my intoxication began to deepen, as the cloud colours grow richer after the sun is down. I felt I had let the moment of moments slip by. What an awful coward I had been! She must have left me in sheer disgust at my qualms – and she was right!

While I was tingling all over with these reflections, a servant came in and announced Amulya, one of our boys. I felt like sending him away for the time, but he stepped in before I could make up my mind. Then we fell to discussing the news of the fights which were raging in different quarters over cloth and sugar and salt; and the air was soon clear of all fumes of intoxication. I felt as if awakened from a dream. I leapt to my feet feeling quite ready for the fray – *Bande Mataram!*

The news was various. Most of the traders who were tenants of Harish Kundu had come over to us. Many of Nikhil's officials were also secretly on our side, pulling the wires in our interest. The Marwari shopkeepers were offering to pay a penalty, if only allowed to clear their present stocks. Only some Mahomedan traders were still obdurate.

One of them was taking home some German-made shawls for his family. These were confiscated and burnt by one of our village boys. This had given rise to trouble. We offered to buy him Indian woollen stuffs in their place. But where were cheap Indian woollens to be had? We could not very well indulge him in Cashmere shawls! He came and complained to Nikhil, who advised him to go to law. Of course Nikhil's men saw to it that the trial should come to nothing, even his law-agent being on our side!

The point is, if we have to replace burnt foreign clothes with Indian cloth every time, and on the top of that fight through a law-suit, where is the money to come from? And the beauty of it is that this destruction of foreign goods is increasing their demand and sending up the foreigner's profits – very like what happened to the fortunate shopkeeper whose chandeliers the nabob delighted in smashing, tickled by the tinkle of the breaking glass.

The next problem is – since there is no such thing as cheap and gaudy Indian woollen stuff, should we be rigorous in our boycott of foreign flannels and merinos, or make an exception in their favour?

'Look here!' said I at length on the first point, 'we are not going to keep on making presents of Indian stuff to those who have got their foreign purchases confiscated. The penalty is intended to fall on them, not on us. If they go to law, we must retaliate by burning down their granaries! – What startles you, Amulya? It is not the prospect of a grand illumination that delights me! You must remember, this is War. If you are afraid of causing suffering, go in for lovemaking, you will never do for this work!'

The second problem I solved by deciding to allow no compromise with foreign articles, in any circumstance whatever. In the good old days, when these gaily coloured foreign shawls were unknown, our peasantry used to manage well enough with plain cotton quilts – they must learn to do so again. They may not look as gorgeous, but this is not the time to think of looks.

Most of the boatmen had been won over to refuse to carry foreign goods, but the chief of them, Mirjan, was still insubordinate.

'Could you not get his boat sunk?' I asked our manager here.

'Nothing easier, sir,' he replied. 'But what if afterwards I am held responsible?'

'Why be so clumsy as to leave any loophole for responsibility? However, if there must be any, my shoulders will be there to bear it.'

Mirjan's boat was tied near the landing-place after its freight had been taken over to the market-place. There was no one on it, for the manager had arranged for some entertainment to which all had been invited. After dusk the boat, loaded with rubbish, was holed and set adrift. It sank in mid-stream.

Mirjan understood the whole thing. He came to me in tears to beg for mercy. 'I was wrong, sir –' he began.

'What makes you realize that all of a sudden?' I sneered.

He made no direct reply. 'The boat was worth two thousand rupees,' he said. 'I now see my mistake, and if excused this time I will never . . .' with which he threw himself at my feet.

I asked him to come ten days later. If only we could pay him that two thousand rupees at once, we could buy him up body and soul. This is just the sort of man who could render us immense service, if won over. We shall never be able to make any headway unless we can lay our hands on plenty of money.

As soon as Bimala came into the sitting-room, in the evening, I said as I rose up to receive her: 'Queen! Everything is ready, success is at hand, but we must have money.'

'Money? How much money?'

'Not so very much, but by hook or by crook we must have it!'

'But how much?'

'A mere fifty thousand rupees will do for the present.'

Bimala blenched inwardly at the figure, but tried not to show it. How could she again admit defeat?

'Queen!' said I, 'you only can make the impossible possible. Indeed you have already done so. Oh, that I could show you the extent of your achievement – then you would know it. But the time for that is not now. Now we want money!'

'You shall have it,' she said.

I could see that the thought of selling her jewels had occurred to her. So I said: 'Your jewels must remain in reserve. One can never tell when they may be wanted.' And then, as Bimala stared blankly at me in silence, I went on: 'This money must come from your husband's treasury.'

Bimala was still more taken aback. After a long pause she said: 'But how am I to get his money?'

'Is not his money yours as well?'

'Ah, no!' she said, her wounded pride hurt afresh.

'If not,' I cried, 'neither is it his, but his country's, whom he has deprived of it, in her time of need!'

'But how am I to get it?' she repeated.

'Get it you shall and must. You know best how. You must get it for Her to whom it rightfully belongs. *Bande Mataram!*

These are the magic words which will open the door of his iron safe, break through the walls of his strong-room, and confound the hearts of those who are disloyal to its call. Say *Bande Mataram*, Bee!'

'*Bande Mataram!*'

CHAPTER SEVEN

Sandip's Story

VIII

WE ARE MEN, we are kings, we must have our tribute. Ever since we have come upon the Earth we have been plundering her; and the more we claimed, the more she submitted. From primeval days have we men been plucking fruits, cutting down trees, digging up the soil, killing beast, bird and fish. From the bottom of the sea, from underneath the ground, from the very jaws of death, it has all been grabbing and grabbing and grabbing – no strong-box in Nature's store-room has been respected or left unrifled.

The one delight of this Earth is to fulfil the claims of those who are men. She has been made fertile and beautiful and complete through her endless sacrifices to them. But for this, she would be lost in the wilderness, not knowing herself, the doors of her heart shut, her diamonds and pearls never seeing the light.

Likewise, by sheer force of our claims, we men have opened up all the latent possibilities of women. In the process of surrendering themselves to us, they have ever gained their true greatness. Because they had to bring all the diamonds of their happiness and the pearls of their sorrow into our royal treasury, they have found their true wealth. So for men to accept is truly to give: for women to give is truly to gain.

The demand I have just made from Bimala, however, is indeed a large one! At first I felt scruples; for is it not the habit of man's mind to be in purposeless conflict with itself? I thought I had imposed too hard a task. My first impulse was to call her back, and tell her I would rather not make her life wretched by dragging her into all these troubles. I forgot, for the moment, that it was the mission of man to be aggressive, to make woman's existence fruitful by stirring up disquiet in the depth of her passivity, to make the whole world blessed by churning up the immeasurable abyss of suffering! This is why man's hands are so strong, his grip so firm.

Bimala had been longing with all her heart that I, Sandip, should demand of her some great sacrifice – should call her to her death. How else could she be happy? Had she not waited all these weary years only for an opportunity to weep out her heart – so satiated was she with the monotony of her placid happiness? And therefore, at the very sight of me, her heart's horizon darkened with the rain clouds of her impending days of anguish. If I pity her and save her from her sorrows, what then was the purpose of my being born a man?

The real reason of my qualms is that my demand happens to be for money. That savours of beggary, for money is man's, not woman's. That is why I had to make it a big figure. A thousand or two would have the air of petty theft. Fifty thousand has all the expanse of romantic brigandage.

Ah, but riches should really have been mine! So many of my desires have had to halt, again and again, on the road to accomplishment simply for want of money. This does not become me! Had my fate been merely unjust, it could be forgiven – but its bad taste is unpardonable. It is not simply a hardship that a man like me should be at his wit's end to pay his house rent, or should have to carefully count out the coins for an Intermediate Class railway ticket – it is vulgar!

It is equally clear that Nikhil's paternal estates are a superfluity to him. For him it would not have been at all unbecoming to be poor. He would have cheerfully pulled in the double harness of indigent mediocrity with that precious master of his.

I should love to have, just for once, the chance to fling about fifty thousand rupees in the service of my country and to the satisfaction of myself. I am a nabob born, and it is a great dream of mine to get rid of this disguise of poverty, though it be for a day only, and to see myself in my true character.

I have grave misgivings, however, as to Bimala ever getting that fifty thousand rupees within her reach, and it will probably be only a thousand or two which will actually come to hand. Be it so. The wise man is content with half a loaf, or any fraction for that matter, rather than no bread.

I must return to these personal reflections of mine later. News comes that I am wanted at once. Something has gone wrong . . .

It seems that the police have got a clue to the man who sank Mirjan's boat for us. He was an old offender. They are on his trail, but he should be too practised a hand to be caught blabbing. However, one never knows. Nikhil's back is up, and his manager may not be able to have things his own way.

'If I get into trouble, sir,' said the manager when I saw him, 'I shall have to drag you in!'

'Where is the noose with which you can catch me?' I asked.

'I have a letter of yours, and several of Amulya Babu's.'

I could not see that the letter marked 'urgent' to which I had been hurried into writing a reply was wanted urgently for this purpose only! I am getting to learn quite a number of things.

The point now is, that the police must be bribed and hush-money paid to Mirjan for his boat. It is also becoming evident that much of the cost of this patriotic venture of ours will find its way as profit into the pockets of Nikhil's manager. However, I must shut my eyes to that for the present, for is he not shouting *Bande Mataram* as lustily as I am?

This kind of work has always to be carried on with leaky vessels which let as much through as they fetch in. We all have a hidden fund of moral judgement stored away within us, and so I was about to wax indignant with the manager, and enter in my diary a tirade against the unreliability of our countrymen. But, if there be a god, I must acknowledge with gratitude to him that he has given me a clear-seeing mind, which allows nothing inside or outside it to remain vague. I may delude others, but never myself. So I was unable to continue angry.

Whatever is true is neither good nor bad, but simply true, and that is Science. A lake is only the remnant of water which has not been sucked into the ground. Underneath the cult of *Bande Mataram*, as indeed at the bottom of all mundane affairs, there is a region of slime, whose absorbing power must be reckoned with. The manager will take what he wants; I also have my own wants. These lesser wants form a part of the wants of the great Cause – the horse must be fed and the wheels must be oiled if the best progress is to be made.

The long and short of it is that money we must have, and that soon. We must take whatever comes the readiest, for we cannot afford to wait. I know that the immediate often swallows up the ultimate; that the five thousand rupees of today may nip in the bud the fifty thousand rupees of tomorrow. But I must accept the penalty. Have I not often twitted Nikhil that they who walk in the paths of restraint have never known what sacrifice is? It is we greedy folk who have to sacrifice our greed at every step!

Of the cardinal sins of man, Desire is for men who are men – but Delusion, which is only for cowards, hampers them. Because delusion keeps them wrapped up in past and future, but is the very deuce for confounding their footsteps in the present. Those who are always straining their ears for the call of the remote, to the neglect of the call of the imminent, are like Sakuntala[1] absorbed in the memories of her lover. The guest comes unheeded, and the curse descends, depriving them of the very object of their desire.

The other day I pressed Bimala's hand, and that touch still stirs her mind, as it vibrates in mine. Its thrill must not be deadened by repetition, for then what is now music will descend to mere argument. There is at present no room in her mind for the question 'why?' So I must not deprive Bimala, who is one of those creatures for whom illusion is necessary, of her full supply of it.

As for me, I have so much else to do that I shall have to be content for the present with the foam of the wine cup of passion. O man of desire! Curb your greed, and practise your hand on the harp of illusion till you can bring out all the delicate nuances of suggestion. This is not the time to drain the cup to the dregs.

IX

OUR WORK PROCEEDS apace. But though we have shouted ourselves hoarse, proclaiming the Mussulmans to be our brethren, we have come to realize that we shall never be able to bring them wholly round to our side. So they must be suppressed altogether and made to understand that we are the masters. They are now showing their teeth, but one day they shall dance like tame bears to the tune we play.

'If the idea of a United India is a true one,' objects Nikhil, 'Mussulmans are a necessary part of it.'

'Quite so,' said I, 'but we must know their place and keep them there, otherwise they will constantly be giving trouble.'

'So you want to make trouble to prevent trouble?'

'What, then, is your plan?'

'There is only one well-known way of avoiding quarrels,' said Nikhil meaningly.

1. Sakuntala, after the king, her lover, went back to his kingdom, promising to send for her, was so lost in thoughts of him, that she failed to hear the call of her hermit guest, who thereupon cursed her, saying that the object of her love would forget all about her.

I know that, like tales written by good people, Nikhil's discourse always ends in a moral. The strange part of it is that with all his familiarity with moral precepts, he still believes in them! He is an incorrigible schoolboy. His only merit is his sincerity. The mischief with people like him is that they will not admit the finality even of death, but keep their eyes always fixed on a hereafter.

I have long been nursing a plan which, if only I could carry it out, would set fire to the whole country. True patriotism will never be roused in our countrymen unless they can visualize the motherland. We must make a goddess of her. My colleagues saw the point at once. 'Let us devise an appropriate image!' they exclaimed. 'It will not do if you devise it,' I admonished them. 'We must get one of the current images accepted as representing the country – the worship of the people must flow towards it along the deep-cut grooves of custom.'

But Nikhil's needs must argue even about this. 'We must not seek the help of illusions,' he said to me some time ago, 'for what we believe to be the true cause.'

'Illusions are necessary for lesser minds,' I said, 'and to this class the greater portion of the world belongs. That is why divinities are set up in every country to keep up the illusions of the people, for men are only too well aware of their weakness.'

'No,' he replied. 'God is necessary to clear away our illusions. The divinities which keep them alive are false gods.'

'What of that? If need be, even false gods must be invoked, rather than let the work suffer. Unfortunately for us, our illusions are alive enough, but we do not know how to make them serve our purpose. Look at the Brahmins. In spite of our treating them as demi-gods, and untiringly taking the dust of their feet, they are a force going to waste.

'There will always be a large class of people, given to grovelling, who can never be made to do anything unless they are bespattered with the dust of somebody's feet, be it on their heads or on their backs! What a pity if after keeping Brahmins saved up in our armoury for all these ages – keen and serviceable – they cannot be utilized to urge on this rabble in the time of our need.'

But it is impossible to drive all this into Nikhil's head. He has such a prejudice in favour of truth – as though there exists such an objective reality! How often have I tried to explain to him that where untruth truly exists, there it is indeed the truth. This was understood in our country in the old days, and so they had the courage to declare that for those of little understanding untruth is the truth. For them, who can truly believe their country to be a goddess, her image will do duty for the truth. With our nature and our traditions we are unable to realize our country as she is, but we can easily bring ourselves to believe in her image. Those who want to do real work must not ignore this fact.

Nikhil only got excited. 'Because you have lost the power of walking in the path of truth's attainment,' he cried, 'you keep waiting for some miraculous boon to drop from the skies! That is why when your service to the country has fallen centuries into arrears all you can think of is, to make of it an image and stretch out your hands in expectation of gratuitous favours.'

'We want to perform the impossible,' I said. 'So our country needs must be made into a god.'

'You mean you have no heart for possible tasks,' replied Nikhil. 'Whatever is already there is to be left undisturbed; yet there must be a supernatural result.'

'Look here, Nikhil,' I said at length, thoroughly exasperated. 'The things you have been saying are good enough as moral lessons. These ideas have served their purpose, as milk for babes, at one stage of man's evolution, but will no longer do, now that man has cut his teeth.

'Do we not see before our very eyes how things, of which we never even dreamt of sowing the seed, are sprouting up on every side? By what power? That of the deity in our country who is becoming manifest. It is for the genius of the age to give that deity its image. Genius does not argue, it creates. I only give form to what the country imagines.

'I will spread it abroad that the goddess has vouchsafed me a dream. I will tell the Brahmins that they have been appointed her priests, and that their downfall has been due to their dereliction of duty in not seeing to the proper performance of her worship. Do you say I shall be uttering lies? No, say I, it is the truth – nay more, the truth which the country has so long been waiting to learn from my lips. If only I could get the opportunity to deliver my message, you would see the stupendous result.'

'What I am afraid of,' said Nikhil, 'is, that my lifetime is limited and the result you speak of is not the final result. It will have after-effects which may not be immediately apparent.'

'I only seek the result,' said I, 'which belongs to today.'

'The result I seek,' answered Nikhil, 'belongs to all time.'

Nikhil may have had his share of Bengal's greatest gift – imagination, but he has allowed it to be overshadowed and nearly killed by an exotic conscientiousness. Just look at the worship of Durga which Bengal has carried to such heights. That is one of her greatest achievements. I can swear that Durga is a political goddess and was conceived as the image of the *Shakti* of patriotism in the days when Bengal was praying to be delivered from Mussulman domination. What other province of India has succeeded in giving such wonderful visual expression to the ideal of its quest?

Nothing betrayed Nikhil's loss of the divine gift of imagination more conclusively than his reply to me. 'During the Mussulman domination,' he said, 'the Maratha and the Sikh asked for fruit from the arms which they themselves took up. The Bengali contented himself with placing weapons in the hands of his goddess and muttering incantations to her; and as his country did not really happen to be a goddess the only fruit he got was the lopped-off heads of the goats and buffaloes of the sacrifice. The day that we seek the good of the country along the path of righteousness, He who is greater than our country will grant us true fruition.'

The unfortunate part of it is that Nikhil's words sound so fine when put down on paper. My words, however, are not meant to be scribbled on paper, but to be scored into the heart of the country. The Pandit records his *Treatise on Agriculture* in printer's ink; but the cultivator at the point of his plough impresses his endeavour deep in the soil.

X

WHEN I NEXT saw Bimala I pitched my key high without further ado. 'Have we been able,' I began, 'to believe with all our heart in the god for whose worship we have been born all these millions of years, until he actually made himself visible to us?

'How often have I told you,' I continued, 'that had I not seen you I never would have known all my country as One. I know not yet whether you rightly understand me. The gods are invisible only in their heaven – on earth they show themselves to mortal men.'

Bimala looked at me in a strange kind of way as she gravely

replied: 'Indeed I understand you, Sandip.' This was the first time she called me plain Sandip.

'Krishna,' I continued, 'whom Arjuna ordinarily knew only as the driver of his chariot, had also His universal aspect, of which, too, Arjuna had a vision one day, and that day he saw the Truth. I have seen your Universal Aspect in my country. The Ganges and the Brahmaputra are the chains of gold that wind round and round your neck; in the woodland fringes on the distant banks of the dark waters of the river, I have seen your collyrium-darkened eyelashes; the changeful sheen of your *sari* moves for me in the play of light and shade amongst the swaying shoots of green corn; and the blazing summer heat, which makes the whole sky lie gasping like a red-tongued lion in the desert, is nothing but your cruel radiance.

'Since the goddess has vouchsafed her presence to her votary in such wonderful guise, it is for me to proclaim her worship throughout our land, and then shall the country gain new life. "Your image make we in temple after temple."[1] But this our people have not yet fully realized. So I would call on them in your name and offer for their worship an image from which none shall be able to withhold belief. Oh give me this boon, this power.'

Bimala's eyelids drooped and she became rigid in her seat like a figure of stone. Had I continued she would have gone off into a trance. When I ceased speaking she opened wide her eyes, and murmured with fixed gaze, as though still dazed: 'O Traveller in the path of Destruction! Who is there that can stay your progress? Do I not see that none shall stand in the way of your desires? Kings shall lay their crowns at your feet; the wealthy shall hasten to throw open their treasure for your acceptance; those who have nothing else shall beg to be allowed to offer their lives. O my king, my god! What you have seen in me I know not, but I have seen the immensity of your grandeur in my heart. Who am I, what am I, in its presence? Ah, the awful power of Devastation! Never shall I truly live till it kills me utterly! I can bear it no longer, my heart is breaking!'

Bimala slid down from her seat and fell at my feet, which she clasped, and then she sobbed and sobbed and sobbed.

This is hypnotism indeed – the charm which can subdue the

---

1. A line from Bankim Chatterjee's national song *Bande Mataram*.

world! No materials, no weapons – but just the delusion of irresistible suggestion. Who says 'Truth shall Triumph'?[1] Delusion
shall win in the end. The Bengali understood this when he conceived the image of the ten-handed goddess astride her lion, and
spread her worship in the land. Bengal must now create a new
image to enchant and conquer the world. *Bande Mataram!*

I gently lifted Bimala back into her chair, and lest reaction
should set in, I began again without losing time: 'Queen! The
Divine Mother has laid on me the duty of establishing her worship in the land. But, alas, I am poor!'

Bimala was still flushed, her eyes clouded, her accents thick,
as she replied: 'You poor? Is not all that each one has yours?
What are my caskets full of jewellery for? Drag away from me
all my gold and gems for your worship. I have no use for them!'

Once before Bimala had offered up her ornaments; I am not
usually in the habit of drawing lines, but I felt I had to draw the
line there.[2] I know why I feel this hesitation. It is for man to
give ornaments to woman; to take them from her wounds his
manliness.

But I must forget myself. Am I taking them? They are for the
Divine Mother, to be poured in worship at her feet. Oh, but it
must be a grand ceremony of worship such as the country has
never beheld before. It must be a landmark in our history. It
shall be my supreme legacy to the Nation. Ignorant men worship
gods. I, Sandip, shall create them.

But all this is a far cry. What about the urgent immediate? At
least three thousand is indispensably necessary – five thousand
would do roundly and nicely. But how on earth am I to mention
money after the high flight we have just taken? And yet time is
precious!

I crushed all hesitation under foot as I jumped up and made

1. A quotation from the Upanishads.
2. There is a world of sentiment attached to the ornaments worn by women in
Bengal. They are not merely indicative of the love and regard of the giver, but
the wearing of them symbolizes all that is held best in wifehood – the constant
solicitude for her husband's welfare, the successful performance of the material
and spiritual duties of the household entrusted to her care. When the husband
dies, and the responsibility for the household changes hands, then are all ornaments cast aside as a sign of the widow's renunciation of worldly concerns. At
any other time the giving up of ornaments is always a sign of supreme distress
and as such appeals acutely to the sense of chivalry of any Bengali who may
happen to witness it.

my plunge: 'Queen! Our purse is empty, our work about to stop!'

Bimala winced. I could see she was thinking of that impossible fifty thousand rupees. What a load she must have been carrying within her bosom, struggling under it, perhaps, through sleepless nights! What else had she with which to express her loving worship? Debarred from offering her heart at my feet, she hankers to make this sum of money, so hopelessly large for her, the bearer of her imprisoned feelings. The thought of what she must have gone through gives me a twinge of pain; for she is now wholly mine. The wrench of plucking up the plant by the roots is over. It is now only careful tending and nurture that is needed.

'Queen!' said I, 'that fifty thousand rupees is not particularly wanted just now. I calculate that, for the present, five thousand or even three will serve.'

The relief made her heart rebound. 'I shall fetch you five thousand,' she said in tones which seemed like an outburst of song – the song which Radhika of the Vaishnava lyrics sang:

For my lover will I bind in my hair
The flower which has no equal in the three worlds!

– it is the same tune, the same song: five thousand will I bring! That flower will I bind in my hair!

The narrow restraint of the flute brings out this quality of song. I must not allow the pressure of too much greed to flatten out the reed, for then, as I fear, music will give place to the questions 'Why?' 'What is the use of so much?' 'How am I to get it?' – not a word of which will rhyme with what Radhika sang! So, as I was saying, illusion alone is real – it is the flute itself; while truth is but its empty hollow. Nikhil has of late got a taste of that pure emptiness – one can see it in his face, which pains even me. But it was Nikhil's boast that he wanted the Truth, while mine was that I would never let go illusion from my grasp. Each has been suited to his taste, so why complain?

To keep Bimala's heart in the rarefied air of idealism, I cut short all further discussion over the five thousand rupees. I reverted to the demon-destroying goddess and her worship. When was the ceremony to be held and where? There is a great annual fair at Ruimari, within Nikhil's estates, where hundreds of thousands of pilgrims assemble. That would be a grand place to inaugurate the worship of our goddess!

Bimala waxed intensely enthusiastic. This was not the burning of foreign cloth or the people's granaries, so even Nikhil could have no objection – so thought she. But I smiled inwardly. How little these two persons, who have been together, day and night, for nine whole years, know of each other! They know something perhaps of their home life, but when it comes to outside concerns they are entirely at sea. They had cherished the belief that the harmony of the home with the outside was perfect. Today they realize to their cost that it is too late to repair their neglect of years, and seek to harmonize them now.

What does it matter? Let those who have made the mistake learn their error by knocking against the world. Why need I bother about their plight? For the present I find it wearisome to keep Bimala soaring much longer, like a captive balloon, in regions ethereal. I had better get quite through with the matter in hand.

When Bimala rose to depart and had neared the door I remarked in my most casual manner: 'So, about the money . . .'

Bimala halted and faced back as she said: 'On the expiry of the month, when our personal allowances become due . . .'

'That, I am afraid, would be much too late.'

'When do you want it then?'

'Tomorrow.'

'Tomorrow you shall have it.'

CHAPTER EIGHT

Nikhil's Story

X

PARAGRAPHS AND LETTERS against me have begun to come out in the local papers; cartoons and lampoons are to follow, I am told. Jets of wit and humour are being splashed about, and the lies thus scattered are convulsing the whole country. They know that the monopoly of mud-throwing is theirs, and the innocent passer-by cannot escape unsoiled.

They are saying that the residents in my estates, from the highest to the lowest, are in favour of *Swadeshi*, but they dare not declare themselves, for fear of me. The few who have been brave enough to defy me have felt the full rigour of my persecution. I am in secret league with the police, and in private communication with the magistrate, and these frantic efforts of mine to add a foreign title of my own earning to the one I have inherited, will not, it is opined, go in vain.

On the other hand, the papers are full of praise for those devoted sons of the motherland, the Kundu and the Chakravarti *zamindars*. If only, say they, the country had a few more of such staunch patriots, the mills of Manchester would have had to sound their own dirge to the tune of *Bande Mataram*.

Then comes a letter in blood-red ink, giving a list of the traitorous *zamindars* whose treasuries have been burnt down because of their failing to support the Cause. Holy Fire, it goes on to say, has been aroused to its sacred function of purifying the country; and other agencies are also at work to see that those who are not true sons of the motherland do cease to encumber her lap. The signature is an obvious *nom-de-plume*.

I could see that this was the doing of our local students. So I sent for some of them and showed them the letter.

The B.A. student gravely informed me that they also had heard that a band of desperate patriots had been formed who would stick at nothing in order to clear away all obstacles to the success of *Swadeshi*.

'If,' said I, 'even one of our countrymen succumbs to these overbearing desperadoes, that will indeed be a defeat for the country!'

'We fail to follow you, Maharaja,' said the history student.

'Our country,' I tried to explain, 'has been brought to death's door through sheer fear – from fear of the gods down to fear of the police; and if you set up, in the name of freedom, the fear of some other bogey, whatever it may be called; if you would raise your victorious standard on the cowardice of the country by means of downright oppression, then no true lover of the country can bow to your decision.'

'Is there any country, sir,' pursued the history student, 'where submission to Government is not due to fear?'

'The freedom that exists in any country,' I replied, 'may be measured by the extent of this reign of fear. Where its threat is confined to those who would hurt or plunder, there the Government may claim to have freed man from the violence of man. But if fear is to regulate how people are to dress, where they shall trade, or what they must eat, then is man's freedom of will utterly ignored, and manhood destroyed at the root.'

'Is not such coercion of the individual will seen in other countries too?' continued the history student.

'Who denies it?' I exclaimed. 'But in every country man has destroyed himself to the extent that he has permitted slavery to flourish.'

'Does it not rather show,' interposed a Master of Arts, 'that trading in slavery is inherent in man – a fundamental fact of his nature?'

'Sandip Babu made the whole thing clear,' said a graduate. 'He gave us the example of Harish Kundu, your neighbouring *zamindar*. From his estates you cannot ferret out a single ounce of foreign salt. Why? Because he has always ruled with an iron hand. In the case of those who are slaves by nature, the lack of a strong master is the greatest of all calamities.'

'Why, sir!' chimed in an undergraduate, 'have you not heard of the obstreperous tenant of Chakravarti, the other *zamindar* close by – how the law was set on him till he was reduced to utter destitution? When at last he was left with nothing to eat, he started out to sell his wife's silver ornaments, but no one dared buy them. Then Chakravarti's manager offered him five rupees for the lot. They were worth over thirty, but he had to accept or starve. After taking over the bundle from him the manager coolly said that those five rupees would be credited towards his rent! We felt like having nothing more to do with Chakravarti or his manager after that, but Sandip Babu told us that if we threw over all the live people, we should have only dead bodies from the burning-grounds to carry on the work with! These live men, he pointed out, know what they want and how to get it – they are born rulers. Those who do not know how to desire for themselves, must live in accordance with, or die by virtue of, the desires of such as these. Sandip Babu contrasted them – Kundu and Chakravarti – with you, Maharaja. You, he said, for all your good intentions, will never succeed in planting *Swadeshi* within your territory.'

'It is my desire,' I said, 'to plant something greater than *Swadeshi*. I am not after dead logs but living trees – and these will take time to grow.'

'I am afraid, sir,' sneered the history student, 'that you will get neither log nor tree. Sandip Babu rightly teaches that in order to get, you must snatch. This is taking all of us some time to learn, because it runs counter to what we were taught at school. I have seen with my own eyes that when a rent-collector of Harish Kundu's found one of the tenants with nothing which could be sold up to pay his rent, he was made to sell his young wife! Buyers were not wanting, and the *zamindar*'s demand was satisfied. I tell you, sir, the sight of that man's distress prevented my getting sleep for nights together! But, feel it as I did, this much I realized, that the man who knows how to get the money he is out for, even by selling up his debtor's wife, is a better man than I am. I confess it is beyond me – I am a weakling, my eyes fill with tears. If anybody can save our country it is these Kundus and these Chakravartis and their officials!'

I was shocked beyond words. 'If what you say be true,' I cried, 'I clearly see that it must be the one endeavour of my life to save the country from these same Kundus and Chakravartis and officials. The slavery that has entered into our very bones is breaking out, at this opportunity, as ghastly tyranny. You have been so used to submit to domination through fear, you have come to believe that to make others submit is a kind of religion. My fight shall be against this weakness, this atrocious cruelty!'

These things, which are so simple to ordinary folk, get so twisted in the minds of our B.A.'s and M.A.'s, the only purpose of whose historical quibbles seems to be to torture the truth!

XI

I AM WORRIED over Panchu's sham aunt. It will be difficult to disprove her, for though witnesses of a real event may be few or even wanting, innumerable proofs of a thing that has not happened can always be marshalled. The object of this move is, evidently, to get the sale of Panchu's holding to me set aside.

Being unable to find any other way out of it, I was thinking of allowing Panchu to hold a permanent tenure in my estates and building him a cottage on it. But my master would not have it. I should not give in to these nefarious tactics so easily, he objected, and offered to attend to the matter himself.

'You, sir!' I cried, considerably surprised.

'Yes, I,' he repeated.

I could not see, at all clearly, what my master could do to counteract these legal machinations. That evening, at the time he usually came to me, he did not turn up. On my making inquiries, his servant said he had left home with a few things packed in a small trunk, and some bedding, saying he would be back in a few days. I thought he might have sallied forth to hunt for witnesses in Panchu's uncle's village. In that case, however, I was sure that his would be a hopeless quest . . .

During the day I forget myself in my work. As the late autumn afternoon wears on, the colours of the sky become turbid, and so do the feelings of my mind. There are many in this world whose minds dwell in brick-built houses – they can afford to ignore the thing called the outside. But my mind lives under the trees in the open, directly receives upon itself the messages borne by the free winds, and responds from the bottom of its heart to all the musical cadences of light and darkness.

While the day is bright and the world in the pursuit of its numberless tasks crowds around, then it seems as if my life wants nothing else. But when the colours of the sky fade away and the blinds are drawn down over the windows of heaven, then my heart tells me that evening falls just for the purpose of shutting out the world, to mark the time when the darkness must be filled with the One. This is the end to which earth, sky, and waters conspire, and I cannot harden myself against accepting its meaning. So when the gloaming deepens over the world, like the gaze of the dark eyes of the beloved, then my whole being tells me that work alone cannot be the truth of life, that work is not the be-all and the end-all of man, for man is not simply a serf – even though the serfdom be of the True and the Good.

Alas, Nikhil, have you for ever parted company with that self of yours who used to be set free under the starlight, to plunge into the infinite depths of the night's darkness after the day's work was done? How terribly alone is he, who misses companionship in the midst of the multitudinousness of life.

The other day, when the afternoon had reached the meeting-point of day and night, I had no work, nor the mind for work, nor was my master there to keep me company. With my empty, drifting heart longing to anchor on to something, I traced my steps towards the inner gardens. I was very fond of chrysanthemums and had rows of them, of all varieties, banked up in pots against one of the garden walls. When they were in flower, it looked like a wave of green breaking into iridescent foam. It was some time since I had been to this part of the grounds, and I was beguiled into a cheerful expectancy at the thought of meeting my chrysanthemums after our long separation.

As I went in, the full moon had just peeped over the wall, her slanting rays leaving its foot in deep shadow. It seemed as if she had come a-tiptoe from behind, and clasped the darkness over the eyes, smiling mischievously. When I came near the bank of chrysanthemums, I saw a figure stretched on the grass in front. My heart gave a sudden thud. The figure also sat up with a start at my footsteps.

What was to be done next? I was wondering whether it would do to beat a precipitate retreat. Bimala, also, was doubtless casting about for some way of escape. But it was as awkward to go as to stay! Before I could make up my mind, Bimala rose, pulled the end of her *sari* over her head, and walked off towards the inner apartments.

This brief pause had been enough to make real to me the cruel load of Bimala's misery. The plaint of my own life vanished from me in a moment. I called out: 'Bimala!'

She started and stayed her steps, but did not turn back. I went round and stood before her. Her face was in the shade, the moonlight fell on mine. Her eyes were downcast, her hands clenched.

'Bimala,' said I, 'why should I seek to keep you fast in this closed cage of mine? Do I not know that thus you cannot but pine and droop?'

She stood still, without raising her eyes or uttering a word.

'I know,' I continued, 'that if I insist on keeping you shackled my whole life will be reduced to nothing but an iron chain. What pleasure can that be to me?'

She was still silent.

'So,' I concluded, 'I tell you, truly, Bimala, you are free. Whatever I may or may not have been to you, I refuse to be your fetters.' With which I came away towards the outer apartments.

No, no, it was not a generous impulse, nor indifference. I had simply come to understand that never would I be free until I could set free. To try to keep Bimala as a garland round my neck, would have meant keeping a weight hanging over my heart. Have I not been praying with all my strength, that if happiness may not be mine, let it go; if grief needs must be my lot, let it come; but let me not be kept in bondage. To clutch hold of that which is untrue as though it were true, is only to throttle oneself. May I be saved from such self-destruction.

When I entered my room, I found my master waiting there. My agitated feelings were still heaving within me. 'Freedom, sir,' I began unceremoniously, without greeting or inquiry, 'freedom is the biggest thing for man. Nothing can be compared to it – nothing at all!'

Surprised at my outburst, my master looked up at me in silence.

'One can understand nothing from books,' I went on. 'We read in the scriptures that our desires are bonds, fettering us as well as others. But such words, by themselves, are so empty. It is only when we get to the point of letting the bird out of its cage that we can realize how free the bird has set us. Whatever we cage, shackles us with desire whose bonds are stronger than those of iron chains. I tell you, sir, this is just what the world has failed to understand. They all seek to reform something outside themselves. But reform is wanted only in one's own desires, nowhere else, nowhere else!'

'We think,' he said, 'that we are our own masters when we get in our hands the object of our desire – but we are really our own masters only when we are able to cast out our desires from our minds.'

'When we put all this into words, sir,' I went on, 'it sounds like some bald-headed injunction, but when we realize even a little of it we find it to be *amrita* – which the gods have drunk and become immortal. We cannot see Beauty till we let go our hold of it. It was Buddha who conquered the world, not Alexander – this is untrue when stated in dry prose – oh when shall we be able to sing it? When shall all these most intimate truths of the universe overflow the pages of printed books and leap out in a sacred stream like the Ganges from the Gangotrie?'

I was suddenly reminded of my master's absence during the last few days and of my ignorance as to its reason. I felt somewhat foolish as I asked him: 'And where have you been all this while, sir?'

'Staying with Panchu,' he replied.

'Indeed!' I exclaimed. 'Have you been there all these days?'

'Yes. I wanted to come to an understanding with the woman who calls herself his aunt. She could hardly be induced to believe that there could be such an odd character among the gentlefolk as the one who sought their hospitality. When she found I really meant to stay on, she began to feel rather ashamed of herself. "Mother," said I, "you are not going to get rid of me, even if you abuse me! And so long as I stay, Panchu stays also. For you see, do you not, that I cannot stand by and see his motherless little ones sent out into the streets?"

'She listened to my talks in this strain for a couple of days without saying yes or no. This morning I found her tying up her bundles. "We are going back to Brindaban," she said. "Let us have our expenses for the journey." I knew she was not going to Brindaban, and also that the cost of her journey would be substantial. So I have come to you.'

'The required cost shall be paid,' I said.

'The old woman is not a bad sort,' my master went on musingly. 'Panchu was not sure of her caste, and would not let her touch the water-jar, or anything at all of his. So they were continually bickering. When she found I had no objection to her touch, she looked after me devotedly. She is a splendid cook!

'But all remnants of Panchu's respect for me vanished! To the last he had thought that I was at least a simple sort of person. But here was I, risking my caste without a qualm to win over the old woman for my purpose. Had I tried to steal a march on her by tutoring a witness for the trial, that would have been a different matter. Tactics must be met by tactics. But stratagem at the expense of orthodoxy is more than he can tolerate!

'Anyhow, I must stay on a few days at Panchu's even after

the woman leaves, for Harish Kundu may be up to any kind of devilry. He has been telling his satellites that he was content to have furnished Panchu with an aunt, but I have gone the length of supplying him with a father. He would like to see, now, how many fathers of his can save him!'

'We may or may not be able to save him,' I said; 'but if we should perish in the attempt to save the country from the thousand-and-one snares — of religion, custom, and selfishness — which these people are busy spreading, we shall at least die happy.'

Bimala's Story

XIV

WHO COULD HAVE thought that so much would happen in this one life? I feel as if I have passed through a whole series of births, time has been flying so fast, I did not feel it move at all, till the shock came the other day.

I knew there would be words between us when I made up my mind to ask my husband to banish foreign goods from our market. But it was my firm belief that I had no need to meet argument by argument, for there was magic in the very air about me. Had not so tremendous a man as Sandip fallen helplessly at my feet, like a wave of the mighty sea breaking on the shore? Had I called him? No, it was the summons of that magic spell of mine. And Amulya, poor dear boy, when he first came to me — how the current of his life flushed with colour, like the river at dawn! Truly have I realized how a goddess feels when she looks upon the radiant face of her devotee.

With the confidence begotten of these proofs of my power, I was ready to meet my husband like a lightning-charged cloud. But what was it that happened? Never in all these nine years have I seen such a far-away, distraught look in his eyes — like the desert sky — with no merciful moisture of its own, no colour reflected, even, from what it looked upon. I should have been so relieved if his anger had flashed out! But I could find nothing in him which I could touch. I felt as unreal as a dream — a dream which would leave only the blackness of night when it was over.

In the old days I used to be jealous of my sister-in-law for her beauty. Then I used to feel that Providence had given me no power of my own, that my whole strength lay in the love which my husband had bestowed on me. Now that I had drained to the dregs the cup of power and could not do without its intoxication, I suddenly found it dashed to pieces at my feet, leaving me nothing to live for.

How feverishly I had sat to do my hair that day. Oh, shame, shame on me, the utter shame of it! My sister-in-law, when passing by, had exclaimed: 'Aha, Chota Rani! Your hair seems ready to jump off. Don't let it carry your head with it.'

And then, the other day in the garden, how easy my husband found it to tell me that he set me free! But can freedom – empty freedom – be given and taken so easily as all that? It is like setting a fish free in the sky – for how can I move or live outside the atmosphere of loving care which has always sustained me?

When I came to my room today, I saw only furniture – only the bedstead, only the looking-glass, only the clothes-rack – not the all-pervading heart which used to be there, over all. Instead of it there was freedom, only freedom, mere emptiness! A dried-up watercourse with all its rocks and pebbles laid bare. No feeling, only furniture!

When I had arrived at a state of utter bewilderment, wondering whether anything true was left in my life, and whereabouts it could be, I happened to meet Sandip again. Then life struck against life, and the sparks flew in the same old way. Here was truth – impetuous truth – which rushed in and overflowed all bounds, truth which was a thousand times truer than the Bara Rani with her maid, Thako and her silly songs, and all the rest of them who talked and laughed and wandered about . . .

'Fifty thousand!' Sandip had demanded.

'What is fifty thousand?' cried my intoxicated heart. 'You shall have it!'

How to get it, where to get it, were minor points not worth troubling over. Look at me. Had I not risen, all in one moment, from my nothingness to a height above everything? So shall all things come at my beck and call. I shall get it, get it, get it – there cannot be any doubt.

Thus had I come away from Sandip the other day. Then as I looked about me, where was it – the tree of plenty? Oh, why does this outer world insult the heart so?

And yet get it I must; how, I do not care; for sin there cannot be. Sin taints only the weak; I with my *Shakti* am beyond its reach. Only a commoner can be a thief, the king conquers and takes his rightful spoil . . . I must find out where the treasury is; who takes the money in; who guards it.

I spent half the night standing in the outer verandah peering at the row of office buildings. But how to get that fifty thousand rupees out of the clutches of those iron bars? If by some *mantram* I could have made all those guards fall dead in their places, I would not have hesitated – so pitiless did I feel!

But while a whole gang of robbers seemed dancing a war-dance within the whirling brain of its Rani, the great house of the Rajas slept in peace. The gong of the watch sounded hour after hour, and the sky overhead placidly looked on.

At last I sent for Amulya.

'Money is wanted for the Cause,' I told him. 'Can you not get it out of the treasury?'

'Why not?' said he, with his chest thrown out.

Alas! had I not said 'Why not?' to Sandip just in the same way? The poor lad's confidence could rouse no hopes in my mind.

'How will you do it?' I asked.

The wild plans he began to unfold would hardly bear repetition outside the pages of a penny dreadful.

'No, Amulya,' I said severely, 'you must not be childish.'

'Very well, then,' he said, 'let me bribe those watchmen.'

'Where is the money to come from?'

'I can loot the bazar,' he burst out, without blenching.

'Leave all that alone. I have my ornaments, they will serve.'

'But,' said Amulya, 'it strikes me that the cashier cannot be bribed. Never mind, there is another and simpler way.'

'What is that?'

'Why need you hear it? It is quite simple.'

'Still, I should like to know.'

Amulya fumbled in the pocket of his tunic and pulled out, first a small edition of the *Gita*, which he placed on the table – and then a little pistol, which he showed me, but said nothing further.

Horror! It did not take him a moment to make up his mind to kill our good old cashier![1] To look at his frank, open face one

[1]. The cashier is the official who is most in touch with the ladies of a *zamindar*'s household, directly taking their requisitions for household stores and doing their shopping for them, and so he becomes more a member of the family than the others.

would not have thought him capable of hurting a fly, but how different were the words which came from his mouth. It was clear that the cashier's place in the world meant nothing real to him; it was a mere vacancy, lifeless, feelingless, with only stock phrases from the *Gita* – *Who kills the body kills naught!*

'Whatever do you mean, Amulya?' I exclaimed at length. 'Don't you know that the dear old man has got a wife and children and that he is . . .'

'Where are we to find men who have no wives and children?' he interrupted. 'Look here, Maharani, the thing we call pity is, at bottom, only pity for ourselves. We cannot bear to wound our own tender instincts, and so we do not strike at all – pity indeed! The height of cowardice!'

To hear Sandip's phrases in the mouth of this mere boy staggered me. So delightfully, lovably immature was he – of that age when the good may still be believed in as good, of that age when one really lives and grows. The Mother in me awoke.

For myself there was no longer good or bad – only death, beautiful alluring death. But to hear this stripling calmly talk of murdering an inoffensive old man as the right thing to do, made me shudder all over. The more clearly I saw that there was no sin in his heart, the more horrible appeared to me the sin of his words. I seemed to see the sin of the parents visited on the innocent child.

The sight of his great big eyes shining with faith and enthusiasm touched me to the quick. He was going, in his fascination, straight to the jaws of the python, from which, once in, there was no return. How was he to be saved? Why does not my country become, for once, a real Mother – clasp him to her bosom and cry out: 'Oh, my child, my child, what profits it that you should save me, if so it be that I should fail to save you?'

I know, I know, that all Power on earth waxes great under compact with Satan. But the Mother is there, alone though she be, to contemn and stand against this devil's progress. The Mother cares not for mere success, however great – she wants to give life, to save life. My very soul, today, stretches out its hands in yearning to save this child.

A while ago I suggested robbery to him. Whatever I may now say against it will be put down to a woman's weakness. They only love our weakness when it drags the world in its toils!

'You need do nothing at all, Amulya, I will see to the money,' I told him finally.

When he had almost reached the door, I called him back. 'Amulya,' said I, 'I am your elder sister. Today is not the Brothers' Day[1] according to the calendar, but all the days in the year are really Brothers' Days. My blessing be with you: may God keep you always.'

These unexpected words from my lips took Amulya by surprise. He stood stock-still for a time. Then, coming to himself, he prostrated himself at my feet in acceptance of the relationship and did me reverence. When he rose his eyes were full of tears . . . O little brother mine! I am fast going to my death – let me take all your sin away with me. May no taint from me ever tarnish your innocence!

I said to him: 'Let your offering of reverence be that pistol!'

'What do you want with it, sister?'

'I will practise death.'

'Right, sister. Our women, also, must know how to die, to deal death!' with which Amulya handed me the pistol.

The radiance of his youthful countenance seemed to tinge my life with the touch of a new dawn. I put away the pistol within my clothes. May this reverence-offering be the last resource in my extremity . . .

The door to the mother's chamber in my woman's heart once opened, I thought it would always remain open. But this pathway to the supreme good was closed when the mistress took the place of the mother and locked it again. The very next day I saw Sandip; and madness, naked and rampant, danced upon my heart.

What was this? Was this, then, my truer self? Never! I had never before known this shameless, this cruel one within me. The snake-charmer had come, pretending to draw this snake

---

1. The daughter of the house occupies a place of specially tender affection in a Bengali household (perhaps in Hindu households all over India) because, by dictate of custom, she must be given away in marriage so early. She thus takes corresponding memories with her to her husband's home, where she has to begin as a stranger before she can get into her place. The resulting feeling, of the mistress of her new home for the one she has left, has taken ceremonial form as the Brothers' Day, on which the brothers are invited to the married sisters' houses. Where the sister is the elder, she offers her blessing and receives the brother's reverence, and vice versa. Presents, called the offerings of reverence (or blessing), are exchanged.

from within the fold of my garment – but it was never there, it was his all the time. Some demon has gained possession of me, and what I am doing today is the play of his activity – it has nothing to do with me.

This demon, in the guise of a god, had come with his ruddy torch to call me that day, saying: 'I am your Country. I am your Sandip. I am more to you than anything else of yours. *Bande Mataram!*' And with folded hands I had responded: 'You are my religion. You are my heaven. Whatever else is mine shall be swept away before my love for you. *Bande Mataram!*'

Five thousand is it? Five thousand it shall be! You want it tomorrow? Tomorrow you shall have it! In this desperate orgy, that gift of five thousand shall be as the foam of wine – and then for the riotous revel! The immovable world shall sway under our feet, fire shall flash from our eyes, a storm shall roar in our ears, what is or is not in front, shall become equally dim. And then with tottering footsteps we shall plunge to our death – in a moment all fire will be extinguished, the ashes will be scattered, and nothing will remain behind.

CHAPTER NINE

Bimala's Story

XV

FOR A TIME I was utterly at a loss to think of any way of getting that money. Then, the other day, in the light of intense excitement, suddenly the whole picture stood out clear before me.

Every year my husband makes a reverence-offering of six thousand rupees to my sister-in-law at the time of the Durga Puja. Every year it is deposited in her account at the bank in Calcutta. This year the offering was made as usual, but it has not yet been sent to the bank, being kept meanwhile in an iron safe, in a corner of the little dressing-room attached to our bedroom.

Every year my husband takes the money to the bank himself. This year he has not yet had an opportunity of going to town. How could I fail to see the hand of Providence in this? The money has been held up because the country wants it — who could have the power to take it away from her to the bank? And how can I have the power to refuse to take the money? The goddess revelling in destruction holds out her blood-cup crying: 'Give me drink. I am thirsty.' I will give her my own heart's blood with that five thousand rupees. Mother, the loser of that money will scarcely feel the loss, but me you will utterly ruin!

Many a time, in the old days, have I inwardly called the Senior Rani a thief, for I charged her with wheedling money out of my trusting husband. After her husband's death, she often used to make away with things belonging to the estate for her own use. This I used to point out to my husband, but he remained silent. I would get angry and say: 'If you feel generous, make gifts by all means, but why allow yourself to be robbed?' Providence must have smiled, then, at these complaints of mine, for tonight I am on the way to rob my husband's safe of my sister-in-law's money.

My husband's custom was to let his keys remain in his pockets when he took off his clothes for the night, leaving them in the dressing-room. I picked out the key of the safe and opened it. The slight sound it made seemed to wake the whole world! A sudden chill turned my hands and feet icy cold, and I shivered all over.

There was a drawer inside the safe. On opening this I found the money, not in currency notes, but in gold rolled up in paper. I had no time to count out what I wanted. There were twenty rolls, all of which I took and tied up in a corner of my *sari*.

What a weight it was. The burden of the theft crushed my heart to the dust. Perhaps notes would have made it seem less like thieving, but this was all gold.

After I had stolen into my room like a thief, it felt like my own room no longer. All the most precious rights which I had over it vanished at the touch of my theft. I began to mutter to myself, as though telling *mantrams*: *Bande Mataram, Bande Mataram*, my Country, my golden Country, all this gold is for you, for none else!

But in the night the mind is weak. I came back into the bedroom where my husband was asleep, closing my eyes as I passed through, and went off to the open terrace beyond, on which I lay prone, clasping to my breast the end of the *sari* tied over the gold. And each one of the rolls gave me a shock of pain.

The silent night stood there with forefinger upraised. I could not think of my house as separate from my country: I had robbed my house, I had robbed my country. For this sin my house had ceased to be mine, my country also was estranged from me. Had I died begging for my country, even unsuccessfully, that would have been worship, acceptable to the gods. But theft is never worship – how then can I offer this gold? Ah me! I am doomed to death myself, must I desecrate my country with my impious touch?

The way to put the money back is closed to me. I have not the strength to return to the room, take again that key, open once more that safe – I should swoon on the threshold of my husband's door. The only road left now is the road in front. Neither have I the strength deliberately to sit down and count the coins. Let them remain behind their coverings: I cannot calculate.

There was no mist in the winter sky. The stars were shining brightly. If, thought I to myself, as I lay out there, I had to steal these stars one by one, like golden coins, for my country – these stars so carefully stored up in the bosom of the darkness – then the sky would be blinded, the night widowed for ever, and my theft would rob the whole world. But was not also this very thing I had done a robbing of the whole world – not only of money, but of trust, of righteousness?

I spent the night lying on the terrace. When at last it was morning, and I was sure that my husband had risen and left the room, then only with my shawl pulled over my head, could I retrace my steps towards the bedroom.

My sister-in-law was about, with her brass pot, watering her plants. When she saw me passing in the distance she cried: 'Have you heard the news, Chota Rani?'

I stopped in silence, all in a tremor. It seemed to me that the rolls of sovereigns were bulging through the shawl. I feared they would burst and scatter in a ringing shower, exposing to all the servants of the house the thief who had made herself destitute by robbing her own wealth.

'Your band of robbers,' she went on, 'have sent an anonymous message threatening to loot the treasury.'

I remained as silent as a thief.

'I was advising Brother Nikhil to seek your protection,' she continued banteringly. 'Call off your minions, Robber Queen! We will offer sacrifices to your *Bande Mataram* if you will but save us. What doings there are these days! – but for the Lord's sake, spare our house at least from burglary.'

I hastened into my room without reply. I had put my foot on quicksand, and could not now withdraw it. Struggling would only send me down deeper.

If only the time would arrive when I could hand over the money to Sandip! I could bear it no longer, its weight was breaking through my very ribs.

It was still early when I got word that Sandip was awaiting me. Today I had no thought of adornment. Wrapped as I was in my shawl, I went off to the outer apartments.

As I entered the sitting-room I saw Sandip and Amulya there, together. All my dignity, all my honour, seemed to run tingling through my body from head to foot and vanish into the ground. I should have to lay bare a woman's uttermost shame in sight of this boy! Could they have been discussing my deed in their meeting place? Had any vestige of a veil of decency been left for me?

We women shall never understand men. When they are bent on making a road for some achievement, they think nothing of breaking the heart of the world into pieces to pave it for the

progress of their chariot. When they are mad with the intoxication of creating, they rejoice in destroying the creation of the
Creator. This heart-breaking shame of mine will not attract even
a glance from their eyes. They have no feeling for life itself –
all their eagerness is for their object. What am I to them but a
meadow flower in the path of a torrent in flood?

What good will this extinction of me be to Sandip? Only five
thousand rupees? Was not I good for something more than only
five thousand rupees? Yes, indeed! Did I not learn that from
Sandip himself, and was I not able in the light of this knowledge
to despise all else in my world? I was the giver of light, of life, of
Shakti, of immortality – in that belief, in that joy, I had burst all
my bounds and come into the open. Had anyone then fulfilled
for me that joy, I should have lived in my death. I should have
lost nothing in the loss of my all.

Do they want to tell me now that all this was false? The psalm
of my praise which was sung so devotedly, did it bring me down
from my heaven, not to make heaven of earth, but only to level
heaven itself with the dust?

XVI

'THE MONEY, QUEEN?' said Sandip with his keen glance full
on my face.

Amulya also fixed his gaze on me. Though not my own
mother's child, yet the dear lad is brother to me; for mother
is mother all the world over. With his guileless face, his gentle
eyes, his innocent youth, he looked at me. And I, a woman – of
his mother's sex – how could I hand him poison, just because
he asked for it?

'The money, Queen!' Sandip's insolent demand rang in my
ears. For very shame and vexation I felt I wanted to fling that
gold at Sandip's head. I could hardly undo the knot of my *sari*, my
fingers trembled so. At last the paper rolls dropped on the table.

Sandip's face grew black . . . He must have thought that the
rolls were of silver . . . What contempt was in his looks. What
utter disgust at incapacity. It was almost as if he could have struck
me! He must have suspected that I had come to parley with him,
to offer to compound his claim for five thousand rupees with a
few hundreds. There was a moment when I thought he would
snatch up the rolls and throw them out of the window, declaring
that he was no beggar, but a king claiming tribute.

'Is that all?' asked Amulya with such pity welling up in his voice that I wanted to sob out aloud. I kept my heart tightly pressed down, and merely nodded my head.

Sandip was speechless. He neither touched the rolls, nor uttered a sound.

My humiliation went straight to the boy's heart. With a sudden, feigned enthusiasm he exclaimed: 'It's plenty. It will do splendidly. You have saved us.' With which he tore open the covering of one of the rolls.

The sovereigns shone out. And in a moment the black covering seemed to be lifted from Sandip's countenance also. His delight beamed forth from his features. Unable to control his sudden revulsion of feeling, he sprang up from his seat towards me. What he intended I know not. I flashed a lightning glance towards Amulya – the colour had left the boy's face as at the stroke of a whip. Then with all my strength I thrust Sandip from me. As he reeled back his head struck the edge of the marble table and he dropped on the floor. There he lay awhile, motionless. Exhausted with my effort, I sank back on my seat.

Amulya's face lightened with a joyful radiance. He did not even turn towards Sandip, but came straight up, took the dust of my feet, and then remained there, sitting on the floor in front of me. O my little brother, my child! This reverence of yours is the last touch of heaven left in my empty world! I could contain myself no longer, and my tears flowed fast. I covered my eyes with the end of my *sari*, which I pressed to my face with both my hands, and sobbed and sobbed. And every time that I felt on my feet his tender touch trying to comfort me my tears broke out afresh.

After a little, when I had recovered myself and taken my hands from my face, I saw Sandip back at the table, gathering up the sovereigns in his handkerchief, as if nothing had happened. Amulya rose to his seat, from his place near my feet, his wet eyes shining.

Sandip coolly looked up at my face as he remarked: 'It is six thousand.'

'What do we want with so much, Sandip Babu?' cried Amulya. 'Three thousand five hundred is all we need for our work.'

'Our wants are not for this one place only,' Sandip replied. 'We shall want all we can get.'

'That may be,' said Amulya. 'But in future I undertake to get you all you want. Out of this, Sandip Babu, please return the extra two thousand five hundred to the Maharani.'

Sandip glanced enquiringly at me.

'No, no,' I exclaimed. 'I shall never touch that money again. Do with it as you will.'

'Can man ever give as woman can?' said Sandip, looking to-wards Amulya.

'They are goddesses!' agreed Amulya with enthusiasm.

'We men can at best give of our power,' continued Sandip. 'But women give themselves. Out of their own life they give birth, out of their own life they give sustenance. Such gifts are the only true gifts.' Then turning to me, 'Queen!' said he, 'if what you have given us had been only money I would not have touched it. But you have given that which is more to you than life itself!'

There must be two different persons inside men. One of these in me can understand that Sandip is trying to delude me; the other is content to be deluded. Sandip has power, but no strength of righteousness. The weapon of his which rouses up life smites it again to death. He has the unfailing quiver of the gods, but the shafts in them are of the demons.

Sandip's handkerchief was not large enough to hold all the coins. 'Queen,' he asked, 'can you give me another?'

When I gave him mine, he reverently touched his forehead with it, and then suddenly kneeling on the floor he made me an obeisance. 'Goddess!' he said, 'it was to offer my reverence that I had approached you, but you repulsed me, and rolled me in the dust. Be it so, I accept your repulse as your boon to me, I raise it to my head in salutation!' with which he pointed to the place where he had been hurt.

Had I then misunderstood him? Could it be that his out-stretched hands had really been directed towards my feet? Yet, surely, even Amulya had seen the passion that flamed out of his eyes, his face. But Sandip is such an adept in setting music to his chant of praise that I cannot argue; I lose my power of seeing truth; my sight is clouded over like an opium-eater's eyes. And so, after all, he gave me back twice as much in return for the blow I had dealt him – the wound on his head ended by making me bleed at heart. When I had received Sandip's obeisance my theft seemed to gain a dignity, and the gold glittering on the table to smile away all fear of disgrace, all stings of conscience.

Like me Amulya also was won back. His devotion to Sandip, which had suffered a momentary check, blazed up anew. The flower-vase of his mind filled once more with offerings for the worship of Sandip and me. His simple faith shone out of his eyes with the pure light of the morning star at dawn.

After I had offered worship and received worship my sin became radiant. And as Amulya looked on my face he raised his folded hands in salutation and cried *Bande Mataram!* I cannot expect to have this adoration surrounding me for ever; and yet this has come to be the only means of keeping alive my self-respect.

I can no longer enter my bedroom. The bedstead seems to thrust out a forbidding hand, the iron safe frowns at me. I want to get away from this continual insult to myself which is rankling within me. I want to keep running to Sandip to hear him sing my praises. There is just this one little altar of worship which has kept its head above the all-pervading depths of my dishonour, and so I want to cleave to it night and day; for on whichever side I step away from it, there is only emptiness.

Praise, praise, I want unceasing praise. I cannot live if my wine-cup be left empty for a single moment. So, as the very price of my life, I want Sandip of all the world, today.

XVII

WHEN MY HUSBAND nowadays comes in for his meals I feel I cannot sit before him; and yet it is such a shame not to be near him that I feel I cannot do that either. So I seat myself where we cannot look at each other's face. That was how I was sitting the other day when the Bara Rani came and joined us.

'It is all very well for you, brother,' said she, 'to laugh away these threatening letters. But they do frighten me so. Have you sent off that money you gave me to the Calcutta bank?'

'No, I have not yet had the time to get it away,' my husband replied.

'You are so careless, brother dear, you had better look out . . .'

'But it is in the iron safe right inside the inner dressing-room,' said my husband with a reassuring smile.

'What if they get in there? You can never tell!'

'If they go so far, they might as well carry you off too!'

'Don't you fear, no one will come for poor me. The real attraction is in your room! But joking apart, don't run the risk of keeping money in the room like that.'

'They will be taking along the Government revenue to Calcutta in a few days now; I will send this money to the bank under the same escort.'

'Very well. But see you don't forget all about it, you are so absent-minded.'

'Even if that money gets lost, while in my room, the loss cannot be yours, Sister Rani.'

'Now, now, brother, you will make me very angry if you talk in that way. Was I making any difference between yours and mine? What if your money is lost, does not that hurt me? If Providence has thought fit to take away my all, it has not left me insensible to the value of the most devoted brother known since the days of Lakshman.[1]

'Well, Junior Rani, are you turned into a wooden doll? You have not spoken a word yet. Do you know, brother, our Junior Rani thinks I try to flatter you. If things came to that pass I should not hesitate to do so, but I know my dear old brother does not need it!'

Thus the Senior Rani chattered on, not forgetting now and then to draw her brother's attention to this or that special delicacy amongst the dishes that were being served. My head was all the time in a whirl. The crisis was fast coming. Something must be done about replacing that money. And as I kept asking myself what could be done, and how it was to be done, the unceasing patter of my sister-in-law's words seemed more and more intolerable.

What made it all the worse was, that nothing could escape my sister-in-law's keen eyes. Every now and then she was casting side glances towards me. What she could read in my face I do not know, but to me it seemed that everything was written there only too plainly.

Then I did an infinitely rash thing. Affecting an easy, amused laugh I said: 'All the Senior Rani's suspicions, I see, are reserved for me – her fears of thieves and robbers are only a feint.'

The Senior Rani smiled mischievously. 'You are right, sister

1. Of the *Ramayana*. The story of his devotion to his elder brother Rama and his brother's wife Sita, has become a byword.

mine. A woman's theft is the most fatal of all thefts. But how can you elude my watchfulness? Am I a man, that you should hoodwink me?'

'If you fear me so,' I retorted, 'let me keep in your hands all I have, as security. If I cause you loss, you can then repay yourself.'

'Just listen to her, our simple little Junior Rani!' she laughed back, turning to my husband. 'Does she not know that there are losses which no security can make good, either in this world or in the next?'

My husband did not join in our exchange of words. When he had finished, he went off to the outer apartments, for nowadays he does not take his mid-day rest in our room.

All my more valuable jewels were in deposit in the treasury in charge of the cashier. Still what I kept with me must have been worth thirty or forty thousand. I took my jewel-box to the Bara Rani's room and opened it out before her, saying: 'I leave these with you, sister. They will keep you quite safe from all worry.'

The Bara Rani made a gesture of mock despair. 'You positively astound me, Chota Rani!' she said. 'Do you really suppose I spend sleepless nights for fear of being robbed by you?'

'What harm if you did have a wholesome fear of me? Does anybody know anybody else in this world?'

'You want to teach me a lesson by trusting me? No, no! I am bothered enough to know what to do with my own jewels, without keeping watch over yours. Take them away, there's a dear, so many prying servants are about.'

I went straight from my sister-in-law's room to the sitting-room outside, and sent for Amulya. With him Sandip came along too. I was in a great hurry, and said to Sandip: 'If you don't mind, I want to have a word or two with Amulya. Would you . . .'

Sandip smiled a wry smile. 'So Amulya and I are separate in your eyes? If you have set about to wean him from me, I must confess I have no power to retain him.'

I made no reply, but stood waiting.

'Be it so,' Sandip went on. 'Finish your special talk with Amulya. But then you must give me a special talk all to myself too, or it will mean a defeat for me. I can stand everything, but not defeat. My share must always be the lion's share. This has been my constant quarrel with Providence. I will defeat the

Dispenser of my fate, but not take defeat at his hands.' With a crushing look at Amulya, Sandip walked out of the room.

'Amulya, my own little brother, you must do one thing for me,' I said.

'I will stake my life for whatever duty you may lay on me, sister.'

I brought out my jewel-box from the folds of my shawl and placed it before him. 'Sell or pawn these,' I said, 'and get me six thousand rupees as fast as ever you can.'

'No, no, Sister Rani,' said Amulya, touched to the quick. 'Let these jewels be, I will get you six thousand all the same.'

'Oh, don't be silly,' I said impatiently. 'There is no time for any nonsense. Take this box. Get away to Calcutta by the night train. And bring me the money by the day after tomorrow positively.'

Amulya took a diamond necklace out of the box, held it up to the light and put it back gloomily.

'I know,' I told him, 'that you will never get the proper price for these diamonds, so I am giving you jewels worth about thirty thousand. I don't care if they all go, but I must have that six thousand without fail.'

'Do you know, Sister Rani,' said Amulya, 'I have had a quarrel with Sandip Babu over that six thousand rupees he took from you? I cannot tell you how ashamed I felt. But Sandip Babu would have it that we must give up even our shame for the country. That may be so. But this is somehow different. I do not fear to die for the country, to kill for the country – that much *Shakti* has been given me. But I cannot forget the shame of having taken money from you. There Sandip Babu is ahead of me. He has no regrets or compunctions. He says we must get rid of the idea that the money belongs to the one in whose box it happens to be – if we cannot, where is the magic of *Bande Mataram*?'

Amulya gathered enthusiasm as he talked on. He always warms up when he has me for a listener. 'The *Gita* tells us,' he continued, 'that no one can kill the soul. Killing is a mere word. So also is the taking away of money. Whose is the money? No one has created it. No one can take it away with him when he departs this life, for it is no part of his soul. Today it is mine, tomorrow my son's, the next day his creditor's. Since, in fact, money belongs to no one, why should any blame attach to our patriots if, instead of leaving it for some worthless son, they take it for their own use?'

When I hear Sandip's words uttered by this boy, I tremble all over. Let those who are snake-charmers play with snakes; if harm comes to them, they are prepared for it. But these boys are so innocent, all the world is ready with its blessing to protect them. They play with a snake not knowing its nature, and when we see them smilingly, trustfully, putting their hands within reach of its fangs, then we understand how terribly dangerous the snake is. Sandip is right when he suspects that though I, for myself, may be ready to die at his hands, this boy I shall wean from him and save.

'So the money is wanted for the use of your patriots?' I questioned with a smile.

'Of course it is!' said Amulya proudly. 'Are they not our kings? Poverty takes away from their regal power. Do you know, we always insist on Sandip Babu travelling First Class? He never shirks kingly honours – he accepts them not for himself, but for the glory of us all. The greatest weapon of those who rule the world, Sandip Babu has told us, is the hypnotism of their display. To take the vow of poverty would be for them not merely a penance – it would mean suicide.'

At this point Sandip noiselessly entered the room. I threw my shawl over the jewel-case with a rapid movement.

'The special-talk business not yet over?' he asked with a sneer in his tone.

'Yes, we've quite finished,' said Amulya apologetically. 'It was nothing much.'

'No, Amulya,' I said, 'we have not quite finished.'

'So exit Sandip for the second time, I suppose?' said Sandip.

'If you please.'

'And as to Sandip's re-entry . . .'

'Not today. I have no time.'

'I see!' said Sandip as his eyes flashed. 'No time to waste, only for special talks!'

Jealousy! Where the strong man shows weakness, there the weaker sex cannot help beating her drums of victory. So I repeated firmly: 'I really have no time.'

Sandip went away looking black. Amulya was greatly perturbed. 'Sister Rani,' he pleaded, 'Sandip Babu is annoyed.'

'He has neither cause nor right to be annoyed,' I said with some vehemence. 'Let me caution you about one thing, Amulya.

Say nothing to Sandip Babu about the sale of my jewels – on your life.'

'No, I will not.'

'Then you had better not delay any more. You must get away by tonight's train.'

Amulya and I left the room together. As we came out on the verandah Sandip was standing there. I could see he was waiting to waylay Amulya. To prevent that I had to engage him. 'What is it you wanted to tell me, Sandip Babu?' I asked.

'I have nothing special to say – mere small talk. And since you have not the time . . .'

'I can give you just a little.'

By this time Amulya had left. As we entered the room Sandip asked: 'What was that box Amulya carried away?'

The box had not escaped his eyes. I remained firm. 'If I could have told you, it would have been made over to him in your presence!'

'So you think Amulya will not tell me?'

'No, he will not.'

Sandip could not conceal his anger any longer. 'You think you will gain the mastery over me?' he blazed out. 'That shall never be. Amulya, there, would die a happy death if I deigned to trample him under foot. I will never, so long as I live, allow you to bring him to your feet!'

Oh, the weak! the weak! At last Sandip has realized that he is weak before me! That is why there is this sudden outburst of anger. He has understood that he cannot meet the power that I wield, with mere strength. With a glance I can crumble his strongest fortifications. So he must needs resort to bluster. I simply smiled in contemptuous silence. At last have I come to a level above him. I must never lose this vantage ground; never descend lower again. Amidst all my degradation this bit of dignity must remain to me!

'I know,' said Sandip, after a pause, 'it was your jewel-case.'

'You may guess as you please,' said I, 'but you will get nothing out of me.'

'So you trust Amulya more than you trust me? Do you know that the boy is the shadow of my shadow, the echo of my echo – that he is nothing if I am not at his side?'

'Where he is not your echo, he is himself, Amulya. And that is where I trust him more than I can trust your echo!'

'You must not forget that you are under a promise to render up all your ornaments to me for the worship of the Divine Mother. In fact your offering has already been made.'

'Whatever ornaments the gods leave to me will be offered up to the gods. But how can I offer those which have been stolen away from me?'

'Look here, it is no use your trying to give me the slip in that fashion. Now is the time for grim work. Let that work be finished, then you can make a display of your woman's wiles to your heart's content – and I will help you in your game.'

The moment I had stolen my husband's money and paid it to Sandip, the music that was in our relations stopped. Not only did I destroy all my own value by making myself cheap, but Sandip's powers, too, lost scope for their full play. You cannot employ your marksmanship against a thing which is right in your grasp. So Sandip has lost his aspect of the hero; a tone of low quarrelsomeness has come into his words.

Sandip kept his brilliant eyes fixed full on my face till they seemed to blaze with all the thirst of the mid-day sky. Once or twice he fidgeted with his feet, as though to leave his seat, as if to spring right on me. My whole body seemed to swim, my veins throbbed, the hot blood surged up to my ears; I felt that if I remained there, I should never get up at all. With a supreme effort I tore myself off the chair, and hastened towards the door.

From Sandip's dry throat there came a muffled cry: 'Whither would you flee, Queen?' The next moment he left his seat with a bound to seize hold of me. At the sound of footsteps outside the door, however, he rapidly retreated and fell back into his chair. I checked my steps near the bookshelf, where I stood staring at the names of the books.

As my husband entered the room, Sandip exclaimed: 'I say, Nikhil, don't you keep Browning among your books here? I was just telling Queen Bee of our college club. Do you remember that contest of ours over the translation of those lines from Browning? You don't?

She should never have looked at me
If she meant I should not love her!
There are plenty . . . men, you call such,
I suppose . . . she may discover

All her soul to, if she pleases,
And yet leave much as she found them:
But I'm not so, and she knew it
When she fixed me, glancing round them.

'I managed to get together the words to render it into Bengali, somehow, but the result was hardly likely to be a "joy forever" to the people of Bengal. I really did think at one time that I was on the verge of becoming a poet, but Providence was kind enough to save me from that disaster. Do you remember old Dakshina? If he had not become a Salt Inspector, he would have been a poet. I remember his rendering to this day . . .

'No, Queen Bee, it is no use rummaging those bookshelves. Nikhil has ceased to read poetry since his marriage – perhaps he has no further need for it. But I suppose "the fever fit of poesy", as the Sanskrit has it, is about to attack me again.'

'I have come to give you a warning, Sandip,' said my husband.

'About the fever fit of poesy?'

My husband took no notice of this attempt at humour. 'For some time,' he continued, 'Mahomedan preachers have been about stirring up the local Mussulmans. They are all wild with you, and may attack you any moment.'

'Are you come to advise flight?'

'I have come to give you information, not to offer advice.'

'Had these estates been mine, such a warning would have been necessary for the preachers, not for me. If, instead of trying to frighten me, you give them a taste of your intimidation, that would be worthier both of you and me. Do you know that your weakness is weakening your neighbouring *zamindars* also?'

'I did not offer you my advice, Sandip. I wish you, too, would refrain from giving me yours. Besides, it is useless. And there is another thing I want to tell you. You and your followers have been secretly worrying and oppressing my tenantry. I cannot allow that any longer. So I must ask you to leave my territory.'

'For fear of the Mussulmans, or is there any other fear you have to threaten me with?'

'There are fears the want of which is cowardice. In the name of those fears, I tell you, Sandip, you must go. In five days I shall be starting for Calcutta. I want you to accompany me. You may of course stay in my house there – to that there is no objecion.'

'All right, I have still five days' time then. Meanwhile, Queen

Bee, let me hum to you my song of parting from your honey-hive. Ah! you poet of modern Bengal! Throw open your doors and let me plunder your words. The theft is really yours, for it is my song which you have made your own – let the name be yours by all means, but the song is mine.' With this Sandip struck up in a deep, husky voice, which threatened to be out of tune, a song in the *Bhairavi* mode:

> 'In the springtime of your kingdom, my Queen,
> Meetings and partings chase each other in their endless hide
>   and seek,
> And flowers blossom in the wake of those that droop and die in
>   the shade.
> In the springtime of your kingdom, my Queen,
> My meeting with you had its own songs,
> But has not also my leave-taking any gift to offer you?
> That gift is my secret hope, which I keep hidden in the
>   shadows of your flower garden,
> That the rains of July may sweetly temper your fiery June.'

His boldness was immense – boldness which had no veil, but was naked as fire. One finds no time to stop it: it is like trying to resist a thunderbolt: the lightning flashes: it laughs at all resistance.

I left the room. As I was passing along the verandah towards the inner apartments, Amulya suddenly made his appearance and came and stood before me.

'Fear nothing, Sister Rani,' he said. 'I am off tonight and shall not return unsuccessful.'

'Amulya,' said I, looking straight into his earnest, youthful face, 'I fear nothing for myself, but may I never cease to fear for you.'

Amulya turned to go, but before he was out of sight I called him back and asked: 'Have you a mother, Amulya?'

'I have.'

'A sister?'

'No, I am the only child of my mother. My father died when I was quite little.'

'Then go back to your mother, Amulya.'

'But, Sister Rani, I have now both mother and sister.'

'Then, Amulya, before you leave tonight, come and have your dinner here.'

'There won't be time for that. Let me take some food for the journey, consecrated with your touch.'

'What do you specially like, Amulya?'

'If I had been with my mother I should have had lots of *Poush* cakes. Make some for me with your own hands, Sister Rani!'

CHAPTER TEN

Nikhil's Story

XII

I LEARNT FROM my master that Sandip had joined forces with Harish Kundu, and there was to be a grand celebration of the worship of the demon-destroying Goddess. Harish Kundu was extorting the expenses from his tenantry. Pandits Kaviratna and Vidyavagish had been commissioned to compose a hymn with a double meaning.

My master has just had a passage at arms with Sandip over this. 'Evolution is at work amongst the gods as well,' says Sandip. 'The grandson has to remodel the gods created by the grandfather to suit his own taste, or else he is left an atheist. It is my mission to modernize the ancient deities. I am born the saviour of the gods, to emancipate them from the thraldom of the past.'

I have seen from our boyhood what a juggler with ideas is Sandip. He has no interest in discovering truth, but to make a quizzical display of it rejoices his heart. Had he been born in the wilds of Africa he would have spent a glorious time inventing argument after argument to prove that cannibalism is the best means of promoting true communion between man and man. But those who deal in delusion end by deluding themselves, and I fully believe that, each time Sandip creates a new fallacy, he persuades himself that he has found the truth, however contradictory his creations may be to one another.

However, I shall not give a helping hand to establish a liquor distillery in my country. The young men, who are ready to offer their services for their country's cause, must not fall into this habit of getting intoxicated. The people who want to exact work by drugging methods set more value on the excitement than on the minds they intoxicate.

I had to tell Sandip, in Bimala's presence, that he must go. Perhaps both will impute to me the wrong motive. But I must free myself also from all fear of being misunderstood. Let even Bimala misunderstand me . . .

A number of Mahomedan preachers are being sent over from Dacca. The Mussulmans in my territory had come to have almost as much of an aversion to the killing of cows as the Hindus. But now cases of cow-killing are cropping up here and there. I had the news first from some of my Mussulman tenants with expressions of their disapproval. Here was a situation which I could see would be difficult to meet. At the bottom was a pretence of fanaticism, which would cease to be a pretence if obstructed. That is just where the ingenuity of the move came in!

I sent for some of my principal Hindu tenants and tried to get them to see the matter in its proper light. 'We can be staunch in our own convictions,' I said, 'but we have no control over those of others. For all that many of us are Vaishnavas, those of us who are Shaktas go on with their animal sacrifices just the same. That cannot be helped. We must, in the same way, let the Mussulmans do as they think best. So please refrain from all disturbance.'

'Maharaja,' they replied, 'these outrages have been unknown for so long.'

'That was so,' I said, 'because such was their spontaneous desire. Let us behave in such a way that the same may become true, over again. But a breach of the peace is not the way to bring this about.'

'No, Maharaja,' they insisted, 'those good old days are gone. This will never stop unless you put it down with a strong hand.'

'Oppression,' I replied, 'will not only not prevent cow-killing, it may lead to the killing of men as well.'

One of them had had an English education. He had learnt to repeat the phrases of the day. 'It is not only a question of orthodoxy,' he argued. 'Our country is mainly agricultural, and cows are . . .'

'Buffaloes in this country,' I interrupted, 'likewise give milk and are used for ploughing. And therefore, so long as we dance frantic dances on our temple pavements, smeared with their blood, their severed heads carried on our shoulders, religion will only laugh at us if we quarrel with Mussulmans in her name, and nothing but the quarrel itself will remain true. If the cow alone is to be held sacred from slaughter, and not the buffalo, then that is bigotry, not religion.'

'But are you not aware, sir, of what is behind all this?' pursued the English-knowing tenant. 'This has only become possible because the Mussulman is assured of safety, even if he breaks the law. Have you not heard of the Pachur case?'

'Why is it possible,' I asked, 'to use the Mussulmans thus, as tools against us? Is it not because we have fashioned them into such with our own intolerance? That is how Providence punishes us. Our accumulated sins are being visited on our own heads.'

'Oh, well, if that be so, let them be visited on us. But we shall have our revenge. We have undermined what was the greatest strength of the authorities, their devotion to their own laws. Once they were truly kings, dispensing justice; now they themselves will become law-breakers, and so no better than robbers. This may not go down to history, but we shall carry it in our hearts for all time . . .'

The evil reports about me which are spreading from paper to paper are making me notorious. News comes that my effigy has been burnt at the river-side burning-ground of the Chakravartis, with due ceremony and enthusiasm; and other insults are in contemplation. The trouble was that they had come to ask me to take shares in a Cotton Mill they wanted to start. I had to tell them that I did not so much mind the loss of my own money, but I would not be a party to causing a loss to so many poor shareholders.

'Are we to understand, Maharaja,' said my visitors, 'that the prosperity of the country does not interest you?'

'Industry may lead to the country's prosperity,' I explained, 'but a mere desire for its prosperity will not make for success in industry. Even when our heads were cool, our industries did not flourish. Why should we suppose that they will do so just because we have become frantic?'

'Why not say plainly that you will not risk your money?'

'I will put in my money when I see that it is industry which prompts you. But, because you have lighted a fire, it does not follow that you have the food to cook over it.'

XIII

WHAT IS THIS? Our Chakua sub-treasury looted! A remittance of seven thousand five hundred rupees was due from there to headquarters. The local cashier had changed the cash at the Government Treasury into small currency notes for convenience in carrying, and had kept them ready in bundles. In the middle of the night an armed band had raided the room, and wounded Kasim, the man on guard. The curious part of it was that they had taken only six thousand rupees and left the rest scattered on the floor, though it would have been as easy to carry that away also. Anyhow, the raid of the dacoits was over; now the police raid would begin. Peace was out of the question.

When I went inside, I found the news had travelled before me. 'What a terrible thing, brother,' exclaimed the Bara Rani. 'Whatever shall we do?'

I made light of the matter to reassure her. 'We still have something left,' I said with a smile. 'We shall manage to get along somehow.'

'Don't joke about it, brother dear. Why are they all so angry with you? Can't you humour them? Why put everybody out?'

'I cannot let the country go to rack and ruin, even if that would please everybody.'

'That was a shocking thing they did at the burning-grounds. It's a horrid shame to treat you so. The Chota Rani has got rid of all her fears by dint of the Englishwoman's teaching, but as for me, I had to send for the priest to avert the omen before I could get any peace of mind. For my sake, dear, do get away to Calcutta. I tremble to think what they may do, if you stay on here.'

My sister-in-law's genuine anxiety touched me deeply.

'And, brother,' she went on, 'did I not warn you, it was not well to keep so much money in your room? They might get wind of it any day. It is not the money – but who knows . . .'

To calm her I promised to remove the money to the treasury at once, and then get it away to Calcutta with the first escort going. We went together to my bedroom. The dressing-room door was shut. When I knocked, Bimala called out: 'I am dressing.'

'I wonder at the Chota Rani,' exclaimed my sister-in-law, 'dressing so early in the day! One of their *Bande Mataram* meetings, I suppose. Robber Queen!' she called out in jest to Bimala. 'Are you counting your spoils inside?'

'I will attend to the money a little later,' I said, as I came away to my office room outside.

I found the Police Inspector waiting for me. 'Any trace of the dacoits?' I asked.

'I have my suspicions.'

'On whom?'

'Kasim, the guard.'

'Kasim? But was he not wounded?'

'A mere nothing. A flesh wound on the leg. Probably self-inflicted.'

'But I cannot bring myself to believe it. He is such a trusted servant.'

'You may have trusted him, but that does not prevent his being a thief. Have I not seen men trusted for twenty years together, suddenly developing . . .'

'Even if it were so, I could not send him to gaol. But why should he have left the rest of the money lying about?'

'To put us off the scent. Whatever you may say, Maharaja, he must be an old hand at the game. He mounts guard during his watch, right enough, but I feel sure he has a finger in all the dacoities going on in the neighbourhood.'

With this the Inspector proceeded to recount the various methods by which it was possible to be concerned in a dacoity twenty or thirty miles away, and yet be back in time for duty.

'Have you brought Kasim here?' I asked.

'No,' was the reply, 'he is in the lock-up. The Magistrate is due for the investigation.'

'I want to see him,' I said.

When I went to his cell he fell at my feet, weeping. 'In God's name,' he said, 'I swear I did not do this thing.'

'I do not doubt you, Kasim,' I assured him. 'Fear nothing. They can do nothing to you, if you are innocent.'

Kasim, however, was unable to give a coherent account of the incident. He was obviously exaggerating. Four or five hundred men, big guns, numberless swords, figured in his narrative. It must have been either his disturbed state of mind or a desire to account for his easy defeat. He would have it that this was Harish Kundu's doing; he was even sure he had heard the voice of Ekram, the head retainer of the Kundus.

'Look here, Kasim,' I had to warn him, 'don't you be dragging other people in with your stories. You are not called upon to make out a case against Harish Kundu, or anybody else.'

XIV

ON RETURNING HOME I asked my master to come over. He shook his head gravely. 'I see no good in this,' said he − 'this setting aside of conscience and putting the country in its place.

All the sins of the country will now break out, hideous and unashamed.'

'Who do you think could have . . .'

'Don't ask me. But sin is rampant. Send them all away, right away from here.'

'I have given them one more day. They will be leaving the day after tomorrow.'

'And another thing. Take Bimala away to Calcutta. She is getting too narrow a view of the outside world from here, she cannot see men and things in their true proportions. Let her see the world – men and their work – give her a broad vision.'

'That is exactly what I was thinking.'

'Well, don't make any delay about it. I tell you, Nikhil, man's history has to be built by the united effort of all the races in the world, and therefore this selling of conscience for political reasons – this making a fetish of one's country, won't do. I know that Europe does not at heart admit this, but there she has not the right to pose as our teacher. Men who die for the truth become immortal: and, if a whole people can die for the truth, it will also achieve immortality in the history of humanity. Here, in this land of India, amid the mocking laughter of Satan piercing the sky, may the feeling for this truth become real! What a terrible epidemic of sin has been brought into our country from foreign lands . . .'

The whole day passed in the turmoil of investigation. I was tired out when I retired for the night. I left over sending my sister-in-law's money to the treasury till next morning.

I woke up from my sleep at dead of night. The room was dark. I thought I heard a moaning somewhere. Somebody must have been crying. Sounds of sobbing came heavy with tears like fitful gusts of wind in the rainy night. It seemed to me that the cry rose from the heart of my room itself. I was alone. For some days Bimala had her bed in another room adjoining mine. I rose up and when I went out I found her in the balcony lying prone upon her face on the bare floor.

This is something that cannot be written in words. He only knows it who sits in the bosom of the world and receives all its pangs in His own heart. The sky is dumb, the stars are mute, the night is still, and in the midst of it all that one sleepless cry!

We give these sufferings names, bad or good, according to the classifications of the books, but this agony which is welling up from a torn heart, pouring into the fathomless dark, has it any name? When in that midnight, standing under the silent stars, I looked upon that figure, my mind was struck with awe, and I said to myself: 'Who am I to judge her?' O life, O death, O God of the infinite existence, I bow my head in silence to the mystery which is in you.

Once I thought I should turn back. But I could not. I sat down on the ground near Bimala and placed my hand on her head. At the first touch her whole body seemed to stiffen, but the next moment the hardness gave way, and the tears burst out. I gently passed my fingers over her forehead. Suddenly her hands groping for my feet grasped them and drew them to herself, pressing them against her breast with such force that I thought her heart would break.

Bimala's Story

XVIII

AMULYA IS DUE to return from Calcutta this morning. I told the servants to let me know as soon as he arrived, but could not keep still. At last I went outside to await him in the sitting-room.

When I sent him off to sell the jewels I must have been thinking only of myself. It never even crossed my mind that so young a boy, trying to sell such valuable jewellery, would at once be suspected. So helpless are we women, we needs must place on others the burden of our danger. When we go to our death we drag down those who are about us.

I had said with pride that I would save Amulya – as if she who was drowning could save others. But instead of saving him, I have sent him to his doom. My little brother, such a sister have I been to you that Death must have smiled on that Brothers' Day when I gave you my blessing – I, who wander distracted with the burden of my own evil-doing.

I feel today that man is at times attacked with evil as with the plague. Some germ finds its way in from somewhere, and then in the space of one night Death stalks in. Why cannot the stricken one be kept far away from the rest of the world? I, at least, have realized how terrible is the contagion – like a fiery torch which burns that it may set the world on fire.

It struck nine. I could not get rid of the idea that Amulya was in trouble, that he had fallen into the clutches of the police.

There must be great excitement in the Police Office – whose are the jewels? – where did he get them? And in the end I shall have to furnish the answer, in public, before all the world.

What is that answer to be? Your day has come at last, Bara Rani, you whom I have so long despised. You, in the shape of the public, the world, will have your revenge. O God, save me this time, and I will cast all my pride at my sister-in-law's feet.

I could bear it no longer. I went straight to the Bara Rani. She was in the verandah, spicing her betel leaves, Thako at her side. The sight of Thako made me shrink back for a moment, but I overcame all hesitation, and making a low obeisance I took the dust of my elder sister-in-law's feet.

'Bless my soul, Chota Rani,' she exclaimed, 'what has come upon you? Why this sudden reverence?'

'It is my birthday, sister,' said I. 'I have caused you pain. Give me your blessing today that I may never do so again. My mind is so small.' I repeated my obeisance and left her hurriedly, but she called me back.

'You never before told me that this was your birthday, Chotie darling! Be sure to come and have lunch with me this afternoon. You positively must.'

O God, let it really be my birthday today. Can I not be born over again? Cleanse me, my God, and purify me and give me one more trial!

I went again to the sitting-room to find Sandip there. A feeling of disgust seemed to poison my very blood. The face of his, which I saw in the morning light, had nothing of the magic radiance of genius.

'Will you leave the room,' I blurted out.

Sandip smiled. 'Since Amulya is not here,' he remarked, 'I should think my turn had come for a special talk.'

My fate was coming back upon me. How was I to take away the right I myself had given. 'I would be alone,' I repeated.

'Queen,' he said, 'the presence of another person does not prevent your being alone. Do not mistake me for one of the crowd. I, Sandip, am always alone, even when surrounded by thousands.'

'Please come some other time. This morning I am . . .'

'Waiting for Amulya?'

I turned to leave the room for sheer vexation, when Sandip drew out from the folds of his cloak that jewel-casket of mine and banged it down on the marble table. I was thoroughly startled. 'Has not Amulya gone, then?' I exclaimed.

'Gone where?'

'To Calcutta?'

'No,' chuckled Sandip.

Ah, then my blessing had come true, in spite of all. He was saved. Let God's punishment fall on me, the thief, if only Amulya be safe.

The change in my countenance roused Sandip's scorn. 'So pleased, Queen!' sneered he. 'Are these jewels so very precious? How then did you bring yourself to offer them to the Goddess? Your gift was actually made. Would you now take it back?'

Pride dies hard and raises its fangs to the last. It was clear to me I must show Sandip I did not care a rap about these jewels. 'If they have excited your greed,' I said, 'you may have them.'

'My greed today embraces the wealth of all Bengal,' replied Sandip. 'Is there a greater force than greed? It is the steed of the great ones of the earth, as is the elephant, Airauat, the steed of Indra. So then these jewels are mine?'

As Sandip took up and replaced the casket under his cloak, Amulya rushed in. There were dark rings under his eyes, his lips were dry, his hair tumbled: the freshness of his youth seemed to have withered in a single day. Pangs gripped my heart as I looked on him.

'My box!' he cried, as he went straight up to Sandip without a glance at me. 'Have you taken that jewel-box from my trunk?'

'Your jewel-box?' mocked Sandip.

'It was my trunk!'

Sandip burst out into a laugh. 'Your distinctions between mine and yours are getting rather thin, Amulya,' he cried. 'You will die a religious preacher yet, I see.'

Amulya sank on a chair with his face in his hands. I went up to him and placing my hand on his head asked him: 'What is your trouble, Amulya?'

He stood straight up as he replied: 'I had set my heart, Sister Rani, on returning your jewels to you with my own hand. Sandip Babu knew this, but he forestalled me.'

'What do I care for my jewels?' I said. 'Let them go. No harm is done.'

'Go? Where?' asked the mystified boy.

'The jewels are mine,' said Sandip. 'Insignia bestowed on me by my Queen!'

'No, no, no,' broke out Amulya wildly. 'Never, Sister Rani! I brought them back for you. You shall not give them away to anybody else.'

'I accept your gift, my little brother,' said I. 'But let him, who hankers after them, satisfy his greed.'

Amulya glared at Sandip like a beast of prey, as he growled: 'Look here, Sandip Babu, you know that even hanging has no terrors for me. If you dare take away that box of jewels . . .'

With an attempt at a sarcastic laugh Sandip said: 'You also ought to know by this time, Amulya, that I am not the man to be afraid of you.

'Queen Bee,' he went on, turning to me, 'I did not come here today to take these jewels, I came to give them to you. You would have done wrong to take my gift at Amulya's hands. In order to prevent it, I had first to make them clearly mine. Now these my jewels are my gift to you. Here they are! Patch up any understanding with this boy you like. I must go. You have been at your special talks all these days together, leaving me out of them. If special happenings now come to pass, don't blame me.

'Amulya,' he continued, 'I have sent on your trunks and things to your lodgings. Don't you be keeping any belongings of yours in my room any longer.' With this parting shot, Sandip flung out of the room.

XIX

'I HAVE HAD no peace of mind, Amulya,' I said to him, 'ever since I sent you off to sell my jewels.'

'Why, Sister Rani?'

'I was afraid lest you should get into trouble with them, lest they should suspect you for a thief. I would rather go without that six thousand. You must now do another thing for me – go home at once, home to your mother.'

Amulya produced a small bundle and said: 'But, sister, I have got the six thousand.'

'Where from?'

'I tried hard to get gold,' he went on, without replying to my question, 'but could not. So I had to bring it in notes.'

'Tell me truly, Amulya, swear by me, where did you get this money?'

'That I will not tell you.'

Everything seemed to grow dark before my eyes. 'What terrible thing have you done, Amulya?' I cried. 'Is it then . . .'

'I know you will say I got this money wrongly. Very well, I admit it. But I have paid the full price for my wrong-doing. So now the money is mine.'

I no longer had any desire to learn more about it. My very blood-vessels contracted, making my whole body shrink within itself.

'Take it away, Amulya,' I implored. 'Put it back where you got it from.'

'That would be hard indeed!'

'It is not hard, brother dear. It was an evil moment when you first came to me. Even Sandip has not been able to harm you as I have done.'

Sandip's name seemed to stab him.

'Sandip!' he cried. 'It was you alone who made me come to know that man for what he is. Do you know, sister, he has not spent a pice out of those sovereigns he took from you? He shut himself into his room, after he left you, and gloated over the gold, pouring it out in a heap on the floor. "This is not money," he exclaimed, "but the petals of the divine lotus of power; crystallized strains of music from the pipes that play in the paradise of wealth! I cannot find it in my heart to change them, for they seem longing to fulfil their destiny of adorning the neck of Beauty. Amulya, my boy, don't you look at these with your fleshly eye, they are Lakshmi's smile, the gracious radiance of Indra's queen. No, no, I can't give them up to that boor of a manager. I am sure, Amulya, he was telling us lies. The police haven't traced the man who sank that boat. It's the manager who wants to make something out of it. We must get those letters back from him."

'I asked him how we were to do this; he told me to use force or threats. I offered to do so if he would return the gold. That, he said, we could consider later. I will not trouble you, sister, with all I did to frighten the man into giving up those letters and burn them – it is a long story. That very night I came to Sandip and said: "We are now safe. Let me have the sovereigns to return them tomorrow to my sister, the Maharani." But he cried, "What infatuation is this of yours? Your precious sister's skirt bids fair to hide the whole country from you. Say *Bande Mataram* and exorcize the evil spirit."

'You know, Sister Rani, the power of Sandip's magic. The gold remained with him. And I spent the whole dark night on the bathing-steps of the lake muttering *Bande Mataram*.

'Then when you gave me your jewels to sell, I went again to Sandip. I could see he was angry with me. But he tried not to show it. "If I still have them hoarded up in any box of mine you may take them," said he, as he flung me his keys. They were nowhere to be seen. "Tell me where they are," I said. "I will do so," he replied, "when I find your infatuation has left you. Not now."

'When I found I could not move him, I had to employ other methods. Then I tried to get the sovereigns from him in exchange for my currency notes for six thousand rupees. "You shall have them," he said, and disappeared into his bedroom, leaving me waiting outside. There he broke open my trunk and came straight to you with your casket through some other passage. He would not let me bring it, and now he dares call it his gift. How can I tell how much he has deprived me of? I shall never forgive him.

'But, oh sister, his power over me has been utterly broken. And it is you who have broken it!'

'Brother dear,' said I, 'if that is so, then my life is justified. But more remains to be done, Amulya. It is not enough that the spell has been destroyed. Its stains must be washed away. Don't delay any longer, go at once and put back the money where you took it from. Can you not do it, dear?'

'With your blessing everything is possible, Sister Rani.'

'Remember, it will not be your expiation alone, but mine also. I am a woman; the outside world is closed to me, else I would have gone myself. My hardest punishment is that I must put on you the burden of my sin.'

'Don't say that, sister. The path I was treading was not your path. It attracted me because of its dangers and difficulties. Now that your path calls me, let it be a thousand times more difficult and dangerous, the dust of your feet will help me to win through. Is it then your command that this money be replaced?'

'Not my command, brother mine, but a command from above.'

'Of that I know nothing. It is enough for me that this command from above comes from your lips. And, sister, I thought I had an invitation here. I must not lose that. You must give me your *prasad*[1] before I go. Then, if I can possibly manage it, I will finish my duty in the evening.'

Tears came to my eyes when I tried to smile as I said: 'So be it.'

1. Food consecrated by the touch of a revered person.

CHAPTER ELEVEN

Bimala's Story

XX

WITH AMULYA'S DEPARTURE my heart sank within me. On what perilous adventure had I sent this only son of his mother? O God, why need my expiation have such pomp and circumstance? Could I not be allowed to suffer alone without inviting all this multitude to share my punishment? Oh, let not this innocent child fall victim to Your wrath.

I called him back – 'Amulya!'

My voice sounded so feebly, it failed to reach him.

I went up to the door and called again: 'Amulya!'

He had gone.

'Who is there?'

'Rani Mother!'

'Go and tell Amulya Babu that I want him.'

What exactly happened I could not make out – the man, perhaps, was not familiar with Amulya's name – but he returned almost at once followed by Sandip.

'The very moment you sent me away,' he said as he came in, 'I had a presentiment that you would call me back. The attraction of the same moon causes both ebb and flow. I was so sure of being sent for, that I was actually waiting out in the passage. As soon as I caught sight of your man, coming from your room, I said: "Yes, yes, I am coming, I am coming at once!" – before he could utter a word. That up-country lout was surprised, I can tell you! He stared at me, open-mouthed, as if he thought I knew magic.

'All the fights in the world, Queen Bee,' Sandip rambled on, 'are really fights between hypnotic forces. Spell cast against spell – noiseless weapons which reach even invisible targets. At last I have met in you my match. Your quiver is full, I know, you artful warrior Queen! You are the only one in the world who has been able to turn Sandip out and call Sandip back, at your sweet will. Well, your quarry is at your feet. What will you do with him now? Will you give him the *coup de grâce*, or keep him in your cage? Let me warn you beforehand, Queen, you will find the beast as difficult to kill outright as to keep in bondage. Anyway, why lose time in trying your magic weapons?'

Sandip must have felt the shadow of approaching defeat, and this made him try to gain time by chattering away without waiting for a reply. I believe he knew that I had sent the messenger for Amulya, whose name the man must have mentioned. In spite of that he had deliberately played this trick. He was now trying to avoid giving me any opening to tell him that it was Amulya I wanted, not him. But his stratagem was futile, for I could see his weakness through it. I must not yield up a pin's point of the ground I had gained.

'Sandip Babu,' I said, 'I wonder how you can go on making these endless speeches, without a stop. Do you get them up by heart, beforehand?'

Sandip's face flushed instantly.

'I have heard,' I continued, 'that our professional reciters keep a book full of all kinds of ready-made discourses, which can be fitted into any subject. Have you also a book?'

Sandip ground out his reply through his teeth. 'God has given you women a plentiful supply of coquetry to start with, and on the top of that you have the milliner and the jeweller to help you; but do not think we men are so helpless . . .'

'You had better go back and look up your book, Sandip Babu. You are getting your words all wrong. That's just the trouble with trying to repeat things by rote.'

'You!' shouted Sandip, losing all control over himself. 'You to insult me thus! What is there left of you that I do not know to the very bottom? What . . .' He became speechless.

Sandip, the wielder of magic spells, is reduced to utter powerlessness, whenever his spell refuses to work. From a king he fell to the level of a boor. Oh, the joy of witnessing his weakness! The harsher he became in his rudeness, the more did this joy well up within me. His snaky coils, with which he used to snare me, are exhausted – I am free. I am saved, saved. Be rude to me, insult me, for that shows you in your truth; but spare me your songs of praise, which were false.

My husband came in at this juncture. Sandip had not the elasticity to recover himself in a moment, as he used to do before. My husband looked at him for a while in surprise. Had this happened some days ago I should have felt ashamed. But today I was pleased – whatever my husband might think. I wanted to have it out to the finish with my weakening adversary.

Finding us both silent and constrained, my husband hesitated a little, and then took a chair. 'Sandip,' he said, 'I have been looking for you, and was told you were here.'

'I *am* here,' said Sandip with some emphasis. 'Queen Bee sent for me early this morning. And I, the humble worker of the hive, left all else to attend her summons.'

'I am going to Calcutta tomorrow. You will come with me.'

'And why, pray? Do you take me for one of your retinue?'

'Oh, very well, take it that you are going to Calcutta, and that I am your follower.'

'I have no business there.'

'All the more reason for going. You have too much business here.'

'I don't propose to stir.'

'Then I propose to shift you.'

'Forcibly?'

'Forcibly.'

'Very well, then, I will make a move. But the world is not divided between Calcutta and your estates. There are other places on the map.'

'From the way you have been going on, one would hardly have thought that there was any other place in the world except my estates.'

Sandip stood up. 'It does happen at times,' he said, 'that a man's whole world is reduced to a single spot. I have realized my universe in this sitting-room of yours, that is why I have been a fixture here.'

Then he turned to me. 'None but you, Queen Bee,' he said, 'will understand my words – perhaps not even you. I salute you. With worship in my heart I leave you. My watchword has changed since you have come across my vision. It is no longer *Bande Mataram* (Hail Mother), but Hail Beloved, Hail Enchantress. The mother protects, the mistress leads to destruction – but sweet is that destruction. You have made the anklet sounds of the dance of death tinkle in my heart. You have changed for me, your devotee, the picture I had of this Bengal of ours – "the soft breeze-cooled land of pure water and sweet fruit".[1] You have no pity, my beloved. You have come to me with your poison

---

1. Quotation from the National Song – *Bande Mataram*.

cup and I shall drain it, either to die in agony or live triumphing over death.

'Yes,' he continued. 'The mother's day is past. O love, my love, you have made as naught for me the truth and right and heaven itself. All duties have become as shadows: all rules and restraints have snapped their bonds. O love, my love, I could set fire to all the world outside this land on which you have set your dainty feet, and dance in mad revel over the ashes . . . These are mild men. These are good men. They would do good to all – as if this all were a reality! No, no! There is no reality in the world save this one real love of mine. I do you reverence. My devotion to you has made me cruel; my worship of you has lighted the raging flame of destruction within me. I am not righteous. I have no beliefs, I only believe in her whom, above all else in the world, I have been able to realize.'

Wonderful! It was wonderful, indeed. Only a minute ago I had despised this man with all my heart. But what I had thought to be dead ashes now glowed with living fire. The fire in him is true, that is beyond doubt. Oh why has God made man such a mixed creature? Was it only to show his supernatural sleight of hand? Only a few minutes ago I had thought that Sandip, whom I had once taken to be a hero, was only the stage hero of melodrama. But that is not so, not so. Even behind the trappings of the theatre, a true hero may sometimes be lurking.

There is much in Sandip that is coarse, that is sensuous, that is false, much that is overlaid with layer after layer of fleshly covering. Yet – yet it is best to confess that there is a great deal in the depths of him which we do not, cannot understand – much in ourselves too. A wonderful thing is man. What great mysterious purpose he is working out only the Terrible One[1] knows – meanwhile we groan under the brunt of it. Shiva is the Lord of Chaos. He is all Joy. He will destroy our bonds.

I cannot but feel, again and again, that there are two persons in me. One recoils from Sandip in his terrible aspect of Chaos – the other feels that very vision to be sweetly alluring. The sinking ship drags down all who are swimming round it. Sandip is just such a force of destruction. His immense attraction gets hold of one before fear can come to the rescue, and then, in the twinkling of an eye, one is drawn away, irresistibly, from all

1. Rudra, the Terrible, a name of Shiva.

light, all good, all freedom of the sky, all air that can be breathed – from lifelong accumulations, from everyday cares – right to the bottom of dissolution.

From some realm of calamity has Sandip come as its messenger; and as he stalks the land, muttering unholy incantations, to him flock all the boys and youths. The mother, seated in the lotus-heart of the Country, is wailing her heart out; for they have broken open her store-room, there to hold their drunken revelry. Her vintage of the draught for the immortals they would pour out on the dust; her time-honoured vessels they would smash to pieces. True, I feel with her; but, at the same time, I cannot help being infected with their excitement.

Truth itself has sent us this temptation to test our trustiness in upholding its commandments. Intoxication masquerades in heavenly garb, and dances before the pilgrims saying: 'Fools you are that pursue the fruitless path of renunciation. Its way is long, its time passing slow. So the Wielder of the Thunderbolt has sent me to you. Behold, I the beautiful, the passionate, I will accept you – in my embrace you shall find fulfilment.'

After a pause Sandip addressed me again: 'Goddess, the time has come for me to leave you. It is well. The work of your nearness has been done. By lingering longer it would only become undone again, little by little. All is lost, if in our greed we try to cheapen that which is the greatest thing on earth. That which is eternal within the moment only becomes shallow if spread out in time. We were about to spoil our infinite moment, when it was your uplifted thunderbolt which came to the rescue. You intervened to save the purity of your own worship – and in so doing you also saved your worshipper. In my leave-taking today your worship stands out the biggest thing. Goddess, I, also, set you free today. My earthen temple could hold you no longer – every moment it was on the point of breaking apart. Today I depart to worship your larger image in a larger temple. I can gain you more truly only at a distance from yourself. Here I had only your favour, there I shall be vouchsafed your boon.'

My jewel-casket was lying on the table. I held it up aloft as I said: 'I charge you to convey these my jewels to the object of my worship – to whom I have dedicated them through you.'

My husband remained silent. Sandip left the room.

XXI

I HAD JUST sat down to make some cakes for Amulya when the Bara Rani came upon the scene. 'Oh dear,' she exclaimed, 'has it come to this that you must make cakes for your own birthday?'

'Is there no one else for whom I could be making them?' I asked.

'But this is not the day when you should think of feasting others. It is for us to feast you. I was just thinking of making something up[1] when I heard the staggering news which completely upset me. A gang of five or six hundred men, they say, has raided one of our treasuries and made off with six thousand rupees. Our house will be looted next, they expect.'

I felt greatly relieved. So it was our own money after all. I wanted to send for Amulya at once and tell him that he need only hand over those notes to my husband and leave the explanations to me.

'You *are* a wonderful creature!' my sister-in-law broke out, at the change in my countenance. 'Have you then really no such thing as fear?'

'I cannot believe it,' I said. 'Why should they loot our house?'

'Not believe it, indeed! Who could have believed that they would attack our treasury, either?'

I made no reply, but bent over my cakes, putting in the cocoa-nut stuffing.

'Well, I'm off,' said the Bara Rani after a prolonged stare at me. 'I must see Brother Nikhil and get something done about sending off my money to Calcutta, before it's too late.'

She was no sooner gone than I left the cakes to take care of themselves and rushed to my dressing-room, shutting myself inside. My husband's tunic with the keys in its pocket was still hanging there – so forgetful was he. I took the key of the iron safe off the ring and kept it by me, hidden in the folds of my dress.

Then there came a knocking at the door. 'I am dressing,' I called out. I could hear the Bara Rani saying: 'Only a minute ago I saw her making cakes and now she is busy dressing up. What next, I wonder! One of their *Bande Mataram* meetings is on, I

---

1. Any dainties to be offered ceremonially should be made by the lady of the house herself.

suppose. I say, Robber Queen,' she called out to me, 'are you taking stock of your loot?'

When they went away I hardly know what made me open the safe. Perhaps there was a lurking hope that it might all be a dream. What if, on pulling out the inside drawer, I should find the rolls of gold there, just as before? . . . Alas, everything was empty as the trust which had been betrayed.

I had to go through the farce of dressing. I had to do my hair up all over again, quite unnecessarily. When I came out my sister-in-law railed at me: 'How many times are you going to dress today?'

'My birthday!' I said.

'Oh, any pretext seems good enough,' she went on. 'Many vain people have I seen in my day, but you beat them all hollow.'

I was about to summon a servant to send after Amulya, when one of the men came up with a little note, which he handed to me. It was from Amulya. 'Sister,' he wrote, 'you invited me this afternoon, but I thought I should not wait. Let me first execute your bidding and then come for my *prasad*. I may be a little late.'

To whom could he be going to return that money? into what fresh entanglement was the poor boy rushing? O miserable woman, you can only send him off like an arrow, but not recall him if you miss your aim.

I should have declared at once that I was at the bottom of this robbery. But women live on the trust of their surroundings – this is their whole world. If once it is out that this trust has been secretly betrayed, their place in their world is lost. They have then to stand upon the fragments of the thing they have broken, and its jagged edges keep on wounding them at every turn. To sin is easy enough, but to make up for it is above all difficult for a woman.

For some time past all easy approaches for communion with my husband have been closed to me. How then could I burst on him with this stupendous news? He was very late in coming for his meal today – nearly two o'clock. He was absent-minded and hardly touched any food. I had lost even the right to press him to take a little more. I had to avert my face to wipe away my tears.

I wanted so badly to say to him: 'Do come into our room and rest awhile; you look so tired.' I had just cleared my throat with a little cough, when a servant hurried in to say that the Police Inspector had brought Panchu up to the palace. My husband, with the shadow on his face deepened, left his meal unfinished and went out.

A little later the Bara Rani appeared. 'Why did you not send me word when Brother Nikhil came in?' she complained. 'As he was late I thought I might as well finish my bath in the meantime. However did he manage to get through his meal so soon?'

'Why, did you want him for anything?'

'What is this about both of you going off to Calcutta to-morrow? All I can say is, I am not going to be left here alone. I should get startled out of my life at every sound, with all these dacoits about. Is it quite settled about your going tomorrow?'

'Yes,' said I, though I had only just now heard it; and though, moreover, I was not at all sure that before tomorrow our history might not take such a turn as to make it all one whether we went or stayed. After that, what our home, our life would be like, was utterly beyond my ken – it seemed so misty and phantom-like.

In a very few hours now my unseen fate would become visible. Was there no one who could keep on postponing the flight of these hours, from day to day, and so make them long enough for me to set things right, so far as lay in my power? The time during which the seed lies underground is long – so long indeed that one forgets that there is any danger of its sprouting. But once its shoot shows up above the surface, it grows and grows so fast, there is no time to cover it up, neither with skirt, nor body, nor even life itself.

I will try to think of it no more, but sit quiet – passive and callous – let the crash come when it may. By the day after tomorrow all will be over – publicity, laughter, bewailing, questions, explanations – everything.

But I cannot forget the face of Amulya – beautiful, radiant with devotion. He did not wait, despairing, for the blow of fate to fall, but rushed into the thick of danger. In my misery I do him reverence. He is my boy-god. Under the pretext of his playfulness he took from me the weight of my burden. He would save me by taking the punishment meant for me on his own head. But how am I to bear this terrible mercy of my God?

Oh, my child, my child, I do you reverence. Little brother mine, I do you reverence. Pure are you, beautiful are you, I do you reverence. May you come to my arms, in the next birth, as my own child – that is my prayer.

XXII

RUMOUR BECAME busy on every side. The police were continually in and out. The servants of the house were in a great flurry.

Khema, my maid, came up to me and said: 'Oh, Rani Mother! for goodness' sake put away my gold necklace and armlets in your iron safe.' To whom was I to explain that the Rani herself had been weaving all this network of trouble and had got caught in it, too? I had to play the benign protector and take charge of Khema's ornaments and Thako's savings. The milk-woman, in her turn, brought along and kept in my room a box in which were a Benares *sari* and some other of her valued possessions. 'I got these at your wedding,' she told me.

When, tomorrow, my iron safe will be opened in the presence of these – Khema, Thako, the milk-woman and all the rest . . . Let me not think of it! Let me rather try to think what it will be like when this third day of Magh comes round again after a year has passed. Will all the wounds of my home life then be still as fresh as ever? . . .

Amulya writes that he will come later in the evening. I cannot remain alone with my thoughts, doing nothing. So I sit down again to make cakes for him. I have finished making quite a quantity, but still I must go on. Who will eat them? I shall distribute them amongst the servants. I must do so this very night. Tonight is my limit. Tomorrow will not be in my hands.

I went on untiringly, frying cake after cake. Every now and then it seemed to me that there was some noise in the direction of my rooms, upstairs. Could it be that my husband had missed the key of the safe, and the Bara Rani had assembled all the servants to help him to hunt for it? No, I must not pay heed to these sounds. Let me shut the door.

I rose to do so, when Thako came panting in: 'Rani Mother, oh, Rani Mother!'

'Oh get away!' I snapped out, cutting her short. 'Don't come bothering me.'

'The Bara Rani Mother wants you,' she went on. 'Her nephew has brought such a wonderful machine from Calcutta. It talks like a man. Do come and hear it!'

I did not know whether to laugh or to cry. So, of all things, a gramophone needs must come on the scene at such a time, repeating at every winding the nasal twang of its theatrical songs! What a fearsome thing results when a machine apes a man.

The shades of evening began to fall. I knew that Amulya would not delay to announce himself – yet I could not wait. I summoned a servant and said: 'Go and tell Amulya Babu to come straight in here.' The man came back after a while to say that Amulya was not in – he had not come back since he had gone.

'Gone!' The last word struck my ears like a wail in the gathering darkness. Amulya gone! Had he then come like a streak of light from the setting sun, only to be gone for ever? All kinds of possible and impossible dangers flitted through my mind. It was I who had sent him to his death. What if he was fearless? That only showed his own greatness of heart. But after this how was I to go on living all by myself?

I had no memento of Amulya save that pistol – his reverence-offering. It seemed to me that this was a sign given by Providence. This guilt which had contaminated my life at its very root – my God in the form of a child had left with me the means of wiping it away, and then vanished. Oh the loving gift – the saving grace that lay hidden within it!

I opened my box and took out the pistol, lifting it reverently to my forehead. At that moment the gongs clanged out from the temple attached to our house. I prostrated myself in salutation.

In the evening I feasted the whole household with my cakes. 'You have managed a wonderful birthday feast – and all by yourself too!' exclaimed my sister-in-law. 'But you must leave something for us to do.' With this she turned on her gramophone and let loose the shrill treble of the Calcutta actresses all over the place. It seemed like a stable full of neighing fillies.

It got quite late before the feasting was over. I had a sudden longing to end my birthday celebration by taking the dust of my husband's feet. I went up to the bedroom and found him fast asleep. He had had such a worrying, trying day. I raised the edge of the mosquito curtain very very gently, and laid my head near his feet. My hair must have touched him, for he moved his legs in his sleep and pushed my head away.

I then went out and sat in the west verandah. A silk-cotton tree, which had shed all its leaves, stood there in the distance, like a skeleton. Behind it the crescent moon was setting. All of a sudden I had the feeling that the very stars in the sky were afraid of me – that the whole of the night world was looking askance at me. Why? Because I was alone.

There is nothing so strange in creation as the man who is alone. Even he whose near ones have all died, one by one, is not alone – companionship comes for him from behind the screen of death. But he, whose kin are there, yet no longer near, who has dropped out of all the varied companionship of a full home – the starry universe itself seems to bristle to look on him in his darkness.

Where I am, I am not. I am far away from those who are around me. I live and move upon a world-wide chasm of separation, unstable as the dew-drop upon the lotus leaf.

Why do not men change wholly when they change? When I look into my heart, I find everything that was there, still there – only they are topsy-turvy. Things that were well-ordered have become jumbled up. The gems that were strung into a necklace are now rolling in the dust. And so my heart is breaking.

I feel I want to die. Yet in my heart everything still lives – nor even in death can I see the end of it all: rather, in death there seems to be ever so much more of repining. What is to be ended must be ended in this life – there is no other way out.

Oh forgive me just once, only this time, Lord! All that you gave into my hands as the wealth of my life, I have made into my burden. I can neither bear it longer, nor give it up. O Lord, sound once again those flute strains which you played for me, long ago, standing at the rosy edge of my morning sky – and let all my complexities become simple and easy. Nothing save the music of your flute can make whole that which has been broken, and pure that which has been sullied. Create my home anew with your music. No other way can I see.

I threw myself prone on the ground and sobbed aloud. It was for mercy that I prayed – some little mercy from somewhere, some shelter, some sign of forgiveness, some hope that might bring about the end. 'Lord,' I vowed to myself, 'I will lie here, waiting and waiting, touching neither food nor drink, so long as your blessing does not reach me.'

I heard the sound of footsteps. Who says that the gods do not show themselves to mortal men? I did not raise my face to look up, lest the sight of it should break the spell. Come, oh come, come and let your feet touch my head. Come, Lord, and set your foot upon my throbbing heart, and at that moment let me die.

He came and sat near my head. Who? My husband! At the first touch of his presence I felt that I should swoon. And then the pain at my heart burst its way out in an overwhelming flood of tears, tearing through all my obstructing veins and nerves. I strained his feet to my bosom – oh, why could not their impress remain there for ever?

He tenderly stroked my head. I received his blessing. Now I shall be able to take up the penalty of public humiliation which will be mine tomorrow, and offer it, in all sincerity, at the feet of my God.

But what keeps crushing my heart is the thought that the festive flutes which were played at my wedding, nine years ago, welcoming me to this house, will never sound for me again in this life. What rigour of penance is there which can serve to bring me once more, as a bride adorned for her husband, to my place upon that same bridal seat? How many years, how many ages, aeons, must pass before I can find my way back to that day of nine years ago?

God can create new things; but has even He the power to create afresh that which has been destroyed?

CHAPTER TWELVE

Nikhil's Story

XV

TODAY WE ARE going to Calcutta. Our joys and sorrows lie heavy on us if we merely go on accumulating them. Keeping them and accumulating them alike are false. As master of the house I am in an artificial position – in reality I am a wayfarer on the path of life. That is why the true Master of the House gets hurt at every step and at last there comes the supreme hurt of death.

My union with you, my love, was only of the wayside; it was well enough so long as we followed the same road; it will only hamper us if we try to preserve it further. We are now leaving its bonds behind. We are started on our journey beyond, and it will be enough if we can throw each other a glance, or feel the touch of each other's hands in passing. After that? After that there is the larger world-path, the endless current of universal life.

How little can you deprive me of, my love, after all? Whenever I set my ear to it, I can hear the flute which is playing, its fountain of melody gushing forth from the flute-stops of separation. The immortal draught of the goddess is never exhausted. She sometimes breaks the bowl from which we drink it, only to smile at seeing us so disconsolate over the trifling loss. I will not stop to pick up my broken bowl. I will march forward, albeit with unsatisfied heart.

The Bara Rani came and asked me: 'What is the meaning, brother, of all these books being packed up and sent off in box-loads?'

'It only means,' I replied, 'that I have not yet been able to get over my fondness for them.'

'I only wish you would keep your fondness for some other things as well! Do you mean you are never coming back home?'

'I shall be coming and going, but shall not immure myself here any more.'

'Oh indeed! Then just come along to my room and see how many things I have been unable to shake off *my* fondness for.' With this she took me by the hand and marched me off.

In my sister-in-law's rooms I found numberless boxes and bundles ready packed. She opened one of the boxes and said: 'See, brother, look at all my *pan*-making things. In this bottle I have catechu powder scented with the pollen of screw-pine blossoms. These little tin boxes are all for different kinds of spices. I have not forgotten my playing cards and draught-board either. If you two are over-busy, I shall manage to make other friends there, who will give me a game. Do you remember this comb? It was one of the *Swadeshi* combs you brought for me . . .'

'But what is all this for, Sister Rani? Why have *you* been packing up all these things?'

'Do you think I am not going with you?'

'What an extraordinary idea!'

'Don't you be afraid! I am not going there to flirt with you, nor to quarrel with the Chota Rani! One must die sooner or later, and it is just as well to be on the bank of the holy Ganges before it is too late. It is too horrible to think of being cremated in your wretched burning-ground here, under that stumpy banian tree – that is why I have been refusing to die, and have plagued you all this time.'

At last I could hear the true voice of home. The Bara Rani came into our house as its bride, when I was only six years old. We have played together, through the drowsy afternoons, in a corner of the roof-terrace. I have thrown down to her green *amras* from the tree-top, to be made into deliciously indigestible chutneys by slicing them up with mustard, salt and fragrant herbs. It was my part to gather for her all the forbidden things from the store-room to be used in the marriage celebration of her doll; for, in the penal code of my grandmother, I alone was exempt from punishment. And I used to be appointed her messenger to my brother, whenever she wanted to coax something special out of him, because he could not resist my importunity. I also remember how, when I suffered under the rigorous régime of the doctors of those days – who would not allow anything except warm water and sugared cardamom seeds during feverish attacks – my sister-in-law could not bear my privation and used to bring me delicacies on the sly. What a scolding she got one day when she was caught!

And then, as we grew up, our mutual joys and sorrows took on deeper tones of intimacy. How we quarrelled! Sometimes conflicts of worldly interests roused suspicions and jealousies, making breaches in our love; and when the Chota Rani came in between us, these breaches seemed as if they would never be mended, but it always turned out that the healing forces at bottom proved more powerful than the wounds on the surface.

So has a true relationship grown up between us, from our childhood up till now, and its branching foliage has spread and broadened over every room and verandah and terrace of this great house. When I saw the Bara Rani make ready, with all her belongings, to depart from this house of ours, all the ties that bound us, to their wide-spreading ends, felt the shock.

The reason was clear to me, why she had made up her mind to drift away towards the unknown, cutting asunder all her life-long bonds of daily habit, and of the house itself, which she had never left for a day since she first entered it at the age of nine. And yet it was this real reason which she could not allow to escape her lips, preferring rather to put forward any other paltry excuse.

She had only this one relationship left in all the world, and the poor, unfortunate, widowed and childless woman had cherished it with all the tenderness hoarded in her heart. How deeply she had felt our proposed separation I never realized so keenly as when I stood amongst her scattered boxes and bundles.

I could see at once that the little differences she used to have with Bimala, about money matters, did not proceed from any sordid worldliness, but because she felt that her claims in regard to this one relationship of her life had been overridden and its ties weakened for her by the coming in between of this other woman from goodness knows where! She had been hurt at every turn and yet had not the right to complain.

And Bimala? She also had felt that the Senior Rani's claim over me was not based merely on our social connection, but went much deeper; and she was jealous of these ties between us, reaching back to our childhood.

Today my heart knocked heavily against the doors of my breast. I sank down upon one of the boxes as I said: 'How I should love, Sister Rani, to go back to the days when we first met in this old house of ours.'

'No, brother dear,' she replied with a sigh, 'I would not live my life again – not as a woman! Let what I have had to bear end with this one birth. I could not bear it over again.'

I said to her: 'The freedom to which we pass through sorrow is greater than the sorrow.'

'That may be so for you men. Freedom is for you. But we women would keep others bound. We would rather be put into bondage ourselves. No, no, brother, you will never get free from our toils. If you needs must spread your wings, you will have to take us with you; we refuse to be left behind. That is why I have gathered together all this weight of luggage. It would never do to allow men to run too light.'

'I can feel the weight of your words,' I said laughing, 'and if we men do not complain of your burdens, it is because women pay us so handsomely for what they make us carry.'

'You carry it,' she said, 'because it is made up of many small things. Whichever one you think of rejecting pleads that it is so light. And so with much lightness we weigh you down . . . When do we start?'

'The train leaves at half past eleven tonight. There will be lots of time.'

'Look here, do be good for once and listen to just one word of mine. Take a good nap this afternoon. You know you never get any sleep in the train. You look so pulled down, you might go to pieces any moment. Come along, get through your bath first.'

As we went towards my room, Khema, the maid, came up and with an ultra-modest pull at her veil told us, in deprecatingly low tones, that the Police Inspector had arrived with a prisoner and wanted to see the Maharaja.

'Is the Maharaja a thief, or a robber,' the Bara Rani flared up, 'that he should be set upon so by the police? Go and tell the Inspector that the Maharaja is at his bath.'

'Let me just go and see what is the matter,' I pleaded. 'It may be something urgent.'

'No, no,' my sister-in-law insisted. 'Our Chota Rani was making a heap of cakes last night. I'll send some to the Inspector, to keep him quiet till you're ready.' With this she pushed me into my room and shut the door on me.

I had not the power to resist such tyranny – so rare is it in this world. Let the Inspector while away the time eating cakes. What if business is a bit neglected?

The police had been in great form these last few days arresting now this one, now that. Each day some innocent person or other would be brought along to enliven the assembly in my office-room. One more such unfortunate, I supposed, must have been brought in that day. But why should the Inspector alone be re-galed with cakes? That would not do at all. I thumped vigorously on the door.

'If you are going mad, be quick and pour some water over your head – that will keep you cool,' said my sister-in-law from the passage.

'Send down cakes for two,' I shouted. 'The person who has been brought in as the thief probably deserves them better. Tell the man to give him a good big helping.'

I hurried through my bath. When I came out, I found Bimal sitting on the floor outside.[1] Could this be my Bimal of old, my proud, sensitive Bimal?

What favour could she be wanting to beg, seated like this at my door? As I stopped short, she stood up and said gently with downcast eyes: 'I would have a word with you.'

'Come inside then,' I said.

'But are you going out on any particular business?'

'I was, but let that be. I want to hear . . .'

'No, finish your business first. We will have our talk after you have had your dinner.'

I went off to my sitting-room, to find the Police Inspector's plate quite empty. The person he had brought with him, how-ever, was still busy eating.

'Hullo!' I ejaculated in surprise. 'You, Amulya?'

'It is I, sir,' said Amulya with his mouth full of cake. 'I've had quite a feast. And if you don't mind, I'll take the rest with me.' With this he proceeded to tie up the remaining cakes in his handkerchief.

'What does this mean?' I asked, staring at the Inspector.

The man laughed. 'We are no nearer, sir,' he said, 'to solving the problem of the thief: meanwhile the mystery of the theft deepens.' He then produced something tied up in a rag, which when untied disclosed a bundle of currency notes. 'This, Maha-raja,' said the Inspector, 'is your six thousand rupees!'

'Where was it found?'

'In Amulya Babu's hands. He went last evening to the

---

1. Sitting on the bare floor is a sign of mourning, and so, by association of ideas, of an abject attitude of mind.

manager of your Chakna sub-office to tell him that the money had been found. The manager seemed to be in a greater state of trepidation at the recovery than he had been at the robbery. He was afraid he would be suspected of having made away with the notes and of now making up a cock-and-bull story for fear of being found out. He asked Amulya to wait, on the pretext of getting him some refreshment, and came straight over to the Police Office. I rode off at once, kept Amulya with me, and have been busy with him the whole morning. He refuses to tell us where he got the money from. I warned him he would be kept under restraint till he did so. In that case, he informed me he would have to lie. Very well, I said, he might do so if he pleased. Then he stated that he had found the money under a bush. I pointed out to him that it was not quite so easy to lie as all that. Under what bush? Where was the place? Why was he there? – All this would have to be stated as well. "Don't you worry," he said, "there is plenty of time to invent all that."'

'But, Inspector,' I said, 'why are you badgering a respectable young gentleman like Amulya Babu?'

'I have no desire to harass him,' said the Inspector. 'He is not only a gentleman, but the son of Niparan Babu, my school-fellow. Let me tell you, Maharaja, exactly what must have happened. Amulya knows the thief, but wants to shield him by drawing suspicion on himself. That is just the sort of bravado he loves to indulge in.' The Inspector turned to Amulya. 'Look here, young man,' he continued, 'I also was eighteen once upon a time, and a student in the Ripon College. I nearly got into gaol trying to rescue a hack driver from a police constable. It was a near shave.' Then he turned again to me and said: 'Maharaja, the real thief will now probably escape, but I think I can tell you who is at the bottom of it all.'

'Who is it, then?' I asked.

'The manager, in collusion with the guard, Kasim.'

When the Inspector, having argued out his theory to his own satisfaction, at last departed, I said to Amulya: 'If you will tell me who took the money, I promise you no one shall be hurt.'

'I did,' said he.

'But how can that be? What about the gang of armed men? . . .'

'It was I, by myself, alone!'

What Amulya then told me was indeed extraordinary. The

manager had just finished his supper and was on the verandah
rinsing out his mouth. The place was somewhat dark. Amulya
had a revolver in each pocket, one loaded with blank cartridges,
the other with ball. He had a mask over his face. He flashed a
bull's-eye lantern in the manager's face and fired a blank shot.
The man swooned away. Some of the guards, who were off
duty, came running up, but when Amulya fired another blank
shot at them they lost no time in taking cover. Then Kasim, who
was on duty, came up whirling a quarterstaff. This time Amulya
aimed a bullet at his legs, and finding himself hit, Kasim collapsed
on the floor. Amulya then made the trembling manager, who
had come to his senses, open the safe and deliver up six thousand
rupees. Finally, he took one of the estate horses and galloped off
a few miles, there let the animal loose, and quietly walked up
here, to our place.

'What made you do all this, Amulya?' I asked.

'There was a grave reason, Maharaja,' he replied.

'But why, then, did you try to return the money?'

'Let her come, at whose command I did so. In her presence I
shall make a clean breast of it.'

'And who may "she" be?'

'My sister, the Chota Rani!'

I sent for Bimala. She came hesitatingly, barefoot, with a
white shawl over her head. I had never seen my Bimal like this
before. She seemed to have wrapped herself in a morning light.

Amulya prostrated himself in salutation and took the dust of
her feet. Then, as he rose, he said: 'Your command has been
executed, sister. The money is returned.'

'You have saved me, my little brother,' said Bimal.

'With your image in my mind, I have not uttered a single lie,'
Amulya continued. 'My watchword *Bande Mataram* has been cast
away at your feet for good. I have also received my reward, your
prasad, as soon as I came to the palace.'

Bimal looked at him blankly, unable to follow his last words.
Amulya brought out his handkerchief, and untying it showed
her the cakes put away inside. 'I did not eat them all,' he said. 'I
have kept these to eat after you have helped me with your own
hands.'

I could see that I was not wanted here. I went out of the
room. I could only preach and preach, so I mused, and get my
effigy burnt for my pains. I had not yet been able to bring back

a single soul from the path of death. They who have the power, can do so by a mere sign. My words have not that ineffable meaning. I am not a flame, only a black coal, which has gone out. I can light no lamp. That is what the story of my life shows — my row of lamps has remained unlit.

XVI

I RETURNED SLOWLY towards the inner apartments. The Bara Rani's room must have been drawing me again. It had become an absolute necessity for me, that day, to feel that this life of mine had been able to strike some real, some responsive chord in some other harp of life. One cannot realize one's own existence by remaining within oneself – it has to be sought outside.

As I passed in front of my sister-in-law's room, she came out saying: 'I was afraid you would be late again this afternoon. However, I ordered your dinner as soon as I heard you coming. It will be served in a minute.'

'Meanwhile,' I said, 'let me take out that money of yours and have it kept ready to take with us.'

As we walked on towards my room she asked me if the Police Inspector had made any report about the robbery. I somehow did not feel inclined to tell her all the details of how that six thousand had come back. 'That's just what all the fuss is about,' I said evasively.

When I went into my dressing-room and took out my bunch of keys, I did not find the key of the iron safe on the ring. What an absurdly absent-minded fellow I was, to be sure! Only this morning I had been opening so many boxes and things, and never noticed that this key was not there.

'What has happened to your key?' she asked me.

I went on fumbling in this pocket and that, but could give her no answer. I hunted in the same place over and over again. It dawned on both of us that it could not be a case of the key being mislaid. Someone must have taken it off the ring. Who could it be? Who else could have come into this room?

'Don't you worry about it,' she said to me. 'Get through your dinner first. The Chota Rani must have kept it herself, seeing how absent-minded you are getting.'

I was, however, greatly disturbed. It was never Bimal's habit to take any key of mine without telling me about it. Bimal was not present at my meal-time that day: she was busy feasting

Amulya in her own room. My sister-in-law wanted to send for her, but I asked her not to do so.

I had just finished my dinner when Bimal came in. I would have preferred not to discuss the matter of the key in the Bara Rani's presence, but as soon as she saw Bimal, she asked her: 'Do you know, dear, where the key of the safe is?'

'I have it,' was the reply.

'Didn't I say so!' exclaimed my sister-in-law triumphantly. 'Our Chota Rani pretends not to care about these robberies, but she takes precautions on the sly, all the same.'

The look on Bimal's face made my mind misgive me. 'Let the key be, now,' I said. 'I will take out that money in the evening.'

'There you go again, putting it off,' said the Bara Rani. 'Why not take it out and send it to the treasury while you have it in mind?'

'I have taken it out already,' said Bimal.

I was startled.

'Where have you kept it, then?' asked my sister-in-law.

'I have spent it.'

'Just listen to her! Whatever did you spend all that money on?'

Bimal made no reply. I asked her nothing further. The Bara Rani seemed about to make some further remark to Bimala, but checked herself. 'Well, that is all right, anyway,' she said at length, as she looked towards me. 'Just what I used to do with my husband's loose cash. I knew it was no use leaving it with him – his hundred and one hangers-on would be sure to get hold of it. You are much the same, dear! What a number of ways you men know of getting through money. We can only save it from you by stealing it ourselves! Come along now. Off with you to bed.'

The Bara Rani led me to my room, but I hardly knew where I was going. She sat by my bed after I was stretched on it, and smiled at Bimal as she said: 'Give me one of your *pans*, Chotie darling – what? You have none! You have become a regular mem-sahib. Then send for some from my room.'

'But have you had your dinner yet?' I anxiously enquired.

'Oh long ago,' she replied – clearly a fib.

She kept on chattering away there at my bedside, on all manner of things. The maid came and told Bimal that her dinner had been served and was getting cold, but she gave no sign of having heard it. 'Not had your dinner yet? What nonsense! It's fearfully late.' With this the Bara Rani took Bimal away with her.

I could divine that there was some connection between the taking out of this six thousand and the robbing of the other. But I have no curiosity to learn the nature of it. I shall never ask.

Providence leaves our life moulded in the rough – its object being that we ourselves should put the finishing touches, shaping it into its final form to our taste. There has always been the hankering within me to express some great idea in the process of giving shape to my life on the lines suggested by the Creator. In this endeavour I have spent all my days. How severely I have curbed my desires, repressed myself at every step, only the Searcher of the Heart knows.

But the difficulty is, that one's life is not solely one's own. He who would create it must do so with the help of his surroundings, or he will fail. So it was my constant dream to draw Bimal to join me in this work of creating myself. I loved her with all my soul; on the strength of that, I could not but succeed in winning her to my purpose – that was my firm belief.

Then I discovered that those who could simply and naturally draw their environment into the process of their self-creation belonged to one species of the genus 'man', – and I to another. I had received the vital spark, but could not impart it. Those to whom I have surrendered my all have taken my all, but not myself with it.

My trial is hard indeed. Just when I want a helpmate most, I am thrown back on myself alone. Nevertheless, I record my vow that even in this trial I shall win through. Alone, then, shall I tread my thorny path to the end of this life's journey . . .

I have begun to suspect that there has all along been a vein of tyranny in me. There was a despotism in my desire to mould my relations with Bimala in a hard, clear-cut, perfect form. But man's life was not meant to be cast in a mould. And if we try to shape the good, as so much mere material, it takes a terrible revenge by losing its life.

I did not realize all this while that it must have been this unconscious tyranny of mine which made us gradually drift apart. Bimala's life, not finding its true level by reason of my pressure from above, has had to find an outlet by undermining its banks at the bottom. She has had to steal this six thousand rupees because she could not be open with me, because she felt that, in certain things, I despotically differed from her.

Men, such as I, possessed with one idea, are indeed at one with those who can manage to agree with us; but those who do not, can only get on with us by cheating us. It is our unyielding obstinacy, which drives even the simplest to tortuous ways. In trying to manufacture a helpmate, we spoil a wife.

Could I not go back to the beginning? Then, indeed, I should follow the path of the simple. I should not try to fetter my life's companion with my ideas, but play the joyous pipes of my love and say: 'Do you love me? Then may you grow true to yourself in the light of your love. Let my suggestions be suppressed, let God's design, which is in you, triumph, and my ideas retire abashed.'

But can even Nature's nursing heal the open wound, into which our accumulated differences have broken out? The covering veil, beneath the privacy of which Nature's silent forces alone can work, has been torn asunder. Wounds must be bandaged – can we not bandage our wound with our love, so that the day may come when its scar will no longer be visible? It is not too late? So much time has been lost in understanding; it has taken right up to now to come to an understanding; how much more time will it take for the correcting? What if the wound does eventually heal? – can the devastation it has wrought ever be made good?

There was a slight sound near the door. As I turned over I saw Bimala's retreating figure through the open doorway. She must have been waiting by the door, hesitating whether to come in or not, and at last have decided to go back. I jumped up and bounded to the door, calling: 'Bimal.'

She stopped on her way. She had her back to me. I went and took her by the hand and led her into our room. She threw herself face downwards on a pillow, and sobbed and sobbed. I said nothing, but held her hand as I sat by her head.

When her storm of grief had abated she sat up. I tried to draw her to my breast, but she pushed my arms away and knelt at my feet, touching them repeatedly with her head, in obeisance. I hastily drew my feet back, but she clasped them in her arms, saying in a choking voice: 'No, no, no, you must not take away your feet. Let me do my worship.'

I kept still. Who was I to stop her? Was I the god of her worship that I should have any qualms?

Bimala's Story

XXIII

COME, COME! Now is the time to set sail towards that great confluence, where the river of love meets the sea of worship. In that pure blue all the weight of its muddiness sinks and disappears.

I now fear nothing – neither myself, nor anybody else. I have passed through fire. What was inflammable has been burnt to ashes; what is left is deathless. I have dedicated myself to the feet of him, who has received all my sin into the depths of his own pain.

Tonight we go to Calcutta. My inward troubles have so long prevented my looking after my things. Now let me arrange and pack them.

After a while I found my husband had come in and was taking a hand in the packing.

'This won't do,' I said. 'Did you not promise me you would have a sleep?'

'I might have made the promise,' he replied, 'but my sleep did not, and it was nowhere to be found.'

'No, no,' I repeated, 'this will never do. Lie down for a while, at least.'

'But how can you get through all this alone?'

'Of course I can.'

'Well, you may boast of being able to do without me. But frankly I can't do without you. Even sleep refused to come to me, alone, in that room.' Then he set to work again.

But there was an interruption, in the shape of a servant, who came and said that Sandip Babu had called and had asked to be announced. I did not dare to ask whom he wanted. The light of the sky seemed suddenly to be shut down, like the leaves of a sensitive plant.

'Come, Bimal,' said my husband. 'Let us go and hear what Sandip has to tell us. Since he has come back again, after taking his leave, he must have something special to say.'

I went, simply because it would have been still more embarrassing to stay. Sandip was staring at a picture on the wall. As we entered he said: 'You must be wondering why the fellow has returned. But you know the ghost is never laid till all the rites are complete.' With these words he brought out of his pocket something tied in his handkerchief, and laying it on the table, undid the knot. It was those sovereigns.

'Don't you mistake me, Nikhil,' he said. 'You must not imagine that the contagion of your company has suddenly turned me honest; I am not the man to come back in slobbering repentance to return ill-gotten money. But . . .'

He left his speech unfinished. After a pause he turned towards Nikhil, but said to me: 'After all these days, Queen Bee, the ghost of compunction has found an entry into my hitherto untroubled conscience. As I have to wrestle with it every night, after my first sleep is over, I cannot call it a phantom of my imagination. There is no escape even for me till its debt is paid. Into the hands of that spirit, therefore, let me make restitution. Goddess! From you, alone, of all the world, I shall not be able to take away anything. I shall not be rid of you till I am destitute. Take these back!'

He took out at the same time the jewel-casket from under his tunic and put it down, and then left us with hasty steps.

'Listen to me, Sandip,' my husband called after him.

'I have not the time, Nikhil,' said Sandip as he paused near the door. 'The Mussulmans, I am told, have taken me for an invaluable gem, and are conspiring to loot me and hide me away in their graveyard. But I feel that it is necessary that I should live. I have just twenty-five minutes to catch the North-bound train. So, for the present, I must be gone. We shall have our talk out at the next convenient opportunity. If you take my advice, don't you delay in getting away either. I salute you, Queen Bee, Queen of the bleeding hearts, Queen of desolation!'

Sandip then left almost at a run. I stood stock-still; I had never realized in such a manner before, how trivial, how paltry, this gold and these jewels were. Only a short while ago I was so busy thinking what I should take with me, and how I should pack it. Now I felt that there was no need to take anything at all. To set out and go forth was the important thing.

My husband left his seat and came up and took me by the hand. 'It is getting late,' he said. 'There is not much time left to complete our preparations for the journey.'

At this point Chandranath Babu suddenly came in. Finding us both together, he fell back for a moment. Then he said, 'Forgive me, my little mother, if I intrude. Nikhil, the Mussulmans are out of hand. They are looting Harish Kundu's treasury. That does not so much matter. But what is intolerable is the violence that is being done to the women of their house.'

'I am off,' said my husband.

'What can you do there?' I pleaded, as I held him by the hand. 'Oh, sir,' I appealed to his master. 'Will you not tell him not to go?'

'My little mother,' he replied, 'there is no time to do anything else.'

'Don't be alarmed, Bimal,' said my husband, as he left us.

When I went to the window I saw my husband galloping away on horseback, with not a weapon in his hands.

In another minute the Bara Rani came running in. 'What have you done, Chotie darling,' she cried. 'How could you let him go?

'Call the Dewan at once,' she said, turning to a servant.

The Ranis never appeared before the Dewan, but the Bara Rani had no thought that day for appearances.

'Send a mounted man to bring back the Maharaja at once,' she said, as soon as the Dewan came up.

'We have all entreated him to stay, Rani Mother,' said the Dewan, 'but he refused to turn back.'

'Send word to him that the Bara Rani is ill, that she is on her death-bed,' cried my sister-in-law wildly.

When the Dewan had left she turned on me with a furious outburst. 'Oh, you witch, you ogress, you could not die your-self, but needs must send him to his death! . . .'

The light of the day began to fade. The sun set behind the feathery foliage of the blossoming *Sajna* tree. I can see every different shade of that sunset even today. Two masses of cloud on either side of the sinking orb made it look like a great bird with fiery-feathered wings outspread. It seemed to me that this fateful day was taking its flight, to cross the ocean of night.

It became darker and darker. Like the flames of a distant village on fire, leaping up every now and then above the horizon, a distant din swelled up in recurring waves into the darkness.

The bells of the evening worship rang out from our temple. I knew the Bara Rani was sitting there, with palms joined in silent prayer. But I could not move a step from the window.

The roads, the village beyond, and the still more distant fringe of trees, grew more and more vague. The lake in our grounds looked up into the sky with a dull lustre, like a blind man's eye. On the left the tower seemed to be craning its neck to catch sight of something that was happening.

The sounds of night take on all manner of disguises. A twig snaps, and one thinks that somebody is running for his life. A door slams, and one feels it to be the sudden heart-thump of a startled world.

Lights would suddenly flicker under the shade of the distant trees, and then go out again. Horses' hoofs would clatter, now and again, only to turn out to be riders leaving the palace gates.

I continually had the feeling that, if only I could die, all this turmoil would come to an end. So long as I was alive my sins would remain rampant, scattering destruction on every side. I remembered the pistol in my box. But my feet refused to leave the window in quest of it. Was I not awaiting my fate?

The gong of the watch solemnly struck ten. A little later, groups of lights appeared in the distance and a great crowd wound its way, like some great serpent, along the roads in the darkness, towards the palace gates.

The Dewan rushed to the gate at the sound. Just then a rider came galloping in. 'What's the news, Jata?' asked the Dewan.

'Not good,' was the reply.

I could hear these words distinctly from my window. But something was next whispered which I could not catch.

Then came a palanquin, followed by a litter. The doctor was walking alongside the palanquin.

'What do you think, doctor?' asked the Dewan.

'Can't say yet,' the doctor replied. 'The wound in the head is a serious one.'

'And Amulya Babu?'

'He has a bullet through the heart. He is done for.'

PLAYS

The Post Office

Dramatis Personae

MADHAV
AMAL
his adopted child

SUDHA
a little flower girl

DOCTOR
DAIRYMAN
WATCHMAN
GAFFER
HEADMAN
a bully

KING'S HERALD
ROYAL PHYSICIAN
A TROOP OF BOYS

ACT I

MADHAV's *House*

MADHAV What a state I am in! Before he came, nothing mattered; I felt so free. But now that he has come, goodness knows from where, my heart is filled with his dear self, and my home will be no home to me when he leaves. Doctor, do you think he –

DOCTOR If there's life in his fate, then he will live long. But what the medical scriptures say, it seems –

MADHAV Great heavens, what?

DOCTOR The scriptures have it: 'Bile or palsey, cold or gout spring all alike.'

MADHAV Oh, get along, don't fling your scriptures at me; you only make me more anxious; tell me what I can do.

DOCTOR (*Taking snuff*) The patient needs the most scrupulous care.

MADHAV That's true; but tell me how.

DOCTOR I have already mentioned, on no account must he be let out of doors.

MADHAV Poor child, it is very hard to keep him indoors all day long.

DOCTOR What else can you do? The autumn sun and the damp are both very bad for the little fellow – for the scriptures have it:

'In wheezing, swoon or in nervous fret,
In jaundice or leaden eyes –'

MADHAV Never mind the scriptures, please. Eh, then we must shut the poor thing up. Is there no other method?

DOCTOR None at all: for, 'In the wind and in the sun –'

MADHAV What will your 'in this and in that' do for me now? Why don't you let them alone and come straight to the point? What's to be done then? Your system is very, very hard for the poor boy; and he is so quiet too with all his pain and sickness. It tears my heart to see him wince, as he takes your medicine.

DOCTOR The more he winces, the surer is the effect. That's why the sage Chyabana observes: 'In medicine as in good advices, the least palatable ones are the truest.' Ah, well! I must be trotting now. (*Exit*)

GAFFER enters

MADHAV Well, I'm jiggered, there's Gaffer now.

GAFFER Why, why, I won't bite you.

MADHAV No, but you are a devil to send children off their heads.

GAFFER But you aren't a child, and you've no child in the house; why worry then?

MADHAV Oh, but I have brought a child into the house.

GAFFER Indeed, how so?

MADHAV You remember how my wife was dying to adopt a child?

GAFFER Yes, but that's an old story; you didn't like the idea.

MADHAV You know, brother, how hard all this getting money in has been. That somebody else's child would sail in and waste all this money earned with so much trouble – Oh, I hated the idea. But this boy clings to my heart in such a queer sort of way –

GAFFER So that's the trouble! and your money goes all for him and feels jolly lucky it does go at all.

MADHAV Formerly, earning was a sort of passion with me; I simply couldn't help working for money. Now, I make money and as I know it is all for this dear boy, earning becomes a joy to me.

GAFFER Ah, well, and where did you pick him up?

MADHAV He is the son of a man who was a brother to my wife by village ties. He has had no mother since infancy; and now the other day he lost his father as well.

GAFFER Poor thing: and so he needs me all the more.

MADHAV The doctor says all the organs of his little body are at loggerheads with each other, and there isn't much hope for his life. There is only one way to save him and that is to keep him out of this autumn wind and sun. But you are such a terror! What with this game of yours at your age, too, to get children out of doors!

GAFFER God bless my soul! So I'm already as bad as autumn wind and sun, eh! But, friend, I know something, too, of the game of keeping them indoors. When my day's work is over I am coming in to make friends with this child of yours. (*Exit*)

AMAL enters

AMAL Uncle, I say, Uncle!

MADHAV Hullo! Is that you, Amal?

AMAL Mayn't I be out of the courtyard at all?

MADHAV No, my dear, no.

AMAL See, there where Auntie grinds lentils in the quirn, the squirrel is sitting with his tail up and with his wee hands he's picking up the broken grains of lentils and crunching them. Can't I run up there?

MADHAV No, my darling, no.

AMAL Wish I were a squirrel! – it would be lovely. Uncle, why won't you let me go about?

MADHAV Doctor says it's bad for you to be out.

AMAL How can the doctor know?

MADHAV What a thing to say! The doctor can't know and he reads such huge books!

AMAL Does his book-learning tell him everything?

MADHAV Of course, don't you know!

AMAL (*With a sigh*) Ah, I am so stupid! I don't read books.

MADHAV Now, think of it; very, very learned people are all like you; they are never out of doors.

AMAL Aren't they really?

MADHAV No, how can they? Early and late they toil and moil at their books, and they've eyes for nothing else. Now, my little man, you are going to be learned when you grow up; and then you will stay at home and read such big books, and people will notice you and say, 'He's a wonder.'

AMAL No, no, Uncle; I beg of you by your dear feet – I don't want to be learned, I won't.

MADHAV Dear, dear; it would have been my saving if I could have been learned.

AMAL No, I would rather go about and see everything that there is.

MADHAV Listen to that! See! What will you see, what is there so much to see?

AMAL See that far-away hill from our window – I often long to go beyond those hills and right away.

MADHAV Oh, you silly! As if there's nothing more to be done but just get up to the top of that hill and away! Eh! You don't talk sense, my boy. Now listen, since that hill stands there upright as a barrier, it means you can't get beyond it. Else, what was the use in heaping up so many large stones to make such a big affair of it, eh!

AMAL Uncle, do you think it is meant to prevent your crossing over? It seems to me because the earth can't speak it raises its hands into the sky and beckons. And those who live far and sit alone by their windows can see the signal. But I suppose the learned people –

MADHAV No, they don't have time for that sort of nonsense. They are not crazy like you.

AMAL Do you know, yesterday I met someone quite as crazy as I am.

MADHAV Gracious me, really, how so?

AMAL He had a bamboo staff on his shoulder with a small bundle at the top, and a brass pot in his left hand, and an old pair of shoes on; he was making for those hills straight across that meadow there. I called out to him and asked, 'Where are you going?' He answered, 'I don't know, anywhere!' I asked again, 'Why are you going?' He said, 'I'm going out to seek work.' Say, Uncle, have you to seek work?

MADHAV Of course I have to. There's many about looking for jobs.

AMAL How lovely! I'll go about, like them too, finding things to do.

MADHAV Suppose you seek and don't find. Then –

AMAL Wouldn't that be jolly? Then I should go farther! I watched that man slowly walking on with his pair of worn-out shoes. And when he got to where the water flows under the fig tree, he stopped and washed his feet in the stream. Then he took out from his bundle some gram-flour, moistened it with water and began to eat. Then he tied up his bundle and shouldered it again; tucked up his cloth above his knees and crossed the stream. I've asked Auntie to let me go up to the stream, and eat my gram-flour just like him.

MADHAV And what did your Auntie say to that?

AMAL Auntie said, 'Get well and then I'll take you over there.' Please, Uncle, when shall I get well?

MADHAV It won't be long, dear.

AMAL Really, but then I shall go right away the moment I'm well again.

MADHAV And where will you go?

AMAL Oh, I will walk on, crossing so many streams, wading through water. Everybody will be asleep with their doors shut in the heat of the day and I will tramp on and on seeking work far, very far.

MADHAV I see! I think you had better be getting well first; then –

AMAL But then you won't want me to be learned, will you, Uncle?

MADHAV What would you rather be then?

AMAL I can't think of anything just now; but I'll tell you later on.

MADHAV Very well. But mind you, you aren't to call out and talk to strangers again.

AMAL But I love to talk to strangers!

MADHAV Suppose they had kidnapped you?

AMAL That would have been splendid! But no one ever takes me away. They all want me to stay in here.

MADHAV I am off to my work – but, darling, you won't go out, will you?

AMAL No, I won't. But, Uncle, you'll let me be in this room by the roadside.

Exit MADHAV

DAIRYMAN Curds, curds, good nice curds.

AMAL Curdseller, I say, Curdseller.

DAIRYMAN Why do you call me? Will you buy some curds?

AMAL How can I buy? I have no money.

DAIRYMAN What a boy! Why call out then? Ugh! What a waste of time.

AMAL I would go with you if I could.

DAIRYMAN With me?

AMAL Yes, I seem to feel homesick when I hear you call from far down the road.

DAIRYMAN (*Lowering his yoke-pole*) Whatever are you doing here, my child?

AMAL The doctor says I'm not to be out, so I sit here all day long.

DAIRYMAN My poor child, whatever has happened to you?

AMAL I can't tell. You see I am not learned, so I don't know what's the matter with me. Say, Dairyman, where do you come from?

DAIRYMAN From our village.

AMAL Your village? Is it very far?

DAIRYMAN Our village lies on the river Shamli at the foot of the Panch-mura hills.

AMAL Panch-mura hills! Shamli river! I wonder. I may have seen your village. I can't think when though!

DAIRYMAN Have you seen it? Been to the foot of those hills?

AMAL Never. But I seem to remember having seen it. Your village is under some very old big trees, just by the side of the red road – isn't that so?

DAIRYMAN That's right, child.

AMAL And on the slope of the hill cattle grazing.

DAIRYMAN How wonderful! Aren't there cattle grazing in our village! Indeed, there are!

AMAL And your women with red sarees fill their pitchers from the river and carry them on their heads.

DAIRYMAN Good, that's right. Women from our dairy village do come and draw their water from the river; but then it isn't everyone who has a red saree to put on. But, my dear child, surely you must have been there for a walk some time.

AMAL Really, Dairyman, never been there at all. But the first day doctor lets me go out, you are going to take me to your village.

DAIRYMAN I will, my child, with pleasure.

AMAL And you'll teach me to cry curds and shoulder the yoke like you and walk the long, long road?

DAIRYMAN Dear, dear, did you ever? Why should you sell curds? No, you will read big books and be learned.

AMAL No, I never want to be learned – I'll be like you and take my curds from the village by the red road near the old banyan tree, and I will hawk it from cottage to cottage. Oh, how do you cry – 'Curd, curd, good nice curd!' Teach me the tune, will you?

DAIRYMAN Dear, dear, teach you the tune; what an idea!

AMAL Please do. I love to hear it. I can't tell you how queer I feel when I hear you cry out from the bend of that road, through the line of those trees! Do you know I feel like that when I hear the shrill cry of kites from almost the end of the sky?

DAIRYMAN   Dear child, will you have some curds? Yes, do.

AMAL   But I have no money.

DAIRYMAN   No, no, no, don't talk of money! You'll make me so happy if you have a little curds from me.

AMAL   Say, have I kept you too long?

DAIRYMAN   Not a bit; it has been no loss to me at all; you have taught me how to be happy selling curds. (*Exit*)

AMAL   (*Intoning*) Curds, curds, good nice curds – from the dairy village – from the country of the Panch-mura hills by the Shamli bank. Curds, good curds; in the early morning the women make the cows stand in a row under the trees and milk them, and in the evening they turn the milk into curds. Curds, good curds. Hello, there's the watchman on his rounds. Watchman, I say, come and have a word with me.

WATCHMAN   What's all this row you are making? Aren't you afraid of the likes of me?

AMAL   No, why should I be?

WATCHMAN   Suppose I march you off then?

AMAL   Where will you take me to? Is it very far, right beyond the hills?

WATCHMAN   Suppose I march you straight to the King?

AMAL   To the King! Do, will you? But the doctor won't let me go out. No one can ever take me away. I've got to stay here all day long.

WATCHMAN   Doctor won't let you, poor fellow! So I see! Your face is pale and there are dark rings round your eyes. Your veins stick out from your poor thin hands.

AMAL   Won't you sound the gong, Watchman?

WATCHMAN   Time has not yet come.

AMAL   How curious! Some say time has not yet come, and some say time has gone by! But surely your time will come the moment you strike the gong!

WATCHMAN   That's not possible; I strike up the gong only when it is time.

AMAL   Yes, I love to hear your gong. When it is midday and our meal is over, Uncle goes off to his work and Auntie falls asleep reading her Rāmayana, and in the courtyard under the shadow of the wall our doggie sleeps with his nose in his curled-up tail; then your gong strikes out, 'Dong, dong, dong!' Tell me why does your gong sound?

WATCHMAN My gong sounds to tell the people, Time waits for none, but goes on forever.

AMAL Where, to what land?

WATCHMAN That none knows.

AMAL Then I suppose no one has ever been there! Oh, I do wish to fly with the time to that land of which no one knows anything.

WATCHMAN All of us have to get there one day, my child.

AMAL Have I too?

WATCHMAN Yes, you too!

AMAL But doctor won't let me out.

WATCHMAN One day the doctor himself may take you there by the hand.

AMAL He won't; you don't know him. He only keeps me in.

WATCHMAN One greater than he comes and lets us free.

AMAL When will this great doctor come for me? I can't stick in here any more.

WATCHMAN Shouldn't talk like that, my child.

AMAL No. I am here where they have left me – I never move a bit. But when your gong goes off, dong, dong, dong, it goes to my heart. Say, Watchman?

WATCHMAN Yes, my dear.

AMAL Say, what's going on there in that big house on the other side, where there is a flag flying high up and the people are always going in and out?

WATCHMAN Oh, there? That's our new Post Office.

AMAL Post Office? Whose?

WATCHMAN Whose? Why, the King's surely!

AMAL Do letters come from the King to his office here?

WATCHMAN Of course. One fine day there may be a letter for you in there.

AMAL A letter for me? But I am only a little boy.

WATCHMAN The King sends tiny notes to little boys.

AMAL Oh, how lovely! When shall I have my letter? How do you guess he'll write to me?

WATCHMAN Otherwise why should he set his Post Office here right in front of your open window, with the golden flag flying?

AMAL But who will fetch me my King's letter when it comes?

WATCHMAN The King has many postmen. Don't you see them run about with round gilt badges on their chests?

AMAL Well, where do they go?

WATCHMAN Oh, from door to door, all through the country.

AMAL I'll be the King's postman when I grow up.

WATCHMAN Ha! ha! Postman, indeed! Rain or shine, rich or poor, from house to house delivering letters – that's very great work!

AMAL That's what I'd like best. What makes you smile so? Oh, yes, your work is great too. When it is silent everywhere in the heat of the noonday, your gong sounds, Dong, dong, dong, – and sometimes when I wake up at night all of a sudden and find our lamp blown out, I can hear through the darkness your gong slowly sounding, Dong, dong, dong!

WATCHMAN There's the village headman! I must be off. If he catches me gossiping with you there'll be a great to do.

AMAL The headman? Whereabouts is he?

WATCHMAN Right down the road there; see that huge palm-leaf umbrella hopping along? That's him!

AMAL I suppose the King's made him our headman here?

WATCHMAN Made him? Oh, no! A fussy busy-body! He knows so many ways of making himself unpleasant that everybody is afraid of him. It's just a game for the likes of him, making trouble for everybody. I must be off now! Mustn't keep work waiting, you know! I'll drop in again to-morrow morning and tell you all the news of the town. (*Exit*)

AMAL It would be splendid to have a letter from the King every day. I'll read them at the window. But, oh! I can't read writing. Who'll read them out to me, I wonder! Auntie reads her Rāmayana; she may know the King's writing. If no one will, then I must keep them carefully and read them when I'm grown up. But if the postman can't find me? Headman, Mr. Headman, may I have a word with you?

HEADMAN Who is yelling after me on the highway? Oh, you wretched monkey!

AMAL You're the headman. Everybody minds you.

HEADMAN (*Looking pleased*) Yes, oh yes, they do! They must!

AMAL Do the King's postmen listen to you?

HEADMAN They've got to. By Jove, I'd like to see –

AMAL Will you tell the postman it's Amal who sits by the window here?

HEADMAN What's the good of that?

AMAL In case there's a letter for me.

HEADMAN A letter for you! Whoever's going to write to you?

AMAL If the King does.

HEADMAN Ha! ha! What an uncommon little fellow you are! Ha! ha! the King indeed, aren't you his bosom friend, eh! You haven't met for a long while and the King is pining, I am sure. Wait till to-morrow and you'll have your letter.

AMAL Say, Headman, why do you speak to me in that tone of voice? Are you cross?

HEADMAN Upon my word! Cross, indeed! You write to the King! Madhav is devilish swell nowadays. He's made a little pile; and so kings and padishahs are everyday talk with his people. Let me find him once and I'll make him dance. Oh, you snipper-snapper! I'll get the King's letter sent to your house – indeed I will!

AMAL No, no, please don't trouble yourself about it.

HEADMAN And why not, pray! I'll tell the King about you and he won't be very long. One of his footmen will come along presently for news of you. Madhav's impudence staggers me. If the King hears of this, that'll take some of his nonsense out of him. (*Exit*)

AMAL Who are you walking there? How your anklets tinkle! Do stop a while, dear, won't you?

SUDHA *enters*

SUDHA I haven't a moment to spare; it is already late!

AMAL I see, you don't wish to stop; I don't care to stay on here either.

SUDHA You make me think of some late star of the morning! Whatever's the matter with you?

AMAL I don't know; the doctor won't let me out.

SUDHA Ah me! Don't then! Should listen to the doctor. People'll be cross with you if you're naughty. I know, always looking out and watching must make you feel tired. Let me close the window a bit for you.

AMAL No, don't, only this one's open! All the others are shut. But will you tell me who you are? Don't seem to know you.

SUDHA I am Sudha.

AMAL   What Sudha?

SUDHA   Don't you know? Daughter of the flower-seller here.

AMAL   What do you do?

SUDHA   I gather flowers in my basket.

AMAL   Oh, flower gathering! That is why your feet seem so glad and your anklets jingle so merrily as you walk. Wish I could be out too. Then I would pick some flowers for you from the very topmost branches right out of sight.

SUDHA   Would you really? Do you know more about flowers than I?

AMAL   Yes, I do, quite as much. I know all about Champa of the fairy tale and his seven brothers. If only they let me, I'll go right into the dense forest where you can't find your way. And where the honey-sipping hummingbird rocks himself on the end of the thinnest branch, I will flower out as a champa. Would you be my sister Parul?

SUDHA   You are silly! How can I be sister Parul when I am Sudha and my mother is Sasi, the flower-seller? I have to weave so many garlands a day. It would be jolly if I could lounge here like you!

AMAL   What would you do then, all the day long?

SUDHA   I could have great times with my doll Benay the bride, and Meni the pussycat and – but I say it is getting late and I mustn't stop, or I won't find a single flower.

AMAL   Oh, wait a little longer; I do like it so!

SUDHA   Ah, well – now don't you be naughty. Be good and sit still and on my way back home with the flowers I'll come and talk with you.

AMAL   And you'll let me have a flower then?

SUDHA   No, how can I? It has to be paid for.

AMAL   I'll pay when I grow up – before I leave to look for work out on the other side of that stream there.

SUDHA   Very well, then.

AMAL   And you'll come back when you have your flowers?

SUDHA   I will.

AMAL   You will, really?

SUDHA   Yes, I will.

AMAL   You won't forget me? I am Amal, remember that.

SUDHA   I won't forget you, you'll see. (*Exit*)

A TROOP OF BOYS *enter*

AMAL Say, brothers, where are you all off to? Stop here a little.

BOYS We're off to play.

AMAL What will you play at, brothers?

BOYS We'll play at being ploughmen.

FIRST BOY (*Showing a stick*) This is our ploughshare.

SECOND BOY We two are the pair of oxen.

AMAL And you're going to play the whole day?

BOYS Yes, all day long.

AMAL And you'll come back home in the evening by the road along the river bank?

BOYS Yes.

AMAL Do you pass our house on your way home?

BOYS You come out to play with us, yes do.

AMAL Doctor won't let me out.

BOYS Doctor! Suppose the likes of you mind the doctor. Let's be off; it is getting late.

AMAL Don't. Why not play on the road near this window? I could watch you then.

THIRD BOY What can we play at here?

AMAL With all these toys of mine lying about. Here you are, have them. I can't play alone. They are getting dirty and are of no use to me.

BOYS How jolly! What fine toys! Look, here's a ship. There's old mother Jatai: say, chaps, ain't he a gorgeous sepoy? And you'll let us have them all? You don't really mind?

AMAL No, not a bit; have them by all means.

BOYS You don't want them back?

AMAL Oh, no, I shan't want them.

BOYS Say, won't you get a scolding for this?

AMAL No one will scold me. But will you play with them in front of our door for a while every morning? I'll get you new ones when these are old.

BOYS Oh, yes, we will. Say, chaps, put these sepoys into a line. We'll play at war; where can we get a musket? Oh, look here, this bit of reed will do nicely. Say, but you're off to sleep already.

AMAL I'm afraid I'm sleepy. I don't know, I feel like it at times. I have been sitting a long while and I'm tired; my back aches.

BOYS It's only early noon now. How is it you're sleepy? Listen! The gong's sounding the first watch.

AMAL Yes, dong, dong, dong, it tolls me to sleep.

BOYS We had better go then. We'll come in again to-morrow morning.

AMAL I want to ask you something before you go. You are always out – do you know of the King's postmen?

BOYS Yes, quite well.

AMAL Who are they? Tell me their names.

BOYS One's Badal, another's Sarat. There's so many of them.

AMAL Do you think they will know me if there's a letter for me?

BOYS Surely, if your name's on the letter they will find you out.

AMAL When you call in to-morrow morning, will you bring one of them along so that he'll know me?

BOYS Yes, if you like.

ACT II

AMAL *in Bed*

AMAL Can't I go near the window to-day, Uncle? Would the doctor mind that too?

MADHAV Yes, darling, you see you've made yourself worse squatting there day after day.

AMAL Oh, no, I don't know if it's made me more ill, but I always feel well when I'm there.

MADHAV No, you don't; you squat there and make friends with the whole lot of people round here, old and young, as if they are holding a fair right under my eaves – flesh and blood won't stand that strain. Just see – your face is quite pale.

AMAL Uncle, I fear my fakir'll pass and not see me by the window.

MADHAV Your fakir, whoever's that?

AMAL He comes and chats to me of the many lands where he's been. I love to hear him.

MADHAV How's that? I don't know of any fakirs.

AMAL This is about the time he comes in. I beg of you, by your dear feet, ask him in for a moment to talk to me here.

GAFFER *enters in a* FAKIR's *Guise*

AMAL There you are. Come here, Fakir, by my bedside.

MADHAV Upon my word, but this is –

GAFFER (*Winking hard*) I am the fakir.

MADHAV It beats my reckoning what you're not.

AMAL Where have you been this time, Fakir?

FAKIR To the Isle of Parrots. I am just back.

MADHAV The Parrots' Isle!

FAKIR Is it so very astonishing? Am I like you, man? A journey doesn't cost a thing. I tramp just where I like.

AMAL (*Clapping*) How jolly for you! Remember your promise to take me with you as your follower when I'm well.

FAKIR Of course, and I'll teach you such secrets too of travelling that nothing in sea or forest or mountain can bar your way.

MADHAV What's all this rigmarole?

FAKIR   Amal, my dear, I bow to nothing in sea or mountain; but if the doctor joins in with this uncle of yours, then I with all my magic must own myself beaten.

AMAL   No. Uncle shan't tell the doctor. And I promise to lie quiet; but the day I am well, off I go with the Fakir and nothing in sea or mountain or torrent shall stand in my way.

MADHAV   Fie, dear child, don't keep on harping upon going! It makes me so sad to hear you talk so.

AMAL   Tell me, Fakir, what the Parrots' Isle is like.

FAKIR   It's a land of wonders; it's a haunt of birds. There's no man; and they neither speak nor walk, they simply sing and they fly.

AMAL   How glorious! And it's by some sea?

FAKIR   Of course. It's on the sea.

AMAL   And green hills are there?

FAKIR   Indeed, they live among the green hills; and in the time of the sunset when there is a red glow on the hillside, all the birds with their green wings flock back to their nests.

AMAL   And there are waterfalls!

FAKIR   Dear me, of course; you don't have a hill without its waterfalls. Oh, it's like molten diamonds; and, my dear, what dances they have! Don't they make the pebbles sing as they rush over them to the sea. No devil of a doctor can stop them for a moment. The birds looked upon me as nothing but a man, quite a trifling creature without wings – and they would have nothing to do with me. Were it not so I would build a small cabin for myself among their crowd of nests and pass my days counting the sea waves.

AMAL   How I wish I were a bird! Then –

FAKIR   But that would have been a bit of a job; I hear you've fixed up with the dairyman to be a hawker of curds when you grow up; I'm afraid such business won't flourish among birds; you might land yourself into serious loss.

MADHAV   Really this is too much. Between you two I shall turn crazy. Now, I'm off.

AMAL   Has the dairyman been, Uncle?

MADHAV   And why shouldn't he? He won't bother his head running errands for your pet fakir, in and out among the nests in his Parrots' Isle. But he has left a jar of curd for you saying that he is rather busy with his niece's wedding in the village, and he has got to order a band at Kamlipara.

AMAL   But he is going to marry me to his little niece.

FAKIR   Dear me, we are in a fix now.

AMAL   He said she would find me a lovely little bride with a pair of pearl drops in her ears and dressed in a lovely red saree; and in the morning she would milk with her own hands the black cow and feed me with warm milk with foam on it from a brand new earthen cruse; and in the evenings she would carry the lamp round the cow-house, and then come and sit by me to tell me tales of Champa and his six brothers.

FAKIR   How delicious! The prospect tempts even me, a hermit! But never mind, dear, about this wedding. Let it be. I tell you when you wed there'll be no lack of nieces in his household.

MADHAV   Shut up! This is more than I can stand. (*Exit*)

AMAL   Fakir, now that Uncle's off, just tell me, has the King sent me a letter to the Post Office?

FAKIR   I gather that his letter has already started; but it's still on the way.

AMAL   On the way? Where is it? Is it on that road winding through the trees which you can follow to the end of the forest when the sky is quite clear after rain?

FAKIR   That's so. You know all about it already.

AMAL   I do, everything.

FAKIR   So I see, but how?

AMAL   I can't say; but it's quite clear to me. I fancy I've seen it often in days long gone by. How long ago I can't tell. Do you know when? I can see it all: there, the King's postman coming down the hillside alone, a lantern in his left hand and on his back a bag of letters climbing down for ever so long, for days and nights, and where at the foot of the mountain the waterfall becomes a stream he takes to the footpath on the bank and walks on through the rye; then comes the sugarcane field and he disappears into the narrow lane cutting through the tall stems of sugarcanes; then he reaches the open meadow where the cricket chirps and where there is not a single man to be seen, only the snipe wagging their tails and poking at the mud with their bills. I can feel him coming nearer and nearer and my heart becomes glad.

FAKIR   My eyes aren't young; but you make me see all the same.

AMAL   Say, Fakir, do you know the King who has this Post Office?

FAKIR   I do; I go to him for my alms every day.

AMAL   Good! When I get well, I must have my alms too from him, mayn't I?

FAKIR   You won't need to ask, my dear, he'll give it to you of his own accord.

AMAL   No, I would go to his gate and cry, 'Victory to thee, O King!' and dancing to the tabor's sound, ask for alms. Won't it be nice?

FAKIR   It would be splendid, and if you're with me, I shall have my full share. But what'll you ask?

AMAL   I shall say, 'Make me your postman, that I may go about lantern in hand, delivering your letters from door to door. Don't let me stay at home all day!'

FAKIR   What is there to be sad for, my child, even were you to stay at home?

AMAL   It isn't sad. When they shut me in here first I felt the day was so long. Since the King's Post Office I like it more and more being indoors, and as I think I shall get a letter one day, I feel quite happy and then I don't mind being quiet and alone. I wonder if I shall make out what'll be in the King's letter?

FAKIR   Even if you didn't wouldn't it be enough if it just bore your name?

MADHAV *enters*

MADHAV   Have you any idea of the trouble you've got me into, between you two?

FAKIR   What's the matter?

MADHAV   I hear you've let it get rumoured about that the King has planted his office here to send messages to both of you.

FAKIR   Well, what about it?

MADHAV   Our headman Panchanan has had it told to the King anonymously.

FAKIR   Aren't we aware that everything reaches the King's ears?

MADHAV   Then why don't you look out? Why take the King's name in vain? You'll bring me to ruin if you do.

AMAL   Say, Fakir, will the King be cross?

FAKIR   Cross, nonsense! And with a child like you and a fakir such as I am. Let's see if the King be angry, and then won't I give him a piece of my mind.

AMAL   Say, Fakir, I've been feeling a sort of darkness coming over my eyes since the morning. Everything seems like a dream. I long to be quiet. I don't feel like talking at all. Won't the King's letter come? Suppose this room melts away all on a sudden, suppose –

FAKIR (*Fanning Amal*) The letter's sure to come to-day, my boy.

DOCTOR *enters*

DOCTOR And how do you feel to-day?

AMAL Feel awfully well to-day, Doctor. All pain seems to have left me.

DOCTOR (*Aside to Madhav*) Don't quite like the look of that smile. Bad sign that, his feeling well! Chakradhan has observed –

MADHAV For goodness' sake, Doctor, leave Chakradhan alone. Tell me what's going to happen?

DOCTOR Can't hold him in much longer, I fear! I warned you before – This looks like a fresh exposure.

MADHAV No, I've used the utmost care, never let him out of doors; and the windows have been shut almost all the time.

DOCTOR There's a peculiar quality in the air to-day. As I came in I found a fearful draught through your front door. That's most hurtful. Better lock it at once. Would it matter if this kept your visitors off for two or three days? If someone happens to call unexpectedly – there's the back door. You had better shut this window as well, it's letting in the sunset rays only to keep the patient awake.

MADHAV Amal has shut his eyes. I expect he is sleeping. His face tells me – Oh, Doctor, I bring in a child who is a stranger and love him as my own, and now I suppose I must lose him!

DOCTOR What's that? There's your headman sailing in! – What a bother! I must be going, brother. You had better stir about and see to the doors being properly fastened. I will send on a strong dose directly I get home. Try it on him – it may save him at last, if he can be saved at all. (*Exeunt* MADHAV *and* DOCTOR.)

The HEADMAN *enters*

HEADMAN Hello, urchin!

GAFFER (*Rising hastily*) 'Sh, be quiet.

AMAL No, Fakir, did you think I was asleep? I wasn't. I can hear everything; yes, and voices far away. I feel that mother and father are sitting by my pillow and speaking to me.

MADHAV *enters*

HEADMAN I say, Madhav, I hear you hobnob with bigwigs nowadays.

MADHAV Spare me your jests, Headman, we are but common people.

HEADMAN But your child here is expecting a letter from the King.

MADHAV Don't you take any notice of him, a mere foolish boy!

HEADMAN Indeed, why not! It'll beat the King hard to find a better family! Don't you see why the King plants his new Post Office right before your window? Why there's a letter for you from the King, urchin.

AMAL (*Starting up*) Indeed, really!

HEADMAN How can it be false? You're the King's chum. Here's your letter (*showing a blank slip of paper*). Ha, ha, ha! This is the letter.

AMAL Please don't mock me. Say, Fakir, is it so?

FAKIR Yes, my dear. I as Fakir tell you it is his letter.

AMAL How is it I can't see? It all looks so blank to me. What is there in the letter, Mr. Headman?

HEADMAN The King says, 'I am calling on you shortly; you had better arrange puffed rice offerings for me. – Palace fare is quite tasteless to me now.' Ha! ha! ha!

MADHAV (*With folded palms*) I beseech you, Headman, don't you joke about these things –

FAKIR Cutting jokes indeed, dare he!

MADHAV Are you out of your mind too, Gaffer?

FAKIR Out of my mind, well then I am; I can read plainly that the King writes he will come himself to see Amal, with the state physician.

AMAL Fakir, Fakir, 'sh, his trumpet! Can't you hear?

HEADMAN Ha! ha! ha! I fear he won't until he's a bit more off his head.

AMAL Mr. Headman, I thought you were cross with me and didn't love me. I never could think you would fetch me the King's letter. Let me wipe the dust off your feet.

HEADMAN This little child does have an instinct of reverence. Though a little silly, he has a good heart.

AMAL It's hard on the fourth watch now, I suppose – Hark the gong, 'Dong, dong, ding.' 'Dong, dong, ding.' Is the evening star up? How is it I can't see –

FAKIR Oh, the windows are all shut, I'll open them.

A knocking outside

MADHAV What's that? – Who is it – what a bother!

KING'S HERALD (*From outside*) Open the door.

MADHAV Say, Headman – Hope they're not robbers.

HEADMAN Who's there? – It's Panchanan, the headman, calls – Aren't you afraid of the like of me? Fancy! The noise has ceased! Panchanan's voice carries far. – Yes, show me the biggest robbers!

MADHAV (*Peering out of the window*) I should think the noise has ceased. They've smashed the door.

The KING'S HERALD *enters*

KING'S HERALD Our Sovereign King comes to-night!

HEADMAN My God!

AMAL At what hour of the night, Herald?

KING'S HERALD On the second watch.

AMAL When from the city gates my friend the watchman will strike his gong, 'ding dong ding, ding dong ding' – then?

KING'S HERALD Yes, then. The King sends his greatest physician to attend on his young friend.

ROYAL PHYSICIAN *enters*

ROYAL PHYSICIAN What's this? How close it is here! Open wide all the doors and windows. (*Feeling Amal's body*) How do you feel, my child?

AMAL I feel very well, Doctor, very well. All pain is gone. How fresh and open! I can see all the stars now twinkling from the other side of the dark.

ROYAL PHYSICIAN Will you feel well enough to leave your bed with the King when he comes in the middle watches of the night?

AMAL Of course, I'm dying to be about for ever so long. I'll ask the King to find me the polar star. – I must have seen it often, but I don't know exactly which it is.

ROYAL PHYSICIAN He will tell you everything. (*To Madhav*) Will you go about and arrange flowers through the room for the King's visit? (*Indicating the Headman*) We can't have that person in here.

AMAL No, let him be, Doctor. He is a friend. It was he who brought me the King's letter.

ROYAL PHYSICIAN Very well, my child. He may remain if he is a friend of yours.

MADHAV (*Whispering into Amal's ear*) My child, the King loves you. He is coming himself. Beg for a gift from him. You know our humble circumstances.

AMAL Don't you worry, Uncle. – I've made up my mind about it.

MADHAV What is it, my child?

AMAL I shall ask him to make me one of his postmen that I may wander far and wide, delivering his message from door to door.

MADHAV (*Slapping his forehead*) Alas, is that all?

AMAL What'll be our offerings to the King, Uncle, when he comes?

KING'S HERALD He has commanded puffed rice.

AMAL Puffed rice! Say, Headman, you're right. You said so. You knew all we didn't.

HEADMAN If you send word to my house then I could manage for the King's advent really nice –

ROYAL PHYSICIAN No need at all. Now be quiet all of you. Sleep is coming over him. I'll sit by his pillow; he's dropping into slumber. Blow out the oil-lamp. Only let the star-light stream in. Hush, he slumbers.

MADHAV (*Addressing* GAFFER) What are you standing there for like a statue, folding your palms. – I am nervous. – Say, are they good omens? Why are they darkening the room? How will star-light help?

GAFFER Silence, unbeliever.

SUDHA enters

SUDHA Amal!

ROYAL PHYSICIAN He's asleep.

SUDHA I have some flowers for him. Mayn't I give them into his own hand?

ROYAL PHYSICIAN Yes, you may.

SUDHA When will he be awake?

ROYAL PHYSICIAN Directly the King comes and calls him.

SUDHA Will you whisper a word for me in his ear?

ROYAL PHYSICIAN What shall I say?

SUDHA Tell him Sudha has not forgotten him.

Red Oleanders

The curtain rises on a window covered by a network of intricate pattern in front of the Palace.

NANDINI *and* KISHÔR, *a digger boy, come in.*

KISHÔR Have you enough flowers, Nandini? Here, I have brought some more.

NANDINI Run away, Kishôr, do, – back to your work, quick! You'll be late again.

KISHÔR I must steal some time from my digging and digging of nuggets to bring out flowers to you.

NANDINI But they'll punish you, my boy, if they know.

KISHÔR You said you *must* have red oleanders. I am glad they're hard to find in this place. Only one tree I discovered after days of search, nearly hidden away behind a rubbish heap.

NANDINI Show it me. I'll go and gather the flowers myself.

KISHÔR Don't be cruel, Nandini. This tree is my one secret which none shall know. I've always envied Bishu, he can sing to you songs that are his own. From now I shall have flowers which you'll have to take only from my hands.

NANDINI But it breaks my heart to know that those brutes punish you.

KISHÔR It makes these flowers all the more preciously mine. They come from my pain.

NANDINI It pains me to accept anything which brings you hurt.

KISHÔR I dream of dying one day for your sake, Nandini.

NANDINI Is there nothing I can give you in return?

KISHÔR Promise that you will accept flowers only from me every morning.

NANDINI I will. But do be careful.

KISHÔR No, no, I shall be rash and defy their blows. My homage shall be my daily triumph. (*Goes.*)

PROFESSOR *comes in*

PROFESSOR Nandini!

NANDINI Yes, Professor!

PROFESSOR Why do you come and startle one, now and again, and then pass by? Since you awaken a cry in our hearts, what harm if you stop a moment in answer to it? Let us talk a little.

NANDINI What need have you of me?

PROFESSOR If you talk of need, look over there! – You'll see our tunnel-diggers creeping out of the holes like worms, with loads of things of need. In this Yaksha Town all our treasure is of gold, the secret treasure of the dust. But the gold which is you, beautiful one, is not of the dust, but of the light which never owns any bond.

NANDINI Over and over again you say this to me. What makes you wonder at me so, Professor?

PROFESSOR The sunlight gleaming through the forest thickets surprises nobody, but the light that breaks through a cracked wall is quite a different thing. In Yaksha Town, you are this light that startles. Tell me, what d'you think of this place?

NANDINI It puzzles me to see a whole city thrusting its head underground, groping with both hands in the dark. You dig tunnels in the underworld and come out with dead wealth that the earth has kept buried for ages past.

PROFESSOR The *Jinn* of that dead wealth we invoke. If we can enslave him the whole world lies at our feet.

NANDINI Then again, you hide your king behind a wall of netting. Is it for fear of people finding out that he's a man?

PROFESSOR As the ghost of our dead wealth is fearfully potent so is our ghostly royalty, made hazy by this net, with its inhuman power to frighten people.

NANDINI All you say is a kind of made-up talk.

PROFESSOR Of course made-up. The naked is without a credential, it's the made-up clothes that define us. It delights me immensely to discuss philosophy with you.

NANDINI That's strange! You who burrow day and night in a mass of yellow pages, like your diggers in the bowels of the earth, – why waste your time on me?

PROFESSOR The privilege of wasting time proves one's wealth of time. We poor drudges are insects in a hole in this solid toil, you are the evening star in the rich sky of leisure. When we see you, our wings grow restless. Come to my room. For a moment allow me to be reckless in my waste of time.

NANDINI No, not now. I have come to see your king, in *his* room.

PROFESSOR How can you enter through the screen?

NANDINI I shall find my way through the network.

PROFESSOR Do you know, Nandini, I too live behind a network of scholarship. I am an unmitigated scholar, just as our king is an unmitigated king.

NANDINI You are laughing at me, Professor. But tell me, when they brought me here, why didn't they bring my Rañjan also?

PROFESSOR It's their way to snatch things by fractions. But why should you want to drag your life's treasure down amongst this dead wealth of ours?

NANDINI Because I know he can put a beating heart behind these dead ribs.

PROFESSOR Your own presence is puzzling enough for our governors here; if Rañjan also comes they will be in despair.

NANDINI They do not know how comic they are, – Rañjan will bring God's own laughter in their midst and startle them into life.

PROFESSOR Divine laughter is the sunlight that melts ice, but not stones. Only the pressure of gross muscle can move our governors.

NANDINI My Rañjan's strength is like that of your river, Sankhini, – it can laugh and yet it can break. Let me tell you a little secret news of mine. I shall meet Rañjan to-day.

PROFESSOR Who told you that?

NANDINI Yes, yes, we shall meet. The news has come.

PROFESSOR Through what way could news come and yet evade the Governor?

NANDINI Through the same way that brings news of the coming Spring.

PROFESSOR You mean it's in the air, – like the rumours which flush in the colour of the sky, or flutter in the dance of the wind?

NANDINI I won't say more now. When Rañjan comes you'll see for yourself how rumours in the air come down on earth.

PROFESSOR Once she begins to talk of Rañjan there's no stopping Nandini's mouth! Well, well, I have my books, let me take my shelter behind them, – I dare not go on with this. (*Coming back after going a little way.*) Nandini. Let me ask you one thing. Aren't you frightened of our Yaksha Town?

NANDINI Why should I feel afraid?

PROFESSOR All creatures fear an eclipse, not the full sun. Yaksha Town is a city under eclipse. The Shadow Demon, who lives in the gold caves, has eaten into it. It is not whole itself, neither does it allow any one else to remain whole. Listen to me, don't stay here. When you go, these pits will yawn all the wider for us, I know, – yet I say to you, fly; go and live happily with Rañjan where people in their drunken fury don't tear the earth's veil to pieces. (*Going a little way and then coming back.*) Nandini, will you give me a flower from your chain of red oleanders?

NANDINI Why, what will you do with it?

PROFESSOR How often have I thought that there is some omen in these ornaments of yours.

NANDINI I don't know of any.

PROFESSOR Perhaps your fate knows. In that red there is not only beauty, but also the fascination of fear.

NANDINI Fear! Even in me?

PROFESSOR I don't know what event you have come to write with that crimson tint. There was the gardenia and the tuberose, there was white jasmine, – why did you leave them all and choose this flower? Do you know, we often choose our own fate thus, without knowing it!

NANDINI Rañjan sometimes calls me Red Oleander. I feel that the colour of his love is red, – that red I wear on my neck, on my breast, on my arms.

PROFESSOR Well, just give me one of those flowers, – a moment's gift, – let me try to understand the meaning of its colour.

NANDINI Here, take it. Rañjan is coming to-day, – out of my heart's delight I give it to you. (PROFESSOR *goes.*)

GÔKUL, *a digger, comes in*

GÔKUL Turn this way, woman! Who are you? I've never yet been able to understand you.

NANDINI I'm nothing more than what you see. What need have you to understand me?

GÔKUL I don't trust what I can't understand. For what purpose has the King brought you here?

NANDINI Because I serve no purpose of his.

GÔKUL You know some spell, I'm sure. You're snaring

everybody here. You're a witch! Those who are bewitched
by your beauty will come to their death.

NANDINI That death will not be yours, Gôkul, never fear!
You'll die digging.

GÔKUL Let me see, let me see, what's that dangling over your
forehead?

NANDINI Only a tassel of red oleanders.

GÔKUL What does it mean?

NANDINI It has no meaning at all.

GÔKUL I don't believe you, one bit! You're up to some trick-
ery. Some evil will befall us before the day is out. That's why
you have got yourself up like this. Oh you terrible, terrible
witch!

NANDINI What makes you think me so terrible?

GÔKUL You're looking like an ominous torch.

NANDINI The autumn song:

> *Hark, 'tis Autumn calling:*
> *'Come, O, come away!'–*
> *Her basket is heaped with corn.*

Don't you see the September sun is spreading the glow of
the ripening corn in the air?

> *Drunken with the perfumed wine of wind,*
> *the sky seems to sway among the*
> *shivering corn,*
> *its sunlight trailing on the fields*

You too come out, King! – out into the fields.

VOICE Fields! What could I do there?

NANDINI The work there is much simpler than your work in
Yaksha Town.

VOICE It's the simple which is impossible for me. A lake cannot
run out dancing, like a frolicsome waterfall. Leave me now,
I have no time.

NANDINI The day you let me into your store-house the blocks
of gold did not surprise me, – what amazed me was the immense strength with which you lifted and arranged them. But
can blocks of gold ever answer to the swinging rhythm of
your arms in the same way as fields of corn? Are you not
afraid, King, of handling the dead wealth of the earth?

VOICE What is there to fear?

NANDINI The living heart of the earth gives itself up in love
and life and beauty, but when you rend its bosom and disturb
the dead, you bring up with your booty the curse of its dark
demon, blind and hard, cruel and envious. Don't you see
everybody here is either angry, or suspicious, or afraid?

VOICE Curse?

NANDINI Yes, the curse of grabbing and killing.

VOICE But we bring up strength. Does not my strength please
you, Nandini?

NANDINI Indeed it does. Therefore I ask you, come out into
the light, step on the ground, let the earth be glad.

VOICE Do you know, Nandini, you too are half-hidden behind
an evasion, – you mystery of beauty! I want to pluck you
out of it, to grasp you within my closed fist, to handle you,
scrutinize you, – or else to break you to pieces.

NANDINI Whatever do you mean?

VOICE Why can't I strain out the tint of your oleanders and
build a dream out of it to keep before my eyes? Those few
frail petals guard it and hinder me. Within you there is the
same hindrance, so strong because so soft. Nandini, will you
tell me what you think of me?

NANDINI Not now, you have no time. Let me go.

VOICE No, no, don't go. Do tell me what you think of me.

NANDINI Have I not told you often enough? I think you are
wonderful. Strength swelling up in your arms, like rolling
clouds before a storm, – it makes my heart dance within me.

VOICE And when your heart dances to see Rañjan, is that also –

NANDINI Let that be, – you have no time.

VOICE There is time, – for this; only tell me, then go.

NANDINI That dance rhythm is different, you won't understand.

VOICE I will, I must understand.

NANDINI I can't explain it clearly. Let me go.

VOICE Tell me, at least, whether you like me.

NANDINI Yes, I like you.

VOICE The same as Rañjan?

NANDINI Again the same question! I tell you, you don't understand these things.

VOICE I *do* understand, a little. I know what the difference is
between Rañjan and me. In me there is only strength, in
Rañjan there is magic.

NANDINI What d'you mean by magic?

VOICE Shall I explain? Underground there are blocks of stone, iron, gold, – there you have the image of strength. On the surface grows the grass, the flower blossoms, – there you have the play of magic. I can extract gold from the fearsome depths of secrecy, but to wrest that magic from the near at hand I fail.

NANDINI You have no end of things, yet why always covet?

VOICE All I possess is so much dead weight. No increase of gold can create a particle of a touchstone, no increase of power can ever come up to youth. I can only guard by force. If I had Rañjan's youth I could leave you free and yet hold you fast. My time is spent in knotting the binding rope, but, alas, everything else can be kept tied, except joy.

NANDINI It is you who entangle yourself in your own net, then why keep on fretting?

VOICE You will never understand. I, who am a desert, stretch out my hand to you, a tiny blade of grass, and cry: I am parched, I am bare, I am weary. The flaming thirst of this desert licks up one fertile field after another, only to enlarge itself, – it can never annex the life of the frailest of grasses.

NANDINI One would never think you were so tired.

VOICE One day, Nandini, in a far-off land, I saw a mountain as weary as myself. I could not guess that all its stones were aching inwardly. One night I heard a noise, as if some giant's evil dream had moaned and moaned and suddenly snapped asunder. Next morning I found the mountain had disappeared in the chasm of a yawning earthquake. That made me understand how overgrown power crushes itself inwardly by its own weight. I see in you something quite opposite.

NANDINI What is it you see in me?

VOICE The dance rhythm of the All.

NANDINI I don't understand.

VOICE The rhythm that lightens the enormous weight of matter. To that rhythm the bands of stars and planets go about dancing from sky to sky, like so many minstrel boys. It is that rhythm, Nandini, that makes you so simple, so perfect. How small you are compared to me, yet I envy you.

NANDINI You have cut yourself off from everybody and so deprived yourself.

VOICE I keep myself apart, that it may become easy for me to plunder the world's big treasure-houses. Nevertheless there are gifts that your little flower-like fingers can easily reach, but not all the strength of my body, – gifts hidden in God's closed hand. That hand I must force open some day.

NANDINI When you talk like that, I don't follow you. Let me go.

VOICE Go then; but here, I stretch out this hand of mine from my window, place your hand on it for a moment.

NANDINI Only a hand, and the rest of you hidden? It frightens me!

VOICE Everybody flies from me because they only see my hand. But if I wished to hold you with all of me, would you come to me, Nandini?

NANDINI Why talk like this when you wouldn't even let me come into your room?

VOICE My busy time, overloaded with work, dragged along against obstruction, is not for you. On the day when you can arrive, full sail before the wind, into the bosom of my full.

PHÁGULAL Isn't it our holiday? Yesterday was the fast day of the War Goddess. To-day they worship the Flag.

CHANDRÁ Must you drink just because it's a holiday? In our village home, on feast days, you never –

PHÁGULAL Freedom itself was enough for the holidays in our village. The caged bird spends its holiday knocking against the bars. In Yaksha Town holidays are more of a nuisance than work.

CHANDRÁ Let's go back home, then.

PHÁGULAL The road to our home is closed for ever.

CHANDRÁ How's that?

PHÁGULAL Our homes don't yield them any profit.

CHANDRÁ But are we closely fitted to their profits only, – like husks to grains of corn, – with nothing of us left over?

PHÁGULAL Our mad Bishu says: to remain whole is useful only for the lamb itself; those who eat it prefer to leave out its horns and hooves, and even object to its bleating when butchered.

There's the madcap, singing as he goes.

CHANDRÁ It's only the last few days that his songs have burst forth.

PHÁGULAL That's true.

CHANDRÁ He's been possessed by Nandini. She draws his heart and his songs too.

PHÁGULAL No wonder.

CHANDRÁ Indeed! You'd better be careful. She'll next be bringing out songs from *your* throat, – which would be rough on our neighbours. The witch is up to all kinds of tricks, and is sure to bring misfortune.

PHÁGULAL Bishu's misfortune is nothing recent, he knew Nandini long before coming here.

CHANDRÁ (*calling out*) I say, Bishu, come this way. Maybe you'll find somebody here also to listen to your singing, – it won't be altogether thrown away.

BISHU *comes in, singing*

BISHU (*sings*)

> Boatman of my dreams,
> The sail is filled with a boisterous breeze
>   and my mad heart sings
> to the lilt of the rocking of thy boat,
> at the call of the far-away landing.

CHANDRÁ I know who the boatman of your dreams is.

BISHU How should you know from outside? You haven't seen from inside my boat.

CHANDRÁ Your boat is going to get wrecked one of these days, let me tell you, – by that pet Nandini of yours.

GÔKUL, *the digger, comes in*

GÔKUL I say, Bishu, I don't quite trust your Nandini.

BISHU Why, what has she done?

GÔKUL She does nothing, that's the rub. I don't understand the way she goes on.

CHANDRÁ To see her flaunting her prettiness all over the place makes me sick.

GÔKUL We can trust features that are plain enough to understand.

BISHU I know the atmosphere of this place breeds contempt for beauty. There must be beauty even in hell; but nobody there can understand it, that's their cruellest punishment.

CHANDRÁ Maybe we are fools, but even our Governor here can't stand her – d'you know that?

BISHU Take care, Chandrá, lest you catch the infection of our
Governor's eyes – then perhaps yours too will redden at the
sight of us. What say you, Phágulal?

PHÁGULAL To tell you the truth, brother, when I see Nandini,
I feel ashamed to think of myself. I can't utter a word when
she's there.

GÓKUL The day will come when you'll know her to your cost,
– perhaps too late. (*Goes.*)

PHÁGULAL Bishu, your friend Chandrá wants to know why
we drink.

BISHU God in his mercy has everywhere provided a liberal allowance of drink. We men with our arms supply the output
of our muscles, you women with yours supply the wine of
embraces. In this world there is hunger to force us to work;
but there's also the green of the woods, the gold of the sunshine, to make us drunk with their holiday-call.

CHANDRÁ You call these things *drink*?

BISHU Yes, drinks of life, an endless stream of intoxication.
Take my case. I come to this place; I am set to work bur-
gling the underworld; for me nature's own ration of spirits
is stopped; so my inner man craves the artificial wine of the
market place. (*Sings.*)

> *My life, your sap has run dry,*
> *Fill then the cup with the wine of death,*
> *That flushes all emptiness with its laughter.*

CHANDRÁ Come, brother, let us fly from here.

BISHU To that boundless tavern, underneath the blue canopy?
Alas, the road is closed, and we seek consolation in the stolen
wine of the prison house. No open sky, no leisure for us;
so we have distilled the essence of all the song and laughter,
all the sunlight of the twelve hours' day into one draught of
liquid fire. (*Sings.*)

> *Thy sun is hidden amid a mass of murky cloud.*
> *Thy day has smudged itself black in dusty toil.*
> *Then let the dark night descend*
> *   the last comrade of drunken oblivion,*
> *Let it cover thy tired eyes with the mist*
> *   that will help thee desperately to lose thyself.*

CHANDRÁ Well, well, Bishu, you men have gone to the dogs

in Yaksha Town, if you like, but we women haven't changed at all.

BISHU Haven't you? Your flowers have faded, and you are all slavering for gold.

CHANDRÁ No, never!

BISHU I say, yes. That Phágulal toils for hours over and above the twelve, – why? For a reason unknown to him, unknown even to you. But I know. It's your dream of gold that lashes him on to work, more severely than the foreman's whip.

CHANDRÁ Very well. Then why don't we fly from here, and go back home?

BISHU Your Governor has closed the way as well as the will to return. If you go there to-day you will fly back here to-morrow, like a caged bird to its cage, hankering for its drugged food.

PHÁGULAL I say, Bishu, once upon a time you came very near spoiling your eyesight poring over books; how is it they made you ply the spade along with the rest of us stupid boors?

CHANDRÁ All this time we've been here, we haven't got from Bishu the answer to this particular question.

PHÁGULAL Yet we all know it.

BISHU Well, out with it then!

PHÁGULAL They employed you to spy on us.

BISHU If you knew that, how is it you let me off alive?

PHÁGULAL But, we knew also, that game was not in your line.

CHANDRÁ How is it you couldn't stick to such a comfortable job, brother?

BISHU Comfortable job? To stick to a living being like a car-buncle on his back?

I said: 'I must go home, my health is failing.'

'Poor thing,' said the Governor, 'how can you go home in such a state? However, there's no harm in your trying.'

Well, I did try. And then I found that, as soon as one enters the maw of Yaksha Town, its jaws shut fast, and the one road that remains open leads withinwards. Now I am swamped in that interior without hope and without light, and the only difference between you and me is, that the Governor looks down upon me even worse than upon you. Man despises the broken pot of his own creation more than the withered leaf fallen from the tree.

PHÁGULAL What does that matter, Bishu? You have risen high in our esteem.

BISHU Discovery only means death. Where your favour falls there falls the Governor's glance. The more noisily the yellow frogs welcome the black toad, the sooner their croaking points him out to the boa-constrictor.

CHANDRÁ But when will your work be finished?

BISHU The calendar never records the last day. After the first day comes the second, after the second the third. There's no such thing as getting finished here. We're always digging – one yard, two yards, three yards. We go on raising gold nuggets, – after one nugget another, then more and more and more. In Yaksha Town figures follow one another in rows and never arrive at any conclusion. That's why we are not men to them, but only numbers. – Phágu, what's yours?

PHÁGULAL I'm No. 47 V.

BISHU I'm 69 Ng.

CHANDRÁ Brother, they've hoarded such heaps of gold, can't they stop digging now?

BISHU There's always an end to things of need, no doubt; so we stop when we've had enough to eat. But we don't need drunkenness, therefore there's no end to it. These nuggets are the drink – the solid drink – of our Gold King. Don't you see?

CHANDRÁ No, I don't.

BISHU Cups in hand, we forget that we are chained to our limits. Gold blocks in hand, our master fancies he's freed from the gravitation of the commonplace, and is soaring in the rarest of upper heights.

CHANDRÁ In this season the villages are preparing for their harvest festival. Let's go home.

PHÁGULAL Don't worry me, Chandrá. A thousand times over have I told you that in these parts there are high roads to the market, to the burning ground, to the scaffold, – everywhere except to the homeland.

CHANDRÁ If we were to go to the Governor, and just tell him –

BISHU Hasn't your woman's wit seen through the Governor yet?

CHANDRÁ Why, he seems to be so nice and –

BISHU Yes, nice and polished, like the crocodile's teeth, which fit into one another with so thorough a bite that the King himself can't unlock the jaw, even if he wants to.

CHANDRÁ There comes the Governor.

BISHU Then it's all up with us. He's sure to have overheard –

CHANDRÁ Why, we haven't said anything so very –

BISHU Sister, we can only say the words, – they put in the meaning.

The GOVERNOR *comes in*

CHANDRÁ Sir Governor!

GOVERNOR Well, my child?

CHANDRÁ Grant us leave to go home for a little.

GOVERNOR Why, aren't the rooms we have given you excellent, much better than the ones at home? We have even kept a state watchman for your safety.

Hullo, 69 Ng, to see you amongst these people reminds one of a heron come to teach paddy birds how to cut capers.

BISHU Sir, your jesting does not reassure me. Had my feet the strength to make others dance, would I not have run away from here, first thing? Especially after the striking examples I've seen of the fate that overtakes dancing masters in this country. As things are, one's legs tremble even to walk straight.

CHANDRÁ Give us leave, Sir Governor, do give us leave. Let us go just for once, and see our waving fields of barleycorn in the ear, and the ample shade of our banian tree with its hanging roots. I cannot tell you how our hearts ache. Don't you see that your men here work all day in the dark, and in the evening steep themselves in the denser dark of drunkenness? Have you no pity for them?

GOVERNOR My dear child, surely you know of our constant anxiety for their welfare. That is exactly why I have sent for our High Preacher, Kenarám Gosain himself, to give moral talks to the men. Their votive fees will pay for his upkeep. Every evening the Gosain will come and –

PHÁGULAL That won't do, sir! Now, at worst, we get drunk of an evening, but if we are preached to every night, there'll be manslaughter!

BISHU Hush, hush, Phágulal.

Preacher GOSAIN *comes in*

GOVERNOR Talk of the Preacher and he appears. Your Holiness, I do you reverence. These workmen of ours sometimes feel disturbed in their weak minds. Deign to whisper in their ears some texts of peace. The need is urgent.

GOSAIN These people? Are they not the very incarnation of the sacred Tortoise of our scripture, that held up the sinking earth on its back? Because they meekly suppress themselves underneath their burden, the upper world can keep its head aloft. The very thought sends a thrill through my body!

Just think of it, friend 47 V, yours is the duty of supplying food to this mouth which chants the holy name. With the sweat of your brow have you woven this wrap printed with the holy name, which exalts this devoted body. Surely that is no mean privilege. May you remain for ever undisturbed, is my benediction, for then the grace of God will abide with you likewise.

My friends, repeat aloud the holy name of Hari, and all your burdens will be lightened. The name of Hari shall be taken in the beginning, in the middle, and at the end, – so say the scriptures.

CHANDRÁ How sweet! It's long since I have heard such words! Give, oh give me a little dust off your feet!

PHÁGULAL Stop this waste of money, Governor. If it's our offerings you want, we can stand it, but we're fairly sick of this cant.

BISHU Once Phágulal runs amok it's all over with the lot of you. Hush, hush, Phágulal!

CHANDRÁ Are you bent on spoiling your chances both in this world and the next, you wretched man? You were never like this before. Nandini's ill wind has blown upon you, – and no mistake.

GOSAIN What charming naiveté, Sir Governor! What's in their heart is always on their lips. What can we teach them? – it's they who'll teach us a lesson. You know what I mean.

GOVERNOR I know where the root of the trouble is. I'll have to take them in hand myself, I see. Meanwhile, pray go to the next parish and chant them the holy name, – the sawyers there have taken to grumbling, somewhat.

GOSAIN Which parish did you say?

GOVERNOR   Parish T-D. No. 71 T is headman there. It ends to the left of where No. 65 of Row M lives.

GOSAIN   My son, though Parish T-D may not yet be quieted, the whole Row of M's have lately become steeped in a beautiful spirit of meekness. Still it is better to keep an extra police force posted in the parish some time longer. Because, as you know our scripture says, – pride is our greatest foe. After the strength of the police has helped to conquer pride, then comes our turn. I take my leave.

CHANDRÁ   Forgive these men, Your Holiness, and give them your blessing, that they may follow the right path.

GOSAIN   Fear not, good woman, they'll all end thoroughly pacified. (*The* GOSAIN *goes.*)

GOVERNOR   I say, 69 Ng, the temper of your parish seems to be somewhat strained.

BISHU   That's nothing strange. The Gosain called them the incarnation of the Tortoise. But, according to scripture, incarnations change; and, when the Tortoise gave place to the Boar, in place of hard shell came out aggressive teeth, so that all-suffering patience was transformed into defiant obstinacy.

CHANDRÁ   But, Sir Governor, don't forget my request.

GOVERNOR   I have heard it and will bear it in mind. (*He goes.*)

CHANDRÁ   Ah now, didn't you see how nice the Governor is? How he smiles every time he talks!

BISHU   Crocodile's teeth begin by smiling and end by biting.

CHANDRÁ   Where does his bite come in?

BISHU   Don't you know he's going to make it a rule not to let the workmen's wives accompany them here?

CHANDRÁ   Why?

BISHU   We have a place in their account book as numbers, but women's figures do not mate with figures of arithmetic.

CHANDRÁ   O dear! but have they no women-folk of their own?

BISHU   Their ladies are besotted with the wine of gold, even worse than their husbands.

CHANDRÁ   Bishu, you had a wife at home, – what's become of her?

BISHU   So long as I filled the honoured post of spy, they used to invite her to those big mansions to play cards with their ladies. Ever since I joined Phágulal's set, all that was stopped, and she left me in a huff at the humiliation.

CHANDRÁ   For shame! But look, brother Bishu, what a grand

procession! One palanquin after another! Don't you see the sparkle of the jewelled fringes of the elephant-seats? How beautiful the out-riders on horseback look, as if they had bits of sunlight pinned on the points of their spears!

BISHU Those are the Governor's and Deputy Governor's ladies, going to the Flag-worship.

CHANDRÁ Bless my soul, what a gorgeous array and how fine they look!

I say, Bishu, if you hadn't given up that job, would you have gone along with that set in this grand style? – and that wife of yours surely –

BISHU Yes, we too should have come to just such a pass.

CHANDRÁ Is there no way going back, – none whatever?

BISHU There is, – through the gutter.

A DISTANT VOICE Bishu, my mad one!

BISHU Yes, my mad girl!

PHÁGULAL There's Nandini. There'll be no more of Bishu for us, for the rest of the day.

CHANDRÁ Tell me, Bishu, what does she charm you with?

BISHU The charm of sorrow.

CHANDRÁ Why do you talk so topsy-turvy?

BISHU She reminds me that there are sorrows, to forget which is the greatest of sorrow.

PHÁGULAL Please to speak plainly, Bishu, otherwise it becomes positively annoying!

BISHU The pain of desire for the near belongs to the animal, the sorrow of aspiration for the far belongs to man. That far-away flame of my eternal sorrow is revealed through Nandini.

CHANDRÁ Brother, we don't understand these things. But one thing I do understand and that is, – the less you men can make out a girl, the more she attracts you! We simple women, – our price is not so high, but we at least keep you on the straight path. I warn you, once for all, that girl with her noose of red oleanders will drag you to perdition. (CHANDRÁ *and* PHÁGULAL *go*.)

NANDINI *comes in*

NANDINI My mad one, did you hear their autumn songs this morning?

BISHU Is my morning like yours that I should hear singing? Mine is only a swept-away remnant of the weary night.

NANDINI In my gladness of heart I thought I'd stand on the rampart and join in their song. But the guards would not let me, so I've come to you.

BISHU I am not a rampart.

NANDINI You are *my* rampart. When I come to you I seem to climb high, I find the open light.

BISHU Ever since coming to Yaksha Town the sky has dropped out of my life. I felt as if they had pounded me in the same mortar with all the fractions of men here, and rolled us into a solid lump.

Then you came and looked into my face in a way that made me sure some light could still be seen through me.

NANDINI In this closed fort a bit of sky survives only between you and me, my mad one.

BISHU Through that sky my songs can fly towards you. (*Sings.*)

> *You keep me awake that I may sing to you,*
> *O Breaker of my sleep!*
> *And so my heart you startle with your call,*
> *O Waker of my grief!*
> *The shades of evening fall,*
> *the birds come to their nest.*
> *The boat arrives ashore,*
> *yet my heart knows no rest,*
> *O Waker of my grief!*

NANDINI The waker of your grief, Bishu?

BISHU Yes, you are my messenger from the unreachable shore. The day you came to Yaksha Town a gust of salt air knocked at my heart.

NANDINI But I never had any message of this sorrow of which you sing.

BISHU Not even from Rañjan?

NANDINI No, he holds an oar in each hand and ferries me across the stormy waters; he catches wild horses by the mane and rides with me through the woods; he shoots an arrow between the eyebrows of the tiger on the spring, and scatters my fear with loud laughter. As he jumps into our Nagai river and disturbs its current with his joyous splashing, so he disturbs me with his tumultuous life. Desperately he stakes his all on the game and thus has he won me.

You also were there with us, but you held aloof, and at last something urged you one day to leave our gambling set. At the time of your parting you looked at my face in a way I could not quite make out. After that I've had no news of you for long. Tell me where you went off to then.

BISHU My boat was tied to the bank; the rope snapped; the wild wind drove it into the tackles unknown.

NANDINI But who dragged you back from there to dig for nuggets here in Yaksha Town?

BISHU A woman. Just as a bird on the wing is brought to the ground by a chance arrow, so did she bring me down to the dust. I forgot myself.

NANDINI How could she touch you?

BISHU When the thirsty heart despairs of finding water it's easy enough for it to be deluded by a mirage, and driven in barren quest from desert to desert.

One day, while I was gazing at the sunset clouds, she had her eye upon the golden spire of the Governor's palace. Her glance challenged me to take her over there. In my foolish pride I vowed to do so. When I did bring her here, under the golden spire, the spell was broken.

NANDINI I've come to take you away from here.

BISHU Since you have moved even the king of this place, what power on earth can prevent you? Tell me, don't you feel afraid of him?

NANDINI I did fear him from outside that screen. But now I've seen him inside.

BISHU What was he like?

NANDINI Like a man from the epics, – his forehead like the gateway of a tower, his arms the iron bolts of some inaccessible fortress.

BISHU What did you see when you went inside?

NANDINI A falcon was sitting on his left wrist. He put it on the perch and gazed at my face. Then, just as he had been stroking the falcon's wings, he began gently to stroke my hand. After a while he suddenly asked: 'Don't you fear me, Nandini?'

'Not in the least,' said I.

Then he buried his fingers in my unbound hair and sat long with closed eyes.

BISHU How did you like it?

NANDINI I liked it. Shall I tell you how? It was as if he were a thousand-year-old banyan tree, and I a tiny little bird; when I lit on a branch of his and had my little swing, he needs must have felt a thrill of delight to his very marrow. I loved to give that bit of joy to that lonely soul.

BISHU Then what did he say?

NANDINI Starting up and fixing his spear-point gaze on my face, he suddenly said: 'I want to know you.'

I felt a shiver run down my body and asked: 'What is there to know? – I am not a manuscript!'

'I know all there is in manuscripts,' said he, 'but I don't know you.' Then he became excited and cried: 'Tell me all about Rañjan. Tell me how you love him.'

I talked on: 'I love Rañjan as the rudder in the water might love the sail in the sky, answering its rhythm of wind in the rhythm of waves.'

He listened quietly, staring like a big greedy boy. All of a sudden he startled me by exclaiming: 'Could you die for him?'

'This very moment,' I replied.

'Never,' he almost roared, as if in anger.

'Yes, I could,' I repeated.

'What good would that do you?'

'I don't know,' said I.

Then he writhed and shouted: 'Go away from my room, go, go at once, don't disturb me in my work.'

I could not understand what that meant.

BISHU He gets angry when he can't understand.

NANDINI Bishu, don't you feel pity for him?

BISHU The day when God will be moved to pity for him, he will die.

NANDINI No, no, you don't know how desperately he wants to live.

BISHU You will see this very day what his living means. I don't know whether you'll be able to bear the sight.

NANDINI There, look, there's a shadow. I am sure the Governor has secretly heard what we've been saying.

BISHU This place is dark with the Governor's shadow, it is everywhere. How do you like him?

NANDINI I have never seen anything so lifeless, – like a cane stick cut from the cane bush, – no leaves, no roots, no sap in the veins.

BISHU Cut off from life, he spends himself in repressing life.

NANDINI Hush, he will hear you.

BISHU He hears even when you are silent, which is all the more dangerous. When I am with the diggers I am careful in my speech, so much so that the Governor thinks I'm the sorriest of the lot, and spares me out of sheer contempt. But, my mad girl, when I am with you my mind scorns to be cautious.

NANDINI No, no, you must not court danger. There comes the Governor.

The GOVERNOR *comes in*

GOVERNOR Hallo, 69 Ng! you seem to be making friends with everybody, without distinction.

BISHU You may remember that I began by making friends even with you, only it was the distinction that stood in the way.

GOVERNOR Well, what are we discussing now?

BISHU We are discussing how to escape from this fortress of yours.

GOVERNOR Really? So recklessly, that you don't even mind confessing it?

BISHU Sir Governor, it doesn't need much cleverness to know that when a captive bird pecks at the bars it's not in the spirit of caress. What does it matter whether that's openly confessed or not?

GOVERNOR The captives' want of love we were aware of, but their not fearing to admit it has become evident only recently.

NANDINI Won't you let Rañjan come?

GOVERNOR You will see him this very day.

NANDINI I knew that; still, for your message of hope I wish you victory. Governor, take this garland of *kunda* flowers.

GOVERNOR Why throw away the garland thus, and not keep it for Rañjan?

NANDINI There is a garland for him.

GOVERNOR Aha, I thought so! I suppose it's the one hanging round your neck. The garland of victory may be of *kunda* flowers, the gift of the hand; but the garland of welcome is of red oleanders, the gift of the heart. Well, let's be quick in accepting what comes from the hand, for that will fade; as for the heart's offering, the longer it waits the more precious it grows. (*The* GOVERNOR *goes.*)

NANDINI (*knocking at the window*) Do you hear? Let me come into your room.

VOICE (*from behind the scenes*) Why always the same futile request? Who is that with you? A pair to Rañjan?

BISHU No, King, I am the obverse side of Rañjan, on which falls the shadow.

VOICE What use has Nandini for you?

BISHU The use which music has for the hollow of the flute.

VOICE Nandini, what is this man to you?

NANDINI He's my partner in music. My heart soars in his voice, my pain cries in his tunes, – that's what he tells me. (*Sings.*)

> 'I love, I love,' – 'Tis the cry that breaks out
> from the bosom of earth and water.

VOICE So that's your partner! What if I dissolved your partnership this very minute?

NANDINI Why are you so cross? Haven't you any companion yourself?

VOICE Has the mid-day sun any companion?

NANDINI Well, let's change the subject. What's that? What's that in your hand?

VOICE A dead frog.

NANDINI What for?

VOICE Once upon a time this frog got into a hole in a stone, and in that shelter it existed for three thousand years. I have learnt from it the secret of continuing to exist, but to live it does not know. To-day I felt bored and smashed its shelter. I've thus saved it from existing for ever. Isn't that good news?

NANDINI Your stone walls will also fall away from around me to-day, – I shall meet Rañjan.

VOICE I want to see you both together.

NANDINI You won't be able to see from behind your net.

VOICE I shall let you sit inside my room.

NANDINI What will you do with us?

VOICE Nothing, I only want to know you.

NANDINI When you talk of knowing, it frightens me.

VOICE Why?

NANDINI I feel that you have no patience with things that cannot be known, but can only be felt.

VOICE I dare not trust such things lest they should play me false. Now go away, don't waste my time. – No, no, wait a little. Give me that tassel of red oleanders which hangs from your hair.

NANDINI What will you do with it?

VOICE When I look at those flowers it seems to me as if the red light of my evil star has appeared in their shape. At times I want to snatch them from you and tear them to pieces. Again I think that if Nandini were ever to place that spray of flowers on my head, with her own hands, then –

NANDINI Then what?

VOICE Then perhaps I might die in peace.

NANDINI Some one loves red oleanders and calls me by that name. It is in remembrance of him that I wear these flowers.

VOICE Then, I tell you, they're going to be *his* evil star as well as *mine*.

NANDINI Don't say such things for shame! I am going.

VOICE Where?

NANDINI I shall go and sit near the gate of your fort.

VOICE Why?

NANDINI When Rañjan comes he'll see I am waiting for him.

VOICE I should like to tread hard on Rañjan and grind him in the dust.

NANDINI Why pretend to frighten me?

VOICE Pretend, you say? Don't you know I am really fearsome?

NANDINI You seem to take pleasure in seeing people frightened at you. In our village plays Srikantha takes the part of a demon; when he comes on the stage, he is delighted if the children are terrified. You are like him. Do you know what I think?

VOICE What is it?

NANDINI The people here trade on frightening others. That's why they have put you behind a network and dressed you fantastically. Don't you feel ashamed to be got up like a bogeyman?

VOICE How dare you!

NANDINI Those whom you have scared all along will one day feel ashamed to be afraid. If my Rañjan were here, he would have snapped his fingers in your face, and not been afraid even if he died for it.

VOICE Your impudence is something great. I should like to stand you up on the top of a heap of everything I've smashed throughout my life. And then –

NANDINI Then what?

VOICE Then, like a squeezed bunch of grapes with its juice running out from between the gripping fingers, if I could but hold you tight with these two hands of mine, – and then – go, go, run away, at once, at once!

NANDINI If you shout at me so rudely, I'll stay on, do what you will!

VOICE I long savagely to prove to you how cruel I am. Have you never heard moans from inside my room?

NANDINI I have. Whose moaning was it?

VOICE The hidden mystery of life, wrenched away by me, bewails its torn ties. To get fire from a tree you have to burn it. Nandini, there is fire within you too, red fire. One day I shall burn you and extract that also.

NANDINI Oh, you are cruel!

VOICE I must either gather or scatter. I can feel no pity for what I do not get. Breaking is a fierce kind of getting.

NANDINI But why thrust out your clenched fist like that?

VOICE Here, I take away my fist. Now fly, as the dove flies from the shadow of a hawk.

NANDINI Very well, I will go, and not vex you any more.

VOICE Here, listen, come back, Nandini!

NANDINI What is it?

VOICE On your face, there is the play of life in your eyes and lips; at the back of you flows your black hair, the silent fall of death. The other day when my hands sank into it they felt the *soft calm of dying*. I long to sleep with my face hidden inside those thick black clusters. You don't know how tired I am!

NANDINI Don't you ever sleep?

VOICE I feel afraid to sleep.

NANDINI Let me sing you the latest song that I've learnt. (*Sings.*)

> *'I love, I love' is the cry that breaks out from*
> *the bosom of earth and water.*
> *The sky broods like an aching heart, the horizon is*
> *tender like eyes misted with tears.*

VOICE Enough! Enough! stop your singing!

NANDINI (*sings on*)

> *A lament heaves and bursts*
> *on the shore of the sea,*
> *The whispers of forgotten days*
> *are born in new leaves to die again.*

See, Bishu, he has left the dead frog there and disappeared. He is afraid of songs.

BISHU The old frog in his heart yearns to die when it hears singing, that's why he feels afraid. My mad girl, why is there a strange light on your face to-day, like the glow of a distant torch in the sky?

NANDINI News has reached me, Rañjan is coming to-day.

BISHU How? ·

NANDINI Let me tell you. Every day a pair of blue-throats come and sit on the pomegranate tree in front of my window. Every night, before I sleep, I salute the pole star and say: Sacred star of constancy, if a feather from the wings of the blue-throats finds its way into my room, then I will know my Rañjan is coming. This morning, as soon as I woke, I found a feather on my bed. See, here it is under my breast-cloth. When I meet him I shall put this feather on his crest.

BISHU They say blue-throats' wings are an omen of victory.

NANDINI Rañjan's way to victory lies through my heart.

BISHU No more of this; let me go to my work.

NANDINI I shan't let you work to-day.

BISHU What must I do then?

NANDINI Sing that song of waiting.

BISHU (*sings*)

> *He who ever wants me through the ages, –*
> *is it not he who sits to-day by my wayside?*
> *I seem to remember a glimpse I had of his face,*
> *in the twilight dusk of some ancient year.*
> *Is it not he who sits to-day by the wayside?*

NANDINI Bishu, when you sing I cannot help feeling that I owe you much, but have never given anything to you.

BISHU I shall decorate my forehead with the mark of your never-giving, and go my way. No little-giving for me, in return for my song! Where will you go now?

NANDINI To the wayside by which Rañjan is coming. (*They go.*)

The GOVERNOR *and a* HEADMAN *come in*

GOVERNOR No, we can't possibly allow Rañjan to enter this parish.

HEADMAN I put him to work in the tunnels of Vajragarh.

GOVERNOR Well, what happened?

HEADMAN He said he was not used to being made to work. The Headman of Vajragarh came with the police, but the fellow doesn't know what fear is. Threaten him, he bursts out laughing. Asked why he laughs, he says solemnity is the mask of stupidity and he has come to take it off.

GOVERNOR Did you set him to work with the diggers?

HEADMAN I did, I thought that pressure would make him yield. But on the contrary it seemed to lift the pressure from the diggers' minds also. He cheered them up, and asked them to have a digger's dance!

GOVERNOR Digger's dance! What on earth is that?

HEADMAN Rañjan started singing. Where were they to get drums? – they objected. Rañjan said, if there weren't any drums, there were spades enough. So they began keeping time with the spades, making a joke of their digging up of nuggets.

The Headman himself came over to reprimand them. 'What style of work is this?' he thundered.

'I have unbound the work,' said Rañjan. 'It won't have to be dragged out by main force any more, it will run along of itself, dancing.'

GOVERNOR The fellow is mad, I see.

HEADMAN Hopelessly mad. 'Use your spade properly,' shouted I. 'Much better give me a guitar,' said he, smiling.

GOVERNOR But how did he manage to escape from Vajragarh and come up here?

HEADMAN That I do not know. Nothing seems to fasten on to him. His boisterousness is infectious. The diggers are getting frisky.

GOVERNOR Hallo, isn't that Rañjan himself, – going along the road, thrumming on an old guitar? Impudent rascal! He doesn't even care to hide.

HEADMAN Well, I never! Goodness alone knows how he broke through the wall!

GOVERNOR Go and seize him instantly! He must not meet Nandini in this parish, for anything.

Enters ASSISTANT GOVERNOR

GOVERNOR Where are you going?

ASSISTANT GOVERNOR To arrest Rañjan.

GOVERNOR Where is the Deputy Governor?

ASSISTANT GOVERNOR He is so much amused by this fellow that he doesn't want to lay hands on him. He says the man's laugh shows us what queer creatures we governors have grown into.

GOVERNOR I have an idea. Don't arrest Rañjan. Send him on to the King's sanctum.

ASSISTANT GOVERNOR He refuses to obey our call, even in the King's name.

GOVERNOR Tell him the King has made a slave-girl of his Nandini.

ASSISTANT GOVERNOR But if the King –

GOVERNOR Don't you worry. Come on, I'll go with you myself. (*They go.*)

Enter PROFESSOR *and* ANTIQUARIAN

ANTIQUARIAN I say, what is this infernal noise going on inside?

PROFESSOR The King, probably in a temper with himself, is engaged in breaking some of his own handiwork.

ANTIQUARIAN It sounds like big pillars crashing down one after another.

PROFESSOR There was a lake, at the foot of our hill over there, in which the waters of this Sankhini river used to gather. One day, suddenly, the rock to its left gave way, and the stored-up water rushed out laughing like mad. To see the King now-a-days, it strikes me that his treasure lake has grown weary of its rock wall.

ANTIQUARIAN What did you bring me here for, Professor?

PROFESSOR Latterly he has begun to get angry with my science. He says it only burgles through one wall to reveal another behind it, and never reaches the inner chamber of the

Life spirit. I thought that, perhaps in the study of antiquity, he might explore the secret of Life's play. My knapsack has been rifled empty, now he can go on pocket-picking history.

ANTIQUARIAN A girl wearing a grass-green robe.

PROFESSOR She has for her mantle the green joy of the earth. That is our Nandini. In this Yaksha Town there are governors, foremen, headmen, tunnel-diggers, scholars like myself; there are policemen, executioners, and undertakers, – altogether a beautiful assortment! Only *she* is out of element. Midst the clamour of the market place she is a tuned-up lyre. There are days when the mesh of my studies is torn by the sudden breeze of her passing by, and through that rent my attention flies away *swish*, like a bird.

ANTIQUARIAN Good heavens, man! Are even your well-seasoned bones subject to these poetic fits?

PROFESSOR Life's attraction, like the tidal wave, tears away mind from its anchorage of books.

ANTIQUARIAN Tell me, where am I to meet the King?

PROFESSOR There's no means of meeting him. You'll have to talk to him from outside this network.

ANTIQUARIAN We're to converse with this net between us?

PROFESSOR Not the kind of whispered talk that may take place through a woman's veil, but solidly concentrated conversation. Even the cows in his stall don't dare to give milk, they yield their butter straight off!

ANTIQUARIAN Admirable! To extract the essential from the diluted, is what scholars aim at.

PROFESSOR But not what God in His creation aims at. He respects the fruit stones that are hard, but rejoices in the pulp that is sweet.

ANTIQUARIAN Professor, I see that your grey science is galloping fast towards grass-green. But I wonder how you can stand this King of yours.

PROFESSOR Shall I tell you the truth? I love him.

ANTIQUARIAN You don't mean to say so?

PROFESSOR He is so great that even what is wrong with him will not be able to spoil him.

The GOVERNOR *comes in*

GOVERNOR I say, man of science, so this is the person you

volunteered to bring here. Our King flew into a passion at the very mention of his special subject.

ANTIQUARIAN   May I ask why?

GOVERNOR   The King says there is no age of history which may be called old. It is always an eternal extension of the present.

ANTIQUARIAN   Can the front exist without the back?

GOVERNOR   What he said was: 'Time proceeds by revealing the new on his front; but the men of learning, suppressing that fact, will have it that Time ever carries the burden of the old on his back.'

NANDINI *comes in hurriedly*

NANDINI   What is happening? Who are they?

GOVERNOR   Hallo, Nandini, is that you? I shall wear your *kunda* chain late in the evening. When three-quarters of me can hardly be seen for the dark, then perchance a flower garland might become even me.

NANDINI   Look over there – what a piteous sight! Who are those people, going along with the guards, filing out from the backdoor of the King's apartments?

GOVERNOR   We call them the King's leavings.

NANDINI   What does that mean?

GOVERNOR   Some day you too will know its meaning; let it be for to-day.

NANDINI   But are these men? Have they flesh and marrow, life and soul?

GOVERNOR   Maybe they haven't.

NANDINI   Had they never any?

GOVERNOR   Maybe they had.

NANDINI   Where then is it all gone now?

GOVERNOR   Man of science, explain it if you can, I'm off. (*He goes.*)

NANDINI   Alas, alas! I see amongst these shadows faces that I know. Surely that is our Anup and Upamanyu?

Professor, they belong to our neighbouring village. Two brothers as tall as they were strong. They used to come and race their boats in our river on the fourteenth day of the moon in rainy June. Oh, who has brought them to this miserable plight?

See, there goes Shaklu, – in sword play he used to win the prize garland before all the others. Anu-up! Sha-klu-u! look this way; it's I, your the principle underlying all rise to greatness.

NANDINI It's a fiendish principle!

PROFESSOR It's no use getting annoyed with a principle. Principles are neither good nor bad. That which happens *does* happen. To go against it, is to knock your head against the law of being.

NANDINI If this is the way of man's being, I refuse to *be*, I want to depart with those shadows, – show me the way.

PROFESSOR When the time comes for showing us out, the great ones themselves will point the way. Before that, there's no such nuisance as a way at all! You see how our Antiquarian has quietly slipped off, thinking he'll fly and save himself. After going a few steps, he'll soon discover that there's a wire network stretched from post to post, from country to country.

Nandini, I see, your temper is rising. The red oleanders against your flaming cheek are beginning to look like evening storm clouds gathering for a night of terror.

NANDINI (*knocking at the net window*) Listen, listen!

PROFESSOR Whom are you calling?

NANDINI That King of yours, shrouded in his mist of netting.

PROFESSOR The door of the inner room has been closed. He won't hear you.

NANDINI (*calling out*) Bishu, mad brother mine!

PROFESSOR What d'you want with him?

NANDINI Why hasn't he come back yet? I feel afraid.

PROFESSOR He was with you only a little while ago.

NANDINI The Governor said he was wanted to identify Rañjan. I tried to go with him, but they wouldn't let me. Whose groaning is that?

PROFESSOR It must be that wrestler of ours.

NANDINI What wrestler?

PROFESSOR The world-famous Gajju, whose brother, Bhajan, had the bravado to challenge the King to a wrestling match, since when not even a thread of his loin cloth is anywhere to be seen. That put Gajju on his mettle, and he came on with great sound and fury. I told him at the outset that, if he wanted to dig in the tunnels underneath this kingdom, he was welcome, – he could at least drag on a dead and alive existence for some time. But if he wanted to make a show of heroics, that would not be tolerated for a moment.

NANDINI Does it at all make for their well-being thus to keep watch and ward over these man-traps night and day?

PROFESSOR Well-being! There's no question of 'well' in it at all, – only 'being'. That *being* of theirs has expanded so terribly that, unless millions of men are pressed into service, who's going to support its weight? So the net is spreading farther and farther. They must exist, you see.

NANDINI Must they? If it is necessary to die in order to live like men, what harm in dying?

PROFESSOR Again that anger, the wild cry of red oleander? It is sweet, no doubt, yet what is true is true. If it gives you pleasure to say that one must die to live, well, say so by all means; but those who say that others must die that they themselves may live, – it's only they who are actually alive. You may cry out that this shows a lack of humanity, but you forget, in your indignation, that this is what humanity itself happens to be. The tiger does not feed on the tiger, it's only man who fattens on his fellow-man.

The WRESTLER *totters in*

NANDINI Oh poor thing, see how he comes, staggering. Wrestler, lie down here. Professor, do see where he's hurt.

PROFESSOR You won't see any outward sign of a wound.

WRESTLER All-merciful God, grant me strength once more in my life, if only for one little day!

PROFESSOR Why, my dear fellow?

WRESTLER Just to wring that Governor's neck!

PROFESSOR What has the Governor done to you?

WRESTLER It's he who brought about the whole thing. I never wanted to fight. Now, after egging me on, he goes about saying it's my fault.

PROFESSOR Why, what interest had he in your fighting?

WRESTLER They only feel safe when they rob the whole world of strength. Lord of Mercy, grant that I may be able to gouge his eyes out some day, to tear asunder his lying tongue!

NANDINI How do you feel now, Wrestler?

WRESTLER Altogether hollowed out! These demons know the magic art of sucking away not only strength but hope.

If only once I could somehow, – O good God, but once, – everything is possible to Thy mercy, – if only I could fasten my teeth for once in the Governor's throat!

NANDINI Professor, help me to raise him.

PROFESSOR That would be a crime, Nandini, according to the custom of this land.

NANDINI Wouldn't it be a crime to let the man perish?

PROFESSOR That which there is none to punish may be a sin, but never a crime. Nandini, come away, come right away out of this. The tree spreads its root-fingers and does its grabbing underground, but there it does not bring forth its flowers. Flowers bloom on the branches which reach towards the light. My sweet Red Oleander, don't try to probe our secrets in the depths of their dust. Be for us swaying in the air above, that we may gaze upwards to see you.

There comes the Governor. He hates to see me talk to you. So I must go.

NANDINI Why is he so dead against me?

PROFESSOR I can guess. You have touched his heart-strings. The longer it takes to tune them up, the more awful the discord meanwhile.

The PROFESSOR *goes, the* GOVERNOR *comes in*

NANDINI Sir Governor!

GOVERNOR Nandini, when our Gosain saw that *kunda* garland of yours in my room, both his eyes, – but here he comes – (*The* GOSAIN *comes in*).

Your Holiness, accept my reverence. That garland was given to me by our Nandini here.

GOSAIN Ah indeed! the gift of a pure heart! God's own white *kunda* flowers! Their beauty remains unsullied even in the hands of a man of the world. This is what gives one faith in the power of virtue, and hope for the sinners' redemption.

NANDINI Please do something for this man, Your Reverence. There's very little life left in him.

GOSAIN The Governor is sure to keep him as much alive as it is necessary for him to be. But, my child, these discussions ill become your lips.

NANDINI So in this kingdom you follow some calculation in apportioning life?

GOSAIN Of course, – for mortal life has its limits. Our class of
people have their great burden to bear, therefore we have to
claim a larger portion of life's sustenance for our share. That's
according to Almighty God's own decree.

NANDINI Reverend Sir, may I know what good God has so
heavily charged you to do to these people?

GOSAIN The life that is unlimited gives no provocation to fight
for its distribution. We Preachers have the charge of turning these people towards this unlimited life. So long as they
remain content with that, we are their friends.

NANDINI Let me come over to the Headman's quarters to help
you.

WRESTLER No. Don't add to my troubles, I beg of you. (*The*
WRESTLER *goes.*)

NANDINI Governor, stay, tell me, whither have you taken my
Bishu?

GOVERNOR Who am I that I should take him? The wind carries off the clouds, – if you think that to be a crime, make
enquiries as to who is behind the wind.

NANDINI Dear me, what an awful place! You are not men, and
those you drive are not men, either, – you are winds and they
are clouds!

Reverend Gosain, I am sure, *you* know where my Bishu is.

GOSAIN I know, for sure, that wherever he is, it's for the best.

NANDINI For whose best?

GOSAIN That you won't understand –

Oh, I say, leave off, let go of that, it's my rosary. – Hallo,
Governor, what wild girl is this you have –

GOVERNOR The girl has somehow managed to ensconce herself in a niche, safe from the laws of this land, and we can't lay
hands on her. Our King himself –

GOSAIN Good heavens, now she'll tear off my wrap of the Holy
Name too. What unspeakable outrage! (*The* GOSAIN *flies.*)

NANDINI Governor, you *must* tell me where you have taken
Bishu.

GOVERNOR They have summoned him to the court of judgement. That's all that there is to tell you. Let me go.

NANDINI Because I am a woman, you are not afraid of me?
God sends His thunderbolt through His messenger, the lightning spark – that bolt I have borne here with me; it will
shatter the golden spire of your mastery.

GOVERNOR Then let me tell you the truth before I go. It's you
who have dragged Bishu into danger.

NANDINI I?

GOVERNOR Yes, you! He was so long content to be quietly
burrowing away underground like a worm. It's you who
taught him to spread the wings of death. O fire of the gods,
you'll yet draw forth many more to their fate. – Then at
length will you and I come to our understanding, and that
won't be long.

NANDINI So may it be. But tell me one thing before you go.
Will you not let Rañjan come and see me?

GOVERNOR No, never.

NANDINI Never, you say! I defy you to do your worst. This
very day I am sure, absolutely sure, that he and I will meet!
(GOVERNOR *goes.*)

NANDINI (*knocking and tugging at the network*) Listen, listen,
King! Where's your court of judgement? Open its door to
me. (KISHÔR *comes in.*)

Who is that? My boy, Kishôr! Do you know where
Bishu is?

KISHÔR Yes, Nandini, be ready to see him. I don't know how
it was, the Chief of the Guard took a fancy to my youthfulness and yielded to my entreaties. He has consented to take
him along by this path.

NANDINI Guard! Take him along? Is he then –

KISHÔR Yes, here they come.

NANDINI What! Handcuffs on your wrists? Friend of my heart,
where are they taking you like that?

BISHU *comes in under arrest*

BISHU It's nothing to be anxious about! – Guards, please wait a
little, let me say a few words to her. – My wild girl, my heart's
joy, at last I am free.

NANDINI What do you mean, Singer of my heart? I don't understand your words.

BISHU When I used to be afraid, and try to avoid danger at
every step, I seemed to be at liberty; but that liberty was the
worst form of bondage.

NANDINI What offence have you committed that they should
take you away thus?

BISHU I spoke out the truth to-day, at last.

NANDINI What if you did?

BISHU No harm at all!

NANDINI Then why did they bind you like this?

BISHU What harm in that either? These chains will bear witness to the truth of my freedom.

NANDINI Don't they feel ashamed of themselves to lead you along the road chained like a beast? Aren't they men too?

BISHU They have a big beast inside them, that's why their heads are not lowered by the indignity of man, rather the inner brute's tail swells and wags with pride at man's downfall.

NANDINI O dear heart! Have they been hurting you? What are these marks on your body?

BISHU They have whipped me, with the whips they use for their dogs. The string of that whip is made with the same thread which goes to the stringing of their Gosain's rosary. When they tell their beads they don't remember that; but probably their God is aware of it.

NANDINI Let them bind me like that too, and take me away with you, my heart's joy! Unless I share some of your punishment I shan't be able to touch food from to-day.

KISHÔR I'm sure I can persuade them to take me in exchange for you. Let me take your place, Bishu.

BISHU Don't be silly!

KISHÔR Punishment won't hurt me. I am young. I shall bear it with joy.

NANDINI No, no, do not talk like that.

KISHÔR Nandini, my absence has been noticed, their blood-hounds are after me. Allow me to escape the indignity awaiting me by taking shelter in a punishment I joyfully accept.

BISHU No, it won't do for you to be caught – not for a while yet. There's work for you, dear boy, and dangerous work too. Rañjan has come. You must find him out.

KISHÔR Then I bid you farewell, Nandini. What is your message when I meet Rañjan?

NANDINI This tassel of red oleanders. (*Hands it to him.*) (KISHÔR *goes.*)

BISHU May you both be united once again.

NANDINI That union will give me no pleasure now. I shall never be able to forget that I sent you away empty-handed. And what has that poor boy, Kishôr, got from me?

BISHU All the treasure hidden in his heart has been revealed to him by the fire you have lighted in his life. Nandini, I remind you, it's for you to put that blue-throat's feather on Rañjan's crest. – There, do you hear them singing the harvest song?

NANDINI I do, and it wrings my heart, to tears.

BISHU The play of the fields is ended now, and the field-master is taking the ripe corn home. Come on, Guards, let's not linger any more. (*Sings.*)

> *Mow the corn of the last harvest,*
> *bind it in sheaves.*
> *The remainder, let it return*
> *as dust unto the dust.*

They go

The GOVERNOR *and a* DOCTOR *come in*

DOCTOR I've seen him. I find the King.

GOVERNOR My wife will be driving out to-day. The post will be changed near your village, and you must see that she's not detained.

HEADMAN There's a plague on the cattle of our parish, and not a single ox can be had to draw the car. Never mind, we can press the diggers into service.

GOVERNOR You know where you have to take her? To the garden-house, where the feast of the Flag-worship is to be held.

HEADMAN I'll see to it at once, but let me tell you one thing before I go. That 69 Ng, whom they call mad Bishu, – it's high time to cure his madness.

GOVERNOR Why, how does he annoy you?

HEADMAN Not so much by what he says or does, as by what he implies.

GOVERNOR There's no need to worry about him any further. You understand!

HEADMAN Really! That's good news, indeed! Another thing. That 47 V, he's rather too friendly with 69 Ng.

GOVERNOR I have observed that.

HEADMAN Your Lordship's observation is ever keen. Only, as you have to keep an eye on so many things, one or two may perchance escape your notice. For instance, there's our No.

95, a distant connection of mine by marriage, ever ready to make sandals for the feet of Your Lordship's sweeper out of his own ribs, – so irrepressibly loyal is he that even his wife hangs her head for very shame, – and yet up to now –

GOVERNOR His name has been entered in the High Register.

HEADMAN Ah, then his lifelong service will at last receive its reward! The news must be broken to him gently, because he gets epileptic fits, and supposing suddenly –

GOVERNOR All right, we'll see to that. Now be off, there's no time.

HEADMAN Just a word about another person, – though he's my own brother-in-law. When his mother died, my wife brought him up with her own hands; yet for my master's sake –

GOVERNOR You can tell me about him another time. Run away now.

HEADMAN There comes His Honour the Deputy Governor. Please speak a word to him on my behalf. He doesn't look upon me with favour. I suspect that when 69 Ng used to enjoy the favour of free entry into the palace, he must have been saying things against me.

GOVERNOR I assure you, he never even mentioned your name.

HEADMAN That's just his cleverness! What can be more damaging than to suppress the name of a man, whose name is his best asset? These schemers have their different ways. No. 33 of our parish has an incurable habit of haunting Your Lordship's private chamber. One is always afraid of his inventing goodness knows what calumnies about other people. And yet if one knew the truth about his own –

GOVERNOR There's positively no time to-day. Get away with you, quick!

HEADMAN I make my salute. (*Coming back.*) Just one word more lest I forget. No. 88 of our neighbouring parish started work on a miserable pittance, and before two years are out his income has run into thousands, not to speak of extras! Your Lordship's mind is like that of the gods – a few words of hypocritical praise are enough to draw down the best of your boons.

GOVERNOR All right, all right, – that can keep for to-morrow.

HEADMAN I'm not so mean as to suggest taking away the bread from his mouth. But Your Lordship should seriously consider whether it's wise to keep him on at the Treasury. Our Vishnu Dutt knows him inside out. If you send –

GOVERNOR   I shall send for him this very day. But begone, – not another word!

HEADMAN   Your Lordship, my third son is getting to be quite a big boy. He came the other day to prostrate himself at your feet. After two days of dancing attendance outside, he had to go away without gaining admission to you. He feels it very bitterly. My daughter-in-law has made with her own hands an offering of sweet pumpkin for Your Lordship –

GOVERNOR   Oh confound you! Tell him to come day after to-morrow, he will be admitted. *Now, will you –*

HEADMAN *goes. The* DEPUTY GOVERNOR *comes in*

DEPUTY GOVERNOR   I've just sent on the dancing girls and musicians to the garden.

GOVERNOR   And that little matter about Rañjan, – how far –?

DEPUTY GOVERNOR   That kind of work is not in my line. The Assistant Governor has taken it upon himself to do the job. By this time his –

GOVERNOR   Does the King –?

DEPUTY GOVERNOR   The King can't possibly have understood. Some lie told by our men has goaded Rañjan to frenzy, and he's rushing to the usual fate of – I detest the whole business. Moreover, I don't think it right to deceive the King like this.

GOVERNOR   That responsibility is mine. Now then, that girl must be –

DEPUTY GOVERNOR   Don't talk of all that to me. The Headman who has been put on duty is the right man, – he doesn't stick at any dirtiness whatever.

GOVERNOR   Does that man Gosain know about this affair?

DEPUTY GOVERNOR   I'm sure he can guess, but he's careful not to know for certain.

GOVERNOR   What's his object?

DEPUTY GOVERNOR   For fear of there being no way left open for saying: 'I don't believe it.'

GOVERNOR   But what makes him take all this trouble?

DEPUTY GOVERNOR   Don't you see? The poor man is really two in one, clumsily joined, – Priest on the skin, Governor at the marrow. He has to take precious care to prevent the Governor part of him coming up to the surface, lest it should clash too much with his telling of beads.

GOVERNOR He might have dropped the beads altogether.

DEPUTY GOVERNOR No, for whatever his blood may be, his mind, in a sense, is really pious. If only he can tell his beads in his temple, and revel in slave-driving in his dreams, he feels happy. But for him, the true complexion of our God would appear too black. In fact, Gosain is placed here only to help our God to feel comfortable.

GOVERNOR My friend, I see the instinct of the Ruler doesn't seem to match with the colour of your own blood, either!

DEPUTY GOVERNOR There's hope still. Human blood is fast drying up. But I can't stomach your No. 321 yet. When I'm obliged to embrace him in public, no holy water seems able to wash out the impurity of his touch.

Here comes Nandini.

GOVERNOR Come away, I don't trust you. I know the spell of Nandini has fallen on your eyes.

DEPUTY GOVERNOR I know that as well as you do. But you don't seem to know that a tinge of her oleanders has got mixed with the colour of duty in *your* eyes too – that's what makes them so frightfully red.

GOVERNOR That may be. Fortunately for us, our mind knows not its own secret. Come away. (*They go.*)

NANDINI *comes in*

NANDINI (*knocking and pushing at the network*) Listen, listen, listen!

The GOSAIN *comes in*

GOSAIN Whom are you prodding like that?

NANDINI That boa-constrictor of yours, who remains in hiding and swallows men.

GOSAIN Lord, lord! When Providence wishes to destroy the small, it does so by putting big words into their little mouths.

See here, Nandini, believe me when I tell you that I aim at your welfare.

NANDINI Try some more real method of doing me good.

GOSAIN Come to my sanctuary, let me chant you the Holy Name for a while.

NANDINI What have I to do with the name?

GOSAIN You will gain peace of mind.

NANDINI Shame, shame on me if I do! I shall sit and wait here at the door.

GOSAIN You have more faith in men than in God?

NANDINI Your God of the Flagstaff, – he will never unbend. But the man who is lost to sight behind the netting, will he also remain bound in his network for ever? Go, go. It's your trade to delude men with words, after filching away their lives. (*The* GOSAIN *goes.*)

Enter PHÁGULAL *and* CHANDRÁ

PHÁGULAL Our Bishu came away with you, where is he now? Tell us the truth.

NANDINI He has been made prisoner and taken away.

CHANDRÁ You witch, you must have given information against him. You are their spy.

NANDINI You don't really believe that!

CHANDRÁ What else are you doing here?

PHÁGULAL Every person suspects every other person in this cursed place. Yet I have always trusted you, Nandini. In my heart I used to – However, let that pass. But to-day it looks very very strange, I must say.

NANDINI Perhaps it does. It may really be even as you say. Bishu has got into trouble for coming with me. He used to be quite safe in your company, he said so himself.

CHANDRÁ Then why did you decoy him away, you evil-omened creature?

NANDINI Because he said he wanted to be free.

CHANDRÁ A precious kind of freedom you have given him!

NANDINI I could not understand all that he said, Chandrá. Why did he tell me that freedom could only be found by plunging down to the bottom of danger? – Phágulal, how could I save him who wanted to be free from the tyranny of safety?

CHANDRÁ We don't understand all this. If you can't bring him back, you'll have to pay for it. I'm not to be taken in by that coquettish prettiness of yours.

PHÁGULAL What's the use of idle bickering? Let's gather a big crowd from the workmen's lines, and then go and smash the prison gate.

NANDINI   I'll come with you.

PHÁGULAL   What for?

NANDINI   To join in the breaking.

CHANDRÁ   As if you haven't done quite enough breaking already, you sorceress!

GÔKUL *comes in*

GÔKUL   That witch must be burnt alive, before everything else.

CHANDRÁ   That won't be punishment enough. First knock off that beauty of hers, with which she goes about ruining people. Weed it out of her face as the grass is weeded with a hoe.

GÔKUL   That I can do. Let this hammer just have a dance on her nose tip –

PHÁGULAL   Beware! If you dare touch her –

NANDINI   Stop, Phágulal. He's a coward; he wants to strike me because he's afraid of me. I don't fear his blows one bit.

GÔKUL   Phágulal, you haven't come to your senses yet. You think the Governor alone is your enemy. Well, I admire a straightforward enemy. But that sweet-mouthed beauty of yours –

NANDINI   Ah, so you too admire the Governor, as the mud beneath his feet admires the soles of his shoes!

PHÁGULAL   Gôkul, the time has at length come to show your prowess, but not by fighting a girl. Come along with me. I'll show you what to fight. (PHÁGULAL, CHANDRÁ, *and* GÔKUL *go.*)

A band of MEN *come in*

NANDINI   Where are you going, my good men?

FIRST MAN   We carry the offering for the Flag-worship.

NANDINI   Have you seen Rañjan?

SECOND MAN   I saw him once, five days ago, but not since. Ask those others who follow us.

NANDINI   Who are they?

THIRD MAN   They are bearing wine for the Governors' feast.

The first batch goes, another comes in

NANDINI Look here, red-caps, have you seen Rañjan?

FIRST MAN I saw him the other day at the house of Headman
Sambhu.

NANDINI Where is he now?

SECOND MAN D'you see those men taking the ladies' dresses
for the feast? Ask them. They hear a lot of things that don't
reach our ears.

Second batch goes, a third come in

NANDINI Do *you* know, my men, where they have kept
Rañjan?

FIRST MAN Hush, hush!.

NANDINI I am sure you know. You *must* tell me.

SECOND MAN What enters by our ears doesn't come out by
our mouths, that's why we are still alive. Ask one of the men
who are carrying the weapons.

They go, others come in

NANDINI Oh do stop a moment and listen to me. Tell me,
where is Rañjan?

FIRST MAN The auspicious hour draws near. It's time for the
King himself to come for the Flag-worship. Ask him about
it when he steps out. We only know the beginning, not the
end. (*They go.*)

NANDINI (*shaking the network violently*) Open the door. The
time has come.

VOICE (*behind the scenes*) But not for you. Go away from
here.

NANDINI You must hear *now* what I have to say. It cannot wait
for another time.

VOICE You want Rañjan, I know. I have asked the Governor
to fetch him at once. But don't remain standing at the door
when I come out for the worship, for then you'll run great
risk.

NANDINI I have cast away all fear. You can't drive me away.
Happen what may, I'm not going to move till your door is
opened.

VOICE To-day's for the Flag-worship. Don't distract my mind. Get away from my door.

NANDINI The gods have all eternity for their worship, they're not pressed for time. But the sorrows of men cannot wait.

KING Deceived! These traitors have deceived me, – perdition take them! My own machine refuses my sway! Call the Governor – bring him to me handcuffed –

NANDINI King, they all say you know magic. Make him wake up for my sake.

KING My magic can only put an end to waking. – Alas! I know not how to awaken.

NANDINI Then lull me to sleep, – the same sleep! Oh, why did you work this havoc? I cannot bear it any more.

KING I have killed youth. Yes, I have indeed killed youth, – all these years, with all my strength. The curse of youth, dead, is upon me.

NANDINI Did he not take my name?

KING He did, – in such a way that every vein in my body was set on fire.

NANDINI (to RAÑJAN) My love, my brave one, here do I place this blue-throat's feather in your crest. Your victory has begun from today, and I am its bearer. Ah, here is that tassel of my flowers in his hand. Then Kishôr must have met him – But where is he? King, where is that boy?

KING Which boy?

NANDINI The boy who brought these flowers to Rañjan.

KING That absurd little child! He came to defy me with his girlish face.

NANDINI And then? Tell me! Quick!

KING He burst himself against me, like a bubble.

NANDINI King, the Time is indeed now come!

KING Time for what?

NANDINI For the last fight between you and me.

KING But I can kill you in no time, – this instant.

NANDINI From that very instant that death of mine will go on killing you every single moment.

KING Be brave, Nandini, trust me. Make me your comrade to-day.

NANDINI What would you have me do?

KING To fight against me, but with your hand in mine. That fight has already begun. There is my flag. First I break the

Flagstaff, – thus! Next it's for you to tear its banner. Let your hand unite with mine to kill me, utterly kill me. That will be my emancipation.

GUARDS (*rushing up*) What are you doing, King? You dare break the Flagstaff, the holiest symbol of our divinity? The Flagstaff which has its one point piercing the heart of the earth and the other that of heaven! What a terrible sin, – on the very day of the Flag-worship! Comrades, let us go and inform our Governors. (*They run off.*)

KING A great deal of breaking remains to be done. You will come with me, Nandini?

NANDINI I will.

PHÁGULAL *comes in*

PHÁGULAL They won't hear of letting Bishu off. I am afraid, they'll – Who is this? The King!

Oh you wicked witch, – conspiring with the King him-self! O vile deceiver!

KING What is the matter with you? What is that crowd out for?

PHÁGULAL To break the prison gate. We may lose our lives, but we shan't fall back.

KING Why should you fall back? I too am out for breaking. Behold the first sign – my broken Flagstaff!

PHÁGULAL What! This is altogether beyond us simple folk.

Be merciful, Nandini, don't deceive me. Am I to believe my eyes?

NANDINI Brother, you have set out to win death. You have left no chance for deception to touch you.

PHÁGULAL You too come along with us, our own Nandini!

NANDINI That is what I'm still alive for, Phágulal. I wanted to bring my Rañjan amongst you. Look there, he has come, my hero, braving death!

PHÁGULAL Oh, horror! Is that Rañjan lying there, silent?

NANDINI Not silent. He leaves behind him in death his con-quering call. He will live again, he cannot die.

PHÁGULAL Ah, my Nandini, my beautiful one, was it for this you were waiting all these eager days?

NANDINI I *did* await his coming, and he *did* come. I still wait to prepare for his coming again, and he *shall* come again. Where is Chandrá?

PHÁGULAL She has gone with her tears and prayers to the Governor, accompanied by Gôkul. I'm afraid Gôkul is seeking to take up service with the Governor. He will betray us.
King, are you sure you don't mistake us? We are out to break your own prison, I tell you!

KING Yes, it is my *own* prison. You and I must work together, for you cannot break it alone.

PHÁGULAL As soon as the Governor hears of it, he will march with all his forces to prevent us.

KING Yes, my fight is against them.

PHÁGULAL But the soldiers will not obey you.

KING You will be on my side!

PHÁGULAL Shall we be able to win through?

KING We shall at least be able to die! At last I have found the meaning of death. I am saved!

PHÁGULAL King, do you hear the tumult?

KING There comes the Governor with his troops. How could he be so quick about it? He must have been prepared beforehand. They have used my own power against me.

PHÁGULAL My men have not yet turned up.

KING They will never come. The Governor is sure to get round them.

NANDINI I had my last hope that they would bring my Bishu to me. Will that never be?

KING No hope of that, I'm afraid.

PHÁGULAL Then come along, Nandini, let us take you to a safe place first. The Governor will see red, if he but catches sight of you.

NANDINI You want to banish me into the solitary exile of safety? (*Calling out*) Governor! Governor! – He has swung up my garland of *kunda* flowers on his spear-head. I will dye that garland the colour of my oleanders with my heart's blood. – Governor! He has seen me! Victory to Rañjan! (*Runs off.*)

KING (*calling after her*) Nandini! (*Follows her.*)

The PROFESSOR *comes in*

PHÁGULAL Where are you hurrying to, Professor?

PROFESSOR Some one said that the King has at last had tidings of the secret of Life, and has gone off in quest of it. I have thrown away my books to follow him.

PHÁGULAL The King has just gone off to his death. He has heard Nandini's call.

PROFESSOR The network is torn to shreds! Where is Nandini?

PHÁGULAL She has gone before them all. We can't reach her any more.

PROFESSOR It is only now that we shall reach her. She won't evade us any longer.

PROFESSOR *rushes out,* BISHU *comes in*

BISHU Phágulal, where is Nandini?

PHÁGULAL How did you get here?

BISHU Our workmen have broken into the prison. There they are, – running off to fight. I came to look for Nandini. Where is she?

PHÁGULAL She has gone in advance of us all.

BISHU Where?

PHÁGULAL To the last freedom. Bishu, do you see who is lying there?

BISHU Rañjan!

PHÁGULAL You see the red streak?

BISHU I understand, – then red marriage.

PHÁGULAL They are united.

BISHU Now it is for me to take my last lonely journey. – Perhaps we may meet. – Perhaps she may want me to sing. – My mad girl, O my mad girl! –
    Come, brother, on to the fight!

PHÁGULAL To the fight! Victory to Nandini!

BISHU Victory to Nandini!

PHÁGULAL Here is her wristlet of red oleanders. She has bared her arm to-day, – and left us.

BISHU Once I told her I would not take anything from her hand. I break my word and take this. Come along! (*They go.*)

Song in the distance

Hark 'tis Autumn calling, –
    Come, O come away!
The earth's mantle of dust is filled with ripe corn!
    O the joy! the joy!

ESSAYS

Nationalism in the West

MAN'S HISTORY IS being shaped according to the difficulties it encounters. These have offered us problems and claimed their solutions from us, the penalty of non-fulfilment being death or degradation.

These difficulties have been different in different peoples of the earth, and in the manner of our overcoming them lies our distinction.

The Scythians of the earlier period of Asiatic history had to struggle with the scarcity of their natural resources. The easiest solution that they could think of was to organize their whole population, men, women, and children, into bands of robbers. And they were irresistible to those who were chiefly engaged in the constructive work of social cooperation.

But fortunately for man the easiest path is not his truest path. If his nature were not as complex as it is, if it were as simple as that of a pack of hungry wolves, then, by this time, those hordes of marauders would have overrun the whole earth. But man, when confronted with difficulties, has to acknowledge that he is man, that he has his responsibilities to the higher faculties of his nature, by ignoring which he may achieve success that is immediate, perhaps, but that will become a death trap to him. For what are obstacles to the lower creatures are opportunities to the higher life of man.

To India has been given her problem from the beginning of history – it is the race problem. Races ethnologically different have come in this country in close contact. This fact has been and still continues to be the most important one in our history. It is our mission to face it and prove our humanity in dealing with it in the fullest truth. Until we fulfil our mission all other benefits will be denied us.

There are other peoples in the world who have obstacles in their physical surroundings to overcome, or the menace of their powerful neighbours. They have organized their power till they are not only reasonably free from the tyranny of Nature and human neighbours, but have a surplus of it left in their hands to employ against others. But in India, our difficulties being internal, our history has been the history of continual social adjustment and not that of organized power for defence and aggression.

Neither the colourless vagueness of cosmopolitanism, nor the fierce self-idolatry of nation-worship is the goal of human history. And India has been trying to accomplish her task through social regulation of differences, on the one hand, and the spiritual recognition of unity, on the other. She has made grave errors in setting up the boundary walls too rigidly between races, in perpetuating the results of inferiority in her classifications; often she has crippled her children's minds and narrowed their lives in order to fit them into her social forms; but for centuries new experiments have been made and adjustments carried out.

Her mission has been like that of a hostess to provide proper accommodation to her numerous guests whose habits and requirements are different from one another. It is giving rise to infinite complexities whose solution depends not merely upon tactfulness but sympathy and true realization of the unity of man. Towards this realization have worked from the early time of the Upanishads up to the present moment, a series of great spiritual teachers, whose one object has been to set at naught all differences of man by the overflow of our consciousness of God. In fact, our history has not been of the rise and fall of kingdoms, of fights for political supremacy. In our country records of these days have been despised and forgotten. For they in no way represent the true history of our people. Our history is that of our social life and attainment of spiritual ideals.

But we feel that our task is not yet done. The world-flood has swept over our country, new elements have been introduced, and wider adjustments are waiting to be made.

We feel this all the more, because the teaching and example of the West have entirely run counter to what we think was given to India to accomplish. In the West the national machinery of commerce and politics turns out neatly compressed bales of humanity which have their use and high market value; but they are bound in iron hoops, labelled and separated off with scientific care and precision. Obviously God made man to be human; but this modern product has such marvellous square-cut finish, savouring of gigantic manufacture, that the Creator will find it difficult to recognize it as a thing of spirit and a creature made in his own divine image.

But I am anticipating. What I was about to say is this, take it in whatever spirit you like, here is India, of about fifty centuries at least, who tried to live peacefully and think deeply, the India devoid of all politics, the India of no nations, whose one ambition has been to know this world as of soul, to live here every moment of her life in the meek spirit of adoration, in the glad consciousness of an eternal and personal relationship with it. This is the remote portion of humanity, childlike in its manner, with the wisdom of the old, upon which burst the Nation of the West.

Through all the fights and intrigues and deceptions of her earlier history India had remained aloof. Because her homes, her fields, her temples of worship, her schools, where her teachers and students lived together in the atmosphere of simplicity and devotion and learning, her village self-government with its simple laws and peaceful administration – all these truly belonged to her. But her thrones were not her concern. They passed over her head like clouds, now tinged with purple gorgeousness, now black with the threat of thunder. Often they brought devastations in their wake, but they were like catastrophes of nature whose traces are soon forgotten.

But this time it was different. It was not a mere drift over her surface of life, – drift of cavalry and foot soldiers, richly caparisoned elephants, white tents and canopies, strings of patient camels bearing the loads of royalty, bands of kettledrums and flutes, marble domes of mosques, palaces and tombs, like the bubbles of the foaming wine of extravagance; stories of treachery and loyal devotion, of changes of fortune, of dramatic surprises of fate. This time it was the Nation of the West driving its tentacles of machinery deep down into the soil.

Therefore, I say to you, it is we who are called as witnesses to give evidence as to what the Nation has been to humanity. We had known the hordes of Moghals and Pathans who invaded India, but we had known them as human races, with their own religions and customs, likes and dislikes, – we had never known them as a nation. We loved and hated them as occasions arose; we fought for them and against them, talked with them in a language which was theirs as well as our own, and guided the destiny of the Empire in which we had our active share. But this time we had to deal, not with kings, not with human races, but with a nation, – we, who are no nation ourselves.

Now let us from our own experience answer the question, What is this Nation?

A nation, in the sense of the political and economic union of a people, is that aspect which a whole population assumes when organized for a mechanical purpose. Society as such has no ulterior purpose. It is an end in itself. It is a spontaneous self-expression of man as a social being. It is a natural regulation of human relationships, so that men can develop ideals of life in cooperation with one another. It has also a political side, but this is only for a special purpose. It is for self-preservation. It is merely the side of power, not of human ideals. And in the early days it had its separate place in society, restricted to the professionals. But when with the help of science and the perfecting of organization this power begins to grow and brings in harvests of wealth, then it crosses its boundaries with amazing rapidity. For then it goads all its neighbouring societies with greed of material prosperity, and consequent mutual jealousy, and by the fear of each other's growth into powerfulness. The time comes when it can stop no longer, for the competition grows keener, organization grows vaster, and selfishness attains supremacy. Trading upon the greed and fear of man, it occupies more and more space in society, and at last becomes its ruling force.

It is just possible that you have lost through habit consciousness that the living bonds of society are breaking up, and giving place to merely mechanical organization. But you see signs of it everywhere. It is owing to this that war has been declared between man and woman, because the natural thread is snapping which holds them together in harmony; because man is driven to professionalism, producing wealth for himself and others, continually turning the wheel of power for his own sake or for the sake of the universal officialdom, leaving woman alone to wither and to die or to fight her own battle unaided. And thus there where cooperation is natural has intruded competition. The very psychology of men and women about their mutual relation is changing and becoming the psychology of the primitive fighting elements rather than of humanity seeking its completeness through the union based upon mutual self-surrender. For the elements which have lost their living bond of reality have lost the meaning of their existence. They, like gaseous particles, forced into a too narrow space, come in continual conflict with each other till they burst the very arrangement which holds them in bondage.

Then look at those who call themselves anarchists, who resent the imposition of power, in any form whatever, upon the individual. The only reason for this is that power has become too abstract – it is a scientific product made in the political laboratory of the Nation, through the dissolution of the personal humanity.

And what is the meaning of these strikes in the economic world, which like the prickly shrubs in a barren soil shoot up with renewed vigour each time they are cut down? What, but that the wealth-producing mechanism is incessantly growing into vast stature, out of proportion to all other needs of society, – and the full reality of man is more and more crushed under its weight. This state of things inevitably gives rise to eternal feuds among the elements freed from the wholeness and wholesomeness of human ideals, and interminable economic war is waged between capital and labour. For greed of wealth and power can never have a limit, and compromise of self-interest can never attain the final spirit of reconciliation. They must go on breeding jealousy and suspicion to the end – the end which only comes through some sudden catastrophe or a spiritual rebirth.

When this organization of politics and commerce, whose other name is the Nation, becomes all powerful at the cost of the harmony of the higher social life, then it is an evil day for humanity. When a father becomes a gambler and his obligations to his family take the secondary place in his mind, then he is no longer a man, but an automaton led by the power of greed. Then he can do things which, in his normal state of mind, he would be ashamed to do. It is the same thing with society. When it allows itself to be turned into a perfect organization of power, then there are few crimes which it is unable to perpetrate. Because success is the object and justification of a machine, while goodness only is the end and purpose of man. When this engine of organization begins to attain a vast size, and those who are mechanics are made into parts of the machine, then the personal man is eliminated to a phantom, everything becomes a revolution of policy carried out by the human parts of the machine, requiring no twinge of pity or moral responsibility. It is not unusual that even through this apparatus the moral nature of man tries to assert itself, but the whole series of ropes and pulleys creak and cry, the forces of the human heart become entangled among the forces of the human automaton, and only with difficulty can the moral purpose transmit itself into some tortured shape of result.

This abstract being, the Nation, is ruling India. We have seen in our country some brand of tinned food advertised as entirely made and packed without being touched by hand. This description applies to the governing of India, which is as little touched by the human hand as possible. The governors need not know our language, need not come into personal touch with us except as officials; they can aid or hinder our aspirations from a disdainful distance, they can lead us on a certain path of policy and then pull us back again with the manipulation of office red tape; the newspapers of England, in whose columns London street accidents are recorded with some decency of pathos, need but take the scantiest notice of calamities happening in India over areas of land sometimes larger than the British Isles.

But we, who are governed, are not a mere abstraction. We, on our side, are individuals with living sensibilities. What comes to us in the shape of a mere bloodless policy may pierce into the very core of our life, may threaten the whole future of our people with a perpetual helplessness of emasculation, and yet may never touch the chord of humanity on the other side, or touch it in the most inadequately feeble manner. Such wholesale and universal acts of fearful responsibility man can never perform, with such a degree of systematic unawareness, where he is an individual human being. These only become possible where the man is represented by an octopus of abstractions, sending out its wriggling arms in all directions of space, and fixing its innumerable suckers even into the far-away future. In this reign of the nation, the governed are pursued by suspicions; and these are the suspicions of a tremendous mass of organized brain and muscle. Punishments are meted out, leaving a trail of miseries across a large bleeding tract of the human heart; but these punishments are dealt by a mere abstract force, in which a whole population of a distant country has lost its human personality.

I have not come here, however, to discuss the question as it affects my own country, but as it affects the future of all humanity. It is not about the British Government, but the government by the Nation – the Nation which is the organized self-interest of a whole people, where it is the least human and the least spiritual. Our only intimate experience of the Nation is with the British Nation, and as far as the government by the Nation goes there are reasons to believe that it is one of the best. Then again we have to consider that the West is necessary to the East. We are complementary to each other because of our different outlooks upon life which have given us different aspects of truth. Therefore if it be true that the spirit of the West has come upon our fields in the guise of a storm it is all the same scattering living seeds that are immortal. And when in India we shall be able to assimilate in our life what is permanent in Western civilization we shall be in the position to bring about a reconciliation of these two great worlds. Then will come to an end the one-sided dominance which is galling. What is more, we have to recognize that the history of India does not belong to one particular race but is of a process of creation to which various races of the world contributed – the Dravidians and the Aryans, the ancient Greeks and the Persians, the Mohamedans of the West and those of central Asia. At last now has come the turn of the English to become true to this history and bring to it the tribute of their life, and we neither have the right nor the power to exclude this people from the building of the destiny of India. Therefore what I say about the Nation has more to do with the history of Man than specially with that of India.

This history has come to a stage when the moral man, the complete man, is more and more giving way, almost without knowing it, to make room for the political and the commercial man, the man of the limited purpose. This, aided by the wonderful progress in science, is assuming gigantic proportion and power, causing the upset of man's moral balance, obscuring his human side under the shadow of soul-less organization. Its iron grip we have felt at the root of our life, and for the sake of humanity we must stand up and give warning to all, that this nationalism is a cruel epidemic of evil that is sweeping over the human world of the present age, eating into its moral vitality.

I have a deep love and a great respect for the British race as human beings. It has produced great-hearted men, thinkers of great thoughts, doers of great deeds. It has given rise to a great literature. I know that these people love justice and freedom, and hate lies. They are clean in their minds, frank in their manners, true in their friendships; in their behaviour they are honest and reliable. The personal experience which I have had of their literary men has roused my admiration not merely for their power of thought or expression but for their chivalrous humanity. We have felt the greatness of this people as we feel the sun; but as for the Nation, it is for us a thick mist of a stifling nature covering the sun itself.

This government by the Nation is neither British nor anything else; it is an applied science and therefore more or less similar in its principles wherever it is used. It is like a hydraulic press, whose pressure is impersonal and on that account completely effective. The amount of its power may vary in different engines. Some may even be driven by hand, thus leaving a margin of comfortable looseness in their tension, but in spirit and in method their differences are small. Our government might have been Dutch, or French, or Portuguese, and its essential features would have remained much the same as they are now. Only perhaps, in some cases, the organization might not have been so densely perfect, and, therefore, some shreds of the human might still have been clinging to the wreck, allowing us to deal with something which resembles our own throbbing heart.

Before the Nation came to rule over us we had other governments which were foreign, and these, like all governments, had some element of the machine in them. But the difference between them and the government by the Nation is like the difference between the hand loom and the power loom. In the products of the hand loom the magic of man's living fingers finds its expression, and its hum harmonizes with the music of life. But the power loom is relentlessly lifeless and accurate and monotonous in its production.

We must admit that during the personal government of the former days there have been instances of tyranny, injustice and extortion. They caused sufferings and unrest from which we are glad to be rescued. The protection of law is not only a boon, but it is a valuable lesson to us. It is teaching us the discipline which is necessary for the stability of civilization and continuity of progress. We are realizing through it that there is a universal standard of justice to which all men irrespective of their caste and colour have their equal claim.

This reign of law in our present Government in India has established order in this vast land inhabited by peoples different in their races and customs. It has made it possible for these peoples to come in closer touch with one another and cultivate a communion of aspiration.

But this desire for a common bond of comradeship among the different races of India has been the work of the spirit of the West, not that of the Nation of the West. Wherever in Asia the people have received the true lesson of the West it is in spite of the Western Nation. Only because Japan had been able to resist the dominance of this Western Nation could she acquire the benefit of the Western Civilization in fullest measure. Though China has been poisoned at the very spring of her moral and physical life by this Nation, her struggle to receive the best lessons of the West may yet be successful if not hindered by the Nation. It was only the other day that Persia woke up from her age-long sleep at the call of the West to be instantly trampled into stillness by the Nation. The same phenomenon prevails in this country also, where the people are hospitable but the nation has proved itself to be otherwise, making an Eastern guest feel humiliated to stand before you as a member of the humanity of his own motherland.

In India we are suffering from this conflict between the spirit of the West and the Nation of the West. The benefit of the Western civilization is doled out to us in a miserly measure by the Nation trying to regulate the degree of nutrition as near the zero point of vitality as possible. The portion of education allotted to us is so raggedly insufficient that it ought to outrage the sense of decency of a Western humanity. We have seen in these countries how the people are encouraged and trained and given every facility to fit themselves for the great movements of commerce and industry spreading over the world, while in India the only assistance we get is merely to be jeered at by the Nation for lagging behind. While depriving us of our opportunities and reducing our education to a minimum required for conducting a foreign government, this Nation pacifies its conscience by calling us names, by sedulously giving currency to the arrogant cynicism that the East is east and the West is west and never the twain shall meet. If we must believe our schoolmaster in his taunt that after nearly two centuries of his tutelage, India not only remains unfit for self-government but unable to display originality in her intellectual attainments, must we ascribe it to something in the nature of Western culture and our inherent incapacity to receive it or to the judicious niggardliness of the Nation that has taken upon itself the white man's burden of civilizing the East? That Japanese people have some qualities which we lack we may admit, but that our intellect is naturally unproductive compared to theirs we cannot accept even from them whom it is dangerous for us to contradict.

The truth is that the spirit of conflict and conquest is at the origin and in the centre of the Western nationalism; its basis is not social cooperation. It has evolved a perfect organization of power but not spiritual idealism. It is like the pack of predatory creatures that must have its victims. With all its heart it cannot bear to see its hunting grounds converted into cultivated fields. In fact, these nations are fighting among themselves for the extension of their victims and their reserve forests. Therefore the Western Nation acts like a dam to check the free flow of the Western civilization into the country of the No-Nation. Because this civilization is the civilization of power, therefore it is exclusive, it is naturally unwilling to open its sources of power to those whom it has selected for its purposes of exploitation.

But all the same moral law is the law of humanity, and the exclusive civilization which thrives upon others who are barred from its benefit carries its own death sentence in its moral limitations. The slavery that it gives rise to unconsciously drains its own love of freedom dry. The helplessness with which it weighs down its world of victims exerts its force of gravitation every moment upon the power that creates it. And the greater part of the world which is being denuded of its self-sustaining life by the Nation will one day become the most terrible of all its burdens ready to drag it down into the bottom of destruction. Whenever Power removes all checks from its path to make its career easy, it triumphantly rides into its ultimate crash of death. Its moral brake becomes slacker every day without its knowing it, and its slippery path of ease becomes its path of doom.

Of all things in Western civilization, those which this Western Nation has given us in a most generous measure are law and order. While the small feeding bottle of our education is nearly dry, and sanitation sucks its own thumb in despair, the military organization, the magisterial offices, the police, the Criminal Investigation Department, the secret spy system, attain to an abnormal girth in their waists, occupying every inch of our country. This is to maintain order. But is not this order merely a negative good? Is it not for giving people's life greater opportunities for the freedom of development? Its perfection is the perfection of an egg-shell whose true value lies in the security it affords to the chick and its nourishment and not in the convenience it offers to the person at the breakfast table. Mere administration is unproductive, it is not creative, not being a living thing. It is a steam-roller, formidable in its weight and power, having its uses, but it does not help the soil to become fertile. When after its enormous toil it comes to offer us its boon of peace we can but murmur under our breath that 'peace is good but not more so than life which is God's own great boon'.

On the other hand, our former governments were woefully lacking in many of the advantages of the modern government. But because those were not the governments by the Nation, their texture was loosely woven, leaving big gaps through which our own life sent its threads and imposed its designs. I am quite sure in those days we had things that were extremely distasteful to us. But we know that when we walk barefooted upon a ground strewn with gravel, gradually our feet come to adjust themselves to the caprices of the inhospitable earth; while if the tiniest particle of a gravel finds its lodgement inside our shoes we can never forget and forgive its intrusion. And these shoes are the government by the Nation, – it is tight, it regulates our steps with a closed-up system, within which our feet have only the slightest liberty to make their own adjustments. Therefore, when you produce your statistics to compare the number of gravels which our feet had to encounter in former days with the paucity in the present régime, they hardly touch the real points. It is not the numerousness of the outside obstacles but the comparative powerlessness of the individual to cope with them. This narrowness of freedom is an evil which is more radical not because of its quantity but because of its nature. And we cannot but acknowledge this paradox, that while the spirit of the West marches under its banner of freedom, the Nation of the West forges its iron chains of organization which are the most relentless and unbreakable that have ever been manufactured in the whole history of man.

When the humanity of India was not under the government of the Organization, the elasticity of change was great enough to encourage men of power and spirit to feel that they had their destinies in their own hands. The hope of the unexpected was never absent, and a freer play of imagination, both on the part of the governor and the governed, had its effect in the making of history. We were not confronted with a future which was a dead white wall of granite blocks eternally guarding against the expression and extension of our own powers, the hopelessness of which lies in the reason that these powers are becoming atrophied at their very roots by the scientific process of paralysis. For every single individual in the country of the no-nation is completely in the grip of a whole nation, – whose tireless vigilance, being the vigilance of a machine, has not the human power to overlook or to discriminate. At the least pressing of its button the monster organization becomes all eyes, whose ugly stare of inquisitiveness cannot be avoided by a single person amongst the immense multitude of the ruled. At the least turn of its screw, by the fraction of an inch, the grip is tightened to the point of suffocation around every man, woman and child of a vast population, for whom no escape is imaginable in their own country, or even in any country outside their own.

It is the continual and stupendous dead pressure of this unhuman upon the living human under which the modern world is groaning. Not merely the subject races, but you who live under the delusion that you are free, are every day sacrificing your freedom and humanity to this fetish of nationalism, living in the dense poisonous atmosphere of world-wide suspicion and greed and panic.

I have seen in Japan the voluntary submission of the whole people to the trimming of their minds and clipping of their freedom by their government, which through various educational agencies regulates their thoughts, manufactures their feelings, becomes suspiciously watchful when they show signs of inclining toward the spiritual, leading them through a narrow path not toward what is true but what is necessary for the complete welding of them into one uniform mass according to its own recipe. The people accept this all-pervading mental slavery with cheerfulness and pride because of their nervous desire to turn themselves into a machine of power, called the Nation, and emulate other machines in their collective worldliness.

When questioned as to the wisdom of its course the newly converted fanatic of nationalism answers that 'so long as nations are rampant in this world we have not the option freely to develop our higher humanity. We must utilize every faculty that we possess to resist the evil by assuming it ourselves in the fullest degree. For the only brotherhood possible in the modern world is the brotherhood of hooliganism.' The recognition of the fraternal bond of love between Japan and Russia, which has lately been celebrated with an immense display of rejoicing in Japan, was not owing to any sudden recrudescence of the spirit of Christianity or of Buddhism, – but it was a bond established according to the modern faith in a surer relationship of mutual menace of bloodshedding. Yes, one cannot but acknowledge that these facts are the facts of the world of the Nation, and the only moral of it is that all the peoples of the earth should strain their physical, moral and intellectual resources to the utmost to defeat one another in the wrestling match of powerfulness. In the ancient days Sparta paid all her attention to becoming powerful – and she did become so by crippling her humanity, and she died of the amputation.

But it is no consolation to us to know that the weakening of humanity from which the present age is suffering is not limited to the subject races, and that its ravages are even more radical because insidious and voluntary in peoples who are hypnotized into believing that they are free. This bartering of your higher aspirations of life for profit and power has been your own free choice, and I leave you there, at the wreckage of your soul, contemplating your protuberant prosperity. But will you never be called to answer for organizing the instincts of self-aggrandizement of whole peoples into perfection, and calling it good? I ask you what disaster has there ever been in the history of man, in its darkest period, like this terrible disaster of the Nation fixing its fangs deep into the naked flesh of the world, taking permanent precautions against its natural relaxation?

You, the people of the West, who have manufactured this abnormality, can you imagine the desolating despair of this haunted world of suffering man possessed by the ghastly abstraction of the organizing man? Can you put yourself into the position of the peoples, who seem to have been doomed to an eternal damnation of their own humanity, who not only must suffer continual curtailment of their manhood, but even raise their voices in paeans of praise for the benignity of a mechanical apparatus in its interminable parody of providence?

Have you not seen, since the commencement of the existence of the Nation, that the dread of it has been the one goblin-dread with which the whole world has been trembling? Wherever there is a dark corner, there is the suspicion of its secret malevolence; and people live in a perpetual distrust of its back where it has no eyes. Every sound of footstep, every rustle of movement in the neighbourhood, sends a thrill of terror all around. And this terror is the parent of all that is base in man's nature. It makes one almost openly unashamed of inhumanity. Clever lies become matters of self-congratulation. Solemn pledges become a farce, – laughable for their very solemnity. The Nation, with all its paraphernalia of power and prosperity, its flags and pious hymns, its blasphemous prayers in the churches, and the literary mock thunders of its patriotic bragging, cannot hide the fact that the Nation is the greatest evil for the Nation, that all its precautions are against it, and any new birth of its fellow in the world is always followed in its mind by the dread of a new peril. Its one wish is to trade on the feebleness of the rest of the world, like some insects that are bred in the paralysed flesh of victims kept just enough alive to make them toothsome and nutritious. Therefore it is ready to send its poisonous fluid into the vitals of the other living peoples, who, not being nations, are harmless. For this the Nation has had and still has its richest pasture in Asia. Great China, rich with her ancient wisdom and social ethics, her discipline of industry and self-control, is like a whale awakening the lust of spoil in the heart of the Nation. She is already carrying in her quivering flesh harpoons sent by the unerring aim of the Nation, the creature of science and selfishness. Her pitiful attempt to shake off her traditions of humanity, her social ideals, and spend her last exhausted resources to drill herself into modern efficiency, is thwarted at every step by the Nation. It is tightening its financial ropes round her, trying to drag her up on the shore and cut her into pieces, and then go and offer public thanksgiving to God for supporting the one existing evil and shattering the possibility of a new one. And for all this the Nation has been claiming the gratitude of history, and all eternity for its exploitation; ordering its band of praise to be struck up from end to end of the world, declaring itself to be the salt of the earth, the flower of humanity, the blessing of God hurled with all his force upon the naked skulls of the world of no nations.

I know what your advice will be. You will say, form yourselves into a nation, and resist this encroachment of the Nation. But is this the true advice? that of a man to a man? Why should this be a necessity? I could well believe you, if you had said, Be more good, more just, more true in your relation to man, control your greed, make your life wholesome in its simplicity and let your consciousness of the divine in humanity be more perfect in its expression. But must you say that it is not the soul, but the machine, which is of the utmost value to ourselves, and that man's salvation depends upon his disciplining himself into a perfection of the dead rhythm of wheels and counterwheels? that machine must be pitted against machine, and nation against nation, in an endless bull-fight of politics?

You say, these machines will come into an agreement, for their mutual protection, based upon a conspiracy of fear. But will this federation of steam-boilers supply you with a soul, a soul which has her conscience and her God? What is to happen to that larger part of the world, where fear will have no hand in restraining you? Whatever safety they now enjoy, those countries of no nation, from the unbridled licence of forge and hammer and turn-screw, results from the mutual jealousy of the powers. But when, instead of being numerous separate machines, they become riveted into one organized gregariousness of gluttony, commercial and political, what remotest chance of hope will remain for those others, who have lived and suffered, have loved and worshipped, have thought deeply and worked with meekness, but whose only crime has been that they have not organized?

But, you say, 'That does not matter, the unfit must go to the wall – they shall *die*, and this is science.'

No, for the sake of your own salvation, I say, they shall *live*, and this is truth. It is extremely bold of me to say so, but I assert that man's world is a moral world, not because we blindly agree to believe it, but because it is so in truth which would be dangerous for us to ignore. And this moral nature of man cannot be divided into convenient compartments for its preservation. You cannot secure it for your home consumption with protective tariff walls, while in foreign parts making it enormously accommodating in its free trade of licence.

Has not this truth already come home to you now, when this cruel war has driven its claws into the vitals of Europe? when her hoard of wealth is bursting into smoke and her humanity is shattered into bits on her battlefields? You ask in amazement what has she done to deserve this? The answer is, that the West has been systematically petrifying her moral nature in order to lay a solid foundation for her gigantic abstractions of efficiency. She has all along been starving the life of the personal man into that of the professional.

In your medieval age in Europe, the simple and the natural man, with all his violent passions and desires, was engaged in trying to find out a reconciliation in the conflict between the flesh and the spirit. All through the turbulent career of her vigorous youth the temporal and the spiritual forces both acted strongly upon her nature, and were moulding it into completeness of moral personality. Europe owes all her greatness in humanity to that period of discipline, – the discipline of the man in his human integrity.

Then came the age of intellect, of science. We all know that intellect is impersonal. Our life is one with us, also our heart, but our mind can be detached from the personal man and then only can it freely move in its world of thoughts. Our intellect is an ascetic who wears no clothes, takes no food, knows no sleep, has no wishes, feels no love or hatred or pity for human limitations, who only reasons, unmoved through the vicissitudes of life. It burrows to the roots of things, because it has no personal concern with the thing itself. The grammarian walks straight through all poetry and goes to the root of words without obstruction. Because he is not seeking reality, but law. When he finds the law, he is able to teach people how to master words. This is a power, – the power which fulfils some special usefulness, some particular need of man.

Reality is the harmony which gives to the component parts of a thing the equilibrium of the whole. You break it, and have in your hands the nomadic atoms fighting against one another, therefore unmeaning. Those who covet power try to get mastery of these aboriginal fighting elements and through some narrow channels force them into some violent service for some particular needs of man.

This satisfaction of man's needs is a great thing. It gives him freedom in the material world. It confers on him the benefit of a greater range of time and space. He can do things in a shorter time and occupies a larger space with more thoroughness of advantage. Therefore he can easily outstrip those who live in a world of a slower time and of space less fully occupied.

This progress of power attains more and more rapidity of pace. And, for the reason that it is a detached part of man, it soon outruns the complete humanity. The moral man remains behind, because it has to deal with the whole reality, not merely with the law of things, which is impersonal and therefore abstract.

Thus, man with his mental and material power far outgrowing his moral strength, is like an exaggerated giraffe whose head has suddenly shot up miles away from the rest of him, making normal communication difficult to establish. This greedy head, with its huge dental organization, has been munching all the topmost foliage of the world, but the nourishment is too late in reaching his digestive organs, and his heart is suffering from want of blood. Of this present disharmony in man's nature the West seems to have been blissfully unconscious. The enormity of its material success has diverted all its attention toward self-congratulation on its bulk. The optimism of its logic goes on basing the calculations of its good fortune upon the indefinite prolongation of its railway lines toward eternity. It is superficial enough to think that all to-morrows are merely to-days with the repeated additions of twenty-four hours. It has no fear of the chasm, which is opening wider every day, between man's ever-growing storehouses and the emptiness of his hungry humanity. Logic does not know that, under the lowest bed of endless strata of wealth and comforts, earthquakes are being hatched to restore the balance of the moral world, and one day the gaping gulf of spiritual vacuity will draw into its bottom the store of things that have their eternal love for the dust.

Man in his fulness is not powerful, but perfect. Therefore, to turn him into mere power, you have to curtail his soul as much as possible. When we are fully human, we cannot fly at one another's throats; our instincts of social life, our traditions of moral ideals stand in the way. If you want me to take to butchering human beings, you must break up that wholeness of my humanity through some discipline which makes my will dead, my thoughts numb, my movements automatic, and then from the dissolution of the complex personal man will come out that abstraction, that destructive force, which has no relation to human truth, and therefore can be easily brutal or mechanical. Take away man from his natural surroundings, from the fulness of his communal life, with all its living associations of beauty and love and social obligations, and you will be able to turn him into so many fragments of a machine for the production of wealth on a gigantic scale. Turn a tree into a log and it will burn for you, but it will never bear living flowers and fruit.

This process of dehumanizing has been going on in commerce and politics. And out of the long birth-throes of mechanical energy has been born this fully developed apparatus of magnif-icent power and surprising appetite, which has been christened in the West as the Nation. As I have hinted before, because of its quality of abstraction it has, with the greatest ease, gone far ahead of the complete moral man. And having the conscience of a ghost and the callous perfection of an automaton, it is causing disasters of which the volcanic dissipations of the youthful moon would be ashamed to be brought into comparison. As a result, the suspicion of man for man stings all the limbs of this civilization like the hairs of the nettle. Each country is casting its net of espionage into the slimy bottom of the others, fishing for their secrets, the treacherous secrets brewing in the oozy depths of diplomacy. And what is their secret service but the nation's underground trade in kidnapping, murder and treachery and all the ugly crimes bred in the depth of rottenness? Because each nation has its own history of thieving and lies and broken faith, therefore there can only flourish international suspicion and jealousy, and international moral shame becomes anaemic to a degree of ludicrousness. The nation's bagpipe of righteous indignation has so often changed its tune according to the variation of time and to the altered groupings of the alliances of diplomacy, that it can be enjoyed with amusement as the variety performance of the political music hall.

I am just coming from my visit to Japan, where I exhorted this young nation to take its stand upon the higher ideals of humanity and never to follow the West in its acceptance of the organized selfishness of Nationalism as its religion, never to gloat upon the feebleness of its neighbours, never to be unscrupulous in its behaviour to the weak, where it can be gloriously mean with impunity, while turning its right cheek of brighter humanity for the kiss of admiration to those who have the power to deal it a blow. Some of the newspapers praised my utterances for their poetical qualities while adding with a leer that it was the poetry of a defeated people. I felt they were right. Japan had been taught in a modern school the lesson how to become powerful. The schooling is done and she must enjoy the fruits of her lessons. The West in the voice of her thundering cannon had said at the door of Japan, Let there be a Nation – and there was a Nation. And now that it *has* come into existence, why do you not feel in your heart of hearts a pure feeling of gladness and say that it is good? Why is it that I saw in an English paper an expression of bitterness at Japan's boasting of her superiority of civilization – the thing that the British, along with other nations, has been carrying on for ages without blushing? Because the idealism of selfishness must keep itself drunk with a continual dose of self-laudation. But the same vices which seem so natural and innocuous in its own life make it surprised and angry at their unpleasantness when seen in other nations. Therefore when you see the Japanese nation, created in your own image, launched in its career of national boastfulness you shake your head and say it is not good. Has it not been one of the causes that raise the cry on these shores for preparedness to meet one more power of evil with a greater power of injury? Japan protests that she has her *bushido*, that she can never be treacherous to America to whom she owes her gratitude. But you find it difficult to believe her, – for the wisdom of the Nation is not in its faith in humanity but in its complete distrust. You say to yourself that it is not with Japan of the *bushido*, the Japan of the moral ideals, that you have to deal – it is with the abstraction of the popular selfishness, it is with the Nation; and Nation can only trust Nation where their interests coalesce, or at least do not conflict. In fact your instinct tells you that the advent of another people into the arena of nationality makes another addition to the evil which contradicts all that is highest in Man and proves by its success that unscrupulousness is the way to prosperity, – and goodness is good for the weak and God is the only remaining consolation of the defeated.

Yes, this is the logic of the Nation. And it will never heed the voice of truth and goodness. It will go on in its ring-dance of moral corruption, linking steel unto steel, and machine unto machine; trampling under its tread all the sweet flowers of simple faith and the living ideals of man.

But we delude ourselves into thinking that humanity in the modern days is more to the front than ever before. The reason of this self-delusion is because man is served with the necessaries of life in greater profusion and his physical ills are being allevi-ated with more efficacy. But the chief part of this is done, not by moral sacrifice, but by intellectual power. In quantity it is great, but it springs from the surface and spreads over the surface. Knowledge and efficiency are powerful in their outward effect, but they are the servants of man, not the man himself. Their service is like the service in a hotel, where it is elaborate, but the host is absent; it is more convenient than hospitable.

Therefore we must not forget that the scientific organizations vastly spreading in all directions are strengthening our power, but not our humanity. With the growth of power the cult of the self-worship of the Nation grows in ascendency; and the individual willingly allows the nation to take donkey rides upon his back; and there happens the anomaly which must have its disastrous effects, that the individual worships with all sacrifices a god which is morally much inferior to himself. This could never have been possible if the god had been as real as the individual.

Let me give an illustration of this in point. In some parts of India it has been enjoined as an act of great piety for a widow to go without food and water on a particular day every fortnight. This often leads to cruelty, unmeaning and inhuman. And yet men are not by nature cruel to such a degree. But this piety being a mere unreal abstraction completely deadens the moral sense of the individual, just as the man who would not hurt an animal unnecessarily, would cause horrible suffering to a large number of innocent creatures when he drugs his feelings with the abstract idea of 'sport'. Because these ideas are the creations of our intellect, because they are logical classifications, therefore they can so easily hide in their mist the personal man.

And the idea of the Nation is one of the most powerful anaes-thetics that man has invented. Under the influence of its fumes the whole people can carry out its systematic programme of the most virulent self-seeking without being in the least aware of its moral perversion, – in fact feeling dangerously resentful if it is pointed out.

But can this go on indefinitely? continually producing bar-renness of moral insensibility upon a large tract of our living nature? Can it escape its nemesis forever? Has this giant power of mechanical organization no limit in this world against which it may shatter itself all the more completely because of its terrible strength and velocity? Do you believe that evil can be perma-nently kept in check by competition with evil, and that confer-ence of prudence can keep the devil chained in its makeshift cage of mutual agreement?

This European war of Nations is the war of retribution. Man, the person, must protest for his very life against the heaping up of things where there should be the heart, and systems and policies where there should flow living human relationship. The time has come when, for the sake of the whole outraged world, Europe should fully know in her own person the terrible absurdity of the thing called the Nation.

The Nation has thriven long upon mutilated humanity. Men,

the fairest creations of God, came out of the National manufactory in huge numbers as war-making and money-making puppets, ludicrously vain of their pitiful perfection of mechanism. Human society grew more and more into a marionette show of politicians, soldiers, manufacturers and bureaucrats, pulled by wire arrangements of wonderful efficiency.

But the apotheosis of selfishness can never make its interminable breed of hatred and greed, fear and hypocrisy, suspicion and tyranny, an end in themselves. These monsters grow into huge shapes but never into harmony. And this Nation may grow on to an unimaginable corpulence, not of a living body, but of steel and steam and office buildings, till its deformity can contain no longer its ugly voluminousness, – till it begins to crack and gape, breathe gas and fire in gasps, and its death-rattles sound in cannon roars. In this war, the death-throes of the Nation have commenced. Suddenly, all its mechanism going mad, it has begun the dance of the furies, shattering its own limbs, scattering them into the dust. It is the fifth act of the tragedy of the unreal.

Those who have any faith in Man cannot but fervently hope that the tyranny of the Nation will not be restored to all its former teeth and claws, to its far-reaching iron arms and its immense inner cavity, all stomach and no heart; that man will have his new birth, in the freedom of his individuality, from the enveloping vagueness of abstraction.

The veil has been raised, and in this frightful war the West has stood face to face with her own creation, to which she had offered her soul. She must know what it truly is.

She had never let herself suspect what slow decay and decomposition were secretly going on in her moral nature, which often broke out in doctrines of scepticism, but still oftener and in still more dangerously subtle manner showed itself in her unconsciousness of the mutilation and insult that she had been inflicting upon a vast part of the world. Now she must know the truth nearer home.

And then there will come from her own children those who will break themselves free from the slavery of this illusion, this perversion of brotherhood founded upon self-seeking, those who will own themselves as God's children and as no bondslaves of machinery, which turns souls into commodities and life into compartments, which, with its iron claws, scratches out the heart of the world and knows not what it has done.

And we of no nations of the world, whose heads have been bowed to the dust, will know that this dust is more sacred than the bricks which build the pride of power. For this dust is fertile of life, and of beauty and worship. We shall thank God that we were made to wait in silence through the night of despair, had to bear the insult of the proud and the strong man's burden, yet all through it, though our hearts quaked with doubt and fear, never could we blindly believe in the salvation which machinery offered to man, but we held fast to our trust in God and the truth of the human soul. And we can still cherish the hope, that, when power becomes ashamed to occupy its throne and is ready to make way for love, when the morning comes for cleansing the bloodstained steps of the Nation along the highroad of human-ity, we shall be called upon to bring our own vessel of sacred water – the water of worship – to sweeten the history of man into purity, and with its sprinkling make the trampled dust of the centuries blessed with fruitfulness.

Nationalism in India

OUR REAL PROBLEM in India is not political. It is social. This is a condition not only prevailing in India, but among all nations. I do not believe in an exclusive political interest. Politics in the West have dominated Western ideals, and we in India are trying to imitate you. We have to remember that in Europe, where peoples had their racial unity from the beginning, and where natural resources were insufficient for the inhabitants, the civilization has naturally taken the character of political and commercial aggressiveness. For on the one hand they had no internal complications, and on the other they had to deal with neighbours who were strong and rapacious. To have perfect combination among themselves and a watchful attitude of animosity against others was taken as the solution of their problems. In former days they organized and plundered, in the present age the same spirit continues – and they organize and exploit the whole world.

But from the earliest beginnings of history, India has had her own problem constantly before her – it is the race problem. Each nation must be conscious of its mission and we, in India, must realize that we cut a poor figure when we are trying to be political, simply because we have not yet been finally able to accomplish what was set before us by our providence.

This problem of race unity which we have been trying to solve for so many years has likewise to be faced by you here in America. Many people in this country ask me what is happening as to the caste distinctions in India. But when this question is asked me, it is usually done with a superior air. And I feel tempted to put the same question to our American critics with a slight modification, 'What have you done with the Red Indian and the Negro?' For you have not got over your attitude of caste toward them. You have used violent methods to keep aloof from other races, but until you have solved the question here in America, you have no right to question India.

In spite of our great difficulty, however, India has done something. She has tried to make an adjustment of races, to acknowledge the real differences between them where these exist, and yet seek for some basis of unity. This basis has come through our

saints, like Nanak, Kabir, Chaitanya and others, preaching one
God to all races of India.

In finding the solution of our problem we shall have helped
to solve the world problem as well. What India has been, the
whole world is now. The whole world is becoming one country
through scientific facility. And the moment is arriving when you
also must find a basis of unity which is not political. If India
can offer to the world her solution, it will be a contribution to
humanity. There is only one history – the history of man. All
national histories are merely chapters in the larger one. And we
are content in India to suffer for such a great cause.

Each individual has his self-love. Therefore his brute instinct
leads him to fight with others in the sole pursuit of his self-
interest. But man has also his higher instincts of sympathy and
mutual help. The people who are lacking in this higher moral
power and who therefore cannot combine in fellowship with
one another must perish or live in a state of degradation. Only
those peoples have survived and achieved civilization who have
this spirit of cooperation strong in them. So we find that from
the beginning of history men had to choose between fighting
with one another and combining, between serving their own
interest or the common interest of all.

In our early history when the geographical limits of each
country and also the facilities of communication were small, this
problem was comparatively small in dimension. It was sufficient
for men to develop their sense of unity within their area of segregation. In those days they combined among themselves and
fought against others. But it was this moral spirit of combination
which was the true basis of their greatness, and this fostered their
art, science and religion. At that early time the most important
fact that man had to take count of was the fact of the members
of one particular race of men coming in close contact with one
another. Those who truly grasped this fact through their higher
nature made their mark in history.

The most important fact of the present age is that all the different races of men have come close together. And again we are
confronted with two alternatives. The problem is whether the
different groups of peoples shall go on fighting with one another
or find out some true basis of reconciliation and mutual help;
whether it will be interminable competition or cooperation.

I have no hesitation in saying that those who are gifted with the moral power of love and vision of spiritual unity, who have the least feeling of enmity against aliens, and the sympathetic insight to place themselves in the position of others will be the fittest to take their permanent place in the age that is lying before us, and those who are constantly developing their instinct of fight and intolerance of aliens will be eliminated. For this is the problem before us, and we have to prove our humanity by solving it through the help of our higher nature. The gigantic organizations for hurting others and warding off their blows, for making money by dragging others back, will not help us. On the contrary, by their crushing weight, their enormous cost and their deadening effect upon the living humanity they will seriously impede our freedom in the larger life of a higher civilization.

During the evolution of the Nation the moral culture of brotherhood was limited by geographical boundaries, because at that time those boundaries were true. Now they have become imaginary lines of tradition divested of the qualities of real ob-stacles. So the time has come when man's moral nature must deal with this great fact with all seriousness or perish. The first impulse of this change of circumstance has been the churning up of man's baser passions of greed and cruel hatred. If this persists indefinitely and armaments go on exaggerating themselves to un-imaginable absurdities, and machines and store-houses envelop this fair earth with their dirt and smoke and ugliness, then it will end in a conflagration of suicide. Therefore man will have to exert all his power of love and clarity of vision to make another great moral adjustment which will comprehend the whole world of men and not merely the fractional groups of nationality. The call has come to every individual in the present age to prepare himself and his surroundings for this dawn of a new era when man shall discover his soul in the spiritual unity of all human beings.

If it is given at all to the West to struggle out of these tangles of the lower slopes to the spiritual summit of humanity, then I cannot but think that it is the special mission of America to fulfil this hope of God and man. You are the country of expectation, desiring something else than what is. Europe has her subtle habits of mind and her conventions. But America, as yet, has come to no conclusions. I realize how much America is untrammelled by the traditions of the past, and I can appreciate that experimen-talism is a sign of America's youth. The foundation of her glory is in the future, rather than in the past; and if one is gifted with the power of clairvoyance, one will be able to love the America that is to be.

America is destined to justify Western civilization to the East. Europe has lost faith in humanity, and has become distrustful and sickly. America, on the other hand, is not pessimistic or blasé. You know, as a people, that there is such a thing as a better and a best; and that knowledge drives you on. There are habits that are not merely passive but aggressively arrogant. They are not like mere walls but are like hedges of stinging nettles. Europe has been cultivating these hedges of habits for long years till they have grown round her dense and strong and high. The pride of her traditions has sent its roots deep into her heart. I do not wish to contend that it is unreasonable. But pride in every form breeds blindness at the end. Like all artificial stimulants its first effect is a heightening of consciousness and then with the increasing dose it muddles it and brings in exultation that is misleading. Europe has gradually grown hardened in her pride of all her outer and inner habits. She not only cannot forget that she is Western, but she takes every opportunity to hurl this fact against others to humiliate them. This is why she is growing incapable of imparting to the East what is best in herself, and of accepting in a right spirit the wisdom that the East has stored for centuries.

In America national habits and traditions have not had time to spread their clutching roots round your hearts. You have constantly felt and complained of its disadvantages when you compared your nomadic restlessness with the settled traditions of Europe – the Europe which can show her picture of greatness to the best advantage because she can fix it against the background of the Past. But in this present age of transition, when a new era of civilization is sending its trumpet call to all peoples of the world across an unlimited future, this very freedom of detachment will enable you to accept its invitation and to achieve the goal for which Europe began her journey but lost herself midway. For she was tempted out of her path by her pride of power and greed of possession.

Not merely your freedom from habits of mind in the individuals but also the freedom of your history from all unclean entanglements fits you in your career of holding the banner of civilization of the future. All the great nations of Europe have their victims in other parts of the world. This not only deadens their moral sympathy but also their intellectual sympathy, which is so necessary for the understanding of races which are different from one's own. Englishmen can never truly understand India because their minds are not disinterested with regard to that country. If you compare England with Germany or France you will find she has produced the smallest number of scholars who have studied Indian literature and philosophy with any amount of sympathetic insight or thoroughness. This attitude of apathy and contempt is natural where the relationship is abnormal and founded upon national selfishness and pride. But your history has been disinterested and that is why you have been able to help Japan in her lessons in Western civilization and that is why China can look upon you with her best confidence in this her darkest period of danger. In fact you are carrying all the responsibility of a great future because you are untrammelled by the grasping miserliness of a past. Therefore of all countries of the earth America has to be fully conscious of this future, her vision must not be obscured and her faith in humanity must be strong with the strength of youth.

A parallelism exists between America and India – the parallelism of welding together into one body various races.

In my country, we have been seeking to find out something common to all races, which will prove their real unity. No nation looking for a mere political or commercial basis of unity will find such a solution sufficient. Men of thought and power will discover the spiritual unity, will realize it, and preach it.

India has never had a real sense of nationalism. Even though from childhood I had been taught that the idolatry of Nation is almost better than reverence for God and humanity, I believe I have outgrown that teaching, and it is my conviction that my countrymen will gain truly their India by fighting against that education which teaches them that a country is greater than the ideals of humanity.

The educated Indian at present is trying to absorb some lessons from history contrary to the lessons of our ancestors. The East, in fact, is attempting to take unto itself a history which is not the outcome of its own living. Japan, for example, thinks she is getting powerful through adopting Western methods, but, after she has exhausted her inheritance, only the borrowed weapons of civilization will remain to her. She will not have developed herself from within.

Europe has her past. Europe's strength therefore lies in her history. We, in India, must make up our minds that we cannot borrow other people's history, and that if we stifle our own, we are committing suicide. When you borrow things that do not belong to your life, they only serve to crush your life.

And therefore I believe that it does India no good to compete with Western civilization in its own field. But we shall be more than compensated if, in spite of the insults heaped upon us, we follow our own destiny.

There are lessons which impart information or train our minds for intellectual pursuits. These are simple and can be acquired and used with advantage. But there are others which affect our deeper nature and change our direction of life. Before we accept them and pay their value by selling our own inheritance, we must pause and think deeply. In man's history there come ages of fireworks which dazzle us by their force and movement. They laugh not only at our modest household lamps but also at the eternal stars. But let us not for that provocation be precipitate in our desire to dismiss our lamps. Let us patiently bear our present insult and realize that these fireworks have splendour but not permanence, because of the extreme explosiveness which is the cause of their power, and also of their exhaustion. They are spending a fatal quantity of energy and substance compared to their gain and production.

Anyhow our ideals have been evolved through our own history and even if we wished we could only make poor fireworks of them, because their materials are different from yours, as is also their moral purpose. If we cherish the desire of paying our all for buying a political nationality it will be as absurd as if Switzerland had staked her existence in her ambition to build up a navy powerful enough to compete with that of England. The mistake that we make is in thinking that man's channel of greatness is only one – the one which has made itself painfully evident for the time being by its depth of insolence.

We must know for certain that there is a future before us and that future is waiting for those who are rich in moral ideals and not in mere things. And it is the privilege of man to work for fruits that are beyond his immediate reach, and to adjust his life not in slavish conformity to the examples of some present success or even to his own prudent past, limited in its aspiration, but to an infinite future bearing in its heart the ideals of our highest expectations.

We must, however, know it is providential that the West has come to India. Yet, some one must show the East to the West, and convince the West that the East has her contribution to make in the history of civilization. India is no beggar of the West. And yet even though the West may think she is, I am not for thrusting off Western civilization and becoming segregated in our independence. Let us have a deep association. If Providence wants England to be the channel of that communication, of that deeper association, I am willing to accept it with all humility. I have great faith in human nature, and I think the West will find its true mission. I speak bitterly of Western civilization when I am conscious that it is betraying its trust and thwarting its own purpose. The West must not make herself a curse to the world by using her power for her own selfish needs, but by teaching the ignorant and helping the weak, by saving herself from the worst danger that the strong is liable to incur by making the feeble to acquire power enough to resist her intrusion. And also she must not make her materialism to be the final thing, but must realize that she is doing a service in freeing the spiritual being from the tyranny of matter.

I am not against one nation in particular, but against the general idea of all nations. What is the Nation?

It is the aspect of a whole people as an organized power. This organization incessantly keeps up the insistence of the population on becoming strong and efficient. But this strenuous effort after strength and efficiency drains man's energy from his higher nature where he is self-sacrificing and creative. For thereby man's power of sacrifice is diverted from his ultimate object, which is moral, to the maintenance of this organization, which is mechanical. Yet in this he feels all the satisfaction of moral exaltation and therefore becomes supremely dangerous to humanity. He feels relieved of the urging of his conscience when he can transfer his responsibility to this machine which is the creation of his intellect and not of his complete moral personality. By this device the people which loves freedom perpetuates slavery in a large portion of the world with the comfortable feeling of pride of having done its duty; men who are naturally just can be cruelly unjust both in their act and their thought, accompanied by a feeling that they are helping the world in receiving its deserts;

men who are honest can blindly go on robbing others of their human rights for self-aggrandizement, all the while abusing the deprived for not deserving better treatment. We have seen in our everyday life even small organizations of business and profession produce callousness of feeling in men who are not naturally bad, and we can well imagine what a moral havoc it is causing in a world where whole peoples are furiously organizing themselves for gaining wealth and power.

Nationalism is a great menace. It is the particular thing which for years has been at the bottom of India's troubles. And inasmuch as we have been ruled and dominated by a nation that is strictly political in its attitude, we have tried to develop within ourselves, despite our inheritance from the past, a belief in our eventual political destiny.

There are different parties in India, with different ideals. Some are struggling for political independence. Others think that the time has not arrived for that, and yet believe that India should have the rights that the English colonies have. They wish to gain autonomy as far as possible.

In the beginning of our history of political agitation in India there was not that conflict between parties which there is to-day. In that time there was a party known as the Indian Congress; it had no real programme. They had a few grievances for redress by the authorities. They wanted larger representation in the Council House, and more freedom in the Municipal government. They wanted scraps of things, but they had no constructive ideal. Therefore I was lacking in enthusiasm for their methods. It was my conviction that what India most needed was constructive work coming from within herself. In this work we must take all risks and go on doing our duties which by right are ours, though in the teeth of persecution; winning moral victory at every step, by our failure, and suffering. We must show those who are over us that we have the strength of moral power in ourselves, the power to suffer for truth. Where we have nothing to show, we only have to beg. It would be mischievous if the gifts we wish for were granted to us *right* now, and I have told my countrymen, time and time again, to combine for the work of creating opportunities to give vent to our spirit of self-sacrifice, and not for the purpose of begging.

The party, however, lost power because the people soon came to realize how futile was the half policy adopted by them.

The party split, and there arrived the Extremists, who advocated independence of action, and discarded the begging method, – the easiest method of relieving one's mind from his responsibility towards his country. Their ideals were based on Western history. They had no sympathy with the special problems of India. They did not recognize the patent fact that there were causes in our social organization which made the Indian incapable of coping with the alien. What would we do if, for any reason, England was driven away? We should simply be victims for other nations. The same social weaknesses would prevail. The thing we, in India, have to think of is this – to remove those social customs and ideals which have generated a want of self-respect and a complete dependence on those above us, – a state of affairs which has been brought about entirely by the domination in India of the caste system, and the blind and lazy habit of relying upon the authority of traditions that are incongruous anachronisms in the present age.

Once again I draw your attention to the difficulties India has had to encounter and her struggle to overcome them. Her problem was the problem of the world in miniature. India is too vast in its area and too diverse in its races. It is many countries packed in one geographical receptacle. It is just the opposite of what Europe truly is, namely one country made into many. Thus Europe in its culture and growth has had the advantage of the strength of the many, as well as the strength of the one. India, on the contrary, being naturally many, yet adventitiously one has all along suffered from the looseness of its diversity and the feebleness of its unity. A true unity is like a round globe, it rolls on, carrying its burden easily; but diversity is a many-cornered thing which has to be dragged and pushed with all force. Be it said to the credit of India that this diversity was not her own creation; she has had to accept it as a fact from the beginning of her history. In America and Australia, Europe has simplified her problem by almost exterminating the original population. Even in the present age this spirit of extermination is making itself manifest, by inhospitably shutting out aliens, through those who themselves were aliens in the lands they now occupy. But India tolerated difference of races from the first, and that spirit of toleration has acted all through her history.

Her caste system is the outcome of this spirit of toleration. For India has all along been trying experiments in evolving a social unity within which all the different peoples could be held together, yet fully enjoying the freedom of maintaining their own differences. The tie has been as loose as possible, yet as close as the circumstances permitted. This has produced something like a United States of a social federation, whose common name is Hinduism.

India had felt that diversity of races there must be and should be whatever may be its drawback, and you can never coerce nature into your narrow limits of convenience without paying one day very dearly for it. In this India was right; but what she failed to realize was that in human beings differences are not like the physical barriers of mountains, fixed forever – they are fluid with life's flow, they are changing their courses and their shapes and volume.

Therefore in her caste regulations India recognized differences, but not the mutability which is the law of life. In trying to avoid collisions she set up boundaries of immovable walls, thus giving to her numerous races the negative benefit of peace and order but not the positive opportunity of expansion and movement. She accepted nature where it produces diversity, but ignored it where it uses that diversity for its world-game of infinite permutations and combinations. She treated life in all truth where it is manifold, but insulted it where it is ever moving. Therefore Life departed from her social system and in its place she is worshipping with all ceremony the magnificent cage of countless compartments that she has manufactured.

The same thing happened where she tried to ward off the collisions of trade interests. She associated different trades and professions with different castes. It had the effect of allaying for good the interminable jealousy and hatred of competition – the competition which breeds cruelty and makes the atmosphere thick with lies and deception. In this also India laid all her emphasis upon the law of heredity, ignoring the law of mutation, and thus gradually reduced arts into crafts and genius into skill.

However, what Western observers fail to discern is that in her caste system India in all seriousness accepted her responsibility to solve the race problem in such a manner as to avoid all friction, and yet to afford each race freedom within its boundaries. Let us admit in this India has not achieved a full measure of success. But this you must also concede, that the West, being more favourably situated as to homogeneity of races, has never given her attention to this problem, and whenever confronted with it she has tried to make it easy by ignoring it altogether. And this is the source of her anti-Asiatic agitations for depriving the aliens of their right to earn their honest living on these shores. In most of your colonies you only admit them on condition of their accepting the menial position of hewers of wood and drawers of water. Either you shut your doors against the aliens or reduce them into slavery. And this is your solution of the problem of race-conflict. Whatever may be its merits you will have to admit that it does not spring from the higher impulses of civilization, but from the lower passions of greed and hatred. You say this is human nature – and India also thought she knew human nature when she strongly barricaded her race distinctions by the fixed barriers of social gradations. But we have found out to our cost that human nature is not what it seems, but what it is in truth; which is in its infinite possibilities. And when we in our blindness insult humanity for its ragged appearance it sheds its disguise to disclose to us that we have insulted our God. The degradation which we cast upon others in our pride or self-interest degrades our own humanity – and this is the punishment which is most terrible because we do not detect it till it is too late.

Not only in your relation with aliens but also with the different sections of your own society you have not brought harmony of reconciliation. The spirit of conflict and competition is allowed the full freedom of its reckless career. And because its genesis is the greed of wealth and power it can never come to any other end but a violent death. In India the production of commodities was brought under the law of social adjustments. Its basis was cooperation having for its object the perfect satisfaction of social needs. But in the West it is guided by the impulse of competition whose end is the gain of wealth for individuals. But the individual is like the geometrical line; it is length without breadth. It has not got the depth to be able to hold anything permanently. Therefore its greed or gain can never come to finality. In its lengthening process of growth it can cross other lines and cause entanglements, but will ever go on missing the ideal of completeness in its thinness of isolation.

In all our physical appetites we recognize a limit. We know that to exceed that limit is to exceed the limit of health. But has this lust for wealth and power no bounds beyond which is death's dominion? In these national carnivals of materialism are not the Western peoples spending most of their vital energy in merely producing things and neglecting the creation of ideals? And can a civilization ignore the law of moral health and go on in its endless process of inflation by gorging upon material things? Man in his social ideals naturally tries to regulate his appetites, subordinating them to the higher purpose of his nature. But in the economic world our appetites follow no other restrictions but those of supply and demand which can be artificially fostered, affording individuals opportunities for indulgence in an endless feast of grossness. In India our social instincts imposed restrictions upon our appetites, – maybe it went to the extreme of repression, – but in the West, the spirit of the economic organization having no moral purpose goads the people into the perpetual pursuit of wealth; – but has this no wholesome limit?

The ideals that strive to take form in social institutions have two objects. One is to regulate our passions and appetites for harmonious development of man, and the other is to help him in cultivating disinterested love for his fellow-creatures. Therefore society is the expression of moral and spiritual aspirations of man which belong to his higher nature.

Our food is creative, it builds our body; but not so wine, which stimulates. Our social ideals create the human world, but when our mind is diverted from them to greed of power then in that state of intoxication we live in a world of abnormality where our strength is not health and our liberty is not freedom. Therefore political freedom does not give us freedom when our mind is not free. An automobile does not create freedom of movement, because it is a mere machine. When I myself am free I can use the automobile for the purpose of my freedom.

We must never forget in the present day that those people who have got their political freedom are not necessarily free, they are merely powerful. The passions which are unbridled in them are creating huge organizations of slavery in the disguise of freedom. Those who have made the gain of money their highest end are unconsciously selling their life and soul to rich persons or to the combinations that represent money. Those who are enamoured of their political power and gloat over their extension of dominion over foreign races gradually surrender their own freedom and humanity to the organizations necessary for holding other peoples in slavery. In the so-called free countries the majority of the people are not free, they are driven by the minority to a goal which is not even known to them. This becomes possible only because people do not acknowledge moral and spiritual freedom as their object. They create huge eddies with their passions and they feel dizzily inebriated with the mere velocity of their whirling movement, taking that to be freedom. But the doom which is waiting to overtake them is as certain as death – for man's truth is moral truth and his emancipation is in the spiritual life.

The general opinion of the majority of the present day nationalists in India is that we have come to a final completeness in our social and spiritual ideals, the task of the constructive work of society having been done several thousand years before we were born, and that now we are free to employ all our activities in the political direction. We never dream of blaming our social inadequacy as the origin of our present helplessness, for we have accepted as the creed of our nationalism that this social system has been perfected for all time to come by our ancestors who had the superhuman vision of all eternity, and supernatural power for making infinite provision for future ages. Therefore for all our miseries and shortcomings we hold responsible the historical surprises that burst upon us from outside. This is the reason why we think that our one task is to build a political miracle of freedom upon the quicksand of social slavery. In fact we want to dam up the true course of our own historical stream and only borrow power from the sources of other peoples' history.

Those of us in India who have come under the delusion that mere political freedom will make us free have accepted their lessons from the West as the gospel truth and lost their faith in humanity. We must remember whatever weakness we cherish in our society will become the source of danger in politics. The same inertia which leads us to our idolatry of dead forms in social institutions will create in our politics prison houses with immovable walls. The narrowness of sympathy which makes it possible for us to impose upon a considerable portion of humanity the galling yoke of inferiority will assert itself in our politics in creating tyranny of injustice.

When our nationalists talk about ideals, they forget that the basis of nationalism is wanting. The very people who are upholding these ideals are themselves the most conservative in their social practice. Nationalists say, for example, look at Switzerland, where, in spite of race differences, the peoples have solidified into a nation. Yet, remember that in Switzerland the races can mingle, they can intermarry, because they are of the same blood. In India there is no common birthright. And when we talk of Western Nationality we forget that the nations there do not have that physical repulsion, one for the other, that we have between different castes. Have we an instance in the whole world where a people who are not allowed to mingle their blood shed their blood for one another except by coercion or for mercenary purposes? And can we ever hope that these moral barriers against our race amalgamation will not stand in the way of our political unity?

Then again we must give full recognition to this fact that our social restrictions are still tyrannical, so much so as to make men cowards. If a man tells me he has heterodox ideas, but that he cannot follow them because he would be socially ostracized, I excuse him for having to live a life of untruth, in order to live at all. The social habit of mind which impels us to make the life of our fellow-beings a burden to them where they differ from us even in such a thing as their choice of food is sure to persist in our political organization and result in creating engines of coercion to crush every rational difference which is the sign of life. And tyranny will only add to the inevitable lies and hypocrisy in our political life. Is the mere name of freedom so valuable that we should be willing to sacrifice for its sake our moral freedom?

The intemperance of our habits does not immediately show its effects when we are in the vigour of our youth. But it gradually consumes that vigour, and when the period of decline sets in then we have to settle accounts and pay off our debts, which leads us to insolvency. In the West you are still able to carry your head high though your humanity is suffering every moment from its dipsomania of organizing power. India also in the heyday of her youth could carry in her vital organs the dead weight of her social organizations stiffened to rigid perfection, but it has been fatal to her, and has produced a gradual paralysis of her living nature. And this is the reason why the educated community of India has become insensible of her social needs. They are taking the very immobility of our social structures as the sign of their perfection, – and because the healthy feeling of pain is dead in the limbs of our social organism they delude themselves into thinking that it needs no ministration. Therefore they think that all their energies need their only scope in the political field. It is like a man whose legs have become shrivelled and useless, trying to delude himself that these limbs have grown still because they have attained their ultimate salvation, and all that is wrong about him is the shortness of his sticks.

So much for the social and the political regeneration of India. Now we come to her industries, and I am very often asked whether there is in India any industrial regeneration since the advent of the British Government. It must be remembered that at the beginning of the British rule in India our industries were suppressed and since then we have not met with any real help or encouragement to enable us to make a stand against the monster commercial organizations of the world. The nations have decreed that we must remain purely an agricultural people, even forgetting the use of arms for all time to come. Thus India is being turned into so many predigested morsels of food ready to be swallowed at any moment by any nation which has even the most rudimentary set of teeth in its head.

India, therefore, has very little outlet for her industrial originality. I personally do not believe in the unwieldy organizations of the present day. The very fact that they are ugly shows that they are in discordance with the whole creation. The vast powers of nature do not reveal their truth in hideousness, but in beauty. Beauty is the signature which the Creator stamps upon his works when he is satisfied with them. All our products that insolently ignore the laws of perfection and are unashamed in their display of ungainliness bear the perpetual weight of God's displeasure. So far as your commerce lacks the dignity of grace it is untrue. Beauty and her twin brother Truth require leisure, and self-control for their growth. But the greed of gain has no time or limit to its capaciousness. Its one object is to produce and consume. It has neither pity for beautiful nature, nor for living human beings. It is ruthlessly ready without a moment's hesitation to crush beauty and life out of them, moulding them into money. It is this ugly vulgarity of commerce which brought upon it the censure of contempt in our earlier days when men had leisure to have an unclouded vision of perfection in humanity. Men in those times were rightly ashamed of the instinct of mere money-making. But in this scientific age money, by its very abnormal bulk, has won its throne. And when from its eminence of piled-up things it insults the higher instincts of man, banishing beauty and noble sentiments from its surroundings, we submit. For we in our meanness have accepted bribes from its hands and our imagination has grovelled in the dust before its immensity of flesh.

But its unwieldiness itself and its endless complexities are its true signs of failure. The swimmer who is an expert does not exhibit his muscular force by violent movements, but exhibits some power which is invisible and which shows itself in perfect grace and reposefulness. The true distinction of man from animals is in his power and worth which are inner and invisible. But the present-day commercial civilization of man is not only taking too much time and space but killing time and space. Its movements are violent, its noise is discordantly loud. It is carrying its own damnation because it is trampling into distortion the humanity upon which it stands. It is strenuously turning out money at the cost of happiness. Man is reducing himself to his minimum, in order to be able to make amplest room for his organizations. He is deriding his human sentiments into shame because they are apt to stand in the way of his machines.

In our mythology we have the legend that the man who performs penances for attaining immortality has to meet with temptations sent by Indra, the Lord of the Immortals. If he is lured by them he is lost. The West has been striving for centuries after its goal of immortality. Indra has sent her the temptation to try her. It is the gorgeous temptation of wealth. She has accepted it and her civilization of humanity has lost its path in the wilderness of machinery.

This commercialism with its barbarity of ugly decorations is a terrible menace to all humanity. Because it is setting up the ideal of power over that of perfection. It is making the cult of self-seeking exult in its naked shamelessness. Our nerves are more delicate than our muscles. Things that are the most precious in us are helpless as babes when we take away from them the careful protection which they claim from us for their very preciousness. Therefore when the callous rudeness of power runs amuck in the broad-way of humanity it scares away by its grossness the ideals which we have cherished with the martyrdom of centuries.

The temptation which is fatal for the strong is still more so for the weak. And I do not welcome it in our Indian life even though it be sent by the Lord of the Immortals. Let our life be simple in its outer aspect and rich in its inner gain. Let our civilization take its firm stand upon its basis of social cooperation and not upon that of economic exploitation and conflict. How to do it in the teeth of the drainage of our life-blood by the economic dragons is the task set before the thinkers of all oriental nations who have faith in the human soul. It is a sign of laziness and impotency to accept conditions imposed upon us by others who have other ideals than ours. We should actively try to adapt the world powers to guide our history to its own perfect end.

From the above you will know that I am not an economist. I am willing to acknowledge that there is a law of demand and supply and an infatuation of man for more things than are good for him. And yet I will persist in believing that there is such a thing as the harmony of completeness in humanity, where poverty does not take away his riches, where defeat may lead him to victory, death to immortality, and in the compensation of Eternal Justice those who are the last may yet have their insult transmuted into a golden triumph.

Construction versus Creation

CONSTRUCTION IS FOR a purpose, it expresses our wants; but creation is for itself, it expresses our very being. We make a vessel because water has to be fetched. It must answer the question why. But when we take infinite trouble to give it a beautiful form, no reason has to be assigned. It is something which is ultimate; it is for the realization of our own spirit which is free, which is glad. If, in the works of our life, needs make themselves too domineering, purposes too obtrusive, if something of our complete humanity is not expressed at the same time, then these works become ugly and unspiritual.

In love, in goodness, man himself is revealed; these express no want in him; they show the fulness of his nature which flows out of himself and therefore they are purely creative. They are ultimate – therefore, in our judgement of man's civilization, they give us the true criterion of perfection.

Creation is the revelation of truth through the rhythm of forms. It has a dualism consisting of the expression and the material. Of these two wedded companions the material must keep in the background and continually offer itself as a sacrifice to its absolute loyalty to the expression. And this is true of all things, whether in our individual life or in our society.

When the material makes itself too aggressive and furiously multiplies itself into unmeaning voluminousness, then the harmony of creation is disturbed and truth is obscured. If the lamp takes a perverse pride in displaying its oil, then the light remains unrevealed. The material must know that it has no idea of completeness in itself, that it must not hold out temptations to decoy men under its destination away from their creative activities.

The laws of grammar are necessary for the construction of a poem, but the readers must not be made conscious of their constant dictatorship. In classical India we have a Sanskrit poem in which all the complex grammatical rules are deliberately illustrated. This gives continual shocks of delight to a class of readers who, even in a work of art, seek some tangible proof of power almost physical in its manifestation. This proves that by special cultivation a kind of mentality can be produced which is strangely capable of taking delight in contemplating the mere spectacle of power manipulating materials, forgetting that materials are not the truth. And these people of an athletic habit of mind encourage artists to sacrifice art to the vanity of performance, simplicity of truth to the antics of cleverness.

What is the truth of the world? Its truth is not the mass of materials, but their universal relatedness. A drop of water is not a particular assortment of elements, it is their mutuality. In fact matter, as a mass, is an abstraction to us; we know it by a betrayal of secret through science. We do not directly perceive it. We see a flower, but not matter. Matter in a laboratory has its use but no expression. This expression alone is creation; it is an end in itself. So also does our civilization find its completeness when it expresses humanity, not when it displays its power to amass materials.

I have said that the truth of this world is in its law of relatedness, that is to say, the law of keeping step together. For the world is a movement, and this movement must not be retarded in any of its parts by a break of cadence. The world of men is suffering the agony of pain, because its movements are not in harmony with one another, because the relationship of races has not yet been established in a balance of beauty and goodness. This balance cannot be maintained by external regulation. It is a dance which must have music to regulate it. This great music is lacking in the historical meeting of man which has taken place in the present age, and all its movements in their discongruity are creating complexities of pain.

We know of an instance in our own history of India when a great personality[1] struck up in his life and voice the key-note of the solemn music of man-love for all creatures. And that music crossed the sea and the mountain and the desert, and races belonging to different climes and habits and languages were drawn together, not in a clash of arms or in the conflict of exploitation but in co-operation of life, in amity and peace. This was a creation. The great rhythm of this symphony was in the very heart of the world. This rhythm is what metre is to a poem, not a mere enclosure for keeping ideas from running off in disorder, but a vitalizing force, making them indivisible in a unity of creation.

When humanity lacks this music of soul, then society

1. Gautama Buddha.

becomes a mechanical arrangement of compartments, of political and social classifications. Such a machine is a mere aping of creation, and not having unity at its heart it enforces it in its outer structure for mere convenience. In it the life that grows and feels is hurt, and either is crushed into insensibility or breaks out in constant convulsions.

The vital harmony is lacking to-day in unity of man, for the formalness of law and regulation has displaced the living ideal of personality from human affairs, and science has taken the office of religion in man's greatest creative work, his civilization.

The diversion of man's energy to the outside is producing an enormous quantity of materials which may give rise in us to the pride of power but not the joy of life. The hugeness of things is every day overawing the greatness of man, and the gap between matter and life is growing wider. For when things become too many, they refuse to be completely assimilated to life, thus becoming its most dangerous rival, as is an excessively large pile of fuel to the fire.

Expression belongs to a different plane from that of its material. Our physical body has its elaborate mechanism for its various vital needs. Yet the wholeness of our body, where it is an expression, where it is one with our personality, is absolutely different in its aspect and meaning from the muscular, vascular or nervous system, and it keeps its veil strictly drawn. The physiological mechanism as an organ of efficiency carefully exacts from its means and methods their full equivalents in results. But the body is more than this mechanism, it is divine. An exhaustive list of all its functions fails to give us its definiteness. It is a creation and not a mere construction, rising far above its purposes and composition. Creation is infinitely in excess of all measurements, it is the immaterial in matter.

In all art every display of power is vulgar, and a true artist is humble in his creation. He despises making a show of material in his work and a parade of the difficulties of its process. For the power which accumulates things and manipulates them is fundamentally different from the power which transmutes them into the perfection of a creative unity.

And God is humble in His creation. He does not keep His muscles bared, nor does He go out of His way to attract our attention to His store of things or account-book of their cost. He gives out Himself in the abundance of His nature.

It is the final object of man to prove his similarity of nature with God by his fulness of truth, by his creativeness. Whatever he does solely in obedience to natural law, goaded by hunger or other compulsions, he feels at heart to be alien to his own nature. He somehow feels a shame about their evidence in his life and tries to put a cover over it, some cover fashioned by his own creative mind.

For instance, in his necessity for eating there is no difference between man and other creatures, yet he seems unwilling fully to acknowledge this and consequently tries to hide away the hunger element from his meals till it is almost lost to sight. He takes endless care to make his food ornamental and likewise the vessel out of which he takes it. And so, with regulations and designs of his own make, he sets up an elaborate pretension that he is not busy satisfying any legitimate need of the physiological nature.

This is the process by which the unnecessary has assumed an enormously greater proportion than the necessary in our civilization. In its own turn it begets the danger of burdening us with fixed necessities of habit which have not the sanction of nature nor that of our creative freedom but get merely piled up into a refuse heap of conventionality.

It may be said that as life is a growth it cannot have a completeness of expression and, therefore, its only true expression is vigour. As intensity of passion leading to a variety of emotional experiences, and adventures of mind giving rise to a wealth of power and production, constitute what they call living, vigour of feeling and intellect is no doubt a great asset of life. But life, merely taken as a force, is elemental, it is not human. It has its use like steam and electricity, but there is no ideal of perfection in it. Those who make such life an object of their worship lose all pity for the personal man and have no compunction in sacrificing individuals to their blind infatuation for power and experiences. And I repeat it once again that life can only become an end in itself when it is a creation, just as the elements that go to the composition of a flower are fulfilled only when they are a flower.

Growth there must be in life. But growth does not mean an enlargement through additions. Things, such as masonry-structure, which have to be constructed by a gradual building up of materials, do not show their perfection until they are completed. But living things start with their wholeness from the beginning of their growth. Life is a continual process of synthesis. A child is complete in itself; it does not wait for the perfection of its lovability till it has come to the end of its childhood. The enjoyment of a song begins from the beginning of the singing and continually follows its course to the end. But the man whose sole concern is the acquisition of power or material deals with a task which is cursed with eternal incompleteness. For things find no meaning in themselves when their magnitude consists solely of accumulated bulk. They acquire truth only when they are assimilated to a living idea. This assimilation becomes impossible so long as the passion for acquisition occupies all our mind, when there is no large leisure for life force to pursue its own great work of self-creation.

There was a time when commerce was restricted to a narrow circle in society, and was meek enough to acknowledge its limitations. In spite of its usefulness men treated it with condescension, even with disrespect. This was because man tried to maintain an imperious aloofness from all exacting needs, and, while accepting their services, he refused to do homage to them. I believe and hope that in the range of all literature and art there is no single instance of a monied man being glorified for the mere sake of his money. Our Laxmi[1] is not the goddess of the cash balance in the bank: she is the symbol of that ideal plenitude which is never dissociated from goodness and beauty.

But in recent centuries has come a devastating change in our mentality with regard to the acquisition of money. We not only pursue it but bend our knees to it. For us its call has become the loudest of all voices, reaching even the sanctuaries of our temples. That it should be allowed a sufficiently large place in society there can be no question, but it becomes an outrage when it occupies those seats which are specially reserved for the immortals, by bribing us, by tampering with our moral pride, by recruiting the best strength of society on its side in a traitor's campaign against human ideals, disguising with the help of pageantry and pomp its innate insignificance.

Such a state has come to pass because, with the help of science, the possibility of profit has suddenly become immoderate. The whole of human society throughout its length and breadth

1. The Hindu goddess of abundance and fortune, wife of Vishnu.

has felt the gravitational pull of a giant planet of greed with its concentric rings of innumerable satellites. It has carried to our society a distinct deviation from its moral orbit, its mental balance being upset and its aspirations brought down to the dust. This is why never before in our history have our best instincts and endeavours been so openly flouted as a sickness of a rickety sentimentalism. And what is becoming a constant source of disaster for humanity is the incessant hypnotism of money and its secret action upon the mind. It manufactures opinions, it navigates newspapers through tortuous channels of suppression of truth and exaggeration, it pulls most of the strings of politics, it secretly maintains all kinds of slavery under all varieties of masks. In former times the intellectual and spiritual powers of this earth upheld their dignity of independence, but to-day, as in the fatal stage of disease, the influence of money has got into our brain and affected our heart.

Any impetuosity of passion that tends to overwhelm social equilibrium not only produces moral callousness but destroys our reverence for beauty. The truth of this was made evident to us when I set out from Calcutta on my voyage to Japan. The first thing that shocked me with a sense of personal injury was the sight of the ruthless intrusion of factories on both banks of the Ganges, where they are most unbecoming in their brazen-faced effrontery. The blow which it gave to me was owing to the precious memory of the days of my boyhood when the scenery of this river was the only great thing near my birthplace reminding me of the existence of a world made by God's own hands. You all know that Calcutta is an upstart town with no depth of sentiment in her face or in her manners. It may truly be said about its genesis, that in the beginning there was the spirit of the shop which uttered through its megaphone, 'Let there be the office,' and there was Calcutta. She brought with her no dowry of distinctions, no majesty of a noble or romantic origin. She never gathered round her any great historical associations, annals of brave sufferings or memory of mighty deeds done. The only thing which gave her the sacred baptism of beauty was the river, which carried the voice of the Genius of our race from an immortal past singing of its aspiration of the boundless. I was fortunate enough to be born before the smoke-belching Iron Dragon had devoured the greater part of the life on its banks; when the landing stairs descending into its water, caressed by its tide, appeared to me like the loving arms of the villages clinging to it.

I am afraid my complaint will evoke a feeling of pitying amusement in the minds of all sober people when these words reach them. To condemn the impairing of the beauty of a river bank and to overlook the substantial fact of the production of a prodigious quantity of gunny bags will sound too exquisitely unpractical to be able to cause any serious harm!

But as an instance of the contrast of the different ideal of a different age as incarnated in the form of a town, the memory of my last visit to Benares comes to my mind. What impressed me most deeply while I was there was the mother-call of the river Ganges which ever filled the atmosphere with an 'unheard melody', attracting the whole population to its bosom every hour of the day. I am proud of the fact that India has felt a most profound love for this river which nourished her civilization on its banks, guiding its course from the majestic silence of the Himalayas to the sea with its myriad voices of solitude. This feeling of love is different in a great measure from the modern sentiment of patriotism. It is not too definitely associated with a particular geography or a limited series of political events. It represents the sub-conscious memory of a whole country, of her ages of endeavour after spiritual emancipation.

But what about our gunny bags? Sentiments are fine, but gunny bags are indispensable. I admit it, and am willing to allow them a place in society (but in strictly modest moderation), if my opponent will only admit that even gunny bags should have their limits and acknowledge the full worth of man who needs leisure and space for his joy and worship. But if this concession to humanity be denied or curtailed, and if profit and production are allowed to run amuck, they play havoc with our love of beauty, of truth, of justice and with our love for our fellow-beings. That man is brave, that he is social, that he is religious, that he is the seeker of the unknown – these have some aspect of the complete in them; but that he is a manufacturer of gunny bags and other articles has not in itself any idea of an organic wholeness. Therefore utility should never forget its subordinate position in human affairs: it must not be permitted to occupy more than its legitimate place and powers in society, nor to have the liberty to desecrate the poetry of life, or to deaden our sensitiveness to ideals, bragging of our coarseness as a sign of virility and bespattering with the mud of mockery our spiritual nature. That would be like allowing a rugged boulder to sneer at and browbeat the living perfection of a flower.

We have our out-offices in the back yard of our houses. And because they disturb the unity of the idea which is our home, we keep a line of separateness between the outside help bought with money and services of kinship, between necessity and sentiment. But the home gives way to the office if the necessity becomes overwhelming. This has made our modern civilization all out-offices, to which home is an adjunct. Modern civilization has become Shudra[1] in its character.

For the name Shudra symbolizes one who is merely useful, in whom the man who is above usefulness is not recognized. The word Shudra denotes a classification which includes all named machines who have lost the decency of humanity, be their works manual or intellectual. They are like a walking stomach, or brain, and we feel, in pity, urged to call on God to make them into a man. When man adopted his ideals he did not give success a place of distinction; and even in war he held the ideal of honour above that of success. But success which is Shudra, and whose dwelling is in the office, has arrogantly come into the front. And if through its incessant touch of defilement we contract the ugly habit of deriding sentiments in favour of materials, then the slave dynasty will be confirmed for ever.

This is the root of the struggle of the present age. Man is refusing to accept for good his position as Shudra, and our civilization is feeling ashamed of the degradation imposed upon it by the lust of power and money.

In the old time when commerce was a member of the normal life of man, there ruled the spirit of Laxmi, who with her divine touch of humanity saved wealth from the unseemliness of rampant individualism, mean both in motive and method. Venice had very little that was deformed and discordant; Samarkand and Bokhara had in them the richness of human associations. We can imagine what Delhi and Agra must have been in the time to which they belonged. They manifested in their development some creatively human aspect of a great empire. Whatever might have been its character, even in their decay they still retain their

1. Servile caste whose duty is to serve the three higher castes according to the Hindu code of Manu.

magnificence which was the true product of the self-respect of man.

Then think of Calcutta, which on one side has its squalid congeries of clerks clinging to the meagre and precarious liveli-hood short of all margin for beauty and joy accorded to them in a niggardly spirit of utilitarianism, and on the other its pompously formal rows of buildings sheltering a nomadic swarm of money-mongers – with no human link between them, with no common sharing of social amenities. This is the hideousness of modern commerce – it does not stimulate men into a healthy and normal activity of production but organizes and makes use of them by mixing and mangling their minds; it is shabbily parsimonious in all that is connected with human life and extravagant in all that tends to the multiplying of market wares.

I do not for a moment mean to imply that in any particular period of their history men were free from the disturbances of their lower passions. Selfishness ever had its share in their gov-ernment and trade. Yet there was a struggle for maintaining a balance of forces in our society, and our passions with their rude strength cherished no delusions about their own rank and value, and contrived no clever devices to hoodwink our moral nature. For in those days our intellect was not so tempted to put its weight into the balance on the side of over-greed.

But now our passion for power and money has no equal in the field. It has not only science for its ally, but also other forces that have some semblance of religion, such as nation-worship and the idealizing of self-interest.

Science is producing a habit of mind which is ever weakening in us this spiritual standpoint of truth that has its foundation in our sense of a person as the ultimate and innermost reality of existence. Science has its true sphere in analysing this world as a construction just as a grammarian has his legitimate mission in analysing the syntax of a poem. But the world as a creation is not a construction; it is also more than its syntax. It is a poem, which we are apt to forget when, by exclusive attention, grammar takes complete possession of our mind.

Upon the loss of the sense of religion, the reign of the machine and of method has been firmly established. It is the simplification of man by jettisoning a great part of his treasure; spiritually speaking, he has been made a homeless tramp, getting a freedom which is negative because superficial. Its concentrated hurt had been felt by all the world in the late war. Freed from the bond of spiritual relationship as the medium of the brotherhood of man, the different sections of society are continually being resolved into their elemental character of forces. Labour is a force, and also capital; so are the Government and the people, the man and the woman. It is said that when the forces lying latent even in a handful of dust are liberated from their bond of unity, which is their bond of creation, they can lift St. Paul's Cathedral to the height of a mountain. Such disfranchised forces roving as irresponsible freebooters may be useful to us for certain purposes, but St. Paul's Cathedral is, generally speaking, better for us standing secure on its foundation than shattered into pieces and scattered in the void. To own the secret of mastering these forces is a proud fact for us, but the power of self-control and self-sacrifice within is a truer subject of exultation for mankind. The genii of the *Arabian Nights* may have their lure and fascination for us, but God is infinitely more precious for imparting to our society its spiritual power of creation. But these genii are abroad everywhere; and even after their death-dance in the late war, incantations addressed to them are secretly being muttered, and their red-robed devotees are still getting ready to play tricks upon humanity by suddenly spiriting it away to some hill-top of desolation. The thunder-clouds of revolution which are ominously gathering and flashing their angry teeth and growling, are the outcome of a long process of separation of human personality from human power, reducing man into a ghost of abstraction.

Modern science has outwardly brought all mankind close together. The situation requires the spiritual realization of some great truth of relationship to save human societies from constant conflict of interest and friction of pride. The people who are mere forces, when not organically united, must prove their humanity by some creative transfusion. This is not a mere problem of construction, and therefore does not chiefly fall within the province of science, which deals merely with discovery and invention and not with creation. The outer bonds of telegraph wires and railway lines have helped men all the more efficiently to tear one another to pieces and to rob their weaker fellow-beings of food, of freedom, and of self-respect. Must the sword continue to rule for ever and not the sceptre, and must science after her great achievement of mastering the geography of the earth remain at the head of the administration? Can she establish peace and unity in this world of diverse races? Has it not been sufficiently proved that her material law of ruthless skilfulness can only commandeer the genii of power for her agents but cannot conjure up that spirit of creation which is the love of God and man? And yet science does not show any sign of vacating her seat in favour of humanity or submit to any curtailment of her jurisdiction after her own proper work has been finished. The powerful races who have the scientific mind and method and machinery have taken upon themselves the immense responsibility of the present age. We complain not of their law and government, which are scientifically efficient, but of the desolating deadliness of their machine domination. These people in their dealings with subject races all over the world forget that science and law are not a perfect medium for human communication. They refuse to acknowledge what an ordeal it can be for human beings meekly to have to receive gifts from animated pigeon-holes or condescension from a steam-engine of the latest type. We feel the withering fierceness of the spirit of modern civilization all the more because it beats directly against our human sensibility; and it is we of the Eastern hemisphere who have the right to say that those who represent this great age of great opportunities are furiously building their doom by their renouncement of the divine ideal of personality; for the ultimate truth in man is not in his intellect or in his material wealth; it is in his imagination of sympathy, in his illumination of heart, in his activities of self-sacrifice, in his capacity for extending love far and wide across all barriers of caste and colour, in his realizing this world not as a storehouse of mechanical power but as a habitation of man's soul with its eternal music of beauty and its inner light of a divine presence.

1920

East and West

I

IT IS NOT ALWAYS a profound interest in man that carries travellers nowadays to distant lands. More often it is the facility for rapid movement. For lack of time and for the sake of convenience we generalize and crush our human facts into the packages within the steel trunks that hold our travellers' reports.

Our knowledge of our own countrymen and our feelings about them have slowly and unconsciously grown out of innumerable facts which are full of contradictions and subject to incessant change. They have the elusive mystery and fluidity of life. We cannot define to ourselves what we are as a whole, because we know too much; because our knowledge is more than knowledge. It is an immediate consciousness of personality, any evaluation of which carries some emotion, joy or sorrow, shame or exaltation. But in a foreign land we try to find our compensation for the meagreness of our data by the compactness of the generalization which our imperfect sympathy itself helps us to form. When a stranger from the West travels in the Eastern world he takes the facts that displease him and readily makes use of them for his rigid conclusions, fixed upon the unchallengeable authority of his personal experience. It is like a man who has his own boat for crossing his village stream, but, on being compelled to wade across some strange watercourse, draws angry comparisons as he goes from every patch of mud and every pebble which his feet encounter.

Our mind has faculties which are universal, but its habits are insular. There are men who become impatient and angry at the least discomfort when their habits are incommoded. In their idea of the next world they probably conjure up the ghosts of their slippers and dressing-gowns, and expect the latchkey that opens their lodging-house door on earth to fit their front door in the other world. As travellers they are a failure; for they have grown too accustomed to their mental easy-chairs, and in their intellectual nature love home comforts, which are of local make, more than the realities of life, which, like earth itself, are full of ups and downs, yet are one in their rounded completeness.

The modern age has brought the geography of the earth near

to us, but made it difficult for us to come into touch with man. We go to strange lands and observe; we do not live there. We hardly meet men: but only specimens of knowledge. We are in haste to seek for general types and overlook individuals.

When we fall into the habit of neglecting to use the understanding that comes of sympathy in our travels, our knowledge of foreign people grows insensitive, and therefore easily becomes both unjust and cruel in its character, and also selfish and contemptuous in its application. Such has, too often, been the case with regard to the meeting of Western people in our days with others for whom they do not recognize any obligation of kinship.

It has been admitted that the dealings between different races of men are not merely between individuals; that our mutual understanding is either aided, or else obstructed, by the general emanations forming the social atmosphere. These emanations are our collective ideas and collective feelings, generated according to special historical circumstances.

For instance, the caste-idea is a collective idea in India. When we approach an Indian who is under the influence of this collective idea, he is no longer a pure individual with his conscience fully awake to the judging of the value of a human being. He is more or less a passive medium for giving expression to the sentiment of a whole community.

It is evident that the caste-idea is not creative; it is merely institutional. It adjusts human beings according to some mechanical arrangement. It emphasizes the negative side of the individual – his separateness. It hurts the complete truth in man.

In the West, also, the people have a certain collective idea that obscures their humanity. Let me try to explain what I feel about it.

II

LATELY I WENT to visit some battlefields of France which had been devastated by war. The awful calm of desolation, which still bore wrinkles of pain – death-struggles stiffened into ugly ridges – brought before my mind the vision of a huge demon, which had no shape, no meaning, yet had two arms that could strike and break and tear, a gaping mouth that could devour, and bulging brains that could conspire and plan. It was a purpose, which had a living body, but no complete humanity to temper it. Because it was passion – belonging to life, and yet not having the wholeness of life – it was the most terrible of life's enemies.

Something of the same sense of oppression in a different degree, the same desolation in a different aspect, is produced in my mind when I realize the effect of the West upon Eastern life – the West which, in its relation to us, is all plan and purpose incarnate, without any superfluous humanity.

I feel the contrast very strongly in Japan. In that country the old world presents itself with some ideal of perfection, in which man has his varied opportunities of self-revelation in art, in ceremonial, in religious faith, and in customs expressing the poetry of social relationship. There one feels that deep delight of hospitality which life offers to life. And side by side, in the same soil, stands the modern world, which is stupendously big and powerful, but inhospitable. It has no simple-hearted welcome for man. It is living; yet the incompleteness of life's ideal within it cannot but hurt humanity.

The wriggling tentacles of a cold-blooded utilitarianism, with which the West has grasped all the easily yielding succulent portions of the East, are causing pain and indignation throughout the Eastern countries. The West comes to us, not with the imagination and sympathy that create and unite, but with a shock of passion – passion for power and wealth. This passion is a mere force, which has in it the principle of separation, of conflict.

I have been fortunate in coming into close touch with individual men and women of the Western countries, and have felt with them their sorrows and shared their aspirations. I have known that they seek the same God, who is my God – even those who deny Him. I feel certain that, if the great light of culture be extinct in Europe, our horizon in the East will mourn in darkness. It does not hurt my pride to acknowledge that, in the present age, Western humanity has received its mission to be the teacher of the world; that her science, through the mastery of laws of nature, is to liberate human souls from the dark dungeon of matter. For this very reason I have realized all the more strongly, on the other hand, that the dominant collective idea in the Western countries is not creative. It is ready to enslave or kill individuals, to drug a great people with soul-killing poison, darkening their whole future with the black mist of stupefaction, and emasculating entire races of men to the utmost degree of helplessness. It is wholly wanting in spiritual power to blend and harmonize; it lacks the sense of the great personality of man.

The most significant fact of modern days is this, that the West has met the East. Such a momentous meeting of humanity, in order to be fruitful, must have in its heart some great emotional idea, generous and creative. There can be no doubt that God's choice has fallen upon the knights-errant of the West for the service of the present age; arms and armour have been given to them; but have they yet realized in their hearts the single-minded loyalty to their cause which can resist all temptations of bribery from the devil? The world to-day is offered to the West. She will destroy it, if she does not use it for a great creation of man. The materials for such a creation are in the hands of science; but the creative genius is in Man's spiritual ideal.

III

WHEN I WAS young a stranger from Europe came to Bengal. He chose his lodging among the people of the country, shared with them their frugal diet, and freely offered them his service. He found employment in the houses of the rich, teaching them French and German, and the money thus earned he spent to help poor students in buying books. This meant for him hours of walking in the mid-day heat of a tropical summer; for, intent upon exercising the utmost economy, he refused to hire conveyances. He was pitiless in his exaction from himself of his resources, in money, time, and strength, to the point of privation; and all this for the sake of a people who were obscure, to whom he was not born, yet whom he dearly loved. He did not come to us with a professional mission of teaching sectarian creeds; he had not in his nature the least trace of that self-sufficiency of goodness, which humiliates by gifts the victims of its insolent benevolence. Though he did not know our language, he took every occasion to frequent our meetings and ceremonies; yet he was always afraid of intrusion, and tenderly anxious lest he might offend us by his ignorance of our customs. At last, under the continual strain of work in an alien climate and surroundings, his health broke down. He died, and was cremated at our burning-ground, according to his express desire.

The attitude of his mind, the manner of his living, the object of his life, his modesty, his unstinted self-sacrifice for a people who had not even the power to give publicity to any benefaction bestowed upon them, were so utterly unlike anything we were accustomed to associate with the Europeans in India, that it gave rise in our mind to a feeling of love bordering upon awe.

We all have a realm, a private paradise, in our mind, where dwell deathless memories of persons who brought some divine light to our life's experience, who may not be known to others, and whose names have no place in the pages of history. Let me confess to you that this man lives as one of those immortals in the paradise of my individual life.

He came from Sweden, his name was Hammargren. What was most remarkable in the event of his coming to us in Bengal was the fact that in his own country he had chanced to read some works of my great countryman, Ram Mohan Roy, and felt an immense veneration for his genius and his character. Ram Mohan Roy lived in the beginning of the last century, and it is no exaggeration when I describe him as one of the immortal personalities of modern time. This young Swede had the un-usual gift of a farsighted intellect and sympathy, which enabled him even from his distance of space and time, and in spite of racial differences, to realize the greatness of Ram Mohan Roy. It moved him so deeply that he resolved to go to the country which produced this great man, and offer her his service. He was poor, and he had to wait some time in England before he could earn his passage money to India. There he came at last, and in reckless generosity of love utterly spent himself to the last breath of his life, away from home and kindred and all the inheritances of his motherland. His stay among us was too short to produce any outward result. He failed even to achieve during his life what he had in his mind, which was to found by the help of his scanty earnings a library as a memorial to Ram Mohan Roy, and thus to leave behind him a visible symbol of his devotion. But what I prize most in this European youth, who left no record of his life behind him, is not the memory of any service of goodwill, but the precious gift of respect which he offered to a people who are fallen upon evil times, and whom it is so easy to ignore or to humiliate. For the first time in the modern days this obscure individual from Sweden brought to our country the chivalrous courtesy of the West, a greeting of human fellowship.

The coincidence came to me with a great and delightful sur-prise when the Nobel Prize was offered to me from Sweden. As a recognition of individual merit it was of great value to me, no doubt; but it was the acknowledgement of the East as a collaborator with the Western continents, in contributing its riches to the common stock of civilization, which had the chief significance for the present age. It meant joining hands in comradeship by the two great hemispheres of the human world across the sea.

IV

TO-DAY THE REAL East remains unexplored. The blindness of contempt is more hopeless than the blindness of ignorance; for contempt kills the light which ignorance merely leaves unignited. The East is waiting to be understood by the Western races, in order not only to be able to give what is true in her, but also to be confident of her own mission.

In Indian history, the meeting of the Mussulman and the Hindu produced Akbar, the object of whose dream was the unification of hearts and ideals. It had all the glowing enthusiasm of a religion, and it produced an immediate and a vast result even in his own lifetime.

But the fact still remains that the Western mind, after centuries of contact with the East, has not evolved the enthusiasm of a chivalrous ideal which can bring this age to its fulfilment. It is everywhere raising thorny hedges of exclusion and offering human sacrifices to national self-seeking. It has intensified the mutual feelings of envy among Western races themselves, as they fight over their spoils and display a carnivorous pride in their snarling rows of teeth.

We must again guard our minds from any encroaching distrust of the individuals of a nation. The active love of humanity and the spirit of martyrdom for the cause of justice and truth which I have met with in the Western countries have been a great lesson and inspiration to me. I have no doubt in my mind that the West owes its true greatness, not so much to its marvellous training of intellect, as to its spirit of service devoted to the welfare of man. Therefore I speak with a personal feeling of pain and sadness about the collective power which is guiding the helm of Western civilization. It is a passion, not an ideal. The more success it has brought to Europe, the more costly it will prove to her at last, when the accounts have to be rendered. And the signs are unmistakable, that the accounts have been called for. The time has come when Europe must know that the forcible parasitism which she has been practising upon the two large Continents of the world – the two most unwieldy whales of humanity – must be causing to her moral nature a gradual atrophy and degeneration.

As an example, let me quote the following extract from the concluding chapter of *From the Cape to Cairo*, by Messrs. Grogan and Sharp, two writers who have the power to inculcate their doctrines by precept and example. In their reference to the African they are candid, as when they say, 'We have stolen his land. Now we must steal his limbs.' These two sentences, carefully articulated, with a smack of enjoyment, have been more clearly explained in the following statement, where some sense of that decency which is the attenuated ghost of a buried conscience, prompts the writers to use the phrase 'compulsory labour' in place of the honest word 'slavery'; just as the modern politician adroitly avoids the word 'injunction' and uses the word 'mandate'. 'Compulsory labour in some form,' they say, 'is the corollary of our occupation of the country.' And they add: 'It is pathetic, but it is history,' implying thereby that moral sentiments have no serious effect in the history of human beings.

Elsewhere they write: 'Either we must give up the country commercially, or we must make the African work. And mere abuse of those who point out the impasse cannot change the facts. We must decide, and soon. Or rather the white man of South Africa will decide.' The authors also confess that they have seen too much of the world 'to have any lingering belief that Western civilization benefits native races'.

The logic is simple – the logic of egoism. But the argument is simplified by lopping off the greater part of the premise. For these writers seem to hold that the only important question for the white men of South Africa is, how indefinitely to grow fat on ostrich feathers and diamond mines, and dance jazz dances over the misery and degradation of a whole race of fellow-beings of a different colour from their own. Possibly they believe that moral laws have a special domesticated breed of comfortable concessions for the service of the people in power. Possibly they ignore the fact that commercial and political cannibalism, profitably practised upon foreign races, creeps back nearer home; that the cultivation of unwholesome appetites has its final reckoning with the stomach which has been made to serve it. For, after all, man is a spiritual being, and not a mere living money-bag jump-ing from profit to profit, and breaking the backbone of human races in its financial leapfrog.

Such, however, has been the condition of things for more than a century; and to-day, trying to read the future by the light of the European conflagration, we are asking ourselves every-where in the East: 'Is this frightfully overgrown power really great? It can bruise us from without, but can it add to our wealth of spirit? It can sign peace treaties, but can it give peace?'

It was about two thousand years ago that all-powerful Rome in one of its eastern provinces executed on a cross a simple teacher of an obscure tribe of fishermen. On that day the Roman governor felt no falling off of his appetite or sleep. On that day there was, on the one hand, the agony, the humiliation, the death; on the other, the pomp of pride and festivity in the Gov-ernor's palace.

And to-day? To whom, then, shall we bow the head?

Kasmai devaya havisha vidhema?
(To which God shall we offer oblation?)

We know of an instance in our own history of India, when a great personality, both in his life and voice, struck the keynote of the solemn music of the soul – love for all creatures. And that music crossed seas, mountains, and deserts. Races belonging to different climates, habits, and languages were drawn together, not in the clash of arms, not in the conflict of exploitation, but in harmony of life, in amity and peace. That was creation.

When we think of it, we see at once what the confusion of thought was to which the Western poet, dwelling upon the difference between East and West, referred when he said, 'Never the twain shall meet.' It is true that they are not yet showing any real sign of meeting. But the reason is because the West has not sent out its humanity to meet the man in the East, but only its machine. Therefore the poet's line has to be changed into something like this:

Man is man, machine is machine,
And never the twain shall wed.

You must know that red tape can never be a common human bond; that official sealing-wax can never provide means of mutual attachment; that it is a painful ordeal for human beings to have to receive favours from animated pigeon-holes, and condescensions from printed circulars that give notice but never speak. The presence of the Western people in the East is a human fact. If we are to gain anything from them, it must not be a mere sum-total of legal codes and systems of civil and military services. Man is a great deal more to man than that. We have our human birthright to claim direct help from the man of the West, if he has anything great to give us. It must come to us, not through mere facts in a juxtaposition, but through the spontaneous sacrifice made by those who have the gift, and therefore the responsibility.

Earnestly I ask the poet of the Western world to realize and sing to you with all the great power of music which he has, that the East and the West are ever in search of each other, and that they must meet not merely in the fulness of physical strength, but in fulness of truth; that the right hand, which wields the sword, has the need of the left, which holds the shield of safety.

The East has its seat in the vast plains watched over by the snow-peaked mountains and fertilized by rivers carrying mighty volumes of water to the sea. There, under the blaze of a tropical sun, the physical life has bedimmed the light of its vigour and lessened its claims. There man has had the repose of mind which has ever tried to set itself in harmony with the inner notes of existence. In the silence of sunrise and sunset, and on star-crowded nights, he has sat face to face with the Infinite, waiting for the revelation that opens up the heart of all that there is. He has said, in a rapture of realization:

'Hearken to me, ye children of the Immortal, who dwell in the Kingdom of Heaven. I have known, from beyond darkness, the Supreme Person, shining with the radiance of the sun.'

The man from the East, with his faith in the eternal, who in his soul had met the touch of the Supreme Person – did he never come to you in the West and speak to you of the Kingdom of Heaven? Did he not unite the East and the West in truth, in the unity of one spiritual bond between all children of the Immortal, in the realization of one great Personality in all human persons?

Yes, the East did once meet the West profoundly in the growth of her life. Such union became possible, because the East came to the West with the ideal that is creative, and not with the passion that destroys moral bonds. The mystic consciousness of the Infinite, which she brought with her, was greatly needed by the man of the West to give him his balance.

On the other hand, the East must find her own balance in Science – the magnificent gift that the West can bring to her. Truth has its nest as well as its sky. That nest is definite in structure, accurate in law of construction; and though it has to be changed and rebuilt over and over again, the need of it is never-ending and its laws are eternal. For some centuries the East has neglected the nest-building of truth. She has not been attentive to learn its secret. Trying to cross the trackless infinite, the East has relied solely upon her wings. She has spurned the earth, till, buffeted by storms, her wings are hurt and she is tired, sorely needing help. But has she then to be told that the messenger of the sky and the builder of the nest shall never meet?

A Vision of India's History

WHEN INDIVIDUAL COMMUNITIES, who come to dwell in the same neighbourhood, differ from each other in race and culture the first attempts at unity become too obviously mechanical in their classified compartments. Some system of adjustment is needed in all kinds of Society, but in order that a system should be successful it must completely submit itself to the principle of life and become the organ for the vital functions.

The history of India has been the history of the struggle between the constructive spirit of the machine, which seeks the cadence of order and conformity in social organization, and the creative spirit of man, which seeks freedom and love for its self-expression. We have to watch and see if the latter is still living in India; and also whether the former offers its service and hospitality to life, through which its system can be vitalized.

We know not who were the heroes of the day when the racial strife between Aryan and non-Aryan was at its height. The significant fact is that the names of such conquering heroes have not been sung in Indian epic. It may be that an episode of that race war in India lies enshrouded in the mythical version of King Janamejaya's ruthless serpent sacrifice – the attempted extermination of the entire Nāga race. There is, however, no special glorification of that king on this account. But he who strove to bring about the reconciliation between Aryan and non-Aryan is worshipped to this day as an Avatar.

As the leading figures of the grand movement of that age, which sought to embrace both Aryan and non-Aryan in a larger synthesis, we find the names of three Kshatriyas standing out in the story of the Rāmāyaṇa. There Janaka, Visvāmitra and Rāmachandra are not merely related by bonds of kinship or affection, but through oneness of ideal. What if it be possible that Janaka, Visvāmitra and Rāma may not have been contemporaries as a matter of historical fact? That does not take away from their nearness to one another in the plane of idea. Viewed from the standpoint of intervening space, the distance between the earth and the moon may loom large, and tend to obscure the fact of their relationship. There are many double stars in the firmament of history, whose distance from each other does not affect the truth of their brotherhood. We know, from the suggestion thrown out by the poet of Rāmāyaṇa, that Janaka, Visvāmitra and Rāma, even if actually separated by time, were nevertheless members of such a triple system.

In the history of idea, as distinguished from the history of fact, a hero often comes to mean, for his race, the *ideal*; and ceases to be an individual. In Aryan history, Janaka and Visvāmitra as well as Rāma have become historical symbols. They are composite pictures of numerous personalities having a common purpose. Just as King Arthur, from the Christendom of the Dark Ages, represents the Christian Knight, the valiant champion of the faith against all challengers, so in India we get glimpses of the Kshātra ideal gathering round its champions for a determined and pro-longed crusade against its opponents. Proofs are not wanting that often these opponents were the Brahmins.

The idea, which was behind the neo-Kshatriya movement of old, cannot be known to-day in its full meaning, but still it is possible to make out the lines along which the divergence of Brahmin and Kshatriya had occurred.

The four-headed god Brahmā represents the four Vedas with all their hymns and regulations of sacrifice. The Brahmin Bhrigu, one of the most renowned priests of the ancient days, is said to have sprung from the heart of Brahmā, thereby showing that he occupied a prominent part in the cult of Vedic ceremonialism. It is said in the Bhāgavata Purāṇa that the Kshatriya king, Kār-tavīrya, stole a sacrificial cow from Yamadagni, a priest of the same Bhrigu clan, which was the cause of the class-war led by Parasu-rāma, the son of Yamadagni, against the whole Kshatriya community. Unless the stealing of the sacrificial cow stands for an idea, such a crusade of the Brahmin against the entire Ksha-triya class misses its meaning. It really indicates that among a great body of Kshatriyas there arose a spirit of resistance against sacrificial rites, and this gave rise to a fierce conflict between the two communities.

It has to be noted that the series of battles begun by Parasu-rāma, the descendant of Bhrigu, at last came to their end with his defeat at the hands of Rāma-chandra. This Kshatriya hero, as we all know, is accepted and adored as an incarnation of Vishnu, the deity of the monotheistic sect of Bhāgavatas. It certainly means that this fight was a fight of ideals, which terminated in the triumph of the religion in which, at a later date, Rāma-chandra occupied a central place.

It is well known that Rāma had an intimate relationship with the great king Janaka, which also we consider to be a relationship of ideals. Janaka has won from the people of India the title of Rājarshi, the kingly prophet. It has been said about him in the Bhagavad-Gītā:

कर्मणैव हि संसिद्धि आस्थिता जनकादय: ।[1]

Janaka and others of his kind have attained their fulfilment through the performance of duty. This means that Janaka, and others who had the same faith as he, followed the path of moral action for attaining spiritual perfection. This was specially mentioned because it was not the path of the orthodox religion, which laid stress on ceremonials performed for the sake of averting injuries or acquiring merit or wealth. It was evidently a revolutionary movement, one of whose leaders was Janaka, and Rāma-chandra obtained his inspiration from him. Therefore when we find that it was the Kshatriya Rāma-chandra who defeated the Brahmin Parasu-rāma, we feel certain that the battle which was fought was the battle of two differing ideals.

Those institutions which are static in their nature raise their fixed walls of division. This is why, in the history of religions, priesthood has everywhere hindered the freedom of man and maintained dissensions. The moving principle of life unites. It deals with the varied, and seeks unity in order to be able to deal truly. The Brahmins, who had the static ideals of Society in their charge, spun into elaboration the different forms of ritualism and set up sectarian barriers between clans and classes. Of the two original deities of the Indo-Aryan tribe, the Sun and Fire, the latter specially represented the cult of Brahmins. Round it different forms of sacrifice gathered and grew in number, accompanied by strict rules of incantation; with it came to be intimately associated the pluralism of divinity, since fire had always been made the vehicle of oblation to numerous gods.

The Kshatriyas, on the other hand, as they sallied forth in their endeavour against all obstacles, natural and human, developed in their life the principle which was for expansion and inclusion. Born and bred amidst the clash of forces, hostile and favourable,

1. The *Bhagavad-Gītā*, 3/20.

in the field of life's strenuous conflict, the superfine complexities of the external forms of religious worship could have no special significance for them. With them the Sun-god seems to have a special connection. From him, Manu, the law giver who was a Kshatriya, and also the great kingly line of Raghu, to which belonged Rāma-chandra, are said to have sprung. This Sun-god, in course of time, developed into the personal god Vishnu, the god of the Bhāgavata sect, the god who principally belonged to the Kshatriyas.

From Brahmā's four mouths had issued the four Vedas, revealed for all time, jealously sealed against outsiders, as unchanging as the passive features of Brahmā himself rapt in meditation. This was the symbol of Brahmanism, placid and immutable, profoundly filled with the mystery of knowledge. But the four active arms of Vishnu were busy, proclaiming the sway of the Good; expanding the cycle of unity; maintaining the reign of law; supporting the spirit of beauty and plenitude. All the symbols carried by Vishnu have the different aspects of Kshatriya life for their significance.

Brahma-vidyā, the knowledge of Supreme Truth, had its origin in the seclusion of the primeval forest of India, where the human mind could intensely concentrate itself in the depth of things and the reality of spiritual existence. The world must acknowledge its debt to the contemplative Indo-Aryan for this profound vision of truth which he has revealed to man. This Brahma-vidyā in India has followed two different courses. In the one, the Supreme Soul is viewed as monistic, absolutely negating the phenomenal world; in the other as dualistic in creative imagination, yet one in essence. Unless duality is admitted there can be no worship; but, if at the same time, fundamental unity be not recognized, the worship cannot be intimate and loving.

The original gods of the Vedas were separate from man; they received worship which consisted only of external ceremony, not the homage of love. When the relationship between God and man came to be known as based on their spiritual unity, then only the worship of love became possible. That is how the mystic Brahma-vidyā brought in its train the Religion of Love, of which the god was Vishnu. There is no doubt that the religion of love had its origin, or at least its principal support, among Kshatriyas whose freedom of movement had the effect of liberating their minds from the coils of established forms of sacrifice.

That, naturally, there was a period of struggle between the cult of ritualism supported by the Brahmins, and the religion of love, is evident. The mark of the Brahmin Bhrigu's kick, which Vishnu carries on his breast, is a myth-relic of the original conflict. In the fact that Krishna, a Kshatriya, was not only at the head of the Vaishnava cult, but the object of its worship, that in his teaching, as inculcated in the Bhagavad-Gītā, there are hints of detraction against Vedic verses, we find a proof that this cult was developed by the Kshatriyas. Another proof is found in the fact that the two non-mythical human avatars of Vishnu, Krishna and Rāma-chandra, were both Kshatriyas, and the Vaishnava religion of love was spread by the teaching of the one and the life of the other.

The ideal, which was supported by the Kshatriya opponents of the priesthood, is represented by the Bhagavad-Gītā. It was spoken to the Kshatriya hero Arjuna, by the Kshatriya prophet Krishna. The doctrine of Yoga which it advocates – the doctrine of the disinterested concentration of life, with all its thoughts and deeds, in the Supreme Being – had its tradition, according to Krishna, along the line of the Rājarshis, the kingly prophets. He says:

एवं परम्पराप्राप्तमिमं राजर्षयो विदुः ।
स कालेनेह महता योगो नष्टः परन्तप ।।[1]

> This, handed on down the line, the king-sages knew. This Yoga, by great efflux of time, decayed in the world, O Parantapa.

That this religion of Yoga, as revived by Krishna and inculcated in the Bhagavad-Gītā, was not in harmony with Vedic scriptures is directly affirmed by the Master in his teaching to his disciple Arjuna when he says:

श्रुतिविप्रतिपन्ना ते यदा स्थास्यति निश्चला ।
समाधावचला बुद्धिस्तदा योगमवास्यसि ।।[2]

> When thy mind, bewildered by the scriptures, shall stand immovable in contemplation, then shalt thou attain unto Yoga.

---

1. The *Bhagavad-Gītā*, 4/2.
2. The *Bhagavad-Gītā*, 2/53.

Krishna undoubtedly takes his stand against the traditional cult of sacrificial ceremonies, which according to him distracts our minds from the unity of realization when he speaks thus:

यामिमां पुष्पितां वाचं प्रवदन्त्यविपश्चितः ।
वेदवादरताः पार्थ नान्यदस्तीतिवादिनः ॥
कामात्मानः स्वर्गपरा जन्मकर्मफलप्रदाम् ।
क्रियाविशेषबहुलां भोगैश्वर्यगतिं प्रति ॥
भोगैश्वर्यप्रसक्तानां तयापहृतचेतसाम् ।
व्यवसायात्मिका बुद्धिः समाधौ न विधीयते ॥[1]

> The flowery speech that the unwise utter, O Partha, cling-
> ing to the word of the Veda, saying there is nothing else,
> ensouled by desire and longing after heaven, the speech
> that offereth only rebirth as the ultimate fruit of action,
> that is full of recommendations to various rites for the sake
> of gaining enjoyments and sovereignty – the thoughts of
> those misled by that speech cleaving to pleasures and lord-
> ship, not being inspired with resolution, is not engaged in
> contemplation.

These words are evidently of him, who in his teachings has for his opponents the orthodox multitude, the believers in Vedic texts.

The Kurukshetra war, described in the Mahābhārata, was a war between two parties, one of which had rejected Krishna, the other consisting of his followers, guided by him in the war. The motive of this conflict, which had attracted all the great ruling powers of that age into one or other of the two opposing parties, could not have been a mere scramble for land between cousins. In this latter version of the epic the fact is suppressed that it was an unorthodox religious movement, acknowledging Krishna to be its prophet, that gave rise to the most desperate fight in the an-cient ages in India. The very fact that Krishna was the charioteer of Arjuna is proof enough that it was a war of rival creeds; and for that very reason the battle ground of Kurukshetra has ever remained a sacred spot of pilgrimage.

It is significant to note that the lives of great Brahmins of the olden times, like that of Yājñavalkya, have the association of

---

1. The *Bhagavad-Gītā*, 2/42–44.

intellectual profundity and spiritual achievement, while those of great Kshatriyas represent ethical magnanimity which has love for its guiding principle. It is also significant that the people of India, though entertaining deep veneration for the Brahmin sages, instinctively ascribe divine inspiration to the Kshatriya heroes who actively realized high moral ideals in their personalities. Parasu-rāma, the only historical personage belonging to the Brahmin caste who has been given a place in the list of avatars, has never found a seat in the hearts of the people. This shows that, according to India, the mission of divine power in this country is to bring reconciliation, through moral influence, between races that are different – never to acquire dominance over others through physical prowess and military skill.

The most important aspect of Rāma-chandra's life, which has made the Vaishnava accept him as the incarnation of divine love, has been missed by the current version of the Rāmāyaṇa. There he is depicted merely as an ideal son, brother and husband, a paragon of the domestic virtues, a king who holds that cultivation of popularity is a duty higher than doing justice in the teeth of clamorous disapprobation. I have no doubt that the real story of his life, which has become dim in the course of time and with the growth of conventionalism, is concerned with his sympathy for the despised races, his love for the lowly; and that this made him the ideal of the primitive people whose totem was Hanumān.

The religion represented by the third human avatar of Vishnu, who is Buddha, has in it the same moral quality which we find in the life and teaching of Rāma and Krishna. It clearly shows the tendency of the Kshātra ideal with its freedom and courage of intellect, and above all its heart, comprehensive in sympathy, generous in self-sacrifice.

Foreign critics are too often ready to misread the conservative spirit of India, putting it down as the trade artifice of an interested priestcraft. But they forget that there was no racial difference between Brahmin and Kshatriya. These merely represented two different natural functions of the body politic, which, though from the outside presenting the appearance of antagonism, have as a matter of fact co-operated in the evolution of Indian history. Sowing seed in one's own land and reaping the harvest for distant markets are apparently contradictory. The seed-sowers naturally cling to the soil which they cultivate, while the distributors of the harvest develop a different mentality, being always on the move. The Brahmins were the guardians of the seed of culture in ancient India and the Kshatriyas strove to put into wide use the harvest of wisdom. The principle of stability and the principle of movement, though they depend upon each other for their truth, are, in human affairs, apt to lose their balance and come into fierce conflict. Yet these conflicts, as meteorology tells us in the physical plane, have the effect of purifying the atmosphere and restoring its equilibrium. In fact, perfect balance in these opposing forces would lead to deadlock in creation. Life moves in the cadence of constant adjustment of opposites; it is a perpetual process of reconciliation of contradictions.

The divergence of ideals between the Brahmins, dwellers in the forest, and the Kshatriyas, founders of cities, often led to prolonged fights, a fact which is revealed by the story of the struggle between Vasishtha and Visvāmitra. The Brahmins were not all on one side, nor the Kshatriyas all on the other. Many Kshatriyas espoused the Brahmin cause. We are told how the Brahmanic *Vidyās* as personified in the form of three maidens outraged by Visvāmitra were sore distressed, and how the chivalrous Kshatriya King, Harischandra, came to their rescue, losing his all for their sake. Then again, Krishna in the course of his endeavour to liberate the Kshatriya victims from a dread ceremonial, slew King Jarāsandha with the help of the Pāṇḍava braves. This Jarāsandha, himself a Kshatriya, was on the other side and had defeated and imprisoned many Kshatriya kings. Krishna and the Pāṇḍavas had to disguise themselves as Brahmins in order to gain entrance within the walls of his stronghold. Many other legends bear this out. The spiritual movement started by Krishna had something in it which went against the orthodox forms of worship. This is further hinted at by the legend, belonging to a later period, of his taking the part of the Abhiras against their persecution by Indra, the king of the Vedic gods, and preventing the devastation of the pasture land, Govardhana, held by that tribe.

Anyhow, it is abundantly clear that the ideals represented by Krishna had divided the Aryan community into two rival camps. When King Yudhishthira, as overlord, summoned a Rājasūya Yagña in order to heal those dissensions, King Sisupāla tried to wreck the proceedings by publicly insulting Krishna, the acknowledgement of whose precedence over all assembled Brahmins and Kshatriyas was the object of that great conclave. The main motive behind the devastating Kurukshetra war was this very internal strife within the community – the party which op-posed Krishna being generalled by Drona, the famous Brahmin warrior, with his kinsmen Kripa and Asvatthāmā. It is a notable fact that Drona himself was a disciple of Parasu-rāma; and Karna, one of the most important fighters who stood against Krishna's party, also had Parasu-rāma for his teacher.

There can be no doubt that the period of history covered by the main incidents related in the Rāmāyaṇa, and that of the Kurukshetra war, are widely apart in time. Therefore, we have no other alternative but to admit that Parasu-rāma, who takes part in both the narratives, represents a long continued Brahmin movement, anti-Kshatriya in character; and Rāma and Krishna, who come out victorious in this conflict, have some common ideal, which also had a long period of struggle for its manifesta-tion and development.

Any number of such stories show that the two epics of India were concerned with this same social revolution, that is to say, with the conflict of the new and the old within the Aryan com-munity. We have its analogy in comparatively modern days when the Bengali epic, Kavikankan Chandi, was written. In this poem is also described the conflict of religious ideals, with the god Siva on one side and the goddess Chandī on the other. It represented the tragedy of the downfall of a higher principle of religion which had its devotees in the cultured classes, and the usurpation of its altar by the vindictive deity Chandī, patron of wild animals, who was worshipped by the aboriginal Vyādha tribes, as is described in the poem.

In the age of which the Rāmāyaṇa tells, Rāma-chandra was the champion of the new party. Rāma was born in the orthodox creed at the head of which was Vasishtha, the priest of the royal house. But from his boyhood he was won over by Visvāmitra, the implacable antagonist of Vasishtha. From this Kshatriya sage the Kshatriya prince received his initiation into a path of adventure, which evidently had behind it a mighty movement led by the great personalities of the age. It appears to me that Rāma's banishment had its cause in some conflict of ideals be-tween Vasishtha, who stood as the symbol of the Brahmanic tradition, and Visvāmitra, who had fought against it and had wrenched Rāma-chandra away from the clasp of the unwilling royal household.

When later, for sectarian reasons, the story of the great

movement was retold as the Rāmāyaṇa – a dynastic history – the absurd reason was invented about the weak old king yielding to a favourite wife, who took advantage of a vague promise which could fit itself to any demand of hers, however preposterous. This story merely reveals the later degeneracy of mind, when form assumed a greater value than spirit, and some casual words uttered in a moment of infatuation could be deemed more sacred than the truth which is based upon justice and perfect knowledge.

Janaka is considered to be an embodiment of the kingly virtues of an ideal Kshatriya. In the history of the colonization of India by the Aryans, his life must have served a great purpose. We can guess from his own position in the story of the Rāmāyaṇa that he was the principal inspiration in an enterprise which had a large meaning, and that Rāma accepted his mission of life from Janaka. If we pierce through the mist which has gathered round the original narrative, we shall see that there is a general challenge to all Kshatriyas of that time in the story of Sitā's wedding.

Sitā is said to have been no ordinary mortal. She came out of the soil itself when King Janaka was employed in ploughing, as was his wont. 'Furrow-line' is the meaning which the name 'Sitā' bears. This daughter of the soil he promised to give in marriage to him who could break the bow of Siva. Rāma was led to this trial by Visvāmitra, and he succeeded first in bending the bow and then breaking it, thereupon being declared worthy of receiving Sitā from the hand of Janaka. A great fact of history, which very probably occupied a large expanse of time and was borne along by several generations of heroes, appears to have been condensed in this story. Janaka was one of those sublime figures who could focus in himself all the significance of an epoch-making endeavour, scattered through time and space.

The fact that Janaka's personality comprehended in its inner realization the Brahma-vidyā, and in its outer activity the culti-vation of the soil, indicates that the Kshatriya kings developed the art of agriculture, on which the civilization of the Aryans of India was established. Originally the tending of flocks had been the main occupation of the Aryan tribes. This pastoral life like-wise suited the forest tracts of India, and Brahmins in their forest retreats continued to regard the cow as their principal wealth. But though tending cattle was fit for the nomad life or for that of small groups of individuals living in forests, the concentration of large bodies of men in cities required the organized production of food. Naturally, the necessity of such organization was more keenly felt by Kshatriyas, who were founders of cities, than by the others. Therefore in the life of Janaka, the ideal king of ancient India, are seen, side by side, Brahma-vidyā – the philosophy which, if truly accepted, could be the spiritual support of the unity of races – and Agriculture which could be the material support of the economic union effected by the large communities. And just as the European colonists in America, while cutting down its forests, had to contest every step with the aborigines who depended on the chase for their living, so also in India the pioneers of agriculture encountered the opposition of the non-Aryans living in its wildernesses, whose fierce onslaughts made their task far from easy.

It is interesting to note in this connection that Zarathushtra, the great spiritual master of ancient Iran, had, like Janaka himself, an ideal which combined spiritual wisdom with a faith in agricultural civilization. And it also became his mission to save agriculture from the depredation of nomadic hordes.

Let me quote from 'Zarathushtra in Gathas', translated from Dr. Geiger's book on the subject, a passage which bears strong analogy to the aspect of the old Aryan history in India as revealed by the legend of Janaka. He says:

> The Iranian people of the Gathic period were, in fact, subdivided into husbandmen and nomads, and in the sharp opposition which obtained between the two, the prophet Zarathushtra played a prominent part. In a number of Gathic passages we see him standing as an advocate of the settled husbandmen. He admonishes them not to be tired of their good work, to cultivate diligently the fields and to devote to their cattle that fostering care which they deserve. And far and wide spreads the dominion of husbandmen and the settlements of the pious people increase, in spite of all molestations, all persecutions and violence, which they have to suffer from the nomads who attack their settlements in order to desolate their son fields and to deprive them of their herds.

King Janaka reigned over Mithila, which shows that the Aryan colonies had extended along the North to the easternmost natural boundary of India. But the Vindhya hills were then inaccessible, and the forest regions to their South remained intact. Here the Dravidian culture had reached its height, proving a formidable rival to that of the Aryans, and here the puissant Rāvaṇa had established the Dravidian god, Siva, defeating Indra and other Vedic deities.

The question which then arose in the Aryan community as to who should be the champion of their civilization, proving his competency to carry his standard forward by success in the preliminary trial of the breaking of *Haradhanu*, Siva's bow, is to be read in the same light. He who could break the strong resistance of the Siva-worshippers and carry into the South the civilization which had Brahma-Vidyā for its spirit, and for its body Agriculture, would verily win, for his spouse, Janaka's earth-born daughter Sītā.

When Rāma-chandra set out under his master Visvāmitra on what became his life-mission he started, even at that early age, by emerging triumphant through three severe tests. First, he slew the foremost of the obstructive barbarians in the vicinity. Next, at his skilled touch, the desert soil which had lain for long years bound in the hardness of stone − becoming Ahalyā, not fit for ploughing − resumed the bloom of life. It was the self-same soil which Rishi Gautama, the foremost of the early Aryan pioneers who had striven to drive the plough southwards, had found treacherous and had abandoned in despair. Thirdly, to the prowess and wisdom of this disciple of the Kshatriya sage was due the subduing of the virulence of the anti-Kshatriya movement personified in the Brahmin Parasu-rāma.

Both in the Rāmāyaṇa and Mahābhārata, the wedding of the principal heroes is connected with the story of a preliminary trial. This is not a mere chance coincidence. It is the crystallization, in the memory of the race, of a great fact which had an epoch-making character. In both cases, it was the acknowledgement of a difficult ideal which involved the heroic responsibility of upholding it in the teeth of desperate opposition. In both cases the bride was not a mortal woman, but a great mission. The trial described in the Mahābhārata is the piercing of a disc in the sky, difficult to discern, fixed in the centre of a revolving wheel, which has to be reached by concentrating one's attention on its shadow reflected in a vessel of water. This trial is obviously of a spiritual nature. The fixed centre of Truth in the heart of the revolving wheel of the World (*Samsāra*) is reflected in the depth of our own being, which can be reached by the one-pointed concentration of Yoga. Is not this the doctrine of the Gītā in the language of a picture? The symbolism of the piercing of the target is well known to us, as it is used in the Upanishad:

प्रणवोधनु: शरो ह्यात्माब्रह्म तत् लक्ष्यमुच्यते ।[1]

> The bow is omkāra, – the utterance of the sound Om, which helps mental concentration, – the soul is the arrow, and the Infinite the target.

Though it was Arjuna who originally won the maiden whose name was Krishṇā, she was accepted in marriage by all the brothers. It is ridiculous to try to establish, on the strength of this fact, that the Pāṇḍava clan came from the Himalayan regions, where polyandry is tolerated. As a matter of fact, it was a sacred rite of ideal polyandry which came to be shared by all the brothers. Krishṇā is the impersonation of the truth taught by Krishna himself, which had some association with the Sun-worship which was the original meaning of Vishnu-worship. It is related in the epic that in the vessel carried by Krishṇā food would become inexhaustible when she invoked the sun to help her. This must refer to the unlimited spiritual food ready for all guests who chose to come and enjoy it.

Evidently, the Pāñchāla kingdom was one of the great centres of this unorthodox religion led by the Kshatriyas. It is to be noted that it was in Pāñchāla that the Brahmin student, Svetaketu, went to the Kshatriya King, Pravāhana Jaibāli, for instruction in the mystic philosophy consisting in the doctrine that the creative process going on in the world of stars, in sky and earth, and in man himself, is a perpetual ceremony of sacrifice, for which the sacrificial fire appears in different aspects and forms. We know the story of how the Brahmin Drona had a grudge against the King of Pāñchāla owing to the latter not recognizing the right of his Brahmin comrade to an equal share in his kingly wealth and power. It is not unlikely that in this legend lies hidden the history of the conflict between the power of the priesthood and that of the religious movement started by the Kshatriyas.

It can be surmised that it was from the province of Pāñchāla, in the close neighbourhood of Mathurā, that the Pāṇḍava brothers received the new creed preached by Krishna. It is significant that the Brahmin Drona, who originated the quarrel, was the

---

1. The *Mundakopanishad*, 2/2/36.

first general on the side of the Kurus. Krishṇā was insulted by
the Kuru brothers, as was Sītā by Rāvaṇa, and she was rescued
from her humiliation by Krishna. It was proved to those who
tried to expose her to indignities that her veil of honour was of
unlimited length, just as the food in her vessel was inexhaustible.
It was proved, in like manner, that Rāvaṇa had not the power
to defile Sītā, though, for a time, she was under his dominance,
for ideal truth is inviolable even though it may remain for a
time in obscurity. That the hero of the Rāmāyaṇa, the rescuer
of Sītā, and the hero of the Mahābhārata, the friend of Krishṇā,
both occupied the same exalted position in the later Vaishnava
religion, is not a mere accident. This fact itself gives us the clue
that the original narration in the case of both the epics had for its
motive the great fight for the ideal, which ushered in a new age
with its new outlook upon life.

It is evident that the sun, which is the one source of light
and life to us, had led the thoughts of the Indo-Aryan sages towards the monotheistic ideal of worship. The following prayer
addressed to the sun, with which the Ishopanishad is concluded,
is full of the mystic yearning of the soul:

हिरण्मयेन पात्रेण सत्यस्यापिहितं मुखम् ।
तत्त्वं पूषन्नपावृणु सत्यधर्माय दृष्टये ।। [1]

> O Sun, nourisher of the world, Truth's face lies hidden in thy
> golden vessel. Take away thy cover for his eyes, who is a
> devotee of Truth.

According to the Chāndogya Upanishad, the teacher Ghora,
after having explained to his disciple Krishna, who had become
apipāsa, free from desire, the consecration ceremony which leads
to giving oneself a new spiritual birth, and in which *austerity*,
almsgiving, harmlessness, truthfulness are one's gifts for the priests,
winds up his teaching with these words: 'In the final hour one
should take refuge in these three thoughts: *You are the Indestructible; you are the Unshaken, you are the very Essence of Life.*' On this
point there are these two Rig verses:

---

1. The *Ishopanishad*, 15.

आदित् प्रत्नस्य रेतसो
ज्योतिष्पश्यन्ति वासरम्
परो यदिध्यते दिवि ।
उदवयं तमसस्परि
ज्योतिष्पश्यन्त उत्तरम्
–स्व: पश्यन्त उत्तरम्–
देव देवत्रा सूर्यम्
अगन्म ज्योतिरुत्तममिति
      –ज्योतिरुत्तममिति । ।[1]

Proceeding from primeval seed,
The early morning light they see,
That gleameth higher than the heaven,
From out of darkness all around,
We, gazing on the higher light –
Yea, gazing on the higher light –
To Surya, god among the gods,
We have attained the highest light!
      – Yea, the highest light![2]

We find a hint here of the teaching which was developed by Krishna into a great religious movement which preached freedom from desire and absolute devotion to God, and which spiritualized the meaning of ceremonies. That this religion had some association with the sun can be inferred from the legend of Krishṇā finding an inexhaustible store of food in her vessel after her worship of the sun, and also the one about the piercing of the target of the disc by Arjuna, which very likely was the mystic disc of the sun, the golden vessel that holds Truth hidden in it, the Truth which has to be attained by piercing the cover.

It is interesting to see how in the history of religion the sun has also had a strong monotheistic suggestion in civilizations other than the Aryan. The great Egyptian King, Akhenaten, belonging to the 14th century BC, struggled against the congregated might of the priestly polytheistic ceremonials, substituting for them the purer form of worship of 'the radiant energy of the sun'. Here

1. Quoted in the *Chhāndogya Upanishad* 3/17/7 from the *Rigveda* (8/6/30 and 1/50/10) with slight changes.
2. *The Thirteen Principal Upanishads*, translated by R. E. Hume, 1921, pp. 212–13.

also we find the significant analogy of a religious revolution, initiated by one belonging to the kingly caste, against the opposition of the orthodox priestly sect of the land. This Egyptian King, like other prophets of his type, speaks of the truth coming to him as a personal revelation when he sings:

> Thou art in my heart, there is none
> Who knoweth thee excepting thy son;
> Thou causest that he should have understanding,
> In thy ways and in thy might.

'In ethics a great change also marks this age,' says Prof. Flinders Petrie. 'The motto "Living in Truth" is constantly put forward as the keynote to the king's character, and to his changes in various lines.'[1] Thus we find that History is a plagiarist that steals its own ideals over and over again.

In connection with this we have to note that the spiritual religion which Krishna preached must have ignored the exclusiveness of priestly creeds and extended its invitation to peoples of all classes, Aryans and non-Aryans alike. The legend of his intimate relationship with the shepherd tribes supports this view, and we still find the religion, of which Krishna is the centre, to be the great refuge of the lower castes and outcastes of the present Indian population. The most significant fact of Indian history is that all the human avatars of Vishnu had, by their life and teaching, broken the barriers of priestcraft by acknowledging the relation of fellowship between the privileged classes and those that were despised.

There came the day when Rāma-chandra, the Kshatriya of royal descent, embraced as his friend and comrade the lowest of the low, the untouchable *chandāla*, Guhaka – an incident in his career which to this day is cited as proof of the largeness of his soul. During the succeeding period of conservative reaction, an attempt was made to suppress this evidence of Rāma-chandra's liberality of heart in a supplemental canto of the epic, which is an evident interpolation; and in order to fit it with the later ideal, its votaries did not hesitate to insult his memory by having it in their rendering of the episode that Rāma beheaded with his own hands an ambitious Sudra for presuming to claim equal status in the attainment of spiritual excellence. It is like the ministers of

1. W. M. Flinders Petrie, *A History of Egypt*, p. 218.

the Christian religion, in the late war, taking Christ's name for justifying the massacre of men.

However that may be, India has never forgotten that Rāma-chandra was the beloved comrade of a *chandāla*; that he appeared as divine to the primitive tribes, some of whom had the totem of monkey, some that of bear. His name is remembered with reverence because he won over his antagonists as his allies and built the bridge of love between Aryan and non-Aryan.

This is the picture we see of one swing of the pendulum in the Aryan times. We shall never know India truly unless we study the manner in which she reacted to the pull of the two opposite principles, that of self-preservation represented by the Brahmin, and that of self-expansion represented by the Kshatriya.

When the first overtures towards social union were being made, it became necessary for the Aryans to come to an under-standing with the non-Aryan religion as well. In the beginning, as we have seen, there was a state of war between the followers of Siva and the worshippers of the Vedic gods. The fortune of arms favoured sometimes one side, sometimes the other. Even Krishna's valiant comrade, Arjuna, had once to acknowledge defeat at the hands of Siva of the *Kirātas*, a hunter tribe. Then there is the well-known record of a refusal to give Siva place in a great Vedic sacrifice, which led to the breaking up of the ceremony by the non-Aryans. At last, by the identification of Siva with the Vedic Rudra, an attempt had to be made to bring this constant religious antagonism to an end. And yet in the Mahābhārata we find the later story of a battle between Rudra and Vishnu, which ended in the former acknowledging the latter's superiority. Even in Krishna worship we find the same struggle, and therefore in the popular recitation of Krishna leg-ends we often hear of Brahmā's attempt at ignoring Krishna, till at last the ancestor god of the Aryans is compelled to pay homage to the later divinity of the populace. These stories reveal the per-sisting self-consciousness of the newcomers even after they had been admitted to the privileges of the old-established pantheon.

The advent of the two great Kshatriya founders of religion, Buddha and Mahāvīra, in the same eastern part of India where once Janaka had his seat, brought into being a spirit of simpli-fication. They exercised all their force against the confusing maze of religions and doctrines, which had beset the bewildered country and through which it could not find its goal. Amidst the ceremonial intricacies on the one hand, and the subtleties of metaphysical speculation on the other, the simple truth was overlooked that creeds and rites have no value in themselves; that human welfare is the one object towards which religious enthusiasm has to be directed. These two Kshatriya *sannyāsins* refused to admit that any distinctions between man and man were inherent and perpetual; according to their teaching, man could only be saved by realizing truth, and not by social conformity or non-ethical practice. It was wonderful how the triumph of these Kshatriya teachers rapidly overcame all obstacles of tradition and habit, and swept over the whole country.

Long before the full flood of the Buddhistic influence had subsided, most of the protecting walls had been broken down, and the banks of the discipline through which the forces of unification had been flowing in a regulated stream had been obliterated. In fact, in departing, Buddhism left all the numerous aboriginal diversities of India to rear their heads unchecked, because one of the two guiding forces of Indian history had been enfeebled, which with its spirit of resistance had been helping the process of assimilation.

In the midst of the Buddhistic revolution only the Brahmins were able to keep themselves intact, because the maintaining of exclusiveness had all along been their function. But the Kshatriyas had become merged into the rest of the people, and so in the succeeding age we find that most of the kings had ceased to belong to Kshatriya dynasties. Then there were the Sakas and the Hunas whose repeated hordes flowed into India and got mixed with the elder inhabitants. The Aryan civilization, thus stricken to the quick, put forth all its life force in a supreme attempt at recovery, and its first effort was directed to regaining its race consciousness, which had been overwhelmed.

During the long period of this social and religious revolution, which had the effect of rubbing out the individual features of the traditional Aryan culture, the question 'What am I?' came to the forefront. The rescue of the racial personality from beneath the prevailing chaos became the chief endeavour. Aroused by the powerful shock of a destructive opposition, it was then, for the first time, that India sought to define her individuality. When she now tried to know and name herself, she called to mind the empire of Bhārata, a legendary suzerain of by-gone days, and defining her boundaries accordingly, she called herself

Bhāratavarsha. She tried to pick up the lost threads of her earlier achievements in order to restore the fabric of her original civilization. Thus collection and compilation, not new creation, were characteristics of this age. The great sage of this epoch, Vyāsa, who is reported to have performed this function, may not have been one real person, but he was, at any rate, the personification of the spirit of the times.

The movement began with the compilation of the Vedas. Now that it had become necessary to have some common unifying agent, the Vedas, as the oldest part of Aryan lore, had to be put on a pedestal for the purpose, in order to serve as a fixed centre of reference round which the distracted community could rally.

Another task undertaken by this age was the gathering and arranging of historical material. In this process, spread over a long period of time, all the scattered myths and legends were brought together, and not only these but also the beliefs and discussions of every kind which still lingered in the racial memory. And thus a great literacy image of the Aryan India of old was formed which was called the Mahābhārata – the great Bhārata. The very name shows the awakened consciousness of the unity of the people struggling to find its expression and permanent record.

The eager effort to gather all the drifting fragments from the wreck resulted in the overloading with indiscriminate miscellanies of the central narrative of the epic. The natural desire of the artist to impart an aesthetic relevancy to the story was swamped by the exigency of the time. The most important need of the age was for an immortal epic, a majestic ship fit to cross the sea of time, to serve the purpose of carrying various materials for the building of a permanent shelter for the race mind.

Therefore, though the Mahābhārata may not be history in the modern western definition of the term, it is, nevertheless, a receptacle of the historical records which had left their impress upon the living memory of the people for ages. Had any competent person attempted to sift and sort and analyse this material into an ordered array of facts, we should have lost the changing picture of Aryan society which they present, a picture in which the lines are vivid or dim, connected or confusedly conflicting, according to the lapses of memory, changes of ideal, and variations of light and shade incident to time's perspective. Self-recording annals of history, as they are imprinted on the living tablet of ages, are bared before our sight in this great work.

The genius of that extraordinary age did not stop short at the discovery of the thread of unity on which were strung the variegated materials scattered through its history; it also searched out the unity of a spiritual philosophy running through all contradictions that are to be found in the metaphysical speculations of the Vedas. The outline presentation of this philosophy was made by the same Vyāsa, who had not only the industry to gather and piece together details, but also the power to visualize the whole in its completeness. His compilation is a creative synthesis.

One thing which remains significant is the fact that this age of compilation has insisted upon the sacredness of the Brahmins and Brahminic lore by constant reiteration in exaggerated language. It proves that there was a militant spirit fighting against odds, and that a complete loss of faith in the freedom of intellect and conscience of the people had come about. Its analogy can be found in the occasional distrust of democracy which we observe among some modern intellectuals of Europe.

The main reason for this was that, during the period of alternating ascendancy of Brahmin and Kshatriya, the resulting synthesis had its unity of Aryan character, but when during the Buddhist period not only non-Aryans but also non-Indians from outside gained free access, it became difficult to maintain organic coherence. A strong undercurrent of race-mingling and religious compromise had set in, and as the mixed races and beliefs began to make themselves felt, the Aryan forces of self-preservation struggled to put up wall beyond wall in order to prevent successive further encroachments. Only those intrusions which could not be resisted found a place within extended barriers.

Let no one imagine, however, that the non-Aryan contributions were taken in by sheer force of circumstance only, and that they had no value of their own. As a matter of fact, the old Dravidian culture was by no means to be despised, and the result of its combination with the Aryan, which formed the Hindu civilization, was that the latter acquired both richness and depth under the influence of its Dravidian component. Dravidians might not be introspective or metaphysical, but they were artists, and they could sing, design and construct. The transcendental thought of the Aryan by its marriage with the emotional and creative art of the Dravidian gave birth to an offspring which was neither fully Aryan, nor Dravidian, but Hindu.

With its Hindu civilization, India attained the gift of being able to realize in the commonplaceness of life, the infinity of the Universal. But on the other hand, by reason of the mixed strain in its blood, whenever Hinduism has failed to take its stand on the reconciliation of opposites which is of its essence, it has fallen a prey to incongruous folly and blind superstition. This is the predicament in which Hindu India has been placed by its birthright. Where the harmony between the component differences has been organically effected, there beauty has blossomed; so long as it remains wanting, there is no end to deformities. Moreover, we must remember that not only the Dravidian civilization, but things appertaining to primitive non-Aryan tribes also, found entrance into the Aryan polity; and the torment of these unassimilable intrusions has been a darkly cruel legacy left to the succeeding Hindu society.

When the non-Aryan gods found place in the Aryan pantheon, their inclusion was symbolized by the Trinity, Brahmā, Vishnu and Siva – Brahmā standing for the ancient tradition, exclusive externalism; Vishnu for the transition when the original Vedic Sun-god became humanized and emerged from the rigid enclosure of scriptural texts into the world of the living human heart; and Siva for the period when the non-Aryan found entrance into the social organization of the Aryan. But though the Aryan and non-Aryan thus met, they did not merge completely. Like the Ganges and the Jumna at their confluence, they flowed on together in two separately distinguishable streams.

In spite of Siva's entry amongst the Aryan gods, his Aryan and non-Aryan aspects remained different. In the former, he is the lord of ascetics, who, having conquered desire, is rapt in the bliss of *nirvāṇa*, as bare of raiment as of worldly ties. In the latter, he is terrible, clad in raw, bleeding elephant hide, intoxicated by the hemp decoction. In the former, he is the replica of Buddha, and as such has captured many a Buddhist shrine; in the latter, he is the overlord of demons, spirits and other dreadful beings, who haunt the places of the dead, and as such has appropriated to himself the worshippers of the phallus, and of snakes, trees and other totems. In the former, he is worshipped in the quietude of meditation; in the latter, in frenzied orgies of self-torture.

Similarly in the Vaishnava cult, Krishna, who became the mythological god of the non-Aryan religious legends, was not the same in character as the brave and sagacious ruler of Dvārakā who acted as the guide, philosopher and friend of the valiant Arjuna. Alongside the heights of the Song Celestial are ranged the popular religious stories of the cowherd tribes.

But in spite of all that was achieved, it was quite impossible, even for the Aryan genius, to bring into harmony with itself and assimilate each and every one of the practices, beliefs and myths of innumerable non-Aryan tribes. More and more of what was non-Aryan came to be not merely tolerated, but welcomed in spite of incongruities, as the non-Aryan element became increasingly predominant in the race mixture. This led to the formulation of the principle that any religion which should satisfy the capacity of a particular sect was enough for its salvation. But in consequence, the organizing force was reduced to the mere compulsion of some common customs, some repetition of external practices, which barely served loosely to hold together these heterogeneous elements. For the mind which has lost its vigour, all external habits become tyrannical. The result for India is that the tie of custom which is extraneous has become severely tight, hardly leaving any freedom of movement even in insignificant details of life. This has developed in the people an excessively strong sense of responsibility to the claims of the class tradition which divides, but not the conviction of that inner moral responsibility which unites.

We have seen how, after the decline of Buddhism, a path had to be cleared through the jungle of rank undergrowth which had been allowed to run wild during the prolonged inaction of the Brahmanic hierarchy. At the latter end of its career in India the mighty stream of Buddhism grew sluggish and lost itself in morasses of primitive superstitions and promiscuous creeds and practices, which had their root in non-Aryan crudities. It had lost its depth of philosophy and breadth of humanity, which had their origin in the Aryan mind.

Therefore the time came for the Brahmins to assert themselves and bring back into the heart of all this incongruity some unity of ideal, which it had always been their function to maintain. It was now a difficult task for them because of the varied racial strains which had become part of the constitution of the Indian people. And so, in order to save their ideals from the attack of this wild exuberance of heterogeneous life, they fixed them in a permanent rigidity. This had the reactionary effect of making their own ideals inert, and unfit for adaptation to changes of time; while it left to all the living elements of the different races included in the people their freedom of growth, unguided by any dictates of reason. The result has been our huge medley of customs, ceremonials and creeds, some of which are the ruins of the old, and some merely the anomalies of the living outgrowths which continue clinging to them and smothering them in the process.

And yet the genius of India went on working, albeit through the tremendous obstacle of the shackled mind of the people. In the Vedic times, as we have seen, it was mainly the Kshatriyas who repeatedly brought storms of fresh thought into the atmosphere of the people's life whenever it showed signs of stagnation. In later ages, when the Kshatriyas had lost their individuality, the message of the spiritual freedom and unity of man mainly sprang from the obscure strata of the community, where belonged the castes that were despised. Though it has to be admitted that in the medieval age the Brahmin Rāmānanda was the first to give voice to the cry of unity, which is India's own, and in consequence lost his honoured privileges as a Brahmin guru, yet it is none the less true that most of our great saints of that time, who took up this cry in their life and teaching and songs, came from the lower classes, one of them being a Muhammadan weaver, one a cobbler, and several coming from ranks of society whose touch would pollute the drinking water of the respectable section of Hindus. And thus the living voice of India ever found its medium even in the darkest days of our downfall, the voice which proclaimed that he only knows Truth who knows the unity of all beings in the spirit.

The age in which we now live, we cannot see clearly in its true features, as from without. Yet we feel that the India of to-day has roused herself once more to search out her truth, her harmony, her oneness, not only among her own constituent elements, but with the great world. The current of her life, which had been dammed up in stagnation, has found some breach in the wall and can feel the pulse of the tidal waves of humanity outside. We shall learn that we can reach the great world of man, not through the effacement but through the expansion of our own individuality. We shall know for certain that just as it is futile mendicancy to covet the wealth of others in place of our own, so also to keep ourselves segregated and starved by refusing the gift which is the common heritage of man because it is brought to us by a foreign messenger, only makes for utter destitution.

Our western critics, whose own people, whenever confronted with non-western races in a close contact, never know any other solution of the problem but extermination or expulsion by physical force, and whose caste feeling against darker races is brutally aggressive and contemptuous, are ready to judge us with a sneering sense of superiority when comparing India's history with their own. They never take into consideration the enormous burden of difficulty which Indian civilization has taken upon itself from its commencement. India is the one country in the world where the Aryan colonizers had to make constant social adjustments with peoples who vastly outnumbered them, who were physically and mentally alien to their own race, and who were for the most part distinctly inferior to the invaders. Europe, on the other hand, is one in mind; her dress, custom, culture, and with small variations her habits, are one. Yet her inhabitants, although only politically divided, are perpetually making preparations for deadly combats, wherein entire populations indulge in orgies of wholesale destruction unparalleled in ferocity in the history of the barbarian. It is not merely such periodic irruptions of bloody feuds that are the worst characteristic of the relationship between the countries of Europe, even after centuries of close contact and intellectual co-operation, but there is also the intense feeling of mutual suspicion generating diplomatic deceitfulness and shameless moral obliquities.

India's problem has been far more complex than that of the West, and I admit that our rigid system of social regulation has not solved it. For, to bring order and peace at the cost of life is terribly wasteful, whether in the policy of government or of society. But all the same, I believe that we have cause to be proud of the fact that for a long series of centuries beset with vicissitudes of stupendous proportions, crowded with things that are incongruous and facts that are irrelevant, India still keeps alive the inner principle of her own civilization against the cyclonic fury of contradictions and the gravitational pull of the dust.

This has been the great function of the Brahmins of this land, to keep the lamp lighted when the storm has been raging on all sides. It has been their endeavour gradually to permeate the tremendous mass of obstructive material with some quickening ideal of their own that would transmute it into the life-stuff of a composite civilization; to discover some ultimate meaning in the inarticulate primitive forms struggling for expression, and to give it a voice. In a word, it was the mission of the Brahmin to comprehend by the light of his own mature understanding the undeveloped minds of the people.

It would be wrong for us, when we judge the historical career of India, to put all the stress upon the accumulated heap of refuse, gross and grotesque, that has not yet been assimilated in one consistent cultural body. Our great hope lies there, where we realize that something positively precious in our achievements still persists in spite of circumstances that are inclement. The best of us still have our aspiration for the supreme end of life, which is so often mocked at by the prosperous people who hold their sway over the present-day world. We still believe that the world has a deeper meaning than what is apparent, and that therein the human soul finds its ultimate harmony and peace. We still know that only in this spiritual wealth and welfare does civilization attain its end, and not in a prolific production of materials, not in the competition of intemperate power with power.

It has certainly been unfortunate for us that we have neglected the cult of *Anna Brahma*, the infinite as manifested in the material world of utility, and we are dearly paying for it. We have set our mind upon realizing the eternal in the intensity of spiritual consciousness so long, that we have overlooked the importance of realizing the infinite in the world of extension by ever pursuing a path which is endless. And in this great field of adventure the West has attained its success, for which humanity has to be immensely grateful to it.

But the true happiness and peace are awaiting the children of the West in the *tapasyā*, which is for realizing Brahma in spirit, for acquiring the luminous inner vision before which the sphere of immortality reveals itself. If ever that time comes, if the western world does not meet its catastrophic end under the trampling tread of contending commerce and politics, of monstrous greed and hatred, then the world will owe its gratitude to the Brahmins for the faith in the infinitude of the human spirit which they have upheld in the face of forces that spurned it, exultingly counting the skulls of their victims.

I love India, not because I cultivate the idolatry of geography, not because I have had the chance to be born in her soil, but because she has saved through tumultuous ages the living words that have issued from the illuminated consciousness of her great sons: *Satyam, Jñānam, Anantam Brahma*, Brahma is truth, Brahma is wisdom, Brahma is infinite; *Sāntam, Sivam, Advaitam*, peace is in Brahma, goodness is in Brahma, and the unity of all beings.

ब्रह्मनिष्ठोगृहस्थः स्यात् तत्त्वज्ञानपरायणः ।
यद्यत् कर्म प्रकुर्वीत तद्ब्रह्मणि समर्पयेत् ॥[1]

> The householder shall have his life established in Brahma, shall pursue the deeper truth of all things and in all activities of life dedicate his works to the Eternal Being.

Thus we have come to know that what India truly seeks is not a peace which is in negation or in some mechanical adjustment, but that which is in *Sivam*, in goodness, which is in *Advaitam*, in the truth of perfect union; that India does not enjoin her children to cease from *karma*, but to perform their *karma* in the presence of the Eternal, with the pure knowledge of the spiritual meaning of existence; that this is the true prayer of Mother India:

य एकोऽवर्णोबहुधा शक्तियोगाद्
वर्णाननेकान्निहितार्थोदधाति ।
विचैति चान्ते विश्वमादौ सदेवः
सनोबुद्ध्या शुभया संयुनक्तु ॥[2]

> He who is one, who is above all colour distinctions, who dispenses the inherent needs of men of all colours, who comprehends all things from their beginning to the end, let Him unite us to one another with the wisdom which is the wisdom of goodness.

1923

---

1. The *Mahānirvān Tantra*, 8/23.
2. The *Svetāsvataropanishad*, 4/1.
All the translations of the verses from the *Bhagavad-Gītā* are in the words of Annie Besant.

The Educational Mission of the Visva-Bharati

I HAVE BEEN asked to speak this evening to my invisible audience about the educational mission to which I have devoted my life and I am thankful for this opportunity.

I am an artist and not a man of science, and therefore my institution necessarily has assumed the aspect of a work of art and not that of a pedagogical laboratory. And this is the reason why I find it difficult to give you a distinct idea of my work which is continually growing for the last thirty years. With it my own mind has grown, and my own ideal of education found freedom to reach its fullness through a vital process so elusive that the picture of its unity cannot be analysed.

Children's minds are sensitive to the influences of the great world to which they have been born. This delicate receptivity of their passive mind helps them, without their feeling any strain, to master language, that most complex instrument of expression full of ideas that are indefinable and symbols that deal with abstractions. Through their natural gift of guessing, children learn the meaning of the words which we cannot explain.

But it is just at this critical period that the child's life is brought into the education factory, lifeless, colourless, dissociated from the context of the universe, with bare white walls staring like eyeballs of the dead. The children have to sit inert whilst lessons are pelted at them like hailstones on flowers.

I believe that children should be surrounded with the things of nature that have their own educational value. Their minds should be allowed to stumble on and be surprised at everything that happens before them in the life of to-day. The new to-morrow will stimulate their attention with new facts of life.

The minds of the adults are crowded; the stream of lessons perpetually flowing from the heart of nature does not fully touch them; they choose those that are useful, rejecting the rest as inadmissible. The children have no such distractions. With them every new fact comes to a mind that is always open, with an abundant hospitality. And through this exuberant, indiscriminate acceptance they learn innumerable facts within a short time, amazing compared to our own slowness. These are the most important lessons of life that are thus learnt in the first few years of our career.

Because, when I was young I underwent the mechanical pressure of a teaching process, one of man's most cruel, and most wasteful mistakes, I felt it my duty to found a school where the children might be free in spite of the school.

At the age of twelve I was first coerced into learning English. Most of you in this country are blissfully unconscious of the mercilessness of your own language. You will admit, however, that neither its spelling, nor its syntax, is perfectly rational. The penalty for this I had to pay, without having done anything to deserve it, with the exception of being born ignorant.

When in the evening my English teacher used to come I was dragged to my daily doom at a most unsympathetic desk and an unprepossessing text book containing lessons that are followed by rows of separated syllables with accent-marks like soldiers' bayonets.

As for that teacher, I can never forgive him. He was so inordinately conscientious! He insisted on coming every single evening, – there never seemed to be either illness or death in his family. He was so preposterously punctual too. I remember how the fascination for the frightful attracted me every evening to the terrace facing the road; and just at the right moment, his fateful umbrella, – for bad weather never prevented him from coming, – would appear at the bend of our lane.

Remembering the experience of my young days, of the school masters and the class rooms, also knowing something of the natural school which Nature herself supplies to all her creatures, I established my institution in a beautiful spot, far away from the town, where the children had the greatest freedom possible under the shade of ancient trees and the field around open to the verge of horizon.

From the beginning I tried to create an atmosphere which I considered to be more important than the class teaching. The atmosphere of nature's own beauty was there waiting for us from a time immemorial with her varied gifts of colours and dance, flowers and fruits with the joy of her mornings and the peace of her starry nights. I wrote songs to suit the different seasons, to celebrate the coming of Spring and the resonant season of the rains following the pitiless months of summer. When nature herself sends her message we ought to acknowledge its compelling invitation. While the kiss of rain thrills the heart of the surrounding trees if we pay all our dutiful attention to mathematics we are ostracized by the spirit of universe. Our holidays are unexpected like Nature's own. Clouds gather above the rows of the palm trees without any previous notice; we gladly submit to its sudden suggestion and run wildly away from our Sanskrit grammar. To alienate our sympathy from the world of birds and trees is a barbarity which is not allowed in my institution.

I invited renowned artists from the city to live at the school, leaving them free to produce their own work which the boys and girls watch if they feel inclined. It is the same with my own work. I compose my songs and poems, the teachers sit round me and listen. The children are naturally attracted and they peep in and gather, even if they do not fully understand, something fresh from the heart of the composer.

From the commencement of our work we have encouraged our children to be of service to our neighbours from which has grown up a village reconstruction work in our neighbourhood unique in the whole of India. Round our educational work the villages have grouped themselves in which the sympathy for nature and service for man have become one. In such extension of sympathy and service our mind realizes its true freedom.

Along with this has grown an aspiration for even a higher freedom, a freedom from all racial and national prejudice. Children's sympathy is often deliberately made narrow and distorted making them incapable of understanding alien peoples with different languages and cultures. This causes us, when our growing souls demand it, to grope after each other in ignorance, to suffer from the blindness of this age. The worst fetters come when children lose their freedom of heart in love.

We are building up our institution upon the ideal of the spiritual unity of all races. I hope it is going to be a great meeting place for individuals from all countries who believe in the divine humanity, and who wish to make atonement for the cruel disloyalty displayed against her by men. Such idealists I have frequently met in my travels in the West, often unknown persons, of no special reputation, who suffer and struggle for a cause generally ignored by the clever and the powerful. These individuals, I am sure, will alter the outlook for the future. By them will be ushered a new sunrise of truth and love, like that great personality, who had only a small number of disciples from among the insignificant, and who at the end of his career presented a pitiful picture of utter failure. He was reviled by those in power, unknown by the larger world, and suffered an inglorious death, and yet through the symbol of this utmost failure he conquers and lives for ever.

For some time past education has lacked idealism in its mere exercise of an intellect which has no depth of sentiment. The one desire produced in the heart of the students has been an ambition to win success in the world, not to reach some inner standard of perfection, not to obtain self-emancipation.

Let me confess this fact, that I have my faith in higher ideals. At the same time, I have a great feeling of delicacy in giving utterance to them, because of certain modern obstacles. We have now-a-days to be merely commonplace. We have to wait on the reports in the newspapers, representative of the whole machinery which has been growing up all over the world for the making of life superficial. It is difficult to fight through such obstructions and to come to the centre of humanity.

However I have this one satisfaction that I am at least able to put before you the mission to which these last years of my life have been devoted. As a servant of the great cause I must be frank and strong in urging upon you this mission. I represent in my institution an ideal of brotherhood where men of different countries and different languages can come together. I believe in the spiritual unity of man, and therefore I ask you to accept this task from me. Unless you come and say, 'We also recognize this ideal', I shall know that this mission has failed. Do not merely discuss me as a guest, but as one who has come to ask your love, your sympathy and your faith in the following of a great cause.

II

THERE IS NO meaning in such words as spiritualizing[1] the machine, we can spiritualize our own being which makes use of the machine, just as there is nothing good or bad in our bodily organs, but the moral qualities are in our mind. When the temptation is small our moral nature easily overcomes it, but when the bribe that is offered to our soul is too big we do not even realize

1. In reply to the question whether Machines can be spiritualized.

that its dignity is offended. To-day the profit that the machine brings to our door is too big and we do not hesitate to scramble for it even at the cost of our humanity. The shrinking of the man in us is concealed by the augmentation of things outside and we lack the time to grieve over the loss. We can only hope that science herself will help us to bring back sanity to the human world by lessening the opportunity to gamble with our fortune. The means of production constructed by science in her attempts to gain access into nature's storehouse are tremendously complex which only proves her own immaturity just as simplicity is wanting in the movements of a swimmer who is inexpert. It is this cumbersome complexity in the machinery which makes it not only unavailable to the majority of mankind but also compels us to centralize it in monster factories, uprooting the workers' life from its natural soil and creating unhappiness. I do not see any other way to extricate us from these tangled evils except to wait for science to simplify our means of production and thus lessen the enormity of individual greed.

I believe that the social unrest prevalent to-day all over the world is owing to the anarchy of spirit in the modern civilization.

What is called progress is the progress in the mechanical contrivances; it is in fact an indefinite extension of our physical limbs and organs which, owing to the enormous material advantage that it brings to us, has tempted the modern man away from his inner realm of spiritual values. The attainment of perfection in human relationship through the help of religion, and cultivation of our social qualities occupied the most important place in our civilization up till now. But to-day our homes have dissolved into hotels, community life is stifled in the dense and dusty atmosphere of the office, men and women are afraid of love, people clamour for their rights and forget their obligations, and they value comfort more than happiness and the spirit of display more than that of beauty.

Great civilizations in the East as well as in the West, have flourished in the past because they produced food for the spirit of man for all time; they tried to build their life upon the faith in ideals, the faith which is creative. These great civilizations were at last run to death by men of the type of our precocious schoolboys of modern times, smart and superficially critical, worshippers of self, shrewd bargainers in the market of profit and power, efficient in their handling of the ephemeral, who presume to buy human souls with their money and throw them into their dust bins when they have been sucked dry, and who, eventually, driven by suicidal forces of passion, set their neighbours' houses on fire and are themselves enveloped by the flame.

It is some great ideal which creates great societies of men; it is some blind passion which breaks them to pieces. They thrive so long as they produce food for life; they perish when they burn up life in insatiate self-gratification. We have been taught by our sages that it is Truth and not things which saves man from annihilation.

The reward of truth is peace, the reward of truth is happiness. The people suffer from the upsetting of equilibrium when power is there and no inner truth to which it is related, like a motor car in motion whose driver is absent.

1930

The Religion of Man

PREFACE

THE CHAPTERS INCLUDED in this book, which comprises the Hibbert Lectures delivered in Oxford, at Manchester College, during the month of May 1930, contain also the gleanings of my thoughts on the same subject from the harvest of many lectures and addresses delivered in different countries of the world over a considerable period of my life.

The fact that one theme runs through all only proves to me that the Religion of Man has been growing within my mind as a religious experience and not merely as a philosophical subject. In fact, a very large portion of my writings, beginning from the earlier products of my immature youth down to the present time, carry an almost continuous trace of the history of this growth. To-day I am made conscious of the fact that the works that I have started and the words that I have uttered are deeply linked by a unity of inspiration whose proper definition has often remained unrevealed to me.

In the present volume I offer the evidence of my own personal life brought into a definite focus. To some of my readers this will supply matter of psychological interest; but for others I hope it will carry with it its own ideal value important for such a subject as religion.

My sincere thanks are due to the Hibbert Trustees, and especially to Dr. W. H. Drummond, with whom I have been in constant correspondence, for allowing me to postpone the delivery of these Hibbert Lectures from the year 1928, when I was too ill to proceed to Europe, until the summer of 1930. I have also to thank the Trustees for their very kind permission given to me to present the substance of the lectures in this book in an enlarged form by dividing the whole subject into chapters instead of keeping strictly to the lecture form in which they were delivered in Oxford. May I add that the great kindness of my hostess, Mrs. Drummond, in Oxford, will always remain in my memory along with these lectures as intimately associated with them?

In the Appendix I have gathered together from my own writings certain parallel passages which bring the reader to the heart of my main theme. Furthermore, two extracts, which contain historical material of great value, are from the pen of my esteemed colleague and friend, Professor Kshiti Mohan Sen. To him I would express my gratitude for the help he has given me in bringing before me the religious ideas of medieval India which touch the subject of my lectures.[1]

September 1930   RABINDRANATH TAGORE

---

1 The Appendices have been omitted from this edition.

The eternal Dream
    is borne on the wings of ageless Light
    that rends the veil of the vague
        and goes across time
    weaving ceaseless patterns of Being.

The mystery remains dumb,
    the meaning of this pilgrimage,
    the endless adventure of existence
whose rush along the sky
    flames up into innumerable rings of paths,
till at last knowledge gleams out from the dusk
        in the infinity of human spirit,
    and in that dim lighted dawn
    she speechlessly gazes through the break in the mist
        at the vision of Life and of Love
    rising from the tumult of profound pain and joy.

Santiniketan
16 September 1929

[*Composed for the Opening Day Celebrations
of the Indian College, Montpelier, France.*]

CHAPTER ONE
MAN'S UNIVERSE

LIGHT, AS THE radiant energy of creation, started the ring-dance of atoms in a diminutive sky, and also the dance of the stars in the vast, lonely theatre of time and space. The planets came out of their bath of fire and basked in the sun for ages. They were the thrones of the gigantic Inert, dumb and desolate, which knew not the meaning of its own blind destiny and majestically frowned upon a future when its monarchy would be menaced.

Then came a time when life was brought into the arena in the tiniest little monocycle of a cell. With its gift of growth and power of adaptation it faced the ponderous enormity of things, and contradicted the unmeaningness of their bulk. It was made conscious not of the volume but of the value of existence, which it ever tried to enhance and maintain in many-branched paths of creation, overcoming the obstructive inertia of Nature by obeying Nature's law.

But the miracle of creation did not stop here in this isolated speck of life launched on a lonely voyage to the Unknown. A multitude of cells were bound together into a larger unit, not through aggregation, but through a marvellous quality of complex inter-relationship maintaining a perfect co-ordination of functions. This is the creative principle of unity, the divine mystery of existence, that baffles all analysis. The larger co-operative units could adequately pay for a greater freedom of self-expression, and they began to form and develop in their bodies new organs of power, new instruments of efficiency. This was the march of evolution ever unfolding the potentialities of life.

But this evolution which continues on the physical plane has its limited range. All exaggeration in that direction becomes a burden that breaks the natural rhythm of life, and those creatures that encouraged their ambitious flesh to grow in dimensions have nearly all perished of their cumbrous absurdity.

Before the chapter ended Man appeared and turned the course of this evolution from an indefinite march of physical aggrandizement to a freedom of a more subtle perfection. This has made possible his progress to become unlimited, and has enabled him to realize the boundless in his power.

The fire is lighted, the hammers are working, and for laborious days and nights amidst dirt and discordance the musical instrument is being made. We may accept this as a detached fact and follow its evolution. But when the music is revealed, we know that the whole thing is a part of the manifestation of music in spite of its contradictory character. The process of evolution, which after ages has reached man, must be realized in its unity with him; though in him it assumes a new value and proceeds to a different path. It is a continuous process that finds its meaning in Man; and we must acknowledge that the evolution which Science talks of is that of Man's universe. The leather binding and title-page are parts of the book itself; and this world that we perceive through our senses and mind and life's experience is profoundly one with ourselves.

The divine principle of unity has ever been that of an inner inter-relationship. This is revealed in some of its earliest stages in the evolution of multicellular life on this planet. The most perfect inward expression has been attained by man in his own body. But what is most important of all is the fact that man has also attained its realization in a more subtle body outside his physical system. He misses himself when isolated; he finds his own larger and truer self in his wide human relationship. His multicellular body is born and it dies; his multi-personal humanity is immortal. In this ideal of unity he realizes the eternal in his life and the boundless in his love. The unity becomes not a mere subjective idea, but an energizing truth. Whatever name may be given to it, and whatever form it symbolizes, the consciousness of this unity is spiritual, and our effort to be true to it is our religion. It ever waits to be revealed in our history in a more and more perfect illumination.

We have our eyes, which relate to us the vision of the physical universe. We have also an inner faculty of our own which helps us to find our relationship with the supreme self of man, the universe of personality. This faculty is our luminous imagination, which in its higher stage is special to man. It offers us that vision of wholeness which for the biological necessity of physical survival is superfluous; its purpose is to arouse in us the sense of perfection which is our true sense of immortality. For perfection dwells ideally in Man the Eternal, inspiring love for this ideal in the individual, urging him more and more to realize it.

The development of intelligence and physical power is equally necessary in animals and men for their purposes of living; but what is unique in man is the development of his consciousness which gradually deepens and widens the realization of his immortal being, the perfect, the eternal. It inspires those creations of his that reveal the divinity in him – which is his humanity – in the varied manifestations of truth, goodness and beauty, in the freedom of activity which is not for his use but for his ultimate expression. The individual man must exist for Man the great, and must express him in disinterested works, in science and philosophy, in literature and arts, in service and worship. This is his religion, which is working in the heart of all his religions in various names and forms. He knows and uses this world where it is endless and thus attains greatness, but he realizes his own truth where it is perfect and thus finds his fulfilment.

The idea of the humanity of our God, or the divinity of Man the Eternal, is the main subject of this book. This thought of God has not grown in my mind through any process of philosophical reasoning. On the contrary, it has followed the current of my temperament from early days until it suddenly flashed into my consciousness with a direct vision. The experience which I have described in one of the chapters which follow convinced me that on the surface of our being we have the ever-changing phases of the individual self, but in the depth there dwells the Eternal Spirit of human unity beyond our direct knowledge. It very often contradicts the trivialities of our daily life, and upsets the arrangements made for securing our personal exclusiveness behind the walls of individual habits and superficial conventions. It inspires in us works that are the expressions of a Universal Spirit; it invokes unexpectedly in the midst of a self-centred life a supreme sacrifice. At its call, we hasten to dedicate our lives to the cause of truth and beauty, to unrewarded service of others, in spite of our lack of faith in the positive reality of the ideal values.

During the discussion of my own religious experience I have expressed my belief that the first stage of my realization was through my feeling of intimacy with Nature – not that Nature which has its channel of information for our mind and physical relationship with our living body, but that which satisfies our personality with manifestations that make our life rich and stimulate our imagination in their harmony of forms, colours, sounds and movements. It is not that world which vanishes into abstract symbols behind its own testimony to Science, but that which lavishly displays its wealth of reality to our personal self having its own perpetual reaction upon our human nature.

I have mentioned in connection with my personal experience some songs which I had often heard from wandering village singers, belonging to a popular sect of Bengal, called Baüls, who have no images, temples, scriptures, or ceremonials, who declare in their songs the divinity of Man, and express for him an intense feeling of love. Coming from men who are unsophisticated, living a simple life in obscurity, it gives us a clue to the inner meaning of all religions. For it suggests that these religions are never about a God of cosmic force, but rather about the God of human personality.

At the same time it must be admitted that even the impersonal aspect of truth dealt with by Science belongs to the human Universe. But men of Science tell us that truth, unlike beauty and goodness, is independent of our consciousness. They explain to us how the belief that truth is independent of the human mind is a mystical belief, natural to man but at the same time inexplicable. But may not the explanation be this, that ideal truth does not depend upon the individual mind of man, but on the universal mind which comprehends the individual? For to say that truth, as we see it, exists apart from humanity is really to contradict Science itself; because Science can only organize into rational concepts those facts which man can know and understand, and logic is a machinery of thinking created by the mechanic man.

The table that I am using with all its varied meanings appears as a table for man through his special organ of senses and his special organ of thoughts. When scientifically analysed the same table offers an enormously different appearance to him from that given by his senses. The evidence of his physical senses and that of his logic and his scientific instruments are both related to his own power of comprehension; both are true and true for him. He makes use of the table with full confidence for his physical purposes, and with equal confidence makes intellectual use of it for his scientific knowledge. But the knowledge is his who is a man. If a particular man as an individual did not exist, the table would exist all the same, but still as a thing that is related to the human mind. The contradiction that there is between the table of our sense perception and the table of our scientific knowledge has its common centre of reconciliation in human personality.

The same thing holds true in the realm of idea. In the scientific idea of the world there is no gap in the universal law of causality. Whatever happens could never have happened otherwise. This is a generalization which has been made possible by a quality of logic which is possessed by the human mind. But this very mind of Man has its immediate consciousness of will within him which is aware of its freedom and ever struggles for it. Every day in most of our behaviour we acknowledge its truth; in fact, our conduct finds its best value in its relation to its truth. Thus this has its analogy in our daily behaviour with regard to a table. For whatever may be the conclusion that Science has unquestionably proved about the table, we are amply rewarded when we deal with it as a solid fact and never as a crowd of fluid elements that represent a certain kind of energy. We can also utilize this phenomenon of the measurement. The space represented by a needle when magnified by the microscope may cause us no anxiety as to the number of angels who could be accommodated on its point or camels which could walk through its eye. In a cinema-picture our vision of time and space can be expanded or condensed merely according to the different technique of the instrument. A seed carries packed in a minute receptacle a future which is enormous in its contents both in time and space. The truth, which is Man, has not emerged out of nothing at a certain point of time, even though seemingly it might have been manifested then. But the manifestation of Man has no end in itself – not even now. Neither did it have its beginning in any particular time we ascribe to it. The truth of Man is in the heart of eternity, the fact of it being evolved through endless ages. If Man's manifestation has round it a background of millions of light-years, still it is his own background. He includes in himself the time, however long, that carries the process of his becoming, and he is related for the very truth of his existence to all things that surround him.

Relationship is the fundamental truth of this world of appearance. Take, for instance, a piece of coal. When we pursue the fact of it to its ultimate composition, substance which seemingly is the most stable element in it vanishes in centres of revolving forces. These are the units, called the elements of carbon, which can further be analysed into a certain number of protons and electrons. Yet these electrical facts are what they are, not in their detachment, but in their inter-relationship, and though possibly some day they themselves may be further analysed, nevertheless the pervasive truth of inter-relation which is manifested in them will remain.

We do not know how these elements, as carbon, compose a piece of coal; all that we can say is that they build up that appearance through a unity of inter-relationship, which unites them not merely in an individual piece of coal, but in a comradeship of creative co-ordination with the entire physical universe.

Creation has been made possible through the continual self-surrender of the unit to the universe. And the spiritual universe of Man is also ever claiming self-renunciation from the individual units. This spiritual process is not so easy as the physical one in the physical world, for the intelligence and will of the units have to be tempered to those of the universal spirit.

It is said in a verse of the Upanishad that this world which is all movement is pervaded by one supreme unity, and therefore true enjoyment can never be had through the satisfaction of greed, but only through the surrender of our individual self to the Universal Self.

There are thinkers who advocate the doctrine of the plurality of worlds, which can only mean that there are worlds that are absolutely unrelated to each other. Even if this were true it could never be proved. For our universe is the sum total of what Man feels, knows, imagines, reasons to be, and of whatever is knowable to him now or in another time. It affects him differently in its different aspects, in its beauty, its inevitable sequence of happenings, its potentiality; and the world proves itself to him only in its varied effects upon his senses, imagination and reasoning mind.

I do not imply that the final nature of the world depends upon the comprehension of the individual person. Its reality is associated with the universal human mind which comprehends all time and all possibilities of realization. And this is why for the accurate knowledge of things we depend upon Science that represents the rational mind of the universal Man, and not upon that of the individual who dwells in a limited range of space and time and the immediate needs of life. And this is why there is such a thing as progress in our civilization; for progress means that there is an ideal perfection which the individual seeks to reach by extending his limits in knowledge, power, love, enjoyment, thus approaching the universal. The most distant star, whose faint message touches the threshold of the most powerful telescopic vision, has its sympathy with the understanding mind of man, and therefore we can never cease to believe that we shall probe further and further into the mystery of their nature. As we know the truth of the stars we know the great comprehensive mind of man.

We must realize not only the reasoning mind, but also the creative imagination, the love and wisdom that belong to the Supreme Person, whose Spirit is over us all, love for whom comprehends love for all creatures and exceeds in depth and strength all other loves, leading to difficult endeavours and martyrdoms that have no other gain than the fulfilment of this love itself.

The *Isha* of our Upanishad, the Super Soul, which permeates all moving things, is the God of this human universe whose mind we share in all our true knowledge, love and service, and whom to reveal in ourselves through renunciation of self is the highest end of life.

CHAPTER TWO
THE CREATIVE SPIRIT

ONCE, DURING THE improvisation of a story by a young child, I was coaxed to take my part as the hero. The child imagined that I had been shut in a dark room locked from the outside. She asked me, 'What will you do for your freedom?' and I answered, 'Shout for help.' But, however desirable that might be if it succeeded immediately, it would be unfortunate for the story. And thus she in her imagination had to clear the neighbourhood of all kinds of help that my cries might reach. I was compelled to think of some violent means of kicking through this passive resistance; but for the sake of the story the door had to be made of steel. I found a key, but it would not fit, and the child was delighted at the development of the story jumping over obstructions.

Life's story of evolution, the main subject of which is the opening of the doors of the dark dungeon, seems to develop in the same manner. Difficulties were created, and at each offer of an answer the story had to discover further obstacles in order to carry on the adventure. For to come to an absolutely satisfactory conclusion is to come to the end of all things, and in that case the great child would have nothing else to do but to shut her curtain and go to sleep.

The Spirit of Life began her chapter by introducing a simple living cell against the tremendously powerful challenge of the vast Inert. The triumph was thrillingly great which still refuses to yield its secret. She did not stop there, but defiantly courted difficulties, and in the technique of her art exploited an element which still baffles our logic.

This is the harmony of self-adjusting inter-relationship impossible to analyse. She brought close together numerous cell units and, by grouping them into a self-sustaining sphere of co-operation, elaborated a larger unit. It was not a mere agglomeration. The grouping had its caste system in the division of functions and yet an intimate unity of kinship. The creative life summoned a larger army of cells under her command and imparted into them, let us say, a communal spirit that fought with all its might whenever its integrity was menaced.

This was the tree which has its inner harmony and inner movement of life in its beauty, its strength, its sublime dignity of endurance, its pilgrimage to the Unknown through the tiniest gates of reincarnation. It was a sufficiently marvellous achievement to be a fit termination to the creative venture. But the creative genius cannot stop exhausted; more windows have to be opened; and she went out of her accustomed way and brought another factor into her work, that of locomotion. Risks of living were enhanced, offering opportunities to the daring resourcefulness of the Spirit of Life. For she seems to revel in occasions for a fight against the giant Matter, which has rigidly prohibitory immigration laws against all new-comers from Life's shore. So the fish was furnished with appliances for moving in an element which offered its density for an obstacle. The air offered an even more difficult obstacle in its lightness; but the challenge was accepted, and the bird was gifted with a marvellous pair of wings that negotiated with the subtle laws of the air and found in it a better ally than the reliable soil of the stable earth. The Arctic snow set up its frigid sentinel; the tropical desert uttered in its scorching breath a gigantic 'No' against all life's children. But those peremptory prohibitions were defied, and the frontiers, though guarded by a death penalty, were triumphantly crossed.

This process of conquest could be described as progress for the kingdom of life. It journeyed on through one success to another by dealing with the laws of Nature through the help of the invention of new instruments. This field of life's onward march is a field of ruthless competition. Because the material world is the world of quantity, where resources are limited and victory waits for those who have superior facility in their weapons, therefore success in the path of progress for one group most often runs parallel to defeat in another.

It appears that such scramble and fight for opportunities of living among numerous small combatants suggested at last an imperialism of big bulky flesh – a huge system of muscles and bones, thick and heavy coats of armour and enormous tails. The idea of such indecorous massiveness must have seemed natural to life's providence; for the victory in the world of quantity might reasonably appear to depend upon the bigness of dimension. But such gigantic paraphernalia of defence and attack resulted in an utter defeat, the records of which every day are being dug up from the desert sands and ancient mud flats. These represent the fragments that strew the forgotten paths of a great retreat in the battle of existence. For the heavy weight which these creatures carried was mainly composed of bones, hides, shells, teeth and claws that were non-living, and therefore imposed its whole huge pressure upon life that needed freedom and growth for the perfect expression of its own vital nature. The resources for living which the earth offered for her children were recklessly spent by these megalomaniac monsters of an immoderate appetite for the sake of maintaining a cumbersome system of dead burdens that thwarted them in their true progress. Such a losing game has now become obsolete. To the few stragglers of that party, like the rhinoceros or the hippopotamus, has been allotted a very small space on this earth, absurdly inadequate to their formidable strength and magnitude of proportions, making them look forlornly pathetic in the sublimity of their incongruousness. These and their extinct forerunners have been the biggest failures in life's experiments. And then, on some obscure dusk of dawn, the experiment entered upon a completely new phase of a disarmament proposal, when little Man made his appearance in the arena, bringing with him expectations and suggestions that are unfathomably great.

We must know that the evolution process of the world has made its progress towards the revelation of its *truth* – that is to say some inner value which is not in the extension in space and duration in time. When life came out it did not bring with it any new materials into existence. Its elements are the same which are the materials for the rocks and minerals. Only it evolved a value in them which cannot be measured and analysed. The same thing is true with regard to mind and the consciousness of self; they are revelations of a great meaning, the self-expression of a truth. In man this truth has made its positive appearance, and is struggling to make its manifestation more and more clear. That which is eternal is realizing itself in history through the obstructions of limits.

The physiological process in the progress of Life's evolution seems to have reached its finality in man. We cannot think of any noticeable addition or modification in our vital instruments which we are likely to allow to persist. If any individual is born, by chance, with an extra pair of eyes or ears, or some unexpected limbs like stowaways without passports, we are sure to do our best to eliminate them from our bodily organization. Any new chance of a too obviously physical variation is certain to meet with a determined disapproval from man, the most powerful veto being expected from his aesthetic nature, which peremptorily refuses to calculate advantage when its majesty is offended by any sudden licence of form. We all know that the back of our body has a wide surface practically unguarded. From the strategic point of view this oversight is unfortunate, causing us annoyances and indignities, if nothing worse, through unwelcome intrusions. And this could reasonably justify in our minds regret for retrenchment in the matter of an original tail, whose memorial we are still made to carry in secret. But the least attempt at the rectification of the policy of economy in this direction is indignantly resented. I strongly believe that the idea of ghosts had its best chance with our timid imagination in our sensitive back – a field of dark ignorance; and yet it is too late for me to hint that one of our eyes could profitably have been spared for our burden-carrier back, so unjustly neglected and haunted by undefined fears.

Thus, while all innovation is stubbornly opposed, there is every sign of a comparative carelessness about the physiological efficiency of the human body. Some of our organs are losing their original vigour. The civilized life, within walked enclosures, has naturally caused in man a weakening of his power of sight and hearing along with subtle sense of the distant. Because of our habit of taking cooked food we give less employment to our teeth and a great deal more to the dentist. Spoilt and pampered by clothes, our skin shows lethargy in its function of adjustment to the atmospheric temperature and in its power of quick recovery from hurts.

The adventurous Life appears to have paused at a crossing in her road before Man came. It seems as if she became aware of wastefulness in carrying on her experiments and adding to her inventions purely on the physical plane. It was proved in Life's case that four is not always twice as much as two. In living things it is necessary to keep to the limit of the perfect unit within which the inter-relationship must not be inordinately strained. The ambition that seeks power in the augmentation of dimension is doomed; for that perfection which is in the inner quality of harmony becomes choked when quantity overwhelms it in a fury of extravagance. The combination of an exaggerated nose and arm that an elephant carries hanging down its front has its advantage. This may induce us to imagine that it would double the advantage for the animal if its tail also could grow into an additional trunk. But the progress which greedily allows Life's field to be crowded with an excessive production of instruments becomes a progress towards death. For Life has its own natural rhythm which a multiplication table has not; and proud progress that rides roughshod over Life's cadence kills it at the end with encumbrances that are unrhythmic. As I have already mentioned, such disasters did happen in the history of evolution.

The moral of that tragic chapter is that if the tail does not have the decency to know where to stop, the drag of this dependency becomes fatal to the body's empire.

Moreover, evolutionary progress on the physical plane inevitably tends to train up its subjects into specialists. The camel is a specialist of the desert and is awkward in the swamp. The hippopotamus which specializes in the mudlands of the Nile is helpless in the neighbouring desert. Such one-sided emphasis breeds professionalism in Life's domain, confining special efficiencies in narrow compartments. The expert training in the aerial sphere is left to the bird; that in the marine is particularly monopolized by the fish. The ostrich is an expert in its own region and would look utterly foolish in an eagle's neighbourhood. They have to remain permanently content with advantages that desperately cling to their limits. Such mutilation of the complete ideal of life for the sake of some exclusive privilege of power is inevitable;

for that form of progress deals with materials that are physical and therefore necessarily limited.

To rescue her own career from such a multiplying burden of the dead and such constriction of specialization seems to have been the object of the Spirit of Life at one particular stage. For it does not take long to find out that an indefinite pursuit of quantity creates for Life, which is essentially qualitative, complexities that lead to a vicious circle. These primeval animals that produced an enormous volume of flesh had to build a gigantic system of bones to carry the burden. This required in its turn a long and substantial array of tails to give it balance. Thus their bodies, being compelled to occupy a vast area, exposed a very large surface which had to be protected by a strong, heavy and capacious armour. A progress which represented a congress of dead materials required a parallel organization of teeth and claws, or horns and hooves, which also were dead.

In its own manner one mechanical burden links itself to other burdens of machines, and Life grows to be a carrier of the dead, a mere platform for machinery, until it is crushed to death by its interminable paradoxes. We are told that the greater part of a tree is dead matter; the big stem, except for a thin covering, is lifeless. The tree uses it as a prop in its ambition for a high position and the lifeless timber is the slave that carries on its back the magnitude of the tree. But such a dependence upon a dead dependant has been achieved by the tree at the cost of its real freedom. It had to seek the stable alliance of the earth for the sharing of its burden, which it did by the help of secret underground entanglements making itself permanently stationary.

But the form of life that seeks the great privilege of movement must minimize its load of the dead and must realize that life's progress should be a perfect progress of the inner life itself and not of materials and machinery; the non-living must not continue outgrowing the living, the armour deadening the skin, the armament laming the arms.

At last, when the Spirit of Life found her form in Man, the effort she had begun completed its cycle, and the truth of her mission glimmered into suggestions which dimly pointed to some direction of meaning across her own frontier. Before the end of this cycle was reached, all the suggestions had been external. They were concerned with technique, with life's apparatus, with the efficiency of the organs. This might have exaggerated itself into an endless boredom of physical progress. It can be conceded that the eyes of the bee possessing numerous facets may have some uncommon advantage which we cannot even imagine, or the glow-worm that carries an arrangement for producing light in its person may baffle our capacity and comprehension. Very likely there are creatures having certain organs that give them sensibilities which we cannot have the power to guess.

All such enhanced sensory powers merely add to the mileage in life's journey on the same road lengthening an indefinite distance. They never take us over the border of physical existence.

The same thing may be said not only about life's efficiency, but also life's ornaments. The colouring and decorative patterns on the bodies of some of the deep sea creatures make us silent with amazement. The butterfly's wings, the beetle's back, the peacock's plumes, the shells of the crustaceans, the exuberant outbreak of decoration in plant life, have reached a standard of perfection that seems to be final. And yet if it continues in the same physical direction, then, however much variety of surprising excellence it may produce, it leaves out some great element of unuttered meaning. These ornaments are like ornaments lavished upon a captive girl, luxuriously complete within a narrow limit, speaking of a homesickness for a far away horizon of emancipation, for an inner depth that is beyond the ken of the senses. The freedom in the physical realm is like the circumscribed freedom in a cage. It produces a proficiency which is mechanical and a beauty which is of the surface. To whatever degree of improvement bodily strength and skill may be developed they keep life tied to a persistence of habit. It is closed, like a mould, useful though it may be for the sake of safety and precisely standardized productions. For centuries the bee repeats its hive, the weaver-bird its nest, the spider its web; and instincts strongly attach themselves to some invariable tendencies of muscles and nerves never being allowed the privilege of making blunders. The physical functions, in order to be strictly reliable, behave like some model schoolboy, obedient, regular, properly repeating lessons by rote without mischief or mistake in his conduct, but also without spirit and initiative. It is the flawless perfection of rigid limits, a cousin – possibly a distant cousin – of the inanimate.

Instead of allowing a full paradise of perfection to continue its tame and timid rule of faultless regularity the Spirit of Life boldly declared for a further freedom and decided to eat of the fruit of the Tree of Knowledge. This time her struggle was not against the Inert, but against the limitation of her own overburdened agents. She fought against the tutelage of her prudent old prime minister, the faithful instinct. She adopted a novel method of experiment, promulgated new laws, and tried her hand at moulding Man through a history which was immensely different from that which went before. She took a bold step in throwing open her gates to a dangerously explosive factor which she had cautiously introduced into her council – the element of Mind. I should not say that it was ever absent, but only that at a certain stage some curtain was removed and its play was made evident, even like the dark heat which in its glowing intensity reveals itself in a contradiction of radiancy.

Essentially qualitative, like life itself, the Mind does not occupy space. For that very reason it has no bounds in its mastery of space. Also, like Life, Mind has its meaning in freedom, which it missed in its earliest dealings with Life's children. In the animal, though the mind is allowed to come out of the immediate limits of livelihood, its range is restricted, like the freedom of a child that might run out of its room but not out of the house; or, rather, like the foreign ships to which only a certain port was opened in Japan in the beginning of her contact with the West in fear of the danger that might befall if the strangers had their uncontrolled opportunity of communication. Mind also is a foreign element for Life; its laws are different, its weapons powerful, its moods and manners most alien.

Like Eve of the Semitic mythology, the Spirit of Life risked the happiness of her placid seclusion to win her freedom. She listened to the whisper of a tempter who promised her the right to a new region of mystery, and was urged into a permanent alliance with the stranger. Up to this point the interest of life was the sole interest in her own kingdom, but another most powerfully parallel interest was created with the advent of this adventurer Mind from an unknown shore. Their interests clash, and complications of a serious nature arise. I have already referred to some vital organs of Man that are suffering from neglect. The only reason has been the diversion created by the Mind interrupting the sole attention which Life's functions claimed in the halcyon days of her undisputed monarchy. It is no secret that Mind has the habit of asserting its own will for its expression against life's will to live and enforcing sacrifices from her. When lately some adventurers accepted the dangerous enterprise to climb Mount Everest, it was solely through the instigation of the arch-rebel Mind. In this case Mind denied its treaty of cooperation with its partner and ignored Life's claim to help in her living. The immemorial privileges of the ancient sovereignty of Life are too often flouted by the irreverent Mind; in fact, all through the course of this alliance there are constant cases of interference with each other's functions, often with unpleasant and even fatal results. But in spite of this, or very often because of this antagonism, the new current of Man's evolution is bringing a wealth to his harbour infinitely beyond the dream of the creatures of monstrous flesh.

The manner in which Man appeared in Life's kingdom was in itself a protest and a challenge, the challenge of Jack to the Giant. He carried in his body the declaration of mistrust against the crowding of burdensome implements of physical progress. His Mind spoke to the naked man, 'Fear not'; and he stood alone facing the menace of a heavy brigade of formidable muscles. His own puny muscles cried out in despair, and he had to invent for himself in a novel manner and in a new spirit of evolution. This at once gave him his promotion from the passive destiny of the animal to the aristocracy of Man. He began to create his further body, his outer organs – the workers which served him and yet did not directly claim a share of his life. Some of the earliest in his list were bows and arrows. Had this change been undertaken by the physical process of evolution, modifying his arms in a slow and gradual manner, it might have resulted in burdensome and ungainly apparatus. Possibly, however, I am unfair, and the dexterity and grace which Life's technical instinct possesses might have changed his arm into a shooting medium in a perfect manner and with a beautiful form. In that case our lyrical literature to-day would have sung in praise of its fascination, not only for a consummate skill in hunting victims, but also for a similar mischief in a metaphorical sense. But even in the service of lyrics it would show some limitation. For instance, the arms that would specialize in shooting would be awkward in wielding a pen or stringing a lute. But the great advantage in the latest method of human evolution lies in the fact that Man's additional new limbs, like bows and arrows, have become detached. They never tie his arms to any exclusive advantage of efficiency.

The elephant's trunk, the tiger's paws, the claws of the mole, have combined their best expressions in the human arms, which are much weaker in their original capacity than those limbs I have mentioned. It would have been a hugely cumbersome practical joke if the combination of animal limbs had had a simultaneous location in the human organism through some overzeal in biological inventiveness.

The first great economy resulting from the new programme was the relief of the physical burden, which means the maximum efficiency with the minimum pressure of taxation upon the vital resources of the body. Another mission of benefit was this, that it absolved the Spirit of Life in Man's case from the necessity of specialization for the sake of limited success. This has encouraged Man to dream of the possibility of combining in his single person the fish, the bird and the fleet-footed animal that walks on land. Man desired in his completeness to be the one great representative of multiform life, not through wearisome subjection to the haphazard gropings of natural selection, but by the purposeful selection of opportunities with the help of his reasoning mind. It enables the schoolboy who is given a pen-knife on his birthday to have the advantage over the tiger in the fact that it does not take him a million years to obtain its possession, nor another million years for its removal, when the instrument proves unnecessary or dangerous. The human mind has compressed ages into a few years for the acquisition of steel-made claws. The only cause of anxiety is that the instrument and the temperament which uses it may not keep pace in perfect harmony. In the tiger, the claws and the temperament which only a tiger should possess have had a synchronous development, and in no single tiger is any maladjustment possible between its nails and its tigerliness. But the human boy, who grows a claw in the form of a pen-knife, may not at the same time develop the proper temperament necessary for its use which only a man ought to have. The new organs that to-day are being added as a supplement to Man's original vital stock are too quick and too numerous for his inner nature to develop its own simultaneous concordance with them, and thus we see everywhere innumerable schoolboys in human society playing pranks with their own and other people's lives and welfare by means of newly acquired pen-knives which have not had time to become humanized.

One thing, I am sure, must have been noticed – that the original plot of the drama is changed, and the mother Spirit of Life has retired into the background, giving full prominence, in the third act, to the Spirit of Man – though the dowager queen, from her inner apartment, still renders necessary help. It is the consciousness in Man of his own creative personality which has ushered in this new regime in Life's kingdom. And from now onwards Man's attempts are directed fully to capture the government and make his own Code of Legislation prevail without a break. We have seen in India those who are called mystics, impatient of the continued regency of mother Nature in their own body, winning for their will by a concentration of inner forces the vital regions with which our masterful minds have no direct path of communication.

But the most important fact that has come into prominence along with the change of direction in our evolution, is the possession of a Spirit which has its enormous capital with a surplus far in excess of the requirements of the biological animal in Man. Some overflowing influence led us over the strict boundaries of living, and offered to us an open space where Man's thoughts and dreams could have their holidays. Holidays are for gods who have their joy in creation. In Life's primitive paradise, where the mission was merely to live, any luck which came to the creatures entered in from outside by the donations of chance; they lived on perpetual charity, by turns petted and kicked on the back by physical Providence. Beggars never can have harmony among themselves; they are envious of one another, mutually suspicious, like dogs living upon their master's favour, showing their teeth, growling, barking, trying to tear one another. This is what Science describes as the struggle for existence. This beggar's paradise lacked peace; I am sure the suitors for special favour from fate lived in constant preparedness, inventing and multiplying armaments.

But above the din of the clamour and scramble rises the voice of the Angel of Surplus, of leisure, of detachment from the compelling claim of physical need, saying to men, 'Rejoice'. From his original serfdom as a creature Man takes his right seat as a creator. Whereas, before, his incessant appeal has been to get, now at last the call comes to him to give. His God, whose help he was in the habit of asking, now stands Himself at his door and asks for his offerings. As an animal, he is still dependent upon Nature; as a Man, he is a sovereign who builds his world and rules it.

And there, at this point, comes his religion, whereby he realizes himself in the perspective of the infinite. There is a remarkable verse in the Atharva Veda which says: 'Righteousness, truth, great endeavours, empire, religion, enterprise, heroism and prosperity, the past and the future, dwell in the surpassing strength of the surplus.'

What is purely physical has its limits like the shell of an egg; the liberation is there in the atmosphere of the infinite, which is indefinable, invisible. Religion can have no meaning in the enclosure of mere physical or material interest; it is in the surplus we carry around our personality – the surplus which is like the atmosphere of the earth, bringing to her a constant circulation of light and life and delightfulness.

I have said in a poem of mine that when the child is detached from its mother's womb it finds its mother in a real relationship whose truth is in freedom. Man in his detachment has realized himself in a wider and deeper relationship with the universe. In his moral life he has the sense of his obligation and his freedom at the same time, and this is goodness. In his spiritual life his sense of the union and the will which is free has its culmination in love. The freedom of opportunity he wins for himself in Nature's region by uniting his power with Nature's forces. The freedom of social relationship he attains through owning responsibility to his community, thus gaining its collective power for his own welfare. In the freedom of consciousness he realizes the sense of his unity with his larger being, finding fulfilment in the dedicated life of an ever-progressive truth and ever-active love.

The first detachment achieved by Man is physical. It represents his freedom from the necessity of developing the power of his senses and limbs in the limited area of his own physiology, having for itself an unbounded background with an immense result in consequence. Nature's original intention was that Man should have the allowance of his sight-power ample enough for his surroundings and a little over. But to have to develop an astronomical telescope on our skull would cause a worse crisis of bankruptcy than it did to the Mammoth whose densely foolish body indulged in an extravagance of tusks. A snail carries its house on its back and therefore the material, the shape and the weight have to be strictly limited to the capacity of the body. But fortunately Man's house need not grow on the foundation of his bones and occupy his flesh. Owing to this detachment, his ambition knows no check to its daring in the dimension and strength of his dwellings. Since his shelter does not depend upon his body, it survives him. This fact greatly affects the man who builds a house, generating in his mind a sense of the eternal in his creative work. And this background of the boundless surplus of time encourages architecture, which seeks a universal value overcoming the miserliness of the present need.

I have already mentioned a stage which Life reached when the units of single cells formed themselves into larger units, each consisting of a multitude. It was not merely an aggregation, but had a mysterious unity of inter-relationship, complex in character, with differences within of forms and function. We can never know concretely what this relation means. There are gaps between the units, but they do not stop the binding force that permeates the whole. There is a future for the whole which is in its growth, but in order to bring this about each unit works and dies to make room for the next worker. While the unit has the right to claim the glory of the whole, yet individually it cannot share the entire wealth that occupies a history yet to be completed.

Of all creatures Man has reached that multicellular character in a perfect manner, not only in his body but in his personality. For centuries his evolution has been the evolution of a consciousness that tries to be liberated from the bonds of individual separateness and to comprehend in its relationship a wholeness which may be named Man. This relationship, which has been dimly instinctive, is ever struggling to be fully aware of itself. Physical evolution sought for efficiency in a perfect communication with the physical world; the evolution of Man's consciousness sought for truth in a perfect harmony with the world of personality.

There are those who will say that the idea of humanity is an abstraction, subjective in character. It must be confessed that the concrete objectiveness of this living truth cannot be proved to its own units. They can never see its entireness from outside; for they are one with it. The individual cells of our body have their separate lives; but they never have the opportunity of observing the body as a whole with its past, present and future. If these cells have the power of reasoning (which they may have for aught we know) they have the right to argue that the idea of the body has no objective foundation in fact, and though there is a mysterious sense of attraction and mutual influence running through them, these are nothing positively real; the sole reality which is provable is in the isolation of these cells made by gaps that can never be crossed or bridged.

We know something about a system of explosive atoms whirling separately in a space which is immense compared to their own dimension. Yet we do not know why they should appear to us a solid piece of radiant mineral. And if there is an onlooker who at one glance can have the view of the immense time and space occupied by innumerable human individuals engaged in evolving a common history, the positive truth of their solidarity will be concretely evident to him and not the negative fact of their separateness.

The reality of a piece of iron is not provable if we take the evidence of the atom; the only proof is that I see it as a bit of iron, and that it has certain reactions upon my consciousness. Any being from, say, Orion, who has the sight to see the atoms and not the iron, has the right to say that we human beings suffer from an age-long epidemic of hallucination. We need not quarrel with him but go on using the iron as it appears to us. Seers there have been who have said *Vedāhamētam*, 'I see', and lived a life according to that vision. And though our own sight may be blind we have ever bowed our head to them in reverence.

However, whatever name our logic may give to the truth of human unity, the fact can never be ignored that we have our greatest delight when we realize ourselves in others, and this is the definition of love. This love gives us the testimony of the great whole, which is the complete and final truth of man. It offers us the immense field where we can have our release from the sole monarchy of hunger, of the growling voice, snarling teeth and tearing claws, from the dominance of the limited material means, the source of cruel envy and ignoble deception, where the largest wealth of the human soul has been produced through sympathy and co-operation; through disinterested pursuit of knowledge that recognizes no limit and is unafraid of all time-honoured *taboos*; through a strenuous cultivation of intelligence for service that knows no distinction of colour and clime. The Spirit of Love, dwelling in the boundless realm of the surplus, emancipates our consciousness from the illusory bond of the separateness of self; it is ever trying to spread its illumination in the human world. This is the spirit of civilization, which in all its best endeavour invokes our supreme Being for the only bond of unity that leads us to truth, namely, that of righteousness:

Ya ēkō varnō bahudhā saktiyogāt
varnān anēkān nihitārthō dadhāti
vichaitti chānte visvamādau sa dēvah
sa nō budhyā subhayā samyunaktu.

He who is one, above all colours, and who with his manifold power supplies the inherent needs of men of all colours, who is in the beginning and in the end of the world, is divine, and may he unite us in a relationship of good will.

CHAPTER THREE
THE SURPLUS IN MAN

THERE ARE CERTAIN verses from the Atharva Veda in which the poet discusses his idea of Man, indicating some transcendental meaning that can be translated as follows:

> Who was it that imparted form to man, gave him majesty, movement, manifestation and character, inspired him with wisdom, music and dancing? When his body was raised upwards he found also the oblique sides and all other directions in him – he who is the Person, the citadel of the infinite being.

Tasmād vai vidvān purushamidan brahmēti manyatē.
And therefore the wise man knoweth this person as Brahma.

Sanātanam ēnam āhur utādya syāt punarnavah.
Ancient they call him, and yet he is renewed even now to-day.

In the very beginning of his career Man asserted in his bodily structure his first proclamation of freedom against the established rule of Nature. At a certain bend in the path of evolution he refused to remain a four-footed creature, and the position which he made his body to assume carried with it a permanent gesture of insubordination. For there could be no question that it was Nature's own plan to provide all land-walking mammals with two pairs of legs, evenly distributed along their lengthy trunk heavily weighted with a head at the end. This was the amicable compromise made with the earth when threatened by its conservative downward force, which extorts taxes for all movements. The fact that man gave up such an obviously sensible arrangement proves his inborn mania for repeated reforms of constitution, for pelting amendments at every resolution proposed by Providence.

If we found a four-legged table stalking about upright upon two of its stumps, the remaining two foolishly dangling by its sides, we should be afraid that it was either a nightmare or some supernormal caprice of that piece of furniture, indulging in a practical joke upon the carpenter's idea of fitness. The like absurd behaviour of Man's anatomy encourages us to guess that he was born under the influence of some comet of contradiction that forces its eccentric path against orbits regulated by Nature. And it is significant that Man should persist in his foolhardiness, in spite of the penalty he pays for opposing the orthodox rule of animal locomotion. He reduces by half the help of an easy balance of his muscles. He is ready to pass his infancy tottering through perilous experiments in making progress upon insufficient support, and followed all through his life by liability to sudden downfalls resulting in tragic or ludicrous consequences from which law-abiding quadrupeds are free. This was his great venture, the relinquishment of a secure position of his limbs, which he could comfortably have retained in return for humbly salaaming the all-powerful dust at every step.

This capacity to stand erect has given our body its freedom of posture, making it easy for us to turn on all sides and realize ourselves at the centre of things. Physically, it symbolizes the fact that while animals have for their progress the prolongation of a narrow line Man has the enlargement of a circle. As a centre he finds his meaning in a wide perspective, and realizes himself in the magnitude of his circumference.

As one freedom leads to another, Man's eyesight also found a wider scope. I do not mean any enhancement of its physical power, which in many predatory animals has a better power of adjustment to light. But from the higher vantage of our physical watch-tower we have gained our *view*, which is not merely information about the location of things but their inter-relation and their unity.

But the best means of the expression of his physical freedom gained by Man in his vertical position is through the emancipation of his hands. In our bodily organization these have attained the highest dignity for their skill, their grace, their useful activities, as well as for those that are above all uses. They are the most detached of all our limbs. Once they had their menial vocation as our carriers, but raised from their position as *shudras*, they at once attained responsible status as our helpers. When instead of keeping them underneath us we offered them their place at our side, they revealed capacities that helped us to cross the boundaries of animal nature.

This freedom of view and freedom of action have been accompanied by an analogous mental freedom in Man through his imagination, which is the most distinctly human of all our faculties. It is there to help a creature who has been left unfinished by his designer, undraped, undecorated, unarmoured and without weapons, and, what is worse, ridden by a Mind whose energies for the most part are not tamed and tempered into some difficult ideal of completeness upon a background which is bare. Like all artists he has the freedom to make mistakes, to launch into desperate adventures contradicting and torturing his psychology or physiological normality. This freedom is a divine gift lent to the mortals who are untutored and undisciplined; and therefore the path of their creative progress is strewn with debris of devastation, and stages of their perfection haunted by apparitions of startling deformities. But, all the same, the very training of creation ever makes clear an aim which cannot be in any isolated freak of an individual mind or in that which is only limited to the strictly necessary.

Just as our eyesight enables us to include the individual fact of ourselves in the surrounding view, our imagination makes us intensely conscious of a life we must live which transcends the individual life and contradicts the biological meaning of the instinct of self-preservation. It works at the surplus, and extending beyond the reservation plots of our daily life builds there the guest chambers of priceless value to offer hospitality to the world-spirit of Man. We have such an honoured right to be the host when our spirit is a free spirit not chained to the animal self. For free spirit is godly and alone can claim kinship with God.

Every true freedom that we may attain in any direction broadens our path of self-realization, which is in superseding the self. The unimaginative repetition of life within a safe restriction imposed by Nature may be good for the animal, but never for Man, who has the responsibility to outlive his life in order to live in truth.

And freedom in its process of creation gives rise to perpetual suggestions of something further than its obvious purpose.
For freedom is for expressing the infinite; it imposes limits in its
works, not to keep them in permanence but to break them over
and over again, and to reveal the endless in unending surprises.
This implies a history of constant regeneration, a series of fresh
beginnings and continual challenges to the old in order to reach
a more and more perfect harmony with some fundamental ideal
of truth.

Our civilization, in the constant struggle for a great Further,
runs through abrupt chapters of spasmodic divergences. It nearly
always begins its new ventures with a cataclysm; for its changes
are not mere seasonal changes of ideas gliding through varied pe-
riods of flowers and fruit. They are surprises lying in ambuscade
provoking revolutionary adjustments. They are changes in the
dynasty of living ideals – the ideals that are active in consolidating
their dominion with strongholds of physical and mental habits,
of symbols, ceremonials and adornments. But however violent
may be the revolutions happening in whatever time or country, they never completely detach themselves from a common
centre. They find their places in a history which is one.

The civilizations evolved in India or China, Persia or Judaea,
Greece or Rome, are like several mountain peaks having different altitude, temperature, flora and fauna, and yet belonging to
the same chain of hills. There are no absolute barriers of communication between them; their foundation is the same and they
affect the meteorology of an atmosphere which is common to
us all. This is at the root of the meaning of the great teacher
who said he would not seek his own salvation if all men were
not saved; for we all belong to a divine unity, from which our
great-souled men have their direct inspiration; they feel it immediately in their own personality, and they proclaim in their
life, 'I am one with the Supreme, with the Deathless, with
the Perfect.'

Man, in his mission to create himself, tries to develop in his
mind an image of his truth according to an idea which he believes
to be universal, and is sure that any expression given to it will
persist through all time. This is a mentality absolutely superfluous
for biological existence. It represents his struggle for a life which
is not limited to his body. For our physical life has its thread of
unity in the memory of the past, whereas this ideal life dwells

in the prospective memory of the future. In the records of past civilizations, unearthed from the closed records of dust, we find pathetic efforts to make their memories uninterrupted through the ages, like the effort of a child who sets adrift on a paper boat his dream of reaching the distant unknown. But why is this desire? Only because we feel instinctively that in our ideal life we must touch all men and all times through the manifestation of a truth which is eternal and universal. And in order to give expression to it materials are gathered that are excellent and a manner of execution that has a permanent value. For we mortals must offer homage to the Man of the everlasting life. In order to do so, we are expected to pay a great deal more than we need for mere living, and in the attempt we often exhaust our very means of livelihood, and even life itself.

The ideal picture which a savage imagines of himself requires glaring paints and gorgeous fineries, a rowdiness in ornaments and even grotesque deformities of over-wrought extravagance. He tries to sublimate his individual self into a manifestation which he believes to have the majesty of the ideal Man. He is not satisfied with what he is in his natural limitations; he irresistibly feels something beyond the evident fact of himself which only could give him worth. It is the principle of power, which, according to his present mental stage, is the meaning of the universal reality whereto he belongs, and it is his pious duty to give expression to it even at the cost of his happiness. In fact, through it he becomes one with his God, for him his God is nothing greater than power. The savage takes immense trouble, and often suffers tortures, in order to offer in himself a representation of power in conspicuous colours and distorted shapes, in acts of relentless cruelty and intemperate bravado of self-indulgence. Such an appearance of rude grandiosity evokes a loyal reverence in the members of his community and a fear which gives them an aesthetic satisfaction because it illuminates for them the picture of a character which, as far as they know, belongs to ideal humanity. They wish to see in him not an individual, but the Man in whom they all are represented. Therefore, in spite of their sufferings, they enjoy being overwhelmed by his exaggerations and dominated by a will fearfully evident owing to its magnificent caprice in inflicting injuries. They symbolize their idea of unlimited wilfulness in their gods by ascribing to them physical and moral enormities in their anatomical idiosyncrasy and virulent vindictiveness crying for the blood of victims, in personal preferences indiscriminate in the choice of recipients and methods of rewards and punishments. In fact, these gods could never be blamed for the least wavering in their conduct owing to any scrupulousness accompanied by the emotion of pity so often derided as sentimentalism by virile intellects of the present day.

However crude all this may be, it proves that Man has a feeling that he is truly represented in something which exceeds himself. He is aware that he is not imperfect, but incomplete. He knows that in himself some meaning has yet to be realized. We do not feel the wonder of it, because it seems so natural to us that barbarism in Man is not absolute, that its limits are like the limits of the horizon. The call is deep in his mind – the call of his own inner truth, which is beyond his direct knowledge and analytical logic. And individuals are born who have no doubt of the truth of this transcendental Man. As our consciousness more and more comprehends it, new valuations are developed in us, new depths and delicacies of delight, a sober dignity of expression through elimination of tawdriness, of frenzied emotions, of all violence in shape, colour, words, or behaviour, of the dark mentality of Ku-Klux-Klanism.

Each age reveals its personality as dreamer in its great expressions that carry it across surging centuries to the continental plateau of permanent human history. These expressions may not be consciously religious, but indirectly they belong to Man's religion. For they are the outcome of the consciousness of the greater Man in the individual men of the race. This consciousness finds its manifestation in science, philosophy and the arts, in social ethics, in all things that carry their ultimate value in themselves. These are truly spiritual and they should all be consciously co-ordinated in one great religion of Man, representing his ceaseless endeavour to reach the perfect in great thoughts and deeds and dreams, in immortal symbols of art, revealing his aspiration for rising in dignity of being.

I had the occasion to visit the ruins of ancient Rome, the relics of human yearning towards the immense, the sight of which teases our mind out of thought. Does it not prove that in the vision of a great Roman Empire the creative imagination of the people rejoiced in the revelation of its transcendental humanity? It was the idea of an Empire which was not merely for opening an outlet to the pent-up pressure of over-population, or widening its field of commercial profit, but which existed as a concrete representation of the majesty of Roman personality, the soul of the people dreaming of a world-wide creation of its own for a fit habitation of the Ideal Man. It was Rome's titanic endeavour to answer the eternal question as to what Man truly was, as Man. And any answer given in earnest falls within the realm of religion, whatever may be its character; and this answer, in its truth, belongs not only to any particular people but to us all. It may be that Rome did not give the most perfect answer possible when she fought for her place as a world-builder of human history, but she revealed the marvellous vigour of the indomitable human spirit which could say, *Bhumaiva sukkam*, 'Greatness is happiness itself'. Her Empire has been sundered and shattered, but her faith in the sublimity of man still persists in one of the vast strata of human geology. And this faith was the true spirit of her religion, which had been dim in the tradition of her formal theology, merely supplying her with an emotional pastime and not with spiritual inspiration. In fact this theology fell far below her personality, and for that reason it went against her religion, whose mission was to reveal her humanity on the background of the eternal. Let us seek the religion of this and other people not in their gods but in Man, who dreamed of his own infinity and majestically worked for all time, defying danger and death.

Since the dim nebula of consciousness in Life's world became intensified into a centre of self in Man, his history began to unfold its rapid chapters; for it is the history of his strenuous answers in various forms to the question rising from this conscious self of his, 'What am I?' Man is not happy or contented as the animals are; for his happiness and his peace depend upon the truth of his answer. The animal attains his success in a physical sufficiency that satisfies his nature. When a crocodile finds no obstruction in behaving like an orthodox crocodile he grins and grows and has no cause to complain. It is truism to say that Man also must behave like a man in order to find his truth. But he is sorely puzzled and asks in bewilderment: 'What is it to be like a man? What am I?' It is not left to the tiger to discover what is his own nature as a tiger, nor, for the matter of that, to choose a special colour for his coat according to his taste.

But Man has taken centuries to discuss the question of his

own true nature and has not yet come to a conclusion. He has been building up elaborate religions to convince himself, against his natural inclinations, of the paradox that he is not what he is but something greater. What is significant about these efforts is the fact that in order to know himself truly Man in his religion cultivates the vision of a Being who exceeds him in truth and with whom also he has his kinship. These religions differ in details and often in their moral significance, but they have a common tendency. In them men seek their own supreme value, which they call divine, in some personality anthropomorphic in character. The Mind, which is abnormally scientific, scoffs at this; but it should know that religion is not essentially cosmic or even abstract; it finds itself when it touches the Brahma in man; otherwise it has no justification to exist.

It must be admitted that such a human element introduces into our religion a mentality that often has its danger in aberrations that are intellectually blind, morally reprehensible and aesthetically repellent. But these are wrong answers; they distort the truth of man and, like all mistakes in sociology, in economics or politics, they have to be fought against and overcome. Their truth has to be judged by the standard of human perfection and not by some arbitrary injunction that refuses to be confirmed by the tribunal of the human conscience. And great religions are the outcome of great revolutions in this direction causing fundamental changes of our attitude. These religions invariably made their appearance as a protest against the earlier creeds which had been unhuman, where ritualistic observances had become more important and outer compulsions more imperious. These creeds were, as I have said before, cults of power; they had their value for us, not helping us to become perfect through truth, but to grow formidable through possessions and magic control of the deity.

But possibly I am doing injustice to our ancestors. It is more likely that they worshipped power not merely because of its utility, but because they, in their way, recognized it as truth with which their own power had its communication and in which it found its fulfilment. They must have naturally felt that this power was the power of will behind nature, and not some impersonal insanity that unaccountably always stumbled upon correct results. For it would have been the greatest depth of imbecility on their part had they brought their homage to an abstraction, mindless, heartless and purposeless; in fact, infinitely below them in its manifestation.

CHAPTER FOUR
SPIRITUAL UNION

WHEN MAN'S PREOCCUPATION with the means of livelihood became less insistent he had the leisure to come to the mystery of his own self, and could not help feeling that the truth of his personality had both its relationship and its perfection in an endless world of humanity. His religion, which in the beginning had its cosmic background of power, came to a higher stage when it found its background in the human truth of personality. It must not be thought that in this channel it was narrowing the range of our consciousness of the infinite.

The negative idea of the infinite is merely an indefinite enlargement of the limits of things; in fact, a perpetual postponement of infinitude. I am told that mathematics has come to the conclusion that our world belongs to a space which is limited. It does not make us feel disconsolate. We do not miss very much and need not have a low opinion of space even if a straight line cannot remain straight and has an eternal tendency to come back to the point from which it started. In the Hindu Scripture the universe is described as an egg; that is to say, for the human mind it has its circular shell of limitation. The Hindu Scripture goes still further and says that time also is not continuous and our world repeatedly comes to an end to begin its cycle once again. In other words, in the region of time and space infinity consists of ever-revolving finitude.

But the positive aspect of the infinite is in *advaitam*, in an absolute unity, in which comprehension of the multitude is not as in an outer receptacle but as in an inner perfection that permeates and exceeds its contents, like the beauty in a lotus which is ineffably more than all the constituents of the flower. It is not the magnitude of extension but an intense quality of harmony which evokes in us the positive sense of the infinite in our joy, in our love. For *advaitam* is *anandam*; the infinite One is infinite Love. For those among whom the spiritual sense is dull, the desire for realization is reduced to physical possession, an actual grasping in space. This longing for magnitude becomes not an aspiration

towards the great, but a mania for the big. But true spiritual realization is not through augmentation of possession in dimension
or number. The truth that is infinite dwells in the ideal of unity
which we find in the deeper relatedness. This truth of realization
is not in space, it can only be realized in one's own inner spirit.

> *Ekadhaivanudrashtavyam etat aprameyam dhruvam.*
> This infinite and eternal has to be known as One.

Ākasat aja ātmā – 'this birthless spirit is beyond space'. For it is
Purushah, it is the 'Person'.

The special mental attitude which India has in her religion is
made clear by the word *Yoga*, whose meaning is to effect union.
Union has its significance not in the realm of *to have*, but in that
of *to be*. To *gain* truth is to admit its separateness, but to *be* true is
to become one with truth. Some religions, which deal with our
relationship with God, assure us of reward if that relationship be
kept true. This reward has an objective value. It gives us some
reason outside ourselves for pursuing the prescribed path. We
have such religions also in India. But those that have attained a
greater height aspire for their fulfilment in union with *Narayana*,
the supreme Reality of Man, which is divine.

Our union with this spirit is not to be attained through the
mind. For our mind belongs to the department of economy in
the human organism. It carefully husbands our consciousness for
its own range of reason, within which to permit our relationship
with the phenomenal world. But it is the object of *Yoga* to help
us to transcend the limits built up by Mind. On the occasions
when these are overcome, our inner self is filled with joy, which
indicates that through such freedom we come into touch with
the Reality that is an end in itself and therefore is bliss.

Once man had his vision of the infinite in the universal Light,
and he offered his worship to the sun. He also offered his service
to the fire with oblations. Then he felt the infinite in Life, which
is Time in its creative aspect, and he said, *Yat kincha yadidam
sarvam prana ejati nihsritam*, 'all that there is comes out of life
and vibrates in it'. He was sure of it, being conscious of Life's
mystery immediately in himself as the principle of purpose, as
the organized will, the source of all his activities. His interpretation of the ultimate character of truth relied upon the suggestion
that Life had brought to him, and not the non-living which is
dumb. And then he came deeper into his being and said '*Raso*

vai sah', 'the infinite is love itself', – the eternal spirit of joy. His religion, which is in his realization of the infinite, began its journey from the impersonal *dyaus*, 'the sky', wherein light had its manifestation; then came to Life, which represented the force of self-creation in time, and ended in *purushah*, the 'Person', in whom dwells timeless love. It said, *Tam vedyam purusham vedah*, 'Know him the Person who is to be realized', *Yatha ma vo mrityug parivyathah* – 'So that death may not cause you sorrow'. For this Person is deathless in whom the individual person has his immortal truth. Of him it is said: *Eskha devo visvakarmā mahātmā sadā janānam hridaye sannivishatah*. 'This is the divine being, the world-worker, who is the Great Soul ever dwelling inherent in the hearts of all people.'

Ya etad vidur amritas te bhavanti. 'Those who realize him, transcend the limits of mortality' – not in duration of time, but in perfection of truth.

Our union with a Being whose activity is world-wide and who dwells in the heart of humanity cannot be a passive one. In order to be united with Him we have to divest our work of selfishness and become *visvakarmā*, 'the world-worker', we must work for all. When I use the words 'for all', I do not mean for a countless number of individuals. All work that is good, however small in extent, is universal in character. Such work makes for a realization of *Visvakarmā*, 'the World-Worker' who works for all. In order to be one with this Mahatma, 'the Great Soul', one must cultivate the greatness of soul which identifies itself with the soul of all peoples and not merely with that of one's own. This helps us to understand what Buddha has described as *Brahmavihāra*, 'living in the infinite'. He says:

'Do not deceive each other, do not despise anybody anywhere, never in anger wish anyone to suffer through your body, words or thoughts. Like a mother maintaining her only son with her own life, keep thy immeasurable loving thought for all creatures.

'Above thee, below thee, on all sides of thee, keep on all the world thy sympathy and immeasurable loving thought which is without obstruction, without any wish to injure, without enmity.

'To be dwelling in such contemplation while standing, walking, sitting or lying down, until sleep overcomes thee, is called living in Brahma.'

This proves that Buddha's idea of the infinite was not the idea of a spirit of an unbounded cosmic activity, but the infinite whose meaning is in the positive ideal of goodness and love, which cannot be otherwise than human. By being charitable, good and loving, you do not realize the infinite, in the stars or rocks, but the infinite revealed in Man. Buddha's teaching speaks of Nirvana as the highest end. To understand its real character we have to know the path of its attainment, which is not merely through the negation of evil thoughts and deeds but through the elimination of all limits to love. It must mean the sublimation of self in a truth which is love itself, which unites in its bosom all those to whom we must offer our sympathy and service.

When somebody asked Buddha about the original cause of existence he sternly said that such questioning was futile and ir- relevant. Did he not mean that it went beyond the human sphere as our goal – that though such a question might legitimately be asked in the region of cosmic philosophy or science, it had nothing to do with man's *dharma*, man's inner nature, in which love finds its utter fulfilment, in which all his sacrifice ends in an eternal gain, in which the putting out of the lamplight is no loss because there is the all-pervading light of the sun. And did those who listened to the great teacher merely hear his words and understand his doctrines? No, they directly felt in him what he was preaching, in the living language of his own person, the ultimate truth of Man.

It is significant that all great religions have their historic origin in persons who represented in their life a truth which was not cosmic and unmoral, but human and good. They rescued reli- gion from the magic stronghold of demon force and brought it into the inner heart of humanity, into a fulfilment not confined to some exclusive good fortune of the individual but to the wel- fare of all men. This was not for the spiritual ecstasy of lonely souls, but for the spiritual emancipation of all races. They came as the messengers of Man to men of all countries and spoke of the salvation that could only be reached by the perfecting of our relationship with Man the Eternal, Man the Divine. Whatever might be their doctrines of God, or some dogmas that they bor- rowed from their own time and tradition, their life and teaching had the deeper implication of a Being who is the infinite in Man, the Father, the Friend, the Lover, whose service must be realized through serving all mankind. For the God in Man depends upon men's service and men's love for his own love's fulfilment

The question was once asked in the shade of the ancient forest of India:

Kasmai devāya havishā vidhema?
Who is the God to whom we must bring our oblation?

That question is still ours, and to answer it we must know in the depth of our love and the maturity of our wisdom what man is – know him not only in sympathy but in science, in the joy of creation and in the pain of heroism; *tena tyaktena bhunji-tha*, 'enjoy him through sacrifice' – the sacrifice that comes of love; *ma gridhah*, 'covet not'; for greed diverts your mind to that illusion in you in which you represent the *parama purushah*, 'the supreme Person'.

Our greed diverts our consciousness to materials away from that supreme value of truth which is the quality of the universal being. The gulf thus created by the receding stream of the soul we try to replenish with a continuous stream of wealth, which may have the power to fill but not the power to unite and re-create. Therefore the gap is dangerously concealed under the glittering quicksand of things, which by their own weight cause a sudden subsidence while we are in the depths of sleep.

The real tragedy, however, does not lie in the risk of our material security but in the obscuration of Man himself in the human world. In the creative activities of his soul Man realizes his surroundings as his larger self, instinct with his own life and love. But in his ambition he deforms and defiles it with the callous handling of his voracity. His world of utility assuming a gigantic proportion, reacts upon his inner nature and hyp-notically suggests to him a scheme of the universe which is an abstract system. In such a world there can be no question of *mukti*, the freedom in truth, because it is a solidly solitary fact, a cage with no sky beyond it. In all appearance our world is a closed world of hard facts; it is like a seed with its tough cover. But within this enclosure is working our silent cry of life for *mukti*, even when its possibility is darkly silent. When some huge overgrown temptation tramples into stillness this living aspira-tion then does civilization die like a seed that has lost its urging for germination. And this *mukti* is in the truth that dwells in the ideal man.

CHAPTER FIVE
THE PROPHET

IN MY INTRODUCTION I have stated that the universe to which we are related through our sense perception, reason or imagination, is necessarily Man's universe. Our physical self gains strength and success through its correct relationship in knowledge and practice with its physical aspect. The mysteries of all its phenomena are generalized by man as laws which have their harmony with his rational mind. In the primitive period of our history Man's physical dealings with the external world were most important for the maintenance of his life, the life which he has in common with other creatures, and therefore the first expression of his religion was physical – it came from his sense of wonder and awe at the manifestations of power in Nature and his attempt to win it for himself and his tribe by magical incantations and rites. In other words his religion tried to gain a perfect communion with the mysterious magic of Nature's forces through his own power of magic. Then came the time when he had the freedom of leisure to divert his mind to his inner nature and the mystery of his own personality gained for him its highest importance. And instinctively his personal self sought its fulfilment in the truth of a higher personality. In the history of religion our realization of its nature has gone through many changes even like our realization of the nature of the material world. Our method of worship has followed the course of such changes, but its evolution has been from the external and magical towards the moral and spiritual significance.

The first profound record of the change of direction in Man's religion we find in the message of the great prophet in Persia, Zarathustra, and as usual it was accompanied by a revolution. In a later period the same thing happened in India, and it is evident that the history of this religious struggle lies embedded in the epic Mahabharata associated with the name of Krishna and the teachings of Bhagavadgita.

The most important of all outstanding facts of Iranian history is the religious reform brought about by Zarathustra. There can be hardly any question that he was the first man we know who gave a definitely moral character and direction to religion and at the same time preached the doctrine of monotheism which offered an eternal foundation of reality to goodness as an ideal of perfection. All religions of the primitive type try to keep men bound with regulations of external observances. Zarathustra was the greatest of all the pioneer prophets who showed the path of freedom to man, the freedom of moral choice, the freedom from the blind obedience to unmeaning injunctions, the freedom from the multiplicity of shrines which draw our worship away from the single-minded chastity of devotion.

To most of us it sounds like a truism to-day when we are told that the moral goodness of a deed comes from the goodness of intention. But it is a truth which once came to Man like a revelation of light in the darkness and it has not yet reached all the obscure corners of humanity. We still see around us men who fearfully follow, hoping thereby to gain merit, the path of blind formalism, which has no living moral source in the mind. This will make us understand the greatness of Zarathustra. Though surrounded by believers in magical rites, he proclaimed in those dark days of unreason that religion has its truth in its moral significance, not in external practices of imaginary value; that its value is in upholding man in his life of good thoughts, good words and good deeds.

'The prophet', says Dr. Geiger, 'qualifies his religion as "unheard of words" (*Yasna* 31. 1) or as a "mystery" (Y.48. 3) because he himself regards it as a religion quite distinct from the belief of the people hitherto. The revelation he announces is to him no longer a matter of sentiment, no longer a merely undefined presentiment and conception of the Godhead, but a matter of intellect, of spiritual perception and knowledge. This is of great importance, for there are probably not many religions of so high antiquity in which this fundamental doctrine, that religion is a knowledge or learning, a science of what is true, is so precisely declared as in the tenets of the Gathas. It is the unbelieving that are unknowing; on the contrary, the believing are learned because they have penetrated into this knowledge.'

It may be incidentally mentioned here, as showing the parallel to this in the development of Indian religious thought, that all through the Upanishad spiritual truth is termed with a repeated emphasis, *vidya*, knowledge, which has for its opposite *avidya*, acceptance of error born of unreason.

The outer expression of truth reaches its white light of simplicity through its inner realization. True simplicity is the physiognomy of perfection. In the primitive stages of spiritual growth, when man is dimly aware of the mystery of the infinite in his life and the world, when he does not fully know the inward character of his relationship with this truth, his first feeling is either of dread, or of greed of gain. This drives him into wild exaggeration in worship, frenzied convulsions of ceremonialism. But in Zarathustra's teachings, which are best reflected in his Gathas, we have hardly any mention of the ritualism of worship. Conduct and its moral motives have there received almost the sole attention.

The orthodox Persian form of worship in ancient Iran included animal sacrifices and offering of *haema* to the *daevas*. That all these should be discountenanced by Zarathustra not only shows his courage, but the strength of his realization of the Supreme Being as spirit. We are told that it has been mentioned by Plutarch that 'Zarathustra taught the Persians to sacrifice to Ahura Mazda, "vows and thanksgivings"'. The distance between faith in the efficiency of the bloodstained magical rites, and cultivation of the moral and spiritual ideals as the true form of worship is immense. It is amazing to see how Zarathustra was the first among men who crossed this distance with a certainty of realization which imparted such a fervour of faith to his life and his words. The truth which filled his mind was not a thing which he borrowed from books or received from teachers; he did not come to it by following a prescribed path of tradition, but it came to him as an illumination of his entire life, almost like a communication of his universal self to his personal self, and he proclaimed this utmost immediacy of his knowledge when he said:

> When I conceived of Thee, O Mazda, as the very First and the Last, as the most Adorable One, as the Father of the Good Thought, as the Creator of Truth and Right, as the Lord Judge of our actions in life, then I made a place for Thee in my very eyes. – *Yasna* 31.8 (Translation D. J. Irani).

It was the direct stirring of his soul which made him say:

> Thus do I announce the Greatest of all! I weave my songs of praise for him through Truth, helpful and beneficent of all that live. Let Ahura Mazda listen to them with his Holy Spirit, for the Good Mind instructed me to adore Him; by his wisdom let Him teach me about what is best. – *Yasna* 45.6 (Translation D. J. Irani).

The truth which is not reached through the analytical process of reasoning and does not depend for proof on some corroboration of outward facts or the prevalent faith and practice of the people – the truth which comes like an inspiration out of context with its surroundings brings with it an assurance that it has been sent from an inner source of divine wisdom, that the individual who has realized it is specially inspired and therefore has his responsibility as a direct medium of communication of Divine Truth.

As long as man deals with his God as the dispenser of benefits only to those of His worshippers who know the secret of propitiating Him, he tries to keep Him for his own self or for the tribe to which he belongs. But directly the moral nature, that is to say, the humanity of God is apprehended, man realizes his divine self in his religion, his God is no longer an outsider to be propitiated for a special concession. The consciousness of God transcends the limitations of race and gathers together all human beings within one spiritual circle of union. Zarathustra was the first prophet who emancipated religion from the exclusive narrowness of the tribal God, the God of a chosen people, and offered it the universal Man. This is a great fact in the history of religion. The Master said, when the enlightenment came to him:

> Verily I believed Thee, O Ahura Mazda, to be the Supreme Benevolent Providence, when Sraosha came to me with the Good Mind, when first I received and became wise with your words. And though the task be difficult, though woe may come to me, I shall proclaim to all mankind Thy message, which Thou declarest to be the best. – *Yasna* 43 (Translation D. J. Irani).

He prays to Mazda:

> This I ask Thee, tell me truly, O Ahura, the religion that is best for all mankind, the religion, which based on truth, should prosper in all that is ours, the religion which establishes our actions in order and justice by the Divine songs of Perfect Piety, which has for its intelligent desire of desires, the desire for Thee, O Mazda. – *Yasna* 44.10 (Translation D. J. Irani).

With the undoubted assurance and hope of one who has got a direct vision of Truth he speaks to the word:

Hearken unto me, Ye who come from near and from far!
Listen for I shall speak forth now; ponder well over all
things, weigh my words with care and clear thought. Never
shall the false teacher destroy this world for a second time,
for his tongue stands mute, his creed exposed. – *Yasna* 45.1
(Translation D. J. Irani).

I think it can be said without doubt that such a high conception
of religion, uttered in such a clear note of affirmation with a sure
note of conviction that it is a truth of the ultimate ideal of perfection which must be revealed to all humanity, even at the cost
of martyrdom, is unique in the history of any religion belonging
to such a remote dawn of civilization.

There was a time when, along with other Aryan peoples,
the Persian also worshipped the elemental gods of Nature,
whose favour was not to be won by any moral duty performed
or service of love. That in fact was the crude beginning of the
scientific spirit trying to unlock the hidden sources of power in
nature. But through it all there must have been some current of
deeper desire, which constantly contradicted the cult of power
and indicated worlds of inner good, infinitely more precious
than material gain. Its voice was not strong at first nor was it
heeded by the majority of the people; but its influences, like the
life within the seed, were silently working.

Then comes the great prophet; and in his life and mind the
hidden fire of truth suddenly bursts out into flame. The best in
the people works for long obscure ages in hints and whispers till
it finds its voice which can never again be silenced. For that voice
becomes the voice of Man, no longer confined to a particular
time or people. It works across intervals of silence and oblivion,
depression and defeat, and comes out again with its conquering
call. It is a call to the fighter, the fighter against untruth, against
all that lures away man's spirit from its high mission of freedom
into the meshes of materialism.

Zarathustra's voice is still a living voice, not alone a matter of
academic interest for historical scholars who deal with the facts
of the past; nor merely the guide of a small community of men
in the daily details of their life. Rather, of all teachers Zarathustra
was the first who addressed his words to all humanity, regardless
of distance of space or time. He was not like a cave-dweller who,
by some chance of friction, had lighted a lamp and, fearing lest

it could not be shared with all, secured it with a miser's care for his own domestic use. But he was the watcher in the night, who stood on the lonely peak facing the East and broke out singing the paeans of light to the sleeping world when the sun came out on the brim of the horizon. The Sun of Truth is for all, he declared – its light is to unite the far and the near. Such a message always arouses the antagonism of those whose habits have become nocturnal, whose vested interest is in the darkness. And there was a bitter fight in the lifetime of the prophet between his followers and the others who were addicted to the ceremonies that had tradition on their side, and not truth.

We are told that 'Zarathustra was descended from a kingly family', and also that the first converts to his doctrine were of the ruling caste. But the priesthood, 'the Kavis and the Karapans, often succeeded in bringing the rulers over to their side'. So we find that, in this fight, the princes of the land divided themselves into two opposite parties as we find in India in the Kurukshetra War.

It has been a matter of supreme satisfaction to me to realize that the purification of faith which was the mission of the great teachers in both communities, in Persia and in India, followed a similar line. We have already seen how Zarathustra spiritualized the meaning of sacrifice, which in former days consisted in external ritualism entailing bloodshed. The same thing we find in the Gita, in which the meaning of the word *Yajna* has been translated into a higher significance than it had in its crude form.

According to the Gita, the deeds that are done solely for the sake of self fetter our soul; the disinterested action, performed for the sake of the giving up of self, is the true sacrifice. For creation itself comes of the self-sacrifice of Brahma, which has no other purpose; and therefore, in our performance of the duty which is self-sacrificing, we realize the spirit of Brahma.

The Ideal of Zoroastrian Persia is distinctly ethical. It sends its call to men to work together with the Eternal Spirit of Good in spreading and maintaining *Kshathra*, the kingdom of righteousness, against all attacks of evil. This ideal gives us our place as collaborators with God in distributing his blessings over the world.

Clear is this to the man of wisdom as to the man who carefully thinks;

He who upholds Truth with all the might of his power,
He who upholds Truth the utmost in his words and deed,
He, indeed, is Thy most valued helper, O Mazda Ahura!

Yasna 31.22 (Translation D. J. Irani)

It is a fact of supreme moment to us that the human world is in an incessant state of war between that which will save us and that which will drag us into the abyss of disaster. Our one hope lies in the fact that Ahura Mazda is on our side if we choose the right course.

The active heroic aspect of this religion reflects the character of the people themselves, who later on spread conquests far and wide and built up great empires by the might of their sword. They accepted this world in all seriousness. They had their zest in life and confidence in their own strength. They belonged to the western half of Asia and their great influence travelled through the neighbouring civilization of Judaea towards the Western Continent. Their ideal was the ideal of the fighter. By force of will and deeds of sacrifice they were to conquer *haurvatat* – welfare in this world, and *ameratat* – immortality in the other. This is the best ideal in the West, the great truth of fight. For paradise has to be gained through conquest. That sacred task is for the heroes, who are to take the right side in the battle, and the right weapons.

There was a heroic period in Indian history, when this holy spirit of fight was invoked by the greatest poet of the Sanskrit Literature. It is not to be wondered at that his ideal of fight was similar to the ideal that Zarathustra preached. The problem with which his poem starts is that paradise has to be rescued by the hero from its invasion by evil beings. This is the eternal problem of man. The evil spirit is exultant and paradise is lost when *Sati*, the spirit of *Sat* (Reality), is disunited from *Siva*, the Spirit of Goodness. The Real and the Good must meet in wedlock if the hero is to take his birth in order to save all that is true and beautiful. When the union was attempted through the agency of passion, the anger of God was aroused and the result was a tragedy of disappointment. At last, by purification through penance, the wedding was effected, the hero was born who fought against the forces of evil and paradise was regained. This is a poem of the ideal of the moral fight, whose first great prophet was Zarathustra.

We must admit that this ideal has taken a stronger hold upon the life of man in the West than in India – the West, where the vigour of life receives its fullest support from Nature and the excess of energy finds its delight in ceaseless activities. But everywhere in the world, the unrealized ideal is a force of disaster. It gathers its strength in secret even in the heart of prosperity, kills the soul first and then drives men to their utter ruin. When the aggressive activity of will, which naturally accompanies physical vigour, fails to accept the responsibility of its ideal, it breeds unappeasable greed for material gain, leads to unmeaning slavery of things, till amidst a raging conflagration of clashing interests the tower of ambition topples down to the dust.

And for this, the prophetic voice of Zarathustra reminds us that all human activities must have an ideal goal, which is an end to itself, and therefore is peace, is immortality. It is the House of Songs, the realization of love, which comes through strenuous service of goodness.

> All the joys of life which Thou holdest, O Mazda, the joys that were, the joys that are, and the joys that shall be, Thou dost apportion all in Thy love for us.

We, on the other hand, in the tropical East, who have no surplus of physical energy inevitably overflowing in outer activities, also have our own ideal given to us. Our course is not so much through the constant readiness to fight in the battle of the good and evil, as through the inner concentration of mind, through pacifying the turbulence of desire, to reach that serenity of the infinite in our being which leads to the harmony in the all. Here, likewise, the unrealized ideal pursues us with its malediction. As the activities of a vigorous vitality may become unmeaning, and thereupon smother the soul with a mere multiplicity of material, so the peace of the extinguished desire may become the peace of death; and the inner world, in which we would dwell, become a world of incoherent dreams.

The negative process of curbing desire and controlling passion is only for saving our energy from dissipation and directing it into its proper channel. If the path of the channel we have chosen runs withinwards, it also must have its expression in action, not for any ulterior reward, but for the proving of its own truth. If the test of action is removed, if our realization grows purely subjective, then it may become like travelling in a desert in the night, going round and round the same circle, imagining all the while that we are following the straight path of purpose.

This is why the prophet of the Gita in the first place says:

> Who so forsakes all desires and goeth onwards free from yearnings, selfless and without egoism, he goeth to peace.

But he does not stop here, he adds:

> Surrendering all actions to me, with Thy thoughts resting on the Supreme Self, from hope and egoism freed, and of mental fever cured, engage in battle.

Action there must be, fight we must have – not the fight of passion and desire, or arrogant self-assertion, but of duty done in the presence of the Eternal, the disinterested fight of the serene soul that helps us in our union with the Supreme Being.

In this, the teaching of Zarathustra, his sacred gospel of fight finds its unity. The end of the fight he preaches is in the House of Songs, in the symphony of spiritual union. He sings:

> Ye, who wish to be allied to the Good Mind, to be friend with Truth, Ye who desire to sustain the Holy Cause, down with all anger and violence, away with all ill-will and strife! Such benevolent men, O Mazda, I shall take to the House of Songs!

The detailed facts of history, which are the battle-ground of the learned, are not my province. I am a singer myself, and I am ever attracted by the strains that come forth from the House of Songs. When the streams of ideals that flow from the East and from the West mingle their murmur in some profound harmony of meaning it delights my soul.

In the realm of material property men are jealously proud of their possessions and their exclusive rights. Unfortunately there are quarrelsome men who bring that pride of acquisition, the worldliness of sectarianism, even into the region of spiritual truth. Would it be sane, if the man in China should lay claim to the ownership of the sun because he can prove the earlier sunrise in his own country?

For myself, I feel proud whenever I find that the best in the world have their fundamental agreement. It is their function to unite and to dissuade the small from bristling-up, like prickly shrubs, in the pride of the minute points of their differences, only to hurt one another.

CHAPTER SIX
THE VISION

I HOPE THAT my readers have understood, as they have read these pages, that I am neither a scholar nor a philosopher. They should not expect from me fruits gathered from a wide field of studies or wealth brought by a mind trained in the difficult exploration of knowledge. Fortunately for me the subject of religion gains in interest and value by the experience of the individuals who earnestly believe in its truth. This is my apology for offering a part of the story of my life which has always realized its religion through a process of growth and not by the help of inheritance or importation.

Man has made the entire geography of the earth his own, ignoring the boundaries of climate; for, unlike the lion and the reindeer, he has the power to create his special skin and temperature, including his unscrupulous power of borrowing the skins of the indigenous inhabitants and misappropriating their fats.

His kingdom is also continually extending in time through a great surplus in his power of memory, to which is linked his immense facility of borrowing the treasure of the past from all quarters of the world. He dwells in a universe of history, in an environment of continuous remembrance. The animal occupies time only through the multiplication of its own race, but man through the memorials of his mind, raised along the pilgrimage of progress. The stupendousness of his knowledge and wisdom is due to their roots spreading into and drawing sap from the far-reaching area of history.

Man has his other dwelling place in the realm of inner realization, in the element of an immaterial value. This is a world where from the subterranean soil of his mind his consciousness often, like a seed, unexpectedly sends up sprouts into the heart of a luminous freedom, and the individual is made to realize his truth in the universal Man. I hope it may prove of interest if I give an account of my own personal experience of a sudden spiritual outburst from within me which is like the underground current of a perennial stream unexpectedly welling up on the surface.

I was born in a family which, at that time, was earnestly developing a monotheistic religion based upon the philosophy of the Upanishad. Somehow my mind at first remained coldly aloof, absolutely uninfluenced by any religion whatever. It was through an idiosyncrasy of my temperament that I refused to accept any religious teaching merely because people in my surroundings believed it to be true. I could not persuade myself to imagine that I had a religion because everybody whom I might trust believed in its value.

Thus my mind was brought up in an atmosphere of freedom – freedom from the dominance of any creed that had its sanction in the definite authority of some scripture, or in the teaching of some organized body of worshippers. And, therefore, the man who questions me has every right to distrust my vision and reject my testimony. In such a case, the authority of some particular book venerated by a large number of men may have greater weight than the assertion of an individual, and therefore I never claim any right to preach.

When I look back upon those days, it seems to me that unconsciously I followed the path of my Vedic ancestors, and was inspired by the tropical sky with its suggestion of an uttermost Beyond. The wonder of the gathering clouds hanging heavy with the unshed rain, of the sudden sweep of storms arousing vehement gestures along the line of coconut trees, the fierce loneliness of the blazing summer noon, the silent sunrise behind the dewy veil of autumn morning, kept my mind with the intimacy of a pervasive companionship.

Then came my initiation ceremony of Brahminhood when the *Gayatri* verse of meditation was given to me, whose meaning, according to the explanation I had, runs as follows:

> Let me contemplate the adorable splendour of Him who created the earth, the air and the starry spheres, and sends the power of comprehension within our minds.

This produced a sense of serene exaltation in me, the daily meditation upon the infinite being which unites in one stream of creation my mind and the outer world. Though to-day I find no difficulty in realizing this being as an infinite personality in whom the subject and object are perfectly reconciled, at that time the idea to me was vague. Therefore the current of feeling that it aroused in my mind was indefinite, like the circulation of air – an atmosphere which needed a definite world to complete itself and satisfy me. For it is evident that my religion is a poet's religion, and neither that of an orthodox man of piety nor that of a theologian. Its touch comes to me through the same unseen and trackless channel as does the inspiration of my songs. My religious life has followed the same mysterious line of growth as has my poetical life. Somehow they are wedded to each other and, though their betrothal had a long period of ceremony, it was kept secret to me.

When I was eighteen, a sudden spring breeze of religious experience for the first time came to my life and passed away leaving in my memory a direct message of spiritual reality. One day while I stood watching at early dawn the sun sending out its rays from behind the trees, I suddenly felt as if some ancient mist had in a moment lifted from my sight, and the morning light on the face of the world revealed an inner radiance of joy. The invisible screen of the commonplace was removed from all things and all men, and their ultimate significance was intensified in my mind; and this is the definition of beauty. That which was memorable in this experience was its human message, the sudden expansion of my consciousness in the super-personal world of man. The poem I wrote on the first day of my surprise was named 'The Awakening of the Waterfall'. The waterfall, whose spirit lay dormant in its ice-bound isolation, was touched by the sun and, bursting in a cataract of freedom, it found its finality in an unending sacrifice, in a continual union with the sea. After four days the vision passed away, and the lid hung down upon my inner sight. In the dark, the world once again put on its disguise of the obscurity of an ordinary fact.

When I grew older and was employed in a responsible work in some villages I took my place in a neighbourhood where the current of time ran slow and joys and sorrows had their simple and elemental shades and lights. The day which had its special significance for me came with all its drifting trivialities of the commonplace life. The ordinary work of my morning had come to its close and before going to take my bath I stood for a moment at my window, overlooking a market place on the bank of a dry river bed, welcoming the first flood of rain along its channel. Suddenly I became conscious of a stirring of soul within me. My world of experience in a moment seemed to become lighted, and facts that were detached and dim found a great unity of meaning. The feeling which I had was like that which a man, groping through a fog without knowing his destination, might feel when he suddenly discovers that he stands before his own house.

I still remember the day in my childhood when I was made to struggle across my lessons in a first primer, strewn with isolated words smothered under the burden of spelling. The morning hour appeared to me like a once-illumined page, grown dusty and faded, discoloured into irrelevant marks, smudges and gaps, wearisome in its moth-eaten meaninglessness. Suddenly I came to a rhymed sentence of combined words, which may be translated thus – 'It rains, the leaves tremble'. At once I came to a world wherein I recovered my full meaning. My mind touched the creative realm of expression, and at that moment I was no longer a mere student with his mind muffled by spelling lessons, enclosed by classroom. The rhythmic picture of the tremulous leaves beaten by the rain opened before my mind the world which does not merely carry information, but a harmony with my being. The unmeaning fragments lost their individual isolation and my mind revelled in the unity of a vision. In a similar manner, on that morning in the village, the facts of my life suddenly appeared to me in a luminous unity of truth. All things that had seemed like vagrant waves were revealed to my mind in relation to a boundless sea. I felt sure that some Being who comprehended me and my world was seeking his best expression in all my experiences, uniting them into an ever-widening individuality which is a spiritual work of art.

To this Being I was responsible; for the creation in me is his as well as mine. It may be that it was the same creative Mind that is shaping the universe to its eternal idea; but in me as a person it had one of its special centres of a personal relationship growing into a deepening consciousness. I had my sorrows that left their memory in a long burning track across my days, but I felt at that moment that in them I lent myself to a travail of creation that ever exceeded my own personal bounds like stars which in their individual firebursts are lighting the history of the universe. It gave me a great joy to feel in my life detachment at the idea of a mystery of a meeting of the two in a creative comradeship. I felt that I had found my religion at last, the religion of Man, in which the infinite became defined in humanity and came close to me so as to need my love and co-operation.

This idea of mine found at a later date its expression in some of my poems addressed to what I called *Jivan devatā*, the Lord of my life. Fully aware of my awkwardness in dealing with a foreign language, with some hesitation I give a translation, being sure that any evidence revealed through the self-recording instrument of poetry is more authentic than answers extorted through conscious questionings:

Thou who art the innermost Spirit of my being,
art thou pleased,
    Lord of my Life?
For I gave to thee my cup
filled with all the pain and delight
that the crushed grapes of my heart had surrendered,
I wove with the rhythm of colours and songs the cover
    for thy bed,
and with the molten gold of my desires
I fashioned playthings for thy passing hours.

I know not why thou chosest me for thy partner,
    Lord of my life!
Didst thou store my days and nights,
my deeds and dreams for the alchemy of thy art,
and string in the chain of thy music my songs of autumn
    and spring,
and gather the flowers from my mature moments for
    thy crown?

I see thine eyes gazing at the dark of my heart,
    Lord of my life,
I wonder if my failures and wrongs are forgiven.
For many were my days without service
and nights of forgetfulness;
futile were the flowers that faded in the shade not
    offered to thee.
Often the tired strings of my lute
slackened at the strain of thy tunes.
And often at the ruin of wasted hours
my desolate evenings were filled with tears.

But have my days come to their end at last,
    Lord of my life,
while my arms round thee grow limp,

my kisses losing their truth?
Then break up the meeting of this languid day.
Renew the old in me in fresh forms of delight;
and let the wedding come once again
in a new ceremony of life.

You will understand from this how unconsciously I had been travelling towards the realization which I stumbled upon in an idle moment on a day in July, when morning clouds thickened on the eastern horizon and a caressing shadow lay on the tremulous bamboo branches, while an excited group of village boys was noisily dragging from the bank an old fishing boat; and I cannot tell how at that moment an unexpected train of thoughts ran across my mind like a strange caravan carrying the wealth of an unknown kingdom.

From my infancy I had a keen sensitiveness which kept my mind tingling with consciousness of the world around me, natural and human. We had a small garden attached to our house; it was a fairyland to me, where miracles of beauty were of everyday occurrence.

Almost every morning in the early hour of the dusk, I would run out from my bed in a great hurry to greet the first pink flush of the dawn through the shivering branches of the palm trees which stood in a line along the garden boundary, while the grass glistened as the dew-drops caught the earliest tremor of the morning breeze. The sky seemed to bring to me the call of a personal companionship, and all my heart – my whole body in fact – used to drink in at a draught the overflowing light and peace of those silent hours. I was anxious never to miss a single morning, because each one was precious to me, more precious than gold to the miser. I am certain that I felt a larger meaning of my own self when the barrier vanished between me and what was beyond myself.

I had been blessed with that sense of wonder which gives a child his right of entry into the treasure house of mystery in the depth of existence. My studies in the school I neglected, because they rudely dismembered me from the context of my world and I felt miserable, like a caged rabbit in a biological institute. This, perhaps, will explain the meaning of my religion. This world was living to me, intimately close to my life, permeated by a subtle touch of kinship which enhanced the value of my own being.

It is true that this world also has its impersonal aspect of truth which is pursued by the man of impersonal science. The father has his personal relationship with his son; but as a doctor he may detach the fact of a son from that relationship and let the child become an abstraction to him, only a living body with its physiological functions. It cannot be said that if through the constant pursuit of his vocations he altogether discards the personal element in his relation to his son he reaches a greater truth as a doctor than he does as a father. The scientific knowledge of his son is information about a fact, and not the realization of a truth. In his intimate feeling for his son he touches an ultimate truth – the truth of relationship, the truth of a harmony in the universe, the fundamental principle of creation. It is not merely the number of protons and electrons which represents the truth of an element; it is the mystery of their relationship which cannot be analysed. We are made conscious of this truth of relationship immediately within us in our love, in our joy; and from this experience of ours we have the right to say that the Supreme One, who relates all things, comprehends the universe, is all love – the love that is the highest truth being the most perfect relationship.

I still remember the shock of repulsion I received as a child when some medical student brought to me a piece of a human windpipe and tried to excite my admiration for its structure. He tried to convince me that it was the source of the beautiful human voice. But I could not bear the artisan to occupy the throne that was for the artist who concealed the machinery and revealed the creation in its ineffable unity. God does not care to keep exposed the record of his power written in geological inscriptions, but he is proudly glad of the expression of beauty which he spreads on the green grass, in the flowers, in the play of the colours on the clouds, in the murmuring music of running water.

I had a vague notion as to who or what it was that touched my heart's chords, like the infant which does not know its mother's name, or who or what she is. The feeling which I always had was a deep satisfaction of personality that flowed into my nature through living channels of communication from all sides.

I am afraid that the scientist may remind me that to lose sight of the distinction between life and non-life, the human and the non-human, is a sign of the primitive mind. While admitting it, let me hope that it is not an utter condemnation, but rather the contrary. It may be a true instinct of Science itself, an instinctive logic, which makes the primitive mind think that humanity has become possible as a fact only because of a universal human truth which has harmony with its reason, with its will. In the details of our universe there are some differences that may be described as non-human, but not in their essence. The bones are different from the muscles, but they are organically one in the body. Our feeling of joy, our imagination, realizes a profound organic unity with the universe comprehended by the human mind. Without minimizing the differences that are in detailed manifestations, there is nothing wrong in trusting the mind, which is occasionally made intensely conscious of an all-pervading personality answering to the personality of man.

The details of reality must be studied in their differences by Science, but it can never know the character of the grand unity of relationship pervading it, which can only be realized immediately by the human spirit. And therefore it is the primal imagination of man – the imagination which is fresh and immediate in its experiences – that exclaims in a poet's verse:

> Wisdom and spirit of the universe!
> Thou soul, that art the eternity of thought,
> And giv'st to forms and images a breath
> And everlasting motion.

And in another poet's words it speaks of

> That light whose smile kindles the universe,
> That Beauty in which all things work and move.

The theologian may follow the scientist and shake his head and say that all that I have written is pantheism. But let us not indulge in an idolatry of name and dethrone living truth in its favour. When I say that I am a man, it is implied by that word that there is such a thing as a general idea of Man which persistently manifests itself in every particular human being, who is different from all other individuals. If we lazily label such a belief as 'pananthropy' and divert our thoughts from its mysteriousness by such a title it does not help us much. Let me assert my faith by saying that this world, consisting of what we call animate and inanimate things, has found its culmination in man, its best expression. Man, as a creation, represents the Creator, and this is why of all creatures it has been possible for him to comprehend this world in his knowledge and in his feeling and in his imagination, to realize in his individual spirit a union with a Spirit that is everywhere.

There is an illustration that I have made use of in which I supposed that a stranger from some other planet has paid a visit to our earth and happens to hear the sound of a human voice on the gramophone. All that is obvious to him and most seemingly active, is the revolving disc. He is unable to discover the personal truth that lies behind, and so might accept the impersonal scientific fact of the disc as final — the fact that could be touched and measured. He would wonder how it could be possible for a machine to speak to the soul. Then, if in pursuing the mystery, he should suddenly come to the heart of the music through a meeting with the composer, he would at once understand the meaning of that music as a personal communication.

That which merely gives us information can be explained in terms of measurement, but that which gives us joy cannot be explained by the facts of a mere grouping of atoms and molecules. Somewhere in the arrangement of this world there seems to be a great concern about giving us delight, which shows that, in the universe, over and above the meaning of matter and forces, there is a message conveyed through the magic touch of personality. This touch cannot be analysed, it can only be felt. We cannot prove it any more than the man from the other planet could prove to the satisfaction of his fellows the personality which remained invisible, but which, through the machinery, spoke direct to the heart.

Is it merely because the rose is round and pink that it gives me more satisfaction than the gold which could buy me the necessities of life, or any number of slaves? One may, at the outset, deny the truth that a rose gives more delight than a piece of gold. But such an objector must remember that I am not speaking of artificial values. If we had to cross a desert whose sand was made of gold, then the cruel glitter of these dead particles would become a terror for us, and the sight of a rose would bring to us the music of paradise.

The final meaning of the delight which we find in a rose can never be in the roundness of its petals, just as the final meaning of the joy of music cannot be in a gramophone disc. Somehow we feel that through a rose the language of love reached our heart. Do we not carry a rose to our beloved because in it is already embodied a message which, unlike our language of words, cannot be analysed. Through this gift of a rose we utilize a universal language of joy for our own purposes of expression.

Fortunately for me a collection of old lyrical poems composed by the poets of the Vaishnava sect came to my hand when I was young. I became aware of some underlying idea deep in the obvious meaning of these love poems. I felt the joy of an explorer who suddenly discovers the key to the language lying hidden in the hieroglyphs which are beautiful in themselves. I was sure that these poets were speaking about the supreme Lover, whose touch we experience in all our relations of love – the love of nature's beauty, of the animal, the child, the comrade, the beloved, the love that illuminates our consciousness of reality. They sang of a love that ever flows through numerous obstacles between men and Man the Divine, the eternal relation which has the relationship of mutual dependence for a fulfilment that needs perfect union of individuals and the Universal.

The Vaishnava poet sings of the Lover who has his flute which, with its different stops, gives out the varied notes of beauty and love that are in Nature and Man. These notes bring to us our message of invitation. They eternally urge us to come out from the seclusion of our self-centred life into the realm of love and truth. Are we deaf by nature, or is it that we have been deafened by the claims of the world, of self-seeking, by the clamorous noise of the market place? We miss the voice of the Lover, and we fight, we rob, we exploit the weak, we chuckle at our cleverness, when we can appropriate for our use what is due to others; we make our lives a desert by turning away from our world that stream of love which pours down from the blue sky and wells up from the bosom of the earth.

In the region of Nature, by unlocking the secret doors of the workshop department, one may come to that dark hall where dwells the mechanic and help to attain usefulness, but through it one can never attain finality. Here is the storehouse of innumerable facts and, however necessary they may be, they have not the treasure of fulfilment in them. But the hall of union is there, where dwells the Lover in the heart of existence. When a man reaches it he at once realizes that he has come to Truth, to immortality, and he is glad with a gladness which is an end, and yet which has no end.

Mere information about facts, mere discovery of power, belongs to the outside and not to the inner soul of things. Gladness is the one criterion of truth, and we know when we have touched Truth by the music it gives, by the joy of greeting it sends forth to the truth in us. That is the true foundation of all religions. It is not as ether waves that we receive light; the morning does not wait for some scientist for its introduction to us. In the same way we touch the infinite reality immediately within us only when we perceive the pure truth of love or goodness, not through the explanations of theologians, not through the erudite discussion of ethical doctrines.

I have already made the confession that my religion is a poet's religion. All that I feel about it is from vision and not from knowledge. Frankly, I acknowledge that I cannot satisfactorily answer any questions about evil, or about what happens after death. Nevertheless, I am sure that there have come moments in my own experience when my soul has touched the infinite and has become intensely conscious of it through the illumination of joy. It has been said in our Upanishad that our mind and our words come away baffled from the Supreme Truth, but he who knows truth through the immediate joy of his own soul is saved from all doubts and fears.

In the night we stumble over things and become acutely conscious of their individual separateness. But the day reveals the greater unity which embraces them. The man whose inner vision is bathed in an illumination of his consciousness at once realizes the spiritual unity reigning supreme over all differences. His mind no longer awkwardly stumbles over individual facts of separateness in the human world, accepting them as final. He realizes that peace is in the inner harmony which dwells in truth and not in any outer adjustments. He knows that beauty carries an eternal assurance of our spiritual relationship to reality, which waits for its perfection in the response of our love.

CHAPTER SEVEN
THE MAN OF MY HEART

AT THE OUTBURST of an experience, which is unusual, such as happened to me in the beginning of my youth, the puzzled mind seeks its explanation in some settled foundation of that which is usual, trying to adjust an unexpected inner message to an organized belief which goes by the general name of a religion. And, therefore, I naturally was glad at that time of youth to accept from my father the post of secretary to a special section of the monotheistic church of which he was the leader. I took part in its services mainly by composing hymns which unconsciously took the many-thumbed impression of the orthodox mind, a composite smudge of tradition. Urged by my sense of duty I strenuously persuaded myself to think that my new mental attitude was in harmony with that of the members of our association, although I constantly stumbled upon obstacles and felt constraints that hurt me to the quick.

At last I came to discover that in my conduct I was not strictly loyal to my religion, but only to the religious institution. This latter represented an artificial average, with its standard of truth at its static minimum, jealous of any vital growth that exceeded its limits. I have my conviction that in religion, and also in the arts, that which is common to a group is not important. Indeed, very often it is a contagion of mutual imitation. After a long struggle with the feeling that I was using a mask to hide the living face of truth, I gave up my connection with our church.

About this time, one day I chanced to hear a song from a beggar belonging to the Baül sect of Bengal. We have in the modern Indian Religion deities of different names, forms and mythology, some Vedic and others aboriginal. They have their special sectarian idioms and associations that give emotional satisfaction to those who are accustomed to their hypnotic influences. Some of them may have their aesthetic value to me and others philosophical significance overcumbered by exuberant distraction of legendary myths. But what struck me in this simple song was a religious expression that was neither grossly concrete, full of crude details, nor metaphysical in its rarefied transcendentalism. At the same time it was alive with an emotional sincerity. It spoke of an intense yearning of the heart for the divine which is in Man and not in the temple, or scriptures, in images and symbols. The worshipper addresses his songs to the Man the ideal, and says:

> Temples and mosques obstruct thy path,
> and I fail to hear thy call or to move,
> when the teachers and priest angrily crowd round me.

He does not follow any tradition of ceremony, but only believes in love. According to him:

> Love is the magic stone, that transmutes by its touch greed
> into sacrifice.

He goes on to say:

> For the sake of this love heaven longs to become earth and
> gods to become man.

Since then I have often tried to meet these people, and sought to understand them through their songs, which are their only form of worship. One is often surprised to find in many of these verses a striking originality of sentiment and diction; for, at their best, they are spontaneously individual in their expressions. One such song is a hymn to the Ever Young. It exclaims:

> O my flower buds, we worship the Young;
> for the Young is the source of the holy Ganges of life;
> from the Young flows the supreme bliss

And it says:

> We never offer ripe corn in the service of the Young,
> nor fruit, nor seed,
> but only the lotus bud which is of our own mind.
> The young hour of the day, the morning,
> is our time for the worship of Him
> from whose contemplation has sprung the Universe.

It calls the Spirit of the Young the *Brahma Kamal*, 'the infinite lotus'. For it is something which has perfection in its heart and yet ever grows and unfolds its petals.

There have been men in India who never wrote learned texts about the religion of Man but had an overpowering desire and practical training for its attainment. They bore in their life the testimony of their intimacy with the Person who is in all persons, of Man the formless in the individual forms of men. Rajjab, poet-saint of medieval India, says of Man:

> God-man (*nara-nārāyana*) is thy definition, it is not a delusion
> but truth. In thee the infinite seeks the finite, the perfect
> knowledge seeks love, and when the form and the Form-
> less (the individual and the universal) are united love is
> fulfilled in devotion.

Ravidas, another poet of the same age, sings:

Thou seest me, O Divine Man (*narahari*), and I see thee, and
our love becomes mutual.

Of this God-man a village poet of Bengal says:

He is within us, an unfathomable reality. We know him
when we unlock our own self and meet in a true love
with all others.

A brother poet of his says:

Man seeks the man in me and I lose myself and run out.

And another singer sings of the Ideal Man, and says:

How could the scripture know the meaning of the Lord who
has his play in the world of human forms?
Listen, O brother man (declares Chandidas), the truth of
man is the highest truth, there is no other truth above it.

All these are proofs of a direct perception of humanity as an
objective truth that rouses a profound feeling of longing and
love. This is very unlike what we find in the intellectual cult of
humanity, which is like a body that has tragically lost itself in the
purgatory of shadows.

Wordsworth says:

We live by admiration, hope and love,
And ever as these are well and wisely fixed
In dignity of being we ascend.

It is for dignity of being that we aspire through the expansion of
our consciousness in a great reality of man to which we belong.
We realize it through admiration and love, through hope that
soars beyond the actual, beyond our own span of life into an
endless time wherein we live the life of all men.

This is the infinite perspective of human personality where
man finds his religion. Science may include in its field of knowledge the starry world and the world beyond it; philosophy may
try to find some universal principle which is at the root of all
things, but religion inevitably concentrates itself on humanity,
which illumines our reason, inspires our wisdom, stimulates our
love, claims our intelligent service. There is an impersonal idea,
which we call law, discoverable by an impersonal logic in its pursuit of the fathomless depth of the hydrogen atom and the distant

virgin worlds clothed in eddying fire. But as the physiology of our beloved is not our beloved, so this impersonal law is not our God, the *Pitritamah pitrinam*, the Father who is ultimate in all fathers and mothers, of him we cannot say:

Tad viddhi pranipatena pariprasnena sevayā –
Realize him by obeisance, by the desire to know, by service –

For this can only be relevant to the God who is God and man at the same time; and if this faith be blamed for being anthropomorphic, then Man is to be blamed for being Man, and the lover for loving his dear one as a person instead of as a principle of psychology. We can never go beyond Man in all that we know and feel, and a mendicant singer of Bengal has said:

> Our world is as it is in our comprehension; the thought and existence are commingled. Everything would be lost in unconsciousness if man were nought; and when response comes to your own call you know the meaning of reality.

According to him, what we call nature is not a philosophical abstraction, not cosmos, but what is revealed to *man* as nature. In fact it is included in himself and therefore there is a commingling of his mind with it, and in that he finds his own being. He is truly lessened in humanity if he cannot take it within him and through it feel the fulness of his own existence. His arts and literature are constantly giving expression to this intimate communion of man with his world. And the Vedic poet exclaims in his hymn to the sun:

> Thou who nourishest the earth, who walkest alone, O Sun, withdraw thy rays, reveal thy exceeding beauty to me and let me realize that the Person who is there is the One who I am.

It is for us to realize the Person who is in the heart of the All by the emancipated consciousness of our own personality. We know that the highest mission of science is to find the universe enveloped by the human comprehension; to see man's *visvarupa*, his great mental body, that touches the extreme verge of time and space, that includes the whole world within itself.

The original Aryans who came to India had for their gods the deities of rain, wind, fire, the cosmic forces which singularly enough found no definite shapes in images. A time came when it was recognized that individually they had no separate, unrelated power of their own, but there was one infinite source of power which was named Brahma. The cosmic divinity developed into an impersonal idea; what was physical grew into a metaphysical abstraction, even as in modern science matter vanishes into mathematics. And Brahma, according to those Indians, could neither be apprehended by mind nor described by words, even as matter in its ultimate analysis proves to be.

However satisfactory that idea might be as the unknowable principle relating to itself all the phenomena that are non-personal, it left the personal man in a void of negation. It cannot be gain-said that we can never realize things in this world from inside, we can but know how they appear to us. In fact, in all knowledge we know our own self in its condition of knowledge. And religion sought the highest value of man's existence in this self. For this is the only truth of which he is immediately conscious from within. And he said:

> *Purushānna parā kinchit*
> *sā kāshthtā sā para gātih*
> Nothing is greater than the Person; he is the supreme, he is the ultimate goal.

It is a village poet of East Bengal who preaches in a song the philosophical doctrine that the universe has its reality in its relation to the Person, which I translate in the following lines:

> The sky and the earth are born of mine own eyes,
> The hardness and softness, the cold and the heat are the products of mine own body,
> The sweet smell and the bad are of my own nostrils.

This poet sings of the Eternal Person within him, coming out and appearing before his eyes, just as the Vedic Rishi speaks of the Person, who is in him, dwelling also in the heart of the sun:

> I have seen the vision,
> the vision of mine own revealing itself,
> coming out from within me.

In India, there are those whose endeavour is to merge completely their personal self in an impersonal entity which is without any quality or definition; to reach a condition wherein mind becomes perfectly blank, losing all its activities. Those who claim the right to speak about it say that this is the purest state of consciousness, it is all joy and without any object or content. This is considered to be the ultimate end of *Yoga*, the cult of union, thus completely to identify one's being with the infinite Being who is beyond all thoughts and words. Such realization of transcendental consciousness accompanied by a perfect sense of bliss is a time-honoured tradition in our country, carrying in it the positive evidence which cannot be denied by any negative argument of refutation. Without disputing its truth I maintain that it may be valuable as a great psychological experience but all the same it is not religion, even as the knowledge of the ultimate state of the atom is of no use to an artist who deals in images in which atoms have taken forms. A certain condition of vacuum is needed for studying the state of things in its original purity, and the same may be said of the human spirit; but the original state is not necessarily the perfect state. The concrete form is a more perfect manifestation than the atom, and man is more perfect as a man than where he vanishes in an original indefiniteness. This is why the Ishopanishat says: 'Truth is both finite and infinite at the same time, it moves and yet moves not, it is in the distant, also in the near, it is within all objects and without them.'

This means that perfection as the ideal is immovable, but in its aspect of the real it constantly grows towards completion, it moves. And I say of the Supreme Man, that he is infinite in his essence, he is finite in his manifestation in us the individuals. As the Ishopanishat declares, a man must live his full term of life and work without greed, and thus realize himself in the Being who is in all beings. This means that he must reveal in his own personality the Supreme Person by his disinterested activities.

CHAPTER EIGHT
THE MUSIC MAKER

A PARTICLE OF sand would be nothing if it did not have its background in the whole physical world. This grain of sand is known in its context of the universe where we know all things through the testimony of our senses. When I say the grain of sand *is*, the whole physical world stands guarantee for the truth which is behind the appearance of the sand.

But where is that guarantee of truth for this personality of mine that has the mysterious faculty of knowledge before which the particle of sand offers its credential of identification? It must be acknowledged that this personal self of mine also has for its truth a background of personality where knowledge, unlike that of other things, can only be immediate and self-revealed.

What I mean by personality is a self-conscious principle of transcendental unity within man which comprehends all the details of facts that are individually his in knowledge and feeling, wish and will and work. In its negative aspect it is limited to the individual separateness, while in its positive aspect it ever extends itself in the infinite through the increase of its knowledge, love and activities.

And for this reason the most human of all facts about us is that we *do* dream of the limitless unattained – the dream which gives character to what *is* attained. Of all creatures man lives in an endless future. Our present is only a part of it. The ideas unborn, the unbodied spirits, tease our imagination with an insistence which makes them more real to our mind than things around us. The atmosphere of the future must always surround our present in order to make it life-bearing and suggestive of immortality. For he who has the healthy vigour of humanity in him has a strong instinctive faith that ideally he is limitless. That is why our greatest teachers claim from us a manifestation that touches the infinite. In this they pay homage to the Supreme Man. And our true worship lies in our indomitable courage to be great and thus to represent the human divine and ever to keep open the path of freedom towards the unattained.

We Indians have had the sad experience in our own part of the world how timid orthodoxy, its irrational repressions and its accumulation of dead centuries, dwarfs man through its idolatry of the past. Seated rigid in the centre of stagnation, it firmly ties the human spirit to the revolving wheels of habit till faintness overwhelms her. Like a sluggish stream choked by rotting weeds, it is divided into shallow slimy pools that shroud their dumbness in a narcotic mist of stupor. This mechanical spirit of tradition is essentially materialistic, it is blindly pious but not spiritual, obsessed by phantoms of unreason that haunt feeble minds in the ghastly disguise of religion. For our soul is shrunken when we allow foolish days to weave repeated patterns of unmeaning meshes round all departments of life. It becomes stunted when we have no object of profound interest, no prospect of heightened life, demanding clarity of mind and heroic attention to maintain and mature it. It is destroyed when we make fire-works of our animal passions for the enjoyment of their meteoric sensations, recklessly reducing to ashes all that could have been saved for permanent illumination. This happens not only to mediocre individuals hugging fetters that keep them irresponsible or hungering for lurid unrealities, but to generations of insipid races that have lost all emphasis of significance in themselves, having missed their future.

The continuous future is the domain of our millennium, which is with us more truly than what we see in our history in fragments of the present. It is in our dream. It is in the realm of the faith which creates perfection. We have seen the records of man's dreams of the millennium, the ideal reality cherished by forgotten races in their admiration, hope and love manifested in the dignity of their being through some majesty in ideals and beauty in performance. While these races pass away one after another they leave great accomplishments behind them carrying their claim to recognition as dreamers – not so much as conquerors of earthly kingdoms, but as the designers of paradise. The poet gives us the best definition of man when he says:

We are the music-makers,
We are the dreamers of dreams.

Our religions present for us the dreams of the ideal unity which is man himself as he manifests the infinite. We suffer from the sense of sin, which is the sense of discord, when any disruptive passion tears gaps in our vision of the One in man, creating isolation in our self from the universal humanity.

The Upanishad says, *mā gridah*, 'covet not'. For coveting diverts attention from the infinite value of our personality to the temptation of materials. Our village poet sings: 'Man will brightly flash into your sight, my heart, if you shut the door of desires.'

We have seen how primitive man was occupied with his physical needs, and thus restricted himself to the present which is the time boundary of the animal; and he missed the urge of his consciousness to seek its emancipation in a world of ultimate human value.

Modern civilization for the same reason seems to turn itself back to that primitive mentality. Our needs have multiplied so

furiously fast that we have lost our leisure for the deeper realization of our self and our faith in it. It means that we have lost
our religion, the longing for the touch of the divine in man,
the builder of the heaven, the music-maker, the dreamer of
dreams. This has made it easy to tear into shreds our faith in
the perfection of the human ideal, in its wholeness, as the fuller
meaning of reality. No doubt it is wonderful that music contains
a fact which has been analysed and measured, and which music
shares in common with the braying of an ass or of a motor-car
horn. But it is still more wonderful that music has a truth, which
cannot be analysed into fractions; and there the difference between it and the bellowing impertinence of a motor-car horn is
infinite. Men of our own times have analysed the human mind,
its dreams, its spiritual aspirations, – most often caught unawares
in the shattered state of madness, disease and desultory dreams –
and they have found to their satisfaction that these are composed
of elemental animalities tangled into various knots. This may
be an important discovery; but what is still more important to
realize is the fact that by some miracle of creation man infinitely
transcends the component parts of his own character.

Suppose that some psychological explorer suspects that man's
devotion to his beloved has at bottom our primitive stomach's
hankering for human flesh, we need not contradict him; for
whatever may be its genealogy, its secret composition, the complete character of our love, in its perfect mingling of physical,
mental and spiritual associations, is unique in its utter difference
from cannibalism. The truth underlying the possibility of such
transmutation is the truth of our religion. A lotus has in common
with a piece of rotten flesh the elements of carbon and hydrogen.
In a state of dissolution there is no difference between them,
but in a state of creation the difference is immense; and it is that
difference which really matters. We are told that some of our
most sacred sentiments hold hidden in them instincts contrary
to what these sentiments profess to be. Such disclosures have the
effect upon certain persons of the relief of a tension, even like the
relaxation in death of the incessant strenuousness of life.

We find in modern literature that something like a chuckle
of an exultant disillusionment is becoming contagious, and the
knights-errant of the cult of arson are abroad, setting fire to our
time-honoured altars of worship, proclaiming that the images
enshrined on them, even if beautiful, are made of mud. They

say that it has been found out that the appearances in human idealism are deceptive, that the underlying mud is real. From such a point of view, the whole of creation may be said to be a gigantic deception, and the billions of revolving electric specks that have the appearance of 'you' or 'me' should be condemned as bearers of false evidence.

But whom do they seek to delude? If it be beings like ourselves who possess some inborn criterion of the real, then to them these very appearances in their integrity must represent reality, and not their component electric specks. For them the rose must be more satisfactory as an object than its constituent gases, which can be tortured to speak against the evident identity of the rose. The rose, even like the human sentiment of goodness, or ideal of beauty, belongs to the realm of creation, in which all its rebellious elements are reconciled in a perfect harmony. Because these elements in their simplicity yield themselves to our scrutiny, we in our pride are inclined to give them the best prizes as actors in that mystery-play, the rose. Such an analysis is really only giving a prize to our own detective cleverness.

I repeat again that the sentiments and ideals which man in his process of self-creation has built up, should be recognized in their wholeness. In all our faculties or passions there is nothing which is absolutely good or bad; they all are the constituents of the great human personality. They are notes that are wrong when in wrong places; our education is to make them into chords that may harmonize with the grand music of Man. The animal in the savage has been transformed into higher stages in the civilized man – in other words has attained a truer consonance with Man the divine, not through any elimination of the original materials, but through a magical grouping of them, through the severe discipline of art, the discipline of curbing and stressing in proper places, establishing a balance of lights and shadows in the background and foreground, and thus imparting a unique value to our personality in all its completeness.

So long as we have faith in this value, our energy is steadily sustained in its creative activity that reveals the eternal Man. This faith is helped on all sides by literature, arts, legends, symbols, ceremonials, by the remembrance of heroic souls who have personified it in themselves.

Our religion is the inner principle that comprehends these endeavours and expressions and dreams through which we approach Him in whose image we are made. To keep alive our faith in the reality of the ideal perfection is the function of civilization, which is mainly formed of sentiments and the images that represent that ideal. In other words, civilization is a creation of art, created for the objective realization of our vision of the spiritually perfect. It is the product of the art of religion. We stop its course of conquest when we accept the cult of realism and forget that realism is the worst form of untruth, because it contains a minimum of truth. It is like preaching that only in the morgue can we comprehend the reality of the human body – the body which has its perfect revelation when seen in life. All great human facts are surrounded by an immense atmosphere of expectation. They are never complete if we leave out from them what might be, what should be, what is not yet proven but profoundly felt, what points towards the immortal. This dwells in a perpetual surplus in the individual, that transcends all the desultory facts about him.

The realism in Man is the animal in him, whose life is a mere duration of time; the human in him is his reality which has life everlasting for its background. Rocks and crystals being complete definitely in what they are, can keep as 'mute insensate things' a kind of dumb dignity in their stolidly limited realism; while human facts grow unseemly and diseased, breeding germs of death, when divested of their creative ideal – the ideal of Man the divine. The difference between the notes as mere facts of sound and music as a truth of expression is immense. For music though it comprehends a limited number of notes yet represents the infinite. It is for man to produce the music of the spirit with all the notes which he has in his psychology and which, through inattention or perversity, can easily be translated into a frightful noise. In music man is revealed and not in a noise.

CHAPTER NINE
THE ARTIST

THE FUNDAMENTAL DESIRE of life is the desire to exist. It claims from us a vast amount of training and experience about the necessaries of livelihood. Yet it does not cost me much to confess that the food that I have taken, the dress that I wear, the house where I have my lodging, represent a stupendous knowledge, practice and organization which I helplessly lack; for I find that I am not altogether despised for such ignorance and inefficiency. Those who read me seem fairly satisfied that I am nothing better than a poet or perhaps a philosopher – which latter reputation I do not claim and dare not hold through the precarious help of misinformation.

It is quite evident in spite of my deficiency that in human society I represent a vocation, which though superfluous has yet been held worthy of commendation. In fact, I am encouraged in my rhythmic futility by being offered moral and material incentives for its cultivation. If a foolish blackbird did not know how to seek its food, to build its nest, or to avoid its enemies, but specialized in singing, its fellow creatures, urged by their own science of genetics, would dutifully allow it to starve and perish. That I am not treated in a similar fashion is the evidence of an immense difference between the animal existence and the civilization of man. His great distinction dwells in the indefinite margin of life in him which affords a boundless background for his dreams and creations. And it is in this realm of freedom that he realizes his divine dignity, his great human truth, and is pleased when I as a poet sing victory to him, to Man the self-revealer, who goes on exploring ages of creation to find himself in perfection.

Reality, in all its manifestations, reveals itself in the emotional and imaginative background of our mind. We know it, not because we can think of it, but because we directly feel it. And therefore, even if rejected by the logical mind, it is not banished from our consciousness. As an incident it may be beneficial or injurious, but as a revelation its value lies in the fact that it offers us an experience through emotion or imagination; we feel ourselves in a special field of realization. This feeling itself is delightful when it is not accompanied by any great physical or moral risk, we love to feel even fear or sorrow if it is detached from all practical consequences. This is the reason of our enjoyment of tragic dramas, in which the feeling of pain rouses our consciousness to a white heat of intensity.

The reality of my own self is immediate and indubitable to me. Whatever else affects me in a like manner is real for myself, and it inevitably attracts and occupies my attention for its own sake, blends itself with my personality, making it richer and larger and causing it delight. My friend may not be beautiful, useful, rich or great, but he is real to me; in him I feel my own extension and my joy.

The consciousness of the real within me seeks for its own corroboration the touch of the Real outside me. When it fails the self in me is depressed. When our surroundings are monotonous and insignificant, having no emotional reaction upon our mind, we become vague to ourselves. For we are like pictures, whose reality is helped by the background if it is sympathetic. The punishment we suffer in solitary confinement consists in the obstruction to the relationship between the world of reality and the real in ourselves, causing the latter to become indistinct in a haze of inactive imagination: our personality is blurred, we miss the companionship of our own being through the diminution of our self. The world of our knowledge is enlarged for us through the extension of our information; the world of our personality grows in its area with a large and deeper experience of our personal self in our own universe through sympathy and imagination.

As this world, that can be known through knowledge, is limited to us owing to our ignorance, so the world of personality, that can be realized by our own personal self, is also restricted by the limit of our sympathy and imagination. In the dim twilight of insensitiveness a large part of our world remains to us like a procession of nomadic shadows. According to the stages of our consciousness we have more or less been able to identify ourselves with this world, if not as a whole, at least in fragments; and our enjoyment dwells in that wherein we feel ourselves thus united. In art we express the delight of this unity by which this world is realized as humanly significant to us. I have my physical, chemical and biological self; my knowledge of it extends through the extension of my knowledge of the physical, chemical and biological world. I have my personal self, which has its communication with our feelings, sentiments and imaginations, which lends itself to be coloured by our desires and shaped by our imageries.

Science urges us to occupy by our mind the immensity of the knowable world; our spiritual teacher enjoins us to comprehend by our soul the infinite Spirit which is in the depth of the moving and changing facts of the world; the urging of our artistic nature is to realize the manifestation of personality in the world of appearance, the reality of existence which is in harmony with the real within us. Where this harmony is not deeply felt, there we are aliens and perpetually homesick. For man by nature is an artist; he never receives passively and accurately in his mind a physical representation of things around him. There goes on a continual adaptation, a transformation of facts into human imagery, through constant touches of his sentiments and imagination. The animal has the geography of its birthplace; man has his country, the geography of his personal self. The vision of it is not merely physical; it has its artistic unity, it is a perpetual creation. In his country, his consciousness being unobstructed, man extends his relationship, which is of his own creative personality. In order to live efficiently man must know facts and their laws. In order to be happy he must establish harmonious relationship with all things with which he has dealings. Our creation is the modification of relationship.

The great men who appear in our history remain in our mind not as a static fact but as a living historical image. The sublime suggestions of their lives become blended into a noble consistency in legends made living in the life of ages. Those men with whom we live we constantly modify in our minds, making them more real to us than they would be in a bare presentation. Men's ideal of womanhood and women's ideal of manliness are created by the imagination through a mental grouping of qualities and conducts according to our hopes and desires, and men and women consciously and unconsciously strive towards its attainment. In fact, they reach a degree of reality for each other according to their success in adapting these respective ideals to their own nature. To say that these ideals are imaginary and therefore not true is wrong in man's case. His true life is in his own creation, which represents the infinity of man. He is naturally indifferent to things that merely exist; they must have some ideal value for him, and then only his consciousness fully recognizes them as real. Men are never true in their isolated self, and their imagination is the faculty that brings before their mind the vision of their own greater being.

We can make truth ours by actively modulating its interrelations. This is the work of art; for reality is not based in the substance of things but in the principle of relationship. Truth is the infinite pursued by metaphysics; fact is the infinite pursued by science, while reality is the definition of the infinite which relates truth to the person. Reality is human; it is what we are conscious of, by which we are affected, that which we express. When we are intensely aware of it, we are aware of ourselves and it gives us delight. We live in it, we always widen its limits. Our arts and literature represent this creative activity which is fundamental in man.

But the mysterious fact about it is that though the individuals are separately seeking their expression, their success is never individualistic in character. Men must find and feel and represent in all their creative works Man the Eternal, the creator. Their civilization is a continual discovery of the transcendental humanity. In whatever it fails it shows the failure of the artist, which is the failure in expression; and that civilization perishes in which the individual thwarts the revelation of the universal. For Reality is the truth of Man, who belongs to all times, and any individualistic madness of men against Man cannot thrive for long.

Man is eager that his feeling for what is real to him must never die; it must find an imperishable form. The consciousness of this self of mine is so intensely evident to me that it assumes the character of immortality. I cannot imagine that it ever has been or can be non-existent. In a similar manner all things that are real to me are for myself eternal, and therefore worthy of a language that has permanent meaning. We know individuals who have the habit of inscribing their names on the walls of some majestic monument of architecture. It is a pathetic way of associating their own names with some works of art which belong to all times and to all men. Our hunger for reputation comes from our desire to make objectively real that which is inwardly real to us. He who is inarticulate is insignificant, like a dark star that cannot prove itself. He ever waits for the artist to give him his fullest worth, not for anything specially excellent in him but for the wonderful fact that he is what he certainly is, that he carries in him the eternal mystery of being.

A Chinese friend of mine while travelling with me in the streets of Peking suddenly exclaimed with a vehement enthusiasm: 'Look, here is a donkey!' Surely it was an utterly ordinary donkey, like an indisputable truism, needing no special introduction from him. I was amused; but it made me think. This animal is generally classified as having certain qualities that are not recommendable and then hurriedly dismissed. It was obscured to me by an envelopment of commonplace associations; I was lazily certain that I knew it and therefore I hardly saw it. But my friend, who possessed the artist mind of China, did not treat it with a cheap knowledge but could see it afresh and recognize it as real. When I say real, I mean that it did not remain at the outskirt of his consciousness tied to a narrow definition, but it easily blended in his imagination, produced a vision, a special harmony of lines, colours and life and movement, and became intimately his own. The admission of a donkey into a drawing-room is violently opposed; yet there is no prohibition against its finding a place in a picture which may be admiringly displayed on the drawing-room wall.

The only evidence of truth in art exists when it compels us to say 'I see'. A donkey we may pass by in Nature, but a donkey in art we must acknowledge even if it be a creature that disreputably ignores all its natural history responsibility, even if it resembles a mushroom in its head and a palm-leaf in its tail.

In the Upanishad it is said in a parable that there are two birds sitting on the same bough, one of which feeds and the other looks on. This is an image of the mutual relationship of the infinite being and the finite self. The delight of the bird which looks on is great, for it is a pure and free delight. There are both of these birds in man himself, the objective one with its business of life, the subjective one with its disinterested joy of vision.

A child comes to me and commands me to tell her a story. I tell her of a tiger which is disgusted with the black stripes on its body and comes to my frightened servant demanding a piece of soap. The story gives my little audience immense pleasure, the pleasure of a vision, and her mind cries out, 'It is here, for I see!' She *knows* a tiger in the book of natural history, but she can *see* the tiger in the story of mine.

I am sure that even this child of five knows that it is an impossible tiger that is out on its untigerly quest of an absurd soap. The delightfulness of the tiger for her is not in its beauty, its usefulness, or its probability; but in the undoubted fact that she can see it in her mind with a greater clearness of vision than she can the walls around her – the walls that brutally shout their evidence of certainty which is merely circumstantial. The tiger in the story is inevitable, it has the character of a complete image, which offers its testimonial of truth in itself. The listener's own mind is the eye-witness, whose direct experience could not be contradicted. A tiger must be like every other tiger in order that it may have its place in a book of Science; there it must be a commonplace tiger to be at all tolerated. But in the story it is uncommon, it can never be reduplicated. We *know* a thing because it belongs to a class; we *see* a thing because it belongs to itself. The tiger of the story completely detached itself from all others of its kind and easily assumed a distinct individuality in the heart of the listener. The child could vividly see it, because by the help of her imagination it became her own tiger, one with herself, and this union of the subject and object gives us joy. Is it because there is no separation between them in truth, the separation being the *Maya*, which is creation?

There come in our history occasions when the consciousness of a large multitude becomes suddenly illumined with the recognition of a reality which rises far above the dull obviousness of daily happenings. The world becomes vivid; we see, we feel it with all our soul. Such an occasion there was when the voice of Buddha reached distant shores across physical and moral impediments. Then our life and our world found their profound meaning of reality in their relation to the central person who offered us emancipation of love. Men, in order to make this great human experience ever memorable, determined to do the impossible; they made rocks to speak, stones to sing, caves to remember; their cry of joy and hope took immortal forms along the hills and deserts, across barren solitudes and populous cities. A gigantic creative endeavour built up its triumph in stupendous carvings, defying obstacles that were overwhelming. Such heroic activity over the greater part of the Eastern continents clearly answers the question: 'What is Art?' It is the response of man's creative soul to the call of the Real.

Once there came a time, centuries ago in Bengal, when the divine love drama that has made its eternal playground in human souls was vividly revealed by a personality radiating its intimate realization of God. The mind of a whole people was stirred by a vision of the world as an instrument, through which sounded out invitation to the meeting of bliss. The ineffable mystery of God's love-call, taking shape in an endless panorama of colours and forms, inspired activity in music that overflowed the restrictions of classical conventionalism. Our Kirtan music of Bengal came to its being like a star flung up by a burning whirlpool of emotion in the heart of a whole people, and their consciousness was aflame with a sense of reality that must be adequately acknowledged.

The question may be asked as to what place music occupies

in my theory that art is for evoking in our mind the deep sense of reality in its richest aspect. Music is the most abstract of all the arts, as mathematics is in the region of science. In fact these two have a deep relationship with each other. Mathematics is the logic of numbers and dimensions. It is therefore employed as the basis of our scientific knowledge. When taken out of its concrete associations and reduced to symbols, it reveals its grand structural majesty, the inevitableness of its own perfect concord. Yet there is not merely a logic but also a magic of mathematics which works at the world of appearance, producing harmony – the cadence of inter-relationship. This rhythm of harmony has been extracted from its usual concrete context, and exhibited through the medium of sound. And thus the pure essence of ex-pressiveness in existence is offered in music. Expressiveness finds the least resistance in sound, having freedom unencumbered by the burden of facts and thoughts. This gives it a power to arouse in us an intimate feeling of reality. In the pictorial, plastic and literary arts, the object and our feelings with regard to it are closely associated, like the rose and its perfumes. In music, the feeling distilled in sound, becoming itself an independent object. It assumes a tune-form which is definite, but a meaning which is undefinable, and yet which grips our mind with a sense of absolute truth.

It is the magic of mathematics, the rhythm which is in the heart of all creation, which moves in the atom and, in its differ-ent measures, fashions gold and lead, the rose and the thorn, the sun and the planets. These are the dance-steps of numbers in the arena of time and space, which weave the *maya*, the patterns of appearance, the incessant flow of change, that ever is and is not. It is the rhythm that churns up images from the vague and makes tangible what is elusive. This is *maya*, this is the art in creation, and art in literature, which is the magic of rhythm.

And must we stop here? What we know as intellectual truth, is that also not a rhythm of the relationship of facts, that weaves the pattern of theory, and produces a sense of convincingness to a person who somehow feels sure that he knows the truth? We believe any fact to be true because of a harmony, a rhythm in reason, the process of which is analysable by the logic of mathematics, but not its result in me, just as we can count the notes but cannot account for the music. The mystery is that I am convinced, and this also belongs to the *maya* of creation, whose one important, indispensable factor is this self-conscious personality that I represent.

And the Other? I believe it is also a self-conscious personality, which has its eternal harmony with mine.

CHAPTER TEN

MAN'S NATURE

FROM THE TIME when Man became truly conscious of his own self he also became conscious of a mysterious spirit of unity which found its manifestation through him in his society. It is a subtle medium of relationship between individuals, which is not for any utilitarian purpose but for its own ultimate truth, not a sum of arithmetic but a value of life. Somehow Man has felt that this comprehensive spirit of unity has a divine character which could claim the sacrifice of all that is individual in him, that in it dwells his highest meaning transcending his limited self, representing his best freedom.

Man's reverential loyalty to this spirit of unity is expressed in his religion; it is symbolized in the names of his deities. That is why, in the beginning, his gods were tribal gods, even gods of the different communities belonging to the same tribe. With the extension of the consciousness of human unity his God became revealed to him as one and universal, proving that the truth of human unity is the truth of Man's God.

In the Sanskrit language, religion goes by the name *dharma*, which in the derivative meaning implies the principle of relationship that holds us firm, and in its technical sense means the virtue of a thing, the essential quality of it; for instance, heat is the essential quality of fire, though in certain of its stages it may be absent.

Religion consists in the endeavour of men to cultivate and express those qualities which are inherent in the nature of Man the Eternal, and to have faith in him. If these qualities were absolutely natural in individuals, religion could have no purpose. We begin our history with all the original promptings of our brute nature which helps us to fulfil those vital needs of ours that are immediate. But deeper within us there is a current of tendencies which runs in many ways in a contrary direction, the life current of universal humanity. Religion has its function in reconciling the contradiction, by subordinating the brute nature to what we consider as the truth of Man. This is helped when our faith in the Eternal Man, whom we call by different names and imagine in different images, is made strong. The contradiction between the two natures in us is so great that men have willingly sacrificed their vital needs and courted death in order to express their *dharma*, which represents the truth of the Supreme Man.

The vision of the Supreme Man is realized by our imagination, but not created by our mind. More real than individual men, he surpasses each of us in his permeating personality which is transcendental. The procession of his ideas, following his great purpose, is ever moving across obstructive facts towards the perfected truth. We, the individuals, having our place in his composition, may or may not be in conscious harmony with his purpose, may even put obstacles in his path bringing down our doom upon ourselves. But we gain our true religion when we consciously co-operate with him, finding our exceeding joy through suffering and sacrifice. For through our own love for him we are made conscious of a great love that radiates from his being, who is Mahātma, the Supreme Spirit.

The great Chinese sage Lao-tze has said: 'One who may die, but will not perish, has life everlasting.' It means that he lives in the life of the immortal Man. The urging for this life induces men to go through the struggle for a true survival. And it has been said in our scripture: 'Through *adharma* (the negation of *dharma*) man prospers, gains what appears desirable, conquers enemies, but he perishes at the root.' In this saying it is suggested that there is a life which is truer for men than their physical life which is transient.

Our life gains what is called 'value' in those of its aspects which represent eternal humanity in knowledge, in sympathy, in deeds, in character and creative works. And from the beginning of our history we are seeking, often at the cost of everything else, the value for our life and not merely success; in other words, we are trying to realize in ourselves the immortal Man, so that we may die but not perish. This is the meaning of the utterance in the Upanishad: *Tam vedyam purusham veda, yatha ma vo mrityuh parivyathah* – 'Realize the Person so that thou mayst not suffer from death.'

The meaning of these words is highly paradoxical, and cannot be proved by our senses or our reason, and yet its influence is so strong in men that they have cast away all fear and greed, defied all the instincts that cling to the brute nature, for the sake of acknowledging and preserving a life which belongs to the Eternal Person. It is all the more significant because many of them do not believe in its reality, and yet are ready to fling away for it all that they believe to be final and the only positive fact.

We call this ideal reality 'spiritual'. That word is vague; nevertheless, through the dim light which reaches us across the barriers of physical existence, we seem to have a stronger faith in the spiritual Man than in the physical; and from the dimmest period of his history, Man has a feeling that the apparent facts of existence are not final; that his supreme welfare depends upon his being able to remain in perfect relationship with some great mystery behind the veil, at the threshold of a larger life, which is for giving him a far higher value than a mere continuation of his physical life in the material world.

Our physical body has its comprehensive reality in the physical world, which may be truly called our universal body, without which our individual body would miss its function. Our physical life realizes its growing meaning through a widening freedom in its relationship with the physical world, and this gives it a greater happiness than the mere pleasure of satisfied needs. We become aware of a profound meaning of our own self at the consciousness of some ideal of perfection, some truth beautiful or majestic which gives us an inner sense of completeness, a heightened sense of our own reality. This strengthens man's faith, effective even if indefinite – his faith in an objective ideal of perfection comprehending the human world. His vision of it has been beautiful or distorted, luminous or obscure, according to the stages of development that his consciousness has attained. But whatever may be the name and nature of his religious creed, man's ideal of human perfection has been based upon a bond of unity running through individuals culminating in a supreme Being who represents the eternal in human personality. In his civilization the perfect expression of this idea produces the wealth of truth which is for the revelation of Man and not merely for the success of life. But when this creative ideal which is *dharma* gives place to some overmastering passion in a large body of men civilization bursts out in an explosive flame, like a star that has lighted its own funeral pyre of boisterous brilliancy.

When I was a child I had the freedom to make my own toys out of trifles and create my own games from imagination. In my happiness my playmates had their full share, in fact the complete enjoyment of my games depended upon their taking part in them. One day, in this paradise of our childhood, entered the temptation from the market world of the adult. A toy brought from an English shop was given to one of our companions; it was perfect, it was big and wonderfully life-like. He became proud of the toy and less mindful of the game; he kept that expensive thing carefully away from us, glorying in his exclusive possession of it, feeling himself superior to his playmates whose toys were cheap. I am sure if he could use the modern language of history he would say that he was more civilized than ourselves to the extent of his owning that ridiculously perfect toy.

One thing he failed to realize in his excitement – a fact which at the moment seemed to him insignificant – that this temptation obscured something a great deal more perfect than his toy, the revelation of the perfect child which ever dwells in the heart of man, in other words, the *dharma* of the child. The toy merely expressed his wealth but not himself, not the child's creative spirit, not the child's generous joy in his play, his identification of himself with others who were his compeers in his play world. Civilization is to express Man's *dharma* and not merely his cleverness, power and possession.

Once there was an occasion for me to motor down to Calcutta from a place a hundred miles away. Something wrong with the mechanism made it necessary for us to have a repeated supply of water almost every half-hour. At the first village where we were compelled to stop, we asked the help of a man to find water for us. It proved quite a task for him, but when we offered him his reward, poor though he was, he refused to accept it. In fifteen other villages the same thing happened. In a hot country, where travellers constantly need water and where the water supply grows scanty in summer, the villagers consider it their duty to offer water to those who need it. They could easily make a business out of it, following the inexorable law of demand and supply. But the ideal which they consider to be their *dharma* has become one with their life. They do not claim any personal merit for possessing it.

Lao-tze, speaking about the man who is truly good, says: 'He quickens but owns not. He acts but claims not. Merit he accomplishes but dwells not in it. Since he does not dwell in it, it will never leave him.' That which is outside ourselves we can sell; but that which is one with our being we cannot sell. This complete assimilation of truth belongs to the paradise of perfection; it lies beyond the purgatory of self-consciousness. To have reached it proves a long process of civilization.

To be able to take a considerable amount of trouble in order to supply water to a passing stranger and yet never to claim merit or reward for it seems absurdly and negligibly simple compared with the capacity to produce an amazing number of things per minute. A millionaire tourist, ready to corner the food market and grow rich by driving the whole world to the brink of starvation, is sure to feel too superior to notice this simple thing while rushing through our villages at sixty miles an hour.

Yes, it is simple, as simple as it is for a gentleman to be a gentleman; but that simplicity is the product of centuries of culture. That simplicity is difficult of imitation. In a few years' time, it might be possible for me to learn how to make holes in thousands of needles simultaneously by turning a wheel, but to be absolutely simple in one's hospitality to one's enemy, or to a stranger, requires generations of training. Simplicity takes no account of its own value, claims no wages, and therefore those who are enamoured of power do not realize that simplicity of spiritual expression is the highest product of civilization.

A process of disintegration can kill this rare fruit of a higher life, as a whole race of birds possessing some rare beauty can be made extinct by the vulgar power of avarice which has civilized weapons. This fact was clearly proved to me when I found that the only place where a price was expected for the water given to us was a suburb at Calcutta, where life was richer, the water supply easier and more abundant and where progress flowed in numerous channels in all directions. It shows that a harmony of character which the people once had was lost – the harmony with the inner self which is greater in its universality than the self that gives prominence to its personal needs. The latter loses its feeling of beauty and generosity in its calculation of profit; for there it represents exclusively itself and not the universal man.

There is an utterance in the Atharva Veda, wherein appears the question as to who it was that gave Man his music. Birds repeat their single notes, or a very simple combination of them, but Man builds his world of music and establishes ever new rhythmic relationship of notes. These reveal to him a universal mystery of creation which cannot be described. They bring to him the inner rhythm that transmutes facts into truths. They give him pleasure not merely for his sense of hearing, but for his deeper being, which gains satisfaction in the ideal of perfect unity. Somehow man feels that truth finds its body in such perfection; and when he seeks for his own best revelation he seeks a medium which has the harmonious unity, as has music. Our impulse to give expression to Universal Man produces arts and literature. They in their cadence of lines, colours, movements, words, thoughts, express vastly more than what they appear to be on the surface. They open the windows of our mind to the eternal reality of man. They are the superfluity of wealth of which we claim our common inheritance whatever may be the country and time to which we belong; for they are inspired by the universal mind. And not merely in his arts, but in his own behaviour, the individual must for his excellence give emphasis to an ideal which has some value of truth that ideally belongs to all men. In other words, he should create a music of expression in his conduct and surroundings which makes him represent the supreme Personality. And civilization is the creation of the race, its expression of the universal Man.

When I first visited Japan I had the opportunity of observing where the two parts of the human sphere strongly contrasted; one, on which grew up the ancient continents of social ideal, standards of beauty, codes of personal behaviour; and the other part, the fluid element, the perpetual current that carried wealth to its shores from all parts of the world. In half a century's time Japan has been able to make her own the mighty spirit of progress which suddenly burst upon her one morning in a storm of insult and menace. China also has had her rousing, when her self-respect was being knocked to pieces through series of helpless years, and I am sure she also will master before long the instrument which hurt her to the quick. But the ideals that imparted life and body to Japanese civilization had been nourished in the reverent hopes of countless generations through ages which were not primarily occupied in an incessant hunt for opportunities. They had those large tracts of leisure in them which are necessary for the blossoming of Life's beauty and the ripening of her wisdom.

On the one hand we can look upon the modern factories in Japan with their numerous mechanical organizations and engines of production and destruction of the latest type. On the other hand, against them we may see some fragile vase, some small piece of silk, some architecture of sublime simplicity, some perfect lyric of bodily movement. We may also notice the Japanese expression of courtesy daily extracting from them a considerable amount of time and trouble. All these have come not from any accurate knowledge of things but from an intense consciousness of the value of reality which takes time for its fulness. What Japan reveals in her skilful manipulation of telegraphic wires and railway lines, of machines for manufacturing things and for killing men, is more or less similar to what we see in other countries which have similar opportunity for training. But in her art of living, her pictures, her code of conduct, the various forms of beauty which her religious and social ideals assume Japan expresses her own personality, her *dharma*, which, in order to be of any worth, must be unique and at the same time represent Man of the Everlasting Life.

Lao-tze has said: 'Not knowing the eternal causes passions to rise; and that is evil.' He has also said: 'Let us die, and yet not perish.' For we die when we lose our physical life, we perish when we miss our humanity. And humanity is the *dharma* of human beings.

What is evident in this world is the endless procession of moving things; but what is to be realized, is the supreme human Truth by which the human world is permeated.

We must never forget to-day that a mere movement is not valuable in itself, that it may be a sign of a dangerous form of inertia. We must be reminded that a great upheaval of spirit, a universal realization of true dignity of man once caused by Buddha's teachings in India, started a movement for centuries which produced illumination of literature, art, science and numerous efforts of public beneficence. This was a movement whose motive force was not some additional accession of knowledge or power or urging of some overwhelming passion. It was an inspiration for freedom, the freedom which enables us to realize *dharma*, the truth of Eternal Man.

Lao-tze in one of his utterances has said: 'Those who have virtue (*dharma*) attend to their obligations; those who have no virtue attend to their claims.' Progress which is not related to an inner *dharma*, but to an attraction which is external, seeks to satisfy our endless claims. But civilization, which is an ideal, gives us the abundant power to renounce which is the power that realizes the infinite and inspires creation.

This great Chinese sage has said: 'To increase life is called a blessing.' For, the increase of life realizes the eternal life and yet does not transcend the limits of life's unity. The mountain pine grows tall and great, its every inch maintains the rhythm of an inner balance, and therefore even in its seeming extravagance it has the reticent grace of self-control. The tree and its productions belong to the same vital system of cadence; the timber, the flowers, leaves and fruits are one with the tree; their exuberance is not a malady of exaggeration, but a blessing.

CHAPTER ELEVEN

THE MEETING

OUR GREAT PROPHETS in all ages did truly realize in themselves the freedom of the soul in their consciousness of the spiritual kinship of man which is universal. And yet human races, owing to their external geographical condition, developed in their individual isolation a mentality that is obnoxiously selfish. In their instinctive search for truth in religion either they dwarfed and deformed it in the mould of the primitive distortions of their own race-mind, or else they shut their God within temple walls and scriptural texts safely away, especially from those departments of life where his absence gives easy access to devil-worship in various names and forms. They treated their God in the same way as in some forms of government the King is treated, who has traditional honour but no effective authority. The true meaning of God has remained vague in our minds only because our consciousness of the spiritual unity has been thwarted.

One of the potent reasons for this – our geographical separation – has now been nearly removed. Therefore the time has come when we must, for the sake of truth and for the sake of that peace which is the harvest of truth, refuse to allow the idea of our God to remain indistinct behind unrealities of formal rites and theological mistiness.

The creature that lives its life screened and sheltered in a dark cave, finds its safety in the very narrowness of its own environment. The economical providence of Nature curtails and tones down its sensibilities to such a limited necessity. But if these cave-walls were to become suddenly removed by some catastrophe, then either it must accept the doom of extinction, or carry on satisfactory negotiations with its wider surroundings.

The races of mankind will never again be able to go back to their citadels of high-walled exclusiveness. They are to-day exposed to one another, physically and intellectually. The shells, which have so long given them full security within their individual enclosures have been broken, and by no artificial process can they be mended again. So we have to accept this fact, even though we have not yet fully adapted our minds to this changed environment of publicity, even though through it we may have to run all the risks entailed by the wider expansion of life's freedom.

A large part of our tradition is our code of adjustment which deals with the circumstances special to ourselves. These traditions, no doubt, variegate the several racial personalities with their distinctive colours – colours which have their poetry and also certain protective qualities suitable to each different environment. We may come to acquire a strong love for our own colourful race speciality; but if that gives us fitness only for a very narrow world, then, at the slightest variation in our outward circumstances, we may have to pay for this love with our life itself.

In the animal world there are numerous instances of complete race-suicide overtaking those who fondly clung to some advantage which later on became a hindrance in an altered dispensation. In fact the superiority of man is proved by his adaptability to extreme surprises of chance – neither the torrid nor the frigid zone of his destiny offering him insuperable obstacles.

The vastness of the race problem with which we are faced to-day will either compel us to train ourselves to moral fitness in the place of merely external efficiency, or the complications arising out of it will fetter all our movements and drag us to our death.

When our necessity becomes urgently insistent, when the resources that have sustained us so long are exhausted, then our spirit puts forth all its force to discover some other source of sustenance deeper and more permanent. This leads us from the exterior to the interior of our store-house. When muscle does not fully serve us, we come to awaken intellect to ask for its help and are then surprised to find in it a greater source of strength for us than physical power. When, in their turn, our intellectual gifts grow perverse, and only help to render our suicide gorgeous and exhaustive, our soul must seek an alliance with some power which is still deeper, yet further removed from the rude stupidity of muscle.

Hitherto the cultivation of intense race egotism is the one thing that has found its fullest scope at this meeting of men. In no period of human history has there been such an epidemic of moral perversity, such a universal churning up of jealousy, greed, hatred and mutual suspicion. Every people, weak or strong, is constantly indulging in a violent dream of rendering itself thoroughly hurtful to others. In this galloping competition of hurtfulness, on the slope of a bottomless pit, no nation dares to stop or slow down. A scarlet fever with a raging temperature has attacked the entire body of mankind, and political passion has taken the place of creative personality in all departments of life.

It is well known that when greed has for its object material gain then it can have no end. It is like the chasing of the horizon by a lunatic. To go on in a competition multiplying millions becomes a steeplechase of insensate futility that has obstacles but no goal. It has for its parallel the fight with material weapons – weapons which must perpetually be multiplied, opening up new vistas of destruction and evoking new forms of insanity in the forging of frightfulness. Thus seems now to have commenced the last fatal adventure of drunken Passion riding on an intellect of prodigious power.

To-day, more than ever before in our history, the aid of spiritual power is needed. Therefore, I believe its resources will surely be discovered in the hidden depths of our being. Pioneers will come to take up this adventure and suffer, and through suffering open out a path to that higher elevation of life in which lies our safety.

Let me, in reference to this, give an instance from the history of Ancient India. There was a noble period in the early days of India when, to a band of dreamers, agriculture appeared as a great idea and not merely useful fact. The heroic personality of Ramachandra, who espoused its cause, was sung in popular ballads, which in a later age forgot their original message and were crystallized into an epic merely extolling some domestic virtues of its hero. It is quite evident, however, from the legendary relics lying entombed in the story, that a new age ushered in by the spread of agriculture came as a divine voice to those who could hear. It lifted up the primeval screen of the wilderness, brought the distant near, and broke down all barricades. Men who had formed separate and antagonistic groups in their sheltered seclusions were called upon to form a united people.

In the Vedic verses, we find constant mention of conflicts between the original inhabitants of Ancient India and the colonists. There we find the expression of a spirit that was one of mutual distrust and a struggle in which was sought either wholesale slavery or extermination for the opponents carried on in the manner of animals who live in the narrow segregation imposed upon them by their limited imagination and imperfect sympathy. This spirit would have continued in all its ferocious vigour of savagery had men failed to find the opportunity for the discovery that man's highest truth was in the union of co-operation and love.

The progress of agriculture was the first external step which led to such a discovery. It not only made a settled life possible for a large number of men living in close proximity, but it claimed for its very purpose a life of peaceful co-operation. The mere fact of such a sudden change from a nomadic to an agricultural condition would not have benefited Man if he had not developed therewith his spiritual sensitiveness to an inner principle of truth. We can realize, from our reading of the Ramayana, the birth of idealism among a section of the Indian colonists of those days, before whose mind's eye was opened a vision of emancipation rich with the responsibility of a higher life. The epic represents in its ideal the change of the people's aspiration from the path of conquest to that of reconciliation.

At the present time, as I have said, the human world has been overtaken by another vast change similar to that which had occurred in the epic age of India. So long men had been cultivating, almost with a religious fervour, that mentality which is the product of racial isolation; poets proclaimed, in a loud pitch of bragging, the exploits of their popular fighters; money-makers felt neither pity nor shame in the unscrupulous dexterity of their pocket-picking; diplomats scattered lies in order to reap concessions from the devastated future of their own victims. Suddenly the walls that separated the different races are seen to have given way, and we find ourselves standing face to face.

This is a great fact of epic significance. Man, suckled at the wolf's breast, sheltered in the brute's den, brought up in the prowling habit of depredation, suddenly discovers that he is Man, and that his true power lies in yielding up his brute power for the freedom of spirit.

The God of humanity has arrived at the gates of the ruined temple of the tribe. Though he has not yet found his altar, I ask the men of simple faith, wherever they may be in the world, to bring their offering of sacrifice to him, and to believe that it is far better to be wise and worshipful than to be clever and supercilious. I ask them to claim the right of manhood to be friends of men, and not the right of a particular proud race or nation which may boast of the fatal quality of being the rulers of men. We should know for certain that such rulers will no longer be tolerated in the new world, as it basks in the open sunlight of mind and breathes life's free air.

In the geological ages of the infant earth the demons of physical force had their full sway. The angry fire, the devouring flood, the fury of the storm, continually kicked the earth into frightful distortions. These titans have at last given way to the reign of life. Had there been spectators in those days who were clever and practical they would have wagered their last penny on these titans and would have waxed hilariously witty at the expense of the helpless living speck taking its stand in the arena of the wrestling giants. Only a dreamer could have then declared with unwavering conviction that those titans were doomed because of their very exaggeration, as are, to-day, those formidable qualities which, in the parlance of schoolboy science, are termed Nordic.

I ask once again, let us, the dreamers of the East and the West, keep our faith firm in the Life that creates and not in the Machine that constructs – in the power that hides its force and blossoms in beauty, and not in the power that bares its arms and chuckles at its capacity to make itself obnoxious. Let us know that the Machine is good when it helps, but not so when it exploits life; that Science is great when it destroys evil, but not when the two enter into unholy alliance.

CHAPTER TWELVE
THE TEACHER

I HAVE ALREADY described how the nebulous idea of the divine essence condensed in my consciousness into a human realization. It is definite and finite at the same time, the Eternal Person manifested in all persons. It may be one of the numerous manifestations of God, the one in which is comprehended Man and his Universe. But we can never know or imagine him as revealed in any other inconceivable universe so long as we remain human beings. And therefore, whatever character our theology may ascribe to him, in reality he is the infinite ideal of Man towards whom men move in their collective growth, with whom they seek their union of love as individuals, in whom they find their ideal of father, friend and beloved.

I am sure that it was this idea of the divine Humanity unconsciously working in my mind, which compelled me to come out of the seclusion of my literary career and take my part in the world of practical activities. The solitary enjoyment of the infinite in meditation no longer satisfied me, and the texts which I used for my silent worship lost their inspiration without my knowing it. I am sure I vaguely felt that my need was spiritual self-realization in the life of Man through some disinterested service. This was the time when I founded an educational institution for our children in Bengal. It has a special character of its own which is still struggling to find its fulfilment; for it is a living temple that I have attempted to build for my divinity. In such a place education necessarily becomes the preparation for a complete life of man which can only become possible by living that life, through knowledge and service, enjoyment and creative work. The necessity was my own, for I felt impelled to come back into a fulness of truth from my exile in a dream-world.

This brings to my mind the name of another poet of ancient India, Kalidasa, whose poem of Meghaduta reverberates with the music of the sorrow of an exile.

It was not the physical home-sickness form which the poet suffered, it was something far more fundamental, the home-sickness of the soul. We feel from almost all his works the oppressive atmosphere of the kings' palaces of those days, dense with things of luxury, and also with the callousness of self-indulgence, albeit an atmosphere of refined culture based on an extravagant civilization.

The poet in the royal court lived in banishment – banishment from the immediate presence of the eternal. He knew it was not merely his own banishment, but that of the whole age to which he was born, the age that had gathered its wealth and missed its well-being, built its storehouse of things and lost its background of the great universe. What was the form in which his desire for perfection persistently appeared in his drama and poems? It was the form of the *tapovana*, the forest-dwelling of the patriarchal community of ancient India. Those who are familiar with Sanskrit literature will know that this was not a colony of people with a primitive culture and mind. They were seekers after truth, for the sake of which they lived in an atmosphere of purity but not of Puritanism, of the simple life but not the life of self-mortification. They never advocated celibacy and they had constant intercommunication with other people who lived the life of worldly interest. Their aim and endeavour have briefly been suggested in the Upanishad in these lines:

Te sarvagam sarvatah prapya dhira
yuktatmanah sarvamevavisanti.
Those men of serene mind enter into the All, having realized and being in union everywhere with the omnipresent
Spirit.

It was never a philosophy of renunciation of a negative character, but a realization completely comprehensive. How the tortured mind of Kalidasa in the prosperous city of Ujjaini, and the glorious period of Vikramaditya, closely pressed by all-obstructing things and all-devouring self, let his thoughts hover round the vision of a *tapovana* for his inspiration of life!

It was not a deliberate copy but a natural coincidence that a poet of modern India also had the similar vision when he felt within him the misery of a spiritual banishment. In the time of Kalidasa the people vividly believed in the ideal of *tapovana*, the forest colony, and there can be no doubt that even in the late age there were communities of men living in the heart of nature, not ascetics fiercely in love with a lingering suicide, but men of serene sanity who sought to realize the spiritual meaning of their life. And, therefore, when Kalidasa sang of the *tapovana*, his poems found their immediate communion in the living faith of his hearers. But to-day the idea has lost any definite outline of reality, and has retreated into the far away phantom-land of legend. Therefore the Sanskrit word in a modern poem would merely be poetical, its meaning judged by a literary standard of appraisement. Then, again, the spirit of the forest-dwelling in the purity of its original shape would be a fantastic anachronism in the present age, and therefore, in order to be real, it must find its reincarnation under modern conditions of life. It must be the same in truth, but not identical in fact. It was this which made the modern poet's heart crave to compose his poem in a language of tangible words.

But I must give the history in some detail. Civilized man has come far away from the orbit of his normal life. He has gradually formed and intensified some habits that are like those of the bees for adapting himself to his hive-world. We often see men suffering from ennui, from world-weariness, from a spirit of rebellion against their environment for no reasonable cause whatever. Social revolutions are constantly ushered in with a suicidal violence that has its origin in our dissatisfaction with our hive-wall arrangement – the too exclusive enclosure that deprives us of the perspective which is so much needed to give us the proper proportion in our art of living. All this is an indication that man has not been moulded on the model of the bee and therefore he becomes recklessly anti-social when his freedom to be more than social is ignored.

In our highly complex modern condition mechanical forces are organized with such efficiency that materials are produced that grow far in advance of man's selective and assimilative capacity to simplify them into harmony with his nature and needs.

Such an intemperate overgrowth of things, like rank vegetation in the tropics, creates confinement for man. The nest is simple, it has an early relationship with the sky; the cage is complex and costly; it is too much itself excommunicated from whatever lies outside. And man is building his cage, fast developing his parasitism on the monster Thing, which he allows to envelop him on all sides. He is always occupied in adapting himself to its dead angularities, limits himself to its limitations, and merely becomes a part of it.

This may seem contrary to the doctrine of those who believe that a constant high pressure of living, produced by an artificially cultivated hunger of things, generates and feeds the energy that drives civilization upon its endless journey. Personally, I do not believe that this has ever been the principal driving force that has led to eminence any great civilization of which we know in history.

I was born in what was once the metropolis of British India. My own ancestors came floating to Calcutta upon the earliest tide of the fluctuating fortune of the East India Company. The unconvential code of life for our family has been a confluence of three cultures, the Hindu, Mohammedan and British. My grandfather belonged to that period when the amplitude of dress and courtesy and a generous leisure were gradually being clipped and curtailed into Victorian manners, economical in time, in ceremonies, and in the dignity of personal appearance. This will show that I came to a world in which the modern city-bred spirit of progress had just begun driving its triumphal car over the luscious green life of our ancient village community. Though the trampling process was almost complete round me, yet the wailing cry of the past was still lingering over the wreckage.

Often I had listened to my eldest brother describing with the poignancy of a hopeless regret a society hospitable, sweet with the old-world aroma of natural kindliness, full of simple faith and the ceremonial-poetry of life. But all this was a vanishing shadow behind me in the dusky golden haze of a twilight horizon – the all-pervading fact around my boyhood being the modern city newly built by a company of western traders and the spirit of the modern time seeking its unaccustomed entrance into our life, stumbling against countless anomalies.

But it always is a surprise to me to think that though this closed-up hardness of a city was my only experience of the world, yet my mind was constantly haunted by the home-sick fancies of an exile. It seems that the sub-conscious remembrance of a primeval dwelling-place, where, in our ancestors' minds, were figured and voiced the mysteries of the inarticulate rocks, the rushing water and the dark whispers of the forest, was constantly stirring my blood with its call. Some shadow-haunting living reminiscence in me seemed to ache for the pre-natal cradle and playground it shared with the primal life in the illimitable magic of the land, water and air. The shrill, thin cry of the high-flying kite in the blazing sun of the dazed Indian midday sent to a solitary boy the signal of a dumb distant kinship. The few coconut plants growing by the boundary wall of our house, like some war captives from an older army of invaders of this earth, spoke to me of the eternal companionship which the great brotherhood of trees has ever offered to man.

Looking back upon those moments of my boyhood days, when all my mind seemed to float poised upon a large feeling of the sky, of the light, and to tingle with the brown earth in its glistening grass, I cannot help believing that my Indian ancestry had left deep in my being the legacy of its philosophy – the philosophy which speaks of fulfilment through our harmony with all things. The founding of my school had its origin in the memory of that longing for the freedom of consciousness, which seems to go back beyond the skyline of my birth.

Freedom in the mere sense of independence has no content, and therefore no meaning. Perfect freedom lies in a perfect harmony of relationship, which we realize in this world not through our response to it in knowing, but in being. Objects of knowledge maintain an infinite distance from us who are the knowers. For knowledge is not union. Therefore the further world of freedom awaits us there where we reach truth, not through feeling it by our senses or knowing it by our reason, but through the union of perfect sympathy.

Children with the freshness of their senses come directly to the intimacy of this world. This is the first great gift they have. They must accept it naked and simple and must never again lose their power of immediate communication with it. For our perfection we have to be vitally savage and mentally civilized; we should have the gift to be natural with nature and human with human society. My banished soul sitting in the civilized isolation of the town-life cried within me for the enlargement of the horizon of its comprehension. I was like the torn-away line of a verse, always in a state of suspense, while the other line, with which it rhymed and which could give it fulness, was smudged by the mist away in some undecipherable distance. The inexpensive power to be happy which, along with other children, I brought to this world, was being constantly worn away by friction with the brick-and-mortar arrangement of life, by monotonously mechanical habits and the customary code of respectability.

In the usual course of things I was sent to school, but possibly my suffering was unusually greater than that of most other children. The non-civilized in me was sensitive; it had the great thirst for colour, for music, for movement of life. Our city-built education took no heed of that living fact. It had its luggage-van waiting for branded bales of marketable result. The relative proportion of the non-civilized to the civilized in man should be in the proportion of the water and the land in our globe, the former predominating. But the school had for its object a continual reclamation of the civilized. Such a drain in the fluid element causes an aridity which may not be considered deplorable under city conditions. But my nature never got accustomed to those conditions, to the callous decency of the pavement. The non-civilized triumphed in me only too soon and drove me away from school when I had just entered my teens. I found myself stranded on a solitary island of ignorance, and had to rely solely upon my own instincts to build up my education from the very beginning.

This reminds me that when I was young I had the great good fortune of coming upon a Bengali translation of *Robinson Crusoe*. I still believe that it is the best book for boys that has ever been written. There was a longing in me when young to run away from my own self and be one with everything in Nature. This mood appears to be particularly Indian, the outcome of a traditional desire for the expansion of consciousness. One has to admit that such a desire is too subjective in its character; but this is inevitable in the geographical circumstances which we have to endure. We live under the extortionate tyranny of the tropics, paying heavy toll every moment for the barest right of existence. The heat, the damp, the unspeakable fecundity of minute life feeding upon big life, the perpetual sources of irritation, visible and invisible, leave very little margin of capital for extravagant experiments. Excess of energy seeks obstacles for its self-realization. That is why we find so often in Western literature a constant emphasis upon the malignant aspect of Nature, in whom the people of the West seem to be delighted to discover an enemy for the sheer enjoyment of challenging her to fight. The reason which made Alexander express his desire to find other worlds to conquer, when his conquest of the world was completed, makes the enormously vital people of the West desire, when they have some respite in their sublime mission of fighting against objects that are noxious, to go out of their way to spread their coat-tails in other people's thoroughfares and to claim indemnity when these are trodden upon. In order to make the thrilling risk of hurting themselves they are ready to welcome endless trouble to hurt others who are inoffensive, such as the beautiful birds which happen to know how to fly away, the timid beasts, which have the advantage of inhabiting inaccessible regions, and – but I avoid the discourtesy of mentioning higher races in this connection.

Life's fulfilment finds constant contradictions in its path; but those are necessary for the sake of its advance. The stream is saved from the sluggishness of its current by the perpetual opposition of the soil through which it must cut its way. It is this soil which forms its banks. The spirit of fight belongs to the genius of life. The tuning of an instrument has to be done, not because it reveals a proficient perseverance in the face of difficulty, but because it helps music to be perfectly realized. Let us rejoice that in the West life's instrument is being tuned in all its different chords owing to the great fact that the West has triumphant pleasure in the struggle with obstacles. The spirit of creation in the heart of the universe will never allow, for its own sake, obstacles to be completely removed. It is only because positive truth lies in that ideal of perfection, which has to be won by our own endeavour in order to make it our own, that the spirit of fight is great. But this does not imply a premium for the exhibition of a muscular athleticism or a rude barbarism of ravenous rapacity.

In *Robinson Crusoe*, the delight of the union with Nature finds its expression in a story of adventure in which the solitary Man is face to face with solitary Nature, coaxing her, co-operating with her, exploring her secrets, using all his faculties to win her help.

This is the heroic love-adventure of the West, the active wooing of the earth. I remember how, once in my youth, the feeling of intense delight and wonder followed me in my railway journey across Europe from Brindisi to Calais, when I realized the chaste beauty of this continent everywhere blossoming in a glow of health and richness under the age-long attention of her chivalrous lover, Western humanity. He had gained her, made her his own, unlocked the inexhaustible generosity of her heart. And I had intently wished that the introspective vision of the universal soul, which an Eastern devotee realizes in the solitude of his mind, could be united with this spirit of its outward expression in service, the exercise of will in unfolding the wealth of beauty and well-being from its shy obscurity to the light.

I remember the morning when a beggar woman in a Bengal village gathered in the loose end of her *sari* the stale flowers that were about to be thrown away from the vase on my table; and with an ecstatic expression of tenderness buried her face in them, exclaiming, 'Oh, Beloved of my Heart!' Her eyes could easily pierce the veil of the outward form and reach the realm of the infinite in these flowers, where she found the intimate touch of her Beloved, the great, the universal Human. But in spite of it all she lacked that energy of worship, that Western form of direct divine service, the service of man, which helps the earth to bring out her flowers and spread the reign of beauty on the desolate dust. I refuse to think that the twin spirits of the East and the West, the Mary and Martha, can never meet to make perfect the realization of truth. And in spite of our material poverty in the East and the antagonism of time I wait patiently for this meeting.

Robinson Crusoe's island comes to my mind when I think of some institution where the first great lesson in the perfect union of Man and Nature, not only through love, but through active communication and intelligent ways, can be had unobstructed. We have to keep in mind the fact that love and action are the only intermediaries through which perfect knowledge can be obtained; for the object of knowledge is not pedantry but wisdom. The primary object of an institution should not be merely to educate one's limbs and mind to be in efficient readiness for all emergencies, but to be in perfect tune in the symphony of response between life and world, to find the balance of their harmony which is wisdom. The first important lesson for children in such a place would be that of improvisation, the constant imposition of the ready-made having been banished from here. It is to give occasions to explore one's capacity through surprises of achievement. I must make it plain that this means a lesson not in simple life, but in creative life. For life may grow complex, and yet if there is a living personality in its centre, it will still have the unity of creation; it will carry its own weight in perfect grace, and will not be a mere addition to the number of facts that only goes to swell a crowd.

I wish I could say that I had fully realized my dream in my school. I have only made the first introduction towards it and have given an opportunity to the children to find their freedom in Nature by being able to love it. For love is freedom; it gives us that fulness of existence which saves us from paying with our soul for objects that are immensely cheap. Love lights up this world with its meaning and makes life feel that it has that 'enough' everywhere which truly is its 'feast'. I know men who preach the cult of simple life by glorifying the spiritual merit of poverty. I refuse to imagine my special value in poverty when it is a mere negation. Only when the mind has the sensitiveness to be able to respond to the deeper call of reality is it naturally weaned away from the lure of the fictitious value of things. It is callousness which robs us of our simple power to enjoy, and dooms us to the indignity of a snobbish pride in furniture and the foolish burden of expensive things. But the callousness of asceticism pitted against the callousness of luxury is merely fighting one evil with the help of another, inviting the pitiless demon of the desert in place of the indiscriminate demon of the jungle.

I tried my best to develop in the children of my school the freshness of their feeling for Nature, a sensitiveness of soul in their relationship with their human surroundings, with the help of literature, festive ceremonials and also the religious teaching which enjoins us to come to the nearer presence of the world through the soul, thus to gain it more than can be measured – like gaining an instrument in truth by bringing out its music.

CHAPTER THIRTEEN
SPIRITUAL FREEDOM

THERE ARE INJURIES that attack our life; they hurt the harmony of life's functions through which is maintained the harmony of our physical self with the physical world; and these injuries are called diseases. There are also factors that oppress our intelligence. They injure the harmony of relationship between our rational mind and the universe of reason; and we call them stupidity, ignorance or insanity. They are uncontrolled exaggerations of passions that upset all balance in our personality. They obscure the harmony between the spirit of the individual man and the spirit of the universal Man; and we give them the name sin. In all these instances our realization of the universal Man, in his physical, rational and spiritual aspects, is obstructed, and our true freedom in the realms of matter, mind and spirit is made narrow or distorted.

All the higher religions of India speak of the training for *Mukti*, the liberation of the soul. In this self of ours we are conscious of individuality, and all its activities are engaged in the expression and enjoyment of our finite and individual nature. In our soul we are conscious of the transcendental truth in us, the Universal, the Supreme Man; and this soul, the spiritual self, has its enjoyment in the renunciation of the individual self for the sake of the supreme soul. This renunciation is not in the negation of self, but in the dedication of it. The desire for it comes from an instinct which very often knows its own meaning vaguely and gropes for a name that would define its purpose. This purpose is in the realization of its unity with some objective ideal of perfections, some harmony of relationship between the individual and the infinite man. It is of this harmony, and not of a barren isolation that the Upanishad speaks, when it says that truth no longer remains hidden in him who finds himself in the All.

Once when I was on a visit to a remote Bengali village, mostly inhabited by Mahomedan cultivators, the villagers entertained me with an operatic performance the literature of which belonged to an obsolete religious sect that had wide influence centuries ago. Though the religion itself is dead, its voice still continues preaching its philosophy to a people, who, in spite of their different culture, are not tired of listening. It discussed according to its own doctrine the different elements, material and transcendental, that constitute human personality, comprehending the body, the self and the soul. Then came a dialogue, during the course of which was related the incident of a person who wanted to make a journey to Brindaban, the Garden of Bliss, but was prevented by a watchman who startled him with an accusation of theft. The thieving was proved when it was shown that inside his clothes he was secretly trying to smuggle into the garden the self, which only finds its fulfilment by its surrender. The culprit was caught with the incriminating bundle in his possession which barred for him his passage to the supreme goal. Under a tattered canopy, supported on bamboo poles and lighted by a few smoking kerosene lamps, the village crowd, occasionally interrupted by howls of jackals in the neighbouring paddy fields, attended with untired interest, till the small hours of the morning, the performance of a drama that discussed the ultimate meaning of all things in a seemingly incongruous setting of dance, music and humorous dialogue.

This illustration will show how naturally, in India, poetry and philosophy have walked hand in hand, only because the latter has claimed its right to guide men to the practical path of their life's fulfilment. What is that fulfilment? It is our freedom in truth, which has for its prayer:

Lead us from the unreal to reality.
For *satyam* is *anandam*, the Real is Joy.

In the world of art, our consciousness being freed from the tangle of self-interest, we gain an unobstructed vision of unity, the incarnation of the real, which is a joy for ever.

As in the world of art, so in the spiritual world, our soul waits for its freedom from the ego to reach that disinterested joy which is the source and goal of creation. It cries for its *mukti*, its freedom in the unity of truth. The idea of *mukti* has affected our lives in India, touched the springs of pure emotions and supplications; for it soars heavenward on the wings of poesy. We constantly hear men of scanty learning and simple faith singing in their prayer to Tara, the Goddess Redeemer:

'For what sin should I be compelled to remain in this dungeon of the world of appearance?'

They are afraid of being alienated from the world of truth, afraid of perpetual drifting amidst the froth and foam of things, of being tossed about by the tidal waves of pleasure and pain and never reaching the ultimate meaning of life. Of these men, one may be a carter driving his cart to market, another a fisherman playing his net. They may not be prompt with an intelligent answer if they are questioned about the deeper import of the song they sing, but they have no doubt in their mind, that the abiding cause of all misery is not so much in the lack of life's furniture as in the obscurity of life's significance. It is a common topic with such to decry an undue emphasis upon 'me' and 'mine', which falsifies the perspective of truth. For have they not often seen men, who are not above their own level in social position or intellectual acquirement, going out to seek Truth, leaving everything that they have behind them?

They know that the object of these adventurers is not betterment in worldly wealth and power − it is *mukti*, freedom. They possibly know some poor fellow villager of their own craft, who remains in the world carrying on his daily vocation and yet has the reputation of being emancipated in the heart of the Eternal. I myself have come across a fisherman singing with an inward absorption of mind, while fishing all day in the Ganges, who was pointed out to me by my boatman, with awe, as a man of liberated spirit. He is out of reach of the conventional prices that are set upon men by society, and which classify them like toys arranged in the shop-windows according to the market standard of value.

When the figure of this fisherman comes to my mind, I cannot but think that their number is not small who with their lives sing the epic of the unfettered soul, but will never be known in history. These unsophisticated Indian peasants know that an Emperor is merely a decorated slave, remaining chained to his Empire, that a millionaire is kept pilloried by his fate in the golden cage of his wealth, while this fisherman is free in the realm of light. When, groping in the dark, we stumble against objects, we cling to them believing them to be our only hope. When light comes, we slacken our hold, finding them to be mere parts of the All to which we are related. The simple man of the village knows what freedom is – freedom from the isolation of self, from the isolation of things, which imparts a fierce intensity to our sense of possession. He knows that this freedom is not the mere negation of bondage, in the bareness of our belongings, but in some positive realization which gives pure joy to our being, and he sings: 'To him who sinks into the deep, nothing remains unattained.' He says again:

Let my two minds meet and combine,
And lead me to the city Wonderful.

When that one mind of ours which wanders in search of things in the outer region of the varied, and the other which seeks the inward vision of unity, are no longer in conflict, they help us to realize the *ajab*, the *anirvachaniya*, the ineffable. The poet saint Kabir has also the same message when he sings:

By saying that Supreme Reality only dwells in the inner realm of spirit, we shame the outer world of matter; and also when we say that he is only in the outside, we do not speak the truth.

According to these singers, truth is in unity, and therefore freedom is in its realization. The texts of our daily worship and meditation are for training our mind to overcome the barrier of separateness from the rest of existence and to realize *advaitam*, the Supreme Unity which is *anantam*, infinitude. It is philosophical wisdom, having its universal radiation in the popular mind in

India, that inspires our prayer, our daily spiritual practices. It has its constant urging for us to go beyond the world of appearances, in which facts as facts are alien to us, like the mere sounds of foreign music; it speaks to us of an emancipation in the inner truth of all things, where the endless *Many* reveal the *One*.

Freedom in the material world has also the same meaning expressed in its own language. When nature's phenomena appeared to us as irrelevant, as heterogeneous manifestations of an obscure and irrational caprice, we lived in an alien world never dreaming of our *swaraj* within its territory. Through the discovery of the harmony of its working with that of our reason, we realize our unity with it, and therefore our freedom.

Those who have been brought up in a misunderstanding of this world's process, not knowing that it is one with themselves through the relationship of knowledge and intelligence, are trained as cowards by a hopeless faith in the ordinance of a destiny darkly dealing its blows. They submit without struggle when human rights are denied them, being accustomed to imagine themselves born as outlaws in a world constantly thrusting upon them incomprehensible surprises of accidents.

Also in the social or political field, the lack of freedom is based upon the spirit of alienation, on the imperfect realization of the One. There our bondage is in the tortured link of union. One may imagine that an individual who succeeds in dissociating himself from his fellow attains real freedom, inasmuch as all ties of relationship imply obligation to others. But we know that, though it may sound paradoxical, it is true that in the human world only a perfect arrangement of interdependence gives rise to freedom. The most individualistic of human beings who own no responsibility are the savages who fail to attain their fulness of manifestation. They live immersed in obscurity, like an ill-lighted fire that cannot liberate itself from its envelope of smoke. Only those may attain their freedom from the segregation of an eclipsed life who have the power to cultivate mutual understanding and co-operation. The history of the growth of freedom is the history of the perfection of human relationship.

It has become possible for men to say that existence is evil, only because in our blindness we have missed something wherein our existence has its truth. If a bird tries to soar with only one of its wings, it is offended with the wind for buffeting it down to the dust. All broken truths are evil. They hurt because they suggest something they do not offer. Death does not hurt us, but disease does, because disease constantly reminds us of health and yet withholds it from us. And life in a halfworld is evil because it feigns finality when it is obviously incomplete, giving us the cup but not the draught of life. All tragedies result from truth remaining a fragment, its cycle not being completed. That cycle finds its end when the individual realizes the universal and thus reaches freedom.

But because this freedom is in truth itself and not in an appearance of it, no hurried path of success, forcibly cut out by the greed of result, can be a true path. And an obscure village poet, unknown to the world of recognized respectability, sings:

> O cruel man of urgent need, must you scorch with fire the mind which still is a bud? You will burst it into bits, destroy its perfume in your impatience. Do you not see that my Lord, the Supreme Teacher, takes ages to perfect the flower and never is in a fury of haste? But because of your terrible greed, you only rely on force, and what hope is there for you, O man of urgent need? 'Prithi', says Madan the poet, 'Hurt not the mind of my Teacher. Know that only he who follows the simple current and loses himself, can hear the voice, O man of urgent need.'

This poet knows that there is no external means of taking freedom by the throat. It is the inward process of losing ourselves that leads to it. Bondage in all its forms has its stronghold in the inner self and not in the outside world; it is in the dimming of our consciousness, in the narrowing of our perspective, in the wrong valuation of things.

Let me conclude this chapter with a song of the Baül sect in Bengal, over a century old, in which the poet sings of the eternal bond of union between the infinite and the finite soul, from which there can be no *mukti*, because love is ultimate, because it is an inter-relation which makes truth complete, because absolute independence is the blankness of utter servility. The song runs thus:

> It goes on blossoming for ages, the soul-lotus, in which I am bound, as well as thou, without escape. There is no end to the opening of its petals, and the honey in it has so much sweetness that thou, like an enchanted bee, canst

never desert it, and therefore thou art bound, and I am, and *mukti* is nowhere.

CHAPTER FOURTEEN
THE FOUR STAGES OF LIFE

I HAVE EXPRESSLY said that I have concentrated my attention upon the subject of religion which is solely related to man, helping him to train his attitude and behaviour towards the infinite in its human aspect. At the same time it should be understood that the tendency of the Indian mind has ever been towards that transcendentalism which does not hold religion to be ultimate but rather to be a means to a further end. This end consists in the perfect liberation of the individual in the universal spirit across the furthest limits of humanity itself.

Such an extreme form of mysticism may be explained to my Western readers by its analogy in science. For science may truly be described as mysticism in the realm of material knowledge. It helps us to go beyond appearances and reach the inner reality of things in principles which are abstractions; it emancipates our mind from the thraldom of the senses to the freedom of reason.

The commonsense view of the world that is apparent to us has its vital importance for ourselves. For all our practical purposes the earth is flat, the sun *does* set behind the western horizon and whatever may be the verdict of the great mathematician about the lack of consistency in time's dealings we should fully trust it in setting our watches right. In questions relating to the arts and our ordinary daily avocations we must treat material objects as they seem to be and not as they are in essence. But the revelations, of science even when they go far beyond man's power of direct perception give him the purest feeling of disinterested delight and a supersensual background to his world. Science offers us the mystic knowledge of matter which very often passes the range of our imagination. We humbly accept it following those teachers who have trained their reason to free itself from the trammels of appearance or personal preferences. Their mind dwells in an impersonal infinity where there is no distinction between good and bad, high and low, ugly and beautiful, useful and useless, where all things have their one common right of recognition, that of their existence.

The final freedom of spirit which India aspires after has a similar character of realization. It is beyond all limits of personality, divested of all moral, or aesthetic distinctions; it is the pure consciousness of Being, the ultimate reality which has an infinite illumination of bliss. Though science brings our thoughts to utmost limit of mind's territory it cannot transcend its own creation made of a harmony of logical symbols. In it the chick has come out of its shell but not out of the definition of its own chickenhood. But in India it has been said by the *yogi* that through an intensive process of concentration and quietude our consciousness *does* reach that infinity where knowledge ceases to be knowledge, subject and object become one, a state of existence that cannot be defined.

We have our personal self. It has its desires which struggle to create a world where they could have their unrestricted activity and satisfaction. While it goes on we discover that our self-realization reaches its perfection in the abnegation of self. This fact has made us aware that the individual finds his meaning in a fundamental reality comprehending all individuals – the reality which is the moral and spiritual basis of the realm of human values. This belongs to our religion. As science is the liberation of our knowledge in the universal reason which cannot be other than human reason, religion is the liberation of our individual personality in the universal Person who is human all the same.

The ancient explorers in psychology in India who declare that our emancipation can be carried still further into a realm where infinity is not bounded by human limitations, are not content with advancing this as a doctrine; they advocate its pursuit for the attainment of the highest goal of man. And for its sake the path of discipline has been planned which should be opened out across our life through all its stages helping us to develop our humanity to perfection so that we may surpass it in a finality of freedom.

Perfection has its two aspects in man which can to some extent be separated, the perfection in being, and perfection in doing. It can be imagined that through some training or compulsion good works may possibly be extorted from a man who personally may not be good. Activities that have fatal risks are often undertaken by cowards even though they are conscious of the danger. Such works may be useful and may continue to exist beyond the lifetime of the individual who produced them. And yet where the question is not that of utility but of moral perfection we hold it important that the individual should be true in his goodness. His outer good work may continue to produce good results but the inner perfection of his personality has its own immense value which for him is spiritual freedom and for humanity is an endless asset though we may not know it. For goodness represents the detachment of our spirit from the exclusiveness of our egoism; in goodness we identify ourselves with the universal humanity. Its value is not merely in some benefit for our fellow beings but in its truth itself through which we realize within us that man is not merely an animal bound by his individual passions and appetites but a spirit that has its unfettered perfection. Goodness is the freedom of our self in the world of man, as is love. We have to be true within, not for worldly duties but for that spiritual fulfilment, which is harmony with the Perfect, in union with the Eternal. If this were not true, then mechanical perfection would be considered to be of higher value than the spiritual. In order to realize his unity with the universal, the individual man must live his perfect life which alone gives him the freedom to transcend it.

Doubtless Nature, for its own biological purposes, has created in us a strong faith in life, by keeping us unmindful of death. Nevertheless, not only our physical existence, but also the environment which it builds up around itself, may desert us in the moment of triumph, the greatest prosperity comes to its end, dissolving into emptiness; the mightiest empire is overtaken by stupor amidst the flicker of its festival lights. All this is none the less true because its truism bores us to be reminded of it.

And yet it is equally true that, though all our mortal relationships have their end, we cannot ignore them with impunity while they last. If we behave as if they do not exist, merely because they will not continue forever, they will all the same exact their dues, with a great deal over by way of penalty. Trying to ignore bonds that are real, albeit temporary, only strengthens and prolongs their bondage. The soul is great, but the self has to be crossed over in order to reach it. We do not attain our goal by destroying our path.

Our teachers in ancient India realized the soul of man as something very great indeed. They saw no end to its dignity, which found its consummation in Brahma himself. Any limited view of man would therefore be an incomplete view. He could not reach his finality as a mere citizen or Patriot, for neither City nor Country nor the bubble called the World, could contain his eternal soul.

Bhartrihari, who was once a king, has said:

> What if you have secured the fountain-head of all desires; what if you have put your foot on the neck of your enemy, or by your good fortune gathered friends around you? What, even, if you have succeeded in keeping mortal bodies alive for ages – *tatah kim*, what then?

That is to say, man is greater than all these objects of his desire. He is true in his freedom.

But in the process of attaining freedom one must bind his will in order to save its forces from distraction and wastage, so as to gain for it the velocity which comes from the bondage itself. Those also, who seek liberty in a purely political plane, constantly curtail it and reduce their freedom of thought and action to that narrow limit which is necessary for making political power secure, very often at the cost of liberty of consciousness.

India had originally accepted the bonds of her social system in order to transcend society, as the rider puts reins on his horse and stirrups on his own feet in order to ensure greater speed towards his goal.

The Universe cannot be so madly conceived that desire should be an interminable song with no finale. And just as it is painful to stop in the middle of the tune, it should be as pleasant to reach its final cadence.

India has not advised us to come to a sudden stop while work is in full swing. It is true that the unending procession of the world has gone on, through its ups and downs, from the beginning of creation till to-day; but it is equally obvious that each individual's connection therewith *does* get finished. Must he necessarily quit it without any sense of fulfilment?

So, in the divisions of man's world-life which we had in India, work came in the middle, and freedom at the end. As the day is divided into morning, noon, afternoon and evening, so India had divided man's life into four parts, following the requirements of his nature. The day has the waxing and waning of its light; so has man the waxing and waning of his bodily powers. Acknowledging this, India gave a connected meaning to his life from start to finish.

First came *brahmacharya*, the period of discipline in education; then *grahasthya*, that of the world's work; then *vanaprasthya*, the retreat for the loosening of bonds; and finally *pravrajya*, the expectant awaiting of freedom across death.

We have come to look upon life as a conflict with death, – the intruding enemy, not the natural ending, – in impotent quarrel with which we spend every stage of it. When the time comes for youth to depart, we would hold it back by main force. When the fervour of desire slackens, we would revive it with fresh fuel of our own devising. When our sense organs weaken, we urge them to keep up their efforts. Even when our grip has relaxed we are reluctant to give up possession. We are not trained to recognize the inevitable as natural, and so cannot give up gracefully that which has to go, but needs must wait till it is snatched from us. The truth comes as conqueror only because we have lost the art of receiving it as guest.

The stem of the ripening fruit becomes loose, its pulp soft, but its seed hardens with provision for the next life. Our outward losses, due to age, have likewise corresponding inward gains. But, in man's inner life, his will plays a dominant part, so that these gains depend on his own disciplined striving; that is why, in the case of undisciplined man, who has omitted to secure such provision for the next stage, it is so often seen that his hair is grey, his mouth toothless, his muscles slack, and yet his stem-hold on life has refused to let go its grip, so much so that he is anxious to exercise his will in regard to worldly details even after death.

But renounce we must, and through renunciation gain, – that is the truth of the inner world.

The flower must shed its petals for the sake of fruition, the fruit must drop off for the re-birth of the tree. The child leaves the refuge of the womb in order to achieve the further growth of body and mind in which consists the whole of the child life; next, the soul has to come out of this self-contained stage into the fuller life, which has varied relations with kinsman and neighbour, together with whom it forms a larger body; lastly comes the decline of the body, the weakening of desire, and, enriched with its experiences, the soul now leaves the narrower life for the universal life, to which it dedicates its accumulated wisdom and itself enters into relationship with the Life Eternal; so that, when finally the decaying body has come to the very end of its tether, the soul views its breaking away quite simply and without regret, in the expectation of its own entry into the Infinite.

From individual body to community, from community to universe, from universe to Infinity, – this is the soul's normal progress.

Our teachers, therefore, keeping in mind goal of this progress, did not, in life's first stage of education, prescribe merely the learning of books of things, but *brahmacharya*, the living in discipline, whereby both enjoyment and its renunciation would come with equal ease to the strengthened character. Life being a pilgrimage, with liberation in Brahma as its object, the living of it was as a spiritual exercise to be carried through its different stages, reverently and with a vigilant determination. And the pupil, from his very initiation, had this final consummation always kept in his view.

Once the mind refuses to be bound by temperate requirements, there ceases to be any reason why it should cry halt at any particular limit; and so, like trying to extinguish fire with oil, its acquisitions only make its desires blaze up all the fiercer. That is why it is so essential to habituate the mind, from the very beginning, to be conscious of, and desirous of, keeping within the natural limits; to cultivate the spirit of enjoyment which is allied with the spirit of freedom, the readiness for renunciation.

After the period of such training comes the period of world-life, – the life of the householder. Manu tells us:

> It is not possible to discipline ourselves so effectively if out of touch with the world, as while pursuing the world-life with wisdom.

That is to say, wisdom does not attain completeness except through the living of life; and discipline divorced from wisdom is not true discipline, but merely the meaningless following of custom, which is only a disguise for stupidity.

Work, especially good work, becomes easy only when desire has learnt to discipline itself. Then alone does the householder's state become a centre of welfare for all the world, and instead of being an obstacle, helps on the final liberation.

The second stage of life having been thus spent, the decline of the bodily powers must be taken as a warning that it is coming to its natural end. This must not be taken dismally as a notice of dismissal to one still eager to stick to his post, but joyfully as maturity may be accepted as the stage of fulfilment.

After the infant leaves the womb, it still has to remain close to its mother for a time, remaining attached in spite of its detachment, until it can adapt itself to its new freedom. Such is the case in the third stage of life, when man though aloof from the world still remains in touch with it while preparing himself for the final stage of complete freedom. He still gives to the world from his store of wisdom and accepts its support; but this interchange is not of the same intimate character as in the stage of the householder, there being a new sense of distance.

Then at last comes a day when even such free relations have their end, and the emancipated soul steps out of all bonds to face the Supreme Soul.

Only in this way can man's world-life be truly lived from one end to the other, without being engaged at every step in trying conclusions with death, not being overcome, when death comes in due course, as by a conquering enemy.

For this fourfold way of life India attunes man to the grand harmony of the universal, leaving no room for untrained desires of a rampant individualism to pursue their destructive career unchecked, but leading them on to their ultimate modulation in the Supreme.

If we really believe this, then we must uphold an ideal of life in which everything else, – the display of individual power, the might of nations, – must be counted as subordinate and the soul of man must triumph and liberate itself from the bond of personality which keeps it in an ever revolving circle of limitation.

If that is not to be, *tatah kim*, what then?

But such an ideal of the utter extinction of the individual separateness has not a universal sanction in India. There are many of us whose prayer is for dualism so that for them the bond of devotion with God may continue forever. For them religion is a truth which is ultimate and they refuse to envy those who are ready to sail for the further shore of existence across humanity. They know that human imperfection is the cause of our sorrow but there is a fulfilment in love within the range of our limitation which accepts all sufferings and yet rises above them.

CHAPTER FIFTEEN
CONCLUSION

IN THE SANSKRIT Language the bird is described as 'twice-born' – once in its limited shell and then finally in the freedom of the unbounded sky. Those of our community who believe in the liberation of man's limited self in the freedom of the spirit retain the same epithet for themselves. In all departments of life man shows this dualism – his existence within the range of obvious facts and his transcendence of it in a realm of deeper meaning.

Having this instinct inherent in his mind which ever suggests to him the crossing of the border, he has never accepted what is apparent as final and his incessant struggle has been to break through the shell of his limitations. In this attempt he often goes against the instincts of his vital nature, and even exults in his defiance of the extreme penal laws of the biological kingdom. The best wealth of his civilization has been achieved by his following the guidance of this instinct in his ceaseless adventure of the Endless Further. His achievement of truth goes far beyond his needs and the realization of his self strives across the frontier of its individual interest. This proves to him his infinity and makes his religion real to him by his own manifestation in truth and goodness. Only for man there can be religion because his evolution is from efficiency in nature towards the perfection of spirit.

According to some interpretations of the Vedanta doctrine Brahman is the absolute Truth, the impersonal It, in which there can be no distinction of this and that, the good and the evil, the beautiful and its opposite, having no other quality except its ineffable blissfulness in the eternal solitude of its consciousness utterly devoid of all things and all thoughts. But, as our religion can only have its significance in this phenomenal world comprehended by our human self, this absolute conception of Brahman is outside the subject of my discussion. What I have tried to bring out in this book is the fact that whatever name may have been given to the divine Reality it has found its highest place in the history of our religion owing to its human character, giving meaning to the idea of sin and sanctity, and offering an eternal background to all the ideals of perfection which have their harmony with man's own nature.

We have the age-long tradition in our country, as I have

already stated, that through the process of *yoga* man can transcend the utmost bounds of his humanity and find himself in a pure state of consciousness of his undivided unity with Parabrahman. There is none who has the right to contradict this belief; for it is a matter of direct experience and not of logic. It is widely known in India that there are individuals who have the power to attain temporarily the state of *Samadhi*, the complete merging of the self in the infinite, a state which is indescribable. While accepting their testimony as true, let us at the same time have faith in the testimony of others who have felt a profound love, which is the intense feeling of union, for a Being who comprehends in himself all things that are human in knowledge, will and action. And he is God, who is not merely a sum total of facts, but the goal that lies immensely beyond all that is comprised in the past and the present.

Crisis in Civilization

TODAY I COMPLETE eighty years of my life. As I look back on the vast stretch of years that lie behind me and see in clear perspective the history of my early development, I am struck by the change that has taken place both in my own attitude and in the psychology of my countrymen – a change that carries within it a cause of profound tragedy.

Our direct contact with the larger world of men was linked up with the contemporary history of the English people whom we came to know in those earlier days. It was mainly through their mighty literature that we formed our ideas with regard to these newcomers to our Indian shores. In those days the type of learning that was served out to us was neither plentiful nor diverse, nor was the spirit of scientific enquiry very much in evidence. Thus their scope being strictly limited, the educated of those days had recourse to English language and literature. Their days and nights were eloquent with the stately declamations of Burke, with Macaulay's long-rolling sentences; discussions centred upon Shakespeare's drama and Byron's poetry and above all upon the large-hearted liberalism of the nineteenth-century English politics.

At the time though tentative attempts were being made to gain our national independence, at heart we had not lost faith in the generosity of the English race. This belief was so firmly rooted in the sentiments of our leaders as to lead them to hope that the victor would of his own grace pave the path of freedom for the vanquished. This belief was based upon the fact that England at the time provided a shelter to all those who had to flee from persecution in their own country. Political martyrs who had suffered for the honour of their people were accorded unreserved welcome at the hands of the English. I was impressed by this evidence of liberal humanity in the character of the English and thus I was led to set them on the pedestal of my highest respect. This generosity in their national character had not yet been vitiated by Imperialist pride. About this time, as a boy in England, I had the opportunity of listening to the speeches of John Bright, both in and outside Parliament. The large-hearted, radical liberalism of those speeches, overflowing all narrow national bounds, had made so deep an impression on my mind that something of it lingers even today, even in these days of graceless disillusionment.

Certainly that spirit of abject dependence upon the charity of our rulers was no matter for pride. What was remarkable, however, was the wholehearted way in which we gave our recognition to human greatness even when it revealed itself in the foreigner. The best and noblest gifts of humanity cannot be the monopoly of a particular race or country; its scope may not be limited nor may it be regarded as the miser's hoard buried underground. That is why English literature which nourished our minds in the past, does even now convey its deep resonance to the recesses of our heart.

It is difficult to find a suitable Bengali equivalent for the English word 'civilization'. That phase of civilization with which we were familiar in this country has been called by Manu '*Sadachar*' (*lit.* proper conduct), that is, the conduct prescribed by the tradition of the race. Narrow in themselves these time-honoured social conventions originated and held good in a circumscribed geographical area, in that strip of land, Brahmavarta by name, bound on either side by the rivers Saraswati and Drisadvati. That is how a pharisaic formalism gradually got the upper hand of free thought and the ideal of 'proper conduct' which Manu found established in Brahmavarta steadily degenerated into socialized tyranny.

During my boyhood days the attitude of the cultured and educated section of Bengal, nurtured on English learning, was charged with a feeling of revolt against these rigid regulations of society. A perusal of what Rajnarain Bose has written describing the ways of the educated gentry of those days will amply bear out what I have said just now. In place of these set codes of conduct we accepted the ideal of 'civilization' as represented by the English term.

In our own family this change of spirit was welcomed for the sake of its sheer rational and moral force and its influence was felt in every sphere of our life. Born in that atmosphere, which was moreover coloured by our intuitive bias for literature, I naturally set the English on the throne of my heart. Thus passed the first chapters of my life. Then came the parting of ways accompanied with a painful feeling of disillusion when I began increasingly to discover how easily those who accepted the highest truths of civilization disowned them with impunity whenever questions of national self-interest were involved.

There came a time when perforce I had to snatch myself away from the mere appreciation of literature. As I emerged into the stark light of bare facts, the sight of the dire poverty of the Indian masses rent my heart. Rudely shaken out of my dreams, I began to realize that perhaps in no other modern state was there such hopeless dearth of the most elementary needs of existence. And yet it was this country whose resources had fed for so long the wealth and mangnificence of the British people. While I was lost in the contemplation of the great world of civilization, I could never have remotely imagined that the great ideals of humanity would end in such ruthless travesty. But today a glaring example of it stares me in the face in the utter and contemptuous indifference of a so-called civilized race to the well-being of crores of Indian people.

That mastery over the machine, by which the British have consolidated their sovereignty over their vast Empire, has been kept a sealed book, to which due access has been denied to this helpless country. And all the time before our very eyes Japan has been transforming herself into a mighty and prosperous nation. I have seen with my own eyes the admirable use to which Japan has put in her own country the fruits of this progress. I have also been privileged to witness, while in Moscow, the unsparing energy with which Russia has tried to fight disease and illiteracy, and has succeeded in steadily liquidating ignorance and poverty, wiping off the humiliation from the face of a vast continent. Her civilization is free from all invidious distinction between one class and another, between one sect and another. The rapid and astounding progress achieved by her made me happy and jealous at the same time. One aspect of the Soviet administration which particularly pleased me was that it provided no scope for unseemly conflict of religious difference nor set one community against another by unbalanced distribution of political favours. That I consider a truly civilized administration which impartially serves the common interests of the people.

While other imperialist powers sacrifice the welfare of the subject races to their own national greed, in the USSR I found a genuine attempt being made to harmonize the interests of the various nationalities that are scattered over its vast area. I saw peoples and tribes, who, only the other day, were nomadic savages being encouraged and indeed trained, to avail themselves freely of the benefits of civilization. Enormous sums are being spent on their education to expedite the process. When I see elsewhere some two hundred nationalities – which only a few years ago were at vastly different stages of development – marching ahead in peaceful progress and amity, and when I look about my own country and see a very highly evolved and intellectual people drifting into the disorder of barbarism, I cannot help contrasting the two systems of government, one based on co-operation, the other on exploitation, which have made such contrary conditions possible.

I have also seen Iran, newly awakened to a sense of national self-sufficiency, attempting to fulfil her own destiny freed from the deadly grinding-stones of two European powers. During my recent visit to that country I discovered to my delight that Zoroastrians who once suffered from the fanatical hatred of the major community and whose rights had been curtailed by the ruling power were now free from this age-long repression, and that civilized life had established itself in the happy land. It is significant that Iran's good fortune dates from the day when she finally disentangled herself from the meshes of European diplomacy. With all my heart I wish Iran well.

Turning to the neighbouring kingdom of Afghanistan I find that though there is much room for improvement in the field of education and social development, yet she is fortunate in that she can look forward to unending progress; for none of the European powers, boastful of their civilization, has yet succeeded in overwhelming and crushing her possibilities.

Thus while these other countries were marching ahead, India, smothered under the dead weight of British administration, lay static in her utter helplessness. Another great and ancient civilization for whose recent tragic history the British cannot disclaim responsibility, is China. To serve their own national profit the British first doped her people with opium and then appropriated a portion of her territory. As the world was about to forget the memory of this outrage, we were painfully surprised by another event. While Japan was quietly devouring North China, her act of wanton aggression was ignored as a minor incident by the veterans of British diplomacy. We have also witnessed from this distance how actively the British statesmen acquiesced in the destruction of the Spanish Republic.

On the other hand, we also noted with admiration how a band of valiant Englishmen laid down their lives for Spain. Even though the English had not aroused themselves sufficiently to their sense of responsibility towards China in the Far East, in their own immediate neighbourhood they did not hesitate to sacrifice themselves to the cause of freedom. Such acts of heroism reminded me over again of the true English spirit to which in those early days I had given my full faith, and made me wonder how imperialist greed could bring about so ugly a transformation in the character of so great a race.

Such is the tragic tale of the gradual loss of my faith in the claims of the European nations to civilization. In India the misfortune of being governed by a foreign race is daily brought home to us not only in the callous neglect of such minimum necessities of life as adequate provision for food, clothing, educational and medical facilities for the people, but in an even unhappier form in the way the people have been divided among themselves. The pity of it is that the blame is laid at the door of our own society. So frightful a culmination of the history of our people would never have been possible, but for the encouragement it has received from secret influences emanating from high places.

One cannot believe that Indians are in any way inferior to the Japanese in intellectual capacity. The most effective difference between these two eastern peoples is that whereas India lies at the mercy of the British, Japan has been spared the shadow of alien domination. We know what we have been deprived of. That which was truly best in their own civilization, the upholding of the dignity of human relationship, has no place in the British administration of this country. If in its place they have established, with baton in hand, a reign of 'law and order', in other words a policeman's rule, such mockery of civilization can claim no respect from us. It is the mission of civilization to bring unity among people and establish peace and harmony. But in unfortunate India the social fabric is being rent into shreds by unseemly outbursts of hooliganism daily growing in intensity, right under the very aegis of 'law and order'. In India, so long as no personal injury is inflicted upon any member of the ruling race, this barbarism seems to be assured of perpetuity, making us ashamed to live under such an administration.

And yet my good fortune has often brought me into close contact with really large-hearted Englishmen. Without the slightest hesitation I may say that the nobility of their character was without parallel – in no country or community have I come across such greatness of soul. Such examples would not allow me wholly to lose faith in the race which produced them. I had the rare blessing of having Andrews – a real Englishman, a real Christian and a true man – for a very close friend. Today in the perspective of death his unselfish and courageous magnanimity shines all the brighter. The whole of India remains indebted to him for innumerable acts of love and devotion. But personally speaking, I am especially beholden to him because he helped me to retain in my old age that feeling of respect for the English race with which in the past I was inspired by their literature and which I was about to lose completely. I count such Englishmen as Andrews not only as my personal and intimate friends but as friends of the whole human race. To have known them has been to me a treasured privilege. It is my belief that such Englishmen will save British honour from shipwreck. At any rate if I had not known them, my despair at the prospect of western civilization would be unrelieved.

In the meanwhile the demon of barbarity has given up all pretence and has emerged with unconcealed fangs, ready to tear up humanity in an orgy of devastation. From one end of the world to the other the poisonous fumes of hatred darken the atmosphere. The spirit of violence which perhaps lay dormant in the psychology of the West, has at last roused itself and desecrates the spirit of Man.

The wheels of Fate will some day compel the English to give up their Indian empire. But what kind of India will they leave behind, what stark misery? When the stream of their centuries' administration runs dry at last, what a waste of mud and filth they will leave behind them! I had at one time believed that the springs of civilization would issue out of the heart of Europe. But today when I am about to quit the world that faith has gone bankrupt altogether.

As I look around I see the crumbling ruins of a proud civilization strewn like a vast heap of futility. And yet I shall not commit the grievous sin of losing faith in Man. I would rather look forward to the opening of a new chapter in his history after the cataclysm is over and the atmosphere rendered clean with the spirit of service and sacrifice. Perhaps that dawn will come from this horizon, from the East where the sun rises. A day will come when unvanquished Man will retrace his path of conquest, despite all barriers, to win back his lost human heritage.

Today we witness the perils which attend on the insolence of might; one day shall be borne out the full truth of what the sages have proclaimed:

'By unrighteousness man prospers, gains what appears desirable, conquers enemies, but perishes at the root.'

1941

Historicality in Literature

I HAVE HEARD it said again and again that we are guided altogether by history, and I have energetically nodded, so to say, in my mind whenever I heard it. I have settled this debate in my own heart where I am nothing but a poet. I am there in the role of a creator all alone and free. There's little to enmesh me there in the net of external events. I find it difficult to put up with the pedantic historian when he tries to force me out of the centre of my creativity as a poet. Let us go back to the inaugural moment of my poetical career.

It's a daybreak in winter. A pale light is beginning to filter through the darkness. We were like the poor in our ways. There was no extravagance about our use of winter garments. One just slipped into a top of some kind on leaving the warmth of the duvet. But there was really no need to rush. Like everyone else I, too, could have stayed happily curled up in bed until at least six in the morning. But it was not possible for me to do so. There was a garden within the inner precincts of our house. Indigent like myself, all it had for its wealth was mostly a row of coconut trees lining the eastern wall. Yet I used to be in such a hurry lest I should miss anything of what I saw every day as the light fell on the trembling coconut fronds and the dewdrops burst into glitter. I used to think that this joy of the welcoming dawn would be of interest to all the other boys as well. If that were true, it would have been easy to explain it in terms of the universality of child behaviour. No other explanation would have been necessary had it been known that I was not set apart from the others by the very force of this excessive curiosity of mine and that I was just as ordinary. But as I grew older I came to realize that there was no other child nearly so keen to see the light vibrating on shrubs and trees. I found out, too, that none of those who had grown up with me fitted into this particular category of madness. Not to speak of them alone, there was nobody in my entire milieu who felt deprived that he hadn't been out, dressed warmly or not, to see the play of light even once. There's nothing in it that comes out of the mould of history. Had that been the case a crowd would have turned up in that miserable garden at dawn with everyone competing to be the first to see and grasp that entire scene by heart. It is precisely in this that one is a poet. One day I had just come back from school at about four-thirty and found a dark blue cumulus suspended high above the third storey of our house. What a marvellous sight that was. Even now I remember that day. But in the history of that day there was no one other than myself who saw those clouds in quite the same way as I did or was similarly thrilled. Rabindranath happened to be all by himself in that instance. Once after school I saw a most amazing spectacle from our western verandah. A donkey – not one of those donkeys manufactured by British imperial policy but the animal that had always belonged to our own society and has not changed in its ways since the beginning of time – one such donkey had come up from the washermen's quarters and was grazing on the grass while a cow fondly licked its body. The attraction of one living being for another that then caught my eye has remained unforgettable for me until today. In the entire history of that day it was Rabindranath alone who witnessed the scene with enchanted eyes. This I know for certain. No one else was instructed by the history of that day in the profound significance of the sight as was Rabindranath. In his own field of creativity Rabindranath has been entirely alone and tied to no public by history. Where history was public, he was there merely as a British subject but not as Rabindranath himself. The bizarre game of political change was being played out there, of course, but the light that glittered on the foliage of coconut palms was not a statist input owing to the British government. It radiated within some mysterious history of my inner soul and manifested itself in its own blissful form every day in various ways. As it has been said in our Upanishads: 'It is not for the sake of the sons, my dear, that they are loved, but for one's own sake that they are loved.' The ātmā wishes to manifest itself as the creator in its love for its son. That is why it values its love for the son so much. The creator gathers some of the material for his creation from historical narratives and some from his social environment. But the material by itself does not make him a creator. It is only by putting it to use that he expresses himself as the creator. There are many events that are there waiting to be known, and it is only by chance that we get to know them. There was a time when I had come to be acquainted with the Buddhist and other historical accounts, and these assumed a pictorial clarity to inspire me with a creative urge. All of a sudden the narratives of *Katha O Kahini* surged like a headspring and branched off in several directions. One could possibly have come to learn about these histories as part of one's education those days. *Katha O Kahini* could therefore be said to be a work that belonged to its time. But it is not because of history that Rabindranath was the only one to be so blissfully moved as he was by the form and aesthetic content of *Katha O Kahini*. The reason lies in his inner soul. Which is why it has been said that the self alone is the agent. To push that in the background and flaunt the raw material of history may be a matter of pride for some. They may even rob the agent of a part of his creative joy for their own benefit. But all this is secondary, as the creator knows. The monk Upagupta emerges from the entire set-up of the history of Buddhism to present himself to Rabindranath alone, and in what glory, what compassion does he do so! Had it been an authentic exercise in historiography, *Katha O Kahini* would have been celebrated throughout the land. No other person had looked at these pictures in the same way until then or since. Indeed it is precisely because of the distinctive character of the poet's creativity that people have come to enjoy it. Once when I used to travel by boat along the rivers of Bengal and came to sense its playful vitality, my inner soul delighted in gathering those wonderful impressions of weal and woe in my heart which were composed into sketches of country life month after month in a way nobody had done before. For the creator works all alone in his studio. Like the Supreme Creator, he, too, creates his work out of his own self. There is no doubt that the rural scenes surveyed by the poet in those days were affected by the conflicts of political history. However, thanks to his creativity, what came to be reflected in *Galpaguccha* was not the image of a feudal order nor indeed any political order at all, but that history of the weal and woe of human life which, with its everyday contentment and misery, has always been there in the peasants' fields and village festivals, manifesting their simple and abiding humanity across all of history – sometimes under Mughal rule, sometimes under British rule. I am not acquainted with at least three-quarters of that far-flung history in which the critics of today wander about so extensively. That is why I guess it upsets me so much. I have it in my mind to say, 'Off with your history.' At the helm of my own vessel of creativity I have the *ātmā* that needs its love for the son in order to express itself. It assimilates to its work the multifarious spectacles of the world with all its happiness and sadness. It takes delight in doing so and sharing its joy with others. I have not been able to put the entire history of my life in words, but that history is of no importance. It is the desire for self-expression on the part of man as the creator that has engaged him in all his long endeavour over the ages. Try and highlight only the history which is piloted by man-as-creator towards the Magnum that lies beyond history and is at the very centre of the human soul. This was known to our Upanishads. The message the Upanishads have for me is what I have taken from them on my own initiative. That stands for an agenthood which is mine alone.

Santiniketan, May 1941

POEMS FOR CHILDREN

THE CAPTIVE HERO

Where the five rivers flow,
The Sikhs awoke to the Guru's word
    With hair knotted in vow –
    No qualms, no fear they knew.
A thousand voices break out, 'Hail, Guru!'
The newly-risen Sikhs, in that new dawn,
Gazed with steady eyes upon the rising sun.

'Hail the unbodied God!' they cried together,
Dispelling every fear, breaking all fetters.
What joyful clamour rings from every sword
As 'Hail the unbodied God!' all Punjab roared.

    The hour is set
For a million hearts grown fearless, owing no man debt,
Flinging aside all care, beneath their feet
Trampling like vanquished slaves both life and death:
On the five rivers' ten banks, a great hour is set.

    In Delhi's castle-keep
The Emperor's son is nightly shaken from his sleep.
Whose voices are those, cleaving through the night?
Whose flaming torches fill the sky with light?

    On the five rivers' shores
O what a tide of blood from pious bodies flows!
    From a million breasts
Flocks of souls take wing, like birds seeking their nests.
    With their life's blood, heroes
Anoint their mother's brow, on the five rivers' shores.

Mughal and Sikh are locked
In death's embrace, clutching each other by the throat:
A serpent struggling with a wounded hawk!
'Hail to the Guru!' deep Sikh voices cry,
     And thirsting for their blood,
'The faith! The faith!' the enraged Mughals reply.

     In the Gurdaspur fort
Banda was taken prisoner by a Turkish force.
They chained him like a lion, brought him thence
     To the Delhi court:
Banda, taken prisoner in Gurdaspur fort.

See the Mughal army, in a cloud of dust
Marching along, severed Sikh heads on spearheads thrust:

And seven hundred Sikhs behind them, stumbling along,
Clanking the chains that bind them: how the people
          throng
The streets, and every window is wide open flung!
Heedless of death, 'Hail to the Guru!' cry the Sikhs.
Mughal and Sikh have stirred the dust of Delhi's streets.

     Now a new strife
Breaks out among the Sikhs – who'll be the first
     To offer up his life?
Each morning they are brought forth, row on row:
A hundred brave hearts utter, 'Hail, Guru!'
     And then lay down
A hundred heads to the executioner's blow.

In seven days, seven hundred lives: when all was done,
The judge put into Banda's clasp Banda's own son.
'Kill him with your own hands,' he said – the little one,
Arms bound, flung on his father's lap: Banda must slay
     His very own son.

He spoke no word,
But slowly drew the little boy close to his heart,
Laid his right hand upon his head for a brief thought,
And placed a single kiss on his red turban-cloth.
Then, bringing out his knife, he said
'Hail to the Guru!' in the boy's ear. 'My son,
　　You mustn't be afraid.'

A flame of courage leaps in the young one's eyes:
His reedy voice 'Hail to the Guru!' cries –
The courtroom trembles: and then, undismayed,
'Father, I'm not afraid.'
　　He looked him in the face;
And Banda, holding him in left embrace,
Plunges the knife with right hand: the boy calls
'Hail to the Guru!' one last time, and falls.

The court was hushed: the grim
Torturer tore Banda limb from limb
With red-hot tongs: without a groan he dies.
The hall was hushed: the courtiers closed their eyes.

THE HERO

Imagine that I'm travelling through
Far-off foreign lands, Mother, with you.
  You're riding in a palanquin
  With doors ajar to peep between,
And I on a great chestnut horse
  That canters by your side:
Its hooves stir up a swirling cloud
  Of red dust as I ride.

It's evening, and the sun is low:
Through the Plain of the Twin Lakes we go.
  There's not a single soul in sight:
  You seem to take a little fright
At such a lonely place, and think
  'Where am I being led?'
'Now, Mother, don't be scared,' I say.
  'That's a dry river-bed.'

The fields are full of prickly grass.
Across them, down a winding track we pass.
  No cow or calf, for all the herds
  At evening have gone villagewards.
We wonder where we're going to –
  One can't tell in the dark.
Then you cry out, 'What is that light?
  I think I saw a spark.'

Just then we hear a 'Ho-ho-ho!'
Who are those people shouting as they go?
  Inside the palanquin you cower,
  Calling to all the gods in prayer;
The trembling bearers run away
  And hide behind a tree.
'Don't be afraid,' I call to you,
  'Just leave it all to me.'

They wave their sticks and toss their mops of hair,
Each with a red hibiscus in his ear.
'Stop!' I call out, 'I'm warning you:
You see this sword? I'll run you through
    If one more step you dare!'
Again they shouted 'Ho-ho-ho!'
    And leapt into the air.

'Khoka, don't go!' you cried in fear.
'Calm down,' I said, 'just see what happens here.'
    I spurred my horse into their midst:
    Shields and sabres clanged and hit.
It really was a fearsome fight —
    You'll shudder when I tell
How many men were scared and fled,
    And heads from bodies fell.

Then, just as to yourself you've said
'In such a fight, my Khoka must be dead!'
    I'd ride up, dripping blood and sweat,
    Calling 'The fight's at end!' And when we've met,
Down from the palanquin you'd step
And kiss and draw me to your lap.
'How lucky Khoka was here,' you'd say,
    'Else I'd have been in dread!'

Each day we hear all kinds of news.
Why can't something like this really come true?
    It would be like the books we read:
    Folk would be stunned to hear the deed.
Dada would say, 'How can it be?
    My puny little brother!'
The neighbours, though, would say, 'What luck
    Khoka was with his mother!'

THE PALM TREE

The palm tree stands
    On one leg, sees
    Past other trees
      Into the sky.
He wants to pierce
    The clouds so grey
    And soar away:
    But can he fly?

At length his wish
    He starts to spread
    Around his head
      In big round fronds:
He thinks they're wings,
    To let him roam
    Away from home,
      Breaking all bonds.

The livelong day
    The branches quiver,
    Sigh and shiver –
      He thinks he flies,
In his own mind
    Skirting the stars,
    Racing afar
      Across the skies.

But when the wind
    Is still at last
    And the leaves hushed,
      Back homeward then
He turns his thoughts,
    And Mother Earth
    That gave him birth
      He loves again.

OUR LITTLE RIVER

Our little river twists and turns:
It's just knee-deep when summer burns.
How easy is it then to cross:
Cattle and carts just ford across.
The banks slope gently, though they're high,
And in the summer, always dry.

No dirt, no mud: it's all so clean.
The sand glints with a golden gleam.
And to one side, there stands a bed
Of kash, with white flowers overspread.
Flocks of mynahs gather there
And with their chatter fill the air,
While deep at night the jackals prowl,
Piercing the silence with their howl.

Groves of palm and mango trees
Upon the other bank one sees.
Nestling beneath their leafy shade
The village houses stand arrayed.
Along the bank the children play,
Splash each other, duck and spray,
Or sometimes, having had their bath,
Catch small fish in bits of cloth.

The village women by that spot
Scrub with sand their pans and pots.
They wash their clothes and have their bath,
Then back they take the homeward path.

And then, after the rains begin,
The river fills up to the brim.
It rushes then upon its course
In muddy whirls and deafening roars.
Upon the banks, among the woods,
A call rings out in joyful mood;
And all the village wakes again
To mark the festival of the rain.

THE RUNAWAY CITY

O what a dream of dreams I had one night!
I could hear Binu crying out in fright,
'Come quickly and you'll see a startling sight:
Our city's rushing in a headlong flight!'

Tottering and lurching
Calcutta goes marching
Beams and joists battling
Doors and windows rattling
Mansion houses dashing
Like brick-built rhinos crashing
Streets and roads jiggling
Like long pythons wriggling
While tumbling on their backs
Tramcars leave their tracks
Shops and marts go sprawling
Rising and then falling
One roof with another
Bang their heads together
Rolls on the Howrah Bridge
Like a giant centipede
Chased by Harrison Road
Breaking the traffic code
See the Monument rock
Like a jumbo run amok
Waving its trunk on high
Against the troubled sky
Even our school in merry scoot
Books of maths in hot pursuit
The maps upon the walls aswing
Like a bird that flaps its wing
The school bell tolls on ding dong ding
Without a sense of when to ring

Thousands of people with Calcutta plead,
'Now stop your madness, where will all this lead?'

The city hurtles on and pays no heed,
Its walls and pillars dance with drunken speed.
But let it wander where it will, I say –
What if Calcutta travels to Bombay?
Agra, Lahore, or Delhi if it goes,
I'll sport a turban and wear nagra shoes.
Or even England if right now it reaches,
I'll turn Englishman in hat, coat and breeches.

Then at some sound, my dream came to a pause
To find Calcutta where it always was.

SONGS

Nothing Has Worked Out

Nothing has worked out;
Overwhelming grief – loud lamentations;
Flowing tears – a pained heart!
Nothing gives peace;
Nothing whets desire!
I'd looked for love; I'd found it too;
I still love – yet what is it that's lacking?

Only Coming and Going

Only coming and going
Only drifting with the tide.
Only tears and laughter in the twilight.
Only stolen glimpses and fleeting touches
And looking back with grief while walking away
Driven on by false aspirations,
Leaving behind belied hopes.
Endless desires possessed of only broken resolve
Endless striving with imperfect results.
Adrift on the river, clutching a broken craft
Deep thoughts find meagre expression.
A half relationship, an unfinished conversation,
In shame, fear, anxiety and doubt,
Only a half-love.

Through Death and Sorrow

Through death and sorrow
there dwells peace
in the heart of the Eternal.
Life's current flows without cease,
the sunlight and starlights
carry the smile of existence
and springtime its songs.
Waves rise and fall,
the flowers blossom and fade
and my heart yearns for its place
at the feet of the Endless.

My Bengal of Gold

I love you, my Bengal of gold,
Your skies and winds will play music in my soul.
O mother, in spring your mango blossoms' heady scent
    drives me wild
How fulfilling it is too, O mother dear
To see your fields smile delightfully in late autumn!

Such beauty and such shades, such warmth and such
    tenderness,
So much of your dress you've spread under bata tree
    canopies and riverbanks;
O mother, your sounds ring in my ear and comfort me
How fulfilling such sights and sounds are, O mother dear!
But when you look sad, how I drown in my tears!

In your nursery I've spent my childhood
I consider life blessed when I daub my body with your
    dust and clay,
And when day ends and evening descends how lovely is
    your light,
How pleasing it is then, O mother dear
Leaving behind all play, how I rush to climb to your lap!

In fields where cattle graze and in ferry ghats;
All day long in shaded village paths reverberating with
    bird songs;
And in your crop-filled fields where we spend our lives;
How fulfilling you make our lives, O mother dear!
Your herd boys and farmhands all become my own then!

O mother, when I lay myself down at your feet;
Bless me with the dust that they tread, for they will
    bejewel me.
O mother dear, what little I have I will lay at your feet,
How fulfilling to stop adorning myself with foreign
    purchases,
To know that even the rope you provide for a noose can
    be my adornment!

Suddenly from the Heart of Bengal

Suddenly from the heart of Bengal
You have stepped out in such amazing beauty!
O Mother, I can't turn my eyes away from you
Your open doors lead today to the golden temple

While the scimitar blazes in your right hand the left
    assails fear
A benign smile lights up your eyes;
The third eye on your forehead is fiery
O Mother, what an awe-inspiring image of you
    I see today!
Your open doors lead to the golden temple
Like cloud clusters your open tresses hide the storm
O sun-clad One, your sari's end drapes the skies!
O Mother, I can't turn my eyes away from you
Your open doors lead to the golden temple

I was careless and didn't turn to you
Thinking of you as a destitute mother
Seeing you lying down and suffering endlessly in a
    decaying house
Where now are your poor weeds, where the sad smile?
The entire sky is dappled by the light from your
    gleaming feet
O Mother, what an awe-inspiring image of you
    I see today!
Your open doors lead this day to the golden temple

Now, in this sad night, float your boat in a current of joy
Your assurance rings in my heart, O heart-conqueror,
O Mother, I can't turn my eyes away from you
Your open doors lead today to the golden temple.

If They Answer Not to Thy Call

If they answer not to thy call walk alone,
If they are afraid and cower mutely facing the wall,
O thou of evil luck,
open thy mind and speak out alone.

If they turn away, and desert you when crossing the
      wilderness,
O thou of evil luck,
trample the thorns under thy tread,
and along the blood-lined track travel alone.

If they do not hold up the light
when the night is troubled with storm,
O thou of evil luck,
with the thunder flame of pain ignite thine own heart
and let it burn alone.

Blessed Am I to Have Been Born in This Land

Blessed am I to have been born in this land
Blessed is my birth O Mother, having loved you
I don't know whether you have as many treasures as
      a queen
All I know is that my body is soothed by your caring
      shade
Can any other forest or flowers have such intense
      fragrance?
In which other sky does the moon rise with such a smile?
When I opened my eyes your light first enchanted me
I'll keep your light in sight till it's time to shut my eyes!

This Stormy Night

This stormy night you will keep tryst in my home,
O my friend, my heart's companion.
   The sky weeps like a soul in despair.
   Sleep has fled my eyes: opening the door,
   I stand, O best-beloved, and look out
      Time and again:
O my friend, my heart's companion.

What may be there outside, I cannot spy:
I think of the lands through which your path may lie:
   How along some distant river-shore,
   Skirting the edge of the dense forest-floor,
   Through a thick pall of darkness, to my door
      You travel on,
O my friend, my heart's companion.

I Know Not How Thou Singest, My Master

I know not how thou singest, my master! I ever listen in silent amazement.

The light of thy music illumines the world. The life breath of thy music runs from sky to sky. The holy stream of thy music breaks through all stony obstacles and rushes on.

My heart longs to join in thy song, but vainly struggles for a voice. I would speak, but speech breaks not into song, and I cry out baffled. Ah, thou hast made my heart captive in the endless meshes of thy music, my master!

The Suit

I have been called to the joy-feast of this earth:
Blessed, O blessed is my human birth.
  My eye surfeited roams
  The palace of all forms,
My ear in sweetest music is immersed.

I have part in your festival:
 I play upon the flute,
Threading my tears and laughter
 Upon my music's note.
  Is it now time to venture forth
  And see you sitting in your court?
Let me cry forth your praise: that is my suit.

When Life Has Withered

When life has withered,
 In a shower of mercy come.
When all sweetness is hidden,
 Come as the nectar of song.
When raging work in all its might
Blots out the world on every side,
 To the heart's borders, silent lord,
  With gentle footsteps come.

When, to its own self niggardly,
My beggared soul in a corner lies,
 Open the gates, O bounteous lord,
  In royal splendour come.
When desire renders blind
In a hail of dust the insensate mind,
 O holy one, unsleeping one,
  In a fierce radiance come.

I'll Overcome You

I'll overcome you not with my beauty but with my love
I'll open doors not with my hands but with my love.
I'll deck myself neither in ornaments nor with flowers
I'll adorn your neck only with a garland made out of love
None will know about the storm swaying my soul
Invisibly, like the tide with the moon, you have me
      rolling!

Light of Mine, O Light

Light of mine, O Light, Light that fills this world!
Light that washes my eyes, Light that steals my heart.
Light that dances, O friend, near my being
Light that plays, O friend, on the veena within me
The sky awakens, the wind races and the entire
      earth smiles
In the stream of light, a thousand butterflies raise
      their sails
In the waves of light, dance mallika and malati
In the clouds that you have touched with gold,
O friend, the gems cannot be counted
In every leaf that smiles, O friend,
There is a pile of merriment
The river of music has submerged its banks
And there is the endless shower of nectar!

Thou Art the Ruler of the Minds of All People

Thou art the ruler of the minds of all people,
Thou Dispenser of India's destiny.
Thy name rouses the hearts
of the Punjab, Sind, Gujarat and Maratha,
of Dravida, Orissa and Bengal.
It echoes in the hills of the Vindhyas and Himalayas,
mingles in the music of Jumna and Ganges,
and is chanted by the waves of the Indian Sea.
They pray for thy blessing and sing thy praise,
Thou dispenser of India's destiny,
Victory, Victory, Victory to thee.

Day and night, thy voice goes out from land to land,
Calling Hindus, Buddhists, Sikhs and Jains round thy
        throne
and Parsees, Mussalmans and Christians.
Offerings are brought to thy shrine by the East and
        the West
to be woven in a garland of love.
Thou bringest the hearts of all peoples into the harmony
        of one life,
Thou Dispenser of India's destiny,
Victory, Victory, Victory to thee.

Eternal Charioteer, thou drivest man's history
along the road rugged with rises and falls of Nations.
Amidst all tribulations and terror
thy trumpet sounds to hearten those that despair
        and droop,
and guide all people in their paths of peril and pilgrimage.
Thou Dispenser of India's destiny,
Victory, Victory, Victory to thee.

When the long dreary night was dense with gloom
and the country lay still in a stupor,
thy Mother's arms held her,
thy wakeful eyes bent upon her face,

till she was rescued from the dark evil dreams
that oppressed her spirit,
Thou Dispenser of India's destiny,
Victory, Victory, Victory to thee.

The night dawns, the sun rises in the East,
the birds sing, the morning breeze brings a stir of
    new life.
Touched by golden rays of thy love
India wakes up and bends her head at thy feet.
Thou King of all Kings,
Thou Dispenser of India's destiny,
Victory, Victory, Victory to thee.

Thou Hast Made Me Endless

Thou hast made me endless, such is thy pleasure. This frail
vessel thou emptiest again and again, and fillest it ever with
fresh life.

This little flute of a reed thou hast carried over hills and
dales, and hast breathed through it melodies eternally new.

At the immortal touch of thy hands my little heart loses
its limits in joy and gives birth to utterance ineffable.

Thy infinite gifts come to me only on these very small
hands of mine. Ages pass, and still thou pourest, and still
there is room to fill.

You Stand on the Other Shore

You stand on the other shore of my song
My tunes find their feet, but I can't find you.
The breeze stirs miraculously, don't keep your boat tied
    any more –
Cross over and come into my soul.
With you I'd frolic in song and frisk across space.
In sorrow I play my flute all day long.
When is it that you will take my flute and sing on it
In the hushed, joyous night's intimate darkness?

The Night My Doors Were Shattered

The night my doors were shattered by the storm,
I did not know you had come to my home.
    The blackness closed about,
    The lamp-flame flickered out:
I raised my hands towards the sky – to whom?

I lay in darkness, thinking it a dream.
How could I know your pennant in the storm?
    Now when the day's at hand,
    At last I see you stand
At the heart of the emptiness that fills my room.

My Lamp Blown Out

My lamp blown out, on my lonely road I fare.
A storm has risen – the storm is now my fellow-traveller.
    The laughter of calamity
    Flashes from the edge of the sky,
Destruction plays about my clothes, my hair.

They have made me lose the path down which I came:
A new path must I seek out in the gloom.
    Perhaps the thunder's roar will speak
    Of the road I now must take,
The city where my night will find its dawn.

Not Your Word Alone

Not your Word alone, my friend, my dear one,
From time to time caress my soul too.
I know not how else it is that I'll overcome
The fatigue of the road, the thirst from a long day –
I would like you to tell me that this darkness is fulfilling.
My soul would like to give and not take all the time,
It carries along in its movements whatever it has stored.
Extend your hand, clasp it in mine –
I'll grasp it, fill it up, and keep it with me,
It will make my lonely journey pleasing.

Forgive My Languor, O Lord

Forgive my languor, O Lord,
if ever I lag behind
  upon life's way.

Forgive my anguished heart
which trembles and hesitates
  in its service.

Forgive my fondness
that lavishes its wealth
  upon an unprofitable past.

Forgive these faded flowers
  in my offering
that wilt in the fierce heat
  of panting hours.

The Cloud Says, 'I Am Going'

The cloud says, 'I am going.'
  Night says, 'I go.'
The ocean says, 'I am at end –
  Here is my shore.'
Grief says, 'I quietly sit
As the imprint of His feet.'
  The self says, 'Now I lose myself:
    I seek no more.'

The world says, 'There's a wedding-garland
  Only for you.'
The sky, 'A million lamps are lit
  Only for you.'
Love says, 'From age to age
For you I have lain awake',
  While Death says, 'The boat
    Of your life I row.'

When My Footprints No Longer Mark
This Road

When my footprints no longer mark this road,
I'll stop rowing my boat to this ghat,
I'll cease all transactions,
I'll settle my accounts and clear all dues.
All business will stop in this mart –
It won't matter if you stop thinking of me then,
Or cease calling me while looking at the stars.

When the strings of my tanpura gather dust,
When prickly shrubs sprout in my doorsteps,
When the garden flowers put on a mantle of weeds,
When moss spreads all over the pond's banks,
It won't matter if you stop thinking of me then,
Or cease calling me while looking at the stars.

Then the flute will play on in this music hall,
Then Time will flow on,
Then days will pass just as they do now.
Then ghats will fill with boats as they do now –
Cattle will graze while cowboys play in that field.
It won't matter if you stop thinking of me then,
Or cease calling me while looking at the stars.

Who can say I won't be there that morning?
I'll be in all your fun and games then – this very me!
You'll name me anew, embracing me as never before,
It won't matter if you stop thinking of me then,
Or cease calling me while looking at the stars.

Beyond Boundaries of Life and Death

Beyond boundaries of life and death
You keep waiting, my dear friend,
In my heart's lonesome sky
Your throne is covered in light
With immense hope and intense delight
I reach out to be one with you.
In the silent darkness of evening
Your footsteps cast their shadow.
What music from your veena
Spreads this night over everything?
The whole world fills with the melody
And I lose myself in the poignant tune!

My Time Flies

My time flies by every evening
In harmonizing my tunes with your tunes.
My one-stringed ektara can't keep up with your
 sad songs.
In vain I take part again and again in this sport
Of harmonizing my tunes with your tunes.
I have tuned my string with the music of the near
But that flute keeps playing on afar.
Can everyone join in the sport of heavenly music?
Can just anyone cross over to the shore of the Universal
 Soul
And cast a net of music
In harmonizing one's tunes with your tunes?

There – in the Lap of the Storm Clouds – the Rain Comes

There – in the lap of the storm clouds – the rain comes,
Its hair loosened, its sari's borders flying!
Its song beats flutter the mango, blackberry, sal and
    rain-trees,
And make their leaves dance and murmur in excitement.
My eyes, moving in beat to its music,
Wander in the falling rain and lose themselves amidst the
    sylvan shades.
Time and again, whose familiar voice calls me in the
    wet wind,
Stirring a storm of anguish in my soul on this lonely day?

Because I Would Sing

Because I would sing, you keep me awake
O sleep breaker.
You startle my soul into song
O source of sorrows.
Darkness spreads and birds nest
Boats moor on banks.
Only my soul finds no solace
O source of sorrows.
When I am in the midst of work
You won't stop the flow of tears and happiness.
Touching me and filling my soul to the brim
You steal away,
Preferring to stay beyond my pain
O source of sorrows.

May Farewell's Platter Be Replete

May farewell's platter be replete with the nectar of
    memories
Only to be returned at the celebration of our reunion
In tearful sadness, in depths of silence,
May life's new resolutions find secret realization
On the path you tread, you are alone,
Before your eyes you see darkness,
But in your mind's eye you see a ray of light
Through the course of the day and in secret
You will refresh your mind with the nectar of
    remembrances
While in the lotus garden of the heart
The farewell strains of the veena play

Stars Fill the Sky

Stars fill the sky, the world teems with life,
    And amidst it all I find my place!
    I wonder, and so I sing.
I feel in my veins the ebb and flow of Earth's eternal tides
      Pulling this Creation
      I wonder and so I sing
    Walking along the forest's grassy paths,
I have been entranced by the sudden scent of a flower,
    Around me lie strewn the gifts of joy
      I wonder, and so I raise my song.
      I have seen, I have heard.
I have poured my being upon the breast of Earth,
    Within the known I have found the unknown.
      I marvel and so I sing.

Has He Come? Or Hasn't He?

Has he come? Or hasn't he?
Hard to say!
Is he a dream image? An illusion?
Or is he merely a delusion?
Can he be caught in beauty's drapes?
Can I catch him in the notes of a song?
He is the always-elusive object of my devotion!
His flute plays a sad tune
A raga blending motifs of union and separation.
Whether in joy or sorrow he can be found,
The restless breeze blowing through my heart
Tells me: he's the true end of all my devotion.

A Slight Caress, a Few Overheard Words

A slight caress, a few overheard words –
With these I weave in my mind my spring songs.
Intoxicated by palash in bloom, by champak flowers too,
I spin my webs of tunes, colours, and desires.
Aroused by what comes my way in fleeting moments,
I paint images in a corner of my mind.
With whatever drifts away, I wander about in tunes,
Thus I let time fly, counting the beat of ankle bells.

POEMS

The Spring Wakes from Its Dream

How have the sun's rays in my heart
Entered this morning! How have the songs
Of morning birds into the dark cave broken!
Who knows why, after long, my soul has woken!

The soul awakes, the waters stir:
I cannot stem my heart's passion, my heart's desire.
    The earth shudders and quakes
    And massive rocks roll down,
    The swollen foaming flood
    Rages with furious groans:
    It rushes here, it rushes there,
    Whirling in a madman's gyre –
Seeks to break out, but cannot see where lies the prison
      door.
    Why is God so stony-hearted?
    Why with his bonds am I begirded?
    Break them, my heart, break every stay –
    Work the will for life today,
Summon wave upon wave, blow upon blow.
    When the soul is roused to gladness,
    What are rocks, and what is darkness?
What need I fear, when longing surges so?
    Then sail again where you would go,
    Give where you will, that you but so
With moment's smile, stopping beside the plain,
Carry away my golden store of grain.

Take on your boat as much as you desire.
And is there more? No more: it's filled entire.
    Layer on layer have I piled
    All that kept my soul beguiled
The long days by the lonely river-shore.
Now, of your mercy, let me come aboard.

No room, there is no room. The little boat
Is full with my own shining harvest-load.
    Wheeling across the monsoon sky
    The laden clouds go roving by –
I lie abandoned on the empty shore,
The golden boat has taken all my store.

I Won't Let You Go

Twelve o'clock: the carriage is at the door.
The autumn sun is steadily growing hotter.
In the empty village streets, the noonday breeze
Scatters the dust. In the peepal's soothing shade
The weary beggar-crone has spread her rags
And gone to sleep. As in a sun-filled night,
Everything silent, lifeless: only no sleep
Or rest within my house. Ashwin is over:
The Puja break has ended, I must go back
To where I work, far off. And so the servants
Are busy with the baggage, tying loads
With great commotion, in this room and that.
My lady of the house, with swimming eyes
And stony weight upon her heart, yet has
No time to weep. She bustles up and down
Arranging my farewell: the more the load,
The less she's satisfied. 'Come, come,' I say,
'These pots and pitchers, bottles, bedding, boxes,
What will I do with all these? Let me take some
And leave the rest behind.'

                    But no one heeds me.
'What if you suddenly need something there?
Where will you find it in that far-off place?
Here's only some good lentils, long-grain rice,
Areca-nuts and betel-leaves; and there
In that pot, a few coconuts and sweets,
And in these two some decent mustard oil.
That's mango jelly, here's two seers of milk,

And medicines in all these jars and cans.
Here are more sweets in this pot: do remember
To eat them.' I knew argument was useless.
The luggage kept on piling like a mountain.
I looked at the clock, then turned again and looked
At my beloved. 'Well then, I'll be off,'
I slowly said. She drew her sari-end across
Her eyes, to hide the inauspicious tears.

Beside the door, wrapped in her thoughts, there sat
My daughter, four years old. On other days
She'd have had her bath before this, and her eyes,
Before she'd swallowed scarce two mouthfuls of
Her mid-day rice, been shut in sleep. Today
Her mother had not seen to her: even now
She had not bathed or eaten, but like a shadow
Hugged my steps all this time, watching each move
With mute unblinking eyes. Worn out at last,
She now sat silently beside the door
With who knows what intent: and when I said
'I'm leaving, little mother,' with sad eyes
And pale look answered, 'I won't let you go.'
She sat where she was, neither clutched my hand
Nor shut the door; only declared the right
Born of her heart's love: 'I won't let you go.'
Yet the time came to an end, and she, alas,
Could not but let me.

                              O my foolish girl,
Who are you? Where could you have drawn such
          strength
To say so boldly, 'I won't let you go'?
Whom in this universe, O arrogant one,
Will you hold back with two small arms, with whom
Grapple, sitting beside the homestead door
With that tired tiny body, only the store
Of that little love-filled breast? Here on this earth
It befits the wounded spirit, with fear and shame,
Only to utter its heart's prayer, to say
'I do not want to let you go.' Who'll say
'I will not'? Hearing from your infant lips

Your love's proud vaunt, the world, taken with mirth,
Snatched me away; only you, vanquished, sat
Like a painted figure tearfully by the door.
I saw and left, dabbing at my own eyes.

As I travel, I see beside the road
The autumn fields bowed down by weight of crops
Bask in the sunshine, the uncaring rows
Of trees along the highway gaze all day
At their own shadow, and the swollen flow
Of the autumn Ganga; sprawled in the blue sky
Tufts of white cloud, like tender new-born calves
Dozing in bliss, replete with mother's milk.
I sigh, seeing the earth to the bright sun
Lie open, stretching to the far horizon,
Weary with time, aeon succeeding aeon.

In what deep grief the whole sky is submerged,
And all the earth: as I move on, I hear
Along the way this one heart-breaking note,
'I will not let you go.' From the world's end
To the remotest corner of the sky
There sounds for ever, without start or end,
'Will not,' and again 'Will not let you go.'
All things call out, 'I will not let you go.'
The mother earth, clutching upon her breast
The tiny blades of grass, cries frantically
'I will not let you go.' The sinking flame
Of the life-spent lamp hears someone draw it back
From the jaws of darkness, calling a hundred times
'I will not let you go.' Through heaven and earth
And the infinite universe, the oldest speech,
The deepest lament, 'I will not let you go.'
And yet, alas, they have to be let go:
They go. It has been so since time began.
Clamouring 'We will not, will not let go',
All things, with arms outstretched and fiery eyes,
Rush down the torrent of creation's tide
Upon destruction's sea; the world's vast shore
Is filled with stricken cries. Each wave calls out
To the one before, 'I will not let you go':

But no one hears or answers.

From all sides
Today, there beats upon my ears that cry
In my daughter's voice, the child-world's foolish call,
Cracking its very heart. Throughout all time
It has lost all it ever gained, but still
It will not loose its clutch; like my girl of four
It still cries, in the pride of unwearied love,
'I will not let go.' Every moment smites
That pride, yet with wan face and tearful eyes,
Love will not be defeated; yet it cries,
With choking voice but with rebellious mien,
'I will not let you go'; and ever quelled,
Ever replies, 'How can the one I love
Be sundered from me? What has the world to show
So fierce, so ardent, so unmatchable
And boundless as my urge?' While proudly thus
It boasts 'I will not let go', on the instant
The treasure of its love is whirled away
Like dross, like driest dust, in just one breath:
Tears flood its eyes, its humbled downcast head
Sinks like an uprooted tree. Yet love
Still says, 'The truth of destiny must stand:
I have received his charter, signed and sealed,
Bond of eternal right.' Hence with proud breast
Standing before the gape of mighty death,
The frail soft flesh can vaunt, 'Death, you are not.'
Death sits and laughs. And so across the world
That death-afflicted everlasting love
Has cast its pall, like the vapour of tears
On grieving eyes, trembling continually
With fervid fears. A weary hope without hope
Has drawn a mist of gloom across the world.
I picture two uncomprehending arms
Enfold the universe in its futile clasp
Movingly, mutely. On the fickle stream
Falls an unchanging shadow, like a dream
Woven by clouds charged with the rain of tears.

And so in the sighing trees today I hear
An anxious longing, even as in idle play
The indifferent noon breeze tosses the dead leaves.
The day wears on: the shadow longer falls
Beneath the peepal tree. To a country tune
The infinite's flute wails on creation's plain;
The earth, transported by that music, sits
With loosened hair among the laden fields
Beside the Ganga, drawing across her bosom
The golden veil of sunshine, her still eyes
Fixed on the far blue sky, lips without speech.
I saw her darkened face: the mute, struck look
Of my four years' girl, sitting beside the door.

Swaying

I will play with my soul today
  A game of death
  Deep in the night.
 Pouring rain, a darkling sky,
 Behold all sides in torrents cry,
 On the world's wave with dire joy
  I float this raft of mine;
 Scorning my bed of dreams I come
  Out in the storm
  In the night-time.

Oh, in the wind, sky, sea today
  What clamouring –
  Swing, swing!
 The frenzied gale hurtles and shoves
 From the rear, 'Ha ha' it laughs
 Like a hundred thousand yaksha children
  Bellowing.
 In heaven and hell, madmen, drunkards
  Rioting –
  Swing, swing.

Roused from its sleep, my soul today
    Sits awake
    So near my breast.
  She trembles almost without rest,
  Presses herself upon my chest,
  In cruel close happy embrace
    My heart dances;
  In terror and delight my soul
    Grows anxious
    So near my breast.

Alas, for long I nurtured her
    With every care
    Upon her bed.
  Lest she feel pain, or sorrows prove,
  Night and day with lavish love
  A nuptial bed I fashioned for her,
    Flower-layered;
  Behind closed doors I kept her there
    In secret room,
    With every care.

How have I caressed and kissed her
    On her eyelids
    Lovingly.
  Beside her have I laid my head
  With soft sweet words, endearments said,
  On moonlight nights have made her
    Lilting melody:
  All that was honeyed I unto
    Her two hands lifted
    Lovingly.

Her happy bed tired her at length –
    Her idle trance,
    Luxuriance.
  No longer did she wake when touched,
  Her flower-garlands weighed too much,
  Sleep and wake were one to her,
    Night one with day.

A numb inert aversion pierced
    Her inwardly,
    Luxuriantly.

Shall I, pouring sweet on sweet,
    My bride forfeit
    Beyond retrieve?
The nuptial lamp flickers and dies:
On every side, my anxious eyes
See only store of withered flowers,
    Heap on heap.
Sunk in my dreams' unfathomed deep,
    I struggle for life:
    Whom do I seek?

Hence have I thought to play today
    A novel game
    In the night-time.
Clutching fast the death-swing's ropes,
The two of us shall nestle close,
The storm will come and give a push
    With laughter high:
We two shall play the swinging game
    At midnight-time,
    My soul and I.

    Swing, swing!
    Swing, swing!
Raise a tempest on this sea!
My lap is full – my bride again
    Has come to me!
My dearest wakens to the noise
    Of dissolution.
In my heart's blood there heaves again
    What agitation!
What clamour rises in my heart
    Without, within!

Her tresses fly, her sari-end,
Her wild-flower garland in the wind –
Her bangles clash, her anklets chime
    In frenzied ring.
    Swing, swing!
Come, O tempest, drive away
My soul-bride's store of piled array –
Despoil her of her veil, unloose
    Each covering:
    Swing, swing!
Face to face, my soul and I
Today, all shame and fear laid by,
Will know each other, breast to breast,
    On rapture's wing:
    Swing, swing!
Breaking out of dreams, today
        Two madmen spring:
        Swing, swing!

The Golden Boat

Clouds rumbling in the sky; teeming rain.
I sit on the river-bank, sad and alone.
The sheaves lie gathered,   harvest has ended,
The river is swollen and fierce in its flow.
As we cut the paddy it started to rain.

One small paddy-field, no one but me –
Flood-waters twisting and swirling everywhere.
Trees on the far bank   smear shadows like ink
On a village painted on deep morning grey.
On this side a paddy-field, no one but me.

Who is this, steering close to the shore,
Singing? I feel that she is someone I know.
The sails are filled wide,   she gazes ahead,
Waves break helplessly against the boat each side.
I watch and feel I have seen her face before.

Oh to what foreign land do you sail?
Come to the bank and moor your boat for a while.
Go where you want to,   give where you care to,
But come to the bank a moment, show your smile –
Take away my golden paddy when you sail.

Take it, take as much as you can load.
Is there more? No, none, I have put it aboard.
My intense labour   here by the river –
I have parted with it all, layer upon layer:
Now take me as well, be kind, take me aboard.

No room, no room, the boat is too small.
Loaded with my gold paddy, the boat is full.
Across the rain-sky   clouds heave to and fro,
On the bare river-bank, I remain alone –
What I had has gone: the golden boat took all.

Now Turn Me Back

The world's busy all day with a hundred tasks:
Only you, like a tetherless truant boy,
Alone in the noontide field, in a tree's sad shade
To the warm sluggish weary woodland breeze
Played all day on your flute. Rouse yourself now!
Somewhere a fire has started: someone blows
A conch to wake the world, while through the skies
A weeping sounds – a shackled orphan-girl
Begs help in some dark prison; from feeble breasts
Bloated insolence, through a hundred thousand mouths,
Sucks out blood. Self-weening unrighteousness
Mocks at pain; the fearful cringing slave
Hides in disguise. See, standing with bowed heads
A silent crowd, long centuries' tales of pain
Writ on their faded faces: weighed down more
And ever more, they trudge on while life lasts,
Then pass their burden down the generations.
They neither carp at fate, nor chide the gods
Nor men, bear no resentment, only draw
Their lives out in affliction, picking at
A few poor grains of rice: when robbed of that,
Or struck at heart by blind pride's tyranny,
They do not know the door to seek redress –
So, calling once upon the poor man's God,
They heave a sigh and wordlessly expire.
To each one of those pale dumb ignorant faces
Speech must be given, those tired withered shattered
          breasts
Made to resound with hope. They must be told,
'Stand together a moment, heads held high,
The evil you fear is more afraid than you:
When you wake and rise, he will run away;
When you confront his path, he'll cringe aside
Like a street cur, stricken with shame and terror.
The gods desert him, no man is his aid:
He rants, but in his heart knows all too well
His own abjection.'

Come then, poet, rise:
If you have life, rally it, sacrifice it.
So much of pain and sorrow – afflicted world,
So poor, so empty, narrow, close and dark.
We want food, we want light, air to breathe free,
And health and strength, a long life lit with joy
And breast made broad by courage. To this penury,
Poet, bring once from heaven an image of hope.

Now turn me back to the shores of the world,
My sportive fancy! Do not from wave to wave,
From breeze to breeze, draw me deceivingly
Or seat me in the melancholy shade
Of the heart's lonely bower. The day is past,
Darkness now falls: the forest sighs and wails
In the uncaring comfortless wind. I pass
From there to the open sky, among the crowds
On the broad dusty highway. Where do you go,
O traveller? Look upon me, a stranger.
Tell me your name: do not distrust me. I
Companionless have dwelt continually,
Night and day, in creation inchoate:
Hence my strange garb, strange conduct; hence my eyes
Dreamily languid, hunger in my heart.
O what mother, when I arrived on earth,
Gave me only this flute to play? And so
Rapt by my own tune, through long days and nights
Far and alone I roamed, past earthly bounds.
If by the joyance of its tune, my flute
Can raise sounds in dejection's songless home,
Or with the music of a death-trouncing hope
Quicken one corner of an idle life
Even for a moment – grant sorrow its language,
Awaken from its sleep the heart's deep thirst
For heaven's immortal nectar – blessed then my song,
The great descant where all griefs find oblivion.

What will you say, what sing? Say, false one's sole joys
And private sorrows: he who, submerged in self,
Turns from the world, has not learnt how to live.
We must race, fearless, dancing on the waves

Of universal life, truth our pole-star.
I do not fear death: torrents of tears will rain
Upon my head in evil days, through which
I'll seek tryst with the one to whom I've pledged
My life, my all, birth after birth. Who she may be
I cannot say: I do not know the face.
I only know, in darkness of the night
Mankind has travelled down that path, through storm
And lightning, from one age towards another,
The heart's flaming lamp borne with care. I know
He who has heard that summoning song runs forth
With fearless soul into disaster's vortex
Laying aside the whole world, bares his breast
To torture's blow. The roar of death he hears
Like music sweet. Fire has devoured him through,
Stakes have impaled him, axes hacked his limbs;
All he loved most he flung unflinchingly
To feed the holy fire of his devotion;
Tore out his heart – blood-lotus, offering
At his last puja, paying the debt of birth
With life in death fulfilled. Princes, I've heard,
Have put on rags, abjured wealth, roamed the streets
Like beggars. Minute to minute, the great-souled man
Has borne life's trivial torments, seen his feet
Pierced through by each day's thorns; foolish wise men
Have held him in distrust, loved ones made mock
In wonted derision; with compassionate eyes
He has forgiven silently, his soul
Bearing within it image of loveliness
Incomparable. The proud has shed his pride
For her, the rich man wealth, the hero life,
The poet framed a hundred thousand songs
And sung them through the world. Her lofty voice
Of benediction rides the ocean winds,
Her trailing robe encinctures the blue sky,
Her world-conquering image of love replete
Blooms at the supreme hour in a loved one's face.
I know, flinging afar all pettiness,
All life's dishonour, as blood-sacrifice
To the love of that world-beloved, I must stand

With head unbowed, not writ upon by fear
Or mired by shame; holding her to my heart,
Must walk life's thorny path silent, alone,
Patient through joy and grief, wiping my tears
In lonely places – every day unsparing
In every day's tasks, making all men happy;
Then at the long road's end, after the toil
Of life's journey, with worn feet, blood-stained clothes,
Ascend one day to a griefless abode
Of peace that soothes all toil. With serene face
The magnanimous goddess will then smile
And garland her devotee: her lotus-touch
Will bring peace to all sorrow and distress,
All evil. Falling at her roseate feet,
I'll bathe them in a lifetime's pent-up tears,
Unfold to her my ever-guarded hope,
Hold out with tears my life's infirmities
And beg eternal pardon. Sorrow's night
May end then, and my lifelong thirst to love
All things, in a single love be satisfied.

The Lord of Life

Lord of my inmost part,
Has all your thirst been slaked at last on coming to my
     heart?
I've filled your cup with all the flow
Of a hundred thousand joys and woes
Wrung from my breast like juice of grapes with cruel
     torment pressed.
From many scents and many hues,
Many verses, many tunes,
Your marriage-bed I've woven with long care,
And fashioned for you every day
New figures for your passing play
By melting down the gold of my desire.

You freely chose me – who knows why? You freely
    sought and wooed.
    Lord of my life, do you delight
    In these my mornings, these my nights,
In all my work, in all my play, amidst your solitude?
    Did you hear from your lonely throne
    The songs that through the spring and rain,
Autumn and winter, sounded in my heart?
    Or filled your lap with flowers of thought,
    And for your neck in garlands wrought,
And wandered with a dreaming soul through the woods
    of my youth?

What do you see, beloved, with your eyes
Fixed on my heart? Have you forgiven all my truancies?
    How often has my prayerless day,
    My slothful night, sped on its way,
My offering-flowers drooped and died among the lonely
    woods.
    How often did my lyre descend
    Below the note that you had tuned:
O poet, can I ever sing the music of your verse?
    To water your garden have I gone,
    Dozed in the shade; when night came on,
With laden eyes conveyed at last the water of my tears.

Lord of my heart, is this the end of all I had to keep –
Beauty, song, life, my waking hours, the drowsy trance
    of sleep?
    My arms have loosened their embrace,
    My kiss does not intoxicate;
In life's grove, does the morning break upon the night of
    love?
    Then shatter this tryst for today,
    Give me new form and new array,
My immemorial self again within your clasp revive:
In a new marriage take me, the bonds of a new life.

A Half-acre of Land

I had forfeited all my land except for one half-acre.
The landlord said, 'Upen, I'll buy it, you must hand it
    over.'
I said, 'You're rich, you've endless land, can't you see
That all I've got is a patch on which to die?'
'Old man,' he sneered, 'you know I've made a garden;
If I have your half-acre its length and breadth will be
    even,
You'll have to sell.' Then I said with my hands on my
    heart
And tears in my eyes, 'Don't take my only plot!
It's more than gold – for seven generations my family
Has owned it: must I sell my own mother through
    poverty?'
He was silent for a while as his eyes grew red with fury.
'All right, we'll see,' he said, smiling cruelly.

Six weeks later I had left and was out on the road;
Everything was sold, debt claimed through a fraudulent
    deed.
For those want most, alas, who already have plenty:
The rich *zamindār* steals the beggar-man's property.
I decided God did not now intend me for worldliness:
In exchange for my land he had given me the universe.
I became disciple to a *sādhu* – I roamed the world:
Many and pleasing were the sights and places I beheld.
But nowhere on mountain or sea, in desert or city could
    I wander
Without thinking, day and night, of that half-acre.
Road, markets, fields – over fifteen years went past;
But finally my homesickness grew too great to resist.

I bow, I bow to my beautiful motherland Bengal!
To your river-banks, to your winds that cool and
    console;
Your plains, whose dust the sky bends down to kiss;
Your shrouded villages, that are nests of shade and peace;
Your leafy mango-woods, where the herd-boys play;
Your deep ponds, loving and cool as the midnight sky;

Your sweet-hearted women returning home with water;
I tremble in my soul and weep when I call you Mother.
Two days later at noon I entered my native village:
The pottery to the right, to the left the festival carriage;
Past temple, market-place, granary, on I came
Till thirsty and tired, at last I arrived at my home.

But shame on you, shame on you, shameless, fallen
    half-acre!
What mother gives herself freely to a chance seducer?
Do you not remember the days when you nursed me
    humbly
With fruits and herbs and flowers held in your sari?
For whom are these lavish garments, these languorous
    airs?
These coloured leaves stitched in your sari, this head of
    flowers?
For you I have wandered, homeless, world-weary, pining,
Whereas you, you witch, have sat here idling and
    laughing.
How a wealthy man's love has turned your head! How wholly
You have changed – all signs of the past have gone
    completely.
You cared for me before, you fed me, your bounty was
    abundant.
You were a goddess; now, for all your wiles, you are
    a servant.

As I paced with my heart in two I looked round and saw
There was still, near the wall, the same old mango-tree.
I sat at its foot and soothed my pain with tears,
And memories rose in my mind of childhood days:
How after a storm that had kept me awake one night
I had dashed out at dawn to gather all the fallen fruit;
Memories of playing truant in the sweet, still noon –
Alas to think those days can never return.
Suddenly a sharp gust of wind shook the branches
    above me
And two ripe mangoes fell to the ground beside me.

I mused: my mother still knows her son, maybe.
I took that gift of love, reverently touched my brow.

Then the gardener appeared from somewhere, like a
    messenger of death –
A topknotted Oṛiyā, abusing me for all he was worth.
I said, 'I gave away everything with scarcely a murmur,
And now when I claim two mangoes there is all this
    uproar.'
He didn't know me, he led me with a stick at his
    shoulders;
The landlord, rod in hand, was fishing with his retainers.
When he heard what had happened he roared, 'I'll kill
    him.'
In each vile thing he said his retainers exceeded him.
I said, 'Two mangoes are all I beg of you, master.'
He sneered, 'He dresses as a *sādhu* but he's a pukka
    robber.'
I wept, but I laughed as well at the irony of life –
For he was now the great *sādhu*, and I was the thief.

Affliction

Although the evening comes with laggard languor,
    Although all music ceases at a sign,
Although the endless sky yields no companion
    And weariness descends on every limb,
Though the horizon's veiled in gloom, amid
    The silent chant of vastly fearful things,
Yet do not even so, O bird, my bird,
    Do not already, sightless, fold your wings.

This is no babble of the murmuring forest
    But swollen seas, stirring in python fury;
No garden decked with show of kunda flowers
    But screaming waves, tossing in foamy flurries.

Where is the shore, laden with leaves and flowers?
　　Where is the nest, with branches sheltering?
Yet do not even so, O bird, my bird,
　　Do not already, sightless, fold your wings.

Enduring night still stretches out before you,
　　The sun sleeps by the mountains where it set.
From its silent lonely seat, the universe
　　Counts every passing hour with bated breath.
Far out on the horizon, a bent moon
　　Slowly across the shoreless darkness swims:
Yet do not even so, O bird, my bird,
　　Do not already, sightless, fold your wings.

There in the sky above, the gazing stars
　　With pointed fingers signalling, regard you;
Seething below, deep and importunate death
　　In a hundred breakers surges up towards you.
Who join their hands in prayer on some far shore
　　And 'Come, O come,' in piteous voices sing?
Then do not even now, O bird, my bird,
　　Do not already, sightless, fold your wings.

You have no fear, no bond of love or longing.
　　You have no hope: hope is a vain deceit.
You have no words, no barren lamentation,
　　Nor any home, or fashioned flowery bed.
Only your wings, the sky's immense arena
　　Darkness-daubed, baffled of dawn's bearings:
Then do not even now, O bird, my bird,
　　Do not already, sightless, fold your wings.

Snatched by the Gods

The news has gradually spread round the villages –
The Brahmin Maitra is going on a pilgrimage
To the mouth of the Ganges to bathe. A party
Of travelling-companions has assembled – old
And young, men and women; his two
Boats are ready at the landing-stage.

Mokṣadā, too, is eager for merit –
She pleads, 'Dear grandfather, let me come with you.'
Her plaintive young widow's eyes cannot see reason;
She entreats him, she is hard to resist. 'There is no
More room,' says Maitra. 'I implore you at your feet,'
She replies, weeping – 'I can find space
For myself somewhere, in a corner.' The Brahmin's
Mind softens, but he still hesitates
And asks, 'But what of your little boy?'
'Rākhāl?' says Mokṣadā, 'he can stay
With his aunt. After he was born I was ill
For a long time with puerperal fever, they despaired
Of my life; Annadā took my baby
And suckled him along with her own – she gave him
Such love that ever since then the boy
Has preferred his aunt's lap to mine. He is so
Naughty, he listens to no one – if you try
And tell him off his aunt comes
And draws him to her breast and weeps and cuddles him.
He will be happier with her than with me.'

Maitra gives in. Mokṣadā immediately
Hurries to get ready – packs her things,
Pays respects to her elders, floods
Her friends with tearful goodbyes. She returns
To the landing-stage – but whom does she see there?
Rākhāl, sitting calmly and happily
On board the boat – he has run there ahead of her.
'What are you doing here?' she cries. He answers,
'I'm going to the sea.' 'You're going to the sea?'
Says his mother, 'You naughty, naughty boy,
Come down at once.' His look is determined,

He says again, 'I'm going to the sea.'
She grabs his arm, but the more she pulls
The more he clings to the boat. In the end
Maitra smiles, says tenderly, 'Let him be,
He can come along.' His mother flares up –
'All right, then, come,' she snaps,
'The sea can have you!' The moment those words
Reach her own ears, her heart cries out,
Repentance runs through it like an arrow; she clenches
Her eyes and murmurs, 'God, God';
She takes her son in her arms, covers him
With loving caresses, blesses him, prays for him.
Maitra draws her aside and whispers,
'For shame, you must never say such things.'
Suddenly Annadā rushes up – people
Have told her that Rākhāl has been allowed
To go with the boats. 'My darling,' she cries,
'Where are you going?' 'I'm going to the sea,'
Says Rākhāl cheerfully, 'but I'll come back again,
Aunt Annadā.' Nearly mad, she shouts to Maitra,
'But who will control him, he is such a mischievous
Boy, my Rākhāl! From the day he was born
He has never been away from his aunt for long –
Where are you taking him? Give him back!'
'Aunt Annadā,' says Rākhāl, 'I'm going to the sea,
But I'll come back again.' The Brahmin says kindly,
Soothingly, 'So long as Rākhāl is with me
You need not fear for him, Annadā. It is winter,
The rivers are calm, there are many other
Pilgrims going – there is no danger
At all. The trip will take two months –
I shall bring your Rākhāl back to you.'
At the auspicious time and with prayers
To Durgā, the boats set sail. Tearful
Womenfolk stay behind on the shore.
The village by the Cūrṇī river seems tearful
Too, with its wintry morning dew.

                           *

The pilgrimage is over and the pilgrims are returning.
Maitra's boat is moored to the bank,

Waiting for the afternoon tide. Rākhāl,
Curiosity satisfied, whimpers with homesick
Longing for his aunt's lap. His heart
Is weary of endless expanses of water.
Sleek and glossy, dark and curving
And cruel and mean and spiteful water,
How like a thousand-headed snake it seems,
So full of deceit, greedy tongues darting,
Hoods rearing, mouths foaming as it hisses and roars
And eternally lusts for the children of Earth!
O Earth, how speechlessly loving you are,
How stable, how certain, how ancient; how smilingly,
Greenly, softly tolerant of all
Upheavals; wherever we are, your invisible
Arms embrace us all, day and night,
Draw us with such huge and rapturous force
Towards your calm, horizon-touching breast!
Every few moments the restless little boy
Comes up to the Brahmin and asks anxiously,
'Grandfather, when will the tide come?'
Suddenly the still waters stir,
Awaking both banks with hope of departure.
The prow of the boat swings round, the cables
Creak as the current pulls; gurgling,
Singing, the sea enters the river
Like a victory-chariot – the tide has come.
The boatman says his prayers and unleashes
The boat on to the northward-racing stream.
Rākhāl comes up to the Brahmin and asks,
'How many days will it take us to get home?'
With four miles gone and the sun still not set
The wind has started to blow more strongly
From the north. At the mouth of the Rūpnārāyaṇ river,
Where a sandbank narrows the channel, a fierce
Seething battle breaks out between the scurrying
Tide and the north wind. 'Get the boat to the shore,'
Cry the passengers repeatedly – but where is the shore?
Everywhere, whipped-up water claps
With a thousand hands its own mad death-dance:
It jeers at the sky in the furious uprush

Of its foam. On one side are glimpses of the distant
Blue line of the woods on the bank; on the other,
Ravenous, gluttonous, murderous waters
Swell in insolent rebellion against the calm
Setting sun. The rudder is useless
As the boat spins and tumbles like a drunkard.
The men and women aboard tremble
And flounder as icy terror mixes
With the piercing winter wind. Some are dumb
With fear; others yell and wail and weep
For their dear ones. Maitra, ashen-faced,
Shuts his eyes and mutters prayers.
Rākhāl hides his face in his mother's breast
And shivers mutely. Desperate now,
The boatman calls out to everyone, 'Someone
Among you has cheated the gods, has not
Given what is owing – hence these waves,
This unseasonal typhoon. I tell you, make good
Your promise now – you must not play games
With angry gods.' The passengers throw money,
Clothes, everything they have into the water,
Recking nothing. But the water surges higher,
Starts to gush into the boat. The boatman
Shouts again, 'I warn you now,
Who is keeping back what belongs to the gods?'

The Brahmin suddenly points to Mokṣadā
And cries, 'This woman is the one, she made
Her own son over to the gods and now
She tries to steal him back.' 'Throw him overboard,'
Scream the passengers with one voice, heartless
In their terror. 'O grandfather,' cries Mokṣadā,
'Spare him, spare him.' With all her heart
And might she squeezes Rākhāl to her breast.
'Am I your saviour?' barks Maitra, his voice
Rising in reproach and bitterness. 'You stupidly
Thoughtlessly gave you own son
To the gods in your anger, and now you expect me
To save him! Pay the gods your debt –
All these people will drown if you break

Your word.' 'I am a foolish, ignorant
Woman,' says Mokṣadā: 'O God, O reader
Of our inmost thoughts, is what I say
In the heat of anger my true word?
Did you not see how far from the truth
It was, O Lord? Do you only listen
To what our mouths say? Do you not hear
The true message of a mother's heart?'

But as they speak the boatman and oarsman
Roughly tear Rākhāl from his mother's clasp.
Maitra turns his face away, shuts his eyes,
Blocks his ears, grits his teeth.
A sharp cry sears his heart like a whiplash
Of lightning, stings like a scorpion – 'Aunt Annadā,
Aunt Annadā, Aunt Annadā!' That helpless, hopeless
Drowning cry stabs Maitra's tightly
Shut ears like a spike of fire. 'Stop!'
He bursts out, 'Save him, save him, save him!'
For an instant he stares at Mokṣadā lying senseless
At his feet; then he turns to the water. The boy's
Agonized eyes show briefly among the frothing
Waves as he splutters 'Aunt Annadā' for the last
Time before the black depths claim him. Only
His frail fist sticks up once in a final
Pathetic grasp at the sky's protection,
But it slips away again, defeated. The Brahmin,
Gasping 'I shall bring you back', leaps
Into the water. He is seen no more. The sun sets.

Where The Mind Is Without Fear

Where the mind is without fear, the head held high;
Where knowledge is free; where through the night
        and day
The homestead walls have not, within their yard,
Shut up in small space a fragmented earth;
Where utterance wells up from the heart's spring;
Where the stream of work with pace unfaltering
From land to land through every quarter goes
With a myriad fulfilments along its course;

> Where desert sands of petty rule have not
> Choked justice's stream, diffusing manly worth
> In a hundred paths; where You, through all our days,
> Lead us in all our labours, thoughts and joys –
> With ruthless blows from your own hand, awaken
> India, O Father, into that heaven.

Death-wedding

Why do you speak so softly, Death, Death,
Creep upon me, watch me so stealthily?
This is not how a lover should behave.
When evening flowers droop upon their tired
Stems, when cattle are brought in from the fields
After a whole day's grazing, you, Death,
Death, approach me with such gentle steps,
Settle yourself immovably by my side.
I cannot understand the things you say.

Alas, will this be how you will take me, Death,
Death? Like a thief, laying heavy sleep
On my eyes as you descend to my heart?
Will you thus let your tread be a slow beat
In my sleep-numbed blood, your jingling ankle-bells
A drowsy rumble in my ear? Will you, Death,
Death, wrap me, finally, in your cold

Arms and carry me away while I dream?
I do not know why you thus come and go.

Tell me, is this the way you wed, Death,
Death? Unceremonially, with no
Weight of sacrament or blessing or prayer?
Will you come with your massy tawny hair
Unkempt, unbound into a bright coil-crown?
Will no one bear your victory-flag before
Or after; will no torches glow like red
Eyes along the river, Death, Death?
Will earth not quake in terror at your step?

When fierce-eyed Śiva came to take his bride,
Remember all the pomp and trappings, Death,
Death: the flapping tiger-skins he wore;
His roaring bull; the serpents hissing round
His hair; the bom-bom sound as he slapped his cheeks;
The necklace of skulls swinging round his neck;
The sudden raucous music as he blew
His horn to announce his coming – was this not
A better way of wedding, Death, Death?

And as that deathly wedding-party's din
Grew nearer, Death, Death, tears of joy
Filled Gaurī's eyes and the garments at her breast
Quivered; her left eye fluttered and her heart
Pounded; her body quailed with thrilled delight
And her mind ran away with itself, Death, Death;
Her mother wailed and smote her head at the thought
Of receiving so wild a groom; and in his mind
Her father agreed calamity had struck.

Why must you always come like a thief, Death,
Death, always silently, at night's end,
Leaving only tears? Come to me festively,
Make the whole night ring with your triumph, blow
Your victory-conch, dress me in blood-red robes,
Grasp me by the hand and sweep me away!
Pay no heed to what others may think, Death,
Death, for I shall of my own free will
Resort to you if you but take me gloriously.

If I am immersed in work in my room
When you arrive, Death, Death, then break
My work, thrust my unreadiness aside.
If I am sleeping, sinking all desires
In the dreamy pleasure of my bed, or I lie
With apathy gripping my heart and my eyes
Flickering between sleep and waking, fill
Your conch with your destructive breath and blow,
Death, Death, and I shall run to you.

I shall go to where your boat is moored,
Death, Death, to the sea where the wind rolls
Darkness towards me from infinity.
I may see black clouds massing in the far
North-east corner of the sky; fiery snakes
Of lightning may rear up with their hoods raised,
But I shall not flinch in unfounded fear –
I shall pass silently, unswervingly
Across that red storm-sea, Death, Death.

Pilgrimage to India

O my soul, on this sacred soil awaken tranquilly
Here, upon India's ocean-shore of great humanity.
  In worship of the human god
    My two hands here I raise:
  In measures free, with ecstasy
    I sing his song of praise.
  These solemn meditating peaks,
  These rivers, rows of prayer-beads
  Clasped by the plains – the sacred earth
    Here you may ever see
On India's ocean-shore of great humanity.

No one knows at whose great call
  Streams of humanity
In a mighty tide flowed who knows whence
  To mingle in that sea.

Aryan and non-Aryan came,
    Chinese, Dravidian,
Scythian, Hun, Mughal, Pathan,
    In body blent as one:
And now the West unfolds its doors,
The world bears bounty from its store –
Give and receive, merge and be merged:
    None will excluded be
From India's ocean-shore of great humanity.

On battle's tide, with clamour wild,
    All those who came in throngs
Through desert and through mountain pass,
    Singing their victory songs,
Within me they all dwell today:
    Not one is alien.
Along my blood their music plays
    In varied unison.
Play on, play on, O veena fierce:
Those who stand far off, still averse,
Will break their bonds, they too will gather
    Round in amity
On India's ocean-shore of great humanity.

Here once arose without a pause
    The mighty sound of Om –
The heart-strings resonated
    With the anthem of the One.
The many being sacrificed
    To the One's holy fire,
Division lost, one great soul rose
    By contemplation's power.
Today that sacrificial hall
Of worship and essay of soul
Is open: all must mingle there,
    Bound in humility
On India's ocean-shore of great humanity.

That holy fire blazes still
    With sorrow's blood-red flames –
It must be borne, burning at heart:
    So destiny ordains.
My soul, O bear this suffering,
    Hear the call of the One:
Conquer all shame, conquer all fear,
    Banish opprobrium.
Once past the intolerable pain,
What vast life will be born again –
The night's at end, the Mother wakes
    In her nest's immensity
On India's ocean-shore of great humanity.

Aryan and non-Aryan come,
    Hindu and Musulman:
Come, O Christian; and today
    Come, O you Englishman.
Come, brahman, with a heart made pure
    Hold hands with one and all:
Come, you outcaste: let your load
    Of insult from you fall.
To the mother's coronation haste:
The sacred pitcher yet awaits
Its holy water, by the touch
    Of all lent sanctity
On India's ocean-shore of great humanity.

The Flying Geese

The Jhelum's curved course, gleaming in evening light,
    Falls into darkness, like a curved scimitar
      Within its sheath. Day's tide has ebbed and gone:
    The night's flood-tide rolls in, bearing along
Star-flowers on its back water; deodars stand
    In rows below the darkling tableland.
        It seemed
    Creation, sunk in a dream,
      Sought utterance but could not clearly speak:
Its massed inarticulate sounds broke through the dark.

Suddenly that instant, in the twilit sky
A lightning-shaft of sound went rushing by –
    Farther and farther, through the plains of space.
      O flying geese,
    Your wings are maddened by the tempest's wine:
      With the resounding laughter of piled-up joy,
Raising waves of wonder, they beat along the sky.
    The rush of wings rose round,
    A dancing nymph composed of sound,
      Breaking the meditation of the silence.
        The mountains sunk in gloom
      Suddenly shuddered, and the deodar woods.

I felt the message of those beating wings
      For an instant bring
    Impulse of motion to the enraptured depths
      Of all that's immobile.
    The mountain yearned to be
The summer's wandering cloud; and the ranked trees,
      Casting earth's bonds aside,
    Directionless on a sudden, longed to glide
      Along that trail of sound
    To seek out the sky's bounds.
    Shattering the evening's dream, a wave of pain
      Arose – O wings
    All-renouncing, heedless of what you are
      In yearning for the far!

A plaintive cry in the heart of endless space
Broke out: 'Not here, not here – in some other place!'

    O flying geese,
You have parted for me tonight the drapes of silence.
    I hear beneath
  The stillness, in the water, sky and earth,
The restless, untameable beating of wings.
    The grass that springs
  Flutters upon the soil's sky, and below
    In subterranean darkness, who can know
What millions of seed-herons spread their wings
    In new seedlings?
  Their pinions freed, today I see this range
  Of mountains, and this forest, fly from strange
To strange realm, isle to isle.
    The pulse of the stars' flight
Startles the dark with the sound of weeping light.

  I heard the words of men flying in flocks
    Along invisible tracks
From the dim past to some new unformed age.
Night and day in my heart have I heard
  With countless other birds, this bird,
Relinquishing its nest, through light and darkness go –
    From what shore to what shore?
The infinite's wings send out their song through space:
  'Not here but elsewhere, elsewhere – in some other
    place.'

.

In Praise of Trees

O Tree, life-founder, you heard the sun
Summon you from the dark womb of earth
At your life's first wakening; your height
Raised from rhythmless rock the first
Hymn to the light; you brought feeling to harsh,
Impassive desert.
                Thus, in the sky,
By mixed magic, blue with green, you flung
The song of the world's spirit at heaven
And the tribe of stars. Facing the unknown,
You flew with fearless pride the victory
Banner of the life-force that passes
Again and again through death's gateway
To follow an endless pilgrim-road
Through time, through changing resting-places,
In ever new mortal vehicles.
Earth's reverie snapped at your noiseless
Challenge: excitedly she recalled
Her daring departure from heaven –
A daughter of God leaving its bright
Splendour, ashy-pale, dressed in humble
Ochre-coloured garments, to partake
Of the joy of heaven fragmented
Into time and place, to receive it
More deeply now that she would often
Pierce it with stabs of grief.
                    O valiant
Child of the earth, you declared a war
To liberate her from that fortress
Of desert. The war was incessant –
You crossed ocean-waves to establish,
With resolute faith, green seats of power
On bare, inaccessible islands;
You bewitched dust, scaled peaks, wrote on stone
In leafy characters your battle
Tales; you spread your code over trackless
Wastes.
          Sky, earth, sea were expressionless

Once, lacking the festival magic
Of the seasons. Your branches offered
Music its first shelter, made the songs
In which the restless wind – colouring
With kaleidoscopic melody
Her invisible body, edging
Her shawl with prismatic tune – first knew
Herself. You were first to describe
On earth's clay canvas, by absorbing
Plastic power from the sun, a living
Image of beauty. You processed light's
Hidden wealth to give colour to light.
When celestial dancing-nymphs shook
Their bracelets in the clouds, shattering
Those misty cups to rain down freshening
Nectar, you filled therewith your vessels
Of leaf and flower to clothe the earth
With perpetual youth.
                                    O profound,
Silent tree, by restraining valour
With patience, you revealed creative
Power in its peaceful form. Thus we come
To your shade to learn the art of peace,
To hear the word of silence; weighed down
With anxiety, we come to rest
In your tranquil blue-green shade, to take
Into our souls life rich, life ever
Juvenescent, life true to earth, life
Omni-victorious. I am certain
My thoughts have borne me to your essence –
Where the same fire as the sun's ritual
Fire of creation quietly assumes
In you cool green form. O sun-drinker,
The fire with which – by milking hundreds
Of centuries of days of sunlight –
You have filled your core, man has received
As your gift, making him world-mighty,
Greatly honoured, rival to the gods:
His shining strength, kindled by your flame,
Is the wonder of the universe

As it cuts through daunting obstacles.
Man, whose life is in you, who is soothed
By your cool shade, strengthened by your power,
Adorned by your garland – O tree, friend
Of man, dazed by your leafy flutesong
I speak today for him as I make
   This verse-homage,
As I dedicate this offering
   To you.

The Child

I

'What of the night?' they ask.
   No answer comes.
   For the blind Time gropes in a maze and knows not
      its path or purpose.
   The darkness in the valley stares like the dead eye-
      sockets of a giant,
   the clouds like a nightmare oppress the sky,
   and the massive shadows lie scattered like the torn
      limbs of the night.
   A lurid glow waxes and wanes on the horizon, –
   is it an ultimate threat from an alien star,
   or an elemental hunger licking the sky?
   Things are deliriously wild,
   they are a noise whose grammar is a groan,
   and words smothered out of shape and sense.
   They are the refuse, the rejections, the fruitless failures
      of life,
   abrupt ruins of prodigal pride, –
   fragments of a bridge over the oblivion of a vanished
      stream,
   godless shrines that shelter reptiles,
   marble steps that lead to blankness.
   Sudden tumults rise in the sky and wrestle
   and a startled shudder runs along the sleepless hours.
   Are they from desperate floods

hammering against their cave walls,
or from some fanatic storms
whirling and howling incantations?
Are they the cry of an ancient forest
flinging up its hoarded fire in a last extravagant
    suicide,
or screams of a paralytic crowd scourged by lunatics
    blind and deaf?
Underneath the noisy terror a stealthy hum creeps up
    like bubbling volcanic mud,
a mixture of sinister whispers, rumours and slanders,
    and hisses of derision.
The men gathered there are vague like torn pages of
    an epic.
Groping in groups or single, their torchlight tattoos
    their faces in chequered lines, in patterns of
    frightfulness.
The maniacs suddenly strike their neighbours on
    suspicion
and a hubbub of an indiscriminate fight bursts forth
    echoing from hill to hill.
The women weep and wail,
they cry that their children are lost in a wilderness of
    contrary paths with confusion at the end.
Others defiantly ribald shake with raucous laughter
their lascivious limbs unshrinkingly loud,
for they think that nothing matters.

2

There on the crest of the hill
stands the Man of faith amid the snow-white silence.
    He scans the sky for some signal of light,
    and when the clouds thicken and the nightbirds
        scream as they fly,
    he cries, 'Brothers, despair not, for Man is great.'
    But they never heed him,
    for they believe that the elemental brute is eternal
    and goodness in its depth is darkly cunning in
        deception.

When beaten and wounded they cry, 'Brother, where
    art thou?'
The answer comes, 'I am by your side.' –
But they cannot see in the dark
and they argue that the voice is of their own desperate
    desire,
that men are ever condemned to fight for phantoms
in an interminable desert of mutual menace.

3

The clouds part, the morning star appears in the East,
a breath of relief springs up from the heart of the earth,
the murmur of leaves ripples along the forest path,
and the early bird sings.
    'The time has come,' proclaims the Man of faith.
    'The time for what?'
    'For the pilgrimage.'
    They sit and think, they know not the meaning,
    and yet they seem to understand according to their
        desires.
    The touch of the dawn goes deep into the soil
    and life shivers along through the roots of all things.
    'To the pilgrimage of fulfilment,' a small voice
    whispers, nobody knows whence.
    Taken up by the crowd
    it swells into a mighty meaning.
    Men raise their heads and look up,
    women lift their arms in reverence,
    children clap their hands and laugh.
    The early glow of the sun shines like a golden garland
    on the forehead of the Man of faith,
    and they all cry: 'Brother, we salute thee!'

4

Men begin to gather from all quarters,
from across the seas, the mountains and pathless wastes.
    They come from the valley of the Nile and the banks
        of the Ganges,
    from the snow-sunk uplands of Thibet,
    from high-walled cities of glittering towers,

from the dense dark tangle of savage wilderness.
Some walk, some ride on camels, horses and
  elephants,
on chariots with banners vying with the clouds of
  dawn.
The priests of all creeds burn incense, chanting verses
  as they go.
The monarchs march at the head of their armies,
lances flashing in the sun and drums beating loud.
Ragged beggars and courtiers pompously decorated,
agile young scholars and teachers burdened with
  learned age jostle each other in the crowd.
Women come chatting and laughing,
mothers, maidens and brides,
with offerings of flowers and fruit,
sandal paste and scented water.
Mingled with them is the harlot,
shrill of voice and loud in tint and tinsel.
The gossip is there who secretly poisons the well of
  human sympathy and chuckles.
The maimed and the cripple join the throng with the
  blind and the sick,
the dissolute, the thief and the man who makes a trade
  of his God for profit and mimics the saint.
'The fulfilment!'
They dare not talk aloud,
but in their minds they magnify their own greed,
and dream of boundless power,
of unlimited impunity for pilfering, and plunder,
and eternity of feast for their unclean gluttonous flesh.

5
The Man of faith moves on along pitiless paths strewn
  with flints over scorching sands and steep
  mountainous tracks.
They follow him, the strong and the weak, the aged
  and young,
the rulers of realms, the tillers of the soil.
Some grow weary and footsore, some angry and
  suspicious.

They ask at every dragging step,
'How much further is the end?'
The Man of faith sings in answer;
they scowl and shake their fists and yet they cannot
  resist him;
the pressure of the moving mass and indefinite hope
  push them forward.
They shorten their sleep and curtail their rest,
they out-vie each other in their speed,
they are ever afraid lest they may be too late for their
  chance
while others be more fortunate.
The days pass,
the ever-receding horizon tempts them with renewed
  lure of the unseen till they are sick.
Their faces harden, their curses grow louder and
  louder.

6

It is night.
  The travellers spread their mats on the ground under
    the banyan tree.
  A gust of wind blows out the lamp
  and the darkness deepens like a sleep into a swoon.
  Someone from the crowd suddenly stands up
  and pointing to the leader with merciless finger breaks
    out:
  'False prophet, thou hast deceived us!'
  Others take up the cry one by one,
  women hiss their hatred and men growl.
  At last one bolder than others suddenly deals him a
    blow.
  They cannot see his face, but fall upon him in a fury
    of destruction
  and hit him till he lies prone upon the ground his life
    extinct.
  The night is still, the sound of the distant waterfall
    comes muffled,
  and a faint breath of jasmine floats in the air.

7

The pilgrims are afraid.
  The women begin to cry, the men in an agony of
      wretchedness
  shout at them to stop.
  Dogs break out barking and are cruelly whipped into
      silence broken by moans.
  The night seems endless and men and women begin
      to wrangle as to who among them was to blame.
  They shriek and shout and as they are ready to
      unsheathe their knives
  the darkness pales, the morning light overflows the
      mountain tops.
  Suddenly they become still and gasp for breath as they
      gaze at the figure lying dead.
  The women sob out loud and men hide their faces in
      their hands.
  A few try to slink away unnoticed,
  but their crime keeps them chained to their victim.
  They ask each other in bewilderment,
  'Who will show us the path?'

  The old man from the East bends his head and says:
  'The Victim.'
  They sit still and silent.
  Again speaks the old man,
  'We refused him in doubt, we killed him in anger,
      now we shall accept him in love,
  for in his death he lives in the life of us all, the great
      Victim.'
  And they all stand up and mingle their voices and sing,
  'Victory to the Victim.'

8

'To the pilgrimage' calls the young,
'to love, to power, to knowledge, to wealth overflowing.'
  'We shall conquer the world and the world beyond
      this,'
  they all cry exultant in a thundering cataract of voices.

The meaning is not the same to them all, but only the
　　impulse,
the moving confluence of wills that recks not death
　　and disaster.
No longer they ask for their way,
no more doubts are there to burden their minds or
　　weariness to clog their feet.
The spirit of the Leader is within them and ever
　　beyond them –
the Leader who has crossed death and all limits.
They travel over the fields where the seeds are sown,
by the granary where the harvest is gathered,
and across the barren soil where famine dwells
and skeletons cry for the return of their flesh.
They pass through populous cities humming with life,
through dumb desolation hugging its ruined past,
and hovels for the unclad and unclean,
a mockery of home for the homeless.
They travel through long hours of the summer day,
and as the light wanes in the evening they ask the man
　　who reads the sky:
'Brother, is yonder the tower of our final hope and
　　peace?'
The wise man shakes his head and says:
'It is the last vanishing cloud of the sunset.'
'Friends,' exhorts the young, 'do not stop.
Through the night's blindness we must struggle into
　　the Kingdom of living light.'
They go on in the dark.
The road seems to know its own meaning
and dust underfoot dumbly speaks of direction.
The stars – celestial wayfarers – sing in silent chorus:
'Move on, comrades!'
In the air floats the voice of the Leader:
'The goal is nigh.'

9

The first flush of dawn glistens on the dew-dripping
    leaves of the forest.
    The man who reads the sky cries:
    'Friends, we have come!'
    They stop and look around.
    On both sides of the road the corn is ripe to the
        horizon,
    – the glad golden answer of the earth to the morning
        light.
    The current of daily life moves slowly
    between the village near the hill and the one by the
        river bank.
    The potter's wheel goes round, the woodcutter brings
        fuel to the market,
    the cow-herd takes his cattle to the pasture,
    and the woman with the pitcher on her head walks to
        the well.
    But where is the King's castle, the mine of gold, the
        secret book of magic,
    the sage who knows love's utter wisdom?
    'The stars cannot be wrong,' assures the reader of the
        sky.
    'Their signal points to that spot.'
    And reverently he walks to a wayside spring
    from which wells up a stream of water, a liquid light,
    like the morning melting into a chorus of tears and
        laughter.
    Near it in a palm grove surrounded by a strange hush
        stands a leaf-thatched hut,
    at whose portal sits the poet of the unknown shore,
        and sings:
    'Mother, open the gate!'

10

A ray of morning sun strikes aslant at the door.
    The assembled crowd feel in their blood the primaeval
        chant of creation:
    'Mother, open the gate!'
    The gate opens.

The mother is seated on a straw bed with the babe on
    her lap,
Like the dawn with the morning star.
The sun's ray that was waiting at the door outside falls
    on the head of the child.
The poet strikes his lute and sings out:
'Victory to Man, the new-born, the ever-living.'
They kneel down, – the king and the beggar, the saint
    and the sinner,
the wise and the fool, – and cry:
'Victory to Man, the new-born, the ever-living.'
The old man from the East murmurs to himself:
'I have seen!'

Question

God, again and again through the ages you have sent
     messengers
  To this pitiless world:
They have said, 'Forgive everyone', they have said, 'Love
     one another –
  Rid your hearts of evil.'
They are revered and remembered, yet still in these dark
     days
We turn them away with hollow greetings, from outside
     the doors of our houses.

And meanwhile I see secretive hatred murdering the
     helpless
  Under cover of night;
And Justice weeping silently and furtively at power
     misused,
  No hope of redress.
I see young men working themselves into a frenzy,
In agony dashing their heads against stone to no avail.

My voice is choked today; I have no music in my flute:
  Black moonless night
Has imprisoned my world, plunged it into nightmare.
     And this is why,
  With tears in my eyes, I ask:
Those who have poisoned your air, those who have
     extinguished your light,
Can it be that you have forgiven them? Can it be that
     you love them?

Unyielding

When I called you in your garden
   Mango blooms were rich in fragrance –
Why did you remain so distant,
   Keep your door so tightly fastened?
Blossoms grew to ripe fruit-clusters –
You rejected my cupped handfuls,
     Closed your eyes to perfectness.

In the fierce harsh storms of Baiśākh
Golden ripened fruit fell tumbling –
   'Dust,' I said, 'defiles such offerings:
   Let your hands be heaven to them.'
     Still you showed no friendliness.

Lampless were your doors at evening,
Pitch-black as I played my vīṇā.
   How the starlight twanged my heartstrings!
   How I set my vīṇā dancing!
     You showed no responsiveness.

Sad birds twittered sleeplessly,
Calling, calling lost companions.
   Gone the right time for our union –
   Low the moon while still you brooded,
     Sunk in lonely pensiveness.

Who can understand another!
Heart cannot restrain its passion.
   I had hoped that some remaining
   Tear-soaked memories would sway you,
     Stir your feet to lightsomeness.

Moon fell at the feet of morning,
Loosened from the night's fading necklace.
   While you slept, O did my vīṇā
   Lull you with its heartache? Did you
     Dream at least of happiness?

I

It is by the colours of my consciousness
    That the emerald is green,
        The ruby red.
I opened my eyes upon the sky,
      And light kindled
          From east to west.
Turning to the rose, I said, 'Beautiful' –
        And it was beautiful.
    You'll say, these are abstractions,
          Not a poet's utterance.
      I'll reply this is truth,
            And therefore poetry.
      This is my pride,
          Pride on behalf of all humanity.
      Human pride is the canvas
          For the divine artificer's cosmic art.
The metaphysician's breath repeats the litany:
        No, no, no –
No emerald, no ruby, no light, no rose,
        No me, no you.
      On the other side, the boundless one himself
    In absorbed endeavour on the bounds of the human:
        That is called 'I'.
    In the depths of that 'I' light and darkness commingled,
      Revealing form, awakening relish;
    Who knows when 'No' blossomed into 'Yes' by
          magic spell
        In line and colour, joy and pain.

Don't say these are abstractions:
    My mind is filled with delight
        In the cosmic I's carnival of workmanship,
          Brush in hand, colours in palette.

        The pundit says –
      The aged moon, with cruel cunning smile,
    Stalks like death's messenger
        Towards the earth's rib-cage.

One day it will give a final tug to ocean and mountain;
   On earth, in the fresh ledger of ravaging Time,
      A zero will fill up the page,
   Swallow up the balance sheet of nights and days;
     Man's achievement will forfeit its fiction
        Of immortality;
     His history will be daubed
        With the blackness of eternal night.
Man's eye, on his day of departure,
   Will mop up all the colour from the cosmos;
Man's mind on his day of departure
     Will strain out all the sap.
Only energy will vibrate in the skies,
    And not a light will kindle anywhere.
In a concert without a veena, the player's fingers will dance
      Without awakening melody.
   On that day God will sit alone, drained of poetry,
    In a sky drained of blue,
   Pondering the mathematics of existence bereft
      Of individuality,
     Then in this vast creation
Through ever-extending boundless countless realm
      beyond realm
     These messages will not resonate anywhere –
      'You are beautiful',
        'I love.'
   Will God begin afresh his absorbed endeavour
      Aeon after aeon,
   Repeat this litany at the twilight hour of doomsday:
     'Speak word, speak word'?
   Will he utter, 'Say "You are beautiful" '?
     Or 'Say "I love" '?

Earth

Accept my homage, Earth, as I make my last obeisance of
the day,
Bowed at the altar of the setting sun.

You are mighty, and knowable only by the mighty;
You counterpoise charm and severity;
Compounded of male and female
You sway human life with unbearable conflict.
The cup that your right hand fills with nectar
Is smashed by your left;
Your playground rings with your mocking laughter.
You make heroism hard to attain;
You make excellence costly;
You are not merciful to those who deserve mercy.
Ceaseless warfare is hidden in your plants:
Their crops and fruits are victory-wreaths won from
struggle.
Land and sea are your cruel battlefields –
Life proclaims its triumph in the face of death.
Civilization rests its foundation upon your cruelty:
Ruin is the penalty exacted for any shortcoming.

In the first chapter of your history Demons were
supreme –
Harsh, barbaric, brutish;
Their clumsy thick fingers lacked art;
With clubs and mallets in hand they rioted over sea and
mountain.
Their fire and smoke churned sky into nightmare;
They controlled the inanimate world;
They had blind hatred of Life.

Gods came next; by their spells they subdued the Demons –
The insolence of Matter was crushed.
Mother Earth spread out her green mantle;
On the eastern peaks stood Dawn;
On the western sea-shore Evening descended,
Dispensing peace from her chalice.

The shackled Demons were humbled;
But primal barbarity has kept its grip on your
history.
It can suddenly invade order with anarchy –
From the dark recesses of your being
It can suddenly emerge like a snake.
Its madness is in your blood.
The spells of the Gods resound through sky and air
and forest,
Sung solemnly day and night, high and low;
But from regions under your surface
Sometimes half-tame Demons raise their serpent-
hoods –
They goad you into wounding your own creatures,
Into ruining your own creation.

At your footstool mounted on evil as well as good,
To your vast and terrifying beauty,
I offer today my scarred life's homage.
I touch your huge buried store of life and death,
Feel it throughout my body and mind.
The corpses of numberless generations of men lie heaped
in your dust:
I too shall add a few fistfuls, the final measure of my joys
and pains:
Add them to that name-absorbing, shape-absorbing,
fame-absorbing
Silent pile of dust.

Earth, clamped into rock or flitting into the clouds;
Rapt in meditation in the silence of a ring of
mountains
Or noisy with the roar of sleepless sea-waves;
You are beauty and abundance, terror and famine.
On the one hand, acres of crops, bent with
ripeness,
Brushed free of dew each morning by delicate sunbeams –
With sunset, too, sending through their rippling
greenness
Joy, joy;

On the other, in your dry, barren, sickly deserts
    The dance of ghosts amid strewn animal-bones.

I have watched your Baiśākh-storms swoop like black
    hawks
    Ripping the horizon with lightning-beaks:
  The whole sky roars like a rampant lion,
    Lashing tail whipping up trees
    Till they crash to the ground in despair;
      Thatched roofs break loose,
  Race before the wind like convicts from their chains.

But I have known, in Phālgun, the warm south breeze
    Spread all the rhapsodies and soliloquies of love
      In its scent of mango-blossom;
Seen the foaming wine of heaven overflow from the
    moon's goblet;
    Heard coppices suddenly submit to wind's importunity
    And burst into breathless rustling.

  You are gentle and fierce, ancient and renewing;
    You emerged from the sacrificial fire of primal
      creation
    Immeasurably long ago.
Your cyclic pilgrimage is littered with meaningless
    remnants of history;
    You abandon your creations without regret; strew
    them layer upon layer,
      Forgotten.

  Guardian of Life, you nurture us
    In little cages of fragmented time,
  Boundaries to all our games, limits to all renown.

Today I stand before you without illusion:
  I do not ask at your door for immortality
    For the many days and nights I have spent weaving
    you garlands.
      But if I have given true value
  To my small seat in a tiny segment of one of the eras
    That open and close like blinks in the millions of
    years

Of your solar round;
If I have won from the trials of life a scrap of success;
    Then mark my brow with a sign made from your
        clay –
            To be rubbed out in time by the night
    In which all signs fade into the final unknown.

        O aloof, ruthless Earth,
            Before I am utterly forgotten
            Let me place my homage at your feet.

Africa

        When, in that turbid first age,
            The Creator, displeased with himself,
    Destroyed his new creations again and again;
        In those days of his shaking and shaking his head in
            irritation
                The angry sea
            Snatched you from the breast of Mother Asia,
                Africa –
    Consigned you to the guard of immense trees,
            To a fastness dimly lit,
        There in your hidden leisure
            You collected impenetrable secrets,
    Learnt the arcane languages of water and earth and
        sky;
                Nature's invisible magic
                    Worked spells in your unconscious
                        mind.
                You ridiculed Horror
                    By making your own appearance
                        hideous;
                You cowed Fear
            By heightening your menacing grandeur,
                By dancing to the drumbeats of chaos.

Alas, shadowy Africa,
Under your black veil
Your human aspect remained unknown,
Blurred by the murk of contempt.
Others came with iron manacles,
With clutches sharper than the claws of your own
wild wolves:
Slavers came,
With an arrogance more benighted than your own
dark jungles.
Civilization's barbarous greed
Flaunted its naked inhumanity.
You wailed wordlessly, muddied the soil of
your steamy jungles
With blood and tears;
The hobnailed boots of your violators
Stuck gouts of that stinking mud
Forever on your stained history.

Meanwhile across the sea in their native parishes
Temple-bells summoned your conquerors to
prayer,
Morning and evening, in the name of a loving
god.
Mothers dandled babies in their laps;
Poets raised hymns to beauty.

Today as the air of the West thickens,
Constricted by imminent evening storm;
As animals emerge from secret lairs
And proclaim by their ominous howls the closing
of the day;
Come, poet of the end of the age,
Stand in the dying light of advancing nightfall
At the door of despoiled Africa
And say, 'Forgive, forgive –'
In the midst of murderous insanity,
May these be your civilization's last, virtuous
words.

The Day My Consciousness Was Freed

The day my consciousness was freed from extinction's
    cave,
I was driven on a resistless wonder-storm
In malefic, hostile weather to the crater-mouth
Of some infernal volcano; in burning smoke
It roared, hissing forth man's deep humiliation.
Its evil resonance shook the earth,
Blackening the air all around. I saw
The sottish suicidal frenzy of our time, on its entire body
The sickening derision of deformity.
On the one hand, insolent brutality,
Unabashed, roaring madness; on the other hand,
The irresolute footsteps of cowardice, clutching to its
    heart
The miser's guarded possessions – like a frightened animal
Growling but for a moment, then at once confessing
In a failing voice its innocuous, mute submission.
Rulers seasoned in power, sitting in council, uncertain,
Unsure, have all kept command and counsel stifled
Under tightly-clamped lips. While monster-birds
    swoop in
Through convulsed ether, across the Baitarani, swarm
    after swarm,
Machine-wings booming, vultures greedy for human
    flesh,
Polluting the skies. Seated on great Time's throne,
O Judge, give me strength – yes, give me strength,
Lend my voice the prophecy of thunder, that I may
Strike at the vile loathsome butchery of woman and child
With condemnation that will reverberate forever
In the heartbeat of shame-racked posterity,
When this terrified, fettered, throttled age
Silently hides itself in the ashes of its own pyre.

Concord

How little I know of this great world.
So many towns and capitals in land on land,
So many human feats, rivers, mountains, deserts, seas,
So many unknown creatures, unfamiliar trees,
Remain unseen. How vast is earth's array;
My mind takes up in it a tiny corner.
This regret drives me to travel-tales in books:
Reading with unflagging zeal, I gather
Words of picturesque accounts, wherever
I find them, trying to replenish
My mind's dearth of knowledge,
As far as I can, with riches begged as alms.

I am the earth's poet. Where its various sounds arise
My flute should sound response, yet diverse voices
Have failed to reach this lifelong discipline
Of melody; there are missing notes.
Imagined or guessed-at, the vast concord of earth
Has in so many silent moments filled my heart.
The impassable snow-clad mountain, singing
An unheard song to the endless, soundless blue,
Has sent its invitation
To my heart again and again.

The unknown star above the South Pole,
Wearing out the long night in the great desert spaces
Has touched with sleeplessness, in unearthly light,
My gazing eyes in the middle of the night.
The distant, overflowing, mighty waterfall
Has sent its music to the depths of my soul.
Many poets from many places pour their songs
Into the current of nature's symphony.
This is my only link with them; I gain
The company of all, and obtain
The feast of joy and the grace
Of the goddess of song in the taste
Of universal music.

He who is most inaccessible in his inmost reaches
Cannot be measured in outward time or space.
He reigns within,
His innerness known only through the heart's union.
I do not find entry to him everywhere,
The fences of my life's course bar the way.
The peasant ploughs the field,
The weaver works the loom, the fisherman casts his net –
On their far-flung, diverse tasks,
The weight of the whole world is set.
In a tiny part of it, exiled by fame,
On society's high dais I sit,
At my narrow window.
Sometimes I have approached those neighbouring
        courtyards,
But lacked all strength to enter.
Song's merchandise goes waste
In counterfeit wares, unless
It can link life to life.
I accept, therefore, the blame
Of my song's incompleteness.
I know that my poems,
Though travelling diverse routes,
Have not gone everywhere.
He who shares the peasant's life,
Earning true kinship through word and deed,
He who lives close to the earth –
It is that poet's voice I strain to hear.
In literature's joyful feast
I search for what I cannot myself provide.
May that be the truth.
May it not only posture to the eye.
To steal literary fame, not paying
Its true price, is wrong: wrong
This fashion of playing the labourer.

Come, poet of the voiceless hearts
Of those unknown:
Deliver their inmost pain,
Fill the dry joyless desert scorched by contempt

In this lifeless land, where songs have ceased,
With rasa:
Set free the spring within its heart.
May those who play on a single string
Find honour in literature's concert-hall.
O gifted one, may we hear the utterance
Of those who are mute in joy and grief,
Heads bowed and silent before the world –
Those who, close at hand, are yet afar.
May you be kin to them,
May your fame be theirs:
Again and again
Shall I salute you then.

The Pall of the Self

Let the pall of this self fall smoothly away,
The clear light of consciousness
Piercing the mist
Reveal the undying shape of truth.
Let the rays of joy
From one eternal man dispersed among all men
Irradiate in my heart.
Let me behold before I go
The peace of the ever-constant
In the silent realm above all worldly agitation.
All that is tangled, meaningless in life,
Transmitting lies prized by society
At a concocted worth –
Thrusting them all far off, a turbulent crowd
Of destitutes,
Let me with lucid eyes
Imbibe the true meaning of this life's birth
Before I pass its bounds.

They Work

Adrift on time's idle current,
The mind gazes into space.
Shadow-pictures rise to my eye on the paths of that great
       void.
How many people, band on band,
Age upon age, have passed
Into the distant past
With furious pace, arrogant in victory.
The Pathans came, lustful of empire,
The Mughals –
The wheels of their triumphal chariots
Blew shrouds of dust, their flags of victory fluttered.
I look at the paths of space:
No trace of them today.
Age after age, the light of sunrise and sunset,
Morning and evening, has reddened that pure blue.
Again across the void
Band on band they came
On iron-bound tracks
In fire-breathing chariots,
The fierce English
Radiating their power.
Time, I know, will flow down their paths too,
Sweep away the encircling fences of empire.
I know that their soldiers, laden with merchandise,
Will leave not the slightest trace on the constellations'
       paths.

When I open my eyes to this world of clay,
I see passing in constant clamour
A great rush of people
On many paths, in many bands,
From age to age, on daily human errands,
In life, in death.
They forever
Bend to the oar, hold the tiller.
In the fields
They sow and reap.

They work
In towns, in the open plains.
The royal canopy falls, the drums of war are silenced,
The pillar of victory, idiot-like, forgets its own meaning,
All those eyes of blood, those hands bearing bloody
      weapons
Hide their faces in children's tales.
They work
At home and abroad,
By the seas and rivers of Bengal, Bihar, Orissa,
In the Punjab, in Bombay and Gujarat.
The passage of their days resounds
In tones now deep, now soft,
Woven into night and day.
Grief and joy, day and night
Make life's great anthem ring.
On the ruins of hundreds and hundreds of empires,
They work.

On the Banks of the Rupnarayan

On the banks of the Rupnarayan I awoke,
And learnt this life
Is not a dream.
I saw my true form
In letters of blood.
I recognized myself
In blow upon blow,
In pain upon pain.
Truth is hard;
I came to love this hardness:
It never deceives.
Life to the end is a meditation of suffering,
To gain the formidable price of truth,
To pay all debts in death.

The First Day's Sun

The first day's sun
Asked at the first appearance of Being,
'Who are you?'
There was no answer.
Year upon year passed,
The day's last sun
Asked the last question on the shore of the western sea
In the hushed evening:
'Who are you?'
It got no answer.

The Path of Your Creation

You have spread the path of your creation
With nets of varied wiles,
O guileful one.
You have laid the snare of false belief
With skilful hands, in simple lives.
By this deceit you have marked greatness out:
Not for him the secret night.
The path your star shows him
Is the path of his heart.
It is ever-clear,
It makes him ever-radiant with simple faith.
Tortuous outside, inwardly it is straight.
In this lies his glory.
People think he is deceived;
He gains truth
In his heart of hearts, washed in its own light.
Nothing can deceive him.
He takes into his store
The last reward.
He who has with ease endured deception,
Gains from your hand
The imperishable right to peace.

Delusions I Did Cherish

Delusions I did cherish
but now I am rid of them.
Tracing the track of false hopes
I trod upon thorns
to know that they are not flowers.

I shall never trifle with love,
never play with heart.
I shall find my refuge in you
on the shore of the troubled sea.

I Thought I Had Something to Say

I thought I had something to say to her when our eyes
    met in the road.
But she passed away, and it rocks day and night
like an idle boat on every wave of the hours –
the thing that I had to say to her.

It seems to sail in the autumn clouds in an endless quest
and to bloom into evening flowers
seeking its lost words in the sunset.

It twinkles like fireflies in my heart to find its own
    meaning
in the dusk of despair –
the thing that I had to say to her.

I Threw Away My Heart

I threw away my heart in the world; you took it up.
I sought for joy and gathered sorrow, you gave me
      sorrow and I found joy.
My heart was scattered in pieces, you picked them up in
      your hand and strung them in a thread of love.
You let me wander from door to door to show me at last
      how near you are.
Your love plunged me into the deep trouble.
When I raised my head I found I was at your door.

My Heart, Like a Peacock

My heart, like a peacock on a rainy day,
spreads its plumes tinged with rapturous colours of
      thoughts,
and in its ecstasy seeks some vision in the sky, –
with a longing for one whom it does not know.
My heart dances.

The clouds rumble from sky to sky –
the shower sweeps horizons,
the doves shiver in silence in their nests,
the frogs croak in the flooded fields, –
and the clouds rumble.

O who is she on the king's tower
that has loosened the braid of her dark hair,
has drawn over her breasts the blue veil?
She wildly starts and runs in the sudden flashes of lightning
and lets the dark hair dance on her bosom.

Ah my heart dances like a peacock,
the rain patters on the new leaves of summer,
the tremor of the crickets' chirp troubles the shade of the
      tree,
the river overflows its bank washing the village meadows.
My heart dances.

I Ask for an Audience

I ask for an audience from you, my King, in your solitary
    chamber.
Call me from the crowd.

When your gate was kept open for all I entered your
    courtyard with the bustling throng, and in the
    confusion found you not.

Now when at night they take up their lanterns and go by
    different roads to their different homes, allow me
    to linger here for a moment, standing at your feet,
    and hold up my lamp and see your face.

Our Master Is a Worker

Our master is a worker and we work with him.
Boisterous is his mirth and we laugh with his laughter.
He beats his drum and we march.
He sings and we dance in its tune.
His play is of life and death. We stake our joys and
    sorrows and play with him.
His call comes like the rumbling of clouds; we set out to
    cross oceans and hills.

The World Today

The world today is wild with the delirium of hatred,
the conflicts are cruel and unceasing in anguish,
crooked are its paths, tangled its bonds of greed.
All creatures are crying for a new birth of thine,
O Thou of boundless life,
save them, rouse thine eternal voice of hope,
Let Love's lotus with its inexhaustible treasure of honey
open its petals in thy light.

O Serene, O Free,
in thine immeasurable mercy and goodness
wipe away all dark stains from the heart of this earth.

Thou giver of immortal gifts
give us the power of renunciation
and claim from us our pride.
In the splendour of a new sunrise of wisdom
let the blind gain their sight
and let life come to the souls that are dead.

O Serene, O Free,
in thine immeasurable mercy and goodness
wipe away all dark stains from the heart of this earth.

Man's heart is anguished with the fever of unrest,
with the poison of self-seeking,
with a thirst that knows no end.
Countries far and wide flaunt on their foreheads
the blood-red mark of hatred.
Touch them with thy right hand,
make them one in spirit,
bring harmony into their life,
bring rhythm of beauty.

O Serene, O Free,
in thine immeasurable mercy and goodness
wipe away all dark stains from the heart of this earth.

Why Deprive Me

Why deprive me, my Fate,
of my woman's right
boldly to conquer the best of life's prizes
with mine own arrogant power,
and not to keep gazing at emptiness,
waiting for some chance drifting towards me
with the withered fruit of weary days of patience?
Send me without pity to the utter risk of my all for
        the treasure
guarded behind rudely forbidding barricades.

Never for me is to steal into the bridal chamber
with the timid tinkling of anklets
in a dim twilight dusk,
but recklessly to rush
into the desperate danger of love,
by some troubled sea,
where its stormy vehemence would snatch away from
        my face
the veil of shrinking maidenliness,
and amidst the ominous shrieks of sea-birds
could be raised to my warrior my cry –
You are mine own.

An Oldish Upcountry Man

An oldish upcountry man tall and lean,
with shaven shrunken cheeks like wilted fruits,
jogging along the road to the market town
in his patched up pair of country-made shoes
and a short tunic made of printed chintz,
a frayed umbrella tilted over his head,
a bamboo stick under his armpit.

Though I Know, My Friend

Though I know, my friend, that we are different
my mind refuses to own it.
For we two woke up in the same sleepless night
while the birds sang,
and the same spell of the spring
entered our hearts.

Though your face is towards the light
and mine in the shade
the delight of our meeting is sweet and secret,
for the flood of youth in its eddying dance
has drawn us close.

With your glory and grace you conquer the world,
my face is pale.
But a magnanimous breath of life
has carried me to your side
and the dark line of our difference
is aglow with the radiance of a dawn.

At the Dusk of the Early Dawn

At the dusk of the early dawn, Ramananda, the great
      Brahmin Teacher, stood in the sacred water of
      the Ganges waiting long for the cleansing touch
      of the stream to flow over his heart.
He wondered why it was not granted him this morning.
The sun rose and he prayed for the divine light to bless
      his thoughts and open his life to truth.
But his mind remained dark and distraught.
The sun climbed high over the *sal* forest and the
      fishermen's boats spread their sails, the milk-maids
      with milk-vessels on head went to the market.
The Guru started up, left the water and walked along the
      sand amidst weeds and rushes and clamorous *saliks*,
      busy digging holes for their nests on the slope of
      the river bank.

He reached the lane which took him to the evil-smelling
  village of the tanners where lean dogs were
  crunching bones at the wayside and kites swooped
  down upon casual morsels of flesh.

Bhajan sat before his cottage door under an ancient
  tamarind tree working at camel's saddle.
His body shrank with awe when he saw the Guru fresh
  from his bath come to the unclean neighbourhood
  and the grizzly old tanner bowed himself down to
  the dust from a distance.
Ramananda drew him to his heart and Bhajan, his eyes
  filled with tears, cried in dismay, 'Master, why
  bringest upon thee such pollution!'
And Master said, 'While on my way to my bath I
  shunned your village and thus my heart missed the
  blessings of the Ganges whose mother's love is
  for all.
'Her own touch comes down at last upon me at the
  touch of your body with mine and I am purified.
'I cried this morning to the Sun, "The divine Person
  who is in thee is also within me but why do I not
  meet thee in my mind?"
'I have met him at this moment when his light descends
  upon your forehead as well as on mine, and there is
  no need for me today to go to the temple.'

The Santal Woman

The Santal woman hurries up and down the gravelled
    path under the *shimool* tree; a coarse grey *sari*
    closely twines her slender limbs, dark and compact;
    its red border sweeping across the air with the
    flaming red magic of the *palash* flower.

Some absent-minded divine designer, while fashioning a
    black bird with the stuff of the July cloud and the
    lightning flash, must have improvised unawares this
    woman's form; her impulsive wings hidden within,
    her nimble steps uniting in them a woman's walk
    and a bird's flight.

With a few lacquer bangles on her exquisitely modelled
    arms and a basket full of loose earth on her head,
    she flits across the gravel-red path under the *shimool*
    tree.

The lingering winter has finished its errand. The casual
    breath of the south is beginning to tease the
    austerity of the cold month. On the *himjhuri*
    branches the leaves are taking the golden tint
    of a rich decay. The ripe fruits are strewn over
    the *amlaki* grove where the rowdy boys crowd
    to pillage them. Swarms of dead leaves and dust
    are capering in a ghastly whirl following sudden
    caprices of the wind.

The building of my mud house has commenced and
    labourers are busy raising the walls. The distant
    whistle announces the passing of the train along
    the railway cutting, and the dingdong of the bell is
    heard from the neighbouring school.

I sit on my terrace watching the young woman toiling
    at her task hour after hour. My heart is touched
    with shame when I feel that the woman's service
    sacredly ordained for her loved ones, its dignity
    soiled by the market price, should have been
    robbed by me with the help of a few pieces of
    copper.

Through the Troubled History of Man

Through the troubled history of man
comes sweeping a blind fury of destruction
and the towers of civilization topple down to dust.
In the chaos of moral nihilism
are trampled underfoot by marauders
the best treasures of Man heroically won by the martyrs
      for ages.

Come, young nations,
proclaim the fight for freedom,
raise up the banner of invincible faith.
Build bridges with your life across the
gaping earth blasted by hatred,
and march forward.

Do not submit yourself to carry the burden of insult
      upon your head,
kicked by terror,
and dig not a trench with falsehood and cunning
to build a shelter for your dishonoured manhood;
offer not the weak as sacrifice to the strong
to save yourself.

Those Who Struck Him Once

Those who struck him once
in the name of their rulers,
are born again in this present age.

They gather in their prayer-halls in a pious garb,
they call their soldiers,
'Kill, kill', they shout;
in their roaring mingles the music of their hymns,
while the Son of Man in His agony prays, 'O God,
fling, fling far away this cup filled with the bitterest of
      poisons.'

NOTES

SHORT STORIES

'The Ghat's Story' (Bengali title 'Ghater Katha') was first published in October–November 1884. This translation by Supriya Chaudhuri is taken from *Rabindranath Tagore: Selected Short Stories*, Oxford Tagore Translations edited by Sukanta Chaudhuri (Oxford University Press, New Delhi, 2000).

'The Postmaster' (Bengali title 'Postmaster') was first published in May–June 1891. This translation by William Radice is from *Rabindranath Tagore: Selected Short Stories*, translated by William Radice (Penguin, London, 1991).

'Little Master's Return' (Bengali title 'Khokababur Pratyabartan') was first published in November–December 1891. This translation by William Radice is from *Rabindranath Tagore: Selected Short Stories*, translated by William Radice.

'Wealth Surrendered' (Bengali title 'Sampatti Samarpan') was first published in December–January 1891–2. This translation by William Radice is from *Rabindranath Tagore: Selected Short Stories*, translated by William Radice.

'The Living and the Dead' (Bengali title 'Jibita o Mrita') was first published in July–August 1892. This translation by William Radice is from *Rabindranath Tagore: Selected Short Stories*, translated by William Radice.

'Kabuliwallah' (Bengali title 'Kabuliwallah') was first published in November–December 1892. This translation by William Radice is from *Rabindranath Tagore: Selected Short Stories*, translated by William Radice.

'Holiday' (Bengali title 'Chhuti') was first published in December–January 1892–3. This translation by William Radice is from *Rabindranath Tagore: Selected Short Stories*, translated by William Radice.

'Giribala' is Tagore's own English rendering of the story 'Man Bhanjan' which was first published in April–May 1895. The English version first appeared in *The Modern Review* (May 1917) and is included in *The English Writings of Rabindranath Tagore*, vol. 2, edited by Sisir Kumar Das (Sahitya Akademi, New Delhi, 1996; reprints 2001, 2004, 2008, 2012, 2014 and 2017).

'The Hungry Stones' (Bengali title 'Khudita Pashan') was first published in July–August 1895. This translation by William Radice is from *Rabindranath Tagore: Selected Short Stories*, translated by William Radice.

'Guest' (Bengali title 'Atithi') was first published in August–September–October–November 1895. This translation by William Radice is from *Rabindranath Tagore: Selected Short Stories*, translated by William Radice.

'The Haldar Family' (Bengali title 'Haldargoshthi') was first published in April–May 1914. This translation by Madhuchchhanda Karlekar is taken from *Rabindranath Tagore: Selected Short Stories*, Oxford Tagore Translations edited by Sukanta Chaudhuri.

'The Wife's Letter' (Bengali title 'Strir Patra') was first published in July–August 1914. This translation by Supriya Chaudhuri is taken from *Rabindranath Tagore: Selected Short Stories*, Oxford Tagore Translations edited by Sukanta Chaudhuri.

'House Number One' (Bengali title 'Paila Number') was first published in June–July 1917. This translation by Shanta Bhattacharya is from *Rabindranath Tagore: Selected Short Stories*, Oxford Tagore Translations edited by Sukanta Chaudhuri.

'The Parrot's Training' first appeared in Bengali in 1917 as 'Tota Kahini'. This translation by Tagore himself is from *The English Writings of Rabindranath Tagore*, vol. 2, edited by Sisir Kumar Das.

'The Patriot' is Tagore's translation of 'Samskar' which was written in May–June 1928 and published in *The Modern Review*. It is included in *The English Writings of Rabindranath Tagore*, vol. 2, edited by Sisir Kumar Das.

'The Laboratory' (Bengali title 'Laboratory') was first published in September–October 1940. This translation by Madhuchchhanda Karlekar is taken from *Rabindranath Tagore: Selected Short Stories*, Oxford Tagore Translations edited by Sukanta Chaudhuri.

'The Story of a Mussalmani' (Bengali title 'Musalmanir Galpa') was first published (posthumously) in June–July 1955 even though the draft was written between 24–25 June 1941. This translation by Palash Baran Pal is taken from *Rabindranath Tagore: Selected Short Stories*, Oxford Tagore Translations edited by Sukanta Chaudhuri.

NOVEL

The Home and the World (Bengali title *Ghare Baire*) was written in 1915. This translation by Surendranath Tagore was first published by Macmillan & Co, Ltd, London, in 1919.

PLAYS

The Post Office (Bengali title *Dak Ghar*) was written in 1912. It was translated into English by Devabrata Mukherjee in 1912.

Red Oleanders (Bengali title *Rakta Karabi*) was written in 1923–4. The English translation was published in 1925, one year before the Bengali original was published as a book. This translation is taken from *The English Writings of Rabindranath Tagore*, vol. 2, edited by Sisir Kumar Das (Sahitya Akademi, New Delhi, 1996; reprints 2001, 2004, 2008, 2012, 2014 and 2017).

ESSAYS

'Nationalism in the West' and 'Nationalism in India' are lectures that Tagore delivered in Japan and in the US. They were published in a volume called *Nationalism* (Macmillan, New York, 1917). Reproduced from *The English Writings of Rabindranath Tagore*, vol. 2, edited by Sisir Kumar Das (Sahitya Akademi, New Delhi, 1996; reprints 2001, 2004, 2008, 2012, 2014 and 2017).

'Construction versus Creation' is an address delivered at the Gujarati Literary Conference in Ahmedabad on 2 April 1920. Source: *The English Writings of Rabindranath Tagore*, vol. 3, edited by Sisir Kumar Das (Sahitya Akademi, New Delhi, 1996; reprints 2003, 2006, 2008 and 2012).

'East and West' is part of the volume *Creative Unity* (Macmillan, New York, 1922). The volume was published after Tagore's third trip to the US (1920–21). Source: *The English Writings of Rabindranath Tagore*, vol. 2, edited by Sisir Kumar Das.

'A Vision of India's History' is a revised English rendering of a Bengali essay 'Bharatbarsher Itihaser Dhara' (1912) which was published in *Viswa-Bharati Quarterly* in 1923. It is reproduced here from *The English Writings of Rabindranath Tagore*, vol. 3, edited by Sisir Kumar Das.

'The Educational Mission of the Visva-Bharati' is the text of a radio talk on Radio New York on 10 November 1930. It was published in *The Modern Review*, June 1931. Source: *The English Writings of Rabindranath Tagore*, vol. 3, edited by Sisir Kumar Das.

The Religion of Man contains the Hibbert Lectures for 1930 which Tagore delivered over three days, 19, 21 and 26 May 1930 at Manchester College, Oxford. It was first published by Allen and Unwin (London, 1930) and reprinted the next year by Macmillan, New York. The original publication included seven appendices ('The Baul Singer of Bengal', 'Notes on the Nature of Reality', 'Dadu and the Mystery of Form', 'The Race Problem', 'Brahma Vidya', 'The East and the West' and 'An Address in the Chapel of Manchester College') which are not included here. Reproduced from *The English Writings of Rabindranath Tagore*, vol. 3, edited by Sisir Kumar Das.

'Crisis in Civilization' was delivered as a public address in Santiniketan on 14 April 1941. Khitish Roy and Krishna Kripalani, two close associates of Tagore, made the English translation which Tagore saw and approved. It was published in *Visva-Bharati News* (vol. ix, no. ii) and in *The Modern Review* (May 1941). Source: *The English Writings of Rabindranath Tagore*, vol. 3, edited by Sisir Kumar Das.

'Historicality in Literature' is the translation of a Bengali piece, 'Sahitye Aitihasikata' that Tagore wrote in May 1941 which makes it the last but one prose piece he wrote. It was translated into English for the first time by Ranajit Guha as an appendix to his book *History at the Limit of World History* (Columbia University Press, New York, 2002).

POEMS FOR CHILDREN

'The Captive Hero' (Bengali title 'Bandi Bir') was written on 15 November 1899 and included in a collection called *Katha* (January 1900) and then in another collection *Katha o Kahini* in 1908. It is now easily available in the latter. The translation is by Sukanta Chaudhuri and is taken from *Rabindranath Tagore: Selected Writings for Children*, Oxford Tagore Translations edited by Sukanta Chaudhuri (Oxford University Press, New Delhi, 2002). The poem is based on a piece of early eighteenth-century Sikh history. The Sikhs then were fighting Mughal absolutism to preserve their independence. After the death of Guru Gobind Singh in 1708, the leadership of the struggle passed to Banda. He built a strong fort in Gurdaspur in the Punjab where he had to fall back after a valiant struggle. The poem describes the aftermath of the retreat.

'The Hero' (Bengali title 'Birpurush') is from the collection *Shishu* (September 1903). The translation is by Sukanta Chaudhuri and is taken from *Rabindranath Tagore: Selected Writings for Children*, Oxford Tagore Translations edited by Sukanta Chaudhuri.

'The Palm Tree' (Bengali title 'Talgachh') is from *Shishu Bholanath* (1922). The translation is by Sukhendu Ray and Sukanta Chaudhuri and is taken from *Rabindranath Tagore: Selected Writings for Children*, Oxford Tagore Translations edited by Sukanta Chaudhuri.

'Our Little River' (Bengali title 'Amader choto nadi') is from *Sahaj Path*, part 1 (April–May 1930). The translation is by Sukhendu Ray and Sukanta Chaudhuri and is taken from *Rabindranath Tagore: Selected Writings for Children*, Oxford Tagore Translations edited by Sukanta Chaudhuri.

'The Runaway City' (Bengali title 'Ek din rate ami Swapna dekhinu') is from *Sahaj Path*, part 2 (April–May 1930). The translation is by Sukhendu Ray and is taken from *Rabindranath Tagore: Selected Writings for Children*, Oxford Tagore Translations edited by Sukanta Chaudhuri.

SONGS

'Nothing Has Worked Out' (Bengali title 'Kichhu to Holo Na') was composed in April–May 1881. This translation by Fakrul Alam is taken from *The Essential Tagore*, edited by Fakrul Alam and Radha Chakravarty (Harvard University Press, Cambridge MA and London, 2011).

'Only Coming and Going' (Bengali title 'Shudhu Jaoa Aasha') was composed in April–May 1892. This translation by Ratna Prakash is taken from *The Essential Tagore*, edited by Fakrul Alam and Radha Chakravarty.

'Through Death and Sorrow' (Bengali title 'Achhe Dukha, Achhe Mrityu') was composed in February–March 1903. This translation is by Rabindranath Tagore himself and is taken from *The English Writings of Rabindranath Tagore*, vol. 1, edited by Sisir Kumar Das (Sahitya Akademi, New Delhi, 1994; reprints 1999, 2001, 2004, 2008, 2011 and 2016).

'My Bengal of Gold' (Bengali title 'Amar Sonar Bangla') was composed in August 1905. This translation by Fakrul Alam is taken from *The Essential Tagore*, edited by Fakrul Alam and Radha Chakravarty. This first verse of the song in the original is the national anthem of Bangladesh.

'Suddenly from the Heart of Bengal' (Bengali title 'Aji Bangladesher Hriday Hotey') was composed in September 1905. This translation by Sanjukta Dasgupta is taken from *The Essential Tagore*, edited by Fakrul Alam and Radha Chakravarty.

'If They Answer Not to Thy Call' (Bengali title 'Jodi Tor Dak Shune') was composed in September 1905. This translation is by Rabindranath Tagore himself and is taken from *The English Writings of Rabindranath Tagore*, vol. 1, edited by Sisir Kumar Das.

'Blessed Am I to Have Been Born in this Land' (Bengali title 'Sharthaka Janam Amar') was composed in October 1905. This translation by Sanjukta Dasgupta is taken from *The Essential Tagore*, by Fakrul Alam and Radha Chakravarty.

'This Stormy Night' (Bengali title 'Aji Jharer Rate') was composed in July–August 1909. This translation by Sukanta Chaudhuri is taken from *Rabindranath Tagore: Selected Poems*, Oxford Tagore Translations edited by Sukanta Chaudhuri (Oxford University Press, New Delhi, 2004).

'I Know Not How Thou Singest, My Master' (Bengali title 'Tumi Kemon Kore Gaan Koro') was composed in August 1909. This translation is by Rabindranath Tagore himself and is taken from *The English Writings of Rabindranath Tagore*, vol. 1, edited by Sisir Kumar Das.

'The Suit' (Bengali title 'Jagater Ananda Yoge Amar Nimantran') was composed in October 1909. This translation by Sukanta Chaudhuri is taken from *Rabindranath Tagore: Selected Poems*, Oxford Tagore Translations edited by Sukanta Chaudhuri.

'When Life Has Withered' (Bengali title' Jiban Jakhan Shukaye Jay') was composed in April 1910. This translation by Sukanta Chaudhuri is taken from *Rabindranath Tagore: Selected Poems*, Oxford Tagore Translations edited by Sukanta Chaudhuri.

'I'll Overcome You' (Bengali title 'Ami Rupey Tomai') was composed in

January 1911. This translation by Fakrul Alam is taken from *The Essential Tagore*, edited by Fakrul Alam and Radha Chakravarty.

'Light of Mine, O Light' (Bengali title 'Aalo Amar Aalo Ogo') was composed in September–October 1911. This translation by Reba Som is taken from *The Essential Tagore*, edited by Fakrul Alam and Radha Chakravarty.

'Thou Art the Ruler of the Minds of All People' (Bengali title 'Jana Gana Mana') was composed in December 1911. This translation is by Rabindranath Tagore himself and is taken from *The English Writings of Rabindranath Tagore*, vol. 1, edited by Sisir Kumar Das. The first verse of the original is the national anthem of India.

'Thou Hast Made Me Endless' (Bengali title 'Amare Tumi Ashesh Korechho') was composed in April 1912. This translation is by Rabindranath Tagore himself and is taken from *The English Writings of Rabindranath Tagore*, vol. 1, edited by Sisir Kumar Das.

'You Stand on the Other Shore' (Bengali title 'Dariye Achho Tumi') was composed in March 1914. This translation by Fakrul Alam is taken from *The Essential Tagore*, edited by Fakrul Alam and Radha Chakravarty.

'The Night My Doors Were Shattered' (Bengali title 'Je Rate More Duarguli Bhanglo') was composed in March 1914. This translation by Sukanta Chaudhuri is taken from *Rabindranath Tagore: Selected Poems,* Oxford Tagore Translations edited by Sukanta Chaudhuri.

'My Lamp Blown Out' (Bengali title 'Jete Jete Ekla Pathe') was composed in September 1914. This translation by Sukanta Chaudhuri is taken from *Rabindranath Tagore: Selected Poems*, Oxford Tagore Translations edited by Sukanta Chaudhuri.

'Not Your Word Alone' (Bengali title 'Shudhu Tomar Bani Noi He') was composed in September 1914. This translation by Fakrul Alam is taken from *The Essential Tagore*, edited by Fakrul Alam and Radha Chakravarty.

'Forgive My Langour, O Lord' (Bengali title 'Klanti Amar Kshama Koro') was composed in October 1914. This translation is by Rabindranath Tagore himself and is taken from *The English Writings of Rabindranath Tagore*, vol. 1, edited by Sisir Kumar Das.

'The Cloud Says, "I Am Going"' (Bengali title 'Megh Balechhe Jabo Jabo') was composed in October 1914. This translation by Sukanta Chaudhuri is taken from *Rabindranath Tagore: Selected Poems*, Oxford Tagore Translations edited by Sukanta Chaudhuri.

'When My Footprints no Longer Mark this Road' (Bengali title 'Jakhan Podbe Na') was composed in April 1916. This translation by Fakrul Alam is taken from *The Essential Tagore*, edited by Fakrul Alam and Radha Chakravarty.

'Beyond Boundaries of Life and Death' (Bengali title 'Jibon o Maraner Simana Chhariye') was composed in April–May 1919. This translation by Fakrul Alam is taken from *The Essential Tagore*, edited by Fakrul Alam and Radha Chakravarty.

'My Time Flies' (Bengali title 'Amar Bela Je Jai') was composed in June–July 1919. This translation by Fakrul Alam is taken from *The Essential Tagore*, edited by Fakrul Alam and Radha Chakravarty.

'There – in the Lap of the Storm Clouds – the Rain Comes' (Bengali title 'Oi Je Jharer Meghe') was composed in August 1922. This translation by Fakrul Alam is taken from *The Essential Tagore*, edited by Fakrul Alam and Radha Chakravarty.

'Because I would Sing' (Bengali title 'Tomai Gaan Shonabo') was composed in March 1923. This translation by Fakrul Alam is taken from *The Essential Tagore*, edited by Fakrul Alam and Radha Chakravarty.

'May Farewell's Platter be Replete' (Bengali title 'Bhora Thak Smriti Sudhaye Bidayer Patrokhani') was composed in April 1923. This translation by Reba Som is taken from *The Essential Tagore*, edited by Fakrul Alam and Radha Chakravarty.

'Stars Fill the Sky' (Bengali title 'Akash Bhara') was composed in September–October 1924. This translation by Ratna Prakash is taken from *The Essential Tagore*, edited by Fakrul Alam and Radha Chakravarty.

'Has He Come? Or Hasn't He?' (Bengali title 'O Ki Elo, O Ki Elo Na') was composed in March 1925. This translation by Fakrul Alam is taken from *The Essential Tagore*, edited by Fakrul Alam and Radha Chakravarty.

'A Slight Caress, a Few Overheard Words' (Bengali title 'Ektuku Chhowan Laage') was composed in February 1928. This translation by Fakrul Alam is taken from *The Essential Tagore*, edited by Fakrul Alam and Radha Chakravarty.

POEMS

'The Spring Wakes From its Dream' (Bengali title 'Nirjharer Swapnabhanga') was written between April and June 1882. This translation by Sukanta Chaudhuri is taken from *Rabindranath Tagore: Selected Poems*, Oxford Tagore Translations edited by Sukanta Chaudhuri (Oxford University Press, New Delhi, 2004).

'I Won't Let You Go' (Bengali title 'Jete Nahi Dibo') was written in 1892. This translation by Sukanta Chaudhuri is taken from *Rabindranath Tagore: Selected Poems*, Oxford Tagore Translations edited by Sukanta Chaudhuri.

'Swaying' (Bengali title 'Jhula') was written in 1893. This translation by Ananda Lal and Sukanta Chaudhuri is taken from *Rabindranath Tagore:*

Selected Poems, Oxford Tagore Translations edited by Sukanta Chaudhuri.

'The Golden Boat' (Bengali title 'Sonar Tari') was written in 1892. This translation is by William Radice and is taken from *Rabindranath Tagore: Selected Poems*, translated by William Radice (Penguin, London, 1985; reprinted 2005).

'Now Turn Me Back' (Bengali title 'Ebar Phirao More') was written in 1894. This translation by Sukanta Chaudhuri is taken from *Rabindranath Tagore: Selected Poems*, Oxford Tagore Translations edited by Sukanta Chaudhuri.

'The Lord of Life' (Bengali title 'Jibandebata') was written in 1896. This translation by Sukanta Chaudhuri is taken from *Rabindranath Tagore: Selected Poems*, Oxford Tagore Translations edited by Sukanta Chaudhuri.

'A Half-acre of Land' (Bengali title 'Dui Bigha Jami') was written in 1896. This translation by William Radice is taken from *Rabindranath Tagore: Selected Poems*, translated by William Radice.

'Affliction' (Bengali title 'Duhsamay') was written in 1897. This translation by Sukanta Chaudhuri is taken from *Rabindranath Tagore: Selected Poems*, Oxford Tagore Translations edited by Sukanta Chaudhuri.

'Snatched by the Gods' (Bengali title 'Devatar Gras') was written in 1897. This translation by William Radice is taken from *Rabindranath Tagore: Selected Poems*, translated by William Radice.

'Where the Mind Is Without Fear' (Bengali first words 'Chitta Jetha Bhayashunya') was written in 1901. This translation by Sukanta Chaudhuri is taken from *Rabindranath Tagore: Selected Poems*, Oxford Tagore Translations edited by Sukanta Chaudhuri.

'Death-wedding' (Bengali title 'Maran Milan') was written in 1902. This translation by William Radice is taken from *Rabindranath Tagore: Selected Poems*, translated by William Radice.

'Pilgrimage to India' (Bengali title 'Bharat Tirtha') was written in 1910. This translation by Sukanta Chaudhuri is taken from *Rabindranath Tagore: Selected Poems*, Oxford Tagore Translations edited by Sukanta Chaudhuri.

'The Flying Geese' (Bengali title 'Balaka') was written in 1915. This translation by Sukanta Chaudhuri is taken from *Rabindranath Tagore: Selected Poems*, Oxford Tagore Translations edited by Sukanta Chaudhuri.

'In Praise of Trees' (Bengali title 'Briksha Bandana') was written in 1927. This translation by William Radice is taken from *Rabindranath Tagore: Selected Poems*, translated by William Radice.

'The Child' was first published by Allen and Unwin, London, in 1931. This is the only major poem by Rabindranath Tagore written directly in English. The poem was written in July 1930 when Rabindranath saw the

Oberammergau passion play in Bavaria, Germany. This had been performed in the village once every ten years since 1634. Source: *The English Writings of Rabindranath Tagore*, vol. 1, edited by Sisir Kumar Das (Sahita Akademi, New Delhi, 1994; reprints 1999, 2001, 2004, 2008, 2011 and 2016).

'Question' (Bengali title 'Prasna') was written in 1932. This translation by William Radice is taken from *Rabindranath Tagore: Selected Poems*, translated by William Radice.

'Unyielding' (Bengali title 'Udasin') was written in 1934. This translation by William Radice is taken from *Rabindranath Tagore: Selected Poems*, translated by William Radice.

'I' (Bengali title 'Ami') was written in 1936. This translation is by Shirshendu Chakrabarti and is taken from *Rabindranath Tagore: Selected Poems*, Oxford Tagore Translations edited by Sukanta Chaudhuri.

'Earth' (Bengali title 'Prithivi') was written in 1935. This translation by William Radice is taken from *Rabindranath Tagore: Selected Poems*, translated by William Radice.

'Africa' (Bengali title 'Africa') was written in 1937. This translation by William Radice is taken from *Rabindranath Tagore: Selected Poems*, translated by William Radice.

'The Day My Consciousness was Freed' (Bengali first words 'Jedin Chaitanya Mor Mukti Pelo') was written in 1937. This translation by Shirshendu Chakrabarti is taken from *Rabindranath Tagore: Selected Poems,* Oxford Tagore Translations edited by Sukanta Chaudhuri.

'Concord' (Bengali title 'Aikatan') was written in 1941. This translation is by Supriya Chaudhuri and is taken from *Rabindranath Tagore: Selected Poems*, Oxford Tagore Translations edited by Sukanta Chaudhuri.

'The Pall of the Self' (Bengali first words 'E Amir Abaran') was written in 1941. This translation by Sukanta Chaudhuri is taken from *Rabindranath Tagore: Selected Poems*, Oxford Tagore Translations edited by Sukanta Chaudhuri.

'They Work' (Bengali first words 'Alas Samaydhara Beye') was written in 1941. This translation by Supriya Chaudhuri is taken from *Rabindranath Tagore: Selected Poems*, Oxford Tagore Translations edited by Sukanta Chaudhuri.

'On the Banks of the Rupnarayan' (Bengali first words 'Rupnarayan Kule') was written in 1941. This translation is by Supriya Chaudhuri and is taken from *Rabindranath Tagore: Selected Poems*, Oxford Tagore Translations edited by Sukanta Chaudhuri.

'The First Day's Sun' (Bengali first words 'Pratham Diner Surja') was written in 1941. This translation is by Supriya Chaudhuri and is taken from

Rabindranath Tagore: Selected Poems, Oxford Tagore Translations edited by Sukanta Chaudhuri.

'The Path of Your Creation' (Bengali first words 'Tomar Srishtir Path') was written in 1941. This translation by Supriya Chaudhuri is taken from *Rabindranath Tagore: Selected Poems*, Oxford Tagore Translations edited by Sukanta Chaudhuri. This was Rabindranath Tagore's last poem composed on 30 July 1941, seven days before his death.

The rest of the poems in this section were translated into English by Rabindranath himself, edited by Krishna Kripalani in collaboration with Amiya Chakravarty, Nirmal Chandra Chattopadhyay and Pulinbihari Sen, and published by Viswa-Bharati in 1942. The poems are unnamed but numbered. The titles/first lines of the Bengali originals are not mentioned in *The English Writings of Rabindranath Tagore*, vol. 1, edited by Sisir Kumar Das from which the following are taken: nos 5, 10, 19, 20, 24, 49, 88, 89, 95, 96, 98, 100, 111 and 112. In this Everyman edition, first lines, in full or part, are used as titles.

CHINUA ACHEBE
The African Trilogy
Things Fall Apart

ISABEL ALLENDE
The House of the Spirits

MARTIN AMIS
London Fields

IVO ANDRIĆ
The Bridge on the Drina

ISAAC ASIMOV
Foundation
Foundation and Empire
Second Foundation
(in 1 vol.)

MARGARET ATWOOD
The Handmaid's Tale

JAMES BALDWIN
Giovanni's Room
Go Tell It on the Mountain

JOHN BANVILLE
The Book of Evidence
The Sea
(in 1 vol.)

JULIAN BARNES
Flaubert's Parrot
A History of the World in
10½ Chapters (in 1 vol.)

GIORGIO BASSANI
The Garden of the Finzi-Continis

SIMONE DE BEAUVOIR
The Second Sex

SAMUEL BECKETT
Molloy, Malone Dies,
The Unnamable

SAUL BELLOW
The Adventures of Augie March

JORGE LUIS BORGES
Ficciones

ELIZABETH BOWEN
Collected Stories

RAY BRADBURY
The Stories of Ray Bradbury

MIKHAIL BULGAKOV
The Master and Margarita

A. S. BYATT
Possession

JAMES M. CAIN
The Postman Always Rings Twice
Double Indemnity
Mildred Pierce
Selected Stories
(1 vol. US only)

ITALO CALVINO
If on a winter's night a traveler

ALBERT CAMUS
The Outsider (UK)
The Stranger (US)
The Plague, The Fall,
Exile and the Kingdom,
and Selected Essays
(in 1 vol.)

PETER CAREY
Oscar and Lucinda
True History of the Kelly Gang
(in 1 vol.)

ANGELA CARTER
The Bloody Chamber,
Wise Children,
Fireworks
(in 1 vol.)

WILLA CATHER
Death Comes for the Archbishop
(US only)
My Ántonia
O Pioneers!

RAYMOND CHANDLER
The novels (2 vols)
Collected Stories

G. K. CHESTERTON
The Everyman Chesterton

KATE CHOPIN
The Awakening

JOSEPH CONRAD
Heart of Darkness
Lord Jim
Nostromo
The Secret Agent
Typhoon and Other Stories
Under Western Eyes
Victory

JULIO CORTÁZAR
Hopscotch
Blow-Up and Other Stories
We Love Glenda So Much and
Other Tales
(in 1 vol.)

ROALD DAHL
Collected Stories

JOAN DIDION
We Tell Ourselves Stories in
Order to Live (US only)

DAPHNE DU MAURIER
Rebecca (US only)

MARGUERITE DURAS
The Lover,
Wartime Notebooks,
Practicalities
(in 1 vol.)

UMBERTO ECO
The Name of the Rose

JAMES ELLROY
The L.A. Quartet
The Underworld U.S.A. Trilogy

J. G. FARRELL
The Siege of Krishnapur
and Troubles

WILLIAM FAULKNER
The Sound and the Fury
(UK only)

F. SCOTT FITZGERALD
The Great Gatsby
This Side of Paradise
(UK only)

PENELOPE FITZGERALD
The Bookshop
The Gate of Angels
The Blue Flower
(in 1 vol.)
Offshore
Human Voices
The Beginning of Spring
(in 1 vol.)

FORD MADOX FORD
The Good Soldier
Parade's End

RICHARD FORD
The Bascombe Novels

E. M. FORSTER
A Room with a View,
Where Angels Fear to Tread
(in 1 vol., US only)
Howards End
A Passage to India

ANNE FRANK
The Diary of a Young Girl
(US only)

GEORGE MACDONALD
FRASER
Flashman
Flash for Freedom!
Flashman in the Great Game

MAVIS GALLANT
The Collected Stories

KAHLIL GIBRAN
The Collected Works

GÜNTER GRASS
The Tin Drum

ROBERT GRAVES
Goodbye to All That

GRAHAM GREENE
Brighton Rock
The Human Factor

VASILY GROSSMAN
Life and Fate

DASHIELL HAMMETT
The Maltese Falcon
The Thin Man
Red Harvest
(in 1 vol.)
The Dain Curse
The Glass Key
and Selected Stories
(in 1 vol.)

JAROSLAV HAŠEK
The Good Soldier Švejk

JOSEPH HELLER
Catch-22

ERNEST HEMINGWAY
A Farewell to Arms
The Collected Stories
(UK only)
The Sun Also Rises

MICHAEL HERR
Dispatches (US only)

PATRICIA HIGHSMITH
The Talented Mr. Ripley
Ripley Under Ground
Ripley's Game
(in 1 vol.)

ALDOUS HUXLEY
Brave New World

KAZUO ISHIGURO
Never Let Me Go
The Remains of the Day

JAMES WELDON JOHNSON
The Autobiography of an
Ex-Colored Man

JAMES JOYCE
Dubliners
A Portrait of the Artist as
a Young Man
Ulysses

FRANZ KAFKA
Collected Stories
The Castle
The Trial

MAXINE HONG KINGSTON
The Woman Warrior and
China Men
(US only)

RUDYARD KIPLING
Collected Stories
Kim

GIUSEPPE TOMASI DI
LAMPEDUSA
The Leopard

NELLA LARSEN
The Complete Fiction
(in 1 vol.)

D. H. LAWRENCE
Collected Stories
The Rainbow
Sons and Lovers
Women in Love

HALLDÓR LAXNESS
Independent People

DORIS LESSING
Stories

PRIMO LEVI
If This is a Man and The Truce
(UK only)
The Periodic Table

NAGUIB MAHFOUZ
The Cairo Trilogy
Three Novels of Ancient Egypt

NADEZHDA MANDELSTAM
Hope Against Hope

THOMAS MANN
Buddenbrooks
Collected Stories (UK only)
Death in Venice and Other Stories
(US only)
Doctor Faustus
Joseph and His Brothers
The Magic Mountain

KATHERINE MANSFIELD
The Garden Party and Other
Stories

GABRIEL GARCÍA MÁRQUEZ
The General in His Labyrinth
Love in the Time of Cholera
One Hundred Years of Solitude

W. SOMERSET MAUGHAM
Collected Stories
Of Human Bondage

CORMAC McCARTHY
The Border Trilogy

IAN McEWAN
Atonement

YUKIO MISHIMA
The Temple of the
Golden Pavilion

NANCY MITFORD
The Pursuit of Love
Love in a Cold Climate
(in 1 vol.)

LORRIE MOORE
Collected Stories

TONI MORRISON
Beloved
Song of Solomon

ALICE MUNRO
Carried Away: A Selection
of Stories

IRIS MURDOCH
The Sea, The Sea
A Severed Head
(in 1 vol.)

VLADIMIR NABOKOV
Lolita
Pale Fire
Pnin
Speak, Memory

V. S. NAIPAUL
A Bend in the River
Collected Short Fiction (US only)
A House for Mr Biswas

R. K. NARAYAN
Swami and Friends, The Bachelor
of Arts, The Dark Room,
The English Teacher
(in 1 vol.)
Mr Sampath – The Printer of
Malgudi, The Financial Expert,
Waiting for the Mahatma
(in 1 vol.)

IRÈNE NÉMIROVSKY
David Golder
The Ball
Snow in Autumn
The Courilof Affair
(in 1 vol.)

FLANN O'BRIEN
The Complete Novels

FRANK O'CONNOR
The Best of Frank O'Connor

BEN OKRI
The Famished Road

MICHAEL ONDAATJE
The English Patient

GEORGE ORWELL
Animal Farm
Nineteen Eighty-Four
Essays
Burmese Days, Keep the Aspidistra
Flying, Coming Up for Air
(in 1 vol.)

ORHAN PAMUK
My Name is Red
Snow

BORIS PASTERNAK
Doctor Zhivago

SYLVIA PLATH
The Bell Jar (US only)

HENRIK PONTOPPIDAN
Lucky Per

MARCEL PROUST
In Search of Lost Time
(4 vols, UK only)

PHILIP PULLMAN
His Dark Materials

ERICH MARIA REMARQUE
All Quiet on the Western Front

MARY RENAULT
The King Must Die
The Bull from the Sea
(in 1 vol.)

JOSEPH ROTH
The Radetzky March
Rebellion

SALMAN RUSHDIE
Midnight's Children

OLIVER SACKS
The Man Who Mistook
His Wife for a Hat

PAUL SCOTT
The Raj Quartet (2 vols)

JANE SMILEY
A Thousand Acres

ALEXANDER SOLZHENITSYN
One Day in the Life of
Ivan Denisovich

MURIEL SPARK
The Prime of Miss Jean Brodie
The Girls of Slender Means
The Driver's Seat
The Only Problem
(in 1 vol.)

CHRISTINA STEAD
The Man Who Loved Children

JOHN STEINBECK
The Grapes of Wrath

ITALO SVEVO
Zeno's Conscience

GRAHAM SWIFT
Waterland

RABINDRANATH TAGORE
The Best of Tagore

JUNICHIRŌ TANIZAKI
The Makioka Sisters

FRED UHLMAN
Reunion

JOHN UPDIKE
The Complete Henry Bech
Rabbit Angstrom

EVELYN WAUGH
(US only)
Black Mischief, Scoop, The Loved
One, The Ordeal of Gilbert
Pinfold (in 1 vol.)
Brideshead Revisited
The Complete Short Stories
Decline and Fall
A Handful of Dust
The Sword of Honour Trilogy
Waugh Abroad: Collected Travel
Writing

H. G. WELLS
The Time Machine,
The Invisible Man,
The War of the Worlds
(in 1 vol.)

EDITH WHARTON
The Age of Innocence
The Custom of the Country
Ethan Frome, Summer,
Bunner Sisters
(in 1 vol.)
The House of Mirth
The Reef

PATRICK WHITE
Voss

COLSON WHITEHEAD
The Intuitionist

OSCAR WILDE
Plays, Prose Writings and Poems

P. G. WODEHOUSE
The Best of Wodehouse

VIRGINIA WOOLF
To the Lighthouse
Mrs Dalloway
Orlando

RICHARD YATES
Revolutionary Road
The Easter Parade
Eleven Kinds of Loneliness
(in 1 vol.)

W. B. YEATS
The Poems (UK only)

This book is set in BEMBO which was cut
by the punch-cutter Francesco Griffo
for the Venetian printer-publisher
Aldus Manutius in early 1495
and first used in a pamphlet
by a young scholar
named Pietro
Bembo.